LOVE AND POWER

The uncertainty came back to Deanna as soon as they got off the motorcycle. "I guess I'm a little nervous about being here."

"Would you rather go out to dinner?" Evan asked. "I'd like us to still be friends in the morning, no regrets."

She didn't want to go out to dinner. She wanted to be back in his arms, back in the dizzy swirl of sensation his kisses generated. She offered him a shy smile. "No regrets."

He hugged her to him in a fierce embrace. His kiss threatened to swamp her with its intensity.

"I thought we were going inside," she gasped, when his mouth left hers to trail scorching kisses down her neck. His hands were already under her sweater, trying to find their way under her thermal underwear.

He went still, his entire body rigid as he just held her against him. His breathing was ragged, the beat of his heart heavy against Deanna's own. "Maybe I'd better let you control this ride," he finally suggested. "If I stay in control, our first time is going to be hard and fast on the garage floor."

Power. The feeling surged through Deanna, as effective an aphrodisiac as his kisses had been. She had the power to make Evan lose complete control. Now he was offering to let her drive. She looked into the heated depths of his hazel eyes and knew it was going to be better than riding the Harley.

IT'S NEVER TOO LATE FOR LOVE AND ROMANCE

JUST IN TIME   (4188, $4.50/$5.50)
by Peggy Roberts

Constantly taking care of everyone around her has earned Remy Dupre the affectionate nickname "Ma." Then, with Remy's husband gone and oil discovered on her Louisiana farm, her sons and their wives decide it's time to take care of her. But Remy knows how to take care of herself. She starts by checking into a beauty spa, buying some classy new clothes and shoes, discovering an antique vase, and moving on to a fine plantation. Next, not one, but two men attempt to sweep her off her well-shod feet. The right man offers her the opportunity to love again.

LOVE AT LAST   (4158, $4.50/$5.50)
by Garda Parker

Fifty, slim, and attractive, Gail Bricker still hadn't found the love of her life. Friends convince her to take an Adventure Tour during the summer vacation she enjoys as an English teacher. At a Cheyenne Indian school in need of teachers, Gail finds her calling. In rancher Slater Kincaid, she finds her match. Gail discovers that it's never too late to fall in love . . . for the very first time.

LOVE LESSONS   (3959, $4.50/$5.50)
by Marian Oaks

After almost forty years of marriage, Carolyn Ames certainly hadn't been looking for a divorce. But the ink is barely dry, and here she is already living an exhilarating life as a single woman. First, she lands an exciting and challenging job. Now Jason, the handsome architect, offers her a fairy-tale romance. Carolyn doesn't care that her ultra-conservative neighbors gossip about her and Jason, but she is afraid to give up her independent life-style. She struggles with the balance while she learns to love again.

A KISS TO REMEMBER   (4129, $4.50/$5.50)
by Helen Playfair

For the past ten years Lucia Morgan hasn't had time for love or romance. Since her husband's death, she has been raising her two sons, working at a dead-end office job, and designing boutique clothes to make ends meet. Then one night, Mitch Colton comes looking for his daughter, out late with one of her sons. The look in Mitch's eye brings back a host of long-forgotten feelings. When the kids come home and spoil the enchantment, Lucia wonders if she will get the chance to love again.

COME HOME TO LOVE   (3930, $4.50/$5.50)
by Jane Bierce

Julia Delaine says good-bye to her skirt-chasing husband Phillip and hello to a whole new life. Julia capably rises to the challenges of her reawakened sexuality, the young man who comes courting, and her new position as the head of her local television station. Her new independence teaches Julia that maybe her time-tested values were right all along and maybe Phillip does belong in her life, with her new terms.

Available wherever paperbacks are sold, or order direct from the Publisher. Send cover price plus 50¢ per copy for mailing and handling to Penguin USA, P.O. Box 999, c/o Dept. 17109, Bergenfield, NJ 07621. Residents of New York and Tennessee must include sales tax. DO NOT SEND CASH.

FOREVER AND A DAY

FAY KILGORE

ZEBRA BOOKS
KENSINGTON PUBLISHING CORP.

ZEBRA BOOKS are published by

Kensington Publishing Corp.
850 Third Avenue
New York, NY 10022

First Printing: March, 1995

Printed in the United States of America

This book is for my family, who sacrificed the most so I could achieve my goals this year, and in loving memory of my grandfather, Ernest Taylor, who taught me to ride motorcycles.

Acknowledgments

Countless numbers of people helped me during the writing of this book. Ralph Frazier is the actual owner of the Harley Davidson dealership in Buford. He not only allowed me to use his store, he answered countless questions about Harley motorcycles. The North Georgia HOG's chapter does meet at his store and are a great group of people. Jorgia Northrup and Claudia Brooks, of Ladies of Harley, talked to me about riding safety and some of the trips the HOGs have made. Mike McMullon and Roger Henley allowed me to prowl through their garages and through their cherished collections of Indian paraphernalia. Tracey Bridges and Lisa Cain, Volunteer Coordinators of Scottish Rite Children's Medical Center, gave me invaluable information on hospital auxiliary work. Sally Danner, Linda Wickham, and Hilda Cyphers all helped me with Buckhead society functions. Gay Mitchell, Gin Ellis,

Donna Deeb, Ann White, and Wanda Fisher reviewed the manuscript and helped me with plotting. And last, and most importantly, my editor, Ann Lafarge, who thought my proposal had great potential. Any mistakes are mine. Please remember that in spite of all the research, this is still a work of fiction.

Thanks to all those named and unnamed who made it possible.

One

Evan Maxwell was accustomed to odd characters. People came into his showroom dressed in everything from torn up blue jeans to business suits, but this woman looked as out of place in his Harley-Davidson dealership as . . . well, as he would look dressed out in his leathers at a society tea. She seemed to know it, as well. She reminded him of a cat trying to walk through a dog pound without attracting too much attention. He took pity on her.

"May I help you?"

Huge brown eyes met his, then flicked over him with wary assessment. "I'm looking for a Mr. Evan Maxwell?"

Her voice was as cultured as her outfit, soft and definitely southern. Evan gave her his most devastating smile. "You've found him." He'd almost added "sugar" but swallowed it abruptly. She wasn't the "sugar" type, even if she was dressed in white from her neck to her toes.

"I have been on the phone all morning, Mr.

Maxwell, and I've been told by several people that you're the man I want . . . um . . . for the job." She flushed slightly. Evan felt his smile widen but didn't comment. "I have an old Indian motorcycle I'd like to have restored."

"Why don't you have a seat in my office," Evan offered, gesturing the way. "I'll get Cloyd to man the counter and be right with you."

"Thank you." Her smile was tight but she seemed relieved to escape the showroom. Evan shut the office door and went to find Cloyd, wondering if she would be willing to sell the motorcycle outright or if she was doing this for a charity function and would try to finagle some free labor out of him. One thing was for sure, she was the classiest thing he'd ever run across, and he'd met his share of classy women.

She wasn't sitting when he entered the office but browsing through the photographs on the walls. "You were in the Air Force?"

"Until three years ago," Evan confirmed. "That's my oldest son Tom and my grandson Tommy. Tom's stationed at McGuire Air Force Base, in New Jersey."

"He's a handsome young man." Her smile seemed more genuine as she turned back to him. "Both of them. Mr. Maxwell, about the Indian—"

"You can call me Evan, Mrs. . . . ?"

"I'm sorry, it's Randolph, Deanna Randolph." She quickly extended a perfectly manicured, soft, white hand to him.

Evan resisted the urge to wipe his hand on his pants leg before taking hers. Her skin was as soft as it looked, but her handshake was firm. "Won't you sit down?"

She glanced skeptically at the chair he indicated, then spoke in a breathless rush. "This really won't take long, Mr. Maxwell. I just need some information on restoring my father's motorcycle— cost, time, its value once restored, that sort of thing."

Evan glanced at the chair she'd refused and at the white suit she was wearing and understood her hesitation. Still, it irritated him somehow. "Mrs. Randolph, why didn't you just call? Without seeing the motorcycle, I could tell you over the phone the information you're asking for."

She flushed again. The lady certainly flustered easily. "I wanted to meet you first, before I decided whether or not to entrust you with the job. I was hoping you could show me some of the motorcycles you've already restored."

"I don't have any of them here." Disappointment pulled at her mouth and clouded her eyes, making Evan want to comfort her somehow. "I can show you some pictures." He pulled a photograph album out of the bottom drawer of his desk and handed it to her, relieved when she eagerly accepted it. She remained standing as she slowly studied the pictures of his work, before, during, and after the restoration process. It gave Evan a chance to study her.

Middle forties, he decided, although it was hard to tell. There were streaks of white in her shoulder-length black hair, but it could just be frosting, or whatever it was women went to beauty shops to have done to their hair. Hair that perfectly poufed, shaped, and sprayed had to come from a beauty shop. Whatever her age, she'd kept her figure and her skin, though he knew rich women could look as young as their surgeons could make them. She had tiny laugh lines near her eyes that made Evan doubt she'd had a face-lift.

Her soft brown eyes seemed to express her every feeling— uncertainty, vulnerability, caution, maybe even a little trepidation. They were honest eyes. She probably couldn't lie if her life depended on it. Her perfectly manicured fingers were toying with a string of pearls as she turned the pages of the album.

She stopped at a page and looked up at him. Those expressive brown eyes were even softer now, slightly misty. "This is it."

He glanced at the picture she indicated and felt a thrill jolt through him. It couldn't be. "Are you sure?"

"Of course I'm sure." There was no hesitation in her voice. "It's a 1953 Chief, just like this one, only maroon instead of black."

"Indian Red," he corrected, his voice strangely hoarse. Did she know what it was worth?

"What?"

Evan cleared his throat and tried to collect his wits. "Indian Red, not maroon. That was the name of the color. How do you know it's a '53?"

"My father bought it on his fiftieth birthday, January 24, 1953. He was very proud of it."

Evan could imagine. His heart was pounding just at the thought. He lowered his eyes and forced himself to sound cool and detached. "Are you wanting to sell it?"

"No, I want to restore it." Evan watched her confidence growing as she talked and felt his own sinking. He had an idea she knew exactly what she had and what it was worth.

He lowered himself into his chair, ignoring protocol, feeling defeated. "What will you do with it once it's restored?"

Her expression, which had become animated while she talked of her father, turned somber. "It's for charity, Mr. Maxwell."

Damn! He hated being right. Still, if money was all she needed . . .

"I'm going to put it in the auction for Children's Hospital. It's an annual event to raise money for the indigent fund," she continued, obviously unaware of the pain she was causing him. "My parents lost a child to cancer, and the hospital has always been my father's favorite charity. He was very proud of that motorcycle, and I know he would be proud to see it going to help children."

To help children. Evan felt like a worm, lusting after a motorcycle when children were dying. Restored, if what she really had was a 1953 Indian Chief, that cycle would bring in over $30,000— probably more at a charity auction. There was no way he could match that kind of money. Hell, he'd probably end up doing the labor for free, and she hadn't even started wheedling him yet. All she had to say was "children," and he went mushy.

Evan opened his eyes to find Deanna Randolph staring at him strangely. He quickly cleared his throat and sat up in his chair. "That's . . . great, Mrs. Randolph, very generous. Of course I'd need to see the bike before I could give you any kind of estimate."

"I can meet you at my mother's, that's where

the bike is, or have it delivered here, whichever you prefer."

Evan stood up, suddenly uncomfortable with sitting while she still stood. "Where is this motorcycle?"

"In the carriage house. I'm afraid it's in sad shape. It hasn't been moved in almost thirty-five years."

"Was it wrecked?"

"Of course not." Her eyes flashed at the very idea.

"Did he ever lay it down?"

She frowned. Maybe she didn't understand the term.

"Laying it down just means he got overbalanced and laid the motorcycle down on its side. It doesn't hurt them usually, but it skins the paint, the chrome, sometimes dents the end of the handlebars."

"My father took exceptional care of that motorcycle, and he was a skilled rider."

She acted as if his questions were an insult to her father's memory. Even so, Evan felt his excitement rising again. "Where's it been stored?"

"In the carriage house," she repeated with deliberate patience.

"Covered?"

"Of course."

"Is the seat cracked?"

She frowned again, now thoughtful. "I don't think so."

Evan could hardly keep his voice calm. "How's the paint? The chrome?"

"I guess the paint's okay." She seemed puzzled by his questions. "It's so dirty it's hard to tell."

Considering the woman's attire and attitude toward his office chair, Evan decided dirty was a relative term. He was also pretty certain she had no idea what a forty-year-old motorcycle in "sad" shape meant to him. Hers sounded like it was in mint condition. He had to stifle the impulse to follow her home.

"I'd rather pick it up myself," he finally said, when he could say it in his business voice. No way was he going to entrust original paint to a delivery service. "What day is good for you?"

"The sooner the better."

A woman after his own heart.

"I have something I want to do . . . um . . . before the auction."

Evan frowned, pulled from his excitement by the return of the hesitant, uncertain woman who'd first entered his shop. He longed to ask her what she planned to do, but it wasn't any of his concern. Still, the way she was acting, he wondered if it was legal. An ugly thought occurred to him, and he quickly scanned her left hand for a wedding ring. The ring she wore was pearls and diamonds, nothing resembling a traditional wedding ring. Was the cycle part of a divorce dispute?

"The shop doesn't open until ten. I can come early in the morning or wait until after we close at six." Stupid suggestion, he thought, scanning the woman again. She probably didn't do anything before noon.

"Is eight o'clock too early?" she asked in a disdainful tone, as if she'd read his thoughts and determined to prove him wrong.

"Eight o'clock is great." He loved determined women and let his approval show in his smile. He watched her eyes widen in surprise. Good, she wasn't immune to him, after all.

"Here's the address." She fumbled in her purse, then handed him a folded piece of paper. "It's in Buckhead. Are you familiar with the area?"

"I know it's inside the perimeter," Evan said, meaning the expressway that ringed the metropolitan Atlanta area. He also knew it was the oldest part of Atlanta— old homes, old money. He had no doubts that this woman had both.

She gave him directions, which he scribbled on the back of the piece of paper where she'd written the address. "It took me about an hour to get here," she concluded.

"I shouldn't have any problems." He smiled at her again.

She was toying with her pearls again. "Um . . . good. I'll meet you there at eight."

Evan was still smiling after Deanna Randolph had left his office. A classy woman and a '53 Indian with its original parts. Life certainly took some interesting turns.

Deanna's mind churned with a clashing, swirling quagmire of confusing emotions as she drove home from Buford and her meeting with Evan Maxwell. She had always prided herself on being pragmatic, self-controlled, well-organized. She wasn't impulsive, didn't take risks, read the fine print. She had three references on Evan Maxwell's integrity, experience, and mechanical skill, but none of them had prepared her for meeting the man.

She'd expected a mechanic, someone wearing a greasy, rumpled uniform who would talk over her head about engines and try to take advantage of the fact that she was a woman and therefore ignorant. She'd been prepared for that. In the hours she'd spent on the phone looking for information she'd learned what the cycle was worth and what she could expect to pay to have it restored. She'd learned Evan Maxwell's advice was sought by Indian collectors and restorers from across the United States. She'd even been prepared for him to try to buy it from her. What she hadn't been prepared for was a bear of a man in neatly pressed khakis with warm hazel eyes and a wolfish grin that had done strange things to her pulse. Was he interested in her as a woman, or was he only interested in her motorcycle?

There was no denying his avarice when he'd learned about it. There were countless stories about women seduced out of their possessions by men with more charm than scruples, especially emotionally vulnerable women, like widows and the recently divorced. Deanna fell into the latter category, a fact that caused her emotions to vacillate between anger and humiliation.

Maybe it was just the natural progression of things. It had been eleven months since Phil had announced his desire for a divorce, five months since the divorce had been made final. In spite of all her friends' encouragement, she had not dated even one man, had not had the desire to date, and, if truth be known, had not had the self-confidence. Phil had shattered that.

Deanna was tired of mourning, tired of letting one egotistical, self-centered man's opin-

ion of her ruin her life. She was going to restore her father's old Indian motorcycle, and
she was going to learn to ride it. Riding with
her father had made her feel more alive than
anything she could remember doing since,
which was a sad realization. She hadn't gone
soul flying with her father in thirty-eight
years. She's been fourteen when he'd put the
motorcycle away for the last time. He'd never
let her drive it, only ride behind. At fourteen,
riding behind had been okay. At fifty-two, it
was no longer acceptable.

So, it was only natural that the first handsome man who smiled at her would elicit a
response. She had crossed a threshold. She was
ready to return to the world of the living. Evan
Maxwell's warm smile was an innocent flirta-
tion, an affirmation that she was still a woman,
still attractive. Nothing would come of it. He
was probably married. He had pictures of his
son and grandson on his wall.

But no wife pictures.

It didn't matter. She was hiring him to restore her father's motorcycle, that made him
her mechanic and totally unacceptable as a romantic interest. Still, it was nice to know that
she wasn't too old to make a handsome man
smile. And she wasn't too old to respond to
that smile.

* * *

Deanna didn't sleep well that night. Her mind churned between memories of her father, the emotional baggage left from her ex-husband, and images of Evan Maxwell. Her father adored her, Phil shattered her self-confidence, and Evan Maxwell smiled at her, made love to her, then rode off on her father's motorcycle, leaving her destitute. At five o'clock Deanna finally gave up on sleep. Getting dressed proved to be more complicated.

Should she dress to impress Evan with her status, show him she wasn't a woman to be trifled with? Should she wear something practical to show him she wasn't above getting her hands dirty? Perhaps she should dress for the hospital, show him she had other important duties to attend to. She had resented his subtle implication that she would find early morning too much of a challenge. He probably shared the common notion that society women sat on a couch and ate bonbons while their maids cleaned their houses.

Irritation gave way to frustration. She needed the man's help, whether she wanted it or not. She could not restore the motorcycle herself, and she didn't know anyone who could teach her to ride it. Her brothers had ridden it in their youth, but, to her knowledge, neither one of them had ridden one since.

She tried not to think about her brothers. Even though neither one of them had shown any interest in the motorcycle the entire time it had sat in the carriage house, she was certain they were going to challenge her right to it. That was one of the reasons she'd made up the auction excuse. The motorcycle belonged to her mother now, as part of the estate willed to her upon her husband's death three years ago.

Her mother had hated that motorcycle. From the moment Joseph Edwards had brought it home to the day he'd finally given in and put it away, Charlotte Edwards had nagged him to get rid of it. It was one of the reasons Deanna had enjoyed riding it so much. It was a small defiance of her mother's efforts to make her into a proper lady, and it gave her a part of her father her mother would never share. Very Freudian, her best friend Georgia would say.

If her mother knew she had no intention of putting the bike in her auction, that she intended to keep it and ride it, she would never give it to her. That's why she needed outside help. That's why she needed Evan Maxwell. Whether Evan Maxwell was a wolf or not, he was necessary to her plan. She needed him to take her seriously. She finally dressed in a pair of practical wool slacks and a sweater.

Deanna had always prided herself on being good with people. Over the years, she had chaired countless fund-raising committees and events. No one was better at sweet talking reluctant patrons into donating toward her causes. She had handled men tougher than Evan Maxwell and come out ahead. All she needed was a little self-confidence and she'd have him donating his labor. He'd definitely reacted to her mention of the Children's Hospital, and he had a grandson. A man soft on children couldn't be totally without scruples.

It wasn't the image of a grandfather she had, though, when she opened her mother's door to him at exactly eight o'clock. He flashed her his easy, slightly lopsided grin which sent her hand immediately to the strand of pearls she always wore around her neck. Worry beads, Georgia called them. The grin widened as he gave her outfit an appraising perusal.

"The carriage house is out back," Deanna said, at a rare loss for words. This wasn't a social visit, she reminded herself as she led the way around the house. He was probably in a hurry and would appreciate her getting right to what he'd come for.

"I'll have my son back the truck closer," Evan said when she'd shown him the way.

He signaled the driver of a late model pickup as he backed a cycle trailer into position in front of the carriage house doors, then introduced Deanna to the young man who got out. "My son, Brian. Brian, this is Mrs. Randolph."

"Dad!" came a child's plaintive cry from inside the pickup.

"And my grandson, Kyle," Evan supplied as Brian walked back to investigate the problem.

"Two sons, two grandsons," Deanna noted, smiling up at him. "Any others?"

"That's all," Evan said, returning her smile. "That's enough."

"I'd turned off the radio," Brian explained Kyle's grievance, rejoining them.

Brian had his father's hazel eyes but seemed to share few other physical traits. Brian was not as tall, his build more wiry. He wore his brown hair slightly long, and though his work clothes were clean, they lacked his father's well-pressed crispness. Both men wore black leather jackets with assorted Harley-Davidson patches and black ball caps with the Harley-Davidson bar and shield. Somehow the jacket seemed to make Evan more imposing than she'd thought him the day before. She could easily imagine him cruising the highway, sitting astride a powerful black motorcycle.

Deanna unlocked the carriage house doors, then the door into the storage room. She had found the cycle at the very back of the storage room, behind boxes of everything any of them had ever owned in their lives, it seemed like. Her father had been a notorious pack rat, never getting rid of anything. Since his death, her mother hadn't been able to part with anything of his. She hadn't been receptive to Deanna digging through his things, until she'd come up with the auction angle.

Her mother's handyman had rearranged boxes into a path just wide enough to get the cycle out. Deanna pointed, intending to stay out of the men's way. With two flat tires, the cycle wasn't going to be easy to move. Her good intentions ended with Evan's reverent, "My God."

"What's wrong?" Deanna tried to peer between the two men, wondering what had happened since she'd last seen the bike, three days before. It looked the same. She cast a worried glance at Evan. "Is it in too bad a shape to fix?"

His sudden laughter did nothing to relieve her fears. Even Brian was grinning as he squatted down to get a closer look at the engine. "You told me it was in sad shape," Evan said, his eyes bright as he watched his son.

Deanna wasn't sure what to think. Brian pointed at an empty bracket. "He took the battery off."

"I'd bet he even drained the gas tank," Evan commented, unscrewing the cap and peering inside. He took a small flashlight out of an inside jacket pocket and shined the light inside the tank to see better.

"Can't you put more in it?" Deanna asked, worrying the strand of pearls around her neck. "And buy a new battery?"

Evan and Brian seemed to find that amusing as they used the flashlight to examine the wiring, the exhaust system, even inside the deep fenders that almost enclosed the wheels. When Evan finally looked at her, Deanna had the impression he wanted to kiss her. He seemed incredibly pleased about something. She took a wary step back and frowned. "What?"

"Any idea when your father last cranked her?"

"No. I never heard him mention the motorcycle again after he quit riding it."

"Are you sure you want to restore it?"

"Can it be restored?"

That set both men off again. "Oh, yeah, it can be restored," Evan said, still grinning ridiculously as he stroked the seat. "Mrs. Randolph, your father took excellent care of this bike. Most Indian owners continued riding their machines long after the company quit manufacturing parts. They replaced worn parts with whatever would fit, and still they rode them. Those that were wrecked or unrepairable were cannibalized for their parts. Then Indian collecting and restoration became popular, and suddenly those ravaged carcasses were worth a lot of money. I have rebuilt three of them that started out as an unrecognizable boxful of engine parts and a bare chassis. The finished machine is a combination of original parts, old 'new' parts, parts robbed off other models of the same year, and new reproduction parts."

He turned back to Deanna's cycle with a look close to love in his eyes. "Unless I totally miss my guess, this one has all its original parts, just the way it came off the wigwam assembly line forty years ago. Not only that, but your father stored it with attention to detail. He removed the battery and drained the gas tank, preventing damage from the deteriorating fluids stored within them. I can get you top dollar for this bike just the way it's sitting here. There are collectors who would kill me for restoring this bike."

The dead air within the storage room rang with the passion of Evan's speech as he waited for Deanna's response. She was too overwhelmed by the zeal radiating from him, the intensity of his hazel-green eyes, to even respond.

"Dad tends to get a little carried away," Brian interceded, standing up. "Why don't we get this loaded?"

Evan was still watching Deanna, waiting for her answer. "I . . . want it restored," she finally managed. Assertiveness. She had to be assertive, not let him take advantage of her.

The disappointment in his eyes made her question her decision. After all, she had hired him because of his knowledge about Indian restoration. But she didn't want to sell the bike to a collector. She wanted to ride it.

He directed his attention back to the bike, turning away from Deanna. She went back outside to give them room to maneuver the bike through the tight maze of boxes. In spite of Evan's words, to Deanna the bike was a pitiful sight exposed to the bright sunlight. Charlotte was waiting for them on the driveway. She, too, shook her head sadly when she saw the motorcycle.

"Really, Deanna, how can you put that old thing in your auction. It's embarrassing."

"Mother, this is Evan and Brian Maxwell," Deanna introduced the two men. "They are going to restore Dad's motorcycle to its original splendor. I think you'll be impressed with the results."

Charlotte did not offer her hand. Her lips were tightly compressed as she took in the men, then turned back to Deanna. "I'll wait for you inside."

Deanna gasped at her mother's rudeness, then turned quickly to Evan, trying to explain. "Please excuse my mother's behavior. She's upset about me taking the motorcycle. It's the first thing of my father's that she has let go since his death, and I'm afraid she isn't dealing with it very well."

There was a hard glint in Evan's eyes as he watched Charlotte's retreating back, then looked at Deanna. "I'm sorry about your father," he said, but Deanna knew he didn't believe her mother's grief was the reason for her behavior. He turned back to help Brian secure the bike on the trailer. Deanna noticed the little boy was watching through the back glass of the pickup with wide-eyed fascination.

Deanna tried to salvage the situation. "How old is Kyle?" she asked, inclining her head toward the little boy.

"He's four."

Deanna waited, but no further information was volunteered. Evan seemed totally preoccupied with the tie-down straps. She noticed he used protective bubble wrap under the woven straps. "I have a three-year-old grandson," she offered, trying to make conversation. "His name's Brady."

He didn't seem to care. Fine. This was a business relationship, not a social one.

"I have the number to your shop. I'll call this afternoon after you've had a chance to look the cycle over. You can give me a quote— "

"Five thousand dollars," Evan interrupted, pulling down hard on the last knot. "That's for labor. I figure another five thousand for parts and the services I have to contract out, like replating the chrome. I'll need that up front. I'll be glad to give you an itemized list of expenses to verify the cost."

Deanna met his cool gaze and matched his even, all-business tone. "I was told the entire restoration shouldn't cost over five thousand dollars, parts and labor included."

Evan smiled, but it wasn't pleasant. "I'm offering you a bargain, lady. I usually charge six thousand just to restore the power plant. If you want a five-thousand-dollar restoration job, then I'll be happy to unload this and you can call the person who gave you the quote."

She hadn't been impressed with the man who'd given her the quote, which was why she had driven all the way to Buford to meet Evan.

"You said it was in remarkably good condition."

"I thought you wanted top-quality work."

Deanna stroked her pearls thoughtfully. "What did you charge for the Indians in the boxes?"

"Nothing."

Deanna hadn't expected that. "Nothing?"

He grinned then, the humor reflected in his eyes. "I bought them for myself."

Deanna frowned. "But when I asked you for examples of your work, you said— "

"I said they weren't at the shop, which they aren't."

"You don't work out of your shop?"

"Nope."

"Why?"

"I don't think Harley-Davidson would approve of Indians being restored in their shop."

"Dad is being deliberately obtuse," Brian said, joining in the conversation. "We own the shop, but it is an authorized Harley-Davidson dealership, which means we follow certain company guidelines. The feud between Indian and Harley-Davidson goes back before the First World War."

"But Indians haven't been built in forty years," Deanna argued. "How can there still be a feud?"

"The War Between the States ended a hundred and thirty years ago," Brian countered, "yet a day doesn't go by that someone doesn't refer to me as 'yankee'— usually in jest."

But not always, Deanna inferred. Well, what did he expect? His accent was broader even than his father's, and their shop was in the middle of rural Georgia.

"I'm considered something of a traitor," Evan added, bringing the conversation back to motorcycles. "A Harley-Davidson dealer shouldn't collect and restore antique Indians. To be fair, I do restore Harleys, also."

Deanna brought the conversation back to their earlier discussion. "For a price."

Evan laughed. "You bet for a price. There's a lot more to this restoration thing than overhauling an old engine."

Deanna played with her pearls, thinking through an idea. "I'll make you a deal, Mr. Maxwell. For my investment of ten thousand dollars you will not only restore my motorcycle to its former glory, but you will teach me to ride it. You will also prove to me that you got the best price on the parts you buy," she finished in a rush, not wanting to give him the opportunity to single out the teaching part. It didn't work.

"You want to ride it?"

Deanna dropped the pearls and met his gaze squarely. "Is that a problem?"

The lopsided smile grew slowly as he considered her offer, becoming the devastating, totally masculine, wolfish grin that once again did strange things to her pulse. "No problem at all."

Two

He probably has fifty women at his beck and call, Deanna thought bitterly as she arranged her cards according to suit. She'd tried all day to get Evan Maxwell off her mind, finally calling Georgia and asking her if she wanted to play bridge. She could always rely on bridge to take her mind off things she'd rather not think about.

Like bedroom eyes and a lopsided, wolfish smile that made her flush warm from the inside out. It was obvious the man was a practiced playboy. She frowned to herself. A man who traveled with his son and grandson didn't exactly fit the image of a playboy.

"Deanna!"

She gave Georgia an irritated glare. "What?"

"Your bid."

"Oh." She wondered how long the others had been waiting. "What's been bid?"

"I passed," Georgia supplied. "South bid two spades."

"Two hearts," Deanna bid quickly.

Georgia looked exasperated. The man in the north seat gave her a haughty look. "You can't bid two hearts following a two spade bid," he said snootily. "Since you've bid hearts, you'll have to go to three."

"No problem." Deanna met his gaze steadily. She didn't have a three heart hand, but he wouldn't know it until the last card fell. Maybe by some miracle, Georgia had the queen.

"Double," he bid, then gave her a tight, taunting smile. Well, she now knew who had the queen. Double was not a bid but an expression of doubt backed by points.

"Pass," Georgia said, rolling her eyes expressively. The rest passed and Deanna was stuck with a bid she'd given no thought to. Another strike against Evan Maxwell.

"That was certainly an interesting evening," Georgia commented on the way home. "What's on your mind instead of bridge?"

"I apologize for that heart bid," Deanna started, but Georgia waved her away.

"Duplicate bridge is always so serious, especially in the evening. Bunch of strangers, no one lets anything slide. Too competitive. Harriet and Darleen would have let you rebid, but not that guy. He wanted his points."

"Doubled," Deanna remembered grimly.

"Yeah, well, he cared and I don't. I'm more interested in why your usual steel-trap mind is not on the game." She twisted in her seat to face Deanna. "What is it on?"

"Billy Adonis called me last week."

"The rock singer? Is there a problem?"

"No, he wanted to make a donation for the auction. Since I'm the chairwoman, he called me."

"That's hardly worthy of getting set— doubled," Georgia said.

"He offered me a 1955 Indian Chief motorcycle."

"That's supposed to impress me, I can tell." Georgia sat sideways in her seat, waiting for Deanna to get to something she wanted to hear.

"He paid twenty-thousand dollars for it five years ago. It's a collector's item. It's fully restored, new paint, new chrome, new seat. It's gorgeous."

"I didn't realize you were into antique motorcycles, Deanna. You're just full of surprises. So, did the two of you ride off into the sunset? Are you planning a walk on the wild side with a heavy metal rock singer?"

Deanna gave her a disgusted look. "Not only is he married, with a baby, he's a kid. I was talking about the motorcycle."

"A motorcycle made you forget thirty-five years of bridge strategy?"

"No, the motorcycle reminded me of Dad's old Indian. He bought a 1953 Indian Chief when I was ten years old. Bragged to anyone who would listen that it was the last year of production, that it would be a collector's item someday. He was right."

Georgia was frowning. "You've lost me. You said Billy offered you a '55."

"He did. It's an English import, sold under the Indian name after the American company stopped production. Billy collects motorcycles. He wants a real Indian, so he's donated this one to our auction on behalf of his daughter, who is now out of intensive care and expected to live a normal life. He wants to express his gratitude, although I'm sure the publicity and the tax write-off is nice, too, and we have a fantastic item to advertise for our auction."

"Listen, Deanna, I know you've been under a lot of stress the last several years, with the loss of your father then that jerk Phil dumping on you like he did. Maybe being auction chairwoman wasn't a good idea this year. We could take a trip, maybe a cruise."

"I've talked Mother into giving me Dad's old bike," Deanna said, ignoring her. "I'm having it restored, just like Billy's, and I'm going to learn to ride it."

Georgia stared thoughtfully out the windshield, watching the late night traffic. "Wouldn't it have been easier just to buy a new motorcycle?" she finally asked. "You can get one of those Gold Wings like Harriet and her husband ride, with the stereo and the intercom."

"I don't plan to take up motorcycle riding," Deanna said. It was hard to explain something to Georgia that was only a half-formed image in her own mind. She just knew she'd seen Billy's Indian and it had unleashed a need within her to prove a point. No man was going to dictate to her again. She needed to prove to her father that she could ride his motorcycle, even if she was a girl. She needed to prove it to herself. She needed to prove it to the world, and especially to Dr. Phillip Randolph.

"It's hard to explain. It's just something I have to do, something tangible to help me work through everything that's happened. You read all those psychology books. I'm sure there's a fancy word for what I'm doing."

"Closure," Georgia supplied. "You're looking for closure with your father, a way of working out your grief." Georgia laid her hand over Deanna's, her blue eyes filled with compassion. "I'm sorry, honey, I know you still miss him."

The tears burned, forming suddenly as they did every time she dwelled on the loss of her father. "Closure's a good term." First her father, then Phil. Then she would be ready to go on with her life.

"I found a man in Buford who's agreed to restore Dad's motorcycle, and he'll teach me to ride it." The tears receded, replaced by heat that warmed her face as she thought about Evan Maxwell. She was grateful it was dark inside the car. Georgia had an uncanny instinct for anything remotely romantic.

"Ahhh," Georgia drawled. "Could we finally be getting to the reason my partner with the steel-trap mind followed a two spades bid with two hearts?"

Deanna sighed, resigned. "His name is Evan Maxwell."

"And? And? Is he young? Old? Cute?"

"He's at least fifty. I don't think 'cute' is quite the right word."

"What word would you use?"

Sexy, but Deanna would never admit it aloud, especially to Georgia.

"Sexy, huh?"

Deanna jumped, jerking the wheel. The heat in her face returned, even hotter. "What are you, clairvoyant?" she demanded when she had the car back under control.

Georgia's smile was smug. "I just know how your mind works. Your silence gave you away."

She snuggled back into her seat. "Sexy is much better than cute."

"He's a mechanic." Deanna intended for that to be the end of the discussion, timing it with their arrival in Georgia's drive.

"Dirty, huh?"

"Well, no . . ."

"Uneducated, not too bright?"

Deanna frowned. His speech had been quite cultured, with a slight New England accent. "He seemed intelligent enough."

"Then what's the problem? Is he going to take your motorcycle and leave the country?"

"He was very interested in it."

"And yourself?"

"Well, of course I'm interested in it. It was— "

"I meant was he interested in you?"

Deanna had turned off the engine, and the silence was heavy and eloquent. Had he been? Or did she just wish he had been?

"It's about time."

"He didn't say anything . . ." Deanna began to protest.

"I don't care about him," Georgia said, laying her hand on Deanna's arm again. "I care about you. I think you find the man intriguing, and that's a wonderful sign. Did you encourage him or did you snub him?"

Deanna couldn't remember doing anything except staring foolishly. "Mother snubbed him. I'm sure he now considers us both to be rich snobs who are afraid he'll get us dirty if we get too close."

"He should see you at the hospital," Georgia said, referring to Deanna's work with the children. Deanna always carried a complete change of clothes and frequently had to utilize them. "That doesn't sound like your mother, either."

"No," Deanna agreed. "Turned out they frightened her to death. Both men wore black leather jackets with Harley-Davidson patches all over them. Mother is convinced I've given Dad's motorcycle over to the Hell's Angels."

"Did you?" Georgia sounded more excited by the prospect than worried.

"Of course not," Deanna snapped. "You, of all people, know better than to stereotype."

Georgia's lushly painted mouth curved into a calculating smile. "Did you mention two men? Is his friend equally sexy?"

Deanna laughed. "His friend is his son, although you might still be interested." She laughed again at the speculative gleam in Georgia's big blue eyes. "And the son has a four-year-old son."

"Wouldn't you know it," Georgia pouted. "So is this hunk married?"

Deanna knew Georgia had dismissed the son and was referring to Evan. "I have no idea. What difference does it make?"

"He sounds like a perfect stud-muffin, although if he's a grandfather, he's a little old."

"A what?"

"A stud-muffin, honey," Georgia repeated. "Every woman needs one after a divorce to prevent rebounding into another bad relationship with a man who reminds her of her husband. A sexy biker is perfect. He'll restore your faith in yourself as a woman while he restores your motorcycle, and when the job's done, you each go your separate ways with no hard feelings."

Deanna stared at her friend in disbelief. "Don't you think that's rather cold?"

"Cold is divorcing a wife of twenty or thirty years for failure to meet his needs when she never knew his needs had changed," Georgia stated, referring to her and Deanna's ex-husbands. "What I'm suggesting is therapy. There's no way an intelligent motorcycle mechanic from Buford is going to think a Buckhead society woman is serious about him. He'll understand it for the game it is, which is more than you're going to be able to do, I can tell from your expression."

Deanna realized she was staring at Georgia with her mouth agape. She clamped it closed and forced her attention out the car window, her fingers automatically finding her pearls and stroking their smooth surface, seeking comfort. She and Georgia had been best friends for years, working together on various projects at Children's Hospital and playing bridge. Usually their minds worked together, one frequently completing a thought the other had started, which made them a formidable bridge team, but Deanna had never shared Georgia's jaded view of men.

"I'm not as tough as you are," Deanna finally said, wanting to put an end to the discussion without insulting her friend, "Nor as free-spirited. I could no more do what you're suggesting than . . . than . . ."

"Fly?"

Soul flying. Wasn't that what she was trying to recapture? What would it be like to ride with Evan, dressed in his black leather? Did he ride a big, black Harley, with flames painted down the gas tank? She would ride behind him— no, that's where the fantasy stopped. She was never riding behind a man again, either figuratively or on a motorcycle.

"Deanna?"

"Right," Deanna agreed quickly, "than fly. Are you coming in the morning to the auction committee meeting?"

"Of course." Georgia opened the car door and slid out, then leaned back in. "When do you see him again?"

"He wants to be paid in advance for the parts, so I guess I'll have to take him a check sometime soon."

"The mail is so unreliable these days," Georgia agreed, her voice thick with mock sympathy.

"I have to monitor his work," Deanna insisted, knowing Georgia wasn't buying it. "What if he's a con-artist?"

"I know you too well, Deanna Randolph. How many references did you contact before you approached him?"

Deanna smiled. Georgia did know her too well. "Three," she admitted, "and I've seen pictures of his work. You should hear him talk, watch him work. He's very conscious of every detail."

"I do like a man who's conscious of every detail," Georgia said, her grin wicked. "You definitely need to keep a close eye on him. See you in the morning."

The car door shut, leaving Deanna sitting in the dark, watching until Georgia had unlocked her door and slipped inside with a final wave. She couldn't play Georgia's game. For all of her fifty-two years of living, twenty-nine years of being married, and a lifetime of mov-

ing in the sophisticated circles of Atlanta society, she wasn't sophisticated enough to flirt
with a man like Evan Maxwell without getting
her heart, and her even more fragile ego, involved. She had known him only two days, but
already his opinion meant too much to her to
risk his rejection.

Deanna could hear the hum of gossip from
the conference room long before she reached
the door. "You know he's been dating Alecia
Weatherby," she heard Julie Stern say in a smug
voice. "She's going to redecorate his office."

"No doubt in black and pink," she heard
Georgia comment with disgust. "The woman
has no taste. Look who she's dating."

Instantly on guard, Deanna stopped outside
the door, eavesdropping shamelessly.

"What's wrong with black and pink?" Harriet Donovan asked.

Deanna smiled. Harriet's guest bathroom
was done in black and pink, and she was very
proud of it.

"Nothing's wrong with black and pink,"
Darleen Carnegie said in a soothing tone.
"Georgia's just defending Deanna."

Georgia, Harriet, Darleen, and Deanna had
played bridge together every Thursday morn-

ing for more years than Deanna cared to think about. They were always defending each other, at auxiliary meetings, at the country club, at parties. Their support had kept Deanna together this past year when she and Phil had been a favorite topic of gossip.

"Really, Georgia," Deanna recognized Susan Whitehead's voice, "I know you feel protective but the man is fair game. They've been separated almost a year. The divorce is final."

"Doesn't make him any less of a jerk," Georgia responded.

"I would never let a man like that get bored if he was married to me." That sultry purr belonged to Connie Tarwater, who Deanna knew was hunting for husband number three.

"I overheard Sylvia Adams compare sleeping with Dr. Randolph to being serviced at Jiffy Lube," Harriet said, in a voice so low Deanna was practically hanging in the doorway to hear it, "fast, efficient, and no frills."

The room erupted in feminine giggles. Deanna couldn't listen to any more. "Good morning, ladies," she called out gaily, entering the room as if she hadn't overheard a word. "It sounds like a party in here."

Greetings were called out, a few faces looking a little sheepish. "Tell us about your visit with Billy Adonis," Georgia invited.

Deanna gave her a grateful look. Even though Georgia had already heard the entire story, none of the other women had. Every one of them would have jumped at the chance to be invited to his home, even though most of them were old enough to be his mother.

"I know it's only four months until the auction," Deanna started, "but Billy's daughter Brittany should be able to go home soon, and he was anxious to show his gratitude. He's offered us his 1955 Indian motorcycle."

She wasn't surprised when her announcement was greeted with puzzled expressions. "Now, I know most of you have no idea what an Indian is, but once you understand I think you will agree with me that his donation is extraordinary and should be utilized as the major drawing card for this year's auction."

She took a deep breath and let it out slowly. No businessman was a harder sell than this group of society women. "Indian motorcycles were last built in America in 1953, leaving Harley-Davidson as the remaining American-built motorcycle. In the last few years, with 'buy American' becoming an increasingly popular theme, collectors have been buying and restoring these old motorcycles, and they are worth a great deal of money. Billy gave twenty thousand for his, a donation worthy of one of our gold sponsors, don't you think?"

That had their attention. Individual gifts of that amount were rare outside of their regular sponsors, and collector's items could be heavily advertised, bringing bidders to the auction who wouldn't come just to support the hospital.

"That's very generous of him," Susan said.

"Yes, it is," Deanna agreed, "which is why I'd like to propose a theme for this year's auction that would build upon his generosity— a fifties theme."

"Fifties?" Julie Stern was the first to voice her dismay. "Fifties themes went out with the seventies."

"There are still some fifties bands hanging around," Georgia said. Again, Deanna sent her a grateful look. "Or even easier, use a DJ and old records, like a high school sock-hop."

"That's so corny, childish even," Connie said, slumping down in her chair to express her disapproval.

Deanna knew Connie lived for formal occasions when she could show off her latest designer gown from New York, sometimes even Paris. A supporting argument came from an unexpected quarter.

"I always did like men in tight jeans and leather jackets." Everyone turned to Hilda

McMullion, age sixty-six, who up until now had been sitting quietly in the corner.

"Oh, me, too," Georgia quickly agreed. "I know a dance instructor who might be persuaded to give jitterbug lessons."

"Motorcycle ownership seems to be making a comeback," Julie put in hesitantly, "especially owning a Harley. David bought one so he could join the Buckhead HOGs."

"Buckhead hogs?" Georgia asked, giving Deanna a meaningful glance.

"It stands for Harley Owner's Group," Julie explained. "They go on that Johnnie Beckman ride for muscular dystrophy every year."

Deanna wondered if there was a Buford HOG and if Evan was a member. The Johnnie Beckman Motorcycle Ride was an annual event to raise funds for muscular dystrophy, but until Julie had mentioned it, she had forgotten about it and the Harley owners' role in it.

"Do you ever ride with David?" Deanna asked Julie, trying to keep the question casual.

"Do I look crazy? I doubled his life insurance the day after he bought the awful thing."

"I'd ride with him," Hilda said, sparking a heated discussion among the other women. Deanna wondered if Julie's daughter rode with him but didn't ask. She rapped on the table to get the meeting back on track.

"So, what do you think about the fifties theme? Any other suggestions, comments?"

"I was hoping we could do the Arabian Nights theme again," Susan put in tentatively. "It works so well with the tent."

"We're using The Depot this year," Harriet reminded her.

"Connie?" Deanna asked.

"Poodle skirts make me look fat."

"That's not all they wore," Darleen pointed out. "Instead of a sock-hop we could do prom night."

Connie brightened at that idea, but Julie disagreed. "You'll get more cooperation from the men if they can wear jeans."

"The auction has always been a formal affair," Darleen reminded everyone. "Remember the Junior League balls we used to throw? We could recreate something like that."

"I like that idea better than high school revisited," Connie said. "We have a reputation to uphold."

That was true. The Children's Hospital auction was one of the gold standards by which charity auctions were compared. Deanna was proud of that fact and felt she had a right to take some of the credit. She'd been the chairwoman for the event more times than anyone else.

"Let's put it to a vote. Anyone disagree with

a 1950s Junior League ballroom theme?" No one did. "Good. Take it back to your committees. Let's get publicity rolling."

The next hour was spent discussing what each subcommittee was accomplishing, who had volunteered for what, and what services were still needed. By the end of the meeting, Deanna was exhausted.

"I'm getting too old to do this anymore," she commented to Georgia as they walked together toward the parking deck.

"Bunch of old cats," Georgia grumbled, referring to the other members. "I find myself with less and less tolerance for them every year."

"Julie's still young and ambitious enough to like the publicity, but I think most of the others do it out of a sincere commitment to the hospital."

"Connie never accepts a job that doesn't involve men, and Susan would shrivel up and die if she didn't get a daily infusion of gossip," Georgia said spitefully. "Yet for all their faults, we could never pull this pony show off every year without them."

"And some of their faults are quite useful," Deanna agreed. "Do you think Phil really is letting Alecia Weatherby redecorate his office?"

Georgia paled, her blue eyes stricken as she

met Deanna's gaze. "Oh, Deanna, how much did you hear?"

Deanna smiled. "Enough. Thanks for the defense, by the way, but answer the question."

"Why?"

They had stopped on the sidewalk in front of the parking deck, and Deanna held the collar of her coat close around her neck against the wind. "It's too complicated to discuss out here in the cold."

"Then follow me over to Tom Tom's and let's discuss it over something loaded with chocolate."

Thirty minutes later, facing each other over dessert and tea, Deanna explained why she was so interested in her ex-husband's office decor. "Do you remember that antique Persian rug I bought Phil when he moved into that office?"

Georgia's spoon arrested halfway to her mouth as realization dawned. Deanna had decorated Phil's office when he'd moved into the new building ten years ago. By redecorating his office, he was completing the removal of Deanna from his life, enlisting the aid of his latest girlfriend.

"She wouldn't," Georgia exclaimed, setting her spoon back in the dish, the dessert momentarily forgotten. "He wouldn't."

Deanna's throat clogged suddenly with unwanted tears at the unexpected revelation in Georgia's expression. She'd been thinking of the rug, not what Phil's removal of the rug signified. It was another step in his year-long effort to rid his life of her boring influence.

"You bought very expensive furniture for his office, Deanna, furniture befitting the city's most prominent pediatric heart surgeon. He'd be a fool to replace all that, though he's already proven he is, but surely his foolishness doesn't extend to redecorating."

"I hope it does," Deanna countered, trying to return to the safer, less personally threatening topic she had intended to discuss. "Ten years is a long time to look at the same decor." Like twenty-nine years was a long time to look at the same wife. She shoved the thought aside, concentrating on her goal. "Antiques or not, I'm sure he's open to the idea of change."

"You think he'll give them to you?"

Deanna knew Georgia had followed her line of thinking, and they were now discussing office furnishings. "I don't know if he'll get rid of everything, but you know what Alecia will do with that Persian rug."

"Tell him it's just a worn out, worthless old rug and have it hauled to the dump."

"Except it will never reach the dump. It will be sold to the next customer who hires her to find him an antique Oriental rug, which she will charge him full price for, plus her commission."

"You gotta admire her resourcefulness," Georgia said, licking chocolate off her spoon.

"Oh, I do," Deanna agreed, finding she had an appetite for her own dessert after all, "but if anyone is going to gouge Phil for that rug, it's going to be me. I saw it— and him— first."

Three

It was close to closing time when Evan noticed the big gray Buick Park Avenue pull up and park a safe distance from the motorcycles lined across the front of the dealership. He watched Deanna Randolph slide out, appraise the line of bikes, then take a deep breath and straighten her shoulders before heading resolutely toward the door. He smiled. It was obvious she had something on her mind and was prepared for a confrontation. He looked forward to it.

A low, appreciative whistle interrupted his thoughts. "Classy lady," Mike Johnson commented from beside him, also watching Deanna as she entered the showroom. "Whatever she's selling, I'd buy. Or is this one of those 'dealer only' perks?"

Mike was in his middle thirties, married with two kids. Still, Evan took exception to his comments about Deanna. "She's not selling anything," Evan said with more heat than he'd intended. He made an effort to modulate his tone. "She's here about an antique motorcycle she's having restored for a charity auction."

"Charity, huh?" Mike asked, finally turning his attention back to Evan. Seeing Evan's expression, Mike's smile faded. He cleared his throat to hide his discomfort, then took refuge in looking at his watch.

"Look at the time. I gotta get. Let me think about those brakes and I'll get back with you." Mike took the long way through the display racks, avoiding Deanna on his way to the door.

Evan shook his head at his own behavior. Deanna Randolph was a customer. He had no cause to get defensive about her with Mike, to the point of running off a potential sale. Evan walked over to intercept her before she made it as far as the counter at the back of the showroom. "Mrs. Randolph."

She turned to face him. "Mr. Maxwell, we need to talk. I hope this isn't an inconvenient time?"

"Not at all." He gestured toward his office.

She wore monochrome gray today, he noticed, following her. Her jacket and skirt were nicely fitted, like the white one she'd worn the last time, subtly emphasizing feminine curves. Her shoes and matching purse were of expensive looking leather. Even her hose and blouse were gray, her strand of pearls adding the only contrast. Where most women would have looked drab dressed like that, Deanna looked elegant. The color darkened her already dark brown eyes and added a radiant glow to her skin, or maybe that was anger. Today she took the chair he offered, perching gingerly at the edge of it, then faced him with a grim set to her mouth.

"First of all, I feel I owe you an apology, or at least an explanation, for Mother's behavior last week."

Evan smiled and waited. She'd had a week to come up with some really clever cover-up for common snobbery.

"She was already upset with me for wanting the motorcycle. Then when you and your son arrived wearing black leather jackets with Harley-Davidson all over them . . ." She paused and seemed to be searching for a tactful way to finish, but Evan knew what she was going to say and that there was no tactful way to say it.

"She thought we were members of the Hell's Angels," he finished for her, the words matter-of-fact. It happened a lot, a misconception the company and the individual HOG chapters worked constantly to correct.

Deanna looked chagrined but defended her mother. "She's seventy-eight years old and has lived a somewhat sheltered life. I've explained who you are, and she asked me to apologize for her."

"You didn't drive all the way up here to apologize for your mother."

"No. I came to deliver the check for the parts and to ask you to reconsider your labor price. Have you had time to look at the cycle?"

Evan leaned back in his chair and folded his arms across his chest. "Why should I reconsider my price? I'm already giving you a discount."

Deanna smiled at him, instantly making him wary. "The motorcycle is for charity, Mr. Maxwell, for the children. I'm willing to donate the parts. Couldn't you at least give us a break on the labor expense?"

First the apology, then the appeal to his conscience. The hard sell would come next, unless he detoured this conversation. "Why do you want to learn to ride it, Mrs. Randolph?"

He watched with satisfaction as flustered color rose in her cheeks and her hand went to the strand of pearls. He was beginning to recognize the pearl stroking as a nervous gesture. It made her more human, evidence of vulnerability. He wondered if she was aware she did it.

"It's hard to explain," she answered, not meeting his eyes. "To prove a point I guess. I always wanted to when I was younger but never could. I suspect my father of sabotaging my efforts."

"How?"

There was a spark of fire in her eyes as she met his gaze. "I'm not stupid, Mr. Maxwell. Motorized vehicles were more complicated back then. They had chokes and clutches and if I'm not mistaken, that motorcycle had a spark advance that had to be set just so prior to starting it, like on the old crank type cars."

No, she wasn't stupid, Evan thought with an impressed smile. "So after you prove you can start it, then what?"

"I want to learn to ride it. That's all you need to know. Last week you said that wasn't a problem. Has it become one?"

Something about Deanna Randolph's challenges did something deep inside Evan. The entire woman was a challenge. He shouldn't care why she wanted to ride the motorcycle, but he wanted to know. There was obviously more to it than proving a point. Or maybe the point she was trying to prove had nothing to do with her old man. The only way to find out was to teach her to ride. He wondered if she'd wear that skirt. It did great things for her legs. Sitting astride a motorcycle . . .

"Mr. Maxwell?"

"Saturday," Evan answered quickly, pulling

his attention back to her face. "Can you be here around ten?"

"This Saturday? You'll have it ready that quickly?" He heard the irritation in her voice and knew she was thinking about his labor fee again.

"You'll start on a little bike, then work up to one of similar weight and handling. I'm not about to let you lay down an antique Indian with original paint." He reached in his desk drawer and tossed a motorcycle handbook at her. "I suggest you read that between now and then. You'll need a learner's permit before you can take the bike out on the road, but Saturday we'll just work on the track out in back of the shop."

"Oh, of course." She picked up the book and slid it into her purse. "Saturday will be fine. Thank you." She stood up to leave, then hesitated.

"About your fee . . ."

"Let's start with parts," Evan compromised, "then see how many hours are involved."

He put the envelope containing her check in his desk drawer, unopened, then walked her to the entrance of the dealership. The shop was closed, the parking lot empty except for her Buick. He locked the door behind her then stood at the window until she was long out of sight.

"Classy lady."

Evan turned at the sound of Cloyd's voice

behind him. "I'm restoring her father's '53 Indian Chief."

"Brian says you're gonna teach her to ride it." There was a knowing gleam in the old man's pale blue eyes that Evan found annoying. He shouldn't have been surprised. It was hard to keep secrets when the three of them worked together as much as they did, and Cloyd had known him most of his life.

"She's paying for lessons," he said to defuse the situation.

"There's schools for such," Cloyd challenged.

"I haven't heard of any that teach people to ride antique motorcycles."

Cloyd took a thoughtful drag on his cigarette and looked out the window. "You sure that's all she wants to ride?"

"What's that supposed to mean?"

"I know you think you're too old for advice, but that woman's trouble."

Evan knew what was coming. "I'm also too old to be some society woman's plaything. Besides, Deanna isn't the type."

"After being married to Pauline you ought to know."

"Deanna's nothing like Pauline was. Deanna's much more serious."

"She's been up here twice, for things that

could'a been handled over the phone or by mail. She widowed or divorced?"

"I haven't asked, and neither has she. It isn't relevant."

"There's no fool like an old fool," Cloyd quoted, shaking his head and walking back up to the counter, leaving Evan to stare out the window at the empty parking lot and wonder.

"I don't think Cloyd likes me," Deanna commented Saturday morning as they walked out to the test track. She'd tried to make small talk with the old man while waiting for Evan but had been rebuffed with short, curt responses. "Are you supposed to be working today?"

"Don't let him get to you. That's just the way Cloyd is." She hadn't worn a skirt, Evan had noticed right away. She was dressed elegantly but practically in wool slacks and low-heeled leather shoes. He wondered if she was wearing the pearls under her jacket, which was zipped to her throat against the wind.

"Doesn't that run off customers?"

Evan laughed at that. "Hardly. People come here from all over to talk to Cloyd. He's been with Harley-Davidson since the war." His eyes sparkled as he looked down at her. "That's World War II."

"Oh." Deanna wasn't sure how else to respond. "How long have you been with him?"

"Cloyd and my dad were partners until Dad's death two years ago. When I retired from the Air Force in '91, Dad wasn't in good health and asked if I was interested in buying him out. I did."

"You had to pay your father?" Deanna was incredulous at the idea.

Evan, rather than taking offense, seemed amused. "I have a younger brother. What we actually did was figure out what Dad's share was worth, then divide it by two. I bought out my brother's share of the dealership. That's where the Indians are I told you I rebuilt for myself. I signed the titles over to him for my share of the dealership. Brian took out a mortgage to buy out my brother's share of the house."

Deanna wasn't sure she understood. "Brian lives with you?" She realized immediately that she'd overstepped polite boundaries. "I'm sorry, I guess it's none of my business."

"Brian is divorced, also," Evan said, smiling at Deanna's flustered state. "Between us two bachelors, we're trying to raise Kyle in as close to a family environment as we can manage. With both of us at the dealership so much, it gets difficult sometimes."

Bachelors. He was divorced, also. Had it been his idea or hers? How long ago? It didn't matter. She had hired him to rebuild her motorcycle and teach her to ride it, nothing more.

"Cloyd's an old bachelor, too," Evan was saying. "He never married, has no children. He's letting Brian buy out his share of the dealership, so one day we'll own it between us." He chuckled then, a deep, rich sound that made Deanna smile with him. "Of course Cloyd's going to have to live to be two hundred at the rate Brian's paying him. How about you? Any kids?"

It was a common enough question. He had shared information about his life, it was only fair to share some of hers. "Three children," Deanna supplied, "all grown now." She didn't understand why, but she didn't want to tell him she was divorced, a woman cast aside by another man. Children were relatively safe topics, though.

"Jeff is in investments with his uncle, my brother, Sherylyn is in her last year of residency to be a pediatric surgeon, and Eric just graduated from the University of Georgia. He's an architect, now working for my other brother." She smiled at him. "I guess we keep everything in the family, too. Is that the motorcycle?"

They had reached the edge of the test track where a small Japanese-made motorcycle waited for them. Evan studied her a moment before answering. "Yes, your first trainer."

Was he wondering why she hadn't mentioned a husband in all that? She was sure he'd noticed she no longer wore a wedding ring. "You won't allow an Indian in your shop but you'll allow a Japanese competitor on your track?"

He smiled at that. "You're very astute." Admiration warmed his hazel eyes and in turn warmed Deanna. "Japanese motorcycles have given Harley some stiff competition. They are highly reliable and much lower in cost, plus come in assorted smaller sizes, like this 250. Harley purists refer to them as rice burners, but since Harley doesn't build anything smaller than 883cc's, I have no choice. This is borrowed, by the way, so don't wreck it. The man who owns it thinks you're crazy to take lessons in December."

"What do the Japanese call Harleys?" Deanna couldn't resist asking.

The question seemed to catch Evan off guard, then he smiled again. "Outrageously overpriced." He immediately switched the subject. "Did you read that handbook I sent home with you?"

"I read it. I'm ready, except for the boots. I'm still shopping for those."

"I was referring to operating the motorcycle."

Deanna gave him a level look. "I'm ready for that, too." It seemed like she was going to have to continuously prove herself to this man.

"Good, let's review the systems then."

He stood very close to her, close enough that she could smell his aftershave and feel his body heat, even though they both wore jackets and gloves. "You did study," he praised, when she'd named all the parts correctly and knew their function. "Throw your leg over it and try it on for size."

Deanna's hand brushed his as she took the handlebars. Rather than move, he continued to hold them, steadying the bike for her to get on. He stood so close, there was no way to mount the bike without her shoulder butting into his side. Her entire body went on alert, compounded by the wanton way her legs straddled the motorcycle. She was now eye level with his belt.

Pay attention, she commanded her brain, as Evan continued his instructions, apparently not as affected by her nearness as she was by his.

"We're not going to start it up right now, but I want you to use the clutch as if it was in gear." He put his left hand over hers.

"Squeeze hard," he instructed, pulling the clutch lever back with her.

He smelled clean, with a hint of spice and the masculine scent of leather. He was a big man, and he surrounded her as he leaned over her, his hands over hers, his upper body leaning into her back. Deanna was glad she'd studied the book so hard, because she was certainly having a difficult time concentrating on what he was saying.

"Your front brake is three-fourths of your braking power," Evan continued, squeezing her right hand and the lever under it. "Feel how it grabs?" He rolled the bike forward slightly, then squeezed the lever again. The bike jerked to a stop. "Now feel the rear brake."

All Deanna could feel was the pounding of her heart. Rear brake— right foot. She put her right foot on the pedal. "I'll hold the bike," Evan promised. "Push forward, then stop, using the rear brake only."

The bike slowed gently, then Evan was back surrounding her again. She was tempted to lean back into him, then straightened herself rigidly. He was trying to teach her to ride a motorcycle and she was behaving like a teenager developing a crush on a handsome teacher.

"Always use both brakes to stop, remembering that the front one is much more powerful.

You grab it too hard, the bike will come to an abrupt halt and you'll go over the handlebars.''

Pleasant thought.

"And never, ever, stop with your front wheel turned. It'll go down like a rock. That's not much of a problem with these little bikes. You can usually hold them up. You overbalance that big Indian, you'll go down with it.''

Another pleasant thought. Deanna sighed. This was more complicated than she'd realized.

"Okay, I'll give you a push. Use both brakes and bring it to a smooth stop.''

Wheel straight, clutch in, squeeze gently. The bike jerked to an abrupt stop, throwing Deanna forward. She clenched her teeth.

"Try it again.''

She did it again, and again, and again after that. He had her push the bike, standing to one side of it. He had her straddle it and push it backward. She was amazed to learn there was no reverse on a motorcycle. By the time they'd been out on the track for two hours, she'd forgotten how warm his presence made her feel. She was cold, she was tired of pushing the motorcycle around, and Evan Maxwell was acting more like a drill sergeant than a benevolent teacher. She still hadn't started the engine.

She understood why the Honda's owner thought she was crazy. It was early December, and in spite of the sunshine, the wind was sharp. Her nose had gone numb, her ears burned, and her hair probably looked like a rat's nest. Her thin kid driving gloves were no match for the cold metal brake and clutch levers. Her legs ached from both the cold and the unaccustomed exercise. She was tempted to run over Evan instead of braking to a stop beside him. She glared at him as she brought the bike to a smooth stop for the third time in a row. She wasn't going to do it again, she didn't care what he said.

"Let's break for lunch," Evan suggested. "You look cold."

Breaking for lunch suggested more drills after lunch. As she'd done all morning, Deanna again reminded herself that she had asked for this, and riding her father's Indian again was worth a few hours of cold and humiliation. Still, she didn't have to do it all in one day.

"I didn't plan to be here all day," she lied, carefully setting the cycle on its stand the way she'd been instructed then facing Evan. "I have things I need to do this afternoon."

Evan regarded her thoughtfully. "Let's get warmed up first." He turned and started for the shop. Deanna followed, not wanting to stand outside in the cold and argue.

"Hot chocolate or coffee?" he asked, holding the door to his office open.

The warmth inside the building was almost painful, and Deanna slid gratefully into the worn leather chair, grease stains being the least of her concerns today. "Hot chocolate please."

"There's a bathroom at the end of the hall," he offered discreetly, then left.

In the bathroom, Deanna washed her hands, reveling in the tingling pain as circulation returned to her cold fingers. Evan must think her a complete idiot. Two hours of drills she couldn't seem to complete to his satisfaction—he wouldn't even trust her to start the thing. She wasn't as strong as she'd thought. This man's rejection was salt in a still open wound. She couldn't take anymore today.

She did the best she could with her windblown hair, applied fresh lipstick to her chapped lips, and wished she had some moisturizer for her face. Promising herself a full facial treatment that night, she returned to the office.

"Hi!" The enthusiastic greeting came from four-year-old Kyle, who was bouncing in his grandfather's lap behind the desk.

"I hope you don't mind if Kyle joins us for hot chocolate?" Evan asked, restraining the energetic child with one arm to keep him from falling. "When we're both here on Saturdays, Kyle comes with us."

Deanna smiled at him. If she concentrated on the child, she wouldn't have to think about how endearing Evan looked, sitting behind his big desk with a four-year-old on his lap. "Hi, Kyle. Do you like hot chocolate?"

"Yup. We made you some."

Deanna noticed the steaming black mug of chocolate sitting on her side of the desk. "Thank you." The first sip warmed her from the inside out, defusing some of her frustration. She unzipped her jacket but didn't remove it. She wasn't staying long.

She'd worn the pearls, Evan noticed immediately, over a soft fuzzy sweater. Her hair was softer, too, the wind having blown out some of the stiffness. She had high color in her cheeks, which Evan knew wasn't all due to chapped skin. She was one frustrated lady, and he had a good idea why.

"You did great out there," he offered.

Deanna wasn't mollified. She picked up her mug and studied the Harley-Davidson emblem stamped on the side. "Is everything motorcycles with you?"

Evan gave a deep sigh and set Kyle off his lap. Undeterred, the child began turning circles in the narrow space between the desk and the wall, accompanied by engine noises. Evan watched him, his hazel eyes filling with tenderness as he spoke.

"Has been for the last three years, I guess. Owning the business is pretty demanding. Doesn't leave much time for other things"

The tenderness in his eyes and the sadness in his voice tugged at Deanna's heart, which irritated her. It was easier to be angry with him, and safer.

When he met her gaze she felt impaled by the emotions she saw, the warmth. It vibrated in his voice. "I know this morning was no fun, but you really did do great. This afternoon we'll start the motorcycle up, and you'll understand the importance of all those drills."

Deanna had already lied about other commitments and had no intention of admitting she had none. Although she resented what she considered his treating her like a child, it made her far less susceptible to his smile. "I can't stay."

"Believe it or not, I'm following the same program used by the state," Evan hastened to assure her. "They spend the entire first session pushing the cycle around, learning to handle it and use the brakes. It's probably less frustrating when you do it in a group rather than one-on-one, but it's necessary for safety reasons."

"I felt like a fool," Deanna finally admitted.

"I know. I don't teach very often, so I probably don't do it well, but I've seen people do handstands on their handlebars and land in front of their motorcycles because they didn't understand how to use the front brake. They felt foolish all the way to the hospital."

"I can do that," Kyle bragged. "Watch me." He did a modified cartwheel, landing in a heap against his grandfather's legs, complete with crash sound effects.

"Go out in the showroom to practice," Evan said, laughing and giving him a playful swat as he stood him back on his feet. "There's not room in here."

Kyle ran out, but not before Evan had caught Deanna smiling at the child's antics. So, she liked kids.

"I seem to remember you mentioning grandchildren," he said, thinking she didn't look old enough to have grandchildren.

"I have a grandson Kyle's age and a new baby granddaughter. They live in Marietta, and I don't see them as often as I'd like. Everyone's so busy it seems. Brady's in gymnastics, too, like Kyle. He's not too good at cartwheels yet, either."

Evan didn't correct her. Kyle's gymnastics were self-taught, mostly from watching the other kids at the preschool and encouraged by his father and grandfather. With Evan's and Brian's long hours at the dealership, there wasn't time for extracurricular activities for Kyle. Evan wondered if that was being fair to Kyle.

It was hard to say which tore at Deanna's heart more, when Evan turned that hungry wolf look on her or when his eyes grew misty watching his grandson. Both made her long to respond to him, a dangerous temptation. She stood up abruptly, mentally knocking the temptation aside.

"Thank you for the chocolate." She set the mug on his desk and stood up, reaching in her jacket pocket for her car keys. "And thank you for the lesson. I'll keep in mind what you said about the handstand."

"Do you at least have time for lunch?" Evan also jumped to his feet, meeting her at the office door. "Buford has a great McDonald's." He flashed her his most charming smile.

He was standing too close and, without anger, as a shield. Deanna felt the impact of his smile clear to her toes. "I really can't," she insisted, fighting panic. "I didn't realize you intended to do this all day, or I wouldn't have made other plans. You know how it is this close to Christmas what with shopping and parties and I always bake cookies for the children."

She was babbling. When she finally met his steady gaze she knew he didn't believe a word she'd said and was taking her rejection personally. His disappointment in her rejection threatened to be her final undoing. "Is there another day we can schedule?"

"How about next Saturday, weather permitting?" he asked evenly.

"Could we start after lunch, when it's a little warmer?" Great, she thought, first babbling, now whining.

"We'll start whenever you get here."

Deanna's hands were shaking when she finally escaped to the relative safety of her car and didn't stop until she was halfway back to Atlanta. She hated Evan thinking of her as a coward and a liar, not to mention a babbling idiot and a whiner. Maybe if he thought poorly of her he'd quit looking at her as if she were a feast to be savored slowly, and he'd quit smiling at her in ways that sent her thoughts in dangerous directions.

Re-entering social life was supposed to involve accepting dinner invitations from eligible men from her own social circle or from friends of hers who had single friends and family members they wanted her to meet. That was safe. That was an environment she understood. She didn't know what to do with a man who touched her so casually, as if it was his right, who yelled at her inexperienced handling of the motorcycle as if she were one of his recruits, whose eyes went misty when he watched his grandson do clumsy cartwheels across his office.

It didn't matter how her body responded to his smile, to the feel of his hand over hers, to the warm scent that came to her when he leaned close. They had nothing in common. Entertaining romantic notions about Evan Maxwell was setting herself up for another bad fall. She needed his professional expertise to restore her motorcycle and to teach her to ride it. No matter how handsome she found the man or how much he reminded her of how long it had been since she'd been intimate with a man, that was all their relationship could ever be— strictly professional.

Four

Charlotte Edwards had been holding court with her family every Sunday for brunch at the country club since Deanna could remember. As the family grew, married, and had families of their own, fewer and fewer of the members attended every week, but they were all expected to come at least once a month to pay their respects, as a family duty. Deanna knew she was in trouble when both her brothers came to church that morning, then positioned themselves one on each side of their mother at the large table the dining room kept reserved for Joseph Edwards's widow. They had hardly started the first course before Charlotte opened Pandora's box.

"You remember that horrid motorcycle your father bought back when you boys were in school?" Charlotte asked conversationally. "Deanna dragged it out a couple of weeks ago to put in her auction. She tells me your father was right, that it's now a collector's item and quite valuable."

Pete and Andrew both stared at Deanna, Pete with accusation, Andrew with surprise. "You would sell Dad's motorcycle?" Pete asked.

Deanna tried to act disinterested, as if the cycle had no personal meaning to her. "Billy Adonis donated one, told me how valuable they had become. I remembered Dad's and thought it would be clever to have two of them in the auction. It's just been sitting out in the carriage house rusting away. I didn't think anyone would care."

"You might have asked," Andrew said, sounding hurt. "You should have asked us if we wanted it before you took it upon yourself to give it away."

"I'm hardly giving it away," Deanna defended herself. "You know how Dad was about Children's Hospital. He was one of their biggest private sponsors, always hoping to improve the health of children."

"Ever since Angelica died there," Charlotte interjected. Angelica had died of leukemia when she was eight, Deanna five. Neither parent had ever gotten over losing her.

"And we've all carried on Dad's legacy," Deanna said. "I thought he'd be proud to know his motorcycle was being put to good use after all these years."

"What kind was it, Mom?" Eric, her youngest, asked. Still single and now working with Andrew, Eric usually attended Sunday brunch with the family. Deanna explained to him about her father's Indian.

"It's so fifties," she concluded, smiling at her grown son. "Big fenders that almost enclose the wheels, big round headlight, it even has an Indian head fender ornament on the front, like the hood ornament of a car. It looked so sad, with two flat tires, all covered with dust. Evan says it's in remarkable shape, but it looks pretty pitiful to me."

"Who's Evan?" her brothers asked almost simultaneously.

Deanna felt her face grow warm.

"He's from the Hell's Angels," her mother said in a low voice, as if someone might overhear. "Deanna says she has references on him, but he came out with a young hoodlum, both of them wearing black leather jackets with Harley-Davidson patches all over them."

Deanna supposed when a woman was seventy-eight she was allowed to be set in her ways, but she was getting tired of defending Evan to her mother. "He owns the Harley-Davidson dealership in Buford. I have three references on him as an expert in Indian restoration, and the hoodlum is his son, who lives with him and works with him and who is raising his four-year-old son without a mother."

The entire family had stopped eating, watching her with curious expressions, as were a few people from surrounding tables. Deanna felt herself blushing again. She'd gotten a little carried away. "I doubt there's even a chapter of Hell's Angels in Atlanta," she finished lamely, then took a long drink of her water.

"So this is a done deal?" Pete asked. "We have nothing to say about it?"

"If the motorcycle was so important, Pete, why haven't you done something about it before now?" Deanna demanded.

"I didn't think I needed to. I didn't think my sister would take it upon herself to give it away."

Pete's wife, Nancy, laid a restraining hand on her husband's arm.

"You're sixty years old, Pete," Deanna pointed out. "When were you going to do something with it?"

"I have two sons," Pete reminded her, "maybe three." He looked down at Nancy, now four months pregnant, then back at Deanna. "Andrew has a son. Did you ask Eric? Or Jeff?"

"Why is it only the sons and grandsons, Pete?" Deanna demanded, irritated as much with her brother's chauvinistic attitude as with his belated concern over a forty-year-old motorcycle. "Why am I not just as entitled to that motorcycle as you or Andrew. Does my being a daughter make me less his child?"

"It's obvious you don't care about the cycle," Pete said. "You're giving it away."

Pete was an investments broker, like their father had been before him and now Deanna's oldest son Jeff. His mind worked in profits and investment potential. Deanna narrowed her eyes at him. "What bothers you most about me having the motorcycle, Pete? The fact that I'm taking it out of the family or the fact that you've just realized it's worth something?"

Pete flushed an angry red, but the others at the table laughed. "I haven't thought about that old motorcycle in years," Andrew said. "What's it worth now, Deanna?"

"Billy gave twenty thousand for his '55 five years ago. He tells me Dad's should be worth more, because it's a '53, the last year they were built in America."

Andrew gave a low, appreciative whistle. "Amazing. The old man was right."

"I didn't mean to start a family feud," Charlotte said, looking at each of her three children. "I'd forgotten about that old motorcycle until Deanna asked for it. Pete's right, Deanna. I should have asked him, as your father's oldest son."

"It's your motorcycle, Mother," Deanna said, frustrated at the unfairness of a society that still taught their women to defer to their men, regardless of their ages. "You may dispose of it as you see fit." But possession was nine-tenths of the law, and Deanna was prepared to fight for her right to keep the Indian, even if she had to put it in the auction and bid on it herself. "Think of it as going to Angelica, Mother."

She caught Pete's glare and knew she was fighting dirty, but so were they, using their gender to sway their mother into taking back something she'd already given Deanna.

"I suppose if we want Dad's motorcycle, we'll have to attend the auction and bid on it," Andrew said calmly, taking a bite of his food as if he'd accepted the situation. "I'd sure like to come see it, though, when you get it restored."

Deanna smiled her gratitude. "Thanks, Andrew. I'll let you know." She turned her attention back to Pete, waiting warily.

"I just wish you'd asked," Pete grouched, which Deanna took as relinquishment of his claim.

"Thanks, Pete. You're right and I'm sorry. I was just so excited, I didn't think." She could afford to be gracious. She'd won.

"So when do we know what the baby is?" she asked Nancy, knowing she'd had an amniocentesis during the past week because of her age. Nancy was thirty-five, Pete's second wife, with two school-age boys from a previous marriage who fidgeted and squirmed through the adult-dominated meal. Deanna had been appalled when she'd learned of her brother's intent to marry a woman so much younger than himself, but over the years she'd grown to love Nancy and her energetic boys. The pregnancy had been quite a surprise to all of them, but Nancy seemed to glow as she talked about it.

"It takes several weeks to get the results back," Nancy said. "The ultrasound looked great, though, the doctor said. He thinks it's a girl."

"After four boys," Pete said, referring to his two now grown sons as well as Nancy's two, "she'll be spoiled rotten."

"I grew up with two older brothers," Deanna said, giving Pete an affectionate smile. "I think she'll survive."

"You were spoiled rotten, too," Pete said, and the family brunch continued with good-natured teasing flowing back and forth.

Deanna supposed she had been spoiled rotten, but she'd never been allowed to go outside the boundaries set by being a girl and being brought up in the rigid social strata that was present in Atlanta during the '50s and '60s. But the times were changing and attitudes were changing, although sometimes it didn't seem like it when she listened to her family argue. Still, the younger generations were having some influence on the old. She'd just challenged her older brothers' right to inherit their father's motorcycle, definitely a masculine asset, and won.

It was a beginning. Tomorrow she would confront Phil in an effort to regain the antiques she'd purchased for his office. She hoped her persuasive reasoning would be as successful with him.

In their twenty-nine years of marriage, Dr. Phillip Randolph had become one of Atlanta's most prominent pediatric heart surgeons. His research had won him national and even international acclaim. He was invited to speak at seminars all over the world, and patients were referred to him from across the nation. He not only did surgery, he taught at the school of medicine and served as mentor to pediatric surgical residents. He spent hours doing research on new and better procedures to help children born with life-threatening heart defects. He was constantly writing and publishing his findings and reading journals to learn what others had found.

For twenty-nine years Deanna had seen to his comforts, organized his life, managed his office, raised children he could be proud of. She had been the perfect hostess when they'd entertained, attended countless events as his gracious and elegant wife, worn his name proudly through years of charity work. She had worn furs and diamonds to display his wealth, acquiesced to his greater wisdom, understood the enormous strain being a brilliant physician put on a man. She had been the perfect society wife, fulfilling the role she'd been trained for from birth.

She'd thought she understood her husband perfectly. She'd tried to anticipate his needs. Apparently, she'd missed a signal somewhere. To Phil's credit, he hadn't cheated on her, not to her knowledge anyway. He had simply come home one day, right after New Year's, told her she was boring and predictable and he wanted a divorce. He'd spent the next two days packing, while Deanna alternated between begging for a better explanation, demanding counseling, and crying over the injustice of the entire situation. He had been infuriatingly unmoved by any of her efforts. Finally, he'd looked down his aristocratic nose at her, told her she was pathetic, and walked out of her life.

Lawyers had done the rest. Deanna had pulled years of experience into play, wrapped herself in a shell of polite propriety, and pretended everything was fine. That's what she'd been taught to do when things were too unpleasant to deal with. She had demanded the house and everything in it, her car, and half of their investments. To her brother Pete's horror, she had refused alimony, preferring to reduce her life-style slightly and to live on her own assets, inherited through her family, than to feel like she owed Phil anything.

Her pride was in shreds, thanks to Phil, but due to her family's holdings she had been able to salvage some of it. Most women she knew in similar situations had been forced to find a job, sell their homes, and live in greatly reduced circumstances unless they remarried or moved in with their children. Deanna had no intention of doing either. She'd thrown herself into her hospital work, played bridge with her friends, and withdrawn from her previously active social life. Then she'd seen Billy's Indian and gotten angry, not at Phil but at herself for believing the labels placed on her by men.

Deanna drove past Phil's office every time she went to Children's Hospital, since it was located in the new medical building across the street. She'd only recently forced herself to stop looking that way every time she drove past it. It felt strange now to deliberately turn into the parking lot. Such a mundane action, both achingly familiar and somewhat threatening.

Deanna brusquely pulled the key from the ignition, knowing that if she started dwelling on the possibility of rejection, she'd lose her nerve. She needed to focus on confidence, not self-doubt. She pulled down the visor to check her reflection in the mirror one last time. She moistened dry lips and carefully fluffed the hair at her temples. Her hair was fine. Her lipstick was fine. The furrow between her brows was not. She forced her face to relax.

"All he can do is tell you no," she told her reflection. "You should be used to hearing that from him by now." She quickly gathered her purse, got out of the car, and locked the door before she could think about what else he could do. The same practiced poise that had carried her through the last year now carried her through the lobby, up the elevator, and to the door with the tasteful brass plaque that read "Phillip J. Randolph, M.D., Pediatric Surgeon." She paused only an instant, then resolutely pushed open the door.

The waiting room was empty, for which

Deanna was grateful. She'd timed her visit to catch Phil between his last morning appointment and lunch. She was also relieved to see that nothing had changed since her last visit. She hoped that meant Alecia hadn't started redecorating yet. A very young receptionist Deanna didn't recognize smiled a greeting at her from behind a counter.

"May I help you?"

"I'm here to see Dr. Randolph," Deanna said in a manner designed to let the girl know she was someone important and not to be taken lightly.

The girl responded with a nervous glance at her appointment book. "Is he expecting you?"

"No, but I'd appreciate it if you'd tell him I'm here. I'm Mrs. Randolph."

Deanna held her polite smile while the receptionist squirmed uncomfortably. "He's with a patient right now, Mrs. Randolph, but I'll let him know you're here."

"Thank you."

Deanna took a seat in one of the comfortable chairs she'd picked out when this waiting room had last needed redecorating. It didn't seem so long ago, but it had been at least five years. She thought her choices had held up rather well, the colors still bright, the fabrics still intact. Alecia would buy things that needed replacing soon, hoping to generate more business in the near future. Deanna stifled a sigh. It wasn't her concern any longer.

The door to the inner office opened and a young couple with a small boy came through. Deanna recognized the features, though not the child. He suffered from Down's syndrome, and Deanna knew from experience that the chromosomal abnormality frequently involved cardiac as well as other internal defects. She quickly scanned the parents' faces, seeking clues to his prognosis. They appeared relaxed, a good sign.

"Hello, Deanna."

Deanna startled, having temporarily forgotten Phil in her effort to seek reassurance about the little boy. She stood up, searching Phil's face for clues even more avidly than she had the unknown couple who'd just left. He was smiling at her, taking her in from head to toe and apparently pleased with what he saw. At least he didn't look down his nose at her, act like he was going to send her packing without hearing what she came for. She had lived with this man for twenty-nine years, yet her heart was pounding nervously and her palms were damp.

"Hello, Phil. I hope this isn't inconvenient, dropping by like this."

"Not at all. Come on back. We can talk in my office."

They were speaking politely, like strangers. Still, they were speaking. Deanna accepted his gesture to precede him down the hall. The eerie feelings returned. Everything was so familiar, unchanged, as if her last visit had been last week, instead of nearly a year ago.

Deanna had decorated the waiting room in a colorful combination designed to be comfortable for the parents as well as entertaining for the children. The examining rooms had been designed to put the children at ease, minimizing the technology and its associated pain. But Phil's office, she had felt, should reassure the parents that Phil was a qualified surgeon and that his advice should be taken seriously. She had done it in rich natural colors and glowing wood. His many degrees and awards were framed and displayed on a prominent wall. Well-read medical volumes filled his bookshelves, and an impressive view of the medical center was visible from the large windows behind his desk. The antique Oriental rug was still on the floor in front of the desk, the twin leather chairs arranged on it, where countless worried parents had sat to discuss the outcome of their child's future.

Deanna sat there now, looking at the man whose life had been entwined with hers for twenty-nine years, who'd become a stranger to her. Her feelings for him were a confusing maelstrom of grief, anger, and even a little guilt. It had been almost a year, and she still wasn't certain what had happened. If she'd seen it coming, could she have prevented it? Did divorcing her give Phil whatever it was he thought he needed?

He was still a handsome man. She wasn't sure what she'd expected, or maybe hoped for— him to go to seed without her nurturing? At fifty-four he was the epitome of a distinguished, mature surgeon. He stood tall and straight, with a slender, boyish frame that would probably never go to fat. He would probably never lose his hair either. It was gradually turning silver, starting at the temples. Instead of making him look old, it made him seem more mature.

He was looking at her as if seeing her for the first time. "You look great, Deanna."

She wondered if his thoughts were similar to hers. Did he think she'd fall apart without him? She almost had, but he'd never know it.

"Thank you." She wasn't going to return the compliment, then remembered her purpose for being here. "I was thinking the same about you."

"Is this a social visit, or is something on your mind?"

A short, nervous laugh escaped Deanna. Phil hated nothing worse than wasting time. As usual, he wanted to skip the amenities and get to the point. This Phil she knew how to talk to.

"I heard you're planning to redecorate. If you're planning to get rid of the rug, I'd like to put it in the auction. There's an incredible market for antique Oriental rugs, even more so than when I bought it."

"Ah, Deanna, ever the crusader." He had not sat down when Deanna had. He stood on the rug under discussion, leaning back against the edge of his desk. He continued to study her with a thoughtful expression that made her nervous.

"I'm afraid Alecia has been talking out of turn. She'd like to redecorate my office, but I haven't agreed. In fact, since she and I are no longer seeing each other, I don't think your rug's in jeopardy."

Deanna couldn't help it. A thrill of malicious pleasure speared through her at his words. He might have rejected her, but at least he hadn't exchanged her for someone like Alecia Weatherby. Then again, Phil's taking up with Alecia would have proven, at least in some circles, that he had taken leave of his senses, absolving Deanna of any wrongdoing.

"I didn't mean to waste your time over idle

gossip, Phil. I just thought that if you were going to get rid of the rug, I should make my interest in it known."

"I'll keep that in mind."

He continued to appraise her. Deanna wished she could read his mind. She stood up to leave, uncomfortable with the situation.

He surprised her by walking her out to her car, talking casually about people they both knew. His eyes caressed her with a warmth that confused her. She could almost believe he was flirting with her. The suspicion was confirmed when she tried to tell him goodbye.

"I'm glad you stopped by today," he said, holding her car door open after she'd slid inside. "It's made me realize I've missed your company. I think you've been avoiding me at the hospital."

Of course she'd been avoiding him at the hospital. He'd made it perfectly clear the last time they'd talked, over the dispensation of their estate, that he wanted nothing more to do with her. Now, she listened to his words with suspicion.

"I know the divorce wasn't your idea, Deanna, but we're adults. We have a lot in common— the children, the hospital."

Twenty-nine years of marriage, Deanna

added silently. He'd certainly taken his time about having second thoughts.

"I've said some unforgivable things, Deanna, but I'd like a chance to talk. Could we have dinner sometime?"

Eleven months ago, she'd made a total fool of herself trying to make him talk to her. Six months ago, she still would have given him a chance, before the divorce was final. Since the divorce, she'd forced herself to begin accepting the situation and she was just now finally making some progress in putting it all behind her. The last thing she needed was another emotional roller coaster ride with Phil Randolph.

"Why, Phil?"

"Just to talk. I'd like to be friends, at least."

"We were never friends." They had been lovers, parents, and partners, but one thing Deanna had been able to figure out in the long months since the divorce was that they had never been friends. The realization had made her sad. His plea for friendship now hurt.

"We still have children, Deanna."

"They're grown, Phil." But she agreed with him. They were still a family, something she felt strongly about. She didn't enjoy sneaking around the hospital, either, trying not to run into him. Giving up her auxiliary work to avoid him was unthinkable.

"Please, Deanna."

Contrition? From Phil? The attitude was such a foreign one, Deanna became even more wary.

"Twenty-nine years of marriage, Deanna, surely that justifies giving a man a second chance."

Deanna frowned. "A second chance at what?"

"To be friends," Phil hastened to explain. "To talk, to have dinner."

"Why, Phil?" she asked again. "Why now? Why today? Why did you wait until I came by your office? You know where I live and you know the phone number."

He looked down at the ground and didn't answer for a moment, trying to come up with something persuasive, Deanna was certain.

"This is going to sound corny as hell," he finally said. "I made a terrible mistake last year, Deanna. I was dissatisfied with my life and I blamed you." He looked up at her, his brown eyes pleading. "But you weren't the problem. I've been even more miserable this past year without you."

If he expected sympathy from her, he must have an even lower opinion of her intelligence than she'd thought. "And you didn't realize it until I walked into your office, right?"

He gave her a sheepish smile. "I told you

it sounded corny. You know how I am, Deanna. From dawn to midnight, and sometimes all night, I have patients, students, phone calls . . ."

Deanna gave him a dubious look. She hadn't spent the past year buried in a hole. Phil's social life was always the latest gossip on the hospital grapevine. He changed tactics.

"Okay, but it's true that you've been avoiding me at the hospital. I haven't seen you in months. Then you walked in today and it just hit me . . . like a revelation from heaven . . ."

"I'd leave heaven out of this, Phil, if I were you."

He squatted down to her level. In his suit pants and his lab coat Dr. Phillip Randolph squatted down in the parking lot beside Deanna and took her hand. "You weren't the problem, Deanna. You were the best thing I had going in my life, and I've been a fool."

Jerk, was the term used to describe him among Deanna's family and friends, but fool was close enough. She just wasn't sure she believed that he believed it. The real question was, did she care? Unfortunately, she did. She'd thought herself over him, but now that he was here, holding her hand and pleading with her, she realized she couldn't get over him until she understood what had happened.

She'd asked him to talk a year ago. It had taken him a year and her stopping by his office, but what was a year after twenty-nine years of marriage? They had children together. They worked in the same hospital, lived in the same town, moved in the same social circles. Deanna's decision to re-enter society and begin dating among her peers meant she would run into Phil from time to time. It would be nice if they could at least be cordial with one another.

"I could pick you up Friday night," he pressed on, obviously taking her silence for acquiescence. "I'll come by the house at seven o'clock. We'll go out to dinner, somewhere nice, and we'll talk."

She nodded her agreement, her stomach a knot of ambivalent feelings. Phil squeezed her hand, then stood up.

"I'm really glad you came by today, Deanna," he said, smiling down at her. "See you Friday." He stepped back to shut her door.

It was just dinner, Deanna thought, driving away. They would talk, he would explain what he should have explained a year ago, and they would part friends. It was nothing to get so upset about. But she was upset. Phil's unexpected behavior had blown her fragile composure. Her hands didn't stop shaking until long after she'd arrived home.

Five

Tuesday morning Deanna played the worst game of bridge since her sorority days in college. The silence during the drive home was almost more than she could take. She'd already apologized three times, but Georgia still wasn't talking, an unheard of situation. Deanna gave up and stared sullenly out the window. She opened the car door as soon as Georgia pulled into her driveway.

"Thanks for driving."

"Deanna, don't go." It was an impassioned plea, filled with anguish. From stony silence to melodrama. Sometimes Georgia was too much.

"It was just a game, Georgia, as you so often—"

"Don't go out with Phil."

Deanna stopped cold and looked at her friend. Her beautiful blue eyes flashed with anger, but Deanna realized it wasn't over their poor bridge game. "Why not?"

"You're too vulnerable, that's why not. Trust

me, honey. I know you and I've been right where you are. He'll hurt you— again."

Deanna leaned back into the leather upholstery with a sigh. "I'm afraid of that, too, but— "

"But nothing." Georgia switched off the engine and twisted to face Deanna. "You're looking for closure— "

"You like that word," Deanna interjected. "First Dad, now Phil?"

"Your daddy adored you and left you grieving over a natural loss. Phil ripped your life apart and left you with a million dangling loose ends."

Deanna had to smile. Georgia loved metaphors. She had to admit, this one was a fair description of how she'd felt, still felt sometimes.

"You are made of too strong a fabric to fray," Georgia continued, "but sometimes you're too analytical for your own good. I've watched you struggle to make sense out of this whole mess. You've raked yourself over the coals with blame for crimes you did not commit. I know what you're thinking. 'If I go out with him Friday night, maybe I'll understand what happened.' "

Deanna winced. Georgia knew her too well and once again her uncanny insight was right on target.

"You're wrong, Deanna. That's not what

will happen Friday night. Phil is and always will be a self-centered, conceited jerk. He's been free just long enough to realize the grass is not greener on the other side of the fence and he wants his comfortable life back."

"He just wants to be friends," Deanna objected, not wanting to believe what Georgia was saying.

"That's what Bill said, too, but what they really want is safe sex and someone to pick their shirts up at the cleaners."

"I would never—"

"Yes, you will," Georgia interrupted. "I did, and from what I've read and from other divorced women I've talked to it's a real common phenomenon." Georgia reached over and grasped Deanna's hand. "You're hurting, honey, and lonely. You miss the intimacy. You need to be held by a man. He's a familiar man and in your heart and mind he's still your husband. Sleep with the biker."

Deanna jerked her head up. Georgia couldn't have shocked her more if she'd slapped her. "What?"

"Sleep with the biker, the one who's fixing your dad's motorcycle. It'll help you put things in perspective."

"That's . . . ludicrous! Not to mention immoral . . . stupid. How about dangerous?"

"Not as dangerous as sleeping with your ex-husband."

Deanna felt herself getting angry. She didn't agree with Georgia's free life-style. It was not discussed between them, by mutual concession. She knew Georgia meant well, but Deanna resented the implication that she would follow in Georgia's footsteps. She pulled her hands out of Georgia's and opened the car door.

"I'm going out to dinner with Phil. You're right about the need to tie up loose ends, but you're wrong about the other. If that's what Phil has in mind, then it's going to be a very short and disappointing night. I'll talk to you tomorrow." Deanna got out and shut the door resolutely, ignoring Georgia's repeated efforts to detain her.

At six-thirty Friday night Deanna stood in front of her mirror in her third outfit. This one was no more appropriate than the first two had been. What did one wear out to dinner with an ex-husband? She wanted to look nice, but she didn't want him to think she was dressing to impress him.

After Georgia's dire prediction, she refused to wear anything even slightly revealing. Everything else made her look severe, dumpy, or overdressed. She finally settled on a black angora sweater dress. It hugged her curves softly but covered her skin from her chin to her knees. She always felt confident in black. It was one of her best colors.

By the time the doorbell sounded, at precisely seven o'clock, she was thoroughly worked up and wished she could call the whole thing off. She clipped on her favorite pearl earrings, fluffed her hair, and fervently wished she hadn't let the housekeeper go. She needed someone to answer the door, stall for time. She wasn't ready for this.

Phil stood on the doorstep of his previous home, looking around as if to see what had changed in his absence. He looked as marvelous as always in a dark blue sport coat with his crisp white shirt and dark silk tie. His eyes darkened appreciatively when he turned and gave her a thorough scrutiny, as he'd done the day she'd gone to his office.

"You always did look marvelous in black."

Deanna was instantly on guard. He'd encouraged her to wear black during their marriage, but not because she looked "marvelous" in it. Usually it was something along the lines of "You don't look as fat." She wished she'd worn the white wool.

"Thank you." Give him a chance, Deanna,

she said to herself. People can change. "I'm ready to go, just let me get my coat. Or do you want to come in?"

He came in, looking at everything. She wondered if he felt as strange as she had coming to his office. Was he reassured, as she had been, by how few changes she'd made since their divorce?

"I've missed this place," he said finally, turning back to her from the center of the living room. "The condo is so . . ." he shrugged, searching for the right word. "It's not home."

"I doubt you're there enough," Deanna suggested.

He looked like he would take exception to her remark, then gave a sad smile. "Maybe you're right. Why should I be? There's no one there to come home to."

Even if someone was there, she doubted he would go home. He was too restless. He thrived on being on the move, being in demand. He had rarely been home when he'd lived with her.

Deanna decided to let it drop. She picked her cashmere coat up off the couch and handed it to him.

"Why don't you wear the fox?" he suggested, not offering to help her into it. "It's cold out tonight."

"It's in storage," where it can stay, she added

silently. Deanna hadn't wanted the expensive silver fox coat, but Phil had insisted. She'd only worn it when they went to power functions, when Phil felt the need to impress someone.

Phil held up the coat, and Deanna slid into it.

"I've made reservations at The Ritz," he said as he held the door open for her. Deanna set the alarm before going through. She stopped in front of the sleek Jaguar sports coupe sitting in her driveway.

It was a new one, though similar to the one he'd brought home four years before. She knew now that his buying an imported sports car after twenty years of driving American-made luxury sedans had been her first clue of impending change. Not for the first time she wondered, if she had understood what was happening, could she have done anything to have made a difference?

"She's a beauty, isn't she?" Phil's statement reminded Deanna of Billy Adonis when he'd shown her his motorcycle. She had thought Billy amusing. Phil's admiration for his car made her angry.

"If men showed as much pride in their women as their cars, there wouldn't be such a high divorce rate in this country." She angled herself into the low-slung car, not expecting

Phil to answer her. Instead of closing her door, he stood there regarding her through intense brown eyes.

"You're right."

Their gazes held for several moments, Deanna totally at a loss as to how to respond. He broke the tension by flashing her a smile, then closing her door.

The car was nice, Deanna had to admit, as Phil maneuvered it through the heavy Friday night traffic. The engine had a pleasant, deep-throated purr that promised power if needed but was equally comfortable gliding along at thirty miles an hour. True to nature, Phil spent the drive to the restaurant demonstrating all the car's features, from the sound system to the map lights, and weighing her down with his knowledge of the car's every detail.

Knowing Phil, he had memorized the owner's manual the night he'd bought it and would follow the maintenance guidelines to the letter. She had always marveled at his ability to retain everything he read or heard. It was part of what made him such a successful surgeon and teacher. He had never learned how to tailor his knowledge to his audience, however, and tended to bog people down with information they cared nothing about. It was funny how she'd forgotten that irritating trait.

He continued to monopolize the conversation throughout dinner, telling her about this year's residents, catching her up on patients she remembered. For Deanna, talking to Phil was like slipping into an old pair of shoes after wearing new ones. There was a reassuring familiarity about it, but the worn places were no longer comfortable. Georgia would love that metaphor.

"Would you like dessert?" Phil asked as the waitress picked up their dinner plates.

"No, thank you," Deanna declined. She hadn't learned a thing about why he'd divorced her and was ready to call it a night.

"I'd like the cobbler with ice cream," Phil told the waitress, "and coffee."

Deanna also ordered coffee, since it was apparent they weren't leaving any time soon. "You said you wanted to talk," she reminded Phil as soon as the waitress left.

Phil looked uncomfortable. He played with his spoon while he talked. "I haven't been very fair to you, Deanna, and I wanted a chance to apologize."

"For what?" Deanna prompted, when he didn't continue right away. Her heart was pounding in her ears in anticipation. Her fingers instinctively sought the strand of pearls around her neck, stroking their smooth surface.

"I went through a bad time last winter, Deanna, and instead of turning to you, I lashed out. I blamed you for things that weren't your fault."

He'd chosen a fine time to learn summation, Deanna thought. "What things, specifically?"

The waitress served his cobbler and poured their coffee.

"Doesn't this look wonderful? Are you sure you don't want some?"

"What things, Phil?" Deanna repeated.

He put down his spoon and reached for her free hand. "You were a good wife, Deanna, a good mother. I felt closed in, trapped. It was more acceptable to blame you than to look at what might be wrong with me."

She'd read that book. He was going to have to be more original. "What's wrong with you?"

Phil looked stunned, then he shook his head with a smile. "You always were smart." He let go of her hand and took a bite of his cobbler. Deanna sipped her coffee and waited.

"I cannot believe that I did something as common as have a midlife crisis," Phil said a few bites later. "I've done some extensive reading on the subject."

Deanna stifled a groan.

"Most men experience it much earlier than

I did. I prefer to think of it as a symptom of professional overload."

Deanna let him explain how overworked he'd gotten with his research, his position as chief of staff, his teaching duties with the residents, his speaking engagements, and his constantly being called in as a consultant on difficult or unusual cases. She listened until he'd finished his cobbler and drank a second cup of coffee.

"Then you don't think I'm boring?" Deanna asked, trying to keep her voice even and unaffected, as if his opinion of her no longer mattered.

Phil frowned, then had the grace to look chagrined. "I was bored, but you were never boring. I was out of line, Deanna. I should never have said that to you."

"How about predictable?"

"I took you for granted. You were always there for me, and I never acknowledged you."

Deanna had a long list of accusations he had spitefully hurled at her. She wondered if he had a glib excuse for every one of them. What hurt the most was that she'd believed him then, and she was having trouble believing him now. She tried to cover her hurt pride with anger, but her question was barely audible.

"How about pathetic, Phil?"

Phil's dark gaze held hers, and she truly believed there was sincere anguish in his. "Let's discuss this somewhere else."

He paid the tab, left a generous tip, and helped Deanna into her coat. He drove back to Deanna's house deep in thought, leaving her to worry her pearls and wonder how much the last eleven months had really changed him. Phil turned into the driveway, cut the engine and the lights, and let the silence descend around them like a wool blanket.

He reached over and captured her hand. "You're going to wear those out."

There was a strange intimacy, sitting so close in the small car, separated only by a console. His hands were warm and strong. His voice was low and caressing, coaxing a response from a deeply buried, long dormant part of her. He brushed a kiss over the backs of her fingers, his eyes never leaving her face. Deanna felt a shiver run through her entire being.

"You were never pathetic, Deanna," he said, his voice still low and caressing, his lips against her fingers. "I was unspeakably cruel. You fought for what you believed in— your home, your family, your marriage."

Deanna felt the tears fill her eyes and overflow. She was shaking uncontrollably now, her throat so tight she couldn't swallow. The last time she'd cried in front of Phil, he'd scorned her and called her pathetic. Now, he was holding her face in his hands and kissing her tears away with soothing endearments that threatened to break her heart all over again. He pulled her into his arms, and she buried her head into his neck.

The console pressed into her ribs, but Deanna was more aware of Phil's hands holding her, stroking her back. When he nudged her chin up to kiss her, she met him halfway. It had been too long. Her body responded with an intensity that threatened to overwhelm her. She tried to move closer, but the console thwarted her efforts.

"We could go inside," Phil said, his voice urgent. He kissed her again, stroking her tongue with his. She groaned in protest when he pulled away. "Come on."

The interior lights came on when he opened his door. He ran around the car quickly to open hers, letting in the cool night air and a measure of sanity. Deanna allowed him to pull her to her feet but resisted his efforts to lead her to the house.

What was she doing?

"Phil, no." She pulled her hand out of his and clutched her coat tighter around her. It took several deep breaths before her heart rate calmed down and her head cleared. Phil moved toward her, and she stepped away. "No."

"No what?" His breathing was still ragged and his irritation at her sudden uncooperative stand obvious. "Deanna, it's cold out here. Can we discuss this inside?"

"No," she repeated again, shaking her head for emphasis. She needed the cold. It was helping clear her mind, even though her love-starved body didn't seem to be cooling off much.

"Deanna." He tried to reach for her again. Again she stepped back.

"Go home, Phil, please." She couldn't look at him. She held herself tightly and prayed he would do as she asked.

"Come on, Deanna. It's not like we're strangers. I won't touch you," he promised when she again evaded his grasp. "Can we please continue this discussion inside?"

Deanna was trembling so hard she could hardly stand up. He was doing it again, ripping her life apart without warning.

"Go home, Phil," she ground out through chattering teeth. "You said you wanted us to talk, to try to be friends. You've talked, but I think we have a different definition of friendship.

"I still love you, Deanna."

She had to get away from him. She groped in her purse desperately, searching for the door key. She didn't believe him, didn't understand his motivation for behaving this way.

"No!" she shouted when he stepped forward to help. She had to calm down, had to regain control of herself. She could fly to pieces later but not in front of Phil. She took several more deep breaths, found her keys, then looked at her ex-husband.

"I remember saying those exact same words to you, Phillip, when you were so determined that all you wanted was a divorce. You would not talk to me. You would not listen to me. You would not consider counseling. I would have done anything, *anything,* if you would have just given me a chance. You refused."

"I've explained that— "

"Not good enough," she cut him off. The cold air was hurting her lungs, but she couldn't seem to get enough of it. "You haven't spoken a civil word to me in a year. Dinner and a glib apology will not make up for that. I have accepted our divorce. I am trying to get on with my life, which you are no longer a part of. I'll be damned if I'm going to be some easy stopgap for you between girlfriends."

She felt the tears and knew she was at the end of her control. Turning away from him, she walked swiftly toward her front door. Thank God he didn't try to follow her but remained on the driveway.

"I'll call you, Deanna," he yelled as she frantically pushed open her door.

She slammed the heavy door closed, entered the code for the alarm, then gave in to the torrent of angry tears. *Damn him!* Damn him for coming back into her life just when she was starting to get it back under control.

"Must have been some party."

So much for Visine and Estee Lauder, Deanna thought, glaring at Evan Maxwell through eyes that hurt just being open. She hadn't slept much the night before. At first she'd been too angry, then she'd lain there and rehashed events from as recently as that night's dinner with Phil to when they'd first met each other. When she'd awakened in the morning, she'd had a hangover worse than anything liquor had ever caused.

As if she didn't have enough on her mind, Georgia's advice kept sneaking into her thoughts. *Sleep with the biker.* She'd almost canceled their lesson this afternoon, but by noon she had been too restless to stay at home. Now, here he was, grinning at her and teasing her about partying too much.

"Are you ready?" she asked, letting him know his observation wasn't appreciated. The effect was somewhat ruined by the thickness of her voice.

"I'll get my jacket." He was still grinning as he walked away. He returned wearing his black leather jacket and gloves and carrying a helmet.

"It's too cold out here to stay long," he said on the walk out to the track. "I thought we'd get you to at least ride it around the track, then work inside on the written exam."

He made her do the braking exercise with the engine off before he showed her how to start it. "Never get on something you don't know how to stop," he advised when she made a face at his request.

Deanna couldn't argue with that. She slid the bike to a smooth, silent stop beside him. Her hands and nose were already uncomfortably cold.

"Okay, let's start 'er up." He turned the key in the ignition which turned on the headlight and the instrument gauges. "See the green light? That and the fact that it rolls freely indicate you're in neutral. This throttle is on a spring, but they aren't all. Make sure it's closed before you start it. This is the choke. This cold you'll need it on full and let the engine run a little while before you cut it back. Kick 'er over."

He stood back, watching Deanna expectantly. She looked down at the kick starter, then nudged it out with her toe. She'd read the book and spent all last Saturday doing powerless drills. It was time to put her knowledge into practice. She took a deep breath, then gave the starter a hard kick. She couldn't hold back a triumphant grin when the little cycle fired to life beneath her.

Evan grinned back, then set the helmet on her head. Deanna winced at the damage it was doing to her hair, but dutifully adjusted the chin strap while he admonished her to start slow, and stay in first gear. "*Ease* out the clutch," he reminded her. "Pop it, and it'll jump out from under you."

Deanna wasn't about to be dropped in the dirt in front of Evan Maxwell. She squeezed the clutch in, toed the gear shift lever down into first, and felt the bike drop into gear. She eased out the clutch. The bike jerked forward and died.

"A little more throttle," Evan suggested.

Deanna bit her lip, suddenly warm inside her wool jacket in spite of the cold. She could do this. She kicked out the starter pedal and prepared to restart it.

"Whoa, hang on." Evan stopped her, then pointed to the instrument panel. "You've either got to be in neutral, or disengage the clutch."

She knew that and said to herself, Think, Deanna, use your head. She took another deep breath and did a quick systems review. Throttle closed, neutral gear, brake on. She kicked it back to life.

"Okay, gently open the throttle a few times until you're comfortable with it, then engage the clutch. Listen to your engine. It'll tell you when it needs more power."

She revved the engine a few times, then slowly engaged the clutch. The bike began to move forward, and the engine bogged down. She opened the throttle a little more.

"That's the way," she heard Evan shout as the engine responded and the bike pulled away from him.

Deanna's entire concentration was on the sound of the engine and its response to the throttle. They moved forward in short, choppy spurts for several yards before she disengaged the clutch and braked to a stop.

"That was great," Evan praised, jogging up beside her. "First gear is real low, so you don't want to stay in it long. Try shifting gears. Keep your speed down, but go on around the track. Listen to your engine."

The first trip around was jerky, her shifting hesitant. By the third trip around, she was feeling more confident. Thirty minutes later, she was nearly frozen from the cold wind, but exhilarated with the feel of the bike responding to her commands.

"This is fantastic!" she shouted as she braked to a smooth stop beside Evan. She took off the helmet, shook out her hair, and tried to warm her ears with her gloved hands. She was certain her hair was a mess and her cheeks scarlet from the wind, but she didn't care.

"Let's go inside for a while," Evan suggested, taking the helmet from her.

Deanna expertly took the bike out of gear, turned off the engine, and set it on its stand. She looked up at Evan, wanting to share the joy of the moment with him. What she saw in his eyes froze her smile and took her breath.

His admiration wasn't that of a teacher toward his pupil. He had that hungry man at a banquet look again. She couldn't tear her gaze away.

Sleep with the biker. Georgia's advice slammed into her as hard now as it had when she'd first heard it. She swallowed hard, forced her attention elsewhere, and ran a self-conscious hand through her hair.

"I must look a mess."

"I like you messed up." His voice was husky, and he sounded as if he, too, was having trouble breathing normally.

Deanna shivered and wrapped her arms around herself. "Do you still serve hot chocolate?" Not waiting for his answer, she began the walk back to the shop.

This is ludicrous, she thought as she ran lukewarm water over her stiff, cold hands. Georgia had put ideas into her head that had no business being there. No, to be fair, she'd had the ideas long before Georgia had put them into words. She'd just dismissed them as inconceivable. She wasn't Georgia, didn't have Georgia's ability to love 'em and leave 'em. Sleeping with Evan Maxwell would not help her put her life in perspective. It would only leave her with more frayed ends.

"Hey, Mrs. Ran-doff."

Kyle greeted her from his grandfather's lap. Evan was trying to drink from his cup without colliding with the bouncing child's head. Deanna smiled at the boy's energy, touched by his effort to learn to pronounce her name properly.

"You can call me Miss Deanna. That's what the children at the hospital call me."

"Are they your chil'ren?" Kyle's bouncing stilled while he awaited her answer.

"No, my children are all grown up." Deanna

took a seat in the now familiar leather chair across from Evan's desk and wrapped her hands around the mug of hot chocolate waiting for her. "These are sick children that have to be in the hospital. I read them stories and play games with them when their parents can't be there with them."

Kyle thought about that while Deanna sipped her chocolate. "Why're they sick?" he finally asked.

Deanna wasn't sure how to explain sick children to an abundantly healthy four-year-old. She looked to Evan for help.

"Like your friend Joey when he broke his arm," Evan offered.

"He has a *cool* cast," Kyle responded, bouncing again. Evan barely managed to get his cup out of harm's way in time. "I wish I could break my arm."

Deanna had to smile at Evan's grimace. "He was in a lot of pain before he got the cast," Evan said, but Kyle was undaunted.

"It's green, and ever'body got to write on it."

"But he can't play on the playground equipment can he?" Evan reminded him.

Kyle stopped bouncing, his little face screwed up as he thought about it. "No, he has to stay by the teacher." That seemed to take some of the fun out of having a broken arm in Kyle's mind.

"Go find your dad," Evan said, setting Kyle off his lap and giving his rear a loving swat to set him in motion. "I have to help Miss Deanna study for her motorcycle test."

Kyle started forward but stopped in front of Deanna, looking up at her with intense hazel eyes similar to Evan's. "Do you only play games with sick chil'ren?"

"No, I have a three-year-old grandson named Brady. He likes to play anything that let's him hit balls."

"Like baseball?"

"Umm-hmm and soccer and tennis and golf."

"What's goff?"

"It's like croquet."

Kyle gave her a blank look.

"It has a little ball that you hit with a stick," Deanna explained, pantomiming. "You use the stick to hit the little ball into a hole. The object is to see who can hit the ball into the holes with the least number of hits."

"Will you play goff with me?"

"Not today, Kyle," Evan interrupted. "Go ask your dad if he knows how to play golf."

Deanna watched Kyle leave, thinking of Brady. "Does Kyle's mother live nearby?" She glanced back at Evan. "I'm sorry, I guess I'm being nosy. He's just such a sweet little boy, I wondered if she ever saw him."

"Not since Kyle was a little over a year old. She wasn't one for responsibility. Brian doesn't talk much about her."

"That's so sad."

"We manage."

"I didn't mean it like that," Deanna said, distressed at having offended him.

Evan smiled. "It's okay. People just seem to worry more when the single parent is a father instead of a mother."

And she'd been angry with her brothers for being sexist. It looked like she had a few biases of her own. "You're right."

"Were you a single mother?" he asked.

Deanna's hand went to her pearls. That's what happened to nosy women. They invited nosy questions back at themselves.

"I couldn't help but notice you don't wear a traditional wedding ring," Evan said when she didn't respond. "You've talked about children and grandchildren but no husband. Or am I the one being nosy now?"

Deanna looked down at the pearl and diamond ring she wore on her left hand. She'd started wearing it after she'd taken her wedding rings off. After twenty-nine years of wearing them, not wearing them was a constant reminder of their absence.

"I'm recently divorced, so, no, I was never a single parent." Although Phil hadn't contributed much. He'd never taken a child to his office on Saturday or shared hot chocolate with them on a cold afternoon. "It's a sad world we live in, isn't it?"

"Yeah," Evan agreed. Deanna was grateful when he left it at that and opened the manual. "What's the most important thing to check on your bike every time you ride it?"

They spent the next hour with Evan asking questions from the manual and Deanna supplying the answers. He didn't stop with rules of the road but quizzed her on motorcycle maintenance and safety as well.

"Next weekend is Christmas," Evan reminded her as he walked her to her car, "and the one after that New Year's. Let's resume three weeks from now."

"Planning a big New Year's bash?" Deanna asked, wanting to tease him.

"Brian, Kyle, and I are flying to New Jersey to spend New Year's with my other son, Tom, and his family. After the divorce, I always let Pauline's family have the boys for Christmas, and I got them for New Year's." He shrugged as if to convey it was no big deal, but Deanna suspected that it was. "After fifteen years, it's become a tradition."

Fifteen years. Deanna suspected a man got pretty cynical toward women after being divorced for fifteen years.

"I take it Tom is still married?"

Evan seemed surprised by her question, then grinned. "Yeah, he's managed to avoid the Maxwell curse, so far. Maybe he's learned from all our mistakes. Someone needs to."

They were at her car. "Have a Merry Christmas, Evan. I hope when we meet again, you'll show me the progress on the Indian."

His eyes were warm as they smiled into hers. "I look forward to it. Go to the driver's license bureau and get your learner's permit in the meantime so we can ride out on the street." He surprised her by taking her hand and giving it a warm squeeze. "Merry Christmas, Deanna."

For the barest instant, Deanna hoped he would kiss her. Her body's response to the look in his eyes, the touch of his hand, guaranteed fireworks from his kiss. Then he moved and she panicked, extracting her hand and hurrying to open her car door.

Evan waved as he re-entered his dealership. Deanna let the engine warm up a minute as she looked back at the shop then out at the test track where the Honda still sat. Evan Maxwell was an enigma. He teased her, he demanded perfection, and he overwhelmed her senses. Three weeks was going to be a long time.

Six

Most of the hospital volunteers took off during the weeks around Christmas, but Deanna knew that was the hardest season for the children. Only the sickest were in the hospital during that time, and they didn't like being there. Deanna took them small presents, things they could read or do in bed, and tried to distract them for a little while.

For three-year-old Charlotte, who insisted on being called Charlie, the biggest challenge was getting her to eat. She was a frequent patient at Children's, where she underwent chemotherapy for leukemia. Deanna usually had better success than most of the staff, or even Charlie's mother.

"I brought 300 gallons of strawberry-banana ice cream with me," Deanna announced loudly as she entered the little girl's room. She carried in a large gallon-sized tin and a huge serving spoon.

"I hate banana," came Charlie's voice from

the bed. She looked more pale than the last time Deanna had seen her, and her voice sounded weaker. But her response told Deanna she was willing to play their game.

"You hate banana?" Deanna asked, feigning dismay. "Then what am I going to do with all this ice cream?"

"You have to take out the bananas," Charlie said soberly, sitting up.

"Then what do I do with them?"

"You have to throw them out the window."

Throwing things was Charlie's favorite activity. Deanna wasn't sure how much was normal childish behavior and how much was an outlet for frustrations too complex for a sick three-year-old to communicate. Whatever the reason, Deanna made sure her games with Charlie included throwing something.

"What if you hit someone on the head?"

"They'll be a banana-head," Charlie said, giving a little giggle.

"What does a banana-head look like?"

"They have bananas growing out of their ears."

"Oh no." Deanna took two small plastic toy bananas out of the container in her lap and stuck them up next to her ears. "Like this?"

Charlie giggled and pointed to Deanna's ears. "You're a banana-head."

Deanna transferred the bananas to Charlie's ears. "No, I'm not. *You're* a banana-head."

"Throw out the bananas!"

Charlie took the toy bananas and threw them toward the door to the hall. Deanna looked up just in time to see one of them land squarely on Dr. Phillip Randolph's nose. He caught it by reflex action, a frown of displeasure pulling his face into fierce lines. Charlie dived behind Deanna for protection with a dramatic, "Uh-oh."

Deanna smiled and wrapped her arm around the child as she addressed Phil. "I didn't realize Charlie was one of your patients."

"She isn't," Phil said, his scowl still in place as he bent over to pick the other banana up off the floor. "I was looking for you."

When she had been married to him, Deanna would have immediately dropped what she was doing to see to whatever Phil needed her to do. But, as she was so frequently and painfully reminded, she was no longer married to him.

"I'll be through here in ten minutes or so."

The scowl deepened. Deanna forcefully kept her pleasant smile in place and waited for his response. It would tell her a lot about whether he had changed or not.

"I'll be out at the nurses' station," he said brusquely, then turned and left.

Deanna let out the breath she'd been holding and realized her pulse was racing. The small victory gave her a heady feeling. She finished her game with Charlie, repeating the banana ritual with plastic strawberries, then continuing with other silliness until she'd coaxed the little girl into eating most of the serving of vanilla ice cream that had gone soft during their game, just the way Charlie liked it. Deanna checked her watch. Phil had been waiting fifteen minutes, if he'd waited at all.

He didn't look pleased, but he'd waited, leaning against the nurses' station. He looked at Deanna, then at his watch, but surprised her by not mentioning the value of his time. Instead, he motioned her toward an empty conference room.

"I'm sorry about the wait, Phil," Deanna apologized, as much from habit as from nervousness. "If I don't play out the entire game, she won't eat."

Phil waved away her explanation, as usual not interested in the games she played with the children. What he'd come to say was more important.

"Christmas is this Sunday," he said, typically without any preamble or amenities. "I understand you and the children will gather at your mother's estate as usual?"

He didn't have to continue. Deanna knew what he wanted.

"I've talked with Sherylyn and the boys," Phil continued when she didn't answer. "They wanted to know if I would be joining the family for Christmas. I told them it was up to you but that I would enjoy that very much."

He knew just where to attack, where she was the most vulnerable. Even though they were all grown and no longer living at home, all three of their children had been devastated by their parents' divorce. They had done everything in their power to encourage a reconciliation and would be ecstatic over Phil's apparent change of attitude. To refuse would make Deanna the villain in her children's eyes. Either decision was going to make Christmas a very uncomfortable occasion.

"It's really up to Mother," Deanna hedged, having no idea how her mother would react to Phil's proposal.

"Would you ask her?" Phil took her hand, caressing it gently between his own. "Please, Deanna?"

Phil's hands were smooth, with long, tapered fingers and perfectly manicured, closely clipped nails. Deanna remembered Evan's hands, strong, rough, warm. She withdrew her hands from Phil's. "I'll ask her, Phil."

"I'll call you," Phil promised. He was gone before Deanna could respond.

Deanna looked down at the tin can she'd set on the floor beside her, at the plastic bananas and strawberries that Charlie got such pleasure out of throwing across the room. The therapy had merit, she decided. She would thoroughly enjoy throwing a few things herself, all of them squishy, and all of them at Dr. Phillip Randolph's distinguished head.

The Edwards' estate was always part of the Christmas tour of homes, another one of the auxiliary's fund-raisers for the hospital. Poinsettias of all colors and pine arrangements of all varieties decorated the house. Candles were everywhere. The large tree in the formal living room was a work of art in itself. Hostessing was what Charlotte Edwards did best, whether it was for hundreds of Atlanta dignitaries or for her large family at Christmas. She had been up since dawn, bustling about, overseeing every detail.

From long experience, Deanna knew better than to interfere. She sat on the floor in the living room, watching her three-year-old grandson Brady and her two-year-old great-niece Tabitha as they played with their bountiful harvest of new toys. Brady's parents and baby sister had gone back to bed after presents had been opened, ostensibly for a morning nap. Deanna sighed. Three-month-old Jamie was napping, but the look in her son's eye as he'd accompanied his wife out with the baby had not been fatigue. Deanna couldn't remember Phil ever taking her back to bed during a baby's nap.

"Hello, Grandma, need some help?"

Deanna smiled at her brother Andrew and accepted the cup of coffee he offered her. "Thanks, Grandpa." He had two more grandchildren than she did. "How did you manage to get through the kitchen to find coffee?"

"Kitchen? Do you think I'm that crazy? There's coffee set up on the sideboard in the dining room, along with anything else anybody could possibly want until dinner." He folded his long legs under him and joined her on the floor, where he was immediately accosted by his granddaughter.

"Whoa, watch the coffee." He held his cup high until Tabitha was settled in his lap with her new baby doll, which was already naked and missing her hair ribbons. He accepted the clothes handed to him and began dressing the doll as if the activity was a familiar one.

Deanna smiled, but it was bittersweet. She

couldn't imagine Phil sitting on the floor dressing a baby doll. Evan would.

"Mom told me Phil's coming for dinner."

Deanna took a sip of her coffee. "He says he wants us to be friends, but I'm beginning to suspect he's hoping for a reconciliation and looking for family support."

"What do you want?" Andrew had their father's piercing blue-green eyes. Deanna couldn't meet them but focused her attention on the child in his lap.

"I don't know." She took another sip of coffee. "Six months ago, I wouldn't have hesitated, but now . . ." she shook her head. "I just want my life back. It would be nice if we could be friends, for the children's sake."

"Do you still love him?"

She met his gaze, the question catching her off guard. "I . . . haven't thought about it."

"That's important, don't you think?" Her doll dressed, Tabitha went off to put it in its new crib.

Deanna thought about Andrew's question. Love had been important in the beginning, but she hadn't thought about it in a long time. Phil had been her husband. She'd trusted his judgment, kept his life as organized and stress-free as possible, raised their children, and con-

ducted her life as befitted her position as Mrs.
Phillip Randolph.

It had been a powerful position, one she'd
taken for granted until it had been abruptly
taken from her. Andrew's question raised an
interesting dilemma. What did she mourn the
loss of, the man or the position? Had her
heart been broken or her self-esteem?

She left Andrew babysitting to see if Phil
had arrived. She found him with their daughter Sherylyn in the den, engrossed in a heated
medical debate. It was their favorite pastime
since Sherylyn had chosen to follow her father
into medicine. After listening for a few moments, Deanna recognized the baby under discussion. Sara Harris had been born with a
life-threatening heart defect. Phil had done
surgery on her, but her only real chance of
survival was a heart transplant.

"It's a waste of the taxpayers' money,"
Sherylyn said.

"The working public pays the bill, whether
it's funded by Medicaid or by insurance," Phil
argued. "If it wasn't funded by third-party
payers, it would be funded by research grants.
The real question we should be addressing is,
are we doing these kids a favor?"

Deanna slipped in and took a seat beside

her daughter, barely receiving a smile of welcome from the two debaters.

"I don't think so," Sherylyn said, shaking her head emphatically. "Even if they receive a heart transplant, it's only good for about ten years, ten years of a very compromised quality of life. The drugs they have to take to avoid rejection leave them open to diseases we never encountered prior to organ transplantation."

"We're encountering them now, in AIDS patients," her father reminded her. "Chemotherapy patients are also immunocompromised. New studies and new drugs are coming out every day. If a heart transplant buys this baby ten years of life, she may live long enough for medical science to find a cure."

"The only cure will be a mechanical heart that won't be rejected by the body and will function as a human heart functions. We're a long way from that."

"Great strides have already been made in that field. How can you deny a patient a chance to live knowing the breakthrough technology could be just around the corner?"

"How can you condone techniques and drugs that contribute to and prolong such an agonizing existence?" Sherylyn shot back. "That baby doesn't even have enough oxygen reserve to cry when she hurts."

"Is she back in the hospital?" Deanna asked, remembering the tiny baby who had touched her heart with more impact than usual from the children she cared for.

"We admitted her last night," Sherylyn answered. "She's dig-toxic."

Deanna had been around medicine long enough to know there was a fine line with digitalis between therapeutic and toxic. The very drug necessary to keep Sara Harris alive could also kill her. Sara Harris might be tiny, but she was a fighter. In spite of her compromised circulation, in spite of all the pain she'd suffered in her short life— or maybe because of it— the baby had looked at Deanna through wise eyes and fought for life with an incredible will.

Medicaid did not pay for heart transplants, still considered an experimental and risky procedure. Deanna's attempts to persuade the indigent fund board to cover the procedure had so far been rebuked, in spite of the fact that the Edwardses and the Randolphs were among the largest individual contributors to the fund. Transplants were expensive, using large sums of money to treat one patient with risky odds of success. The committee argued that the same amount of money could be better utilized to treat several children with better prognoses. Deanna hadn't given up, praying that baby Sara would live until she had convinced the committee and a donor heart was found.

"That mother is a trip," Sherylyn continued. "She didn't even bother to change out of her working clothes when she brought her in. Probably lined up tricks while she sat in the waiting room."

"She's a waitress," Deanna corrected her daughter, frowning in confusion. "What are you talking about, 'lining up tricks in the waiting room'?"

Sherylyn gave her mother a look of disgust. "Well I'm not referring to card tricks. Wake up, Mother. The woman may be a waitress during the day, but she has a more lucrative sideline going at night. She's a prostitute," Sherylyn said baldly, when Deanna continued to look blank.

"No," Deanna said, shaking her head. She had spent hours with this woman during Sara's hospitalization following her surgery. She had listened to Gloria Harris's anguished sobs as she was forced to make decisions that would prolong both her daughter's life and her daughter's suffering.

"She's not even a very classy one," Sherylyn went on. "She was wearing enough makeup to go on stage, all of it smeared with her hysterical crying."

"She loves her daughter," Deanna defended Gloria, upset with Sherylyn's callous observations. "You have no right to make such accusations about her based on outward appearances, especially in the middle of the night when she's afraid her daughter is dying. You should be grateful she recognized that something was wrong before it was too late."

"It's in the social worker's report, Mother. The woman's a prostitute. Her mobile home is a regular truck stop. Social services is investigating whether neglect of the child is involved and if they need to take the baby away from her."

Deanna assimilated the news with a sick heart. The Gloria Harris she had met the day of Sara's surgery was not a prostitute. She was a single mother trying to find a way to keep her only child alive. Gloria was in her late thirties and had shared with Deanna that her pregnancy with Sara had been nothing short of a miracle. Without the money for the heart transplant, she was in danger of losing her miracle child.

"She's doing it for the money," Deanna spoke her realization aloud, sick at heart that Gloria had felt driven to such extremes. Deanna silently vowed to redouble her efforts to persuade the board to vote in favor of Sara's case.

"Of course she's doing it for the money,"

Phil interjected rudely. "Why else would she be doing it?"

"She's doing it for Sara," Deanna said defensively, turning on Phil. "She's desperate to collect money for a transplant in case a donor heart is found."

"Oh, grow up, Deanna," Phil said, exasperation evident in his voice. "She's probably been doing it for years. How do you think she got pregnant? If she hadn't been on Medicaid for the child, she probably would never have been caught."

"How long will Sara be in the hospital?" Deanna asked Sherylyn, ignoring Phil.

"Until she's stable. It's hard to say at this point."

"I'll talk to Gloria. I'll go up there tonight."

"Stay out of this, Deanna," Phil warned. "It doesn't involve you."

Deanna gave him a cool, assessing look. "How would you know, Phil? Gloria Harris is a friend of mine. I won't believe anything until I hear it from her."

"She's one of your charity cases," Phil corrected. "Once the indigent funds committee finds out about her *life-style* they'll never approve your appeal."

"Does her *life-style* automatically make her child unworthy to survive? What if the child had

AIDS instead of hypoplastic left heart? Would her odds of survival be any better? No, of course not. But you wouldn't refuse to treat a child with AIDS, no matter how poor the prognosis. Don't preach ethics to me, Phillip Randolph. A sick child is a sick child, regardless of what made her sick, and it's my job to see that she receives medical care. That Sara Harris's mother loves her enough to sell her body to buy her a chance to live only makes me more determined than ever to see that she has that chance."

Deanna's mother rang the bell announcing dinner being served. Deanna rose to walk to the dining room, the other two following her in strained silence. Deanna felt ill. It was Christmas dinner and instead of a warm family gathering she had instigated a feud. She tried to repair the damage.

"Sherylyn, sit here beside me so your father can sit between you and one of the boys."

Sherylyn smiled and moved to the chair Deanna had indicated for Phil. "I think Daddy came to see you, Mother. I'll sit over here and let the boys sit across from him."

The room continued to fill. Pete's grown sons and their families had come, along with Pete's present young family. Andrew's grown children and their families were finding places to sit.

Deanna's entire crew was in attendance. She smiled around the table at the large family she was part of. This was what Christmas was all about, her elderly mother at one end of the table, infants in high chairs at the other. She was glad she had talked her mother into inviting Phil. He didn't have family of his own, and to exclude him from Christmas with his children and grandchildren would have been cruel.

"This family just keeps getting bigger," Pete commented, holding a chair out for Nancy.

"Well, you're certainly doing your share," Andrew teased him. Everyone laughed as Pete actually blushed.

The table was set with all the elegance at Charlotte Edwards' disposal, the food tastefully prepared and efficiently served by the Jewish family that had been doing this for as far back as Deanna could remember. New generations had been added to their family as well over the years, and they had continued the tradition of cooking and serving Christmas dinner for the Edwards family. Deanna didn't like to think what would happen to all their traditions when her mother was gone.

She thought of Evan. He had talked of their New Year's tradition, but he hadn't mentioned Christmas. Did he and Brian cook? Play Santa Claus for Kyle? Or were they more traditional

bachelors, eating their Christmas dinner at a
restaurant somewhere? She wondered what her
mother's reaction would have been to inviting
them to Christmas dinner. Three more would
have hardly been noticed in this crowd, but then
meeting her family would imply that she and
Evan were friends— more than friends— special
friends. She barely knew the man.

She wasn't thinking of Evan because they
were friends, she tried to contend. She just
hated to think of anyone spending Christmas
alone. Then she thought of Gloria Harris,
spending Christmas sitting in the intensive care
waiting room, not knowing if her child was going to live or not. It was a sobering thought.

"Mother," Eric pulled her back into the conversation flowing around her, "have you seen
Dad's new Jaguar?"

She smiled at her youngest. "Yes, I rode in
it last week. It's very nice."

"He's going to take me for a ride after dinner, maybe let me drive it?" It was a question,
his eyes boyishly bright as they waited for
Phil's response.

To Deanna's surprise, Phil laughed. "I suppose you're old enough. Of course if I let you
drive it, Sherylyn's going to want to."

"You'd better believe it," Sherylyn affirmed.

"There will be no sexist biases allowed in this family."

No, Deanna thought, Sherylyn had never allowed Phil to tell her "no" because she was the daughter. She was the only child who had followed him into medicine. Deanna had watched that decision give Sherylyn an edge over her brothers in the last ten years. Jeff had chosen financial investments and Eric architecture, neither field able to hold their father's interest for any time at all. In fact, Eric's choice of profession had caused heated debates between father and son, Phil viewing architects as only slightly above artists and something to be suspicious of. Eric vacillated between openly defying his father and trying to win his approval in other ways. Apparently today he was trying to win his approval, hence the comment about the car.

"Dad, do you remember that place where we went snorkeling down in the Caribbeans?" Jeff asked.

Deanna frowned. That had been years ago, when the boys were in their early teens.

"I wanted to take Karen there for vacation, if Mom wouldn't mind watching the kids."

"I'd love to watch the kids," Deanna exclaimed. "When?"

"I'm not sure yet," Jeff hedged. "I just wondered if Dad remembered the place so I could get some information."

"We went to the Caymans," Phil supplied. "I don't remember where we stayed, but I'm sure newer places have opened up since we were there."

The kids started remembering stories from the trip, saying, "remember, Mom," every once in a while. When the topic waned they brought up another family vacation, then a third. Deanna began to suspect a plot. She glanced at Andrew and caught his wink. He could see it, too. Her grown children were trying to remind her and Phil of the good times they'd once shared. Their childhood memories tugged at her heart in much stronger ways than Phil's clumsy seduction attempt. She looked at Phil and found his eyes on her, his expression wistful.

Twenty-nine years ago she'd married a dark-haired, brown-eyed man, and between them they had produced three dark-haired, brown-eyed children. Did she love him? There were feelings for him she couldn't deny, but was it love or was it familiarity? Maybe a better question would be, did she like him?

No. She was still angry with him, still hurt by the way he'd treated her and the hateful things he'd said. Could she forgive him? The jury was still out on that one, but they were going to have to reach some level of friendship for their children's sakes.

He was trying, she realized. He was laughing and teasing his children, and they were basking in their father's attention as if they were still six years old. It just proved that no child was too old to need a father. The least Deanna could do was meet him halfway, give him a chance, hope the divorce had opened his eyes to a few character flaws he was willing to work on.

They went outside after dinner was over and Phil swelled like a peacock while his children encouraged him to show them every toy and option on his fancy car. Deanna had to smile. The children were enthralled by the very speech that had bored her. They wanted to hear the stereo and flip on the map lights. He let each one of them drive it, something he hadn't done when he'd brought home the first Jaguar, and seemed to be enjoying being the center of his family's attention. Maybe he had gotten lonely in the last year. Maybe he did realize how much he'd taken them all for granted.

"Come on, Mom, you try it," Eric encouraged when he came back from his drive. "It handles like a dream."

Deanna shook her head. "No thanks."

"Mom's never driven with a clutch," Sherylyn

pointed out. "She wouldn't know how to shift it."

Yes, she had, but it had been a motorcycle, not a sports car. Her daughter's disbelief in her ability rankled. *You can't drive it, honey. You're a girl.* Her father had meant well, but he'd been wrong. She would drive his cantankerous old motorcycle, and she would show her smart aleck daughter that she could drive Phil's fancy sports car.

"Show me how to shift it," she instructed a surprised Phil, sliding into the driver's seat, "and especially how to stop it," she added, remembering Evan's advice about not driving anything she didn't know how to stop.

Her feet worked better than her hands, she discovered. The Jaguar had a stiff-springed racing clutch in it that threatened to drain all the blood out of her left leg, but coordinating the clutch and the gas pedal wasn't as difficult as the motorcycle's hand clutch and throttle. Maybe mastering the mechanics of the motorcycle's clutch had made it easier to learn the foot clutch. One thing was for certain, Evan Maxwell was a better teacher than Phillip Randolph. For all his drill sergeant tactics, he had never criticized her, and he had always put her safety above that of the machine.

"Watch the hole, Deanna," Phil shouted,

pointing to a small defect in the pavement. "Don't shift it yet, can't you hear the engine?"

Not, "Listen to your engine," but "Can't you hear the engine?" The difference was subtle, but Deanna heard it. She pulled the Jaguar into a driveway, shifted into reverse, and turned back toward her mother's house.

"You could have gone farther," Phil said. "You barely went far enough to feel how it handles."

She'd gone far enough to know she didn't enjoy Phil's car, or maybe it was Phil's company. She felt closed in. "I don't like wearing my car," she said to Phil. "I feel claustrophobic driving this."

"It takes a little getting used to, after driving a tank like your Buick, but the handling more than makes up for it. I can take thirty mile-an-hour curves doing forty-five."

"I have no desire to take thirty mile-an-hour curves doing forty-five." Except on a motorcycle, Deanna thought, leaning into them, feeling the wind in her face. She parked the Jaguar in her mother's driveway behind her "tank."

"What'd you think, Mom?" Eric asked, before she'd hardly gotten the door open. "Isn't it great?"

"Your mother doesn't seem to share your appreciation for sports cars, Eric," Phil answered. "Too confining." He came around and hugged Deanna up against him as if it were still his right.

She stiffened, then saw Eric's disappointed expression. She tried to relax against Phil and smiled at her son. "I didn't give it much of a chance," she said to Eric. "I was concentrating too much on learning how to use the clutch."

"You'd look great in a sports car, Mom," Eric said, hugging her from the other side. Deanna slid her arm around her son and hugged him back. Her left arm dangled somewhat awkwardly, so she laid it around Phil's waist, in the interest of family, she told herself.

"A zippy little red convertible," Eric continued as they walked back toward the house. "Course you'd have to change your hair style." He ran a playful hand through her carefully styled hair, making her turn both men loose in an effort to evade him. "And ditch the heels." He was laughing as he danced out of her reach, teasing her about her shoes.

"Heels have very practical uses," Deanna said, chasing him across the lawn. She jerked one off her foot as she ran and threw it at him. "They make great weapons."

He caught it and made a taunting face at her, dangling it by its heel like bait. "You'll ruin your stockings," he said in a falsetto voice.

"Eric Randolph, give me my shoe."

"Damsel in distress! Damsel in distress!" Eric continued in his falsetto voice. "Oh, won't someone help the lady?"

Phil joined in their game by giving her a courtly bow. "Phillip Randolph, at your service, Madame."

"Go slay that idiot dragon and bring back my shoe," Deanna ordered, pointing to Eric.

"Join me, my good fellow, and I'll share my booty," Eric invited, wagging Deanna's shoe. "Better yet, grab the other one."

Phil seemed to consider the request, looking first at Eric then back at Deanna, a smile spreading across his face. Deanna knew when he'd made his decision and began backing away, her hands warning him off.

"Oh, no. No. Don't you dare. Phil!" He scooped her off the ground, his eyes bright with mischief and desire. Eric took advantage of her helpless position and snatched the other shoe off her foot.

"Put me down," she demanded, pushing away from him, but she was laughing too hard to be upset. "Two against one isn't fair."

"Who says I'm on his side?" Phil asked, grinning down at her, "Maybe I intend to keep the princess for myself."

It was a side of Phil Deanna hadn't seen since

their early marriage. The kids circled around them, Eric still the clown, the other two more reserved but laughing at their brother's antics. They entered the house, a boisterous group, causing the others to look up to see what all the commotion was about. Deanna caught her mother's disapproving frown.

Phil caught it, too. He set her down, clearing his throat and straightening his jacket. When they met each other's eyes again, their sheepish expressions both gave way to more laughter. She hadn't laughed with Phil in years. They hadn't played together as a family in years. It gave her a warm satisfaction deep inside her heart.

Later that afternoon, as she held her granddaughter and made silly noises designed to make her smile, Phil came into the den and sat down beside her.

"We've always attended the New Year's Eve party at the country club," he said, making Jamie smile just by looking at her. He smiled back and offered her his finger to grasp. The baby immediately pulled it toward her mouth.

Deanna knew what he was going to ask. Unfortunately, last year's New Year's Eve party had been their last public function together. He had announced his intention to divorce her the following Monday. His deliberate actions told her that he'd been planning for some time, certainly prior to New Year's Eve. He'd probably been planning it for awhile and decided to wait until after the holidays.

As if he knew what her thoughts were, he said, "I know last year isn't a very good memory, but it seems like a good place to start over. I've enjoyed today, Deanna. It's felt good to be a family again."

She searched his eyes. They seemed sincere, but then they always had. Maybe that was something doctors were taught in medical school, how to act sincere when they weren't. She supposed that wasn't being fair, but then she didn't feel like being fair where Phil was concerned. She had also enjoyed the day, but the country club New Year's Eve party with all their friends was a major step. Gossip would fly that they were back together.

Gossip could also fly that she was back in circulation. What better way to re-enter society than escorted by Phil, Atlanta's most eligible bachelor? She would make sure everyone knew they weren't reconciling but desired to remain on good terms with each other. Her friends would all be there, friends who could introduce her to other friends, invite her to dinner parties, introduce her to men who understood about theaters, symphonies, and benefit auctions. Maybe she could even meet one of the Buckhead HOGs.

The thought didn't excite her as much as she'd meant for it to. Unless the man looked, acted, and spoke like Evan Maxwell, she doubted he was going to interest her very much. Still, she had vowed to return to society and the New Year's Eve party seemed as good a way as any.

"I suppose we could go as friends," she said, her focus on the baby in her lap.

She heard Phil sigh. "It's a start, I guess, but I have to warn you, Deanna, I'd like us to be more than friends."

Easy for him to say. He hadn't been the injured party for a year, but she didn't wish to spoil the idyllic day with arguments. "Let's see if we can even be friends first."

Seven

The day after Christmas Deanna found Gloria Harris curled up in a corner of a couch in the waiting room outside the intensive care unit, staring forlornly out the window. Life had not been kind to Gloria, and it showed in the lines of her face, making her look older than she was. Today she looked more haggard than usual. Her short blonde hair was disheveled and her face devoid of makeup. The ill-fitting pink sweats she wore did nothing to flatter her petite figure.

Deanna walked over and laid a gentle hand on Gloria's shoulder. "The nurse tells me Sara's doing much better."

Gloria stared at Deanna, then huge tears formed and spilled over. She took Deanna's hand in both of hers and squeezed it tight. "I'm so glad you're here. I asked the nurses about you, but they said they didn't know the volunteers' schedule."

Deanna sat down on the couch beside

Gloria. Gloria relaxed her grip but didn't let go of Deanna's hand. "I was so scared, Deanna. Sara wouldn't eat and her lips were blue and she was breathing too fast. They said I got her here just in time."

"You were very observant," Deanna praised.

Tears formed again and ran unheeded down Gloria's face. Her voice was barely above a whisper. "They say I'm a bad mother, that they might take her away from me."

"Hush, now," Deanna said, holding Gloria against her, saying comforting words she prayed were true. "No one's going to take Sara away from you. You tell me who I need to talk to, and I'll speak to them."

"It won't . . . do no good." She pulled away from Deanna and huddled back in the corner of the couch. "They say I got to send the men away."

So, it was true, Deanna thought. What hurt Deanna more, Gloria seemed to expect Deanna to shun her now that she'd confessed her sin. Shame radiated from Gloria like heat.

"I had to quit my job," Gloria said. "Sara's not like other children, who can stay at any daycare center. She can't be around sick children or crowds. I didn't know how else to earn the money." Her chin came up with pride then.

"I've saved nearly two thousand dollars for her surgery."

Gloria was practicing the world's oldest profession for what was probably the world's oldest reason— survival. Deanna didn't have an answer, but there had to be a better way.

"Aren't you getting welfare money so you can stay home with Sara?" Deanna asked the question delicately, not wanting Gloria to take offense.

Gloria hugged her knees against her chest and wouldn't meet Deanna's gaze. "It ain't enough, not even to live on. I don't want to do this, Deanna, but what choice do I have?"

She reached over to lay her hand over Gloria's. "I've presented your case to the board in charge of indigent funds. I'll talk to them again after the holidays."

Gloria's smile was bitter. "Won't do no good. Me and Sara, we're just poor white trash. Nobody cares about an ex-Waffle House waitress from Buford, especially one with a kid out of wedlock who's traded her apron for a more personal service."

The name "Buford" struck Deanna like a blow. She hadn't realized Gloria and Evan lived in the same town. Did they know each other? How well? Deanna looked at Gloria's expression of self-disgust and knew that wasn't the issue right now. Gloria needed a friend.

"I care," Deanna said fiercely, giving Gloria's knees a shake. "You care, and a lot of other people care. You wait and see. We're going to find a way to pay for Sara's operation, and you don't need to . . . take in men to earn the money.

"What you're doing is very dangerous," Deanna continued, shaking Gloria again when she didn't respond. "What if one of them gets rough, puts you in the hospital, or hurts Sara because she needs you at the wrong time? What about diseases, Gloria? What if you get AIDS?"

"Don't you think I've thought of all that?" Gloria's teary eyes glittered with anger. "I'm careful, and the men know about Sara. They're very generous."

Deanna refused to concede defeat, but she was fast running out of arguments. "What about social services? What good is all this if they decide to take Sara away from you?"

"I don't use drugs, and I don't abuse my baby." Gloria's chin came up defensively. "Sara's not a normal kid, one they can stick in just any foster home, not that there's a lot of them available. I know worse parents that've been threatened to have their kids taken away, but it don't happen. The state don't want her, they just have to scare me so they look like they're doin' their job."

"You're taking a big gamble, Gloria," Deanna said softly.

"It's my gamble to take." Gloria met Deanna's gaze with proud defiance, and Deanna knew she was right. It wasn't Deanna's decision to make. The most she could do was find resources that would make Gloria's sacrifices unnecessary.

A nurse appeared in the waiting room doorway. "Ms. Harris?"

Gloria was on her feet in an instant. Deanna also rose. The nurse smiled.

"You can see Sara for a few minutes. She's awake and seems much stronger."

Gloria's body sagged with relief. She gave Deanna a quick smile. "Thanks for coming by."

"Tell the nurses if you need me. I told them it was okay to call me."

Gloria thanked her again, then hurried after the nurse. Deanna knew she lived in this waiting room during Sara's hospitalizations, just to be available for moments like this. From long years of experience with other parents and other children, Deanna knew there were many hours of boring, frustrating waiting for every moment they were allowed to spend with their critically ill children.

Gloria Harris was as much a fighter as her daughter, refusing to give up, no matter how discouraging the odds. That she would turn to prostitution rather than sit idly by and hope for a miracle made Deanna even more determined to help them. She had years of experience in fund-raising. There had to be some way of finding Sara a sponsor.

Baby Sara's digoxin level stabilized quickly and by New Year's Eve day, she was discharged home with her mother. Breaking unwritten auxiliary rules, Deanna exchanged phone numbers with Gloria and made her promise to call if anything changed, or if Gloria just needed to talk. Gloria promised, but her expression was guarded. With a heavy heart, Deanna realized that the social gap was probably too great for Gloria to ever really trust her as a friend. She gave baby Sara a last kiss, then handed her back to Gloria. A man Gloria had introduced to Deanna simply as Hank waited to drive them home. Deanna couldn't help wondering if he was one of her generous men, but it was a question she would never ask.

Thoroughly depressed about the uncertain future of baby Sara, Deanna wished she hadn't agreed to attend the New Year's Eve party that night with Phil. She was no longer in a party mood. Re-entering society seemed like a frivolous priority when a baby's life hung in the balance.

Georgia still disapproved of her dating Phil. They had discussed it during their last bridge game at Harriet's. Harriet and Darleen disagreed with Georgia, saying it was a perfect opportunity to put a halt to all the hateful gossip that had spread during the past year. Deanna had taken the brunt of the criticism, been considered an unworthy wife of the highly esteemed Dr. Phillip Randolph. Phil had been heralded as the city's most eligible bachelor. He had dated younger women, career women, even some celebrities, but none of them had held his interest.

Now he was back, admitting he'd made a mistake and courting Deanna again. Darleen had sighed at the romance of it all. Georgia had made a gesture of gagging. Harriet had laughed and asked Deanna what she was going to do. Deanna had reiterated that she just wanted to be Phil's friend, to promote family harmony. Harriet had nodded and said, "uh-huh," as if she didn't believe her. It had given Deanna great pleasure when she and Georgia had trounced the other two soundly at bridge.

Deanna went home from the hospital and

took a long bath. Feeling more relaxed, she stood once again in front of the vast collection of evening wear in her closet. She sighed. In cocktail clothes, she had her choice of black— in every style and fabric imaginable but every one of them black. Phil's opinion of her figure had totally affected her buying habits during their marriage and continued to affect them. She didn't wear black because it gave her confidence. She wore it because she'd been totally brainwashed. She desperately wished she'd thought of that sooner, when she'd had time to do some shopping.

She could have bought something in red sequins.

She was still standing in her closet in her black body smoother and hose when the doorbell sounded. With a sigh of frustration Deanna picked up her robe and slid into it. She was going to have to give serious thought to advertising for a new housekeeper, at least a butler.

"I'm running a little late," she apologized as she opened the door.

Phil looked as dashing as ever in his formal black tuxedo. As was becoming his habit of late, he scanned her boldly from head to toe. "We don't have to go." His voice was husky and his eyes dark, leaving Deanna no doubt as to what he was suggesting.

"Why don't you wait in the living room," Deanna suggested pointedly, not wanting to encourage any thought in that direction. "I'll just be a minute."

"I could help," he offered hopefully.

"I'll just be a minute," Deanna repeated.

She waited until he'd turned toward the living room, shaking her head at his melodramatic sigh, before she returned to her bedroom and selected a simple black, ankle length sheath. It wasn't red, but it left her shoulders bare and showed a considerable amount of cleavage. It also had a matching sequined black jacket, which covered the bare shoulders and considerable cleavage as well as adding class and sparkle. She hesitated a moment over her jewelry, then resolutely fastened on a diamond and ruby necklace, earrings, and bracelet. Phil had given them to her and would probably read too much into her wearing them, but the occasion called for diamonds and what good were diamonds if they weren't worn?

"You've definitely lost weight," Phil said when she rejoined him, his gaze even more appreciative than earlier.

She hadn't done it for him but probably because of him. Depression had done that to her. Of all the compliments he could have offered, that one impressed her least. He'd never been anything but critical of her figure during their marriage, when she'd worked so hard to keep trim for him.

"Where's your coat?"

"This will be fine," Deanna said, indicating her jacket.

Phil studied her silently.

Deanna didn't want to start their evening off with a fight. "It's not as acceptable to wear fur as it used to be, Phil. Every time I wear one, someone makes a comment about dead animals. I'd rather not wear it."

"Seems more wasteful to let it hang in a closet to rot," Phil commented, but he let the subject drop, for which Deanna was grateful.

The bad thing about belonging to the same country club all your life was that everyone knew everyone else's business and felt like they were entitled to know and to offer advice. The club had once been a major part of her life. Now, she only went there for brunch on Sunday with the family after church. Her mother insisted, reminding her that it had been a family tradition long before Phil had come into the picture. That was true, but Deanna resented the fact that every Sunday, no matter how evasive she tried to be, someone found a way to tell her who Phil was currently dating or tried to set her up with some friend or relative of theirs when she hadn't been ready.

When they entered the room, heads turned. Neighbors were nudged as she walked through the crowd on Phil's arm. She could almost see tongues wagging at both ends as the gossipmongers rushed to discuss the significance of this latest development in the Randolph divorce. Deanna smiled and tried not to think vindictive thoughts.

"There's Roger," Phil said, apparently oblivious to the sensation they were causing. Deanna recognized Dr. Roger Gillespie, one of Atlanta's leading gastroenterologists and one of Phil's favorite cronies. When together, the two surgeons tended to monopolize the conversation with detailed discussions on subjects such as the pros and cons of synthetic heart valves and digestion at the cellular level. Roger was sitting with a stunning young woman who could only be the new wife Deanna had heard so much gossip about.

Roger stood up and shook hands with Phil, then greeted Deanna. "Have you met Tricia?" Roger asked, gesturing toward the blonde sitting beside him. "This is my wife and research assistant." His smile was filled with pride as he introduced her. "Tricia, this is Deanna Randolph, Phil's wife."

"Ex-wife, actually," Deanna corrected, extending her hand to Tricia. "It's nice to meet you."

Tricia smiled as she took Deanna's hand. The gossips had referred to Tricia as a barracuda. There was cunning in the cool green eyes that assessed Deanna. Deanna smiled back, refusing to be daunted. After all, Tricia was the newcomer here.

Roger sent Phil an uncomfortable glance. "Won't you join us?" he invited, indicating the vacant chairs at their table. Although Phil held Deanna's chair for her, she could tell he wasn't pleased with her. Too bad. Her status as his ex-wife had been his idea and she had warned him that tonight's date was in friendship only.

"It's beautiful the way they've decorated," Tricia said, trying to make polite conversation.

Deanna looked around at the opulent furnishings, the rich decorations, the designer Christmas tree. It looked the same to her as it looked every year at this time. The same china and silver pattern had been in use here since the club's founding. It was tradition, demanded by some of the oldest families in Atlanta, strictly enforced by some of the oldest money in the South. Deanna realized this was Tricia's first New Year's Eve party at the club.

"Yes, they do a nice job," Deanna responded. She wondered where Ellen, Roger's first wife, was spending New Year's Eve, and with whom. Last New Year's Eve they'd been at the party together. It was almost as if the two physicians had made the decision together. She could imagine their discussion.

"Roger, I've been thinking it's time to get divorced, find me a new wife."

"I've had the same thoughts, Phil, maybe a blonde this time."

"I think we should wait 'til after the holidays, though. Less stress on the family."

"You're right, Phil, good thinking. Let's shoot for January 4th. That's a Monday.

Maybe lawyers had end-of-season discounts, half off if you bring a friend. It was a sad thought.

"Deanna, would you like a drink?" Phil asked, bringing her back to reality.

"What? Oh, yes, white wine, thank you." Ellen Gillespie had taken a course in mountain climbing after their divorce and had spent the summer on an expedition to Mount Everest. She had invited Deanna to join her, but Deanna had declined, preferring to wallow in self-pity, she realized now. She should have gone.

"Would you like to dance or check out the hors d'oeuvres?" Roger asked Tricia.

"Let's dance," Tricia said, jumping to her feet and taking Roger's hand.

"That sounds good to me," Phil said, standing and pulling Deanna to her feet. They were on the dance floor before Deanna realized what had taken place.

Roger, for all his arrogance, had asked Tricia which she preferred. Phil, for all his promised change of attitude, hadn't asked. He never asked. In twenty-nine years of marriage, he'd made decisions and given instructions, expecting Deanna to faithfully carry them out. And damn her, she had.

"Relax," Phil crooned in her ear. "You're as stiff as a mannequin."

"I'm hungry." It came out more baldly than she'd intended, but she was new to this assertiveness behavior. Phil wasn't the only one who needed to change his attitude.

He tried to mold her more intimately against him. "Me, too. We don't have to stay until midnight. We could take a bottle of champagne back and . . ."

"For food, Phil." Deanna shoved away from his advances and tried to put some distance between them. "I haven't eaten since early this morning. I'd like to eat. Now," she added, knowing she wasn't handling this right. She blamed lack of experience.

Phil looked hurt. "Could we at least finish this dance?"

The way he said it made Deanna feel foolish. She forced her body to relax back against his. He led them silently through the dance for several bars, then spoke persuasively near her ear.

"We should do this more often, Deanna, spend more time together. I enjoyed Christmas at your mother's. Maybe we needed some time apart, to realize what we had. I've already admitted I took a lot for granted."

Deanna was also aware of things she'd taken for granted, like her position in society, her worth as a person. Until she'd been labeled "divorced," she'd never given much thought about who she was. She had been Charlotte and Joseph Edwards's daughter right up until the time she became Dr. Phillip Randolph's wife. The last year had given her a painful awakening. On her own, she apparently had little value in the social circles she'd once considered her world.

Because of her family, she hadn't been totally shunned, but invitations had been presented with the stipulation, "bring an escort," either in so many words or implied. Someone was always trying to set her up with some single man they knew. The social world existed for couples, and single women weren't acceptable. At least her charity work at Children's Hospital was her own. There, she was still considered an asset, divorced or not. She had buried the last miserable year of her life there. Now, on this eve of a new year, she was ready for something more.

"Maybe we should take a vacation together," Phil suggested, when she didn't answer him. "Go to Mexico, go to the Caribbean, somewhere warm and sunny. Secluded," he added, nuzzling her ear and making his voice husky and suggestive.

"Haven't you heard? Sun is bad for you." Deanna pulled out of his arms as the music ended. "You promised to feed me." Without waiting for his consent, she worked her way to the buffet table.

It would be very easy to slide back into Phil's arms, back into her old life, chalk this past year up as an interesting experience. He seemed willing, although she was afraid to analyze the reason too closely. The problem was, she wasn't the same woman Phil had divorced a year ago. The only thing she wanted back from her marriage was her status, which made her feel like a mercenary. There was family cohesiveness, of course, but that was hard to justify when none of the children lived at home anymore.

It wouldn't be the same marriage she'd had

before, no matter what they did. She no longer trusted Phil. She was no longer willing to defer to his wishes and answer to his plans. As for desire, his hungry looks didn't do nearly as much to her libido as those of Evan Maxwell, not that she intended to do anything about those, either. It just proved a point. She wasn't too old to enjoy a man's attention.

Deanna selected a generous assortment of appetizers from the variety set up on a side table. She was going to enjoy herself tonight, mingle among life-long friends and make some New Year's resolutions. She was going to rejoin society, accept invitations, meet new people. She was going to buy new clothes in colors she liked and she was going to advertise for a housekeeper, no, a butler. It would be nice to have a man wait on her for a change.

"Deanna, you look marvelous," Susan Whitehead commented as she met Deanna on the way back to her table. "And Phil," she added, taking him in with attentive eyes. "I do hope this means y'all are talking reconciliation."

Susan, the gossip hound. Whatever Deanna said to her at this moment would circulate the room faster than cigar smoke. "There's no reason Phil and I can't be friends, is there?" she asked Susan. "After all, we still have children and our work at the hospital."

"Of course," Susan agreed, her eyes bright. "I think that's lovely, just lovely. Does this mean we'll see you out and about more, Deanna?"

"When it works out," Deanna said, not wanting to sound eager. Susan moved on, and Deanna felt herself launched.

Her satisfaction faded a moment later when Connie Tarwater sailed up to her, the full skirt of her designer gown floating around her like mist. "Deanna! Phil! Don't y'all just look marvelous together again."

"We're here as friends, Connie," Deanna tried to explain, but Connie wasn't interested in explanations.

"I always did like that dress on you, Deanna." Which was Connie's not-so-subtle way of saying "I see you didn't buy a new dress for the occasion." Deanna sighed. That was also part of returning to society.

"Thank you, Connie. I've always liked it, too."

Connie gave her an assessing look, then smiled. She gave Phil an even warmer smile. "I do hope we can dance together later. Ring in the New Year?"

Deanna didn't wait to hear Phil's response. She made it the rest of the way to her table without being further accosted.

She danced again later with Phil, then with

Roger. Then an old friend of hers and Phil's named Sam Dixon asked her to dance. Sam had been widowed for two years, was close to Deanna's age, and had asked her out a couple of times since her divorce. She had refused, telling him she wasn't ready yet. She smiled and accepted his offer to dance, then agreed that he could call her, after the holidays.

She excused herself to go to the ladies' room. She'd wanted back in circulation, but she wasn't as excited about the prospect as she'd thought she'd be. Sam was a perfect escort—a family friend, single, grown children, good job—but his nearness didn't make her want to lean nearer and his conversation didn't make her laugh. She had to quit comparing men to Evan Maxwell. She wasn't planning to marry Sam, just to go out to dinner, attend a party. That's what socializing meant.

She was trying to straighten out her panty hose when two women came into the ladies' room. Their subject of conversation was Phil, and once again Deanna found herself eavesdropping shamelessly, hiding behind the door of her stall.

"What is that proverb?" the one woman asked. "As a dog returns to its vomit, so a fool repeats his folly."

The other woman giggled. "But are you referring to him or her?" They both giggled at that. They sounded very young. Deanna didn't want to hear anymore, but she didn't want them to know she'd overheard them, so she was trapped.

"It's tempting, you know? All that money he makes. But the man makes love like Jiffy Lube—in and out in ten minutes or less." Both girls burst into giggles again. Deanna felt mortifying heat suffuse her face, even though she was alone. She wondered if the one talking was the one Harriet had overheard or if this was another dissatisfied customer. She almost felt sorry for Phil. The man was fifty-four years old and a brilliant surgeon. He shouldn't have to perform for young nymphomaniacs who were only interested in him for his money.

Then resentment set in. The jerk deserved to be laughed at by young nymphomaniacs behind bathroom walls. That's what happened to fifty-four-year-old men who divorced perfectly good, faithful wives and went looking for "one last field to sow in wild oats," as her mother described it.

The girls went into the stalls, still laughing. Deanna went back to her table, where she assessed Phil with a jaundiced eye. Could it be that Georgia was right, that he'd discovered the grass wasn't greener on the bachelor side of the fence? Did he really believe she wasn't boring, or had he decided he preferred boring women, women who offered safe, undemanding sex and dutifully picked up his shirts at the cleaners?

"Phil, did you ever think about buying a motorcycle?" she asked him.

"Why would I want a motorcycle? They're dangerous."

"Harriet and her husband ride one. They go on trips through the mountains together. They have a lot of fun."

He smiled at her paternally, to her irritation, as if she were a silly child. "If we go on vacation, it will be to a resort by airplane. I have no desire to ride a motorcycle through the mountains and camp on the ground or stay in quaint little cabins with linoleum floors. That is not my idea of fun."

"Don't you ever want to do something different? Something a little wild?" Deanna persisted.

His smile became less paternal and more sensual. "The only thing wild I'd like to do is take you home and rekindle old fires."

"But you complained of being bored at home," she reminded him.

"I also told you I've seen the error of my ways. I would like nothing more than to return to the way things were." He offered her his most charming smile, then reached for her hand. "Would you like to dance again, or shall we finish this celebration at home?"

"Let's dance," Deanna said, pulling him to his feet.

She had her answer, and it made her sad. Phil wanted her back for all the same reasons he'd left her. He didn't want to change. He wanted someone who would let him return to his old, comfortable, self-centered ways. Fortunately, Deanna had changed, and she was no longer willing to accept that relationship. She had pulled her self-esteem back together without him, but it would have been nice if he'd truly discovered she was a fun, interesting, sexy woman. Instead, he seemed to believe she was boring, predictable, and pathetic enough to take him back just because he wanted to come back.

The band halted for the countdown to midnight. Confetti flew and everyone screamed "Happy New Year!" including Deanna. Phil grabbed her first and kissed her. She kissed him back, but it was bittersweet. Last year he had kissed her, and he had known it was goodbye. This year it was her turn. She fully intended to have a happy new year, but it wouldn't include Phil Randolph, unless he was willing to accept her as a friend.

Eight

"That society woman comin' today?"

Evan blinked. He'd been sitting behind the counter staring out the front window and hadn't heard Cloyd approach. "Yeah, we're going to take the bikes out on the road today."

"Starin' out the window ain't gonna make her come no faster."

Evan scowled. "I am not staring—"

"You have an unhealthy fascination with dangerous things," Cloyd observed, ignoring Evan's denial. "Airplanes, war zones, fancy women."

"Interesting observation from a man who sets off security gates because of the hardware in his leg from racing motorcycles. I hardly think Deanna compares to a war zone."

"Been my experience that a divorce is real similar to a war zone. You and your daddy both married fancy women, and look what came of that."

"I came from that," Evan reminded him.

"My brother came from that. My sons came from that."

"And all of them sons was raised by their mothers," Cloyd pointed out. "I watched your daddy grieve over not bein' there for your raisin', and I've been watchin' you tryin' to get close to your boys now they're grown. Seems to me you preferred the war zone."

Only Cloyd could get away with talking to him like this, Evan thought, irritated with the old man, knowing he was right. He hadn't liked letting his boys be raised by his ex-wife and her new husband, but the bitter arguments that had ensued had created behavior problems in the boys that he couldn't ignore. So he'd buried himself in his career, spent a lot of time overseas, and tried to be a father through correspondence and phone calls.

Then, when his father had asked him to come and live with him after he'd retired from the Air Force, Evan realized he was as estranged from his sons as he'd been from his father. Adulthood was a difficult time to re-earn the trust of your children, but he was doing everything in his power. That Brian wanted to manage this dealership with him, had asked for his help in raising Kyle, proved he was making inroads. They'd had a wonderful New Year's celebration with his older son

Tom and his family. He was making progress, but the progress only reminded him of how much of their lives he'd missed.

"For a man who's never had kids, you sure seem to know a lot about it," Evan griped.

"I ain't talkin' about the kids, I'm talkin' about learnin' from your mistakes. Fancy women ain't nothin' but trouble."

Evan watched Deanna pull her big Buick into a parking place outside the dealership. It had been three weeks since he'd seen her, and he'd been looking forward to today, until Cloyd had reminded him of his ex-wife. Deanna wasn't anything like Pauline, except that she had a snobby mother and she carried herself like a queen and she wore clothes that cost an average man's paycheck and she abhorred dirt. Evan scowled as the list of similarities grew longer.

"I'm not planning to marry her," he growled at Cloyd as Deanna entered the showroom. "I'm just teaching her to ride her Indian."

"The way you act when she's around, I'd think you was planning on teachin' her to ride a Maxwell." Cloyd gave a bawdy laugh and went to talk to one of the customers, leaving Evan alone behind the counter.

Deanna's smile was radiant when she spotted him, prompting Evan to smile back. Cloyd was right about that, too. He'd like nothing better than to peel away those polite manners and regal airs to disclose the passionate woman he suspected lay buried inside. That kind of thinking was what was going to get him in trouble. Deanna had never given him any encouragement in that direction.

She looked different today. He scanned her, trying to figure out what was unusual. She stopped in front of him, holding out her arms, encouraging his inspection.

"What do you think?" she asked. "They're still pretty stiff, but I was assured they would soften up with use."

He'd never seen her in jeans, he realized. The ones she was wearing were black, crisply new, and enticingly tight. They did incredible things to the flare of her hips and the length of her legs. They ended in a pair of soft leather boots, also black.

"They weren't this tight until I put the ski underwear on under them."

The uncertainty in her voice brought his attention back to her face. She was no longer smiling but watching his reaction with a wary expression. Evan felt mortification warm his neck. He'd been all but drooling. He cleared his throat and forced a smile.

"Very . . . ah . . . practical. They're right. A few washings and they'll soften right up." And mold against her curves even more intimately. He shoved the compelling thought aside and sought for safer ground. "Did you have a good Christmas?"

Deanna's smile made her eyes sparkle. "It was very . . . educational."

Whatever the hell that meant. She was being mysterious. She was also wearing a red sweater with silver designs on it that brightened the brown of her eyes and offset her dark hair. It also defined the feminine curves of her breasts and hugged the flare of her hips, right where the jeans fit the tightest. And he'd thought she looked good in a suit.

Educational. He forced his mind back on track. "Did you take the written test?"

"Yes." The wariness had returned with his perusal, but she smiled again at his question. "I got them all right."

"I didn't expect anything less. Ready to ride?"

"Yes." This smile was closer to the one she'd worn when she'd first spotted him, open and excited. She looked more like an eager kid than a high society lady. Evan felt his own excitement responding to hers.

"Let's go then."

The day was sunny and crisp, the temperature somewhere in the middle forties. It didn't feel bad, standing still, but Evan knew the wind chill on a moving bike was going to be a different story. He fastened his jacket high around his throat and watched Deanna pull on her gloves. The jacket she had put on was also leather, a soft butternut yellow, fashionably cut with wide lapels. It left her throat and upper chest open to the wind, protected only by the thin knit of her turtleneck sweater.

"I think Brian's jacket would fit you," he offered hesitantly. "It would keep you a lot warmer."

"This is leather," Deanna assured him, "and I'm wearing ski underwear under this sweater. If anything, I'm too warm."

Evan smiled. "I'll offer again in half an hour."

They walked outside to where Evan had parked the bikes, the little Honda Deanna had been learning on and his big Harley. Deanna walked reverently around the Harley.

"Is this yours?"

Evan tried to act nonchalant, but it was difficult when Deanna was so obviously impressed. His chest swelled a little with pride and his walk took on a slight swagger. "It's called a Softail," he said, patting the padded passenger seat. "I bought it shortly after I bought into the dealership." It also conjured up images of soft-tailed women, wrapped adoringly around him as he rode it, their full breasts pressed against his back.

"It makes the Honda look like a toy."

Evan forced himself back into teacher mode, clearing his throat and trying to discreetly adjust his jeans. "You won't think so when you start riding it. Start it up and let it warm up while you do your safety check."

Deanna turned on the key, flipped out the kick starter, and tried to start the bike. Evan gave her three unsuccessful attempts before he intervened. Silently, but deliberately, he pulled out the choke. Deanna flushed scarlet. The bike started on her next attempt.

"Take it over to the track and get used to it again before we go out on the road," Evan suggested after she'd finished her safety check. Deanna nodded and put on her helmet. Her mouth was set with grim determination. Evan suspected she wasn't used to learning new skills or to making mistakes. He sincerely hoped she wasn't the type that got too frustrated to learn from them.

He watched her closely when she killed the engine. A smooth start from a standing stop was one of the most difficult skills to learn on a motorcycle, and one of the most critical. Deanna sat for a moment on the silent bike, looking out across the track. He watched her shoulders rise and fall, then she methodically shifted the bike into neutral and restarted it. She shifted into first gear, and the bike moved forward with a jerk. She stopped it and tried again, this time more smoothly. Evan smiled with satisfaction as he watched her repeat the drill several more times. She was frustrated with herself but apparently too determined to learn to ride to let frustration stop her.

Evan loved determined women. It was her determination that had first sparked his interest. She had appealed to him enough to convince him to restore her father's Indian and to teach her to ride it. The more time he spent with her, the more carnal his thoughts were becoming. It was an appeal he was certain was one-sided and doomed to bring him only humiliation. He wasn't used to being on this side of a one-sided attraction. He was much more comfortable being the one pursued.

The sound of the Honda's engine growing closer forced him out of his reverie, no closer to answers to his dilemma. Damn Cloyd for bringing up Pauline. Well, Deanna wasn't Pauline, and he was older and wiser to the ways of women now. He didn't want to marry the woman, just enjoy a mutually satisfying physical relationship for as long as they both found it mutually satisfying. He would just have to move slowly, go with his instincts, and pray those instincts were correct. He was fairly certain that with a woman like Deanna a man only got one chance.

"Comfortable enough to try the road?" he asked, shouting over the noise of her engine.

Comfortable was not the word Deanna would have chosen, but she nodded. She was damp and steamy inside all her layers of clothing, the frustration of her clumsy riding efforts heating her skin in spite of the cool day. The new jeans were stiff and tight, biting into her thighs and the backs of her knees. The new boots were rubbing a blister on her heel. She raised the face shield on her helmet, feeling closed in by the heat of her own breath.

"I think I liked the other helmet better," she shouted, referring to the half-helmet she'd worn the last time.

"No face protection," Evan shouted back. "Go right here," he pointed with his hand, indicating the drive out of the parking lot. "I'll stay behind you. Make a U-turn after you go over the bridge and head back east. Take it slow and pull over to the shoulder when you need a break."

Deanna watched him pull on his helmet, a full face helmet like the one he'd given her, and his gloves and turn the key in the big Harley. His had an electric starter, she noticed as it fired to life with a deep-throated roar that drowned out the softer sound of the Honda. Deanna watched him, mesmerized. She'd thought the black leather jacket changed him. That was nothing compared to what sitting astride the huge black motorcycle did. He checked the headlight and the taillight, let the bike idle for a minute to warm up, then looked over at her, his expression expectant. He gestured for her to lead out.

Deanna licked dry lips and swallowed hard. She wasn't ready for this. She would never sit a bike with Evan's easy confidence. She was frustrated with the little Honda. How did she think she was going to handle her dad's big Indian?

Evan was watching her, waiting. She'd come too far to back out now. The humiliation of quitting would be worse than that of failure. Women her age were climbing mountains and flying airplanes. Motorcycle riding had to be easier than that. She gave the Honda her full concentration, willing it to obey her commands.

"You will not die," she warned the motorcycle through clenched teeth. She slowly opened the throttle and eased out the clutch. The bike moved forward, a little quicker than she'd intended, but it didn't die. Deanna blew out her breath, pulled the clutch back in and stopped at the entrance to the parking lot. Now she had to do it again, this time onto the road.

The entrance to the dealership sloped down from the highway, which meant Deanna was sitting on a fairly steep incline. When she released the front brake to open the throttle, both controlled with her right hand, the bike started rolling backward. To hold the bike with the rear brake meant using her right foot, which only left her with one foot to hold the bike up. Irritation at her lack of knowledge flushed new warmth through her. Why did everything having to do with motorcycles have to be so complicated?

"Hold the bike with your rear brake," Evan instructed, appearing suddenly at her side. "Give it a little more throttle than normal and wait until you feel the clutch engage before you release the brake. Wait until no cars are coming," he added as an afterthought.

"I can't hold it up with one leg," Deanna protested.

"You'd better learn. This one's easy. The Indian is going to be much heavier."

Deanna hesitantly lifted her right foot to the

brake pedal, balancing the bike with her left. Several seconds passed before she could release the front brake.

"You can hold it on a hill with the clutch," Evan shouted, "just like a car. Give it some gas, though, or you'll kill it."

She didn't care to recall her one encounter with the clutch in a car. Besides, she hadn't driven it far enough to need to hold it on a hill. Feeling sweat trickle under her arms, Deanna checked for oncoming traffic, then slowly eased out the clutch. The bike jerked, then died, then threatened to roll back down the hill. Deanna squeezed the front brake, then fought to keep the bike upright. Evan reached out to steady her.

"You're trying too hard," he offered gently. "Feel what the bike is doing. You're fighting with it. Come back down here."

With Evan's support, Deanna let the bike roll back to a level surface. He'd parked the Harley and turned it off. She also noticed several people watching her through the window of the showroom. She felt totally humiliated, a feeling she'd become too familiar with over the last year. She lifted her chin. She would learn how to do this if it killed her.

"Take a deep breath, regroup, then restart the bike."

Deanna did as instructed, raising the face-shield for air. She wished she could take it off, and her jacket as well.

"Let the clutch out just enough to feel the bike move, then stop."

Deanna tried to concentrate on feeling the bike's response as Evan made her do the familiar drill over and over, always stopping before the clutch was fully engaged. "That's how you hold it on a hill," Evan said, "that and your rear brake. And never, ever again hit your brakes with the front wheel turned." The soothing tone had changed to scolding. "You learned that the first day, Deanna. You do that with a big bike and you'll go right down with it. I've seen it happen with bigger men than me. You won't be able to hold it up. You'll be lucky to keep your leg out from under it." He was practically shouting now.

Deanna glared at him, resenting his tone of voice, resenting that she'd put herself in a situation for him to scold her. "I'll remember," she snapped back. "Anything else?"

Evan sucked in air, then paused, as if just realizing he'd been yelling. He let out the breath and gave her a rueful grin. "Sorry, I didn't mean to get so worked up. It's just that mistakes made on a motorcycle are liable to get you killed. I hope I'm not making a mistake, teaching you to ride one."

"If you are, it's my mistake," Deanna assured him, her anger softening. "It's not your fault if I don't remember a drill I worked on for two hours straight."

"I remember you considered it stupid at the time," Evan reminded her, his hazel eyes teasing.

Yes, she had, Deanna remembered, but she refused to admit it to him. Instead she gave him her sweetest smile. "Shall we try again?"

"I'm right behind you." Evan gestured toward the highway, inviting her to lead the way.

I'll do it right this time, Deanna thought, maneuvering the bike to the top of the drive and holding it there with the rear brake. She looked for traffic, then let out the clutch until she felt it start to take hold. She opened up the throttle and felt a surge of triumph as the bike scaled the hill and pulled out on the highway. Her victory was marred by the fact that she almost ran off the other side of the road before she got the bike turned and straightened back out. "God, remind me not to pull out in front of anybody any time soon," she muttered to herself. She shifted into second without too much jerking and felt her racing heart slow down a little. She could do this, it was just going to take some practice. She shifted smoothly into third, welcoming the cold air flowing over her overheated body.

Deanna led the way through the U-turn, then upshifted with much more confidence as they headed east. Evan's dealership was well north of the town of Buford, just off Interstate 85, but basically out in the middle of nowhere. The divided four-lane became a two-lane county road just east of his dealership. It carried very little traffic and had very few curves, for which Deanna was grateful. She kept her speed between thirty and forty, concentrating on keeping the bike where she wanted it in the middle of her lane. For something that had seemed quite simple when she'd read the book, it was proving somewhat difficult to do. Trying to adjust her position on the seat nearly sent her off the shoulder of the road. She knew from her reading and Evan's tutoring that steering the bike was done largely by shifting her weight and leaning the bike, but it seemed that the least little movement sent it in directions she didn't wish to go. After five miles, she pulled over to the shoulder, ready to go back.

Evan pulled off behind her, turned off his engine and walked up beside her. "Finally get cold?"

Deanna realized her teeth were chattering. "Yes, I guess I did. It felt good at first."

"You're doing great."

Deanna didn't think she was, but Evan's smile and the look in his eyes warmed something deep inside her. His face disappeared as steam fogged up her face-shield. She pushed it up impatiently, trying to give the illusion of breathing normally. "Thanks, but I think I'm ready for some hot chocolate."

He knows what he does to me, she thought, watching his eyes darken into that hungry gleam. It would never do to encourage anything more from him than teacher and mechanic.

Sleep with the biker.

She could never do it and keep her pride intact.

"See you back at the store." She lowered her visor and waited for him to step back. He held her gaze another moment, then stepped back, his smile knowing. Deanna took a deep breath, checked for traffic, then pulled her bike out on the road. Her U-turn was a little too wide and very wobbly. Her heartbeat was a little too fast and very shaky. She deliberately concentrated on shifting gears and keeping the bike where she wanted it in the road. Her teeth were chattering again, but she welcomed the cold air. Maybe it would clear her muddled mind.

* * *

It was becoming something of a ritual, Evan realized as he tried to drink hot chocolate with Kyle bouncing in his lap and Deanna spending time in the bathroom, trying to repair the damage to her appearance inflicted by the helmet and the wind. When she appeared in the doorway to his office and smiled at Kyle, he realized he liked the way she looked after riding. Brushed out, her hair looked softer, the cold wind had given her cheeks a healthy color, and the turtleneck sweater and jeans gave her a more relaxed look, even if she was still wearing her pearls.

"I guess I need to buy a helmet of my own," Deanna said, running her hands through her hair. "Do they make one that isn't so hard on hairdos?" She slid into the worn leather chair without reservation, reaching eagerly for the cup of hot chocolate.

"None that I'm aware of. We have plenty around here. Keep trying different ones until you decide which one you prefer."

"The face-shield is nice against the wind, but it kept fogging up and closing me in."

"Only when you're sitting still. They're designed to circulate air when you're moving. If you wear one of the other helmets without the face-shield, you'll need to wear goggles to protect your eyes."

"Joey has a new puppy," Kyle interrupted, having reached his limit of adult conversation.

"Really? What's his name?"

She's good with children, Evan thought, watching Deanna talk effortlessly with Kyle. His presence, his chattering, his rambunctious activity never seemed to bother her. Most of the women who came to the shop either gushed over him or politely tolerated him. Very few ever treated him like a person. It was just one more thing for Evan to admire about Deanna Randolph. He wondered if there was anything about Evan Maxwell that Deanna admired. Maybe he reminded her of her ex-husband. Grim thought.

"You have a dog," Evan reminded Kyle, catching part of the conversation.

"Ghost doesn't like to play, though," Kyle whined. "He just lays there."

"We've been through this. You can play with Joey's puppy. Now run out and let me visit with Miss Deanna."

"You watch, Kyle," Deanna said. "In a year or so, Joey's puppy will grow up and lay around just like Ghost."

Kyle frowned, thinking about that. "I never saw any dog lay around much as Ghost does," he said solemnly. He shook his head sadly as he walked out the office door.

Deanna's gaze met Evan's, her brown eyes filled with suppressed laughter. Evan smiled back at her. "He's right, I'm afraid. If Ghost were a little flatter, we could use him as a rug."

"Looking at puppies yet?" Deanna asked, raising an amused eyebrow.

"No way. We're not home enough. Maybe when Kyle is older." Evan would have enjoyed talking with Deanna about puppies and grandchildren for the rest of the afternoon, but she was here to learn to ride motorcycles. He straightened in his chair and rested his hands on his desk.

"There are some basic skills that you have to do in order to take the road test and get your final license."

"I read about them in the book," Deanna said.

"We need to work on those and you need more time just riding the bike. Once a week isn't going to be enough."

"I came to that conclusion myself this afternoon. It's much harder than it looks."

"The Indian is even more difficult."

"Speaking of which, how's it coming?"

"Why don't you come out tomorrow and see

for yourself? I think you'll be impressed. You can see the Indian, we can do some more riding . . ." I could take you out to dinner. . . . Courage failed him. He left the thought unspoken. She hadn't agreed to the first two suggestions yet.

To his relief, she smiled. "Okay, but it'll be after three. We always have dinner with the family after church on Sunday. Anymore, it's about the only time I see my children and grandchildren." She hesitated, and Evan hoped she was considering inviting him to join them. Instead, she stood up. Disappointment washed through him, then irritation that he'd gotten his hopes up.

"I'd better let you get back to work. Looks like you're busy out front."

"Saturdays are always busy." Evan stood up also and opened the door to his office. "Most people just like to come in and chat, see what's happening. I'll meet you here tomorrow at three. We'll ride first, then you can follow me over to the house to see your bike." He leaned against the doorjamb, deciding not to walk her out to her car this time.

If she was disappointed, it didn't show. She did hesitate for a moment, then pulled herself up straighter. Her smile was cool, polite, distant. "That sounds fine. See you tomorrow."

Even in jeans and boots she walked like a lady, Evan thought, watching her leave. If only he could find a way past that refined lady to the passionate woman he was certain lurked beneath. Tomorrow he'd think of a way to get her on his bike. There was no mistaking her fascination with it, and he doubted even a woman like Deanna could maintain her careful distance when her arms and thighs were wrapped around him, her safety dependent on his skill.

"Hey, Evan, did you order some special pipe for Ernest's old Chopper?" Cloyd's gravelly voice broke into his thoughts.

"Yeah, I'll get it," Evan called back. He turned toward the shop, trying to discreetly adjust for a sudden tightness in the front of his jeans.

Nine

Bundled against the cold weather almost to the point of immobility, Deanna spent what was left of Sunday afternoon learning how to handle the bike in emergency situations. Evan made her practice sudden stops, sharp turns at slow speeds, and evasive maneuvers. Finally, cold to the bone and tired of all of Evan's repetitive drills, Deanna deliberately got too close to him before bringing the bike to a skidding halt. She was quite satisfied with his startled leap to safety. She answered his furious scolding with a malicious smile.

"You did that on purpose," he finally said, realization dawning.

"I'm cold, I'm tired, and I think I can handle this beast in rush hour traffic on 85 in a heavy downpour." Deanna glared at him, daring him to disagree.

He grinned. "Your attitude is improving. Much more positive. Ready to try the Harley?"

Deanna parked the Honda and turned it

off, then dismounted slowly, stiff from cold and too many layers of clothing. "I'd love to try your Harley, just as soon as the temperature gets above fifty."

"Even at fifty, the wind chill is around thirty." Evan held open the door to the dealership. "That's what they make insulated riding suits for."

"I plan to be a fair-weather rider."

It felt strange somehow, being inside the dealership when it was closed. There were no customers to wonder what she was doing there, no metallic clanking from the shop, no Kyle bouncing in Evan's lap when Deanna came into the office. It was just the two of them in the silent building, implying an intimacy that made Deanna self-conscious.

"You're starting to handle that bike like you know what you're doing," Evan commented. "When you're comfortable on the road with it, we'll graduate up to my Harley. There isn't a modern bike that's going to handle anything like the Indian, but at least you'll get used to the size and horsepower. Actually, the Harley is heavier than the Indian, but the wheelbase is similar."

"How's the Indian coming?" Deanna sipped her hot chocolate, warmed by both the drink and Evan's confidence in her ability.

Evan set his cup down, his demeanor instantly changing Deanna's cozy mood.

"What's wrong?" Deanna asked.

"Nothing's wrong," Evan hastened to reassure her. "I'm just at a point I'm not sure how you want me to proceed."

Deanna relaxed. She smiled for him to continue.

"You have a prize in that bike that would be the envy of any collector. It has the incredible distinction of being totally, without exception, factory original, just the way it came off the assembly line forty-one years ago."

His eyes had taken on a fevered shine, Deanna noticed, the way they had when she'd first told him about the bike.

"I've already altered it by overhauling the engine and getting it back into running condition." He made it sound like he'd desecrated a priceless work of art. "I have to tell you I spent extra to buy original parts where I could find them. We'd already agreed about that much."

Deanna nodded, waiting to hear the rest.

"The seat's still good, although I'm not sure how much use it'll take. I've already told you I wouldn't repaint it. If you want to ride it, it has to have new tires."

"What's the problem, Evan?"

Evan sighed. "That's original chrome."

"You said part of the price of restoration was for chrome."

"I know I did, but I can't do it without knowing what you want to do with that bike. If you want to sell it to a collector, a real collector would come after my hide for tampering with original chrome. In fact, I've saved every original part I've taken off that bike. Deanna, you've just got no idea how fanatical some of these collectors are."

If Evan's zeal was any indication, Deanna suspected she was being given a pretty good idea. "What do you suggest?"

"It's too late for what I should have suggested. I should have suggested trailering it from show to show and collecting trophies. You would have an entire nation of Indian collectors falling at your feet, begging just to look at it. It would easily—"

Deanna started laughing, imagining big, hulking bikers groveling at her feet, pleading for permission to look at her rusted relic of a motorcycle. Evan stopped, frowning at her amusement.

"Very wealthy, powerful men take collecting very seriously," he said ominously.

"I'm sure they do." Deanna tried to stifle her smile. "Evan, I'd really like to see what you've done to the bike. Then we'll discuss anything further that should be done. The last time I saw it, it wasn't fit for mouse lodging."

"You could have gotten $30,000 for that bike the way we hauled it out of the carriage house. It takes a collector's eye to see the real beauty of a bike like that."

Deanna was stunned. That was $10,000 more than she'd been quoted for it restored. "I guess you'd better teach me how to see through a collector's eye."

Whatever Deanna had expected when she finally entered Evan's garage, it wasn't disassembled pieces of her motorcycle laid out with great reverence on a clean canvas tarp. Except for the engine, which was sitting on the workbench, there weren't two pieces of the bike still attached to each other.

"You can start that lesson now," Deanna said, somewhat horrified by the sight spread out before her.

"You have to take each part separately, look at how well preserved it is, determine if it's still functional." Evan stepped cautiously onto the tarp. "See the frame? The paint cleaned up well. There's a little bit of rust showing through, mostly around the bolt holes, but the points you'll get for original paint will more than offset any lost by a little rust."

"Points?"

"In judging. One hundred points is a perfect, totally original bike. They're very rare." He turned back, indicating the gas tanks. "The decals are still like new. That alone is reason not to repaint it."

"Why are there two of them?"

"There have always been two of them. They fit together, like this." He held the two tanks together around the upper portion of the frame. "Look more familiar?"

"Hmmm. What about the chrome." Deanna really didn't want to know this much about restoration. She wasn't a collector. She remembered her father's enthusiasm about the bike's value, though. He would have liked Evan Maxwell. She listened patiently while Evan explained about original chrome, wires, and cables.

"You're asking me to put a dull, rusting motorcycle into the auction beside Billy's and expect people to know this one's better?" Deanna finally interrupted to ask. "My mother will never understand."

"Who's Billy? There's another Indian in your auction?"

"Billy Adonis, the rock star. He donated a '55. It's fully restored."

"And that's what you wanted yours to look like." It was a statement, as he realized where her request for restoration had come from.

They were both silent as Deanna looked back over the scattered parts that had once been her father's proud, beautiful motorcycle. Restoring it had been symbolic somehow, as if she could restore her own youth and beauty. Riding it was supposed to prove that she wasn't old, wasn't incapable because she was a woman, wasn't boring.

"If it's buyers you need, all it'll take is a few phone calls and you'll have a genuine bidding war on your hands."

Deanna didn't want a bidding war. She had understood the value of the bike to be $20,000, which she had been willing to pay. Now, Evan was talking $30,000, or higher, and that didn't include his fee for restoring it. Her impulsive decision was snowballing on her.

"It pains me to say this," Evan said, "but it is your bike."

Deanna looked up at him, wondering if her expression was as bleak as her thoughts. "You make me sound like one of those crass people who would paint an antique oak armoire glossy black."

Evan grinned. "Something like that, yeah. Listen, Deanna, you don't have to decide today. When is your auction?"

"March."

"Think about it a week or so. Meanwhile, I'll make those phone calls and— "

"No!" She hadn't meant to shout, but she was feeling backed into a corner. She stroked the pearls around her neck and tried to calm down. Evan was looking at her, his expression perplexed and concerned. She really owed him something of an explanation. "Look, can we go somewhere . . ."

"Do you like Chinese food?" Evan interjected. "There's a place here in Buford."

"That'll be fine."

Deanna spent the ride into Buford trying to word her confession in such a way that she didn't come out looking like a fool. She waited until they were seated across from each other in a cheap, red, vinyl-covered booth and had been served steaming bowls of sizzling rice soup. Evan beat her to the punch.

"You didn't intend to sell the bike," he stated quietly.

There was no accusation in his eyes, only concern. Deanna dropped her gaze. She focused on the peas floating in her soup, dunking them with the little ladle she was supposed to be eating with.

"I didn't give this whole thing much thought. It just sort of evolved." She sighed, then looked back at Evan. "I should start at the beginning." She told him about Billy's daughter and Billy's generous contribution to the auction. "I saw that motorcycle and experienced such a rush of memories. Dad had been so proud of his, so confident of its potential value as a collector's item, and there was proof of his prediction. I knew I had to restore it."

"Your father sounds like he had a good head for investments."

Deanna laughed. "That's an understatement. My father made his own fortune, investing every cent he could earn, then reinvesting every cent he made in profit. My brother Pete took over the firm, but he's more cautious than Dad. He says it's harder to make big money today, and maybe he's right. Dad was the right man for the times."

Deanna knew she was getting wistful, talking about her father. She took a spoonful of her cooling soup. Evan had finished his.

"What made you want to ride it?"

She'd been expecting the question. She wasn't about to reveal all her insecurities to a man like Evan Maxwell, who'd probably never had an insecure moment in his life. No, that wasn't fair. He'd confessed to being divorced for fifteen years. He was asking questions and listening to her talk as if he was genuinely interested. As a mechanic, all he really needed to know was how much she wanted him to do. He was acting more like a friend. Still, she wasn't ready to explain about Phil.

She batted her eyelashes at him. "Oldest reason in the world. Daddy and my brothers always told me I couldn't. I was just a girl."

Evan smiled at her exaggerated southern belle affectation. "A lot of women rode Indians back in the fifties. Still, it wasn't exactly the age of enlightenment."

"No," Deanna agreed. The waiter removed their soup bowls and served the appetizers of egg rolls and deep fried butterfly shrimp.

"Why'd you wait forty years to prove a point?"

That was going to be difficult to answer without dragging in all the other reasons. She gave a nonchalant shrug as she bit into a shrimp. It was not polite to speak with food in one's mouth.

"I'd forgotten about it until I saw Billy's Indian. Like I said earlier, I didn't give this whole thing much thought ahead of time."

"And now I'm clouding the issue by telling you it's more valuable unrestored."

"Putting the bike in the auction was the only way I could think of to get Mother to let me have it. She hated it, nagged at Daddy constantly to get rid of it, swore one of us was going to get killed on it. Then a friend of Andrew's did get killed on one. Andrew's my other brother. His friend was twenty-one at the time. He blew a front tire and lost control of it." The tragedy of the loss was still poignant, making Deanna's throat tight.

"Motorcycles, like cars, have become much safer over the last forty years," Evan put in. His voice was sober, consoling, as if he understood her feelings. When Deanna looked up at him, he gave her a grim smile.

"I've lost a number of friends to motorcycles over the years."

"Yet you still ride them."

His smile widened slightly. "I've lost friends to almost every conceivable cause of death known to man. It's increased my respect for life, but except for giving up cigarettes, it's done little to change my habits. I take it your father was impressed enough to give up riding his."

The appetizer plates were removed and

three mounded platters of steaming food set between them, two entrees and rice.

"I hope you don't expect me to eat all this," Deanna exclaimed, momentarily side-tracked by the enormous portions.

"They provide doggy bags." Evan scooped generous portions of each entree onto his plate. "Actually, Ghost rarely gets Chinese food. I take it to work for lunch."

Deanna had met Ghost briefly on the way to the garage. The huge weimaraner mix had not looked like he lacked for sustenance.

"After Tim got killed, there was no appeasing Mother," Deanna continued after they'd both eaten for awhile. "I was never allowed to ride behind Daddy again, and he rode it less and less until finally he put it away. I'm not sure when he drained the gas and took the battery off of it."

"He really did intend for it to be a collector's item," Evan said. "Gasoline turns to shellac over time, ruining an engine, and of course battery acid is extremely corrosive." He held her gaze for a moment. "What do you think he would want you to do?"

Deanna toyed with her food, unable to hold Evan's intense gaze. "He would want it to go to the children." She laid down her fork and looked across the dining room at the Oriental screens and the framed paintings depicting life in ancient China. "I had a sister who died of leukemia when she was eight years old. The doctors couldn't do anything for her. It tore my father apart. He'd made a fortune, and he would have given every penny of it if it would have made a difference. After Angelica died, he set up a huge research grant through Children's Hospital. It comforted him to know ways were being discovered to fight leukemia, that other children would have a chance."

"And you carry on what he started."

"We all do to some degree. Mother has only recently cut back on the number of hours she used to work there. My daughter, Sherylyn, is specializing in pediatric surgery, like her father." She stopped, realizing she'd shared more than she'd intended.

"And you organize charity auctions," Evan finished smoothly.

"Dad would be pleased to know his efforts were appreciated," Deanna said, steering the conversation back to the Indian. "I guess when I look at it from that standpoint, I should leave it alone, let a collector buy it, someone who'll appreciate the attention Dad gave it."

"You can still learn to ride it."

"And risk scratching original paint?"

Deanna found she had worked through her feelings enough to tease Evan.

Evan smiled back, his eyes warm and appreciative. "What's life without taking a few risks?"

Deanna had the impression he was talking about more than riding an antique motorcycle.

Sleep with the biker.

Life was complicated enough without adding that to it. Looking for a distraction, Deanna snatched up one of the fortune cookies left by their waiter after he'd cleared their table.

Love will come from an unexpected source.

Deanna felt hysterical laughter bubble through her. She crumbled the tiny scrap of paper and shoved it into the side pocket of her purse.

" 'Hasty decisions will make for leisurely regret', " Evan read his out loud. "And they say fortune cookies are a sham. What did yours say?"

"I think you got mine," Deanna hedged, trying to laugh casually. Evan waited expectantly. "Some silly 'Confucius says' nonsense. It didn't make any sense."

Whatever else he was, Evan Maxwell was a gentleman. He took the hint and didn't press the issue. He did give her a long, appraising look before he stood up and held her coat for her to slip into.

"Call those collectors you were telling me

about," Deanna said during the drive back to the dealership, where she'd left her car. "I'll tell my brothers about the situation. I think they were planning on bidding on it as well."

"I take it they aren't pleased that little sister is selling Dad's bike."

"No, they aren't pleased, but like I told them, it was Mother's to do with as she pleased, and she gave it to me."

"To put in the auction."

"To restore and put in the auction. She's going to be so embarrassed when she sees it."

Evan placed his hand over hers on the seat between them. "I'll be happy to explain things to her."

The warmth of Evan's hand, the intimacy of it lying over hers, was so startling, so unexpected, that Deanna jerked her hand away before the ramifications of her actions were even considered. Evan casually put his hand back on the steering wheel, but Deanna could tell by the set of his jaw that she'd committed a major blunder. She might as well have slapped his face. He would never understand how he jumbled her senses.

"Evan—"

"It's okay, Deanna. I was out of line." His voice was hard, not apologetic at all. He was angry and probably thought she was snubbing him. She wasn't sure how to explain without making matters worse.

"You just startled me, that's all. I'm a little out of practice."

Evan pulled into the drive of the dealership and got out to unlock the gate. Deanna sat glumly in her corner of the pickup, worrying her pearls and wondering what else she could say. He got back in and pulled the truck next to her Buick and turned off the engine. The sudden silence was deafening.

"I really enjoyed dinner, Evan. Thanks for taking the time to explain about the motorcycle."

"I should have it back together in a week or two," Evan said, his voice flat. "Come out and ride the Honda any time you want to. Brian has an insulated riding suit you can borrow and there's very little traffic on Friendship Road."

You can learn the rest on your own, was the implied conclusion. Pride be damned, she couldn't end the evening like this. She held out her hand to him.

"Could you try again?"

Evan hesitated, long enough to make Deanna fear that he was going to take advantage of the opportunity to humiliate her in retaliation. His expression was unreadable in the dim light from the Harley-Davidson sign at the front of the dealership. Just as she was ready to withdraw her hand, he grasped it.

"You are the damnedest woman I ever tried to understand."

His hand was as warm as it had been during that first, brief contact, and the impact of his touch just as shattering. His brow was furrowed as if he, too, was trying to understand what was happening between them. Deanna tried to summon a friendly smile and turn the intimate contact into a goodbye handshake.

"I'll try to get out this week."

Evan Maxwell was a gentleman. A Yankee gentleman. An officer and a gentleman, she remembered, from the Air Force. He released her hand without a word and came around to open her door. The cold night air was a welcome balm.

There was no further contact, no further discussion. Deanna got into her car and headed back toward Atlanta, afraid to even think about what had happened with Evan. He was her mechanic, and apparently as aware of the unsuitability of . . . friendly overtures . . . between them as she was. She gave a huge sigh of frustration. Calling Evan a mechanic was hardly fair. He was a retired Air Force officer who was now a businessman and who restored antique motorcycles in his garage. She knew very little about his background, who his parents were, where he grew up.

Was she being a snob, or was she just exercising commendable prudence in a world where casual sex was the equivalent of Russian roulette? Commendable prudence, she decided. She was hardly a snob. Didn't she spend at least three days a week at the hospital doing charity work? It never mattered to her what background a child came from. Look at Sara Harris. Her mother was a prostitute living on welfare.

The phone was ringing when Deanna entered her front door. She disengaged the alarm, knowing the machine would pick up the call.

"Mrs. Randolph, this is Sergeant Smith of the Gwinnett County Sheriff's Department." Deanna grabbed the receiver, disconnecting the machine.

"This is Mrs. Randolph."

"Oh, good, you're there. I hate leaving messages on answering machines. Mrs. Randolph, I'm here with a Gloria Harris. She's been in a slight altercation with one of her boyfriends and needs to go to the emergency room."

Dread apprehension squeezed Deanna's heart. She groped for a chair and sank down into it.

"She gave us your card," the Sergeant continued, "saying you were the only one she would trust with her baby. Would it be possible for you to meet us at the emergency room over at Gwinnett County?"

She had just been there, Deanna thought with disbelief. It had probably happened while she had been at dinner with Evan. She had had no clue. Sara. Was Sara hurt? Was Gloria hurt so badly that she couldn't call. Had they just found Deanna's card on her unconscious body?

The sergeant was still speaking, giving her directions to the hospital. "Wait," Deanna said, searching through her purse for a pen and something to write on. "Yes, I've got it. I'll come right away." She hung up the phone, then realized she still didn't know any details. It didn't matter. She would be there herself in record time.

Ten

Deanna introduced herself at the desk of the emergency room where the policeman on the phone had instructed her to go. The receptionist disappeared, then returned with a harried-looking nurse in tow.

"Mrs. Randolph? I'm Tammy Laurent, the charge nurse. Are you a family member?"

"No, I'm . . . just a personal friend of Gloria's. Is she all right?"

"We don't know. We haven't been able to take any x-rays because of the baby. She may have a concussion, probably a dislocated shoulder. Otherwise just cuts and bruises."

"May I see her?"

The cry of horror that rose in Deanna's throat upon seeing Gloria's appearance was quickly cut off by the defiant glare in Gloria's right eye— the left one was swollen shut— and the stubborn set of her jaw, or what was visible of it beneath the bruises. Deanna struggled to get herself back in control, but her attention kept returning to the terrible damage that had been done to Gloria's face.

"Is Sara all right?" she finally asked.

Gloria sagged back against the raised head of the stretcher. "Yes, thank God." She squeezed the baby tighter against her, only using her left arm. She kept her right arm close against her side. "I'm sorry to call you, but there wasn't no one else who could keep Sara."

"I was glad to come." Gloria looked like she would collapse at any moment. Deanna hurried to take the baby. "I think they want to take you to x-ray."

Gloria relinquished the baby slowly, following her with her good eye. "There's formula in the diaper bag. You remember she has to eat slow."

"I'll take good care of her. We'll be right here when you get back."

"Actually, you'll have to wait in the waiting room," the nurse said. "Visitors aren't allowed back here in the treatment area."

Deanna gave the nurse a superior smile. "Then we'll need somewhere private to wait. This baby cannot be around sick people. She has a heart condition."

The nurse set her lips in disapproval, but she turned and marched out.

"I guess we showed her," Deanna said to Sara, who was staring at her with unblinking fascination.

"You look good in jeans," Gloria said, a weary smile pulling at the cut on the side of her mouth.

Deanna had forgotten about her clothes. She hadn't thought about much of anything except getting here as quickly as possible. "It was the strangest thing . . ."

Gloria leaned back against the stretcher and closed her eye. The visual reminder of Gloria's horror stopped the rest of what Deanna had been going to say. Her earlier visit to Buford seemed a lifetime ago. While Deanna had been struggling over the significance of touching Evan's hand and worrying about her reputation, Gloria had been struggling for her life and worrying about the safety of her child. The differences in their worlds seemed enormous, yet Gloria had reached out to her, knowing Deanna would understand about Sara.

"I'm glad you came, Deanna."

Deanna looked at the woman on the stretcher, then down at the baby in her arms. She felt suddenly overwhelmed with a sense of unworthiness, and a vague sense of guilt. She should have done more to protect Sara and her mother. She should never have allowed them to return to this lifestyle, once she'd known about it. She hadn't known what to do about it. She still didn't, but she knew the situation called for more than polite interest.

Gloria had a mild concussion, a dislocated right shoulder, and some internal injuries, the doctor told Deanna after all the tests were done. There were also multiple cuts and bruises, especially about her face and ribs. The doctor put her arm in a device that held it immobile against her body, wrote her several prescriptions, and told Deanna he would only send her home if someone stayed with her for the next twenty-four hours. Deanna promised.

The nurse showed her how to do pupil checks and what other signs of concussion to watch for, went over all the prescriptions, and finally let them go around two o'clock in the morning. Deanna drove to Gloria's very slowly and carefully, not wanting to jar Gloria and not having a car seat to put Sara in. She parked her Buick next to an ancient Chevrolet Cutlass in front of Gloria's mobile home. The mobile home park was dark and quiet, her neighbors apparently asleep at this hour of the morning. Deanna wondered if any of them had tried to help last night.

Deanna Edwards Randolph had never been inside a mobile home. As she followed Gloria into Sara's bedroom to put the child in her crib, she noticed two things. The mobile home was very small, and Gloria Harris was an immaculate housekeeper.

"Do you want some coffee?" Gloria asked, when they came back into the living area.

The doctor had suggested keeping Gloria awake for several more hours yet, to be certain there were no complications from the concussion. "Coffee would be fine." Deanna followed her into the tiny kitchen. "Would you like me to do that? You don't look very stable on your feet."

Gloria tried to object, but making coffee with only one hand proved more than she could do. She sat at the table and gave Deanna directions. The first sip of hot coffee burned the cut at the side of her mouth, making her jerk the cup back. Deanna found paper towels to clean up the spill.

"I guess I'll be using a straw for a few days," Gloria said, patting up the spilled coffee. Deanna noticed her usually meticulously manicured fingernails were broken and ragged.

"I hope you left the rest of those fingernails in that creep's face."

Gloria stopped mopping up coffee and

looked at her hands as if seeing them for the first time.

"Who called the police?"

Gloria kept her eyes averted. "One of my neighbors, I guess. He broke some lamps and I think I screamed when he dislocated my shoulder."

But not until he'd dislocated her shoulder, Deanna deducted. "Did the police catch him?"

"No. He was long gone by the time they got here."

"Did anyone get— "

"The police already asked all these questions. I'm very tired and I hurt. I know that doctor told you to stay here, but you don't have to." Gloria finally looked at her. "Thanks for stayin' with Sara. I didn't know who else to call."

Fatigue and the swelling made her look like an old woman. Deanna's heart wrenched at the loneliness and the despair in Gloria's voice. But through it all, there was a desperate pride.

Deanna knew she had to appeal to that pride. "I'm pretty exhausted myself," Deanna said, rising and putting the cups in the sink. "Would you mind if I stayed? It's a long drive back to Atlanta and I don't like driving at night."

Gloria seemed to mull that over, as if trying to decide whether Deanna was sincere or not. "If you really want to stay, there's a twin bed in Sara's room. There's a bathroom in there, too."

"That will do fine." Deanna had made some decisions while she waited at the hospital. She intended to stay the night, then in the morning, she and Gloria were going to have a serious discussion. "Do you have an alarm clock? The doctor said I should check you every two hours."

"If you don't tell him, I won't."

Deanna was pleased to see a spark of humor in the brown eye that was still open, a wry smile on her bruised mouth. She smiled back but wouldn't be deterred. "I don't think we should fool around with a concussion."

Gloria sighed but conceded. "It's your loss of sleep."

A fierce pounding jerked Deanna awake the next morning. It took a few seconds to remember where she was, then Sara whimpered from the crib. The sun was shining, and the clock beside the bed said eight-fifteen. The alarm was set for nine o'clock, when Gloria's next pupil check was due. The pounding came again, louder and more insistent this time. Feeling more protective than cautious, Deanna dashed to the front door, hoping to stop the noise before it woke Gloria.

"Stop that this instant!" she demanded as soon as she had the door open. "You'll wake Gloria, and you've already awakened the baby. Is there some sort of emergency?"

The small, wiry woman with wild gray hair and wearing a man's jacket didn't look strong enough to have produced all that noise, but Deanna couldn't see anyone else standing outside. "Who're you?" the woman demanded.

Deanna blinked at the combination of hostility and rudeness. She straightened to her full height and looked down her nose. "I'm Mrs. Phillip Randolph." That wasn't strictly true any longer, but this woman wouldn't know that. "Who are you?"

"Let her in, Deanna," came Gloria's muffled voice from the hallway. "She's Mrs. Lee, my landlady."

Gloria's long, terry cloth robe had seen better days. Her face looked even worse in the morning sunlight.

"You're in no condition to receive callers," Deanna objected, blocking the doorway so Mrs. Lee couldn't see in.

Gloria managed a tired smile. "I guarantee

this ain't no social call." Gloria went into the bedroom to get Sara while Deanna stepped back to let Mrs. Lee enter. Deanna gave the smaller woman a threatening glare before she turned to follow Gloria.

"You can't change a diaper one-handed," Deanna fussed, seeing what Gloria was trying to do. "Go see what Mrs. Lee wants. I'll do this."

"I know what Mrs. Lee wants," Gloria said, but she stood back to give Deanna room. "She was here last night when the police came. She wants me out of here."

"It wasn't your fault. That's not fair."

Gloria just looked at her. Deanna supposed not much in Gloria's life had been fair. "I'll talk to her."

"She won't listen," Gloria warned.

Charming people into her way of thinking was a large part of what Deanna did in her auxiliary work. She had charmed CEOs of international companies out of thousands of dollars. A mobile home park landlady from Buford didn't seem like much of a problem.

"Mrs. Lee." Deanna offered her hand to the woman who eyed her suspiciously, then gave her a grudging handshake. "I'm sorry for my lack of manners earlier. We hadn't been back to sleep long when you knocked so we weren't really prepared for visitors this early in the morning. Would you care for some coffee?"

"No, I wouldn't care for some coffee, and no amount of fancy manners is going to change my mind." Mrs. Lee pointed a gnarled finger at Gloria. "I been warnin' her I wasn't goin' to put up with her runnin' no house of ill repute out of my park. This is what comes of consortin' with that kind of trash. Police havin' to come out here, disturbin' honest folks who have to get up in the morning to go to work. I want her out of here."

"There won't be any more altercations with the police, Mrs. Lee," Deanna promised, keeping her tone soft. "As for a house of ill repute," Deanna gave a disapproving tsk, tsk tsk, "this is Ms. Harris's home. Attractive single ladies always attract gentleman callers. Unfortunately, the one last night wasn't much of a gentleman"

Mrs. Lee gave a rude snort. "I don't know who you are, lady, but you must have a good reason for tryin' to whitewash a piece of white trash like that."

Deanna leapt to her feet, ready for battle. "I have tried to be polite to you, Mrs. Lee, but I will not stand by and allow you to insult my friend. Unless you have proof of your accusations, I suggest you leave."

Instead of being impressed or intimidated, Mrs. Lee laughed, a dry cackle that incited Deanna to visions of violence. "I'll leave, all right," Mrs. Lee said, getting slowly to her feet, "but I'll be back, and I'd better see evidence of a move."

After Mrs. Lee had gone, Deanna sat, thinking furiously about a solution to Gloria's problem. Finally Sara's whimpering and Gloria's clumsy efforts to fix her a bottle brought her back to the problems of the present. "Here, let me do that. Why didn't you say something?"

Gloria sighed as she relinquished the baby. Deanna noticed the wince of pain and the guarding of her side. "Go sit down. Soon as Sara's fed, we'll go get those prescriptions filled."

"You don't have to do that, Deanna. Me and Sara, we're used to takin' care of ourselves."

"I'm sorry to hear that." Deanna sat down with the baby and gave her the bottle. "You're going to have to get used to someone else taking care of you, especially since we're going to be living together."

"You can't stay here," Gloria immediately objected.

"No, and neither can you." The conversation was interrupted by a knock on the door. Gloria got up to answer it.

Gloria's visitor was a tall, thin man who looked to be in his late fifties. He wore jeans and scuffed Western boots and seemed genuinely concerned for Gloria's well-being.

"You can come in for coffee if you'd like," Gloria invited him.

The man stepped inside, then stopped when he saw Deanna. He immediately jerked off his ball cap. "Oh, excuse me, Ma'am. I didn't realize Gloria had company."

Gloria introduced them. "Hank, you remember Mrs. Randolph. She's helping me with Sara today while my arm's in a sling."

Deanna remembered Hank, the man who'd picked Gloria up from the hospital on New Year's Eve. Gloria watched Deanna's reaction with challenge in her one good eye. Hank looked uncomfortable. Apparently Gloria thought Deanna would bail out of this project if she was exposed to Gloria's "business contacts." Deanna looked down at Sara, who had to take breathing breaks while she ate because sucking on a bottle, even one with a special nipple, took more oxygen than her compromised heart could provide. If anything, meeting Gloria's customers increased Deanna's resolve to help this baby.

"Yes, Hank, I remember you." Deanna smiled as if they had been introduced by her best friend during a country club social. "You'll have to help Gloria with the coffee. She doesn't do well with one hand."

Deanna held the smile while Gloria studied her, as if not sure how to interpret Deanna's behavior. Hank went into the kitchen and started fixing the coffee. He carried a thermos bottle with him, Deanna noticed. Gloria's services must include coffee refills.

It also seemed to include breakfast. Deanna finished feeding Sara while Hank cooked breakfast and Gloria supervised. When the dishes were done, Deanna discretely left them alone with the pretense of dressing Sara. Gloria appeared in the doorway a few minutes later.

"Did he pay you anyway?" Deanna asked, picking Sara up. Sara reached for her mother, but Deanna distracted her with a toy.

"Hank's a friend. He was very concerned, wanted the man's name."

"Did you give it to him?"

"No, but I told him who'd referred him to me. He'll find out."

"Have you worked this out mathematically, Gloria?" Deanna had spent her waiting time last night trying to figure out the best argument to use against Gloria's life-style. Since money seemed to be the motivating factor, that seemed the logical enticement. The safety angle would be used as reinforcement.

"How many men will it take to earn the amount of money required for Sara's surgery? How much time will it take to make that much money? Does Sara have that much time?"

Gloria's expression turned cold. "I'm not stupid, you know. I done the arithmetic. I figured if I had some of the money, they'd let me make payments on the rest. I got good credit."

"What if the next man hurts Sara?"

Deanna said it softly and was pleased to observe the desired impact. Gloria's face went white, leaving the bruises in stark relief. Still, she raised her chin defiantly.

"That man was a mistake. He was a referral from another trucker. Word'll get out through Hank, and the other truckers'll take care of him. If I stick to my regular customers, we'll be all right."

"You need hundreds of thousands of dollars, Gloria. Think about it, long-term. Your landlady is threatening eviction. Your daughter, God willing, won't always be a baby. Do you want her shunned because her mother is a prostitute?"

Gloria hung her head. "I have to save my baby. She's all I got, all I'll ever have."

"What are you willing to do to save her?" Deanna asked, being deliberately cruel.

Gloria's head snapped up, her good eye narrowed. "I'll do anything to save my baby."

Deanna smiled, sensing victory. "Even accept help from others?"

Gloria opened her mouth, probably to protest, then closed it. She looked at her daughter, who'd fallen asleep in Deanna's arms during their discussion. "I never thought nobody would care," she finally admitted.

"Well, I care," Deanna stated. "And so does Hank."

While Gloria thought about that, Deanna put Sara down in her crib. "While she takes a nap, I'll go get your prescriptions. You'll have to tell me where to go, since I'm not familiar with Buford." She thought of Evan, who was familiar with Buford, wondering again if he was familiar with Gloria. It probably wasn't a good idea to ask. "I suggest you go back to bed and put a 'closed' sign on your door."

Gloria gave Deanna directions to the nearest pharmacy and insisted that Deanna use her Medicaid card to pay for the prescriptions. Deanna looked at the card, then back at

Gloria. "I don't understand. You'll accept assistance from the government, but you won't accept help from people."

"I been payin' taxes all my life," Gloria defended herself, "so I figured I paid into it. Medicaid was the only way I could get medical care for Sara, and living on welfare is the only way I can stay home and take care of her. I don't like it, but I don't see no other choice."

"Then look at my fund-raising efforts the same way," Deanna advised. "If we want Sara to have a chance, we have no other choice."

That seemed to pacify Gloria some. The next step was to convince her to move, at least temporarily. When Deanna got back from the pharmacy, she noticed a semitractor-trailer rig parked on the shoulder near the mobile home park. She doubted Gloria had gotten much sleep in her absence.

Dusty was cooking pork chops. Gloria seemed to have taken the concept of bed and breakfast into a more personal dimension. Deanna wondered how much of Gloria's profit was reinvested in groceries. Gloria slumped at the table, pain and exhaustion etched into every line of her battered body. Deanna decided she was through with being polite.

She took the bottle of pain pills out of the sack and put two in front of Gloria with a glass of water. "Take those, and go to bed," she instructed in a voice that brooked no argument. "Dusty, I hope you're a fast eater. I expect you to clean up your mess before you go. I also expect you to pass the word among your friends that Gloria's . . . um . . . diner . . . is closed for business. However, I am sponsoring a fund for Baby Sara's heart surgery if any of them wish to donate. Gloria does appreciate your friendship."

Even wearing slept-in jeans, with her hair a mess and only the makeup she carried in her purse, Deanna never doubted her ability to intimidate a man into being a gentleman. Dusty ate his pork chops in record time, washed his dishes, and promised to pass the word. He handed Deanna a $100 bill— "for the fund"— before he made his hasty exit.

Deanna decided to get Sara packed while Gloria slept. She searched the small mobile home for a suitcase, then decided they must be in Gloria's bedroom. Hoping the combination of exhaustion and pain pills would keep Gloria asleep, Deanna tip-toed into the master bedroom.

She had helped Gloria clean up the worst of the damage last night, but the room still caused Deanna to shudder at the violence that had taken place there. Gloria was asleep in the middle of the double bed, buried under a red satin comforter, only her blonde hair visible. Deanna moved silently to one of the double closets and slid back the door. She crouched down to look for a suitcase. The metallic sound of a pistol being cocked froze her instantly.

"One false move, buster, and I blow you to hell."

"Gloria." Deanna's voice squeaked, barely audible, even to her own ears. She wasn't about to move. "Gloria, it's Deanna."

"Deanna?"

Deanna sagged against the closet, feeling faint, gulping air. She sat on the floor and turned toward the bed. Gloria was sitting up, the gun lying harmlessly in her lap. "Where was that last night?"

Gloria shook her head as if trying to clear it. She looked at Deanna, then down at the gun. "God, what did you give me? I could've shot you."

"I won't give you any more," Deanna promised. "Why didn't you use that last night?"

"I couldn't get to it," Gloria said with disgust. "Believe me, I tried." Deanna watched with horrified fascination as Gloria held the gun in her injured hand and unloaded it. "What are you doing down there anyway?"

"Looking for a suitcase so I can pack Sara's clothes." Deanna's attention remained focused on the gun, which Gloria seemed to handle quite efficiently, even injured. "You seem to know how to use that."

"Of course I know how to use it. Only a fool owns a gun without knowing how to use it. I can shoot the balls off a mouse at fifty paces." She put the gun back into the bedside table it had apparently come out of. "There's a trucker out there I'd like to castrate at much closer range."

Deanna flinched at the raw malice and wondered if in addition to the beating, Gloria had been raped. Since the reason for the man's being here in the first place had been for sex, rape was a difficult concept to understand. Thinking about it conjured up images of violence so vivid, Deanna felt ill. There had been blood on the sheets last night, but until now Deanna hadn't given much thought as to the source. Some internal injuries, the doctor had said. She clinched her jaw on the rising nausea and got up off the floor.

"You're coming home with me, right now. Where are your suitcases? I'll pack Sara's things first then come in here to pack yours. You are to stay right there in that bed and do absolutely nothing."

"We can't leave here," Gloria objected as Deanna opened the second closet, still searching for suitcases. "All of Sara's special equipment is here."

"We'll take it with us." Deanna turned, scanning the room for other places to look. There weren't any. "Where do you store your luggage?"

Gloria frowned at her. "I don't have any luggage. It would take a truck to move everything."

Deanna didn't know if Gloria was exaggerating to stall for time or if she was serious. Either way, with Gloria handicapped, Deanna was going to need help. She only knew one other person in Buford, and after last night, she wasn't sure what his response was going to be.

"I have only one question for you." Deanna took a deep breath and prepared for the worst. "Do you know Evan Maxwell?"

"No." Gloria's perplexity seemed genuine. "Is he important?"

Deanna smiled. "Oh, yes. He's very important."

Eleven

Deanna Randolph was the damnedest woman Evan Maxwell had ever met. Every time he thought he knew what to expect, she threw him a curve ball. Gloria Harris and her baby were definitely a curve ball.

Buford was a small community that had experienced a sudden growth spurt over the last ten years. Located strategically between Atlanta and Lake Lanier, with easy interstate access, Buford was rapidly becoming the suburbs. For all its influx of people, though, Buford was still a small town, and there were few secrets. Even a relative newcomer like Evan knew about Gloria Harris, whose mobile home out on the interstate was a regular truck stop. He was angry that he hadn't heard the rest of the story. Instead of throwing sanctimonious stones, he felt the community should have rallied around one of their own, giving Gloria the support that would have made her truck stop unnecessary.

As for Deanna, her appearance amazed him almost as much as her quest. She had on the same clothes she'd had on the day before, her hair was tied up in a ponytail, she had circles under her eyes from lack of sleep, and the only makeup she had on was some lipstick, most of which she'd chewed off. She wasn't even worrying her pearls. In fact, she'd tucked them inside her shirt to keep Sara from pulling on them. Evan watched Deanna's eyes droop as she rocked the frail-looking baby. He thought she was the most incredibly beautiful woman he'd ever seen.

"Let me take her and put her in her crib," Evan offered.

Deanna's eyes opened, then focused slowly on him. "Is she asleep? I'll take her."

"You were both asleep. I can handle a baby," Evan chided her.

Deanna smiled, a tired, beautiful smile. "I know, but she has a special monitor that has to be attached. Besides, her mama carries a gun and can shoot the balls off a mouse at fifty paces."

Evan followed her, wondering if she realized what she'd just said. He stopped in the doorway to the bedroom where he'd set up Sara's crib beside the twin bed where Gloria was asleep. He didn't like the idea of a gun-toting prostitute staying in Deanna's housekeeper's suite. As he stood there, Gloria opened her good eye and raised up to check on Sara.

"You'll call me on the intercom if she wakes up?" Deanna asked.

"If I need you," was all Gloria would concede. "You've done too much already."

"You aren't doing any of us any favors if you reinjure your shoulder. You call me."

"Thanks, Deanna. Thanks again, Evan. It was nice to meet you."

"You, too, Gloria. Goodnight." Evan followed Deanna out of the housekeeper's suite and into the kitchen. Gloria wasn't anything like he'd expected her to be, except for being an aging blonde who'd seen a hard life. She obviously worshiped her tiny daughter and was uncomfortable with everything Deanna was doing for her. If what Deanna had told him was true, she hadn't been hooking for very long, six months max. It was definitely a career chosen out of desperation and lack of resources.

Evan knew where there were resources. With Gloria's permission, he would present their situation to the North Georgia Harley Owner's Group. The chapter met monthly at his dealership, and the next meeting was Thursday night. The members of this HOG chapter were some of the most compassionate people he knew, and some of the most resourceful.

Deanna sagged against the kitchen counter, making Evan wish he could scoop her up and carry her to bed, much the same way she'd carried Sara. She looked much more vulnerable tonight than he'd ever seen her, much more approachable. He decided to risk getting closer.

"I'd like to talk to you about Gloria." Evan stood very close, then waited until Deanna looked up at him. He smiled and brushed stray hairs away from her forehead, then lightly ran his fingertips down the side of her cheek. To his surprise, she leaned into his hand. He folded her easily into his arms, tucking her head against his shoulder. She felt so incredibly good against him.

"You have to be exhausted." He stroked his hands lightly up and down her back, almost afraid to breathe, afraid she'd suddenly bolt. Last night all he'd done was touch her hand, his intentions totally honorable. They were still honorable, but becoming less so the longer he held her. She was so completely relaxed— too relaxed. Evan frowned, pulling back to look down at her. She'd fallen asleep standing up.

"Deanna?"

She blinked up at him. "I'm sorry. I . . ." She blinked several more times and looked around the kitchen, still standing in the circle of his arms. "I was going to offer you coffee."

"You're asleep on your feet. Where's your bedroom?"

That woke her up. She blinked again and pulled away from him. Evan cursed his lack of finesse.

"I didn't get much sleep last night." She tried to smooth the loose hairs back into her ponytail, then gave up with a sigh. "Thanks again for your help, Evan. I couldn't have done it without you, but I guess I'd better say goodnight."

Evan smoothed the errant hairs again, smiling at her with all the desire in his heart— and lower. "I like your hair that way. It makes you look younger, softer." He lowered his mouth closer to hers. "Sexier."

She seemed mesmerized. Maybe she was too tired to realize what was coming, but she let him kiss her. He kept it gentle, just a brushing of lips. She didn't pull away, so he kissed her again, not knowing if she was affected or not, but feeling his own need grow. When he felt her hands slide up his back and her body mold into his, he groaned. He cradled her head in his hand and kissed her with all the longing that had been building inside of him since he'd first watched her walk into his showroom.

Evan stroked gently against her lips with his

tongue, seeking entrance. When Deanna opened to him, then kissed him back, stroking her own sweet tongue against his, Evan thought he'd been granted the keys to heaven. He ran his free hand up the back of her thigh, then cupped her delicious bottom, urging her to press against the most desperate part of himself. He had waited for her so long, but none of that mattered. There would be no stopping now.

Deanna wrenched herself out of his hands with a cry of distress. Evan heard his own cry, felt as if she'd wrenched off a part of his body, instinctively grasped, trying to bring her back. She backed away, her eyes panic-stricken, her hands held out to ward him off. It was the panic in her eyes that stopped him. He struggled to control his breathing. Deanna didn't seem to be doing too well in that department either.

She didn't speak. Other than *what the hell?* Evan wasn't sure what to say either. There was no way she could deny her attraction for him. She'd been a wild woman in his arms, right up to the moment she'd catapulted out.

"Talk to me, Deanna," he finally demanded, hearing the harshness in his voice from thwarted passion. "What's going on?"

"I'm afraid . . ." Her voice was muffled. She cleared her throat and tried again. "I'm afraid I allowed things to progress too far." She studied her hands as she laced her fingers together. "As I told you last night, I'm slightly out of practice. I've only been divorced less than a year, and I haven't felt ready to date yet." She let her hands fall apart as she looked up at him, her brown eyes pleading. "I would hate for this to spoil our friendship."

Evan wavered, wanting to believe her, still aching from wanting to bury himself inside her. He wanted hot, hard, mind-blowing sex, and she wanted friendship. Maybe if he hadn't taken advantage of her exhausted vulnerability, he'd have found that out before he got himself worked up into such a state.

Or maybe she really was the society snob Cloyd had warned him about and friendship was a polite way of saying keep your distance. He studied her, looking for clues. More hair had escaped her ponytail and curled around her face and neck. There was no haughtiness in her expression, just lines of fatigue. Even her usually ramrod straight posture was drooping a little. Evan felt like a consummate jerk.

He tried to smile, but only half his mouth seemed to work. "I would hate for it to spoil our friendship as well. I'll call you in the morning, after you've had some sleep. I would like to discuss Gloria's situation with you."

Deanna closed the door behind Evan, then leaned against it, closing her eyes. She'd known a kiss from Evan would cause fireworks. She hadn't been prepared for an overwhelming assault on her senses that threatened to wipe out every thought from good judgment to self-preservation. Her total body response to his kiss demonstrated his power over her. To become his lover would be to become his slave. There was no way it could ever be a casual affair, a means of avoiding another mistake. Evan Maxwell was nothing like Phil, but she had no doubts that sleeping with him would be a mistake.

Once Evan had made his conquest, she was sure he would become bored with her. They had nothing in common. She couldn't even see the beauty of an unrestored antique motorcycle. Once he became bored with her, he would cast her aside, breaking her heart and shattering her pride more effectively than even Phil Randolph had. Deanna vowed never to put that much power in another man's hands again.

"What a gutsy lady," Georgia commented the next evening, referring to Gloria, "and that baby," Georgia pressed a beringed hand against her heart, "she has the wisdom of the ages in those dark eyes."

"She's suffered a lot for an eight-month-old," Deanna agreed.

Georgia indicated the notepad in front of Deanna. "What's left to do tomorrow?"

"Wait for the results of all the calls we made today." Deanna propped her head on her hand and toyed with the tuna salad on her plate. She and Georgia had been on the phone all day, in addition to taking care of Gloria and Sara. Deanna couldn't remember ever being so tired.

"Your biker is quite the organizer," Georgia commented, scraping up the last bits of tuna from her plate with her fork. "He has more resources than we do."

"He's not *my* biker," Deanna objected. She pushed her unfinished dinner away. She needed sleep, not food. She needed to quit replaying Evan's kiss through her mind—and, worse, through her body. "I can't believe none of the lawyers we called would set up a trust fund."

"At least Evan found one who would. When do I get to meet this hero?"

"He's invited me to come speak to the HOG chapter Thursday night, tell Gloria's story—not the truck stop part, although it sounds like everyone in Buford knows that part already. Gloria was a waitress at the Waffle House for years, so a lot of the residents know her from then. Evan feels strongly that once the situation about Sara is known the community will rally to help one of their own."

"You're going to speak to the Harley Owner's Group?"

Deanna nodded. "Thursday night. Gloria agreed to it. According to Evan the group is made up of a lot of prominent businessmen from Buford and the surrounding area, including Norcross and even Gainesville. He says fund-raising is their primary function. They were third in the state for the muscular dystrophy drive."

Georgia was almost quivering with excitement, listening to Deanna describe the Harley owners. Deanna had to smile. "Wanna come?"

"God, I thought you'd never ask."

Thursday night the parking lot in front of Evan's dealership was packed with vehicles, the shoulder of the highway lined with even more. Deanna parked the Buick the equivalent of a block away. She couldn't remember ever being this nervous before a speaking engagement.

"Where are the motorcycles?" Georgia demanded, scanning the parking lot. "I thought this was a meeting of Harley owners."

"It is January and cold."

The deep-throated sound of a motorcycle caught both women's attention. They watched as a lone rider pulled his bike into the parking lot and found a narrow space to park in. Deanna remembered her one ride in the cold when the sun had been shining. She shivered.

"I think we're overdressed," Georgia commented as they got close enough to see the crowd through the plate glass windows.

A Chanel suit and heels was standard apparel for speaking at fund-raising events, especially to a group of businessmen, so that's what Deanna had insisted they wear. As they surveyed the sea of black leather and blue denim, Deanna silently agreed with Georgia. Still, it was a speaker's obligation to present a professional appearance.

"We'll knock 'em dead, honey," Georgia promised, apparently picking up on Deanna's nervousness.

They certainly got everyone's attention. As soon as they approached the door, it was opened for them. Conversation stopped as everyone in the room turned to look at the two women. Deanna managed a social smile and frantically scanned the crowd for Evan. She spotted him, moving purposefully through the maze of display racks and standing people. He took her hand in a firm grasp, his hazel eyes intense as they searched hers.

Every nerve in Deanna's body remembered his kiss, remembered the urgency of his hands as they'd pressed her against him. One of the earliest lessons Deanna had learned in social etiquette was how to pretend unpleasant things hadn't happened, didn't exist. The problem was that Evan's kiss had not been unpleasant, only the implications of it were. Drawing on a lifetime of experience she managed to keep her smile in place and found a neutral subject.

"It looks like a good turnout."

Evan didn't return her smile, holding her gaze for a moment longer before releasing her hand and scanning back over the room. "Yes, we're expecting around a hundred tonight." They had to move to let some newcomers through the door. "There are chairs for you up front. Everybody I've talked to thinks this is a great project." He turned his attention to Georgia and stuck out his hand. "Evan Maxwell."

Georgia's smile was salacious as she laid her hand in his. "Georgia Howard." Her voice dripped southern honey and Deanna noticed Evan's smile warm appreciatively. She felt a sharp stab of jealousy.

Evan glanced at Deanna and lost the smile. She realized she was glaring daggers at him but couldn't seem to help it. He grinned at her then, as if her reaction pleased him.

"Come on. There's some people I want you to meet." He took her elbow and led her through the crowd, leaving Georgia to follow them on her own. There were curious glances and polite smiles, but mostly everyone had gone back to their conversations. More people were still coming in the door.

Evan separated a man near his own age out of a group near the counter at the front of the showroom and introduced him as Greg Braselton. "Greg is our director," Evan explained. "That's his wife Becky over there taking everybody's money. She's our secretary/treasurer."

"What's she selling?" Georgia asked.

"Raffle tickets," Greg explained. "Every meeting we sell raffle tickets at a dollar each. There's a drawing at the end of the meeting. The winner gets half the pot that's collected. The other half goes toward muscular dystrophy."

"Can anyone participate?" Georgia asked.

"You bet." Greg took Georgia over to meet Becky.

A balding man of medium height approached Deanna and offered his hand. "You must be Mrs. Randolph," he said. "I'm Tony Vigliotti."

"The lawyer I told you about," Evan supplied. Deanna noticed Tony wore suit pants and a white cotton shirt under his black leather jacket. "Tony has an office in Norcross."

"I came here straight from the office," Tony said. "I brought you a stack of business cards. The fund is set up in Sara Harris's name. All donations will be tax deductible. I'll be glad to talk about all that after you tell the folks about the situation."

"We can't thank you enough for what you're doing, Mr. Vigliotti," Deanna said.

"I'd like to meet this little lady," Tony said. Deanna took one of her cards from her purse and handed it to him. "She's staying with me for the time being. I'm sure Ms. Harris would be pleased to have you call on her."

Greg rapped on the counter with a wooden gavel to get everyone's attention. "Would everyone who wants to sit please find a seat. Let's get started, folks. We've got a lot to cover tonight."

Evan seated Deanna and Georgia in the front row of folding chairs that had been arranged in the center of the showroom. Deanna noticed that most of the members preferred to stand along the sides. She also noticed that the lone biker who'd ridden up while they'd been walking in seated himself beside Georgia, with her encouragement. Deanna smiled. Georgia didn't waste any time.

Deanna listened, impressed by the variety of fund-raisers and entertainment activities engaged in by the chapter members. The meeting was incredibly informal, the reports regularly interjected with comments from the group and jokes and teasing of other members. The HOGs might be serious fund-raisers, but they knew how to have a good time, even at a business meeting.

"It's been brought to our attention that one of our Buford families is in need of some serious fund-raising effort," Greg said, and Deanna knew her time had come. "I'd like to introduce Mrs. Deanna Randolph to y'all. She's not from this area, but she's taken it upon herself to see that this baby gets the proper attention from someone. We've invited her here tonight to tell you about this family."

Deanna stood in front of the counter, looking out across the crowd of men and women wearing black leather jackets and vests, wearing black T-shirts, all sporting the Harley-Davidson logo. She didn't have a podium to stand behind or a microphone to speak into, just a compelling story to tell. The crowd who'd been laughing with Greg just a few minutes before now stood or sat quietly, their expressions expectant.

"I met Gloria Harris in the surgical waiting room of Children's Hospital eight months ago," Deanna began. "She had just been discharged from the hospital after having a cesarean section delivery. She sat there alone, having no friends or relatives she could call, waiting to hear if her tiny baby daughter would live."

By the time Deanna was through, most of the women, and even a few of the men, were wiping their eyes with tissues. Greg reclaimed the floor, unashamedly wiping his own eyes with a handkerchief. It was a few seconds before he could speak. "Now, y'all know Evan Maxwell who owns the shop here with Cloyd. He's made a motion that the North Georgia HOGs take on this project to raise money for Baby Sara's heart transplant. Y'all also know muscular dystrophy is our main charity. We can't use MDA funds for this project. It has to be money raised specifically for this purpose.

"Now before I ask for a second . . ."

"I second it!"

"Now, Ernest, just hold on and let me finish. Tony Vigliotti— stand up Tony— has already volunteered his legal services and set up a fund for Baby Sara. This doesn't obligate the HOGs in any way, but a fund has been set up and donations are tax deductible. Mrs. Randolph is on the auxiliary board at Children's Hospital and is working on them to contribute hospital expenses out of the indigent fund. She's also working with the surgeon to see if he'll donate his services. I understand we're looking at a total package of over $100,000. Think about it, folks. That's a lot of money."

"I second it!"

"Thank you, Ernest. All in favor raise your hands."

Deanna couldn't look. She watched Greg and Becky counting votes and felt tears well up in gratitude.

"Keep your hands up, folks. We need an accurate count."

Deanna did turn around then. Almost every member of the chapter had raised a hand, and they were all smiling at Deanna. She felt Georgia grab her hand.

"You did it, honey."

"I haven't done anything until I convince the indigent fund board and Phil to join our cause," Deanna whispered.

"Never underestimate the power of the people," Georgia whispered back.

The rest of the meeting was a blur for Deanna. Volunteers were appointed to come up with various ways to enlist the community's support for their project. The winner of the raffle promptly donated his winnings to Baby Sara. People stayed to talk long after the meeting was officially over.

"Will you be out this weekend to ride the bike?" Evan asked Deanna when the crowd had thinned and he could talk to her.

"I'll try," Deanna hedged, not looking at him. "I don't like leaving Gloria alone for too long. It's hard for her to care for Sara with only one good arm."

"We're talking about holding an open house here at the dealership as a benefit for Sara, maybe put up a big tent over the track. Will you help us organize it?"

Deanna met his gaze, saw his uncertainty, wished she could give this man everything he seemed to want from her. At least she could give him this. "I'm very good at organizing benefits," she agreed with a smile. It would mean working with him more, being with him more. She longed to do that, even though she knew it would make keeping an emotional distance from him more difficult. "I'll draw up a diagram of the committees you'll need and get with you Saturday."

He smiled, but there was a sadness to it. "I'll see you Saturday then."

Twelve

Saturday the weather was cool, but the sun was shining. Gloria asked Deanna to drop her off at her mobile home so she could finish some of the things she hadn't had time for on Monday. Gloria had become quite adept at using just her right hand, keeping the shoulder immobile and the arm secured against her chest. Deanna decided Sara's small size had one advantage. Gloria could carry her with one arm.

Gloria was a very private person, Deanna had discovered. Not only did she not share much about her personal life, she didn't pry into Deanna's, for which Deanna was grateful. As a woman who needed her own personal space, Deanna understood Gloria's request to spend the day alone organizing her home before returning to the house in Buckhead.

Deanna enjoyed having Gloria and Sara living in her housekeeper's suite, but she knew the decision to stay had to be Gloria's. She hoped spending the day alone would help Gloria resolve some of her internal conflicts. Deanna knew her day spent with Evan would probably only make her own more confusing.

Kyle came bounding up to her when she entered the showroom. "Hi, Miss Deanna!"

"Hi, yourself." She bent to scoop him up on his last bounce. Kyle came to her naturally, wrapping his legs around her waist "How's Ghost?"

"Aw, Ghost never changes. You should see Spike, though. He's this big!" Kyle held his hands wide to show her how big Joey's puppy had grown.

"Wow, aren't you afraid of him?" Deanna set Kyle back on the floor. She missed having children underfoot. She didn't see near enough of her grandchildren.

"Naw, I ain't afraid of Spike. He knows me. He scared the pizza man, though. He wouldn't get out'a his car until we put Spike in the house."

"He'll make a good guard dog, then." Deanna noticed Evan coming up the hallway from the shop and cursed the way her heart responded to the sight of him.

"Yeah! Guard dog, that's what we need." Kyle ran off to find Brian. "Dad, we need a guard dog like Spike."

"What he failed to mention is that Spike has chewed all the furniture legs, torn up the bedroom rug, and dug a hole under the back fence." Evan stopped in front of her, his hands on his hips as he smiled down at her. "Hi. Or is it, hey?"

She returned his smile, her pulse accelerating. "Hey."

"You riding in that?"

Deanna looked down at her clothes. She'd worn her ski underwear under her jeans and sweater, just like the last two times, and her leather jacket over that. Evan had been right about her jacket. The open throat didn't do much against the wind. She remembered the outfit the lone biker had been wearing during the chapter meeting.

"I guess I need one of those fleece lined jumpsuits like Kirk had on Thursday night."

"Are you going to do anything with this after you ride the Indian?"

Deanna didn't understand the question. "Do anything with what?"

"Learning to ride. Are you ever going to ride motorcycles again after you learn to ride the Indian?"

"I hadn't given it any thought." She hadn't thought past proving she could ride the Indian. To do so brought to mind some intriguing possibilities. "What would I ride?"

"Anything you wanted to. Anything you could afford."

The next question of course was, where would she ride it? Anywhere she wanted to. Anytime she wanted to. That kind of freedom was more seductive than gold. "What would you suggest?"

"You could go to one of the rallies, test ride the different models. Of course I only recommend Harleys. You want a rice burner, you'll have to go talk to someone else."

"But if I owned my own bike, I'd need the appropriate riding gear," Deanna said thoughtfully, fingering a leather jacket hanging on one of the display racks.

"And you wouldn't want to buy a jacket that said North Georgia HOGs across the back unless you owned a Harley and joined the North Georgia HOGs," Evan added, holding up the jacket so she could see the embroidery on the back.

Deanna wanted the jacket. She wasn't sure she'd ever own a Harley and doubted she would ever officially join the North Georgia HOGs, but she wanted the jacket. Maybe she'd wear it the next time she saw Phil. That would shake him up, show him she wasn't boring or predictable.

"Do you have one in a medium?"

Deanna bought the jacket, a helmet, a T-shirt, and a pair of padded gloves that would take the abuse of driving a motorcycle far better than her thin kid driving gloves. Evan loaned her a pair of leather chaps to protect her legs against the cold and a wool scarf for her neck.

"You're all set," he announced, handing her a key.

"You're not coming?"

"I've taught you everything there is to teach. The rest you learn by riding. If you don't return in an hour, I'll come looking for you."

Seeing Deanna's stricken expression, he smiled. "You'll gain more confidence riding solo, plus I promised a man his bike would be done this afternoon and my mechanic is having some problems with it. I need to stay and help him."

Deanna still felt grave misgivings as he drew a rough map of the local county roads he wanted her to stay on. If she followed his map, she would travel a rectangular route that covered approximately twenty miles and end up back at the dealership.

"As soon as you feel comfortable, we'll take

We've got your authors!

If you seek out the latest historical romances by today's bestselling authors, our new reader's service, KENSINGTON CHOICE, is the club for you.

KENSINGTON CHOICE is the only club where you can find authors like Janelle Taylor, Shannon Drake, Rosanne Bittner, Sylvie Sommerfield, Penelope Neri and Phoebe Conn all in one place...

...and the only service that will deliver their romances direct to your home as soon as they are published—even before they reach the bookstores.

KENSINGTON CHOICE is also the only service that will give you a substantial guaranteed discount off the publisher's prices on every one of those romances.

That's right: Every month, the Editors at Zebra and Pinnacle select four of the newest novels by our bestselling authors and rush them straight to you, usually *before they reach the bookstores*. The publisher's prices for these romances range from $4.99 to $5.99—but they are always yours for the guaranteed low price of just *$4.20!*

That means you'll always save over 20% off the publisher's prices on every shipment you get from KENSINGTON CHOICE!

All books are sent on a 10-day free examination basis, and there is no minimum number of books to buy. (A postage and handling charge of $1.50 is added to each shipment.)

As your introduction to the convenience and value of this new service, we invite you to accept

4 BOOKS FREE

The 4 books, worth up to $23.96, are our welcoming gift. You pay only $1 to help cover postage and handling.

To start your subscription to KENSINGTON CHOICE and receive your introductory package of 4 FREE romances, detach and mail the card at right *today*.

We have 4 FREE BOOKS for you
as your introduction to
KENSINGTON CHOICE
To get your FREE BOOKS, worth
up to $23.96, mail the card below.

FREE BOOK CERTIFICATE

As my introduction to your new KENSINGTON CHOICE reader's service, please send me 4 FREE historical romances (worth up to $23.96), billing me just $1 to help cover postage and handling. As a KENSINGTON CHOICE subscriber, I will then receive 4 brand-new romances to preview each month for 10 days FREE. I can return any books I decide not to keep and owe nothing. The publisher's prices for the KENSINGTON CHOICE romances range from $4.99 to $5.99, but as a subscriber I will be entitled to get them for just $4.20 per book or $16.80 for all four titles. There is no minimum number of books to buy, and I can cancel my subscription at any time. A $1.50 postage and handling charge is added to each shipment.

Name _____

Address _____ Apt. _____

City _____ State _____ Zip _____

Telephone (_____) _____

Signature _____

(If under 18, parent or guardian must sign)

Subscription subject to acceptance. Terms and prices subject to change.

KC0395

We have
4
FREE
Historical
Romances
for you!

(worth up
to $23.96!)

Details inside!

out my Harley. By the time I get the Indian back together, you'll be ready to ride it."

Deanna took the key to the Honda from him, wishing he was going with her. She wasn't sure she was ready to fly solo.

"What happened to the woman who almost ran me down, bragging that she was ready to ride Interstate 85 through Atlanta during rush hour in a rainstorm?"

Deanna raised her chin and met his challenge with defiance in her eyes. She would not be laughed at. She scooped up her new helmet and gloves. "Tell Kyle I'd like my hot chocolate in half an hour."

She remembered to use the choke to start the bike. She remembered to use the rear brake and the clutch on the steep incline out of the dealership. She even managed to stay in her own lane as she pulled out onto Friendship Road. She went right, crossed over the interstate, made the U-turn and waved as she went speeding by in front of the dealership, just in case anyone was watching.

Evan was watching, holding Kyle. Kyle waved back at Deanna, threatening to throw himself out of his grandfather's arms in his enthusiasm. Evan set him down, then checked the time on his watch. He'd give her thirty minutes to make the twenty mile circuit. If she didn't return by then, he'd go looking for her, waiting customer or no waiting customer.

"You're spending a lot of time with Mrs. Randolph," Brian commented, falling in step beside him as he headed back toward the shop. "Should I be worried?"

Evan eyed his son. The question was asked casually, but Evan knew that Brian worried. He and Kyle had come to live with Evan after Brian's wife decided she didn't want to be a wife and mother any longer. It was a major act of trust on Brian's part, to turn to a father who'd not been there for him during his youth except sporadically. Brian's home, his livelihood, the stable environment he wanted for Kyle all now depended on Evan.

When Evan had invited Brian to join him three years ago, Brian had asked what would happen if Evan decided to remarry. Evan had laughed, assuring his son that if a woman hadn't caught him in the twelve years since his divorce, one wasn't likely to. He'd thought Brian would remarry before now. The young man was good-looking, honest, and gainfully employed. He didn't seem to lack for female companionship when he wanted it, but he rarely brought anyone home to meet Kyle, said he hadn't found one he trusted to love Kyle properly. Kyle came first with Brian. Evan was pretty sure the question came more from a concern for Kyle than for himself.

"Mrs. Randolph has made it perfectly clear that she wants nothing more from me than friendship," Evan told Brian, hearing the bitterness in his words. "I wouldn't worry about her changing the dining room wallpaper if I was you."

Brian didn't look convinced. "Would you like her to change the dining room wallpaper?"

Evan wrapped his arm around his son's thin shoulders and turned him away from the window. "Naw, I'm a bachelor to the core. A high-class lady like that, she'd want us to use linen napkins, wouldn't let us clean carburetors on the dining room table, make the dog stay outside."

"Like Mom."

Evan tightened his jaw. He'd been speaking metaphorically. Brian was twisting his words. "Your mother didn't like the Air Force, didn't like my being away from home so much, didn't want to move every few years and be away from her family. I have nothing personal against your mother. Most of my bad habits I've developed in fifteen years of living alone. Now, I'm too old and set in my bachelor ways to desire a change, with any woman."

"Sorry. You just seem different with Mrs. Randolph than with any of the others. It's none of my business."

Evan forced himself to relax. "You worry about Kyle, so that makes changes in my life part of your business. If—and that's a remote 'if'—I ever get serious enough to take up housekeeping with another woman, I'd work something out with you so you and Kyle would keep the house. I'm used to moving. Kyle needs stability. But I wouldn't worry about it any time soon."

"Okay, if you say so. But I have to warn you, I think Kyle's serious about this one."

Deanna did have a way with children, Evan had to admit. Kyle had been angry that Evan had come to see Miss Deanna last Sunday without him. There was no doubt that Baby Sara thought she was special. Evan thought she was pretty special, too, but, as he'd just pointed out to his son, he had nothing to offer her outside of physical pleasure. For some women, that was enough. It obviously wasn't for Deanna Randolph.

Deanna came back into the shop looking frozen and more than a little smug. "I did it," she proclaimed with a triumphant smile. "I leaned into the curves and accelerated out of

them. I didn't kill it once on takeoff. I shifted
it perfectly. I loved it!"

Evan longed to grab her up in a celebratory
hug and swing her around. He forced himself
to be content with offering her a proud smile.
"Ready for the Harley?"

Deanna took off her gloves and jacket and
rubbed her hands together. "I'm ready for hot
chocolate. I'd like to take the Honda out a few
more times before I try a bigger bike."

"Kyle is making it now."

Evan helped Kyle carry in the mugs of
steaming instant hot chocolate mix while
Deanna repaired her hair in the bathroom.
"She sure spends a lot of time in the bathroom, don't she, Grandpa?"

"Doesn't she," Evan corrected automatically,
"and yes, she does. Women are like that. They
don't like for their hair to be messed up."

When Deanna came in and sat down, Kyle
slyly managed to sit in her lap instead of
Evan's. Evan noticed he didn't bounce, but sat
very still, sipping his hot chocolate carefully.
He also noticed Deanna wrap her free arm
around him, holding him securely.

"You make excellent hot chocolate," Deanna
complemented Kyle, "lots of marshmallows."

"My daddy bought me one of those goff
games," Kyle told her. "I was gettin' real good

at hittin' the ball into the hole, then Ghost chewed up my ball."

"Oh, no. I thought Ghost was too lazy to chase balls."

"He didn't chase it. I kinda' forgot and left it out in the yard."

To Deanna's credit, she didn't laugh or scold. She sympathized and told him a story of a book she'd ruined by leaving it out on her patio before a rain storm. "When you do something like that and lose something you care about, it makes you take better care of your other things."

"Ghost chews up a lot of my toys," Kyle complained.

"So what do you do with the ones you really care about?"

Kyle mulled that over for a moment. "I could put them in my toy box. It's got a real heavy lid Ghost can't open."

"That's a smart idea." Deanna gave him a hug, then set him down. "I'd better go ride again or I'm going to run out of time."

Evan stood again at the big plate glass window and watched her ride past the dealership, thinking about her words to Kyle. He'd really loved Pauline, loved his sons, but he hadn't taken good care of them. He'd lost Pauline, he'd almost lost his sons. He was slowly rebuilding a relationship with them now. Since he hadn't been much of a father, he was trying to be a better grandfather. Then there was Deanna.

Did he care about Deanna? Enough to take good care of her, keep her out of the dog's reach, so to speak? She was recently divorced and apparently still hurting. He didn't know the details. He really didn't know much about her at all, didn't know who the dogs were. Maybe it was time to learn. He'd been pleased when she'd turned to him with Gloria, frustrated when she'd reacted with fear to his kiss, proud when she'd found such pleasure in riding the bike. Whatever his feelings were, he wasn't ready to leave her outside in the rain.

The cold air could not dampen Deanna's thrill of being one with the motorcycle. The longer she rode it, the better she handled it. The more confident she got, the harder she leaned into the turns and the tighter she made them. She didn't have to ride fast. It was the control and the responsiveness that gave her such a feeling of flying. Soul flying, only now she was in the pilot's seat.

She arrived back at the dealership too soon, but was cold enough to quit for the day. "Gloria called while you were out," Evan told her as she approached the counter. Deanna's first thought was that something was wrong. "She's fine," Evan hastened to assure her. "A friend of hers named Hank stopped by. She wanted to know if you minded if she had dinner with him. I told her I'd be glad to entertain you for a few hours. She said Hank would help her with Sara."

Hank. He seemed to be a recurring factor in Gloria's life. Deanna hoped Gloria knew what she was doing.

"She's a big girl, Deanna," Evan chided, as if reading her thoughts. "She has to make her own decisions."

"I know." She knew, but what if Gloria made the wrong decisions?

"Come on," Evan said, taking her arm. "You look frozen stiff. Brian took Kyle home. Cloyd can close up. I made some coffee. What do you take in yours?"

"Cream and sugar, thank you." Deanna stripped off her gloves and jacket, sinking gratefully into the leather chair in Evan's office, not bothering to refix her hair. She had shivered herself into exhaustion.

"I don't think I've ever been so cold," she said, eagerly accepting the steaming mug from Evan. "My neck hurts from tensing up, trying not to shiver."

"Few bikers try to ride in cold weather. Usually it's guys like Kirk, whose bike is his only means of transportation. As you noticed, he has the gear for it."

"I wish I could borrow his gear, just until I ride the Indian. By March, the weather should be warmer, but I'll no longer have a bike." It was a sad thought.

"We'll work on that," Evan promised. "Meanwhile, where do we start with this benefit?"

Deanna smiled. "The diagram is out in my car." She stood up to go get it.

Evan stood up also. "I don't know about you, but I'm hungry. We could discuss it over dinner."

She was hungry, she realized. She glanced at her watch. "Okay, if it won't take too long."

Evan took her to the County Seat in Lawrenceville, about fifteen miles from his dealership. The decor was old-fashioned, with framed pictures of historical Lawrenceville and the surrounding area. Their conversation was easy, about motorcycles, grandchildren, and pets. They had more in common than Deanna would have thought.

"I've really enjoyed having Sara in the house," Deanna said. "When I had a housekeeper, I kept Brady more. She watched him when I went to the hospital or had other commitments. Now I get him for occasional weekends. He's three, and almost as energetic as Kyle. He has a baby sister named Jamie who's four months old. I haven't gotten to keep her yet. She still eats at Mom's."

"Where do they live?"

"Marietta. It's only about forty-five minutes away, but everyone seems so busy." Deanna flushed, realizing she had been monopolizing the conversation, talking about grandchildren. Men didn't want to hear about grandchildren. "I'm sorry, we came here to discuss the benefit."

"I like hearing about your family. Are you a proper grandmother with pictures in your purse?"

Deanna stared at Evan in disbelief. Was he being polite or did he really want to see them? No man was that polite. "Of course." She pulled the small photo album out of her purse and handed it to him. He didn't give them a cursory glance, but studied them, comparing features and being suitably impressed.

"I have a new one of Tommy," he said, handing the album back and digging out his wallet. "Got this one and a big one when I went to see them New Year's. He grows so much between my visits. Tom announced there's going to be another one in July."

"How old is Tommy?"

"He'll be five next month. I don't think they meant to wait that long between them, but I guess that's not the sort of thing a son discusses with a father."

Deanna heard the sadness and knew the lack of confidence bothered him. It was an interesting side of him, one which he didn't seem to have as much self-assurance as the other sides she'd seen.

As if sensing she'd seen a weakness in him, he gave her a cocky grin. "So, tell me about this benefit."

Deanna pulled out her diagram and began discussing committees he would need. "The more you can get donated, the more money you'll collect for your cause. Present it to local businesses as a means of advertising, a means of generating public support, a means of showing their community commitment."

Evan listened intently to all her suggestions, making notes and asking questions. "Man, have we got a lot of work to do," he commented an hour later. "Once people are in these committees, can I give them your number? They're going to ask questions I'm not going to have a clue how to answer."

He made her feel important, Deanna realized as they drove back toward the dealership to pick up her car. It was an amazing thing, talking to a man who made her feel important. Most men she talked to either were bored with her conversation or condescended to her as if she were a less than bright child.

"We couldn't do this without you, Deanna," Evan said, parking his pickup next to her Buick.

"I couldn't do it without all of you. Of all the resources I'm used to having for my benefits, none of them were willing to give toward an individual cause. It's frustrating, but I understand. I've always said the same thing myself."

He took her hand and held it in his. She didn't pull away, but reveled in the strength and warmth of the physical contact. "But Sara's different," he finished for her.

"Sara's different," Deanna agreed.

Was she, Deanna thought, or am I the one who's different? She seemed to be looking at life through new eyes lately.

"Anyway, having the HOGs behind me will help when I talk to the indigent fund board Monday. Billy Adonis has agreed to go with me, too." She smiled wickedly. "They can't tell all of us no."

"Billy Adonis," Evan stated, shaking his

head as if in disbelief. "You said he gave you the other Indian."

"He's the one who started this Indian thing." She told him about Billy's donation of the '55. "His daughter Brittany has a heart defect, not as serious as Sara's but serious enough. He could easily become one of the hospital's major sponsors and the board is aware of that. He also wants a genuine, American-made Indian to add to his collection."

"He wants yours?"

"He says he wants one of the police department models with a left-handed throttle." She smiled, remembering the discussion. "I had no idea what he was talking about."

Evan smiled, too. "They wanted left-handed throttles because most of their officers were right-handed. That way they could shoot their guns while they were in hot pursuit."

Deanna laughed. "Can you imagine? That must have been before they worried about innocent bystanders. Now they don't even want the police to initiate hot pursuit, much less shoot guns during one. Anyway, Billy's motorcycle is beautiful, completely restored with new paint and chrome. I have a feeling he won't be as impressed with your completely original restoration as your collectors are."

She hesitated, not certain how to explain the

rest of it. "My brothers are not happy about me putting Dad's bike in the auction. They feel they should have been consulted first."

Evan frowned at that. "Whose bike is it?"

"Legally, it's Mother's. It's part of the estate that Dad willed to her. She's all for it going to auction. She tried to get Dad to sell it from the time he bought it."

A slow grin spread over Evan's face. "Does she know you're learning to ride it?"

"No, and she's not going to know. I'd never hear the end of it. Evan," she pulled her hand out of his and turned more toward him in the seat, "Pete, my older brother, could give your collectors some serious competition. I know you've invited them to the auction with the promise of an authentic Indian—"

"Don't worry about it," Evan interrupted, taking her hand back. "These guys are used to competition. Why do you think Indians are worth so much? Supply and demand. It's for Sara, right?"

Deanna gave a sigh. "I hope so. That's one of the things I'm going to hold over the board's head. Billy has agreed to put that disclaimer on his as well. The money from the bikes is to be used to pay Sara's hospital bills. Not only will they have the money from the Indians, but the Indians will be an incredible drawing card for the rest of the auction." She gave a little shrug. "Everyone wins."

"You should be an ambassador," Evan commented, giving her hand a squeeze before releasing her and opening his door.

"I am an ambassador," Deanna said proudly as she got out of the pickup. "What do you think the women's auxiliary is?"

Evan stood very close, looking down at her with a smile that sent her pulse skittering. She feared he would try to kiss her again. She was even more afraid he wouldn't.

He ran the side of his finger down the bridge of her nose. "Goodnight, Mrs. Ambassador. You come back, and we'll ride a Harley Softail."

Deanna's legs weren't quite steady as she made her way to her car. Evan Maxwell, to use his own expression, was the damnedest man she'd ever met.

Thirteen

"The phone has not stopped ringing," Gloria marveled, sitting in Deanna's bedroom with Sara while Deanna dressed for her dinner with Phil. "Mr. Vigliotti says it's even crazier at his office. I never thought people would respond like this."

The HOGs had been busy the past week. Sara's picture and story were posted all over Buford and in any business owned, patronized, or coerced to participate by a member of the North Georgia HOGs. Not to be outdone by a bunch of motorcycle riders, Gloria's trucker friends were also organizing their own fund-raising efforts.

On Monday, the indigent fund board had capitulated to the combined force of Deanna and Billy. On Wednesday, Gloria had been interviewed on a local news program, holding Sara and generating widespread public sympathy. Now, all that was left was to convince Phil to donate the services of his surgical

team. Deanna had a dinner date with him tonight.

"That's gorgeous," Gloria exclaimed, her
voice awed. "You look dynamite in red."

Deanna smiled and surveyed the new dress
in the full-length mirror. It was a soft jersey
that emphasized her curves without being
tight, then fell in soft folds to just above her
knees. The color made her skin glow and ac-
centuated her dark hair. The cowl neckline
scooped just low enough to reveal her strand
of pearls. The only other jewelry she added
was a pair of emerald-cut ruby ear clips. She
slid her stockinged feet into the new red
leather heels she'd bought to go with the
dress.

"That should do it," Gloria commented,
eyeing the shoes.

"Do what?" Deanna did a final pirouette in
front of the mirror, pleased with the effect.

"Convince Dr. Randolph to do Sara's surgery for free. I'll make sure Sara and I are in
our room when you get home."

Deanna stopped. She did not want Gloria
to think that she was trading sex for favors.
"I'm not sleeping with my ex-husband, Gloria.
We're still friends. I will try to appeal to his
sense of humanity."

"When a woman wears a pair of come-fuck-me red pumps like them, she's gonna appeal to a whole lot more than a man's sense of humanity."

The doorbell chimed. Deanna stood immobile and stared at Gloria, then down at her shoes. She'd bought them because they were sexy, there was no denying that, but was she really issuing a blatant invitation?

Gloria smiled at her bewilderment. "I have a pair, so I know. The men used to request for me to wear them." She paused, the doorbell chimed again. Gloria shrugged. "Course they didn't care nothin' about me wearin' no fancy dress with them. You want me to answer the door?"

"Um . . . yes, the door. Tell Phil I'll just be a minute. You can leave Sara here."

Gloria left to answer the door. Deanna stared at her reflection in the mirror. She had wanted to show Phil she looked good in something other than black. She'd wanted to shake him out of his misconception that she was boring and predictable. It was not her intention to encourage Phil's advances.

She kicked off the shoes and dumped the contents of the matching purse onto her bed. She took off the rubies and put on her favorite pearls. She found a pair of taupe shoes with a modest heel and their matching handbag.

When she stood back in front of the mirror she gave herself a sad grimace. Instead of looking dynamite, she looked merely nice. Nice was safe. Nice was boring. She kicked off the taupe shoes and put the red heels back on.

Gloria's obscene adjective echoed through her mind. There was a name for women who advertised and didn't deliver. It was worse than boring. Deanna took off the red shoes and threw them into the back of her closet. There was always basic black. Black, leather, two-inch pumps went with everything and could in no way be misconstrued as a come-on.

Phil and Gloria were standing in the living room, looking uncomfortable in each other's presence. Phil was scowling. Deanna handed Sara to Gloria, extracting her strand of pearls from the baby's hand.

"You remember Gloria, don't you Phil? And Sara? They're staying here with me until her arm is healed."

Phil turned toward Deanna, his expression softening to admiration as he took in her costume from head to toe. His gaze lingered on her legs, making Deanna grateful to Gloria for her warning. She wanted Phil remorseful, not lascivious.

To insure there would be no conflicts tonight, she had picked up the silver fox coat from storage that afternoon. Knowing his eyes followed her every move, she bent to scoop it off of the couch, then pressed it into his hands. He stroked the soft fur thoughtfully for a moment, then held it up for Deanna to slip into.

"Deanna, why is that woman staying in your house?" Phil demanded as soon as he had the Jaguar out on the road.

Deanna sighed. It didn't sound like wearing the fur was going to offset befriending Gloria. "She's injured, Phil. She has no family, no friends. Since I've cared for Sara in the hospital, it was only logical that I help her. It's not like just anyone can take care of Sara."

"She was injured by one of her johns."

"Well, I wouldn't know." Deanna ignored Phil's irritated tone of voice and feigned innocence. "She's never told me the man's name."

"She's a hooker, Deanna. A prostitute."

"She's a woman, Phil. A mother." And if Sherylyn hadn't said anything, Phil would have never looked at the social worker's report and they wouldn't be having this argument. Deanna dropped the soft, southern drawl and let her irritation show. "She's a single mother trying to survive on welfare with a critically ill baby. I'm ashamed of Sherylyn for spreading idle rumors. Gloria needs help, not condemnation."

Phil drove in silence, then asked, "Are the rumors idle?"

To lie to him would risk the chance of him finding out the truth, which would hurt their cause even more. Deanna had hoped to persuade him with logical appeal, not hot debate. She'd also hoped to soften him up with a couple of Crown Royals before she started.

"She was a waitress for ten years, prior to Sara's birth. For the last six months the truckers she'd met during her job have been helping her earn money toward Sara's surgery. She's a proud woman, Phil. She has no family, and except for the truckers, no close friends. When Sara was first diagnosed and Gloria was told a heart transplant was the only cure, she just focused on earning money whatever way she could."

"Sounds like you're in danger of having your house cleaned."

Resentment threatened Deanna's resolve to keep this evening friendly. Had he always been this narrow-minded and judgmental? Why had she never noticed before? And when had she gotten so protective?

The risk of theft had occurred to her at

first, enough to request a discrete background check the day after she'd moved Gloria in. Now that action provoked feelings of guilt. It was hardly an act of friendship and trust, but a woman had to be careful. Phil's comment implied he didn't trust her judgment.

"Even if she was that type of person, which she's not, there's no need for her to steal. Once her community was made aware of her situation, they rallied to her cause. I've been able to persuade the indigent fund board to cover the hospital bill, with the understanding that the public donations cover supplies and drugs. Now we just need a surgeon." She said it with all the sweetness she could infuse, followed with an expectant smile.

"What you need is a heart." Phil ignored her solicitation efforts, concentrating on his driving as he pulled the Jaguar up in front of the Buckhead Diner. He put the car in neutral, pulled on the brake, then turned to look at her.

"Does your mother know she's living with you?"

Deanna fought the urge to laugh. Fifty-two years old and Phil was threatening her with her mother. Unfortunately, the threat had merit.

"Yes, Mother knows." She'd told Charlotte

that Gloria was her new housekeeper. It was almost the truth. Gloria was living in the housekeeper's suite and was answering the phone and the door.

Once they were seated, Phil ordered his usual Crown and water on-the-rocks. Deanna ordered her usual glass of white wine. In spite of a year's separation, some things didn't change.

"I talked to Andrew today," Deanna said, hoping to sidetrack the conversation until Phil had loosened up a bit. The problem was that Phil never really loosened up. He considered himself on-call at all times. In twenty-nine years of marriage, she'd never seen him drink more than two drinks in an evening, usually only one.

"He's letting Eric design some of the units in that apartment complex he's building. He says Eric has a lot of innovative ideas."

"Which means the kid goes overboard with radical when simple is called for." Phil had never approved of their youngest child going into architecture. A recent college graduate, Eric had been excited when Deanna's brother Andrew, a building contractor, had offered him a job. Phil had viewed it as his son taking his mother's side against him, especially since their oldest son Jeff already worked for

Deanna's older brother. Only Sherylyn had been interested in following in her father's footsteps.

"Andrew says Eric is doing a good job and he's enjoying it. It would be nice if you'd show some enthusiasm for your son's success. It hurts him that you're disappointed in him."

"Eric is a grown man. He hardly needs his father's approval anymore."

Deanna sipped her wine and studied the man across from her. For all his incredible knowledge, he was still sadly lacking in some of the basics. Evan certainly seemed to understand a father's role, but she wasn't here tonight to compare Evan with Phil. Tonight's purpose was to coddle and cajole, to convince him that helping Sara was the only decent thing to do. She would educate him to his role of father later.

"I called Andrew to tell him I had decided not to do the total restoration on Dad's motorcycle," she continued, trying to make conversation. "He and Pete were thinking about bidding on it during the auction. I wanted to let him know he would have some competition."

Phil frowned. "What motorcycle?"

Phil knew nothing about it, she realized. That said a lot about their relationship, considering how much a part of her life it had become recently. "Dad bought a 1953 Indian motorcycle on his fiftieth birthday, sort of the way you bought the Jaguar, only Dad justified his purchase by saying it was destined to be a collector's item someday. Turns out he was right."

"I've never heard of an Indian motorcycle."

She could tell Phil was bored with her discussion. Maybe if he understood its value. "Evan says it's worth $30,000 just the way it is."

"Thirty thousand dollars? For a used motorcycle?"

"With dull paint and pitted chrome. He says the engine doesn't even have to run, but I insisted he at least restore that part."

"Who is Evan?"

Jealousy? From Phil? No, he probably just didn't think she was capable of having a motorcycle appraised without being taken advantage of. "Evan Maxwell owns the Harley-Davidson dealership in Buford and came highly recommended as an Indian restorer." She hoped the subdued lighting would mask the color she could feel flushing her face. "You know, Phil, having merchandise appraised is something I do frequently for the auction. Even Pete knew about the Indian's value. I think he was more upset about the monetary loss than the sentimental value. Now, Andrew—"

"Are you ready to order?"

She was wasting his time. This wasn't going at all the way she'd planned. "The soft-shell crab salad will be fine."

Phil ordered the veal and wild mushroom meatloaf. After their waitress had left, Phil sat back in his chair and studied Deanna. Her fingers found the strand of pearls and stroked them nervously. His intense scrutiny made her self-conscious.

"I like you in red. It's very sexy."

Deanna could feel heat flush her face again. "Thank you. I was tired of black."

"You look good in black, too, but red does something special to your eyes. You should wear more of it or . . . actually less of it . . . more often . . . in private." His voice had taken on a persuasive huskiness, leaving no question as to the direction of his thoughts.

Deanna cleared her throat nervously. "I don't think that would be appropriate, seeing as how we're no longer married."

"I was hoping we could discuss that."

Deanna was grateful when the arrival of their dinner interrupted the conversation. "This looks wonderful, and I'm just starving, aren't you?" Maybe if she made an enthusiastic pretense of eating, he would drop the subject.

His smile said he didn't believe her, and he found her discomfort amusing. "Starving," he echoed, but he made it clear it wasn't food he wanted.

"How's Sherylyn doing?" Discussing the children was always safe.

"Fine." His smile was still amused, but he allowed her to steer the conversation into safer waters. "She would like to be more a part of my research, but I've told her I think she should practice on her own for a few years first. Experience is the best teacher."

"Better than you?" Deanna couldn't help teasing him.

Phil acted affronted. "A different perspective. If she only works with me, then our research efforts won't vary from what I would have done on my own. By working with other surgeons and developing her own style, she'll bring fresh insight into our research."

"Innovative ideas," Deanna said, using the word he'd disdained when they'd been discussing Eric.

Phil frowned. "You can hardly compare medical technology to architecture."

"I was only trying to point out that all of

our children have their own special talents and that one should not be held in higher esteem than another."

"I have never shown favoritism to any of our children."

He said it with such indignity, Deanna knew he believed it. She sighed. She never remembered their conversations as argumentative, yet tonight, when her goal was harmony, every subject they discussed made her want to argue with him. Had he changed or had she?

She tried to remember dinners together when they were married. In the last few years he had been so busy there hadn't been many. When they did go out, he had talked at length about whatever project he was presently working on. None of her activities had interested him, including the children, so they hadn't discussed them. So different from her conversations with Evan.

She wasn't here with Evan. She gave Phil her rapt attention. "So what research are you working on now?" That should keep him off the subject of their relationship. Once he got started talking about his research, he wouldn't quit until after dessert.

He didn't. Deanna sipped her coffee and smiled as he finished his white chocolate banana cream pie and brought his monologue to a conclusion. "You can see how this research will benefit people everywhere, not just children. The government and the insurance companies scream about physician's fees, but their proposed cutbacks would kill research."

Deanna didn't like thinking of Sara as research, but she knew research patients were treated as very special. Funding was hard to get without impressive success statistics.

"I'm glad you brought that up, Phil. Can Sara's transplant surgery be written off as research?"

Phil didn't answer as he signed the credit card receipt. "Ready?" he asked, standing up and pulling out her chair. Deanna let him help her into her coat, knowing he hadn't forgotten her question, he just wasn't ready to answer. He waited until they were back in his car and heading toward Deanna's house.

"It's early yet. We could go dancing."

"Some other time, perhaps. I try not to leave Gloria alone too long. She tries to do too much with her injured shoulder."

"You're going to get hurt, Deanna. It never works, taking in the less fortunate. If you take in this mother, you'll have to take in the next one. They'll take advantage of you, rip you off. You may even get physically hurt. There will always be people in need. You can't sin-gle-handedly save them all."

"I only want to save this one." Deanna felt the defensive anger rising again. It was going to be difficult to sweet talk Phil into helping them when everything he said made her want to bash him in the head.

"Okay, let's look at this from another angle. What if this baby dies while waiting for a heart? She's eight months old and only weighs nine pounds. Her life expectancy without a heart transplant is twelve to eighteen months. What does it do to your credibility with this mother, when you've given her such hope, and her baby dies?"

"Gloria Harris has had nothing but hope for this baby since she found out she was preg-nant with her. That's one of the reasons I got involved. Gloria already had the hope, she just needed some resources. And Sara has enough will to live to survive until a heart is found."

"That sounds real noble, but you are all na-ive if you think it's that simple. Heart trans-plants are very controversial, not totally accepted by the population. Unlike the kid-neys, the heart is considered an integral part of a person, like their soul. To be of any use to the recipient, it must be harvested immedi-ately upon the donor's death, preferably when there is brain death and the heart is still beating.

"Donors tend to be accident victims," Phil continued, ignoring Deanna squeamish flinch. "Unlike adults, children don't have driver's licenses and advance directives that state, 'please harvest any usable organs upon my death.' It requires the signed permission of the parents. Not too many parents want to talk about organ donation when they've just learned their child is dead."

Deanna knew he was being deliberately cruel in an effort to talk her out of her crusade. She refused to be daunted. "The public is slowly becoming more aware of organ transplant. Hypoplastic left heart syndrome is extremely rare. How long can the waiting list be for babies?"

"That's not the only syndrome requiring heart transplant. Not only is there a waiting list, the number of parents willing to donate their dead baby's heart is small. They want their baby buried intact."

"I would want to think some good had come from my child's death."

"Between marriage to a heart surgeon and involvement with the Harrises, I hardly think you qualify as Jane Q. Public."

Phil turned the Jaguar into Deanna's drive

and turned off the engine. Almost reflexively, Deanna unfastened her seatbelt, protective of the fur. Phil unbuckled his as well, then twisted in his seat to face her.

"I'm not refusing to help you, Deanna, I just don't think you realize what all is involved."

"Then help us understand what is involved," Deanna invited.

Phil looked at her a long moment, his expression thoughtful. "Are you going to ask me inside tonight?"

Deanna was instantly suspicious. "To continue discussing what we need for Sara's surgery?"

He reached for her hand across the console, then stroked her fingers in what Deanna was pretty sure he meant to be a seductive manner.

"I had something more pleasant in mind," he said, continuing to caress her hand. "We have lots of time to discuss your baby."

"You just said we didn't have much time."

"I think we have until in the morning," Phil said, his impatience showing through.

"I still have to get Sara ready for bed," she hedged, hoping this conversation wasn't leading where it sounded like it was leading. Phil would never stoop to something that low.

He abruptly released her hand, crossed his

arms over his chest and threw himself back against his seat. "Christ, Deanna, I think you think more of that hooker and her baby than you do of your own family."

"I do not. I have not refused anyone anything since Gloria has moved in here."

"You're refusing me." He glared at her.

Deanna stared back, speechless. He would stoop that low. "You think . . . You want . . ." She couldn't even put it into words she was so upset. "We're not married!" she finally screeched, then winced. Ladies didn't screech.

"I keep trying to discuss that with you, but you keep changing the subject. You want to discuss something tonight, let's discuss that."

"What about Sara?"

"What about her?"

"Are you going to help her?"

"Are you going to listen to reason?"

Deanna stared at him. Blunt, clinical, don't waste my time Phil. He probably thought he should get some sort of medal for the patience he'd already shown her— three dates and Christmas dinner with the family. He also probably thought he was doing this for her own good. God knows a woman wasn't capable of making such a monumental decision without a man's superior intellect to guide her. Damn it! She needed his help.

She was an ambassador, a diplomat, not to mention having fifty-two years of experience in playing polite society games. Deanna gave him her sweetest smile. "Phillip, I've explained that I was willing for us to be friends, for the sake of the children and for harmony at the hospital. What would Gloria think, me letting you spend the night when she knows the purpose for tonight's dinner was to discuss your helping us? She would think I'm no better than her, sleeping with a man I'm not married to and justifying it as necessary to our cause. That would be nothing but prostitution, don't you agree?"

Phil's eyes were nearly black, glaring at her, his jaw clenched with restrained vexation. Deanna pretended not to notice, but she switched the direction of her attack. "You talked so sweet at dinner, about how your research was for the good of mankind and so necessary to show the government how important research is." She laid her hand on the tensed muscles of his arm, soft, helpless, conveying to him how much she needed his superior strength. "I know you'll do this for all the reasons you discussed, and just think of the publicity. The press will make you out to be the hero, not that you care anything about that."

She leaned forward and placed a soft, chaste kiss on his cheek. "I'm glad we're friends again, Phil, working together on these important issues. I could never do it without you."

She opened her car door and slid out before he had a chance to reply. Tomorrow she would tell everyone concerned that Phil had agreed to donate his services. To deny it would make him look heartless. He really wasn't a heartless man. He'd just been raised in a different time, under different priorities. A year ago her own priorities had been much the same as his. If her eyes could be opened, she had every confidence that she could open his.

It was for his own good.

Fourteen

Deanna stared down at the enormous gas tank in front of her and fought panic. She'd ridden horses bigger than Evan's Harley, she tried to remind herself, controlling them with nothing more than a small steel bit in their mouths. At least on the motorcycle her feet touched the ground. That assumption was based on feel alone. She couldn't see the ground.

"I don't think this is a good idea," she told Evan, who stood beside her. "What if I lay it down?"

"I suggest you get your leg out from under it first," Evan said succinctly. "Do the braking drill with the engine off to get used to how it feels."

The bike weighed a ton. It was all she could do to push it into a roll. She braked to a stop and put her feet back down. The bike wobbled, threatening to overpower her.

"It's too heavy," she protested. "Is the Indian really this heavy?"

"You're going to ride it, not carry it," Evan pointed out. "Their weights are similar, but the Indian has a smaller gas tank, so it doesn't seem as massive when you're sitting on it. Once you start riding a bigger bike, you'll never want to go back to a smaller one."

"Why?" Deanna asked, more than a little skeptical.

Evan grinned. "I'll show you."

He motioned for her to trade places with him, started it up and let it idle for a moment. Even the sound of the engine was intimidating, Deanna thought. When it idled without the choke on, he patted the rear seat in invitation.

Deanna's eyes widened in disbelief. Ride behind Evan? That would require wrapping her arms and thighs around him. Heavy riding clothes notwithstanding, it was an intimate position.

He raised his visor and shouted over the engine. "Don't you trust me?"

She trusted him. It was her own response she didn't trust. She approached the bike warily, gingerly using Evan's shoulders for support as she mounted. She clunked him with her helmet as she looked down to position the foot pegs. The bike wasn't so big after all. He was sitting very close between her spread thighs, a very erotic situation, which made Deanna acutely aware of just how totally her body responded to the nearness of his.

"You have to hold on," Evan shouted.

Deanna licked dry lips then laid her hands lightly on Evan's waist. He was a big man, wide in the shoulders and tall, his size made more evident by his close proximity. He gunned the big engine, making it roar, then released the clutch. Deanna was jerked back, instinctively grabbing onto handfuls of his jacket.

"You have to hold on," Evan repeated, stopping at the entrance to the dealership. Deanna did, wrapping her arms and her thighs tightly around him as he launched them out onto the highway. He ran the big bike smoothly through the gears, accelerating across the bridge over the interstate and continuing on west. It was a new direction for Deanna. She sat up straighter to see where they were going.

There was no way to carry on a conversation as they rode. Between the helmets, the noise of the bike, and the wind, communication was impossible. Deanna had nothing to distract her from the nearness of Evan and how totally dependent on his skill her life was at this moment. His body made a wonderful windscreen, as long as she stayed as close to him as possible. Of course staying as close to him as possible produced heat of another source, totally unaffected by the wind.

She sat stiffly at first, resisting his efforts to lean through the curves, her body held rigid against the unaccustomed contact of his. She knew from reading the book and riding her own bike that her actions were making it more difficult for him. She forced herself to relax, to meld her body with his and move as he moved. They were riding a motorcycle. It was only natural that their bodies be touching. If only her body would quit making such a big deal out of it.

He was taking them to Lake Lanier, she realized, recognizing advertisements to familiar places. She had stayed with friends who had homes on the lake, or houseboats, but she hadn't been out here in years. At the stop sign on Peachtree Industrial he raised his visor.

"Feel the difference?"

All Deanna felt was his thighs inside of hers, his back against her breasts, his waist beneath her hands. She felt her face flush. He had brought her on this trip to demonstrate the difference between the little bike and the big bike. She nodded gamely, resolving to pay more attention to the bike and less to the driver. Evan smiled and lowered his visor. Deanna held on as he turned south onto Peachtree Industrial. He went right past the road to the marina.

"Where are we going?" she tried to shout, but her voice carried no farther than inside her own helmet. Where they were going didn't matter, she decided. She was supposed to be comparing bikes.

The heavier bike did give a smoother ride. It dipped gently over low spots in the road, where the little Honda had bounced. It didn't vibrate at road speeds like the little bike, either. The Harley wasn't as fast at acceleration, but Deanna wasn't sure if that was the bike or the way Evan rode it. She did like the sound of the Harley engine. Where the Honda had a softer, higher pitched, buzzing bee sound, the Harley had a deep-throated roar like a big jungle cat.

Evan slowed the bike, then leaned it in a hard right onto Suwanee Dam Road. Suwanee Dam curved and twisted its way through well-kept rural residences set on sprawling lots covered with huge, old trees. There were steep hills and low valleys. The big Harley seemed to float under Deanna, as one with the road and with its riders. She noticed the more she relaxed and moved with Evan, the faster he took the curves, leaning the bike into them, making Deanna feel like she was flying. Soul flying. It was more fantastic with Evan than she remembered it being with her father. Having her entire body on full sensual alert could be a contributing factor. They moved together to the rhythm of the road, her heart beating heavily with excitement. She had never realized motorcycle riding could be sensual.

Evan slowed the bike and downshifted into low gear. He turned onto a road that angled steeply downward and twisted sharply in a series of S-curves. As they rounded the last curve, Deanna saw the river, wide and moving fast below them. To her right the dam loomed above them. Evan parked the bike in a nearly empty parking lot the size of a football field.

"Let's walk around a bit, get warmed back up," Evan suggested, pulling off his helmet.

Deanna pulled her helmet off and tried to fluff her hair. If she was going to ride motorcycles on a routine basis, she was going to have to change her hair style. Evan began stripping off his leather chaps. Even though he was fully dressed beneath them, she found the action as erotic as his sitting between her thighs had been. She licked her lips, her mouth strangely dry.

Evan didn't seem affected. He barely

glanced at her as he folded the chaps and laid them in one of the saddlebags attached to the rear of the bike. "I suggest you do the same," he said. "Now that we're not moving, you'll get hot."

She was already hot. The sun was bright, but somehow Deanna didn't think that was the real reason. She unfastened her chaps, feeling more vulnerable than she should have, considering how many layers she wore beneath them.

"The jacket, too," Evan said, holding out his hand for it. Deanna felt herself blushing as she unzipped it and shrugged out of it. She handed it to him, noticing that his attention was on her sweater, not her jacket— her breasts, actually— his expression wistful. Maybe he wasn't as unaffected as she'd thought.

He turned back to the saddlebags, adding her jacket and securing the locks. "You'll have to carry your helmet," he said, picking his up by the chin strap.

Deanna picked hers up as well, her entire body tuned in to the close proximity of his as they started down the steps to the river. She was slightly winded when they reached the bottom. "That's quite a hike," she said, looking back up to where they'd parked the bike.

Evan chuckled. "Wait 'til we walk back up it."

It was cooler near the river's edge, the rushing water making a pleasant sound as they walked across a picturesque wooden bridge. They stood side by side in the middle of the bridge and looked down at the swirling river.

"So, what did you think?" Evan asked, after they'd stood for several minutes in silence.

That it was getting more and more difficult to keep her thoughts of Evan on a strictly professional, or even friendly, basis. She shivered, then smiled, discrediting the cause.

"I think it's too cold to stand here without our jackets."

Evan smiled back, then wrapped his arm around her shoulders. "Let's go find a warm, sunny rock."

It would be so easy to love this man, Deanna thought, walking in the comfortable security of his embrace. They would share their grandchildren, work together on benefits for the needy, go soul flying on Harley-Davidsons that roared like lions. In an idyllic world, they would live happily ever after.

But it wasn't an idyllic world, Deanna knew. They lived in separate worlds, and it was no more fair for her to give up her world to live in his than it was to ask him to give up his

world to live with her. She didn't even know
if he'd want her in his world, much less if he
would be willing to give up his to live with
her. Men didn't seem to worry about things
like that when they pursued a woman.

Worrying about the future seemed to be a
woman thing, at least where relationships were
concerned. Men seemed to live only in the present. Women were nesters, men hunters, Georgia had explained to her. Nature arranged it
that way to provide a stable environment for
the children. She smiled to herself. She was
long past worrying about a stable environment
for children. A benefit of dating after meno-
pause, Georgia had assured her countless
times.

"This is one of my favorite spots," Evan
said, removing his arm and bringing her back
to the present. He led the way down the steep,
rock-strewn embankment, then offered her his
hand as she followed.

Boulders was more descriptive than rocks,
Deanna thought, picking her way carefully,
grateful for the heavy boots she'd bought for
protection on the motorcycle. Evan settled
onto a large, flat surface near the river's edge
and gestured for her to sit in the space in front
of him. Evan's rock had another rock above it
that formed a backrest. He set his helmet in

a safe niche, then leaned back, stacking his hands behind his head.

"Isn't this great?" he asked. "I like to come here when I need to think or when the pace of my life gets too hectic. There's something soothing about watching a river flow."

The river might be soothing, but there was nothing soothing about sitting between Evan's bent knees, his position and the warm, lazy look in his hazel eyes inviting her to relax back against him. She sat stiffly upright, hugging her knees to her chest. The sun was hot overhead, burning into her skin through all her layers of clothing. She trailed her fingers in the water, then quickly jerked them out.

"Cold?" Evan asked, his voice amused.

"It should be frozen, it's so cold," Deanna commented, drying her hand on her jeans.

"It's probably forty degrees or so, but that's plenty cold. It comes off the bottom of the reservoir. Even in the heat of summer, it's cold enough to take your breath away."

"It amazes me how the air temperature feels standing still versus riding the bike. Even on the bike, it feels like it drops ten degrees when I ride through a shady valley."

"It'll chill your body temperature faster than you realize, too," Evan said. "Hypothermia fogs a biker's ability to interpret. You don't even realize your thinking is impaired, until you don't respond properly to a situation. It can be real dangerous."

"There's so much to think about riding a motorcycle. It's a wonder more people aren't hurt on them."

"Enough are," Evan said, his expression grim. "It's usually rider error, too, though even the most cautious riders get in situations there's no escape from."

"Like what?"

"Friend of mine got rear-ended sitting at a stop light. Guy didn't see him, he claimed. Crushed him into the back of a Lincoln Continental, broke his leg." Evan shrugged. "Stupid stuff like that. It happens all the time. In a car it's a fender bender, a mild case of whiplash. On a motorcycle, there's no protection. He was lucky to only break his leg."

"Does he still ride?" Deanna asked, visions of twisted metal and broken bodies making gooseflesh on her arms in spite of the warm sun.

"He still rides."

Deanna couldn't fathom that. "Why?"

Evan smiled at her reaction. "Why not? People drive cars after accidents. You get back on a horse if you're thrown. People remarry after divorce. Life is full of risks. To avoid all risk is to live a pretty dull life."

There was blatant challenge in his hazel eyes, his gaze intense as it held hers. "None of us is guaranteed a moment past the present one."

"Eat, drink, and be merry, for tomorrow we may die?" Deanna quoted.

"I don't go to that extreme, but I've learned to accept each day as a gift. I try not to waste them or to let my priorities get screwed up with things that won't mean a hill of beans a year from now."

Deanna searched his face, wishing she could ask what had taught him that lesson. Whatever it was, the pain was still evident, like her own from the divorce. If that didn't prove there were no guarantees in life, she didn't know what did.

"So you sell Harley-Davidson motorcycles and repair old Indians and save helpless babies from a system that discriminates against the poor," Deanna commented, trying to get back on a lighter subject.

"Yes," Evan agreed, his expression still serious. "And I call my son in New Jersey every Sunday and talk to my grandson Tommy so I'm not a stranger to him when I see him twice a year. I make sure Brian or I pick Kyle up at his day-care by four o'clock so we can have dinner together and give the kid some sort of family foundation, in spite of being a household of bachelors."

Deanna was impressed. "Even Ghost?"

Evan groaned. "Even Ghost. I suppose the new puppy will be another male, too."

Deanna smiled. "You caved in."

"Brian says I'm overcompensating, but he has no room to talk. Kyle has both of us pretty well wrapped around his finger," he held up his hands, pinkies extended, "one on each hand."

Deanna laughed. "Kyle has the self-confidence of a child who knows he's loved and accepted. You've done a good job, bachelors or not."

Evan smiled but remained thoughtful. "What are your priorities, Deanna?"

Deanna rested her chin on her knees, looking out over the water. Good question. What were her priorities?

"I've spent the last year trying to answer that question," she finally confessed. "Somehow, when I saw Billy's Indian I thought restoring Dad's and learning to ride it would help me figure that out." A pensive smile pulled at her mouth. "I knew who I was and where I wanted to go back then. I had the world by the tail, opportunities spread around my feet like diamonds. Somewhere in the last thirty years I seem to have gotten lost. I didn't realize it until Phil demanded a divorce.''

Evan laid his hands lightly on her shoulders, his caress comforting. "Dr. Randolph, Sara's surgeon?"

"Yes."

"You must still be on good terms, if he's agreed to help Sara."

Deanna choked back a bitter laugh. She'd all but blackmailed him into helping them. "They'll write it off as research or a teaching opportunity. Phil enjoys being a hero, and he doesn't need the money. Everybody wins."

Evan nudged her back against him, still caressing her shoulders. "And what outlet do you use for all this anger?"

"I play a lethal game of bridge."

"And flaunt accepted social mores by riding motorcycles and taking in stray prostitutes?"

Deanna twisted away from him. "If I want a lesson in psychiatric motivating factors, I'll go talk to Georgia. Are you ready to go back?"

"No." Evan's gaze was steady as he looked at her. "I enjoy being with you, Deanna, but I'd like to know where I stand. I'd like to be more than your friend but not if my only appeal is that of forbidden fruit."

She could let him think that and walk out of his life now, removing the temptation of him from hers. The thought left her feeling cold and empty. "You frighten me," she said, barely audible, watching his reaction. "I'm afraid of being hurt again. I couldn't take that."

He didn't try to deny that her getting hurt was a possibility. That alone gave Deanna the confidence to continue— that and the concern in his eyes as he watched her. "I'm afraid I'm not cut out for casual affairs. I could never give my body to a man without my heart being involved."

His expression softened into a rueful smile. "I don't think any affair with you could ever be casual, Deanna. You're too full of passion to allow that."

He saw her as passionate? Her surprise must have shown on her face because his smile widened.

"Does that surprise you? Passion just means you feel things deeply, so deeply no one can mistake the things that matter most to you. Do you know what you've told me means the most to you?"

Deanna slowly shook her head.

"Children are your first passion, I think. I see it when you talk about your grandchildren, when you talk to Kyle, when you hold Sara. I heard it when you moved an entire room full of tough motorcycle riders to tears with your story about a baby who would die without help. That kind of emotion cannot be faked, Deanna. It comes from the deepest part of you.

"Your other passion is freedom," Evan continued, stroking her arm again and making her shiver. "It's there in your fierce determination to learn to ride the motorcycle. It was all over your face when you came in from your first solo ride, frozen to the bone but triumphant." His eyes darkened and his caress took on a more intimate quality. "It was evident the night you kissed me until I lost my mind, then wrenched away from me as if I threatened your soul."

He moved closer. Deanna could only watch him with helpless fascination. "That's what I did, isn't it, Deanna?" he persisted. "And again today, asking you to ride behind me. You're afraid I'll steal your freedom, not your heart."

He was so close, Deanna closed her eyes. She felt the tender pressure of his lips against hers, the warmth of his hand as he cradled her head. She didn't know whether to laugh or cry.

"I promise not to threaten your freedom," Evan said between slow, nibbling kisses. "I only want your heart, that incredible passion that is the essence of you. You already have mine."

Deanna kissed him back, savoring the taste of him, the feel of him, the dizzy kaleidoscope of sensations swirling inside of her at his touch. When Evan groaned and tried to pull her into his lap she struggled to return to sanity. "Evan, this is hardly the place." She glanced around them. Sure enough, a pair of boys were fishing from the bank across the river, watching them avidly. She felt embarrassed heat flush her cheeks.

"You blush more than any woman I ever met," Evan teased her. He kissed her one more time before helping her to her feet. "Warm enough to head back?"

Warm enough to ride naked through a snowstorm, Deanna thought, thoroughly flustered. What would they do now? Brian was at his house and Gloria was at hers. She should have asked Gloria for the key to her mobile home. This wasn't a good idea. There were too many complications, too many ramifications. They would never be able to keep it a secret, and if it was so shameful that it should be kept secret, why was she even considering it? Deanna knew her face was beet red as they climbed back up the steps to the parking lot. Only part of it was from exertion.

"Your turn," Evan said when they got back to the motorcycle. He offered her the key.

Deanna was still trying to breathe normally from the steep climb. She stared at Evan in disbelief. "You aren't serious."

"You have no idea," he said, his gaze boring into hers.

"You'd ride behind me?"

Evan grinned his totally devastating, wolfish grin that had appealed to her from their first meeting. "I'm secure in my manhood. I think I can handle it."

Oh, yes, the man is totally secure in his manhood, Deanna thought, returning his smile and accepting the key.

"Take it around the parking lot a few times," Evan recommended when she was sitting astride the huge machine, once more feeling intimidated by it.

Any doubts she'd had about its acceleration capability were quickly dispelled as the bike threatened to lunge out from under her. Cloying perspiration ran in rivulets as panic threatened to overwhelm her. It was cumbersome to turn, demanding the entire width of the parking lot. It was heavy, requiring more room to stop than the Honda. It kept dying when she tried to take off from a standing stop, much less forgiving than the Honda had ever been.

"You aren't employing any of the skills you learned," Evan scolded when she pulled up beside him, thoroughly discouraged. "The principles are the same, regardless of the size of the bike. Let the bike do the work. You're trying to muscle it into obedience. It outweighs you about five times."

"I've noticed that," Deanna said drily.

"Then quit trying to use your muscles. Use your brain."

Deanna pulled in the clutch and toed it into first gear. She released the clutch and concentrated on becoming one with the bike, making it respond to her commands. She shifted into second and leaned it in a tight turn around the end of the parking lot. She felt much more confident the next time she stopped next to Evan. He was grinning like a fool.

"What do you think now?" he asked.

"I think I like putting this beast through its paces," Deanna said, quirking her eyebrow at him mischievously. "This power thing could become addictive."

"I do like forceful women." His eyes were full of erotic promise.

The thought no longer frightened her, Deanna realized. She returned his smile. "Let

me do a few more runs before you entrust
your life to my driving skills."

It got easier with practice, both handling the
Harley and thinking about Evan as more than
a friend. She had Evan to thank for both, for
teaching her the skills required to handle the
bike, and for giving her the confidence to get
back on a horse she'd been recently and painfully thrown off of. There was always the risk
of being thrown again, but that was the risk
of living a life that was not boring. That was
her third passion, Deanna decided, gliding to
a stop beside Evan, her confidence complete.
She would never be boring again.

Fifteen

The ultimate soul flying— cruising the hills and curves on a big Harley Softail, the sun casting long intimate shadows over the landscape, Evan's arms and thighs wrapped around her, his body moving with hers as she controlled a machine that outweighed her five times. He was right about one thing, she would never be content to ride the little Honda again. She had become a power addict, and nothing was going to satisfy her until she owned one of these for herself.

Instead of riding back to the dealership to pick up her car, Evan directed her toward his house. The uncertainty came back to Deanna as soon as they got off the motorcycle. Evan fished his keys out of his pocket and opened the garage door. The first thing Deanna noticed was her motorcycle, sitting like a proud, aging king.

"You finished it!" She approached it reverently. It didn't look as dilapidated as she'd feared. "Oh, Evan, it's gorgeous." She ran a light finger across the handlebars. "Dad would be so proud."

Evan parked the Harley and came to stand behind her. "They were beautiful bikes. Still disappointed that it doesn't have new paint and chrome like Billy's?"

"No. It wears its age like a true Indian chief. Surviving to an old age should be revered, not painted over to imitate youth."

Evan wrapped his arms around her waist and kissed her neck. "I couldn't agree more, for people as well as motorcycles. Do you know how beautiful you are?"

Deanna let him turn her into his embrace, noting that he had closed the garage door. She slid her arms around his neck and kissed him until they were both breathing heavily.

"Let's go inside," Evan urged.

"What about Brian and Kyle?"

"Kyle is spending the night with Joey. Brian doesn't plan to come home tonight."

Deanna pulled back to eye him suspiciously. "You planned for this?"

"Not this exactly." He tried to kiss her again, then knew he wouldn't get any further without an explanation. "Brian has a lady friend who frequently invites him to stay the night, and I knew we'd be out on the bikes. I wanted to at least be able to invite you to dinner. Joey's mother keeps Kyle frequently. We keep Joey a lot, too."

"How convenient."

"You're not one of those people who can't graciously accept a gift, are you?"

"What gift?"

He tried again to hold her, to appeal to her senses with his deep, husky voice. "We are here, together, alone until morning, at the exact time we both feel we'd like to be more than friends. It's a gift, a moment in time that may never repeat itself."

"Then what happens in the morning?"

Evan dropped his arms with an exasperated sigh. "Damn, woman, you're hell on a man's ego. If I can't seduce you senseless, can we at least go inside instead of standing out here in the garage?"

Deanna felt herself blushing, even as she smiled at his frustration. "I guess I'm a little nervous about being here."

"Would you rather go out to dinner?" Evan asked, his irritation softening into compassion. "I'd like us to still be friends in the morning, no regrets."

She didn't want to go out to dinner. She wanted to go back in his arms, back to the dizzy swirl of sensation his kisses generated. She offered him a shy smile. "No regrets."

He hugged her to him in a fierce embrace. His kiss threatened to swamp her with its intensity.

"I thought we were going inside," she gasped, when his mouth left hers to trail scorching kisses down her neck. His hands were already under her sweater, trying to find their way under her thermal underwear.

He went still, his entire body rigid as he just held her against him. His breathing was ragged, the beat of his heart heavy against Deanna's own. "Maybe I'd better let you control this ride," he finally suggested. "If I stay in control, our first time is going to be hard and fast on the garage floor."

Power. The feeling surged through Deanna, as effective an aphrodisiac as his kisses had been. She had the power to make Evan lose complete control. Now, he was offering to let her drive. She looked into the heated depths of his hazel eyes and knew it was going to be better than riding the Harley.

"Do you think we could find a bed?"

Evan's answer was to scoop her off her feet and carry her through the door into the house, down a hallway and into what she could only assume was his bedroom. Deanna laughed, drunk on exhilaration.

"I thought I was driving."

Evan set her down, then kissed her exuberantly. "You are. I was just showing you the way."

"No more help," Deanna commanded.

"I've created a monster." His eyes sparkled in anticipation. "You really are addicted to this power thing."

"I'm only just realizing how much. Take off your shirt."

Evan grinned wickedly. "Take it off yourself."

Deanna approached him, trying not to show how nervous she was. She'd never been with anyone but Phil, and it had been over a year since she'd been with him. Her fingers fumbled a little as she undid the buttons of his flannel shirt. He waited until she'd reached the bottom, pulled the tail of the shirt out of his jeans, then he held up his hands to let her undo the cuffs.

"You're enjoying this," she said, feeling more confident as she watched the growing warmth in his eyes.

"I thought that was the idea. I warned you I liked forceful women."

"I'll show you force." Deanna stripped the shirt off of him and shoved him down on the bed. She pulled off his boots, then his socks. She hesitated as she eyed his jeans.

"Don't stop now," Evan encouraged. "Aren't you awfully warm in all those clothes?"

She stepped between his knees. "Don't you like my sweater?"

"I like your sweater." He slid his hands under the waistband, slipped it over her head and tossed it into a nearby chair. "I like it better over there. Now, let me show you how you handle those pesky jeans." He unfastened her jeans and shoved them down over her hips. He caressed her skin through the silky ski underwear, pulling her forward so he could nuzzle her belly with his mouth.

Deanna used the position to pull his undershirt up and over his head, leaving his upper torso deliciously bare. She leaned down and kissed him deeply on the mouth. He lay back, bringing her on top of him across the width of the bed. His jeans were erotically rough against the silky material of her underwear. His hands intimately molded her bottom, enticing her to press herself against the hard bulge beneath her.

"Let me help you out here," he offered, unfastening his jeans and shoving them and everything he wore under them off with one swift motion. "I'd hate for you to break a nail."

She raked the maligned talons lightly down the hard muscles of his chest, then burrowed back up through the curling mat of hair. When she reached his nipple, she circled it lightly, teasing it to a hard nub.

He flattened her hand against him with his own, rolling her onto her back so he could loom over her. "I'm at a definite disadvantage here," he growled, tugging at the top to her underwear.

Deanna fought him playfully, squirming away from his seeking hands. "I thought I was in control."

"You are," Evan said, trailing kisses up her midriff. "Take it off."

He let her move away from him. She sat up in the middle of the bed and gave him an assessing look before she removed the top. She had his total attention, his eyes hot and hungry as he waited for her next move. She hesitated, suddenly shy. Her flesh no longer had the firmness of youth. It had been an accepted part of getting older, until now, when she risked rejection from a man whose opinion mattered too much.

Evan seemed to understand. "If I wanted a twenty-year-old, I'd have pursued a twenty-year-old. Be proud of your body, Deanna." His hand caressed her thigh. "You've taken excellent care of it. I promise to worship each and every inch of it."

The thought created a burning deep inside of her. "Could . . . could we at least get under the sheet?"

She scooted over to let him pull down the bedcovers. He slid under them, pulling the sheet up to his waist. He waited expectantly.

Deanna tried to smile. She peeled the top off, then slid beneath the sheet, still wearing her bra and the bottoms of the underwear. Evan reached over to brush her hair back from her face.

"Where would you like me to start?" he asked.

Her smile was more confident this time. She moved against him, her mouth seeking his, his mouth eager in reply. His hands coaxed her back on top of him, where he could use both his hands to stroke her bottom, the backs of her thighs, the curve of her waist. She felt him slide his hands inside the waistband of the underwear and guide it down her body as he continued to caress her. She was hot and slick when he rubbed himself against her. She straddled him, opening herself more intimately, trying to get even closer. She moaned against his mouth at the fire his touch was building inside of her.

Evan used his tongue in imitation of what was to come. He delved deeply, stroking and teasing, then nibbling and tasting. He wrapped his fingers around her ribs, his thumbs moving closer and closer to her sensitive nipples with each caress.

Deanna writhed against him, feeling like she was going to go up in flames. "Evan!"

He unhooked her bra with a deft flick of his fingers, his mouth swooping down on the exposed flesh with a lascivious hunger that caused Deanna to cry out. She moved against him, trying to bring him inside, to assuage the devouring need that threatened to tear her apart. She felt his hands tighten convulsively, felt the throbbing pulsation of him as she took him into the deepest part of herself.

"God, Deanna, stop," he gasped, holding her still as he wrestled with his own raging need.

She waited, feeling the power shift back to her, holding him tight until he regained a small measure of composure, then she moved, milking the length of him with tantalizing, slow strokes, watching his face as he fought for control, tried to hold back.

"No . . . Deanna, I can't . . . *Ahhh!*" It was a deep, harsh cry as he surrendered and pumped into her, holding her hips still against his fevered assault. Deanna felt her own body convulse around him as he gave a last, powerful thrust, exalting in the waves of surging energy that stormed through her. She rode it to the last dying ripple, then collapsed onto his chest. Their skin was slick with perspiration, their breathing labored. Deanna wasn't sure she would ever move again.

Evan didn't move for a long time, either. His breathing gradually slowed, his heart beat returned to a more normal tempo. When he did move, it was to caress her hair, his touch light and achingly tender.

"I knew it would be incredible," he said, his voice soft and intimate.

Deanna didn't know what to say. He had given her control, yet he had sent her spinning out of control, into a realm she'd never reached before. He had a power over her body she'd feared, and now had confirmed. Whatever else happened, she would never be the same again.

"Are you hungry yet?" he asked, returning her to earth, to physical needs of a less carnal nature.

Deanna smiled against his shoulder, then raised up to look at him. "Let's have something delivered, stay here."

"You're in Buford, city woman. The only thing that gets delivered out here is pizza. I can cook, though."

"What a talented man," she teased him.

"I'm only doing it to rebuild your energy reserves. I demand a rematch."

Deanna widened her eyes innocently. "I didn't know we were competing."

He gave her bare bottom a playful swat. "The hell you didn't. Next time, I drive, and we'll see who loses control first."

As a threat, it was filled with delicious possibilities. She smiled, accepting his challenge. "Then by all means, feed me."

He fixed them bacon, egg, and cheese sandwiches on whole wheat toast. Deanna sat at his kitchen table, wearing his terry cloth robe, marveling at her ability to eat something so heavily loaded with fat, salt, and cholesterol, and enjoying every bite.

"Tell me about your ex-husband," Evan asked.

Deanna looked at him, startled. "Why?"

Evan shrugged, trying to act nonchalant about it, but Deanna could tell it bothered him. "Dominant male territorialism, I guess. You haven't been divorced long. You'll be working together for Sara's surgery. You have children together. Should I worry?"

"I thought you promised not to get territorial on me," Deanna teased him. "Freedom and all that."

According to Georgia, a hot affair was supposed to help her know what she wanted in another man. Looking at Evan, remembering his sweet seduction, she couldn't imagine giving him up for another man. But that's how the game was played, or so she'd been told. Neither party was supposed to attach strings. Apparently Evan didn't like that rule, either.

"Don't worry about Phil," Deanna said, laying her hand on his arm. "We've not been together in over a year, and I have no desire to resurrect that part of our life together. What about you? Any girlfriends I should worry about?"

"I wouldn't do that to you, Deanna." He picked up her hand and pressed a kiss to her fingers. "The only people you have to worry about coming between us are Brian and Kyle. I've already promised Brian I'd move out and leave him and Kyle the house. Kyle asked me the other day if we could keep you."

She smiled at his distress. "I would never want to come between you and Brian and Kyle. They're your family. We're just . . . friends." She laughed at his expression. "All right, we're exclusive friends, mutually exclusive."

"Countries use that term to mean they're at war," Evan said.

"I mean I have no intention of carrying on affairs with other men at the same time." She

turned serious, aware that he was not responding to her teasing. "I warned you I wasn't capable of a casual affair, Evan. If you weren't
special to me, I wouldn't be here."

"I just realized how little I know about you,
about your life. You've always come out here."

"You've met Georgia, my best friend and
bridge partner. You've met my mother. You've
been to my house. I've talked your ears off
about my father and my grandchildren. You're
not one of those people who can't graciously
accept a gift, are you?" she asked, taunting
him with his own words.

"What gift?"

"The present." She leaned toward him earnestly. "I'm not trying to make silly puns. I'm
trying to explain things."

Deanna took a deep breath, knowing what
she was about to tell him would risk everything
she had just found. "For twenty-nine years I
lived in a blissful world, raised my children,
took care of my husband, fulfilled my social
obligations through various charities and country club functions, played bridge with my
friends. I coordinated the household help, my
husband's office staff, the committees required
to bring together major benefits. I could hostess an intimate dinner party of four or an ex-

travagant bash for five hundred. That's what I did, and I thought I did it very well."

Evan listened, his eyes never leaving her face, his hand still caressing hers.

Deanna wet her lips. "Then, a year ago, Phil announced he wanted a divorce. Hindsight is great, as they say. The signs were there, but I never saw it coming. He wouldn't discuss it, wouldn't consider counseling, just told me I was boring, predictable, and . . ." she faltered, then forced the word out, "pathetic." She watched a muscle twitch in Evan's jaw and lowered her eyes to where their hands were joined on the table.

"I lost it," she continued. "I withdrew from society and went into mourning. I devoted myself totally to the women's auxiliary at the hospital and my bridge club, neither of which required my being married to a socially prominent physician. I guess I'd pretty much moved past grief and into anger when Billy showed me his motorcycle. I was tired of people telling me I couldn't do things. Daddy telling me I couldn't ride his motorcycle because I was a girl seemed to be where it all began."

She looked back at his face, hoping to soften his dark frown by offering him a rueful smile. "So that's where I am right now, living one day at a time, jumping one hurdle at a time.

I don't know where I'm going, so I can only live in the present. I'd very much like you to be in my present, Evan Maxwell."

Evan was silent a long moment, until Deanna was convinced she should never have said a word. "Is he good?" he finally asked in a flat voice.

Deanna blinked in surprise. "What?"

He met her gaze, the intensity in his hitting her like a physical blow. "Randolph. Is he a good surgeon?"

"One of the best."

"Then I'll wait until after Sara's surgery to beat him to a pulp. After that, I may thank him for letting you go."

Deanna realized her mouth was open. She closed it, not knowing what to say.

"He was a fool to treat you like that. Has he come to his senses? Is that why he's agreed to help Sara?"

Deanna could feel the tell-tale heat suffusing her face, pronouncing her guilty as charged. "We're trying to be friends, for the sake of the children and since we work together for the hospital."

Evan sighed. "I know, accept the gift of the present." His mouth twisted ironically. "You know, it's funny. I thought all I wanted was a mutually satisfying physical relationship, one we could both enjoy for as long as it remained mutually satisfying. Now, here we are. I'm asking for commitment and you're saying let's enjoy it while it lasts."

"I don't want to get hurt, Evan, but I don't want to hurt you, either. I guess I didn't think this through very well. I didn't exactly come out here today to . . . um . . ."

"Have sex?"

Deanna frowned at his bluntness, but at least he was smiling and teasing her again.

"I'm sure I thought about it enough for both of us," Evan said. "I accept your gift, Deanna. I'd like to be in your present. I like having you in mine."

His eyes were dark and hot, causing swirls of their earlier passion to tug at intimate places. She began to tingle and ache just thinking about it. He brought her fingers to his mouth and slowly nibbled her knuckles, then kissed the tip of each finger. She jumped at the surge of sensation when he pulled one into his mouth, sucking hard and stroking the side of it with his tongue.

"Evan!" It was a half-hearted protest.

"I distinctly remember promising to worship each and every inch of your delectable body," he said against her palm, still nibbling, tasting, making her crazy. "I also distinctly remember someone taking over before I had gotten very far." He was to her elbow, making her shiver with his slow, erotic kisses. The long sleeves of the robe blocked further access. Undeterred, he started over with her other hand. "I hope you washed your feet while you were in the bathroom earlier." He raised his eyes to meet hers. "Or I could wash them for you, and whatever else you'd like me to taste."

She silenced his teasing with a kiss full on his mouth. She held him there, splaying her fingers through the short hair at the back of his head, inviting his tongue to duel with hers. She felt him loosen the robe tie and delve inside, his hands roving over the smooth surface of her naked skin. He pulled her out of her chair and into his lap, spreading her thighs wantonly to wrap around his waist. He was already hard, pressing against her intimately through the fleece of his sweat pants.

"Dessert," he said, moving from her mouth to her breasts, suckling each one in turn until Deanna could hardly sit still. "Do you want to be eaten on the table, or would you prefer to be served in bed?"

Deanna could hardly think. While his tongue laved her nipples, his thumbs moved between her legs, parting her swollen flesh and stroking the aching nub of desire. She tried to reach him but had to be content with massaging the hard muscles of his thighs and buttocks through the fleece. There was no way they could finish the job in this position, but to move would be to interrupt the sweet torture.

"The bed . . . Evan . . . *please.*"

He ignored her, sending her over the edge with his hands and his mouth, splintering her into a thousand sparkling shards, her cry echoing through the empty house. Before she had a chance to recover she was on her back on the kitchen floor, the robe beneath her. Evan covered her, then entered her with a long, deep thrust that caused her to cry out again. She couldn't do it again. She would die if she came again.

He was merciless, stoking the fire with slow, languid strokes that went on and on, forcing her to join him, rebuilding the tension until she was clawing at him, demanding release. He complied, increasing the pace. She moved with him, forcing him higher, faster, deeper until he shouted her name and clutched her against him. She clung to him as well, seeking something solid while everything inside of her rocketed out of control.

Former Buckhead Society Woman Found Dead on Kitchen Floor in Home of Promi-

nent Buford Businessman, Overdose Suspected

Deanna envisioned the headlines tomorrow.
An overdose of sex. Her mother would die of
shame. Somehow Deanna didn't think a real
lady allowed herself to be taken on the kitchen
floor. It was a clean floor. One noticed things
like that when one was lying eye level with the
linoleum. It was also cold and hard, but dead
people couldn't do anything about such
things. They didn't have muscles to move them
to a softer surface.

Evan shifted beside her, trying to take some
of the pressure off her leg. "I have a soft,
warm bed just down the hall," he suggested,
his voice near her ear.

"Too late," Deanna said, her throat hoarse.
"I've changed my mind."

Evan sat up, pulling her up beside him. She
glared at him, pulling her robe back around
herself with as much dignity as she could manage under the circumstances.

"You mad?"

She shot him a drop dead look and tried to
get off the floor. She made it as far as the
chair before her legs gave way. Her knees felt
like rubber bands.

He grinned. "You are mad."

Deanna would have cheerfully bashed him over the head, except she didn't think she could lift anything heavier than a dishtowel. He tried hard to look contrite, but the gleam never quite left his eyes.

"What part made you mad, the kitchen floor or the fact that you lost control not once but *twice?*" He was grinning again.

She was going to kill him.

"Ah, Deanna," he stood up, unashamedly naked still, kicked his discarded sweat pants aside and scooped her up in his arms, hugging her against him. "You are a wild woman. I suspected it the day you walked into my dealership, dressed in that prim white suit." He ignored her squeak of protest and carried her down the hall. "You had posture so perfect I thought there was a rod up your . . . spine." He grinned wickedly. "You wouldn't sit in my chair, afraid you'd spoil your clothes, but then you started talking about that motorcycle, and I saw the fire."

He carried her into the bathroom, set her down on the closed lid of the toilet with all the ceremony of setting a queen on her throne. He turned on the taps, filling the tub with hot water. Deanna jerked the edges of her robe together, trying to stay vexed with him, being charmed in spite of herself. The final barrier came down when he opened a cabinet and poured a generous dollop of Mickey Mouse bubble bath into the water. The man had no class sometimes, but he made her laugh.

Sixteen

"Sit up straight, Deanna."

Deanna straightened her spine, then frowned at her mother. She wasn't sure when a person got too old to be told to sit up straight by her mother, but fifty-two was surely too old. She'd been daydreaming or dozing. Either way, she'd lost the thread of conversation.

"He wants each unit to have a balcony and a fireplace," Eric was telling Phil, drawing pictures on a notepad, "but he wants the balconies on the front and fireplaces off the back. I suggested he have the balcony come off the dining room, which is a little different, but it avoids a long, narrow living room."

Phil had joined the family for Sunday brunch at the country club. He really was trying, listening to Eric talk about architecture without one derogatory comment. Knowing Phil was planning to join them this morning was the only reason Deanna was there, tradition notwithstanding. To have not come would have subjected her to an intense interrogation from her mother. There was no way she could explain to Charlotte Edwards where her gently bred daughter had spent the night.

Deanna smiled to herself, drifting again. She had not wanted to leave Evan's warm embrace this morning. He hadn't made it easy for her to leave, either, reminding her that he hadn't worshipped *every* inch of her body yet. It had still been dark when he'd driven her to the dealership, where she'd left her car the day before. It had been covered in frost. Evan had teased her about living such a pampered life that she didn't even own an ice scraper. Then the teasing had stopped when she'd declined his offer to come with her this morning.

She couldn't tell him Phil would be there. It wouldn't have mattered. Her children, her mother would never accept Evan. It was going to make their relationship difficult, she could tell. Evan was a proud man and much too intuitive. Yet she could no more let him come between her and her family than she would ask to come between him and his.

"Deanna!"

Deanna focused on her mother, Charlotte's sharp reprimand telling her she'd missed something again.

"Phil was talking to you. Don't you feel well?

You keep drifting off and you've barely touched your food."

"I'm fine," Deanna said, smiling around the table. They were all watching her curiously. "I just didn't sleep well last night."

"I think you're coming down with something," Charlotte insisted. "Your face is flushed."

Deanna took a sip of water, trying to cool off. Her face seemed to stay flushed lately. "I'll lie down when I get home."

"Let me take you home, Deanna," Phil offered, "make sure nothing's serious."

Deanna was grateful for thirty-five years of practicing composure under duress. "That's sweet, Phil, thank you, but I'm fine. Just tired. Since you're all so concerned though, I'll go straight home now and rest."

There were protests around the table, more expressions of concern, but Deanna kept her resolute smile in place as she kissed her mother and the grandbabies, then took her leave. Sherylyn caught up with her at the door.

"Mom, is something wrong?"

"Sherylyn, really, can't a person be tired? I'm sure as a surgical resident you understand being tired."

Sherylyn walked with her out to the parking lot. "Dad says you've been acting funny lately."

Deanna could understand that. She hadn't jumped this time when he snapped his fingers. To Phil, that was definitely acting funny.

"He's really trying, Mother. Can't you at least talk to him?"

"I do talk to him, Sherylyn. We've been out to dinner several times."

"You know what I mean, Mother. He says you won't even discuss getting back together."

Deanna unlocked her car door, then turned to face her daughter. "Sherylyn, I know you love your father and I trust you love me. I think you're old enough to understand that marriages don't always work out. It's not like you're a child anymore. You still have both parents."

"He made a mistake, Mother," Sherylyn persisted. "Doesn't twenty-nine years of marriage mean more than a mistake?"

"Twenty-nine years of marriage means a great deal," Deanna said, annoyed that Sherylyn was only seeing Phil's side. "If it didn't, I wouldn't even be speaking to him right now. What he did was unspeakably cruel. I'm beginning to realize he did me a favor by insisting on a divorce."

Sherylyn was aghast. "You don't believe that."

"I have agreed to be friends with your father. Considering his behavior last year, I think that's a pretty major concession on my part." Deanna opened her car door and slid inside, exasperated with the entire conversation. "I don't think I'm doing either one of us any favors by encouraging your father into thinking we'll get back together." She shut the door before Sherylyn could offer further arguments on Phil's behalf, turning the ignition with an impatient twist.

She drove home fuming with anger. She resented Phil dragging Sherylyn into their situation. He hadn't worried about the children when he'd cruelly denounced their mother as a failure and divorced her out of hand. He hadn't even worried too much about the children when they'd been small. That had been Deanna's job. She wondered if he would return to his old relationship— which was no relationship— with them when he realized she was serious about not taking him back.

She thought of how Eric looked, practically glowing as his father actually listened to his ideas on apartment design. Would Phil see how important he still was to them, even though they were all now grown? Sherylyn had always worshipped her father. Now she was acting like his campaign manager. Even Jeff, their oldest and most serious child, seemed glad to have Phil back at their family gatherings. She had to make Phil understand that his position as their father was still important, even if he wasn't married to their mother.

And where did Evan fit into all this? At least for the moment, nowhere. It was obvious the children didn't accept the divorce yet. Until they did that, they would never accept a new man in her life. And when they were ready to accept her with another man, would they accept a man like Evan?

One hurdle at a time, she reminded herself, pulling into her driveway. The HOGs' benefit for Sara was a month away, and there was still much to be done. The hospital auction was a month after that. She had a party to organize to thank her workers.

Gloria still wore the arm brace, although there wasn't much of Sara's care she didn't do. All Deanna did was give Sara her bath, usually in the morning. Deanna had offered Gloria the position of housekeeper, but so far Gloria had not made a decision. Deanna knew pride had a lot to do with it, in addition to the lack of independence. She wondered if Hank figured in there somewhere as well. He was becoming a frequent caller.

Gloria had not said a word about Deanna being out all night with Evan. Deanna had called her the night before, so she wouldn't worry, knowing a woman who understood the purpose of red heels would more than understand the significance of Deanna's going out for a motorcycle lesson and not coming home until six A.M. Deanna knew Gloria would never judge her, but Deanna judged herself. She didn't feel she was being a very good role model.

That was presumptive, too, she thought, entering the house and turning off the alarm. Gloria was in her late thirties and could probably teach Deanna a few things. She had already taught Deanna a great deal.

"You're back early," Gloria said, coming out of the housekeeper's suite at the sound of Deanna in the kitchen.

Deanna put water on to boil for tea. "I was tired. I think I'll make a cup of herbal tea and go to bed— unless you need me," Deanna hurried to add, looking at Gloria.

Gloria smiled. "We're fine. We're bored, actually. You're going to have to give me somethin' more to do to earn our keep."

"How's your handwriting? You can address the envelopes for my volunteer appreciation dinner."

"I'd be glad to."

Deanna poured boiling water into a teapot,

warmed it thoroughly, then poured that water out, added her tea leaves and poured fresh boiling water over them. She felt Gloria's eyes on her as she worked. "Is something wrong?" she asked, turning to face her.

Gloria chewed her lip, then spoke hesitantly. "You've been real good to us, Deanna, and I've tried real hard to mind my own business here."

Deanna deliberately got two china cups out of the cabinet. "Would you like some tea?"

Gloria moved closer to Deanna. "What I'm tryin' to say is, I like Evan Maxwell. I know I don't understand very many of the social graces, but I know men. He's a decent man, one a woman can be proud of."

Deanna frowned and stirred sugar into her tea. "I'm not following you. What are you trying to say?"

"You went out Friday night dressed to kill and came home alone and angry. You came in this morning lookin' like you'd ridden a rocket to the moon and back, and you were blushin', stammerin' around here like you had somethin' to be ashamed of. I just wanted to say I think you made the right choice."

Deanna sank down at the kitchen table with her tea, not sure whether to laugh or swear.

Gloria sat down in the chair opposite, ignor-

ing the tea. "I had a man once liked to buy
me fancy things, lived in a fancy house, but
he wasn't good to me. I stayed a long time
because I liked fancy things, but he was a cruel
man. I decided there were worse things than
being a waitress, so I took a job and I moved
out."

A cruel man. Did he beat her, or just belittle
her, as Phil had done?

"Now I got Hank. When I met Hank he
didn't have nothin' except a new truck drivin'
license and a dream, but he treated me like I
was somethin' special." Her face glowed when
she talked about him, Deanna noticed. "We
had an awful fight about the other men, but
he couldn't support us and I didn't think it
was right, anyway, seein' how Sara ain't his."

Deanna smiled. "But now?"

Gloria smiled back. "He's got some money
set by, got a good job. He'd be on the road a
lot, but me and Sara, we're used to bein' by
ourselves."

"So he wants to marry you."

Gloria looked down at the table. "He wants
to, but we can't. I don't like bein' on welfare,
but it's the only way I can stay home with Sara.
If I marry Hank, they'll stop my welfare and
take Sara off Medicaid. Hank's insurance
wouldn't cover her until nine months had

passed, on account of her heart bein' a preexisting condition. We could never afford the doctors for that long. We couldn't even afford her medication. Medicaid pays for her monitors and oxygen equipment, too. You just have no idea."

No, Deanna thought, I have no idea. She'd known there were people who didn't have medical insurance. She'd been on the auction committee that raised money for the indigent fund for most of her adult life. But she'd never understood, not until Gloria, how complicated life could be for these people. It could affect whether they got married or not. Love, even employment, had nothing to do with it, although she was sure it helped.

"We'll have what's important," Gloria said. "If I can convince my landlady that I'm not a threat to the moral fiber of her mobile home park, we'll live there."

"Is that safe?"

Gloria smiled. "That guy has met up with two friends of mine who convinced him of the error of his ways. I understand he's keepin' a low profile. Hank's still lookin' for him."

It wasn't the type of justice Deanna was used to, but Gloria seemed satisfied. "What about the others, Gloria? Will they accept that . . . things have changed?"

"There weren't that many, Deanna. They all know, and they're all helpin' to raise money for Sara. You make it sound like I had some street corner business or somethin'."

Deanna felt the heat in her face. "Sorry. That's not a business I know much about."

Gloria seemed amused by her discomfort. "If it makes you feel any better, neither do I. I'm glad you made me wake up. Maybe gettin' beat up was a blessin' in disguise."

Like my divorce, Deanna thought. "I wouldn't go that far, but I'm glad it's worked out for the good. I wish you'd stay here until your arm is healed though. I'm going to miss you."

"We'll keep in touch," Gloria promised.

"Since you don't have family, maybe you'd let me be Sara's grandma. Children should have at least one grandma."

To Deanna's surprise, Gloria's eyes filled with tears. She grabbed Deanna's hand and squeezed it. "That would be really special. You don't know what it's meant to me, knowin' someone else believes she'll live and have a chance at a normal life."

Deanna knew that even with a heart transplant Sara would never have a normal life, but she could have a productive one. She squeezed Gloria's hand back. "It means a lot to me to have someone else believe being with Evan is the right thing to do. I was having grave misgivings myself."

"So does he want to marry you?" Gloria asked, her brown eyes sparkling with mischief.

Deanna found she could laugh. "It's more complicated than with you and Hank. We can't even live in sin." She was horrified at what she'd just implied. "Oh, Gloria, I didn't mean that like it sounded."

"I knew what you meant. You know, Deanna, you worry too much about bein' proper. You told me you hated that fur coat Dr. Randolph gave you, but you wore it out with him because that was the proper thing to wear."

"That was a diplomatic move to win his favor," Deanna argued. "I wanted him to help us."

"A diplomatic move to win his favor." Gloria said it slowly, trying out each word. "You see what I mean? That's just a fancy way of sayin' you was suckin' up to the man."

Deanna choked on her tea. "It is not."

"Hey, it's okay. It's necessary sometimes. You got the job done and you didn't even resort to sex."

"I told him you wouldn't approve."

Gloria studied her thoughtfully. "You're

right. I would have been disappointed in you. Isn't that a kick in the pants?"

"Especially since you seem to approve of Evan."

"Evan's okay. He knows how to treat a lady."

"And Dr. Randolph doesn't?"

Gloria chewed on her lip again, choosing her words carefully. "Dr. Randolph is real proper, like you, but he's always impatient. When we go see him, I always feel like I'm taking up his valuable time. He's real good lookin' and all, but give me a man who wants to take his time." She shrugged her shoulders suggestively.

Deanna gave the expected laugh, but Gloria's comment was too true to be funny. Phil had been impatient in bed, unwilling to waste time even then. Like being serviced at Jiffy Lube, she thought, then shoved the tacky memory aside. It hadn't always been like that, but they had never engaged in foreplay so hot they'd ended up on the kitchen floor. If gossip could be believed, newer, younger partners hadn't improved his style.

But there was more to a good relationship than good sex. There was mutual respect, caring, common ideals. She was still describing Evan, not Phil. She gave a deep sigh. Why was something that seemed so simple so complicated? Because she wasn't the only one involved. Unlike Gloria, she had family, children, a public image passed down through generations. She wasn't ready to risk losing all that for personal happiness.

This was it, the moment she'd anticipated since she was fourteen years old. She was going to drive the Indian. She just had to concentrate on what Evan was saying and showing her instead of remembering what other things he could do with his mouth and his hands.

"You're going to have to rethink almost everything you've learned in order to drive this," Evan said, standing in his garage with Deanna and the 1953 Indian Chief. "The throttle is in the same place, and the rear brake, but be careful. New motorcycles have seventy-five percent of their braking power on the front brake, the old ones had the majority on the rear, so press gently. It's hand-shifted with a foot clutch, and your front brake is on the left, where you're used to the clutch being."

If Deanna didn't pay attention to the motorcycle instead of to Evan, she was going to do a handstand over the handlebars and wreck a $30,000 collector's item. She closed her eyes, trying to block out the vision.

"What are you doing?" Evan yelled. "I thought you wanted to learn to ride this. Pay attention. I want you to run through the dead engine braking drills before I show you how to shift it and use the spark advance."

More braking drills. That took care of her sensuous thoughts. "What were you in the Air Force, a drill sergeant?"

He seemed surprised at her accusation. "The Air Force doesn't have drill sergeants. I was a squadron leader."

"Well, you're good at giving orders."

Evan's eyes narrowed. "It was my job to keep gung-ho young hot shots from killing themselves with equipment they didn't know how to handle. You hired me to teach you to ride this motorcycle. I'm trying to do that without risking your life."

"I'm just tired of drills," Deanna said, though she wasn't as adamant as she'd been earlier.

"Fine." Evan shrugged. "Let's fire it up and you can figure out how to stop it when the time comes."

"I didn't say I wouldn't do them, just that I was tired of them." She took the bike off its kickstand and rolled it out onto the driveway. Brake on the left, brake on the left, she said to herself over and over. The Indian had foot boards to rest her feet on instead of pegs, which made it awkward to push when sitting astride it. She was ready to quit after three drills.

"I'll go slow," she promised, "but I'm not pushing this beast around anymore."

Evan smiled. "It's your bike and your hide. Okay, let's go over how to use the spark advance."

He showed her how to adjust it, twisting the left handlebar similar to the way the throttle operated. He went into a lengthy discourse on how it worked, when to advance it, when to retard it. By the time he finished, Deanna was having grave misgivings.

"Look down here at your distributor cap," Evan instructed. "This is advanced." He twisted the handlebar. "This is retarded. You want it halfway to start it. Don't ever try to start it fully advanced. It'll kick back like a mule, throw you right over the bike."

Wonderful, Deanna thought.

"Okay, the moment you've been waiting thirty-five years for. Start her up."

Deanna sat astride the bike looking down at the controls. She turned on the key, put the choke on full, set the spark advance halfway, then took several deep breaths. She nudged the kick starter pedal out with her toe, then looked up at Evan. He was smiling down at her. She smiled back, glad Evan was the one sharing this with her, glad they were more than friends as they shared this moment.

She stomped down on the kick starter. The resistance was incredible. The bike didn't even cough.

"She's a bit hard to start," Evan said. "Kick her like you mean business. Show her who's boss."

"It's a he," Deanna corrected him. She kicked it again. It gave a half-hearted rumble. She felt the sweat starting to trickle down inside all her layers of clothing. This was not a lady-like activity.

"If Jane Russell can do it, you can," Evan encouraged.

Deanna paused to look at him. "Jane Russell rode Indians?"

"She sure did. She was one of their spokespeople."

Deanna threw all her weight into the next kick. The engine fired to life with a deafening roar.

"Give it some gas!" Evan yelled over the din.

Deanna twisted the throttle, exhilarated and awed simultaneously. The engine had a rough, raw sound, far less civilized than even Evan's Harley. It was the sound that had sent her run-

ning in her youth, the call to join her father
and go soul flying. It was almost enough just
to hear it run again. Almost, but not quite.

"Always check your oil flow," Evan shouted
over the engine. He opened the cap to the oil
tank, then had her look in while he revved
the engine. Sure enough, oil arced from a
valve back into the tank with every rev. "Now,"
he continued when it began to idle without
the choke on. "There's your clutch. Push forward to disengage, back to engage. You have
three gears, and they're not synchronized, so
they grind like you're tearing the guts out of
it. Ready?"

She doubted it, but she pushed forward on
the clutch and moved the gear shift lever back
toward her into first. She was glad Evan had
warned her. Gears ground and the bike gave
a slight lurch forward.

"You want to roll again, too, don't you,
boy?" Deanna said to the bike. She stepped
back on the clutch gingerly. The bike moved,
taking her out of Evan's driveway and down
the residential street. Deanna ground it into
second and picked up speed. She advanced the
spark slightly as she opened the throttle. At
the end of the street, she slowed, downshifted,
eased it through the tight turn and came back

to Evan's. She felt like her soul had taken wings and soared beside her.

"It's fantastic! Isn't it an incredible machine? It wants to run! Evan, let's take the bikes somewhere. I want to take it out and let it run."

"You'd risk a $30,000 machine out on the road?" Evan asked, but he was smiling at her enthusiasm.

"Not in traffic or anything. I have to do this, Evan. I'll never ride it again."

Evan shook his head, but he was still smiling as he pulled out the key to the Harley. Deanna made several more runs through the neighborhood while he warmed it up. Evan waited until she was coming back toward his house, then pulled out in front of her to lead the way.

He drove toward Friendship Road, past the dealership and on east where the road was good and traffic was light. Evan gave her the lead, and Deanna opened up the throttle and let the old Indian run. The sun was bright, the wind cold, and for the space of an hour, all was right with her world. Where the road was open, they rode side by side. Deanna felt like she would burst from the exhilaration. She looked at Evan riding beside her and felt like her heart, as well as her soul, had taken wing.

Deanna was nearly numb with cold by the

time they returned to Evan's house, but she was still reluctant to park the Indian. Her time with it was so limited.

"I felt like Dad was with me," she told Evan much later, when they were both thoroughly warmed and snuggled together in the aftermath of making love. Brian was working and Kyle was at his day-care, so they had the house to themselves on this bright Friday afternoon. "It was the most incredible experience." She raised up to kiss his mouth. "Thank you."

Evan took his time returning the kiss. "More incredible than making love? I need to work on my technique."

Deanna laid her head back on his shoulder. "Not more incredible, just . . . incredible in its own right. You're pretty incredible, too." She gave him a tight hug for emphasis.

"Is once enough?" He stroked her suggestively.

Deanna turned her head so she could see his face. "Are we discussing the Indian or the Maxwell?"

"Either one. I'm willing."

She gave him a poignant smile. "Once is enough . . . for the Indian, at least. As incredible as it was to ride, I was a nervous wreck, worrying something would go wrong. It's awful to shift, cumbersome to handle compared to your bike, takes bumps worse than the Honda."

"That year had front shocks. You should ride some of the older ones."

"My point is, I've proved my point. I rode Dad's bike and I loved it, but I'm ready for my own."

Evan gave her a slow smile. "Is that right?"

"Yeah, that's right. I want my own Harley so I can take the road test and get my motorcycle license and ride whenever I want to."

"Then we'd better start looking. There aren't too many in the paper right now, since it's January. Most people try to sell in early spring, when cycle fever is highest."

Deanna frowned. "I can't buy one from you? I thought you were a dealer."

"I am a dealer. I have deposits on every new bike I'll receive for the next three years. I'll be glad to add your name to the list, but I thought you wanted one sooner than that."

Deanna was incredulous. "Three years? What about other dealers?"

"Same story. The company is trying to increase production, but they don't want to compromise the quality of the product. With the recent surge in popularity, demand far outstrips supply."

Deanna hadn't even considered she

wouldn't be able to buy one. The news upset her. "I've never bought anything used. I don't want a used bike."

Evan's mouth flattened with reproach. "Haven't you ever bought an antique? They're used." He slid out of the bed, reaching for his jeans. "Sometimes, Deanna, you amaze me. You defy social mores and take a prostitute into your home, but you can't handle the idea of a used motorcycle. I'm okay to sleep with, but I'm not good enough to introduce to your family."

Deanna narrowed her eyes at him in warning. "You can get down off of your sanctimonious high horse, Evan Maxwell. None of those issues have anything to do with each other."

"The hell they don't. You do good things, Deanna, but at heart you're a snob."

Deanna refused to enter a shouting match. She kept her tone deliberate and cold. "You have a very narrow mind sometimes, Evan Maxwell, and apparently a deep-seated prejudice toward . . . society. You make fun of my pampered life-style and criticize my lack of experience. Well that's how I was raised and who I am. Since you have such a problem with that, I suggest we break off this association, then there won't be a need for you to meet my family. I doubt you'd like them anyway. They're even more pampered than I am."

She got out of bed, scooped her clothes off the chair and went into the bathroom, shutting the door with restrained fury. She jerked her clothes on, raked her fingers through her disheveled hair and threw open the door. She would go home and she would never do something this stupid again. She'd learned her lesson. This seemed to be a year of learning lessons, all of them the hard way.

Evan sat at the kitchen table, her jacket and purse on the table in front of him. She intended to grab them up on her way past and leave without speaking to him again. His words stopped her cold.

"My ex-wife is society."

Deanna stood, jacket and purse in hand, listening.

"You're right, I am prejudiced against society people. Pauline is the epitome of a social snob and proud of it. Every time you do anything that even remotely smacks of snobbery, I assume the worst." He looked up at her, his mouth a grim line, his eyes filled with compunction. "I was out of line. I'm sorry."

"Where is she now?"

"Still back in Connecticut with her socially

correct family and her socially correct second husband."

Deanna sank into a chair across the table from him. "I don't understand."

"She didn't like moving every four to five years to wherever I got transferred. She didn't like being home alone and unescorted when I was overseas. To give her credit, she put up with it for twelve years, then I came home on leave to find I'd been displaced. She wanted a divorce so she could marry the man that more closely met her needs."

"I don't mean I don't understand the divorce. I don't understand why you wanted to get involved with me. It's obvious you're still bitter. The first day I walked into your dealership, you should have refused to help me." A sick feeling crawled through Deanna's stomach. "Or is all this some form of retribution, a way to get back for some humiliation Pauline put you through?" She rose slowly, heartsick, on the verge of tears. "I would never have suspected that kind of meanness from you."

She had known getting hurt again was a possibility, but the reality of the pain was overwhelming. She had known having her heart broken by Evan would be worse than having it broken by Phil. She'd been right.

Evan caught her before she had opened the

door, hugging her to him in a fierce embrace. She let her purse and jacket drop to the floor, clinging to him as the tears overflowed. He buried his fingers in her hair and rained kisses over her temple, her eyelids, finally reaching her mouth.

"I never meant to hurt you, Deanna," he said between kisses, his voice anguished. "You're nothing like Pauline. My attraction to you was to you alone. You're a very special lady, and I'm a consummate jerk."

"I seem to have an affinity for jerks," Deanna taunted him, returning his kisses with increasing passion. "Maybe I've developed some sort of masochistic addiction to pain."

"You just show me where it hurts," Evan beguiled her, gently urging her back toward the bedroom. "I'll kiss every little place and make you feel better."

Seventeen

"Your mother called," Gloria told Deanna, reading from a list in her hand. "She ordered the flowers for the appreciation dinner and has the caterer lined up. She said to ask you if crab-stuffed mushroom caps was okay instead of crab-stuffed pastry shells. I told her the invitations went out yesterday."

Deanna hung her coat in the closet, pleasantly tired after her day with the children at the hospital. "You're getting very efficient. Sure you don't want to keep the job? I could keep Sara on the nights Hank is in town."

Gloria just smiled and continued down her list. "Becky called from Buford. She has food donations from a chicken franchise, a pizza franchise, the Chinese restaurant, two hamburger franchises, and three grocery chains. The Ladies of Harley are organizin' a bake sale. You should have tons of food."

Deanna made an appreciative sound. "Evan said they have a bluegrass band lined up, a

Mighty Morphin Power Ranger, and a clown who does balloon animals. It's beginning to sound like a carnival. He got a tent to put over the track."

"Sounds like more fun than the dinner party at your mother's. I don't know how you keep it all straight. I'd end up serving fried chicken to the highfalutin society folks and crab-stuffed mushroom caps to the carnival folks."

"You never know, it might work out better that way."

"Evan called. He's running a little late. I made a meatloaf and put some baked potatoes in with it."

"You're doing too much, Gloria. The doctor said immobile for four to six weeks."

"I keep the shoulder immobile. I just use my hand."

"Which means moving your elbow, which moves the shoulder. It's only been three weeks, Gloria."

"But it doesn't hurt," Gloria said defiantly. "I'm tired of not pullin' my weight around here."

Deanna pointed to the list of phone calls in her hand. "You call that not pulling your weight? Plus you've been here to deal with the cleaning service, the exterminator, and Foster when he comes to work in the yard."

"Those people have been coming here for a year without a housekeeper being here, you said so yourself."

"Which means I've had to deal with them," Deanna rejoined. "I also told you I had decided to hire a new housekeeper."

Gloria grinned. "No, you didn't. You said you wanted a butler, a man to wait on you for a change."

"It's very rude to throw people's words back in their face," Deanna scolded, feigning insult. "I'm going to go take a bath before Evan gets here."

They had so little time together, she mused, sinking up to her neck in soft, scented bubbles. The dealership was open six days a week, Saturday being their busiest day. It wasn't fair to Brian to ask him to work every Saturday so Evan could be off with Deanna. Sundays Deanna was committed to church and brunch with the family until late afternoon. So they stole an occasional afternoon at his house, an occasional evening at hers. Instead of strengthening their relationship, it made it seem more illicit, which she supposed it was. Phil was still coming with the family on Sundays, but he hadn't invited her out since she'd declined his last invitation two weeks ago. He had never handled rejection well.

After her bath, Deanna dressed carefully, having gone shopping for intimate apparel after Evan had shared a fantasy. Gloria frowned in confusion when she came back into the kitchen.

"Are y'all goin' out?"

"No." Deanna smiled to herself as she opened a bottle of red wine and set it aside to breathe. The doorbell rang.

"See you in the mornin'," Gloria said, picking up her plate and heading toward her suite. "I don't plan to leave this room tonight unless there's a fire."

Deanna smiled again. There would be a fire, but it should stay contained in her bedroom.

Evan stepped back in confusion when Deanna opened the door. He'd taken a quick shower and put on clean blue jeans. Deanna was dressed in her fancy white suit, complete with pearls and white stockings, the same outfit she'd worn into his dealership that first day.

"Were we going out?" he asked, knowing he was in trouble if she'd told him and he'd forgotten.

Her smile was mysterious. "No, dinner's in the oven and I opened a bottle of wine." She stepped back to let him in.

He entered, looking around warily. She was up to something. She led the way toward the kitchen, her posture as erect as ever, but with a subtle difference in her walk. He watched her backside, enjoying the way her skirt skimmed over her hips and ended just above the knee. Deanna had great legs, great hips, she looked fantastic in her prim heels. When she stopped in the kitchen he couldn't resist running his hand over the fullness of her bottom.

"I love you in that outfit," he crooned in her ear. Her bottom was incredibly soft and yielding, as if the only thing between his hand and her flesh was the thin material of the skirt. He stroked it again.

"We could have our wine in the den first, unless you're hungry." She turned in his arms, holding the two glasses, then faltered as she met his gaze. He supposed his desire for her was already evident.

"I'm very hungry," he said, taking both of the glasses from her without breaking eye contact. He watched her dark eyes darken even more as she understood his meaning. He set the wine down behind her, then hoisted her up to sit on the countertop, putting her legs within easy reach of his hands.

"I've had fantasies about this skirt." He ran his hands up her thighs, staying outside at first, just skimming, teasing, warming her up. "I saw you wearing it sitting across the motorcycle, the hem hiked up to your hips." He moved the hem upward, feeling her thighs through the silky hose. "I saw you sitting on the edge of my desk." He moved the hem higher, watching her eyes. "Then I would stand here and part your legs, so pure in their white hose." His hand met bare skin, and he stopped, surprised. Deanna was smiling that mysterious, bewitching smile again.

She had on stockings, not panty hose, with white lacy garters. Evan ran his fingers along the soft flesh on the inside of her bare upper thigh and felt a surge of white hot need slam through him. He forgot the rest of the fantasy. His heart was pounding madly as he searched even higher, seeking the treasure that surely lay just ahead. He found it— hot, slick feminine desire without any barriers. No fantasy could match this.

She was sitting too high for him to take her right there, although that's what every male cell in his body was screaming for. Instead he pushed the skirt out of his way and lowered his mouth to taste the tender flesh exposed above the white stockings. He felt her hands move through his hair, urging him closer. Her legs parted even more, inviting him deeper.

He used his hands to lift her off the counter-top, wrapping her legs around his torso as he headed for the floor.

"No, Evan, not the floor," Deanna objected breathlessly.

He ignored her, as he had before, too impatient to reach the bare summit under her skirt. He had a clear approach with her on her back. He pushed the skirt out of his way, used his thumbs to part her folds, then dipped his tongue inside, flicking it over her most sensitive flesh until she moaned and writhed beneath him.

He shoved the skirt up to her waist, then pulled her blouse out of the waistband to give his hands access to her full, soft breasts. She unhooked her bra, arching up, begging him for more. He gave it, rolling her nipples between his finger and thumb as he continued to bring her closer and closer to climax with his tongue. She moved frantically against him, her hands moving restlessly through his hair, over his shoulders, up the length of his arms. He listened to her cries, could feel the spiral of desire winding ever tighter until she came apart, screaming his name. He lifted her buttocks, pulling her even harder into his questing mouth, delving into her essence, prolonging her pleasure until she begged him to stop.

Only then did he give in to his own raging need, raising up on his knees to tear open his jeans, shoving them down only as far as he could reach. He was hard, painfully so, and his penetration wasn't gentle. Deanna didn't seem to mind, moving with him, wrapping her legs around him to urge him deeper, faster, harder. His panting cries mingled with hers. She tightened around him in hot, slick, incredible waves of sensation. He wanted to do this forever. His body demanded release. When it came, he felt like something had been torn from deep inside him, from his belly to his knees. He gave a hoarse cry, momentum carrying him on for several more strokes, then he collapsed on top of her, completely spent.

Reality came back slowly, the soft stroking of her hands along his back, the musky taste in his mouth, the weight of his body crushing hers into the floor. The floor. He vaguely remembered something about her objecting to the floor— again. She was going to kill him.

He rolled to his side, taking her with him so he could linger inside her just a few minutes more. Instead of lambasting him, she used her mouth to place nibbling kisses along his jaw, his neck, his earlobe, making him shiver. He pulled back to look into her eyes. They were soft with adoration, looking back into his.

"I'm sorry about the floor," he said, "but you have to take some of the blame. If you ever wear this suit into my dealership again, I will not be responsible for my actions." He dropped a kiss on the end of her nose, then sat up, pulling her up with him.

She smiled, a totally female smile of satisfaction. "I may never wear this suit again, which would be a shame, considering it's only three months old. I wouldn't be able to wear it without blushing constantly."

"And you blush so becomingly."

She tried to straighten out her skirt. "When I put on a three thousand dollar suit, I expected you to at least wait until I had you on the couch. Really, Evan, this kitchen floor thing has got to stop."

She didn't look too upset. Evan didn't think he'd heard correctly. "What did you say you paid for it?"

"Three thousand dollars."

She said it like that was what everyone paid for a suit. Evan was stunned. "You paid three thousand dollars for one suit?"

"It's Chanel."

Like that explained it. Evan stood up and helped her to her feet, then joined her efforts to smooth her clothing back into place. "I'm glad you didn't tell me that at the door. I would never have touched you."

She smiled that satisfied female smile again, then kissed him lightly on the mouth. "I'm glad I didn't, too. Shall we get cleaned up and see if our dinner is burnt?"

The meatloaf was a little crunchy around the edges, the potatoes a little overdone, but Evan would have been content with cold mush. This woman was having an incredible effect on his mind, on his heart, on his priorities. It almost frightened him, the intensity of his feelings, especially when she didn't seem to reciprocate them to the same degree. He felt like he was on a runaway train, moving faster and faster toward disaster, and there was no way off.

"The HOGs are going on a ride Sunday through Buford to pass out flyers and generate enthusiasm for the benefit. We're going to meet at the dealership at one. Wanna come?" he asked lightly. That way, when she refused, he could act like it was no big deal.

She toyed with her pearls with one hand, her meatloaf with the fork in the other. He could almost hear her internal debate— Evan or family? Who to put first?

"Who gave you those pearls?" he asked, hearing the irritation in his voice, feeling it growing inside himself. He wasn't frustrated with the pearls but with her constantly putting her family before him. Asking about the pearls postponed her answer, telling him once again family had to come first. To be fair, she'd warned him that that was how it had to be, reminding him that his own family also came first with him, but it wasn't the same. He included her in his family, or would if she'd let him.

"They were a gift from my parents on my eighteenth birthday," she answered. "Georgia calls them my worry beads. I seem to have a bad habit of stroking them when I feel . . . I don't know . . . insecure, maybe, worried, too."

She'd taken off the Chanel suit and was wearing the pearls with her robe, a floaty mass of silky pink stuff that swirled around her when she moved. "So what are you insecure about tonight, or is it worry?"

There was a sadness in her liquid brown eyes as she met his gaze. "Both, I guess. I'd like to come with you Sunday, but it means making excuses to my family. I don't want to lie, but I'm not ready to tell them the truth, either. They wouldn't understand."

Evan had to tamp down his irritation, fighting to keep his tone level. "What's not to understand? You've been divorced a year. You're still young. Why can't you have another man in your life?"

"It's more complicated than that."

He waited, but apparently she wasn't going to explain further. Fine, she wanted to be secretive, that was her prerogative. He didn't have to put up with it though.

"Thanks for dinner, and . . ." damn her, she looked at him with those big, dark, vulnerable eyes and he felt like a bully kicking a defenseless dog, "the fantasy." He sat back down and took her hand in his, rubbing his thumb over the back of it. "You make me crazy, do you know that? I have a right to be angry."

"I warned you it would be like this."

"I know. I keep trying to remember I agreed to it, too, but things have changed."

She smiled, a sweet, sad smile. "The only thing that's changed is we're sleeping together. I thought men valued their freedom, resented women who wanted commitment just because sex was involved."

He had been just such a man, avoiding relationships with women who didn't share his desire to keep things light. It was ironic that his main concern about getting involved with Deanna had been his opinion that she was the type of woman who would demand marriage. Instead, he was the one on the verge of demanding marriage. Why? Why was this woman different? Because she brought out the most primitive instincts in him—the need to possess, dominate, protect. He wanted to stake his claim publicly, drag her off to his cave by her hair, kill any man who came sniffing around what was his.

He didn't think Deanna would be flattered by his feelings. She seemed to be doing her utmost to keep him ignorant of any competition he might have. She just kept referring to her family. She probably still considered Phil Randolph family, and not knowing the status of that situation was driving Evan crazy. He considered Randolph a threat, but it was hard to fight a suspicion.

"Do you still see Randolph?" He tried to make the question sound conversational, still rubbing her hand.

Deanna blushed, a bad sign. "I haven't gone out with Phil since we . . . um . . . you and I decided to be more than friends."

What the hell did that mean? That she didn't intend to? That she hadn't had an opportunity? Was she keeping him on a string, comparing notes?

"Is he the problem, Deanna?" It came out more accusatory than he'd intended, but he was beyond caring.

"No." She wouldn't look at him, another bad sign. "My children are. I never asked for the divorce, and now that Phil is apologizing and asking for a second chance, they don't understand why I don't forgive him and let him move back in."

She did look at him then, her eyes pleading for understanding. "They were very angry with their father, almost hated him for what he did. Now, he's trying very hard to convince all of us he's a changed man, he's learned his lesson, he's sorry. I watch my grown children glow in the attention their father has been directing toward them in his campaign, and I can't destroy that, not yet. Maybe it's dishonest, but I keep thinking he'll see for himself how much he means to his children and that they still need him, even if I don't."

She was the damnedest woman he'd ever met. Every time he thought he'd figured her out, she threw him another curve ball. He'd thought Gloria couldn't be topped. Now he wasn't so sure.

"You're playing a dangerous game, Deanna. If he thinks he has a chance, then finds out you've been sleeping with another man, he could destroy you."

"He's not a violent man," Deanna denounced his warning, "and I've told him countless times that I don't want more between us than friendship."

"I'm not talking about just physical violence, although I'm relieved to hear you say that. He can ruin your relationship with the children you're working so hard to protect. Fathers are forgiven for sins of the flesh. Mothers are Madonnas, forever virginal, regardless of how many children they've had. He can also ruin your reputation among your peers, smearing your name and making you forever the subject of tasteless gossip."

She studied him for a long moment, her brown eyes stricken at his words. "I hadn't thought of that. I should have. I knew this whole thing was going to blow up in my face, but I chose to do it anyway."

He waited, letting her think her way through her options. "I have to do this slowly," she finally said, playing with his fingers where their hands were still joined. "I'll come with you Sunday, let Phil do the family thing without me. I'll tell them it's for charity and hope they assume I mean for the hospital."

Evan narrowed his eyes, hoping what she'd said didn't mean what he thought it meant. "They don't know about the benefit for Sara?"

"They know I'm trying to raise money for Sara's surgery. They also know Gloria's hometown is working to raise money."

"But they don't know you're working with the HOGs."

She blushed again, guilty as charged. "They really wouldn't understand that. They don't even know I'm riding motorcycles. You're right about the Madonna image. Jane Russell notwithstanding, I don't think traditional Madonnas ride Harleys, or even antique Indians. I have a rather narrow-minded family."

"They're going to find out, Deanna."

"I know, but hopefully I'll have worked out an explanation by then that will win them over."

Evan lay awake a long time that night, holding Deanna and worrying. They were playing with fire too near the gasoline. Deanna was right. It was all going to blow up in their faces.

Sunday the wind was sharp, but the sun was shining. Thirty HOGs turned out for the publicity ride, most of them riding double so the passenger could hand flyers to anyone standing within reach. Deanna adjusted her helmet while Evan warmed up the Harley. "Halfway through, we switch places, right?" she asked, climbing on behind him and accepting the handful of flyers.

"Not today," Evan shouted back.

"Why not? I thought you were secure in your manhood."

"Not that secure." He pointed to the other bikers, lining up in formation. "Do you see any men riding behind their women? They would tear me apart, razzing me for the next twenty years. Besides, riding in pack formation is not for amateur riders."

As they roared out of the dealership, Deanna understood why. They rode two abreast, with the standard two-second distance between pairs. One mistake and the whole pack would go down.

Evan and Deanna rode near the back. Evan had explained that experienced riders were positioned at the front and rear, the newer riders in the middle, in descending order, the newest nearest the front. Since she wasn't driving, she had the luxury of watching the people's responses to the black leather-clad pack riding their powerful motorcycles in an impressive display of muscle that couldn't be ignored. Some smiled, some frowned, some just stood and watched in awe. Children either waved enthusiastically or clung to their mothers in fear. They rode through shopping center parking lots, handing out flyers and talking to the people. After two hours, thirty cold, tired, exuberant bikers roared north to one of their favorite hangouts, where they could eat barbecue and socialize.

"There's no way we can generate enough publicity by handing out flyers to people who happen to be standing outside when we drive by," Becky, the chapter's secretary/treasurer, told Deanna when they were all seated along the wooden benches. "We have posted the flyers in every business that would let us, plus the collection jars for donations. The week before the benefit, we have radio commercials and newspaper ads scheduled, plus one of the country radio stations has agreed to broadcast live from the dealership the day of the benefit. The TV station that interviewed Gloria is coming to film a spot for their local news, too. We're expecting great things with this."

"You've worked harder than any benefit committee I've ever worked with," Deanna praised them. "Gloria is so touched, she can hardly talk about it without tears in her eyes."

"I wish she could be there. I understand why she can't— Sara's health not safe around crowds and all— but it doesn't seem fair."

"I'm working on that. If we come out to her house or stay at Evan's, we can trade off. One of us can be at the benefit while the other sits with Sara. If we stay at Evan's, Kyle can come home when he gets too tired without Brian or Evan having to come with him."

Becky studied her a moment, then smiled. "You're really good for Evan. He's always seemed so focused on the dealership and Kyle. It's nice to see him enjoying himself with someone special."

Deanna felt uncomfortable, somehow unworthy of Becky's complimentary words. She thanked her and turned to see what the men were doing. They were gathered around a small television set, avidly following the action of a basketball game.

"Do you have children, Deanna?" one of the other ladies asked.

It was a typical gathering of friends, Deanna thought. The men talked of sporting events, hunting, fishing, upcoming rides, and memorable rides from the past. They insulted each other, punched each other playfully, and laughed together. The women joined in some of it, but for the most part they discussed children, careers, plans for the benefit, and shopping. Deanna felt accepted, but she didn't join in, content to watch and listen, and speak when spoken to.

"Always the lady," Evan teased her when they were eating. She had ordered sliced barbecue beef, something she could .eat with a knife and fork. Most of the group had ordered ribs or chicken, disdaining utensils for the primitive pleasure of eating with their fingers and licking the sticky, sweet sauce off afterward. "Here," Evan laid a meaty rib on her plate, dripping with sauce, "wrap your perfectly manicured little fingers around that. Get messy." He wagged his eyebrows suggestively. "I'll lick off any spots you miss."

The conversation around the table had gotten more boisterous as the meal progressed, taunts and insults flying freely, laughter creating a sense of goodwill within Deanna. She should take offense at his teasing, but instead she met the challenge in his eyes and in his wicked leer. She picked the rib up carefully, using only the tips of her fingers, then kept her eyes locked with his as she tore off the meat with her teeth. She watched his eyes darken as she sensuously ran her tongue over her greasy lips.

"Maybe I should let you drive home," he said, his voice low and husky. "It'll be dark, and no one will know where I have my hands."

Deanna felt the warm wetness gather between her legs, her breasts tingling in anticipation. She only hoped he was making himself as uncomfortable as he was making her. She held a sticky finger up to his mouth, inviting him to take it inside and lick it clean. He did, increasing the strain.

"Hey, Maxwell! You want us to leave so y'all can continue in private?"

Deanna felt the heat scalding her face as Evan grinned and released her hand. "You're just jealous, Conway. Go find your own woman."

The teasing continued, then moved on as the group found another subject to harass. It was a long time before Deanna felt like her face was cool again, and the tension of wanting Evan still throbbed within her. She hadn't been this hormone-driven as a teenager.

"Stay tonight," Evan urged her, when the group had disbanded and they stood in front of the silent dealership, the Harley-Davidson sign casting them in a fluorescent glow.

"Brian and Kyle are there," Deanna objected, the yearning inside her not caring.

"I think they know," Evan insisted. He rubbed his body against hers, his hands on her bottom, molding and kneading and increasing her desire.

"Kyle is only four. I wouldn't be comfortable." Her protests were losing strength as she melted against him, her hands seeking the strong contours of his muscles through his jacket. "Let's go to my place."

"That's an hour away," Evan objected.

Deanna stroked lower, running her hands over the backs of his thighs, dipping her fingers along his sensitive inner thighs. "I'll make it worth your while," she whispered, pulling his earlobe between her teeth.

Evan groaned. "Bike or car?"

"Bike," Deanna answered immediately. "I know it's cold, but I can't seem to get enough."

"Of the bike or the biker?"

His kiss was deep and wet, his hands seeking her aching nipples beneath her jacket, beneath her sweater, frustrated at the layers still protecting them. "Both," she gasped, straining toward him. "Evan, this is torture."

"Yeah. It'll help keep you warm for the ride into town."

"I'm plenty warm," she assured him. She was on fire, a fire he continued to fuel with long, deep kisses.

"We could use the back seat of your Buick."

"Never." Unless he continued to kiss her, stroke her, drive her beyond caring where they were.

"Then we'd better get going, or its going to be the asphalt."

She released him reluctantly, straddled his bike with shaky legs, then clung to him with hands that continued to caress, massage, and tantalize, promising incredible pleasure when

the ride was over. They sped through the cold
night air, the traffic light on a Sunday evening, Evan keeping the Harley at the upper
edge of legal. Deanna had visions of opening
the garage, parking the Harley inside, strad-
dling Evan's lap while he straddled the big
bike. Wanton thoughts, not at all the thoughts
of a gently reared lady, but then maybe they
were. Maybe such thoughts just weren't discussed in polite company.

Her hands tightened around Evan in anticipation as they turned down her street. Almost
there. She would tell him her fantasy. His eyes
would darken and he'd reach for her.

Evan turned into her driveway and hit the
brakes hard, throwing Deanna into him,
bumping their helmets together. She righted
herself then looked to see what they'd nearly
collided with. Her heart sank to her knees.
Phil's Jaguar.

Eighteen

Evan parked the Harley next to the garage, turned off the engine, and took off his helmet. Deanna got off slowly, dreading the questions to come. Evan studied the Jaguar, waiting for her to take her helmet off.

"Nice car."

"We could still leave, go back to your place," Deanna suggested, feeling her world crumbling beneath her feet.

Evan turned his attention from the car to her. "Randolph's?"

Deanna sighed, unable to hold his accusing gaze, then nodded.

"I'm not riding back to Buford. Not only am I too cold, but it's obvious your ex is suspicious or he wouldn't be here. It's time to face the music, Deanna. I sure hope you have that winning little explanation speech all rehearsed, because I have one of my own. Mine won't win you any friends, but it'll make the situation clear."

Neanderthals. She was dealing with a pair of Neanderthals, both of them beating their chests and defending their territory. She didn't appreciate it. She didn't belong to either one of them. She was a free agent. It was one of the few advantages to being divorced.

"You will stay out of this, Evan Maxwell. I do not belong to you and I do not belong to Phil. I will not be fought over like a bone between a pair of dogs, do you hear me? One macho, territorial comment and you will be riding back to Buford, no matter how late, no matter how cold."

He narrowed his eyes and glared at her, but she refused to be intimidated. She put her fists on her hips and waited for his acquiescence. It was time to put all that assertiveness training to use.

The muscle in his jaw tightened, but he didn't answer.

"Fine, be stubborn, but you've been warned." Deanna turned and marched toward the front door. She had to take off her gloves to get her keys out of her jacket.

Phil had apparently been waiting in the living room. He strode toward her, his face a thundercloud. He stopped when he saw Evan. Deanna folded her arms defiantly across her chest as he took in their costumes. She decided to take the offensive.

"You're trespassing, Phil. This is my house, free and clear. What did you do to Gloria?"

"Your . . . *housekeeper* . . . knew better than to challenge me. Is that what you wear to charity functions nowadays?"

"Yes, when the charity work is done from the back of a motorcycle, this is the accepted costume." Refusing to let him intimidate her, Deanna moved toward the kitchen. The passion had been hot on the ride in, and her temper was certainly hot now, but her body could feel the effects of an hour's ride in forty degree night air. She was sure Evan was even colder.

Evan followed her. When he came even with Phil he stuck out his hand, still gloved. "Evan Maxwell," he introduced himself. "Deanna seems to have forgotten her manners."

Deanna ignored them, moving toward the kitchen without waiting to see if Phil took Evan's hand or not. She took coffee out of the cupboard and measured it into a filter.

"Dr. Phillip Randolph," she heard Phil say, "Deanna's husband." He must have taken Evan's hand.

"Ex-husband," she reminded him. "Your choice, remember?"

"Deanna— "

She turned and held up her hand, stopping his argument. "Not tonight, Phil. Evan owns the Harley-Davidson dealership in Buford, where Gloria lives. He rebuilt Dad's Indian, that's how I met him. He's also a member of the North Georgia Harley Owner's Group. Their chapter has agreed to take on raising the money for Sara's surgery. The benefit is in two weeks. I went with them today to hand out publicity flyers."

She turned back to pour water into the coffeemaker. "It's been a long day and a cold ride. I promised Evan some coffee. What are you doing here?"

Maybe it was a good thing that she'd never been assertive with Phil. It was obvious he was still angry, but he also seemed a little confused, as if he didn't know how to handle her when she talked to him like that.

"I came to see you," Phil said. "All your little charity friends were at the country club having brunch with their families." *Where you should have been,* she picked up on his insinuation. "They had no idea why you couldn't be there today. I came here to see what was going on. I've wasted my whole afternoon sitting here waiting for you." It was an accusation. He gave Evan a pointed look. "I guess I should be grateful you brought him back here instead of staying in Buford. I could have waited all night."

"You sound like a jealous husband, Phil," Deanna said, refusing to let him bait her, keeping her tone soft. "It was your choice to waste your day here. You should be grateful Gloria didn't call the police and have you forcefully removed, or shoot you." She was about to burn up, between the stress of the situation and enough layers of clothing to withstand forty degree wind. She didn't trust them alone, but she was going to have to get out of some clothes or faint from heat.

"I'm going to go change while that drips through. Evan, you know where the guest bathroom is."

Evan didn't move. Deanna's leaving had presented an opportunity too good to pass up. She continued to amaze him. A born diplomat, he decided. She had Randolph on the defensive, yet she had been nothing but polite. Randolph, on the other hand, was spoiling for a fight, Evan could tell. He, too, was spoiling for a fight. The only thing that stopped him was Deanna's warning. In the mood she was in tonight, she would carry it out.

"That Indian was quite a find," Evan said conversationally, stripping off his gloves. He wasn't going to be accused of throwing the first punch. "I've located two collectors who are coming to the auction. Should bring a good price." He unwound the wool scarf from around his neck.

"Are you a mechanic?" Phil asked, his tone derisive.

Evan hung his jacket on the back of a chair, then unbuckled the leather chaps. "I own the dealership, so that makes me a businessman, but I've always tinkered with engines. Kind of a hobby. Do you mess with engines?"

"No, I'm a pediatric heart surgeon. I would never risk my hands in such a manner."

Evan didn't take offense. Instead, he felt a malicious satisfaction. This guy was going to dig his own grave with his arrogance. Deanna would never tolerate it. Evan continued to peel off layers of clothing, continued the conversational tone, knowing both would drive Randolph nuts. "It sure takes a lot of clothes to ride in January, and even with all that you get cold."

"Don't you own a car?"

"A new GMC pickup, actually, but Deanna prefers the bike." Let him chew on that. Evan was down to his jeans and a thermal undershirt. He folded the discarded clothes and laid them on one of the chairs.

He helped himself to the coffeepot, knowing Deanna was going to kill him for demonstrating his familiarity with her kitchen in front of her ex-husband. He couldn't help it. He wasn't allowed to fight the man, but he could irritate the hell out of him. "You want some of this?"

"I'll get my own."

And the score was tied. It irritated Evan to be reminded that the man had lived in this house as Deanna's husband. He didn't live here now though.

"I'll take Deanna hers," Evan said. She would throw it in his face if she knew the stupid game he and Phil were playing in her kitchen.

"No need," Deanna said, coming back into the kitchen. She'd changed into a soft pink, fuzzy sweat suit and matching socks. Her expression was not soft or fuzzy. She knew exactly what was going on. Evan felt childish. He handed her the coffee. Her look said clearly, "remember my warning." She turned toward Phil.

"So, Phil, did you wait here all afternoon for something specific or were you just spying on me?"

"I wanted to talk to you, Deanna, but apparently this isn't a good time."

"No, it isn't. It's late, and as you can see, I have a guest."

"Is he spending the night?"

Deanna blushed, but she lifted her chin in an affronted manner. "What a rude question,

Phil. It doesn't matter if he is or not, it's no business of yours."

"The hell it isn't. I have a right to know."

Phil stood toe to toe with Deanna, his entire manner threatening. Evan stood rigid. Warning or no warning, if the man laid a hand on her, he would be picking himself up off the floor. He wished he would— just a little push.

"You gave up that right a year ago." To Deanna's credit, she didn't raise her voice. She fought like a lady, her tone even and cold. "I don't remember even once questioning you about your female friends since that time. I would appreciate the same courtesy from you."

Phil glared at Evan, apparently not wanting to continue the argument with a witness. Evan returned the glare with a mocking smile. He wasn't budging.

"I'll call you tomorrow and we'll finish this discussion. I'm warning you, Deanna. He'd better not be spending the night."

"Don't you dare threaten me, Phillip Randolph. What are you going to do, waste some more of your precious time sitting in your car, watching my driveway? That alone would give me reason to let Evan stay. I have lots of guest rooms, but you'd never know, would you? Maybe he came to see Gloria," she taunted him, then lowered her voice suggestively.

"Maybe he has us both, at the same time, in what used to be your bed."

"You're sick, Deanna," Phil determined, backing away from her, pointing his finger at her. "Living with that hooker has warped your mind. I'll call you tomorrow. I trust you'll be more rational by then."

Evan watched as Deanna reset the door alarm after Phil's departure. When she turned back toward him, he could see the lines of fatigue in her expression, in her posture. She wasn't as tough as she liked people to believe. "I need to check on Gloria," she said, noticing him.

"I'll come with you."

But Gloria came into the kitchen just then. "Are you okay?" the women asked each other simultaneously.

"I'm so sorry, Deanna. I should never have opened the door. I didn't think he would barge in like that."

"It's not your fault, Gloria. Phil can be rude and arrogant when he wants to be."

"He made me mad, but I didn't think you'd appreciate me shootin' him or callin' the police. So I just left him to cool his heels in the livin' room."

"You did the right thing," Deanna assured her.

"How long has he been here?" Evan asked.

"Since about four o'clock. I told him Deanna was at a charity function, but he said, 'not likely'."

Deanna picked up coffee cups and rinsed them out in the sink. She started to pour the rest of the coffee out of the pot, then turned to Evan. "Do you want another cup before you head back?"

Anger slammed through Evan, threatening his control.

"I'll go back to my room," Gloria said, giving Evan a nervous glance. "See you in the morning."

"Goodnight, Gloria. We'll talk tomorrow," Deanna said, apparently oblivious to Evan's reaction. He would take care of that.

"What do you mean by, 'before I head back'?"

She seemed startled by the menace in his question. When she spoke her tone was cajoling. "I don't like Phil threatening me, but I don't think your staying tonight is such a good idea."

"The only reason I agreed to ride the bike in here was the promise of a warm bed and a warmer body to make it worth my while. I'm usually a fair-weather biker. I'm too old for riding in this cold, and I'm certainly too old to play stupid games."

She toyed with the neckband of her sweat suit, probably wishing she had her pearls on.

"Can't stand the heat, Deanna? You want out?"

She shook her head. "No." He could barely hear her. "I just resent the fact that everyone, including you," she glared at him, her voice gathering strength, "thinks they have a right to tell me how to live my life. I'm fifty-two years old and divorced. I have a right to choose my own friends, male or female. Phil has no right criticizing you or Gloria or anyone else I care to spend time with, and you," she jabbed a finger into his chest, nearly shouting now, something she hadn't done with Phil, "you have no business telling me how to handle my family. I'll introduce you to them when I'm ready to. I'll be friends with my ex-husband if I want to. I'm a free agent!"

Her shouted declaration echoed off the kitchen walls. He'd known she had a passion for freedom. He'd known, and he'd pushed it anyway, his own needs overriding good judgment. If he pushed it anymore, she was going to explode and he would lose her. A strategic retreat seemed in order, though it went against every masculine instinct he possessed. Retreat, to fight again another day.

"You're right."

That took most of the wind out of her sails. She stared at him in disbelief. "You're just saying that so you don't have to ride back home in the cold."

"I'm saying it because you're right. You're a free agent. I have no hold on you. I agreed to that in the beginning, as you so recently pointed out to me."

"But you don't believe it."

Maybe he was going about this the wrong way. If she thought there was a chance of losing him, would she fight so hard for her freedom? "I do believe it. I hate clinging women. I can't believe I'm trying to do the same. It's undignified, among less flattering adjectives. I won't do it again."

She didn't look convinced. "I'll make you up a bed in the guest room."

He smiled, determined to carry through what he'd started. "Whatever makes you happy." With any luck, she'd get lonely and join him.

Deanna lay awake for a long time, alone in her bed, acutely aware of Evan just down the hall. It would be so easy to go to him. She was certain he would make her glad she had, but morning always followed night and brought reality with it.

She didn't regret her affair with Evan, just the timing of it. She should have resolved things more clearly with Phil, with her children, before she'd allowed another man in her life. That was her first mistake. The second mistake had been getting involved with another possessive, domineering male.

Something had happened to her in the last year. She hadn't tried to change, hadn't deliberately set out to become independent. It had taken place gradually, somewhere between not having a husband and letting the housekeeper go. She hadn't chosen to be divorced, but since becoming so there had been no one to answer to, no one to check in with, no one to care if she played bridge until midnight and ate a bowl of cold cereal for dinner. Sometime during the past year, she had come to enjoy that independence.

Her first clue should have been the divorce settlement. She had accepted the house, her car, and half of their investments. She had some personal investments of her own, handed down through her family. She couldn't live extravagantly, but she could live quite comfortably without ever receiving another cent from Phillip Randolph. Her brother Pete, who handled her finances, had been appalled. After twenty-nine years of marriage and three children, and considering Phil's net worth, he thought she should have demanded a lot more. Call it severance pay and retirement, he'd begged her. She'd declined, not wanting to be beholden to Phil for anything. That had been six months ago. Even then, she'd understood the advantages of independence.

So what to do about Evan? In spite of his noble words tonight, she knew he wouldn't change. He wasn't going to be content to stay in the background and let her keep the two sides of her life separate. Tonight was proof positive. He'd wanted Phil to know they were lovers. That was just his nature. He could no more be subtle when he perceived a threat to his territory than a wild wolf. That raw masculinity was part of his appeal. She wouldn't change him, but she wasn't sure she could live with him, either.

She knew she could no longer live with Phil. If he hadn't divorced her, she would have gone blithely through the rest of her days, content with life as she knew it. But he had divorced her, and her eyes had been opened. Phil had given her three beautiful children, a lavish income, and a very high social status. Now, the children were grown, Deanna's own income was sufficient to meet her needs, and the high social status was of questionable worth when compared to the price.

Phil was impatient, demanding, and totally self-absorbed. He had never been interested in her life, her work, or her accomplishments. He had attended functions with her after all the work was done, but it was more to be seen and exalted among his peers than to please his wife. He'd bought her expensive gifts, not because she wanted them but because he wanted others to see evidence of his worth.

His decision to divorce her had broken her heart. His scornful opinion of her worth had crushed her ego and crippled her self-esteem. Now, she was on her way to recovery, and she didn't need Phil Randolph. If he couldn't accept her as a friend and drop this ridiculous campaign to get her back, then they would just have to go through life uncomfortable in each other's company. Trying to pacify everybody wasn't working.

She would meet him tomorrow— she looked at the clock— she would meet him today and tell him. Over the coming week she would meet with her children and explain things to them. They were all adults. They would understand if they wanted to. She only hoped she could convince Phil that what he'd begun with the children on her behalf was a good thing.

Groggy from lack of sleep, Deanna fixed Evan breakfast the next morning. If he was disappointed that she hadn't joined him, he hid it behind a wall of silence. Since Deanna didn't know what to say to him, breakfast was a stiff, polite meal between two people who acted more like strangers than lovers. Maybe that's what they were, strangers who had become lovers.

"I'll get Georgia to drive me up to get my car," she said, when he was fastening on all the layers required for his ride.

"Fine." He buckled on the chaps and reached for his jacket.

She tried to think of something else to say. *Thanks for the ride* seemed lame. *I'll call you.* Would she? "I really enjoyed yesterday," she finally said, knowing it wasn't enough.

"Yeah, me, too. Right up till the part where the Jaguar was in the driveway." He shrugged as if it didn't matter. "But, hey, shit happens. That's why I wear boots."

He was breaking her heart again, and this time he wouldn't stop and make sweet love to her and apologize, because this time it was her fault. "Evan . . ."

"What?" He had on his gloves, his helmet in his hands, his eyes shuttered against her.

"I'm sorry."

He paused and looked at her. For one heart-stopping minute she thought he might relent, kiss her goodbye, tell her they'd work it out. Then his mouth hardened. "Yeah, me, too. See ya."

She waited until she could no longer hear the sound of the Harley's big engine before she let the tears fall. "See ya," she whispered. There had to be a way to have Evan and her independence both. The thought of living the rest of her life without Evan left her feeling hollow. The thought of sacrificing her independence to have him made her mad.

Nineteen

The HOG's benefit for Sara Harris was held on the Saturday before Valentine's Day. It was a celebration of love and life. Deanna wasn't certain how big Buford was, but it seemed the entire town was milling around in the tent and parking lot around the Harley-Davidson dealership, eating, playing games, enjoying the entertainment— and donating money.

It was early afternoon. Deanna had kept Sara and let Gloria attend during the morning. She wasn't certain how she would be received, having avoided Evan for the past two weeks.

Ernest Price caught her in front of the bandstand, swinging her around in a spontaneous two-step in time to the rollicking bluegrass. "Isn't this a great turnout?" he yelled over the music. "You come over here with me, little lady, cast your vote for the best-looking motorcycle on the road."

Deanna laughed as he wrapped his burly arm around her and led her toward the section roped off for the bikes. Ernest was the chapter's road captain, and he worked hard to fit the Hollywood image of a big, bad biker. She guessed him to stand six foot three inches and to weigh close to three hundred pounds, some of it beer gut, a lot of it brawny muscle. He wore his graying hair and beard long, eagle tattoos on both biceps, and a black vest that left his chest and bulging stomach bare. When he grunted and lunged at children who gawked, they usually ran shrieking. Then he'd laugh when they'd peek back to see if he was still coming, and they'd grin, enjoying the fun.

In keeping with his image, he rode a chopper, the front forks extended to a ridiculous length that made an amateur like Deanna wonder how he controlled it. He'd paid ten dollars to enter it in the motorcycle contest. Votes were cast by the public at one dollar per vote.

"Now, I know you're partial to that little number over there," Ernest crooned in her ear, his arm still around her neck, "but you can surely see who has the best bike. I know you'll vote objectively."

Deanna laughed. The bike he was trying to steer her away from was her Indian. Evan had asked if he could enter it, more for publicity than anything. A placard sat in front of it announcing that it would be donated to Children's Hospital in Sara Harris's name during the auction being held next month. A number was listed for those who were interested.

Deanna fished five dollars out of her purse and voted for Ernest's chopper. He gave her an exuberant smack on her temple, hugging her against him. "Thank you, darlin'. I knew I could count on you to make the right choice."

He left her to harass someone else into voting for his bike, leaving Deanna to wander among the exhibits. She stopped in front of Evan's black Custom Softail, memories twisting through her heart.

"I'll give you a better kiss than Ernest did if you vote for mine, too."

Evan. She couldn't look at him, couldn't yet face what she might see in his eyes. She pulled out another five dollar bill and put it in the jar in front of his bike. Only then did she turn around.

His gaze was hungry as he devoured every detail, from the top of her head to the sole of her boots. "How are you?" he asked.

"Fine." *Awful, terrible, lonely. I can't stop thinking about you.*

"You look good," he said, "but then you always look good."

Maybe she should have worn the white suit. Maybe she should have stayed home. She couldn't think clearly when he looked at her like that, but then she hadn't been thinking clearly for the last two weeks. "How are you?"

"Fine."

"How's Kyle?"

"Kyle's fine. He's been up since six o'clock, helping us set up and tasting everything. Brian just took him home with the optimistic intention of making him take a nap."

"I'm sorry I missed him."

"Do I get the kiss, also, or just the vote?"

Something deep inside Deanna clenched at the thought, at the huskiness of his voice, at the raw hunger in his eyes. She stepped toward him hesitantly, slowly slid her arms around his neck, went up on tiptoe, and plunged into the fire. His kiss was as sweet as her memory, creating a longing ache that only grew more intense as they prolonged the kiss. His tongue caressed hers, she stroked his in return, pulling him closer. She felt his hands burrow through her hair, felt his groan against her mouth.

"Don't you guys have someplace private you can do that? Come on, man, there's children present."

Deanna sprang away from Evan, knowing her face was scarlet. "Conway," Evan drawled, watching Deanna, "we must find you a woman of your own so you'll quit spying on us."

"Spying? I ain't spying. You're standing out here in plain sight of everybody. You were drawing a crowd."

"I don't see a crowd," Evan said, his eyes still locked with Deanna's. "Do you see a crowd?"

She shook her head slowly.

"Come with me. I have something to show you." He ignored Conway and pulled Deanna under his arm, leading her down the line of motorcycles. She laid her arm around his waist, savoring the feel of him against her again.

"This one's for sale," he said, when they stood in front of an immaculate maroon Sportster. "It's a 1992, one lady owner, 8,000 miles. She brings it to me for tune-ups, keeps it in the garage, waxes it to death. You won't find a better cared for bike."

"Why's she selling it?"

"It's an 883. She just bought a Low Rider. Bigger engine," he explained, when she looked blank. "Believe me, it's plenty big enough for you."

"It's beautiful." Deanna walked around it, imagining owning it. She could ride it anytime she wanted, anywhere she wanted.

"Would you like to meet her?"

Deanna looked at him, confused. "The bike?"

Evan laughed. "No, silly, the owner. Her

name's Hazel Sandoval and she's sitting at the bake sale table at this moment."

Hazel Sandoval looked around forty. She was chattering nonstop at the people near her booth, coaxing, challenging, touting her baked goods as the best in the city. People were teasing her, haggling over her prices, refuting her claims, but mostly it looked like they were buying. Evan and Deanna waited for a lull in the activity, then Evan introduced them.

"I can't believe it," Deanna said later, feeling more like dancing than walking. "I own a motorcycle. Not just any motorcycle, a Harley-Davidson. I'm a HOG!"

"You still have to join the chapter to get that distinction," Evan said, but he was laughing with her. "By this summer, you can ride your own bike on our outings. Speaking of which, we're having one in two weeks. We're riding to the Varsity in Athens. You'd still have to ride behind me, but I'd like you to come."

Deanna felt the laughter inside of her die. "Two weeks from today?"

"Is that a problem?"

He'd taken a chance, inviting her out after she'd avoided him for two weeks. She was sure their kiss earlier had something to do with his decision to risk rejection. It was obvious the chemistry between them was still there. Unfortunately, the problems were still there as well.

"I can't. I have a dinner party that night for my volunteers." She met his gaze, pleading with him to understand. "I'd like to come another time though."

He studied her with hard eyes, then took her elbow. "Let's go find somewhere we can talk."

Deanna stumbled after him, finding his invitation somewhat threatening. Maybe he was right. It was time to lay things out on the table.

The only place away from the crowd was his office. Deanna sank into the familiar leather chair. Evan didn't sit but leaned against the edge of his desk with his arms folded over his chest. "Where do we stand, Deanna?"

She resented his towering over her. It was an obvious power move on his part, designed to put her at a disadvantage, just like having their discussion in his office, on his turf. "We're not standing anywhere, you are. If you want to talk to me, sit down."

He acted like he might refuse, then he slowly raised off the desk and moved into his chair. "Okay, I'm sitting."

"I've been busy these last two weeks. I had a long talk with Phil, made it clear to him that I'd like us to be friends, to continue enjoying family events with our children and grandchil-

dren, but that I don't wish to remarry him."
She realized she was twisting her pearls around
her fingers and forced her hands into her lap.

"I've talked to each one of my children, explained to them that their father and I have
grown apart, no longer share the same interests. I expressed my hope that they would continue to seek out both their parents and
understand that we have different needs and
different talents, all of which they can benefit
from. I reminded them that we are both human, that we need friends of our own, just as
they do, in addition to family, and that I trust
them to understand that need."

"And did they?"

"Eric, my youngest, did more than the other
two. Sherylyn is too staunchly her father's
daughter right now. Jeff, the oldest, didn't
want to hear it, but his wife, my daughter-in-
law, was very supportive. I stayed the day with
the grandchildren while she went shopping
with her friends." She smiled, remembering,
then realized she was getting side-tracked.

"Anyway, now I own a motorcycle and I
hope after the auction we can ride together
again. The weather will be warmer, so I'm certain it'll be more pleasant. As soon as I'm comfortable handling it, I'll go take the road tests
and get my license."

He didn't answer for a long time, just sat in his chair with his fingers pressed together in front of him, looking at her. When he did speak, she knew he had decided to let her see how vulnerable she made him feel. "Where do I fit into this whole organizational scheme?"

"I'd like us to be friends, but I warned you the day we went to the river. I just came from a stifling relationship. I'm just learning about a whole other world out there. I don't want commitment right now." She spoke to her lap, her voice soft and low.

"Have I asked for commitment?" Evan asked, his voice equally low.

"You get angry when I don't tell you what I'm doing. You get resentful when I don't invite you into every part of my life. I've only just gotten adjusted to not having someone to answer to. I've decided I like it."

"Sounds lonely to me, Deanna Randolph."

She looked at him then. "That's why I need friends."

"How many friends do you need?"

Deanna frowned, confused. "I don't understand."

"You want me. You want Phil. Who's taking you to the dinner party in two weeks?"

Deanna cursed the telltale flush creeping up

her face. "Why does someone have to take me? It's my party and it's at my mother's."

"You forget, Deanna, I know all about how society works. I was raised in it. I married into it. Just because I chose to leave it doesn't mean I don't remember the rules. You and your mother will both have male escorts, even if they're twenty years old and first-degree relatives."

"That's not true!" Nothing made her more angry than when he started throwing his social prejudice at her.

"Who's your escort?" It wasn't a question, it was a demand.

Deanna glared at him. "See what I mean? It's none of your business. It has nothing to do with you or our friendship."

He surged to his feet, leaning over his desk. "You're right. I want commitment. I thought we had something special, something exclusive, something worthy of making a commitment to each other over. I can't be your friend, Deanna, not one of a string of friends that you call on when it suits you. You don't have to marry me or move to Buford or ask me to move to Buckhead, but I expect to be a part of your life, your whole life. I want you to be proud enough of me as your man that you don't want other men associated with you. But apparently you aren't, so let's just part and leave friendship out of it, shall we?"

Deanna's breath caught in her throat. Tears burned behind her eyes. In her heart, she'd known that was how he'd react, but it still hurt. That's why she'd avoided it for two weeks.

He came around the desk and burrowed his fingers through her hair, pulling her against him. "Oh, Deanna, don't you understand that I love you?"

The tears welled and overflowed. She buried her face against his thigh, hugging him.

"I'm sorry I'm not the open-minded, free-spirited man you want, but I am what I am. It's taken me fifty-six years to understand what I am and what my priorities are. I am willing to love you for all of your charms and all of your faults, but I am not willing to share you with other men."

I don't want other men, her heart screamed. How do you know? her mind asked. You haven't tried.

She had been over and over this in her mind during the last two weeks, discussing it at length with Georgia and Gloria, and had made the logical decision to give it a chance, date other men, put some distance between her and Evan, and see if she still felt the same. So she'd invited a family friend to be her escort to the dinner, one who'd asked her out several times since her divorce. Now, Evan's declaration was threatening all her logical resolve.

That was the problem with the heart, it defied logic. Sometimes she wondered if it wasn't just hormones. When she got around Evan, it was hard to tell them apart. A tissue appeared in her line of vision and she accepted it; wiping her eyes and nose gently. She released him and sat back in her chair.

"I care about you a great deal, Evan, and I've enjoyed our times together more than you'll ever know. I just thought maybe some time away from each other might be a good idea."

He returned to his chair, looking resigned. His hazel eyes were sad, but his voice was even when he spoke.

"Do you still want me to deliver Hazel's Sportster to you?"

She nodded numbly. "Let me pay you for delivery. I need the Indian brought in for the auction, too, so you could just bring them in at the same time. I still need to settle with you on how much I owe for the restoration."

He took an envelope out of his desk drawer and handed it across the table to her. It was the one she'd given him, with her check for the parts still sealed inside. "No charge. Have the hospital give me a receipt for $6,000. That's what a power plant restoration runs.''

New tears gathered, blurring Deanna's vision. ''You don't have to do this,'' she whispered.

''It's for the children,'' he said. ''For Sara.''

''Evan . . .'' Again, words failed her.

''I'll be here, Deanna, if you need anything. If not, I'll see you at the auction.''

The auction. She had a month to either get her head on straight or get over this man. She studied his face, trying to memorize every detail of the hard planes, the hazel eyes that were usually sparkling with mischief or desire, the mouth that smiled so easily, that leered at her with such appeal. It wasn't smiling now but set in a grim line. She sighed and stood up.

''I'll be there,'' she said, referring to the auction. What else to say? *Thank you* was totally inadequate. *I'll never forget you* too final. English was proving to be a totally inept language. A language probably didn't exist that would communicate how she felt to Evan. ''Tell Kyle I'm sorry I missed him.''

''He'll be sorry, too.''

We're all sorry, Deanna thought, walking despondently out of the dealership and toward her car. She passed the line of bikes and stopped to look at her new Sportster again. It didn't give her the thrill it had earlier. Without Evan to ride with, she wondered if she'd even ride it. According to Evan, she wouldn't have any trouble getting her money out of it if she did decide to sell it.

According to Evan. Her whole perspective lately seemed to be according to Evan. She needed a perspective according to Deanna. Making a decision, she walked back over to where Hazel still sat, hawking baked goods.

"Hazel, may I have the key to the Sportster? I'd like to ride it before I go back."

"You're going to take it out of the competition?" Hazel asked, obviously upset at the idea of losing votes.

Deanna smiled. "I'll put fifty dollars in your jar to cover the time it's gone."

"Damn . . . I mean . . . sure, here's the key. It's your bike."

Deanna went to her car and retrieved her helmet and gloves. She was already wearing jeans, jacket, and boots but not her long underwear. The day was pleasant, but the wind on the bike would be cold. It didn't matter. She wouldn't ride long.

The man guarding the voting jars and the bikes approached her as soon as she crossed the ropes. "Hi, Kirk," she said, recognizing the young biker Georgia had been so enamored with. "I just bought this from Hazel." She held up the key. "Thought I'd take it out, try it on."

"Sure, Mrs. Randolph. Let me help you push it out of here."

"Thanks, Kirk, but if I'm going to own one, I guess I'd better learn to push it around myself." Independence. She'd chosen it, she might as well get used to it. She put the promised fifty dollars in the jar before Kirk moved it out of the way.

The Sportster wasn't as overwhelming as Evan's Softail, but it was big enough. She did the safety check the way she'd been taught, then pulled out the choke and pushed the electric starter. Electric was nice, she thought, as the engine fired to life beneath her. She pushed it under the rope Kirk held up for her while the engine warmed up, feeling the eyes of the entire crowd watching her. Maybe this hadn't been such a good idea, but now that everyone had watched her start it, she had no alternative but to ride it.

There was a lot of traffic moving in and out of the parking lot as people continued to arrive and others left. Deanna wasn't used to dodging traffic. She wasn't used to an audience critiquing her riding skills. To add to the pressure, she was wearing a jacket with North Georgia HOGs emblazoned across the back. Official member or not, to this crowd, she represented the North Georgia HOGs. If it died on takeoff, or worse if she lost it on the incline and laid it down, she would die of humiliation on the spot.

She sat on top of the incline, at the entrance of the drive, waiting for traffic to clear. A car pulled up behind her, then another behind it. Perspiration trickled under Deanna's arms, adding to her discomfort. Brains, not muscle, she reminded herself. She held the bike with the rear brake, balancing with her left foot on the ground. Her visor was fogging up. She was going to have to remember to leave the visor open until she was moving.

She didn't kill it, and she didn't lay it down. She eased out the clutch and twisted the throttle. After the cantankerous Indian, the sportster felt as responsive as a kitten. It jumped a little. It purred. It wanted to run and play. Deanna's vision cleared and the cool air soothed away the heat. She was smiling as she crossed over the bridge and passed the turnaround. She was going back to the river below the dam, alone this time, to think.

It was dark when Deanna finally got home, having spent longer at the river than she'd intended. She disengaged the alarm while Gloria carried a sleepy Sara back to her crib.

"You've gotten a million phone calls," Gloria noticed, passing the answering machine.

"They can wait another five minutes while I take off my coat and visit the bathroom." Deanna had just reached into the closet for a hanger when the phone rang. "We're not home yet," she shouted to Gloria. "Let the machine add it to its lineup."

Deanna was halfway down the hall to the bathroom when she recognized her mother's voice. "Deanna Louise Randolph, I am tired of talking to this stupid machine. If you don't call me back— "

"Mother, I'm here. What's wrong?" Deanna's heart was racing with panic. Was one of the children hurt? One of the grandchildren?

"Where have you been all day?" her mother demanded, as if Deanna was still twelve. "Never mind, I saw where you've been all day. Deanna, how could you? Have you taken total leave of your senses? My friends have been calling me all night, 'Was that Deanna we saw on the news?' So I turned it on. This is your father's fault, letting you ride that . . ."

Deanna sank into a chair, numbly listening to her mother go on and on about her unseemly behavior being broadcast on the local news.

"My friends asked me if you'd joined the Hell's Angels. What could I say, Deanna? That awful man kissing you right there on the television, you dressed up in that horrible costume."

Deanna detached herself, wondering if she laid the receiver down and went to the bathroom if her mother would even know she'd been gone. Or she could fuel the fire and tell her mother she'd bought her own motorcycle and spent the afternoon riding it. She'd been so naive, thinking Phil and Evan were the only ones trying to control her life. If the blinking light on her answering machine was any indication, she was surrounded by people trying to control her life.

"It was a benefit, Mother," she finally broke in. "Listen, I just walked in the door and I have to go. I'll pick you up in the morning for church and explain it all then, okay? I love you." She hung up, cutting Charlotte off before the next tirade began. The phone immediately rang again. Deanna ignored it.

She took a long soak in her tub, gave herself a facial, and dressed in her favorite peignoir. She poured herself a glass of wine before she sat down beside the answering machine. With a sigh, she touched the playback button.

Her children were as shocked as her mother.

Her friends' reactions varied from cruelly derisive to surprised. Georgia informed her she looked marvelous. There were several lewd offers from men she barely knew. She sighed again as the last message finished.

"I guess you don't have to worry about your image at the country club anymore," Gloria commented.

Deanna looked up, not having heard Gloria come in. Gloria handed her a plate with a grilled ham and cheese sandwich on it. "What image?"

"The one you told me Phil painted of you after your divorce, you know, dull, boring, predictable." Gloria grinned. "I guess you showed them."

Deanna looked back at the answering machine. "I guess I did. That wasn't my intention."

"Your bike won, by the way. Hazel called while you were in the tub. She said Ernest was fit to be tied, claims you rigged the vote."

Deanna smiled. "I guess I did."

Gloria grew serious. "They brought in over twenty thousand dollars today for Sara. I didn't know what to say."

Deanna laid her hand over Gloria's. "Say thank you. Things won't always be like this for

you and Sara, and you'll be able to help others."

"I want to go back to school, learn to talk
to folks."

Deanna frowned, confused. "You mean give
speeches?"

"Yeah, talk to folks, groups, tell them about
the importance of donating organs. I been
talkin' to the organ bank people. They need
people like that."

"Do they pay for something like that?"

"No, it's volunteer. That's why they need
people. I figure all this money ever'body's
been givin' for Sara is pay enough."

"You still have to eat," Deanna pointed out.

Gloria smiled. "I been thinkin' about this
housekeepin' job I was offered. If I could have
weekends off and buy another crib to put in
the mobile home, me and Sara could move
her monitors and equipment back and forth
in the car."

"There's only one condition to that,"
Deanna said, licking the melted butter from
her sandwich off her fingers.

"What's that?"

"You must learn to cook low fat."

Twenty

Those who hadn't caught Deanna being kissed by Ernest on the local news Saturday night saw the full-color picture in the paper on Sunday morning. To be fair to the newspaper, it was a small picture, and there were plenty of other pictures of the benefit. Deanna personally thought the one of the Power Ranger riding off on his Harley Electra Glide was more interesting, but she was a distinct minority, at least among the congregation at church and the country club members who gathered for brunch. Deanna could hardly pay attention to the criticism from her family for the constant interruptions from her friends.

"You know we have a HOG chapter here in Buckhead," David Stern told her. Deanna remembered Julie talking about them during the one of the auxiliary's auction meetings. "Why didn't you come to us? We're a much classier outfit than those rednecks from Buford."

Deanna smiled, wishing she had the nerve to tell him what the North Georgia HOGs called the Buckhead group. It wasn't nearly as flattering as "rednecks." "Thanks, David, but since Gloria lives in Buford it seemed appropriate that they take on her cause. We could use more help, though, if you'd like me to come talk to your group."

"I'll call you," David said, escaping in such a way that told Deanna he never would.

"I think it's great, Mom," Eric said. "You stood up for what you believed in, took action instead of just whining about how the system fails those it was designed to help."

"She brought a hooker into our house," Sherylyn informed her brother.

Deanna closed her eyes. Sherylyn had done it now.

"A hooker?" Charlotte Edwards voice was a low hiss, not wanting to be overheard by nearby diners. "Your housekeeper is a hooker?"

"No, she isn't," Deanna defended Gloria, giving Sherylyn a sharp look. "Sherylyn made a false assumption based on what Gloria was wearing the night she rushed Sara into the emergency room. Really, Mother, don't you think I have better judgment than that?" She would deal with Sherylyn later.

"I don't know what to think anymore,

Deanna, after seeing that half-naked, hairy beast kiss you last night. And you were smiling!"

"His name is Ernest and he's harmless. He enjoys looking like that so people will have just the reaction to him you're having."

"Dad says you're having an affair with one of them."

The only way to counter being put on the defensive was to take the offensive. Deanna pinned her narrow-minded daughter with a warning glare. "You and your father share a serious personality flaw. You jump to erroneous conclusions based on a single observation. Neither one of you would think of basing a diagnosis on a single symptom, but you're willing to judge people's lives and spread rumors on just such flimsy evidence."

She knew they both had ample evidence on both charges, but she wasn't about to concede that point, not in front of her mother, who looked dangerously pale.

Charlotte glanced at three-year-old Brady to make sure he wasn't paying any attention before she leaned close to Deanna. "Are you having an affair, Deanna?"

"Don't you think I'm old enough?" Deanna shot back, irritated with the whole bunch of them.

"With Ernest?" her brother Andrew asked. He hadn't said much before now, but that idea seemed to bother him.

"It was a rhetorical question, Andrew. Would you listen to all of you? I feel like I'm on trial here."

"Deanna! Aren't you just full of surprises. I couldn't believe that was you on the news last night, but everyone's been talking about it."

"Hi, Susan. Yes, everyone does seem to be talking about it." Deanna threw an accusing glance around the table at her family. "How is your family?"

"Oh, they're fine. Same old stuff. What does Phil think of all these Harley men fawning all over you?"

If Susan Whitehead were a cat, she'd be licking her whiskers. Deanna remembered the night Phil had met Evan. "Phil was quite impressed by the Harley man, actually," she told Susan. "Thanks for stopping by."

Susan took the hint, but she left with a knowing smirk on her face.

"Can we discuss something else," Deanna's older brother Pete asked, clearly bored with Deanna's motorcycle benefit. "Deanna's done charity work her entire life, had her picture in the paper, been on the news before. You remember that body builder you had at the hospital that one time?" he asked Deanna. "They published your picture in a clinch with him and everyone thought it was so cute. You were married then, with small children. Why didn't anyone get upset over that?"

"That was obviously innocent and for a good cause," Charlotte said.

Deanna rolled her eyes. "So is this, Mother," Pete defended her. "Deanna's right. You're meddling."

And Evan wanted to come meet this family, Deanna thought, tuning out the rest of the arguments for and against her. The man didn't realize what she was saving him from. Then she smiled to herself. Knowing Evan, he would hold his own with this bunch just fine, probably better than Phil ever had. She couldn't help thinking she was making a terrible mistake.

It didn't take experience to know Evan Maxwell was a once in a lifetime man. Her logical excuses for putting distance between them became less and less logical the more she analyzed them. It was only a month, a chance to test the waters and be sure. That's what she was, a water-tester, a fine-print-reader, a three-references-please employer. It was a fault, a personality quirk she couldn't seem to override. That quirk was probably what had gotten her labeled as boring and predictable. It wasn't a pleasant thought.

The night of Deanna's dinner party was crisp and clear, allowing the guests to spill out onto the terrace and into the gardens. Inside, the Edwards's home glowed with the warmth of candlelight and a profusion of flowers. Champagne flowed, guests laughed and talked about how beautifully everything was decorated, musicians played softly from a corner of the formal living room. Deanna paced restlessly from group to group, trying to be an attentive hostess, trying not to think about how bored she was.

"You know, her father had just passed away suddenly when Phil up and decided to sow one last field of wild oats before he got too old. I think the combined grief was just too much. She's always been such a delicate child."

Deanna closed her eyes, seeking strength. It had been two weeks since the HOGs's benefit, and Charlotte hadn't let it go yet. She hadn't heard this version before though.

"Mother, really, you make me sound like an invalid or some feeble-minded idiot who should be locked up for her own good. Hello,

Hilda, I'm so glad you could come. You don't believe any of this, do you?"

"I'd like to meet this Ernest," Hilda said, winking at Deanna.

Charlotte made a disgusted noise and stalked off.

"Tell me, did you really buy your own Harley?" Hilda asked conspiratorially.

Deanna blinked, not certain how to answer.

Hilda grinned. "Georgia told me, but I won't tell a soul if you're trying to keep it a secret. I wish I was young enough to ride one."

"There's a lady your age in the North Georgia chapter," Deanna told her. "She started riding when she was fifty. She used to ride behind her husband. When he died, she missed riding almost as much as she missed him, I think. You're not too old, Hilda. You're one of the youngest women I know."

"Thank you, dear, that's sweet, but old bones break easier than young ones, regardless of the state of the mind. I'd better stick with my Cadillac."

Deanna smiled and left Hilda to walk out on the terrace. She had been to thousands of these parties over the years and had always enjoyed them, but tonight she kept thinking about a bluegrass band playing in a parking lot, soft drinks and hot dogs, hog catching contests, and a live auction of the most unique collection of donated items Deanna had ever laid eyes on. The HOG chapter members had worked just as hard if not harder than any of the hospital volunteers, their benefit had been a roaring success, and she was certain that they'd had more fun on their ride today to the Varsity in Athens than she was having to-night. For one thing, Evan was with them.

"Are you okay?" Georgia asked, joining her on the terrace.

Deanna felt immediate remorse. She was the hostess. She shouldn't be out here crying in the rhododendrons, neglecting her guests, es-pecially neglecting her date. "Is Sam looking for me?"

Georgia made a rude noise. "Sam found two others as into this olympics thing as he is. They have a three-way debate going in there, with an audience. You won't be missed until dinnertime."

Georgia gave her a shrewd, assessing look. "So, is it helping?"

"Is what helping?" Deanna asked, turning back to look over the estate's well-manicured landscape, softly lit with small lanterns along the pathway.

"Dating other men. Over Evan yet?"

"One dinner party with Sam hardly constitutes dating other men," Deanna pointed out. It also hadn't helped. Nothing had.

Her ride down to the river hadn't helped. Having the Sportster in her garage at home hadn't helped. Two weeks away from Evan hadn't helped. Deanna missed him, missed his teasing, missed his loving, missed their long talks.

"You are such a collector of metaphors," Deanna said, turning back to Georgia. "You'll love this one. Independence without Evan is like potatoes without butter— healthier for the heart, but who cares?"

"Hey, you're talking to a woman who adds sour cream and bacon in addition to butter," Georgia said. "What's life if you can't enjoy the living of it?"

"I keep saying I don't know what I want. I need time to sort it all out, but you know what, Georgia? I'm fifty-two years old. When do I think I'm going to figure it all out?"

Georgia shrugged. "Beats me. Will you let me know when you do?"

"That's just it. I'm missing the best part while waiting for some sort of revelation to strike me. If I don't know what I want out of life by now, I have serious doubts that I ever will."

"Hey, don't discredit learning. Look at what

you've learned in just the past year, when you were only a year younger."

Deanna lowered her voice, for Georgia's ears only. "I mean, I don't need to date a group of men I've known most of my life to know what I want."

Georgia smiled, a smug, I've-known-it-all-along smile. "What you want wouldn't be about six-foot-two, hazel eyes, short gray hair, military bearing, great shoulders, nice— "

"That's close enough." Deanna was smiling as well.

"I think your family will accept him better than you think."

"Sherylyn, never. Eric, probably. Jeff, he's too busy with his own family to worry about what I'm doing. Pete's divorced and remarried, so he can't say anything. Andrew's pretty open-minded. Did I leave anyone out?"

"Charlotte."

Deanna groaned. "She's in there telling people I'm out of my mind with grief and shouldn't be held responsible for my actions."

"Really? I overheard her tell Susan Whitehead that she was proud of you for not falling for Phil's song and dance about being a changed man. She also said it was too bad how some poor girl was going to fall for his looks and his money only to find out too late she was married to Dr. Frankenstein."

"Dr. Frankenstein? Phil?"

"The man, not the monster. You know the type, dedicated to their research at the expense of all else."

"Yeah, I know the type. I wonder what bit him a year ago, made him want a divorce so suddenly."

"Fear of his own mortality," Georgia said in a voice of grim prophesy. "He noticed the hourglass of his life, that there was more sand on the bottom than the top, and he panicked."

Deanna leaned her backside against the stone wall and crossed her arms over her waist. "So what made him come back?"

"Really, Deanna, give yourself some credit."

"That's not enough."

Georgia looked uncomfortable. "You won't like my theory."

"I don't like my own. I want to know if you concur."

"Tell me yours first. He was your husband."

Deanna twisted her strand of pearls around her index finger. "Phil's looks, his status, got him all the female attention he could handle. Right after the divorce, he was seen with everyone from nursing students to international models. He loved it. His ego swelled to enormous proportions."

"Must have cast a shadow over the city," Georgia interjected sardonically.

Deanna smiled. "Anyway, Phil is not a play-boy. He's a physician, dedicated to his research, alive only when someone's heart is in his hands."

"Ugh. Sorry, continue."

"The novelty of being a prize catch wore off quickly. He wanted someone who would listen to his latest theory, give him a quick . . . um . . . release . . . between watching the eleven o'clock news and catching up on his journal reading. He expected her to wait willing and docile in the wings while he saved humanity, picking up his shirts at the cleaners while they waited and coming when he snapped his fingers. There are no more women like that."

"Yes there are," Georgia argued, "but they usually expect a courtship period so they can say, 'He wasn't like that when we were dating.' Even so, there are women out there who would suck him up in a heartbeat, with their eyes wide open. The money and the status would be enough."

"What upsets me is if he'd gotten tired of the game six months earlier, I would have been the one sucking him up."

"You don't give yourself enough credit, Deanna. I think even then you were aware of which way the wind blew, you were just too unsure of yourself to admit it yet."

Deanna shook her head. "It's amazing what you put up with, gradual changes that don't seem like a big deal, then one day you wake up, and you're pathetic."

"You were never pathetic," Georgia corrected, righteous indignation for her friend flashing from her blue eyes. "If anyone was pathetic, it was Phil."

"Well, I'd gotten pretty complacent, like the frog that gets boiled because the water temperature rises so gradually she never notices. Then one day, she's frog legs."

"I thought you had a lot of independence for a married woman," Georgia disagreed. "You had your children until recently, your auxiliary work, your bridge, garden club, the country club, money to go shopping. The one thing you didn't have was a husband. He was never home."

"And when you think about it, I managed him. No wonder I have such an independent streak."

"So now that you're secure in your independence, what are you going to do about Evan?"

Deanna pondered the question. Her heart urged her to drop everything, drive to Buford, and throw herself in Evan's arms. Then she remembered their last meeting, when he'd delivered her motorcycles. He had been stiffly polite, coolly distant. Her head advised caution. It wasn't like she didn't have anything to do for the next two weeks. A million details needed her attention before the auction. "I don't have time to do anything about Evan until after the auction," she said, knowing Georgia would see right through her. She did.

"Talked yourself into a case of cold feet, didn't you?"

Deanna smiled, a secretive, canary-in-mouth smile as an idea formed in her mind. "Maybe. But I think I have a pair of red shoes that just might take care of the problem."

Pete and Andrew and their families came over to Deanna's after the family brunch the next day to see the Indian. Pete's wife Nancy was now eight months pregnant and not moving very fast, but she wanted to see what all the furor was about. Her sons, aged twelve and eight, were awed. Andrew's wife Delores was more interested in meeting Gloria.

"Will you take us riding?" the boys started asking immediately upon seeing the bike.

"Not right now," Pete said. He scowled at

Deanna. "I cannot believe you are going to give it away. Dad will turn over in his grave."

"Actually, I think he quite approves," Deanna said. "He would have given anything he owned to have saved Angelica. I think a motorcycle is a pretty good trade for a baby's life."

"Are you gonna start it up, Pete?" Nancy's eldest boy asked, practically dancing in anticipation.

"Do you remember how, or would you like me to show you?" Deanna taunted him, handing him the key.

"Very cute," Pete said, not amused. He took the key, straddled the motorcycle and pushed it out of the garage onto the driveway.

"You scratch it, brother, you buy it," Deanna warned him. "It's been forty years since you rode that motorcycle."

She watched closely as Pete and Andrew conferred on all the levers and switches, knowing they wouldn't confess to her if they didn't remember something, but not about to let them tear up her motorcycle. "Test your braking ability before you start it," she instructed Pete.

"What?"

"You should never ride anything you don't know how to stop. With the engine off, roll it forward and try your brakes."

"You're not serious."

Deanna put her hands on her hips. "You haven't ridden in forty years, it's my bike and a collector's item. I have the right to demand a few preliminary drills. Either that or I'll drive it and let you ride behind me."

Pete glowered but he did as she asked. Deanna knew she'd promised they could ride it, but as she watched her sixty-year-old brother try to recall long-forgotten skills she began to regret her decision. She wondered if a man's pride was worth thirty thousand dollars.

"Pete, listen, I took lessons for two months before I rode it. Think about this. You could break a hip, an arm, ruin the motorcycle."

"Run me through the systems," Pete conceded. "It's been a long time and you're right, it's a valuable machine now."

Deanna went through the starting sequence, then reminded him of the levers and clutch. Andrew stood with them, watching everything. Pete finally shook his head.

"Did you remember this thing being so complicated?" he asked Andrew.

"I do now, now that she's pointing everything out. You ridden any of the new ones?"

Deanna assumed he referred to anything built since 1953.

"No. Never had any interest in them." Pete got off the cycle, still not having started it.

"Show off for us, Deanna. I'd hate to be in traction when my daughter makes her appearance next month."

Deanna couldn't believe it. Pete looked resigned, Andrew amused. Deanna grinned at them. "I love you both, you know that?"

"Yeah, yeah," Pete said, embarrassed. "Start the bike."

Deanna started the Indian. She rode it to the end of the block and back, then pulled it back into the driveway and turned it off. Andrew was laughing.

"I'd forgotten about unsynchronized gears. I had a truck that shifted like that. What a dinosaur."

"Do people still ride these, or do they just collect them?" Nancy asked, coming over to join the group now that the engine was quiet.

"They ride them," Deanna supplied. "Some people prefer them to the new ones. There are several chapters of Indian riders, just like Harley riders or Honda Gold Wing riders—people with something in common. They enjoy riding together."

"Take me riding, Aunt Deanna," the boys clamored, having been ignored long enough.

"I'll tell you what," Deanna said, smiling down at the impatient boys. "I'll take you on the Harley. How about that?"

Deanna made them wear her helmet, thinking she should get a second helmet for the children. She had no intention of riding with them any farther than her own quiet residential neighborhood, but they still needed helmets that fit them.

"My turn," Andrew said, when she got back from riding the second child. She thought he meant he wanted to drive it, but he surprised her by climbing on behind her. "I'm not wearing a helmet, so no fancy moves," he yelled at her over the sound of the engine.

"You want to try it?" she asked him when they returned to her driveway.

"You'd trust me with your motorcycle?" Andrew asked.

"It's just a machine, Andrew, repairable, replaceable. You're not. So I guess the question is, do I trust my motorcycle with you?"

"Do you?"

"No." She turned the key off, fighting hard not to smile and spoil the effect.

"Give me that," Andrew demanded, knowing she was pulling his leg.

Deanna laughed and gave him the bike. "Braking drill with the engine off," she demanded. "Those front brakes will throw you right over the handlebars."

It was ten minutes before she let him start

it. He didn't take it far. "I'm too old for such nonsense," he told her when he brought it back. "You're too old for such nonsense, too. Why are you doing this?"

"Because you're only as old as you feel," Deanna told him. "When I'm riding, I'm young, I'm free, and there's nothing I can't do."

"I'll write that on your body cast," Pete predicted direly, "or your headstone."

"Here lies Deanna Randolph," Andrew joined in, pantomiming with his hands, "mother, grandmother, HOG."

"That's enough out of you two." Nancy chided them, herding her crew toward the door.

"We could have her cremated," Pete persisted, holding the door while the others went in. "Pour her ashes in the gas tank and bury them together."

"You're both just jealous," Deanna accused. "You sound like old men."

"Starting over with another family at sixty does that to a man," Pete groaned melodramatically. He wrapped his arms around Nancy and pulled her back against him, contradicting his words.

"Come see this baby, Nancy," Delores called out from the den.

Delores sat on the couch, Sara in her lap,

while Gloria sat nearby. Sara's dark eyes studied Delores with a serious expression. "She stares at you with eyes much too wise for one so young," Delores commented. "And she's so tiny."

"How old is she?" Nancy asked, coming to stand near Delores so she could look at Sara.

"Ten months," Gloria supplied.

"She's a beautiful child," Nancy said, running her fingers over the baby's fine blonde hair.

"I'd better take her back to our room," Gloria said, standing up. "I try to keep her away from groups of people. She doesn't have the normal resistance to common viruses like most folks."

Delores gave Sara up reluctantly. She waited until Gloria had left the room. "I think it's a fine thing, Deanna helping that baby. I can't imagine just letting her die."

Nancy put a protective hand over her own unborn child. "I keep thinking, what if that were our daughter? I would want everything possible done for her."

"I knew Dad would feel the same way," Deanna said, looking at Pete. "I didn't want to give up the Indian until I thought about Dad and how much he grieved for Angelica. It changed the rest of his life. He'd want to see his motorcycle go toward something wonderful, like saving a baby's life."

"No more arguments," Pete conceded, still holding Nancy. "I'm not sure what I would have done with the thing anyway. Certainly nothing as worthwhile as what you're doing with it."

That hurdle cleared, Deanna decided it was time to address the next one. "I've been seeing Evan Maxwell, socially, the man who restored the motorcycle." She looked from face to face, looking for their reaction. "I'd like him to come with us some Sunday, meet the family."

"Sounds serious," Pete said. Nancy was smiling.

"Not serious," Deanna hastened to assure him, "just . . ." she could feel the flush suffusing her face, "well, I don't plan to get married or anything."

"Does Mother know?" Andrew asked, grinning at her.

"No. I wanted to get your reaction first."

"Is he good to you, Deanna?" Andrew asked, serious now.

Deanna smiled. "He's wonderful. He's interested in my work. He loves children. He keeps his grandson with him on weekends when his son is away. He . . ."

The laughter of the others made Deanna

realize she was gushing over Evan like a teenager with her first crush. She stopped, feeling
her face burn hotter.

"We get the picture," Andrew said, still
chuckling. "When do we meet this paragon?"

"At the auction, if you'll help me," Deanna
said, making pleading eyes at her brother.

"Why do you need my help?" Andrew
asked, instantly suspicious.

"I find myself in need of an escort,"
Deanna said. "One who is not a threat, and
one who will know when to find a reason to
leave unexpectedly, requiring someone else to
bring me home."

Twenty-one

Even before the first guest arrived, Deanna knew this year would be the most successful auction the auxiliary had ever pulled off. Three hundred twenty tickets had been sold. The two Indian motorcycles had not only generated interest but stimulated others to donate generously as well. In assessed value alone, this year's donations exceeded any other year. The indigent fund board would never miss the money received from the motorcycles that was earmarked for Sara Harris.

The success of the auction wasn't the reason Deanna couldn't be still. She'd arrived earlier than she needed to, checked on microphones and lighting for the podium that had been checked yesterday, walked through the displays, writing her name and a minimum dollar amount on items she worried wouldn't bring enough without some help. She met with the band leader, the banquet manager, the audiovisual technician from the hospital. She fussed over her committee women as they arrived, questioning what they had left to do.

"You are driving everyone crazy," Georgia warned her, when Deanna checked Harriet's seating chart for the third time. "Go get a drink, sit down, and drink it— slowly. You're going to wear those down to two-inch heels before he gets here and ruin the effect, not to mention not having any friends left."

Deanna looked down at the three-inch red heels on her feet. Her toes were hurting from all her running around, and everyone was seeing to their jobs quite competently. "You're right. I'm just so nervous."

"You look gorgeous. Just relax."

Deanna helped herself to a glass of freshly poured champagne, the servers just getting set up as the first guests arrived. She carried it over to a place at her table that she'd claimed earlier with her purse and wrap. She sat down, eased her shoes off inconspicuously under the tablecloth, and looked out over the huge depot, which they'd rented for the auction. It didn't look anything like a depot, thanks to a talented and resourceful decorating committee.

The Depot had been turned into an elegant ballroom, reminiscent of the old Junior League balls of the Eisenhower era. Linen-covered tables were arranged around a dance floor, the band assembled on a platform. There were even crystal chandeliers hanging from the ceiling, casting a soft, muted light over the dining area, a brighter light over the display tables arranged around the perimeter, where the auction items awaited the bidding.

The Indians sat at the corners of the band platform, proudly displayed as the stars of the program. They would not be included in the silent auction but auctioned live by a local sportscaster as part of the entertainment after dinner. The third major item to be auctioned live was a two-week travel package that included airfare, hotels, entertainment tickets, dinners at exclusive restaurants, even car rental. Deanna herself had put the package together, eliciting donations from travel agents, airlines, hotel chains, car rental agencies, various restaurants, and entertainment spots. The tour covered New England up through Canada, and promised to be a wonderful trip for whoever offered the highest bid.

Deanna sipped her champagne and watched the hostess committee at work near the entrance. She had started at just that level, a young girl, still in high school, escorting guests to their tables at auctions her mother had chaired. This was her world. She'd been cultivated for it since infancy. It was more than her life, it was her work, and she was good at it. The New England tour package was just one example. Evan had chosen to leave it long ago. Doubts began to muddle her mind again. For all their shared interests, they seemed to have some major differences. Maybe they wouldn't be able to work things out after all.

She had dressed carefully for tonight, choosing a deep ruby red satin gown that left her shoulders bare. The skirt was full, calf length as was the style in the fifties. The maligned red shoes that had spent the past month in the back of her closet had been a perfect match. Deanna had made sure of that before she bought the dress. Now, she could only hope Evan understood shoe language and knew the invitation was for him. Differences or not, she was willing to give it a try if he was.

"I thought the chairwoman was supposed to mingle," Andrew said, joining her at their table. "You're missing your own party."

Deanna downed the last of her champagne. "Georgia said I was too tense, told me to come sit down and drink some champagne. I'm better now." She gave him a smile and slid her feet back into her shoes. She stood up and took his arm. "Where shall we start?"

"There's a new set of golf clubs I wouldn't

mind taking home. Let's go see if I've been outbid yet."

"I want the yard service," Deanna said. "I'm not happy with the one I'm using and I thought this was a good way to try out someone new."

They walked toward the displays, stopping frequently to greet people they knew. Deanna upped the bids on several items she didn't care about personally, but that weren't getting much attention. People always responded better if they thought there was competition for their item. Not only that, but merchants who noticed their donations were poorly received, were less likely to donate again the following year. She was pleased to see her committee women were doing the same thing.

She almost didn't recognize Evan when he came in. She had never seen him in a tuxedo before, she realized, and that was a shame. His height, his shoulder width, and his military bearing did wonderful things to a tuxedo. She was not pleased to note other women were also watching him.

Two couples came in with Evan— the Indian collectors, Deanna assumed. The group headed straight to where the Indians were displayed before Deanna had a chance to get Evan's attention. There was plenty of time, she chided herself.

"That's Evan," Deanna said, nudging Andrew, who had been talking cars with Georgia's escort.

"The biggest one, right?" Andrew asked, squinting in the direction Deanna had nodded. "Can I leave now?"

Deanna squeezed his arm reprovingly. "Stop it. You're here representing the Edwards family. Yes, Evan's the tall one. As soon as they start wandering among the auction tables, we'll move into their vicinity and I'll introduce you."

"Then I can leave?"

"You can't leave until after dinner," Deanna hissed. "How would that look?"

"Like I had a real emergency. Emergencies don't wait until after dinner."

"Don't you want to see how the Indians do?"

"You can tell me tomorrow."

"Connie Tarwater at three o'clock," Georgia warned her in a low voice. "Quit drooling, darlin', people will notice."

Deanna felt the heat radiate up her neck. She had been staring toward Evan the entire time she'd been talking to Andrew. She fixed a polite smile on her face before she turned to greet Connie, knowing Georgia's warning had more to do with Connie's date than Connie herself. She'd already been warned through the grapevine that Connie had invited Phil to escort her to the auction. He'd come to be seen and, Deanna was fairly certain, to make sure Deanna saw him escorting Connie. If he expected her to be jealous, he was in for a disappointment.

"This has got to be the best auction we've ever done," Connie gushed to Deanna and Georgia. "It's going to be difficult to top this next year."

"I'm sure we'll think of something," Deanna said confidently. "What a beautiful gown." It was a dark blue fifties recreation with a satin bodice and a sequined net overskirt. Connie swelled with pleasure at the compliment.

"Why, thank you, Deanna. I was about to say the same. I've never seen you in red. You should wear it more often."

"I may do that," Deanna said demurely. "Hello, Phil."

"Hello, Deanna." Phil didn't look pleased as he took in Deanna's costume. He greeted the others perfunctorily before he turned back to Deanna. "May I speak with you in private?"

Deanna exchanged looks with Georgia, knowing what was coming. "If Connie and Andrew don't mind," she told Phil. Connie didn't look pleased, but she assented. Andrew was already talking with someone else. "Excuse us just a minute," Deanna said to the others, then walked with Phil to an area where they wouldn't be overheard.

"When did you start wearing red?" Phil demanded, keeping his voice low.

"You told me yourself that I looked good in red, that I should wear more of it," Deanna said, feigning innocence.

"I'm surprised you're wearing the rubies. You seem to be intent on getting rid of the gifts I gave you."

Deanna answered his snide comment with a cool look. "I like rubies. They go very well with the dress, don't you think?"

"Are those or are those not your fur coats hanging over there among the auction items?" Phil seemed to be having trouble remembering to keep his voice down.

Deanna glanced around them. Her eyes locked with Evan's. He watched them from several yards away, his expression as dark as Phil's. Deanna sent him a reassuring smile and a wave, then turned back to Phil. "They are. They'll bring more money here than if I tried to sell them outright, the donation is tax deductible, and it's for a worthy cause. Add that to the fact that they're costly to maintain, I never wanted them in the first place, and only wore them to please you, and I couldn't see any reason not to donate them."

"I suppose it doesn't matter to you that Lucille Hartwell plans to have the fox remade into a lap rug for that ridiculous antique car they drive all over the country."

Deanna remembered Lucille and Larry Hartwell's restored Hanson, a 1920s vintage roadster that had been built in Atlanta for a limited time. The Hartwells were a retired couple who enjoyed entering car shows and cross-country races, driving the antique automobile dressed in costumes worn in the car's heyday.

"I think a lap rug is a wonderful idea," Deanna said. "Who else likes those old cars? I'll suggest that to them and see if I can get some competition going."

"I don't understand you anymore, Deanna," Phil said, clearly irritated. He turned on his heel and walked away. Deanna smiled. Phil had never understood her, and that had been only one of their many problems. He had just never realized it before now.

"Is that the man's normal demeanor or just the way he is around you?"

Deanna looked up into teasing hazel eyes that melted her heart and made her long to throw herself into Evan's arms. "I think it's me," she answered, her eyes devouring every detail of his face. It had been a month since she'd last seen him. It had been a lifetime. She wasn't going to lose him this time.

She offered her hand. "I'm glad you're here."

Evan took it. "Me, too."

"I want you to meet someone," they said simultaneously, pulling each other in opposite directions, then they laughed.

"Come meet Andrew, then we'll both come meet your friends," Deanna suggested. She felt his arm stiffen as she took it, and smiled to herself. "My brother Andrew has been doing research on Indian collecting, ever since he found out I was restoring Dad's. He's anxious to meet you."

She felt him relax a little at the word "brother." "Won't your date mind?" he asked pointedly.

"Mine won't if yours won't," Deanna said coyly.

Evan glowered at her. "I broke with protocol and came stag."

"Well, as you so painstakingly pointed out to me some time ago, women do not attend these affairs without an escort, even if it's a twenty-year-old first-degree relative. Andrew's fifty-eight, but he was the closest thing I could find on short notice."

Evan grinned at her, his totally devastating, hungry wolf grin that made her pulse beat faster and her whole body go on alert. "Have I told you how incredibly handsome you are in a tuxedo?"

His smile got even warmer. "I'm glad you noticed. I don't wear these monkey suits for just anyone."

Deanna laughed and took his arm, nudging him toward Andrew. He wasn't going to be obvious and tell her she looked gorgeous. He was going to tease her and torment her and make her pay for walking out on him a month ago. She didn't care. He was here and she was here and tonight after the auction she would explain it all to him.

Andrew found her before she could find him. He looked distraught, ignoring Evan. "I just checked in with Delores. I need to get home."

"Is she okay?" Deanna asked, instantly upset.

"She's fine. One of my contractors called. There's a huge sink hole threatening our entire apartment complex. I need to get out there."

He'd been such a convincing actor, Deanna had forgotten about his contrived excuse to leave early. She couldn't believe he couldn't come up with a more original crisis than a sink hole. Not only that, he was supposed to have waited until after dinner.

"Surely your contractors can handle a sink hole," Deanna said, not wanting to make it easy on him after he'd scared her, making her think Delores was hurt. "What are they going to do in the dark."

"I've authorized spotlights, night crews. I'm sorry, Deanna. I know this auction is your big moment, but I really need to be there personally."

"I'd be glad to take over as Deanna's escort," Evan interjected smoothly. Too smoothly. Deanna shot him a quick glance, wondering if Andrew's story was so far-fetched even Evan wasn't believing it. He was watching her, his hazel eyes bright.

"Evan Maxwell," he said, turning back to Andrew and extending his hand. "I rebuilt the Indian. I'll be glad to see Deanna home as well. I understand about business disasters."

"I'll bet you do," Andrew said, mischief playing around the edge of his smile. He glanced at Deanna, then struggled to get it back in control. She let him see she wasn't pleased with his performance. "Uh, right, yeah, what do you think, Deanna? Would that be acceptable to you?"

She was tempted to tell him no, that it

wasn't all right with her, just to make him squirm, but he'd been a real sport about bringing her tonight. He hated big society functions. "I think we're asking a great deal of Mr. Maxwell," she said. "He came with guests."

"Trust me, they won't mind," Evan assured them. "They both brought their wives and I was feeling sort of like a fifth wheel in the middle of them. It's my pleasure."

"Great. Thanks a lot. I'll run then." He was backing away as he spoke. "Deanna, I'll call you tomorrow. Evan, I hope we meet again."

Evan looked down at Deanna. "It's looking that way. Is there really a sink hole threatening his entire apartment complex?"

"He's a building contractor. Sink holes are a well-known risk of the trade."

He waited, a smile teasing the corners of his mouth.

"He is pouring the foundations. I can understand why he'd want to get right out there."

"Maybe we should drive by on our way home, make sure everything's okay."

"It's way out of our way."

"Uh-huh. Why didn't you just call, invite me yourself?"

Deanna looked down at her hands, twisting

her ring around on her finger. "If you'd said 'no', I couldn't have come tonight. It wouldn't have been fair to have asked someone to take my place at the last minute."

"I've never told you 'no'," Evan said softly. "You're the one who's always telling me 'no'."

"This is my life, Evan. This is what I do, like you sell motorcycles."

"I bought the tux, Deanna."

The significance of his words penetrated slowly, like the warmth of the sun on a winter-dormant earth, like the warmth of his gaze on her love-dormant heart.

Georgia cleared her throat behind them, her intent clear. "You're drawing a crowd, young lovers," she warned in a low voice. "I thought that gazing into each other's eyes mush was only in romance novels."

"I need to go back through the items before dinner," Deanna said to Evan, feeling her face burning from Georgia's warning.

"I'll find my friends and explain about the . . . uh . . . sink hole." He grinned at her as he left.

"There's been another sink hole?"

"Only over Andrew's mind," Deanna said, watching Evan.

Over the next two hours, Deanna lost count of how many times she introduced Evan. He'd wanted introduced into her life, he got it to-night in spades. He fit in easily, talking with the men, charming the women, but, most of all, charming Deanna.

Evan sat with Deanna at her table, along with the director of the hospital and Billy Adonis. Billy was impressed with Evan's knowledge of antique motorcycles. Before the night was over, Evan had been invited out to his estate to see Billy's collection. The director was more interested in Evan's military career, having served some time in the army.

"Your brother Pete told me about a friend of his who has a '41 police force Indian," Billy told Deanna while Evan talked to the director. "He didn't know about the throttle, but Evan says it's not that hard to change them over. If I can talk the dude out of it, Evan's promised to go through it for me."

Deanna smiled, pleased for Billy, thinking he was still more kid than adult. Maybe that wasn't all bad.

"It was hard enough riding the Indian with the front brake where I was used to the clutch being," Deanna said. "I can't imagine getting used to a left-handed throttle." It was strange, she mused. When Billy had told her about a left-handed throttle, she hadn't known what he was talking about. Now, she was discussing switching motorcycles and the hazards that incurred from first-hand experience.

"At least the brake lever would be back on the right, where you're used to it," Billy said.

Their dinner was served, prime rib with the perfect amount of pink in the center, parsleyed potatoes, and steamed vegetables that still retained their bright color. The caterers had done a superb job with the dinner, which Deanna had expected. They were serving some of the most powerful money in Atlanta tonight, and the caterers were hoping their donations would catch the attention of future customers. Deanna only wished she could settle down and enjoy her food.

Pride in Evan swelled her heart. Contrition at her lack of faith in him twisted her stomach. Anticipation of their later reconciliation made for a distracting moistness of private places that wouldn't let her sit still. It didn't help that beneath her extravagant gown she wore a lacy red bustier and garter belt, bought specifically with sexy red heels and a sleepless night in mind.

"Would you like to dance?" Evan asked her.

Would you like to cause a scandal and carry me out of here? she thought, smiling into his eyes as she took his hand. She flowed into his arms and followed his lead, breathing in the wonderful scent of him, feeling the heat from his body as it brushed against her own. The band played "Moon River" with all the emotion Audrey Hepburn had first put into it.

Deanna had been dancing at social events since she was sixteen. There should be another word for moving in time to music with Evan Maxwell. Like soul flying with him on the motorcycle, dancing with him was almost a spiritual experience, transformed out of the realm of human, earthly, or ordinary. By the end of the second number, Deanna had forgotten where they were, closing her eyes and letting the music and the feel of Evan's body transport her. She was rudely returned to earth by her brother Pete.

"This must be Evan," Pete interrupted them when the song ended. "Pete Edwards, Deanna's brother. This is my wife Nancy."

"Evan Maxwell," Evan said, his left arm encircling Deanna as he shook hands.

"I'd like to dance with my sister, Maxwell," Pete said.

Deanna smiled at Evan. "It's a ritual. We've been doing this since I was sixteen. Do you mind?"

"You don't have to dance with the pregnant lady," Nancy assured him with a laugh. "We'll go find some fruit juice and talk."

"You look gorgeous tonight, baby sister," Pete said, moving her out onto the dance floor. "I like you in red."

He complimented her work on the auction, the decor, the food, the quality and quantity of donations. Just before the song ended, he got to the subject most on his mind.

"I like seeing you happy, Deanna. I know the last year's been bad, and there wasn't much we could do except berate Phil's behavior. Just be careful. You're a wealthy divorced woman, and there are unscrupulous men out there."

"Evan's not one of them," Deanna assured him.

"I could have him checked out for you, just to be sure."

Deanna smiled. "I already have, before I ever met him, before I asked him to restore Dad's Indian."

Pete smiled down at her. "I should have known you would. You'll have to forgive me for doubting you. It's my right as your brother and your financial manager to worry."

"That's what brothers and financial managers are for," Deanna said, giving him a quick hug as the music ended. "Thanks, Pete."

Her smile faded as she looked up and saw Phil waiting for her. "May I have a dance, as friends?" he said, emphasizing "friends" when Deanna started to refuse. How could she say no, when she'd expressed a desire to remain his friend, when she'd told him she had no desire to remarry him.

"Your mechanic friend is dancing with Connie," Phil said, when Deanna looked around for Evan. Sure enough, she found Evan and Connie not too far away, Evan's expression cold as he watched Deanna and Phil from over Connie's shoulder.

"I thought you said as friends, Phil," Deanna stressed, keeping a platonic distance between them as he positioned his arms around her. "Maligning my other friends is hardly an act of friendship."

"I'm not alone. Most of your friends, your peers, are laughing at you, the way you're making calf eyes over a mechanic."

Deanna broke away from him, vexed beyond caring who noticed. "He's my guest, Phil. That alone should be enough, if people really are my friends. Evan Maxwell is a businessman, with a social pedigree that probably rivals yours. He donated his labor to this cause just as you did, but unlike you he sees Sara as a person, a life worth saving, not a research specimen to further his career."

"I can make life very unpleasant for you, Deanna, at the hospital, at the country club, in your social life, even with the children. At least date someone of your own class."

"Like you, Phil? You can spread rumors and drag my name through the mud, but you will come out sounding like a vindictive, jilted lover, and people will pity you."

They stood at the edge of the dance floor, glaring at each other like a pair of tom cats, each tensed and waiting for the other to make the next aggressive move. Georgia, more the diplomat even than Deanna, stepped between them.

"Deanna, isn't it time to issue the ten minute warning?"

"Yes, of course. I got sidetracked." She sent Phil a last parting glare. Her knees were shaking as she mounted the steps of the platform and took the podium. She took several calming breaths before she spoke.

"Ladies and Gentlemen, I want to thank you for coming out tonight and giving Children's Hospital your generous support. We'd like to give you ten more minutes to make your final bids on the items of your choice. When the bell rings, that will conclude the bidding and we'll begin the entertainment portion of our program."

She walked back down the steps, determined to do her job and not let Phil get her riled. She'd dealt with worse things than an ex-husband over the years, from caterers who changed her menu at the last minute to irate contributors whose name had been inadvertently left off the program. Unfortunately, Phil's attack was of a more personal nature and therefore more difficult to shrug off.

"I thought there was a leash law in this town," Evan said, low and near her ear as they walked back among the displays.

She looked at him, puzzled at first. There was concern in his eyes, but mischief as well. He was referring to Phil.

"Not when they're heart surgeons," she said, in an equally low voice, but the image of Phil on a leash made her smile.

"I'm sure he's not accustomed to making mistakes."

Deanna wasn't following him.

"As a heart surgeon," Evan explained, "he probably has two options when he's made a mistake. He can go back in or he can lose the patient. In your case, he didn't get back in soon enough, and he lost the patient, or the wife, as the case may be."

Deanna laughed. "I'll have to share that with Georgia. She loves metaphors."

His gaze was appreciative as he looked at her. "Have I told you tonight how beautiful you are?"

Deanna felt suddenly shy, but a warm glow formed in her breast from his words. "No, you haven't. I thought maybe you didn't like red."

"Wait until I get you home. I'll show you how much I like red," he promised, his voice low and husky, tickling her ear.

The bell rang, signalling the end of the bidding. The guests all returned to their tables, the director gave his speech and showed his video on the improvements and future plans for the hospital, a demonstration of their donations at work for the children. For entertainment, several local singing groups from the fifties had been located and enticed into performing. There was also a impersonation group that carried the bulk of the show, making the guests laugh with their renditions of Elvis and Buddy Holly, among others of that time frame. Deanna calmed down, a smug sense of satisfaction taking over. Her committee members were right. It was going to be hard to top this year's auction next year.

A local sportscaster named Gordon Forsyth had volunteered his services as auctioneer. The three individual items were auctioned between sets from the entertainers. Deanna's New England tour was auctioned first, bringing in $21,500.

Even Billy had agreed that Deanna's Indian

was worth more than his, which put his ahead of hers in the bidding. Deanna held her breath, knowing she had a guaranteed bid of $20,000 for it, but silently urging the bidding to go higher. Three bidders were still actively upping the bid at $25,000. One dropped out at $28,000. The other two bid back and forth, the pace slowing considerably as the price edged toward $30,000. Deanna noticed one of Evan's collector friends was still in the running, the other man unknown to her. She glanced at Billy, who was watching the proceedings avidly, a big grin on his face. At $31,300, the final bid stood unchallenged. Billy, undaunted by social protocol, jumped to his feet with a shout of triumph. The crowd laughed with him and applauded the winning bidder.

The room seemed unbearably hot to Deanna during the last set, a trio of pseudo-Lennon sisters. She had already grown warm during the bidding over Billy's Indian, wiping her palms on her napkin and drinking ice water. She could barely sit still now, waiting for the bidding to begin on her father's cherished motorcycle. It didn't gleam in the lights from the chandeliers the way Billy's did, but it glowed with a pride all its own, its heritage intact with the patina of age.

"I'm glad Patrick got the '55," Evan said,

when Gordon retook the podium. "Benny wants your father's bad enough to mortgage the house."

"That's good, right?" Deanna asked.

"Benny's wife may not think so."

The bidding started at $20,000. Deanna noticed Pete stayed in the competition until the figure hit $30,000. She wasn't sure if his intention was to buy it or to just make sure it went for the highest possible amount.

"This is a one-of-a-kind antique, ladies and gentlemen," Gordon interjected, when the bidding slowed at $36,500. "Completely original parts, except for the tires and battery. The engine's been overhauled and she's ready to ride. Do I hear thirty-seven?"

He heard thirty-seven, then thirty-seven-five, then after a pause, thirty-seven-seven. "Now I heard a story," Gordon said to the crowd, "that Mrs. Deanna Randolph has been caught riding her father's antique Indian Chief through her neighborhood, scandalously dressed in boots, jeans, and a black leather jacket that says North Georgia HOGs on the back."

Deanna felt her face flush crimson. She closed her eyes and covered her face with her hands, hearing the laughter swell around her. Gordon Forsyth just happened to be a friend of Andrew's. She was going to kill her brother.

"Now, if you're holding back because you aren't sure you can ride one of these side-shifters, I'm sure Mrs. Randolph would be glad to instruct you. How about thirty-eight?"

Evan's friend nodded at thirty-eight. Gordon coaxed the bidding higher, using hundred dollar increments when five hundred dollars got no response. Slowly, the amount went over thirty-nine.

Go for forty, go for forty, Deanna silently urged. Her fists were clenched, her entire body rigid. Three bidders remained, continuing to up each other by one hundred dollars, the pace slowing further, the tension in the crowd a palpable force.

"Forty thousand," said Bennie, standing up, not waiting for Gordon to suggest it, throwing aside social protocol.

"Forty thousand one hundred," said his competitor, also standing.

The crowd and Gordon looked to the third competitor expectantly. He shook his head regretfully.

"Okay, gentleman, do I hear forty thousand five hundred?" Gordon asked.

Apparently smelling the blood of victory, Bennie agreed. The other man faltered.

"Forty thousand five hundred going once,"

Gordon paused dramatically, watching the other man, "going twice,"

"Forty-one," the man said. The crowd groaned. Deanna felt light-headed.

"Forty-two," Bennie said softly.

"He's got it," Evan whispered, on the edge of his own seat.

"Forty-two thousand, for one 1953 antique Indian Chief motorcycle, going once, going twice, *sold!*" The gavel fell and the crowd erupted in shouts and applause. Evan grabbed Deanna out of her chair and whirled her around, then went to congratulate his friend. Then Billy grabbed her in an exuberant hug. Even the director of the hospital shook her hand, his grin almost as wide as Billy's.

"What a great auction this year, Mrs. Randolph. I've never seen anything like it. They'll be talking about this for years." He turned to shake other people's hands.

Deanna made her way to the podium, shook Gordon's hand and fussed at him for telling tales on her, then thanked him again for his contribution to a successful auction. She tried repeatedly to get the crowd's attention, to no avail. Gordon came back and gave a shrill whistle through the microphone. Silence fell immediately.

"Thank you, Gordon. I just want to say on

behalf of Atlanta's Children's Hospital, thank you all for our most successful auction ever. There's a chart in the corner over there with the names of the highest bidders for each item and the amount of their bids. There will be cashiers at the door. Goodnight, and we'll see everyone next year."

The crowd moved slowly, as people claimed their prizes and the cleaning crew began to collect dishes and glasses from the tables. Deanna stood by her father's Indian, now belonging to a collector named Bennie, for an unprecedented sum of forty-two thousand dollars. Still, a sadness wrenched at her heart over the loss, both of the motorcycle and of her father. It had been three years, and still she missed him. She imagined she always would.

"Dad would be proud of you, sis," Pete said, wrapping his arm around her. He stood there with her, just looking at the motorcycle and remembering.

"This is all his fault," Deanna said, feeling tears tightening her throat. "Because of him telling me I couldn't ride it because I was a girl."

"It could have changed the course of history," Pete said. "You might have killed yourself and had a playroom in the hospital donated in your memory instead."

Deanna smiled at his teasing. "If I can handle that beast now, I could have handled it when I was fourteen."

"I don't know, you were a pretty scrawny fourteen-year-old."

Deanna looked over at Billy's Indian, its bright chrome reflecting the light off a hundred chandeliers. "But he didn't let me ride it," Deanna said thoughtfully, "and forty years later look what comes of it— I meet Evan, Sara Harris has a chance at life— "

"And you've just pulled off the most successful auction in hospital history," Pete finished up. "I won't even ask which one of those events carries the most significance."

Deanna turned to see what he was watching. Evan walked toward them through the crowd, his arms around each of his exuberant friends. Deanna smiled. No, it wouldn't be wise to try to prioritize the events of the last four months. It was enough that they'd all come about. The auction was over. She and Evan had just begun. Now, all that remained was to find a donor heart for baby Sara.

Twenty-two

"So," Deanna said, languidly trailing her manicured nails down the length of Evan's bare chest, "tell me about this tuxedo you bought." She was still wearing her rings, the ruby and diamond bracelet that matched the necklace, even the earrings. Her red nail polish gleamed like the rubies as she burrowed through the hair between his nipples, then made teasing circles around the nipples themselves.

"Quit that," Evan instructed, flattening her hand against him with his own, "unless you're ready for round two already."

"I want to hear about the tuxedo first."

"You mean the one I paid six hundred eighty-five dollars and ninety-eight cents for, that is presently scattered all over your house like some massacred scarecrow? That tuxedo?"

Deanna only smiled, remembering how it had come to be scattered all over her house. Actually, the pieces were probably in a pretty direct line from the front door to her bedroom. "That's the one."

His eyes grew serious as he looked at her. "I kept remembering the way you kissed me the day of the benefit. That wasn't the kiss of a lover saying goodbye. That was the kiss of a woman in love and afraid of the consequences. Several years ago, I would have accepted your words of farewell at face value, but I've become something of a risk-taker in my old age." He raised up to claim her mouth in a long kiss. "I decided you were worth the risk. You must have decided the same about me, or do you habitually wear lacy red garters under your fancy ball gowns?" He ran his hand slowly up the inside of her thigh.

"I'm not a risk-taker," Deanna demurred, amazed that her body was capable of responding to him again. "Panty hose aren't healthy."

"I'm so glad to hear that." Evan's hand moved to the other thigh. "What about spike heels?"

"Gloria said you'd like them." He was nibbling her neck, sending shivers through her.

"I disagree."

"You didn't like them?" He'd kissed the instep of her foot when he'd removed them, then peeled the stockings off, kissing and nibbling his way from the tops of her thighs back to the soles of her feet. Just remembering made her insides clench.

"I disagree that you're not a risk-taker." He slid down further in the bed, where he could run his tongue through the valley between her breasts. "Is that necessary?" He frowned at the large ruby dangling at the end of her necklace. It blocked his path.

Deanna reached behind her neck and unclasped the necklace, laying it on the bedside table. "Besides wearing come-fuck-me red pumps to the most important social fund-raiser of my career, what other risks have I taken?"

He raised his head, his hazel eyes bright, his grin spreading wickedly over his face. "Is that what those are? Mrs. Randolph, I'm shocked."

"That's what Gloria called them," Deanna said, reveling in the wanton woman Evan brought out in her. She ran her tongue around the edge of his ear, nipping his earlobe with her teeth.

He groaned in response, then took her nipple full into his mouth and pulled. Desire shafted through Deanna, straight to her core. "Evan, I'm trying to talk to you."

"You have my undivided attention," he said, giving equal time to her other breast. She moved beneath him, feeling the need building again. He was already hard as she reached for

him with her hands. They could talk later, if
either of them had any strength left.

Gloria was in Buford for the weekend, leaving
them with the house to themselves. The sun
had risen long before Evan and Deanna, and
now shone brightly through the kitchen windows while they worked together fixing omelets. He used a cleaver to chop vegetables while
Deanna used a whisk on the eggs. She was elegantly dressed in a black peignoir with matching scuffs on her feet. He was bare-chested and
barefooted, wearing the pants to his tuxedo.

"Why don't you think you're a risk-taker?"
Evan asked her, continuing the conversation
they had abandoned the night before.

"I always have to research everything before
I make a decision," Deanna said.

"It sounds like your decision to restore your
father's Indian was pretty spur of the moment."

"Maybe, but then I spent two days on the
phone talking to Indian collectors and restorers before I came to you, and I had three references on you."

Evan raised an eyebrow at that revelation.
"I'm impressed. Did you also get three references prior to sleeping with me?"

"Don't be crude, of course not. However, I

do remember sitting by a river and discussing the pros and cons at length. That's hardly a decision made in the heat of passion."

"You still took a risk."

Deanna thought about it, then shrugged. "I took a risk getting married. I took a risk having children. As you've mentioned before, life is full of risks. I just tend to stay close to the wall."

"I don't think inviting Gloria into your home and taking on Sara's heart transplant is staying close to the wall," Evan said quietly, laying the cleaver down. "Having your picture taken with me last night for publication in your society magazines wasn't either. Shall we talk about riding thirty thousand dollar antique motorcycles? How about buying a Harley Sportster ten minutes after you'd laid eyes on it?"

Deanna smiled, setting her bowl of beaten eggs down. "You make me sound totally irresponsible."

He came over to wrap his arms around her. She laid her hands against his bare chest, breathing in the masculine scent of him, feeling his heat through her palms. She couldn't seem to get enough of this man.

"You are not irresponsible," he told her, kissing her lightly on her upturned mouth. "What you are is passionate." He kissed her again, taking his time.

"What I am is hungry," Deanna said, pushing him away, "for food. Even a motorcycle has to stop occasionally for fuel."

"Brief stops," Evan said, lunging in for one last kiss. "They get excellent gas mileage."

Deanna ducked him as she reached down to get the omelet pan out of the cabinet beneath the stove. "Did you chop the bell pepper yet?"

"Yes, and the green onions, and the mushrooms. Would you like me to cook the omelets also?"

"No, I want you to grate the cheese and quit acting so mistreated. I'm not a motorcycle."

"I noticed that right off." He slid his hand over her bottom before she could move away. "Even if you do have a soft tail."

"Is that so? Then what are you?"

He leered at her. "I'm an Electra Glide, Road King. You can ride me for hours without stopping."

"I think we've already proven that." Deanna poured the beaten eggs into the hot pan, then smiled at his pout of rejection. She wrapped her arms around his waist, laying her head against his bare chest. "Ah, Evan, what are we going to do?"

"Start with not burning my breakfast." He reached around her to test the edge of the omelet with the spatula. Satisfied with its progress, he sprinkled the vegetables over it, then pulled Deanna back against him. "Then, you could tell me you loved me."

Deanna studied his face. His tone was light and teasing, but his eyes searched hers for answers. "I thought I did," she said, cocking her head to one side.

"When?"

"When I asked you to stand with me in the pictures last night." It had been her way of telling him and anyone who knew her that Evan Maxwell was part of her life, more than just a friend who was kind enough to fill in for Andrew. They held each other's gaze a long time, until Deanna smelled burning egg.

"It's fine," Evan judged, when she jerked the pan off the heat, "just a little crisp around the edge." He sprinkled the cheese over it, then folded it in half and set it back on the burner, turning the fire off.

"Now," he repositioned her back in his arms, "you were saying?"

Deanna smiled. "I love you, Evan Maxwell. I just don't know what to do with you now that I've seduced you back into my life."

"Isn't that enough?"

"Is it?"

"Hmmm." Evan released her, his expression thoughtful as he divided the omelet onto two plates. Deanna poured orange juice into glasses and set them on the little table in the breakfast nook. Neither spoke again until they were seated. Evan chewed a bite of omelet carefully, watching Deanna.

"You're a passable cook," he decided, cutting off another bite with the side of his fork. "I suppose I could offer to marry you, but we'd have to let Brian have the house."

Deanna put down her fork and stared at him. "Evan Maxwell, is that the best you can do for a marriage proposal?"

He examined the piece of omelet he'd been about to put in his mouth, then looked at her. "I guess so, when I expect to be turned down flat." He ate the bite he'd been studying.

"Why do you think I'll turn you down?"

He watched her skeptically. "Will you?"

"Will I what?"

"Will you turn me down?"

Deanna shook her head, confused with the twisted question. "Yes . . . . I think"

He grinned. "I knew if I worded it right, I'd get a yes out of you."

She frowned. "Does that mean your proposal wasn't serious?"

He reached across the table and took her hand. "The proposal's serious and stands as an open option from this day forward. If that's what you want, we'll find a way to make it work out to both of our satisfactions. I didn't think that was what you wanted right now."

"No," Deanna agreed, "I'm not ready for marriage, but I'm not sure what our options are."

He leered at her again. "Want to live together in sin?"

She slapped the top of his hand, then picked up her fork to eat her breakfast before it got cold. "No, I don't want to live together in sin. I don't know where we'd live anyway. My work is here, yours is in Buford."

"We could find a house in Norcross."

Norcross was just outside the Atlanta perimeter, roughly halfway between Buckhead and Buford. "I don't want to live in Norcross. I like it here. And you like Buford," she answered for him, when he didn't. "Your dealership is there, your garage full of tools, and your family."

He sighed, his expression wistful. "That's the real problem. I enticed Brian to come live with me on the promise that I'd help him raise Kyle. I never thought after fifteen years of bachelorhood I'd ever want to marry again, or even be someone's exclusive."

"Oh, I definitely expect to be your exclusive," Deanna assured him. "Can't we do it with separate households?"

"What do you want to do about Kyle?"

Deanna wasn't wearing her pearls. She toyed with the string tie at the neck of her peignoir instead. "You see what I mean? It gets complicated."

"Only if you let it. Kyle enjoys being around you, and except for Joey's mother, he doesn't have too many important women in his life."

"And if I let myself become important in his life, and we decide to go our separate ways someday? What does that do to Kyle?"

"Kyle lost his mother, he's been moved away from his grandmother. He understands more than most older children that life doesn't come with guarantees, that the present must be enjoyed while we have it. Some kids would be bitter or distrustful of relationships, but we're trying hard not to let that happen with Kyle. Just don't make promises to him you don't intend to keep."

It was a warning, and Deanna understood it. "I won't," she promised. "Let's just let things progress naturally, one day at a time."

"Okay," Evan agreed, putting the last bite of his omelet in his mouth. He eyed hers. "Aren't you going to eat any more of that?"

Deanna smiled as she passed him her plate. "I guess Road Kings need more fuel than softails."

He stopped eating, his gaze roaming ove
her with heated, predatory assessment, a slo
smile forming on his mouth. "I guess it a
depends on who's driving."

Deanna felt her own smile, her body re
sponding again to the promise in his eyes
They were refueled, and there was still s
much unexplored territory between them
Holding his heated gaze with her own, sh
rose from her chair, then sank to her knee
in front of his spread thighs. "I'll drive," sh
offered, then reached for the waistband of hi
pants.

Spring exploded across the south in a rio
of color and soft, warm days. Deanna cam
down with a case of motorcycle fever so bad
it threatened to supplant her weekly bridg
game with the girls. Evan finally suggeste
they take the motorcycles on a long weekend
excursion through the North Georgia moun
tains. Deanna had never been camping before
but she was delirious enough to do anything
that involved Evan and the motorcycles.

Evan came over the morning of their trip and
handed her a pair of saddlebags. "Nothing goes
that won't fit inside here," he informed her

'and nothing breakable. I recommend one set of clothes, extra underwear, and a toothbrush."

"For three days?" Deanna asked, incredulous, looking inside the bags. She had bigger purses.

"This is a motorcycle trip, not a motor home trip. We'll use bungie cords to attach the sleeping bag to the passenger seat. You could put some clothes inside the sleeping bag; but you might want a pillow."

He went back out to his pickup to get the sleeping bag while Deanna laid out everything she wanted to take. Just her toiletries filled the saddlebags, and she still had a bed covered with other things she wanted to take.

Evan came back in with the sleeping bag and unrolled it across her bedroom floor. He looked at her assortment of bottles, compacts and tubes, then back at Deanna, his expression thoughtful. "You want to be warm or you want to be beautiful?" he finally asked.

"Those are the bare essentials," Deanna assured him. "The hair dryer wouldn't fit or the curling iron. I was fortunate I had a purse-sized hair spray."

Evan seemed to weigh his words carefully before he spoke. "I don't know what women consider essential, but I've seen you in the mornings, without all that makeup, and didn't run screaming."

"I doubt you had the energy left," Deanna said, quirking her eyebrows suggestively.

Evan smiled. "I'll concede to that point, but the fact remains, you don't have room for all that stuff, and, in my opinion, you don't need it. Chuck the whole kit and caboodle for a good sunscreen with moisturizer."

He dumped the contents of the saddlebag out onto her bed. "This is good," he said, picking up a plastic tube of sunscreen. "You can take this, this, and this." He added her toothbrush, toothpaste and a deodorant stick. "Soap might be useful." He put that in. "Got a couple of washcloths and a towel?"

Deanna stood watching him in silent amazement as he took it upon himself to tell her what she needed for a three-day trip. "Any particular color?" she asked sarcastically.

He looked at her, picking up on her displeasure. "I wouldn't recommend white," he said, almost apologetically.

Deanna flounced out of the bedroom, letting her irritation show. She brought him back two washcloths and a towel— thick, pink, fluffy ones. He regarded them as if she'd handed him a loaded gun.

"Deanna, I know you resent me telling you

how to pack, but let me present this a better way. When you decided to restore your father's Indian, did it ever cross your mind to try to do the work yourself?"

Deanna understood his point, but it only increased her vexation. She didn't like doing things where she was so clearly the novice and he the expert. It seemed their entire relationship had been structured that way— restoring the Indian, riding the Harley, even making love. Just once, she'd like to teach him a thing or two.

As if reading her mind, he asked. "Didn't I defer to your expertise on organizing the benefit for Sara?"

Yes, he had, and very graciously, too. "I still have an empty saddlebag," she conceded, though not very graciously.

He sighed, warning her she wasn't going to like what he said next. "I recommend you put a rain suit in there."

Deanna just stared at him, images too horrible to articulate forming in her mind.

"It is April," Evan reminded her. "It rains a lot in the mountains, especially in the spring. Wet clothes are very cold." He winced at the expression on Deanna's face. "Maybe this trip isn't such a good idea. How about this? We take the pickup, pull the bikes on the trailer, stay in a hotel in Helen or Dahlonega and just ride the bikes during the day when it's pretty."

Deanna sighed. "Why don't you just call me a wimpy princess and be done with it?" She was more aggravated with herself than with Evan. She wanted to ride the motorcycle, but she was whining about the lack of amenities. "A rain suit is a good idea." She hadn't paid much attention to that chapter in her handbook, never imagined herself riding in the rain. She made a mental note to read through it again before they left. "Anything else?"

He helped her arrange her change of clothes inside the sleeping bag, along with the towel and a very small pillow. They would pick up a set of rain gear at the dealership before they left. "You're set," Evan announced, picking up the saddlebags with one hand and the sleeping bag with the other.

Deanna scanned the articles still scattered over her bed wistfully. She had grave misgivings about surviving on what little Evan had allowed her to pack. "What about food and water?" she asked, following him out the front door.

Evan's eyes sparkled with amusement as he looked back at her. "We're not going out in the wilderness. There's restaurants all over the place."

Great. He wouldn't let her bring makeup or

hairspray, but they were going to eat in restaurants all over the place. Evan put down his load and came back to take her in his arms. He placed a comforting kiss on her downturned mouth.

"It's going to be fun. Trust me. It's spring, and the place will be swarming with bikers. You'll fit right in."

She raised her eyes to search his. She didn't want to be with other bikers. "I thought this trip was so we could be alone together."

He smiled, his eyes taking on a carnal gleam. "Oh, we'll be alone as much as you'd like. We can buy groceries and have dinner over a campfire." His voice dropped lower, becoming husky and sensuous. "You can lie naked in your sleeping bag, and I'll feed you brie cheese and sip wine from between your beautiful breasts." He kissed her again, his hands slowly caressing the sides of her breasts through her clothes, making her ache. Her hands sought the contours of his back, urging him closer.

He pulled away reluctantly. "If we don't quit, we aren't going to even leave before noon."

She rubbed her body against his, reveling in his aroused state. "Do we have a plane to catch or something?"

He searched her face, his eyes hot and hungry. "You are the damnedest woman I ever met. Don't you ever get enough?"

"Not of you," she said, returning his salacious gaze with a provocative smile. "Is that a problem?"

He groaned as if in deep pain, then picked her up, wrapping her legs around his waist, and holding her bottom with his hands. "Oh, no," he said, burying his mouth against her neck and working his way back to her mouth. "No problem at all."

They decided to eat lunch at Deanna's, since it was already 11:30 and they still weren't on the road. Deanna had insisted on putting her bedroom back in order, it looking something like the aftermath of a hurricane after their earlier frenzy to clear the bed of the items not packed for their trip. The only shadow over this trip was leaving Gloria and Sara for so long.

"I wish we'd thought about getting one of those cellular phones," Deanna lamented. The one in her car was permanently installed. "I wonder if someone would loan us one."

"We'll be fine," Gloria assured her again. "You'd never hear a phone ring, and where would you carry it?"

Gloria had come out to inspect Deanna's

bike after Evan had installed the saddlebags and strapped on the sleeping bag. She had a point. "You have the number to the lodge?"

Gloria rolled her eyes. "I have the number to the lodge, to the dealership, to Brian's house, to the highway patrol. Even if we get the call that they've found Sara a heart, which is a long shot, there's nothin' you could do."

"I want to be there," Deanna insisted. "Don't put yourself through this alone, Gloria. You have friends now— Georgia, Becky, Delores. Any one of them would come in a heartbeat if you called them."

Gloria smiled. "I know. I still have trouble understandin' it, but I know."

Deanna gave her a quick hug, then hugged Sara and gave her a kiss before she handed the baby back to Gloria. "I'll check in with you tonight," she promised, climbing into the pickup beside Evan.

"If we ever get out of Atlanta," Evan said, his tone pessimistic. They were going to take her bike out to his house on the trailer, then pick up his. They still had to go by the dealership to get her rain gear.

"Just have fun," Gloria advised, waving as they pulled out of the driveway.

"We might as well eat dinner in Buford," Evan commented, frowning at his watch as they finally climbed on the bikes in front of the dealership, an hour and a half later.

"What a grouch," Deanna teased him, checking her packs one last time. She pulled her helmet on, donned her gloves, and turned the key. She looked over at Evan, excitement coursing through her in spite of their delays. He returned her smile, his gaze warm as he held hers for a moment.

"I love you," he said, his helmet visor raised so she could hear him.

"I love you, too." Deanna felt like her heart would burst with it.

He gave her a thumbs up sign. "Let's roll."

Deanna hit the starter, felt as well as heard the powerful engine fire to life beneath her. She revved the throttle a couple of times, just to hear it roar. Headlight on, visor closed, clutch disengaged, she dropped the Sportster into first gear. Evan gave her a wink as he led the way out of the parking lot. Deanna smiled back. She took the incline out of the dealership with barely a pause. She'd come a long way since last December. She still had a long way to go, but she fully intended to enjoy every minute of the journey.

Twenty-three

The mountains challenged every riding skill Deanna had learned and gave her the ultimate definition of the term "soul flying." She longed to toss her helmet aside, to feel the wind in her face and hair as she leaned the responsive Sportster around the hairpin turns, straightening only long enough to lean the other way into the next one. She did raise her visor, shouting down to Evan as she led the way through a switchback that looked out over a lush valley. It felt like they were riding over the top of the world, the valley spread out before them, a verdant carpet liberally sprinkled with white dogwoods and deep pink redbuds. Deanna shouted with the exuberance of being alive, unable to contain the bubbling emotions within herself.

She was still soaring when they reached their campground, a lodge called Two Wheels Only in a tiny town called Suches that sat in the heart of the Chattahoochee National Forest. The lodge sat on three acres of forested property with a stream running behind it. Only motorcycles were allowed to camp there. Evan was right about spring cycle fever. The campgrounds already sported several tents, and more bikers continued to arrive.

Evan and Deanna set up the tiny, two-person tent Evan had brought in an area near the stream, semi-secluded from the other campers. He bought firewood from the lodge owners. Deanna had never been camping. She was charmed by the tiny tent, their sleeping bags stretched out inside, the crackling fire, the enchanting twilight that settled over the forest, creating an intimate environment. Even the two bikes parked near the tent added to the allure.

"I'm glad we decided to buy groceries and eat here," Deanna said, accepting a green stick Evan had peeled for her. Following his lead, she shoved it through the length of a hot dog, only flinching slightly at the feel of skewering the cold meat with the sharpened stick. Evan laughed at her.

"I should have taken you out in the wilderness, shot your dinner, and made you skin it before you roasted it over the fire."

Deanna made a face at him. "One step at a time, if you please. After the stories you seem to delight in telling me, I'm grateful there's a bathroom within walking distance."

"At least I brought bug spray. I could have et you find out about chiggers and wood ticks first hand."

"I appreciate your consideration," Deanna said, offering her hot dog to the flames. "I was promised brie cheese and wine, and here I am roasting hot dogs."

Evan flashed her his wolfish grin. He walked over to his bike and pulled a bottle out of one of the saddlebags.

"Evan Maxwell, you told me I couldn't carry anything breakable."

"I took a chance," he said, pulling his pocket knife out and extracting the cork screw. "You'll have to drink it out of the bottle, though. I drew the line at glasses."

Deanna laughed, feeling carefree and decadent. They ate charred hot dogs and passed the bottle of wine between them like a pair of teenagers. The teasing and laughter grew more lewd as the night grew darker, and colder, and the wine and the anticipation made them giddy. Evan took the bottle, his eyes hot as he looked at Deanna, then dropped his gaze lower.

"I distinctly remember how I promised you I would drink this wine."

Deanna felt a thrill run through her. She

lowered her eyes shyly. "Evan, there are people around. They'll know what we're doing."

"Since most of them are doing the same thing, I doubt they'll notice." He leaned near running his tongue along the hollow of her neck, making her shiver. "Ready for bed?"

She gazed into his eyes, the firelight intensifying the desire reflected in them. "Bring the wine," she said, standing up to lead the way.

Evan picked up the bottle, but he kicked dirt over the fire to put it out before he left it unattended. Then he followed Deanna to their tent. It was too small to enter standing up. The giddiness returned as Deanna crouched down on her hands and knees to crawl into it. Evan took a playful bite of her backside as he crouched down behind her, making her giggle.

They tumbled onto the sleeping bags zipped together to form one large bed they could share. It was pitch dark inside the tent making their love play entirely by feel. Evan continued his teasing bites, chewing on her legs through her jeans, her stomach through her sweater, growling and making Deanna laugh until she couldn't catch her breath.

"I always knew you were a beast," she gasped, trying to fend him off.

He took her sweater in his teeth and shook his head like a dog, then used his hands to ush it out of his way so he could reach the ensitive skin on her bare stomach. His bites ecame sensual licks, edging nearer and earer to the undersides of her breasts. Deanna no longer shoved him away with her ands, but stroked his back, his neck, urging im closer. Her body arched toward his mouth, hungry for his touch, knowing that ouch would only increase the hunger.

His questing hands released her bra, his mouth closed over her breast, and Deanna felt he surge of heat that promised to swamp her enses once again. She stifled her cry, con-cious of the thin walls of the tent. Instead of making her cautious, it heightened the sensu-ality, knowing she had to restrain herself or e heard, as if their lovemaking was forbidden. Evan must have understood the reason for her muffling her cry and taken it as a challenge. The more she tried to restrain her response o him, the more difficult he made her re-traint. He kissed her senseless as he divested er and himself of all the clothing he could each, then he returned to her breasts, laving hem with attention until Deanna could no onger stand the growing need building at her ore. She rolled him onto his back, reaching or the button of his jeans and intending to lo some tormenting of her own.

"Deanna Randolph?"

The hesitant voice outside their tent was a effective as a bucket of ice water. They bot froze. Deanna searched Evan's face, but all sh could see was shadows cast from a flashligh outside their tent. "Yes?" she finally answered

"I have a message for Deanna Randolph," the voice said.

Evan moved first, groping blindly for hi shirt. "We'll be right out," he said, shovin her bra into Deanna's hands.

Panic warred with embarrassment a Deanna dressed quickly in the dark. Sara? He mother? One of her children? She prayed i was Sara, or to be more exact, a heart for Sara Evan found the flap covering the front of th tent and led the way out, on all fours, the wa they'd entered.

Deanna was grateful for the dark as the stood up in front of the proprietor of th lodge. The woman discreetly shone the ligh from her torch toward the ground. "A Glori Harris called, said she couldn't wait but she' leave a message with a Brian Maxwell, tha you'd know the number."

"Yes," Deanna said, emotions clashing within her, demanding action. It had to be heart. It couldn't be anything bad. "May I us your phone?"

"Sure, follow me."

It was all Deanna could do to walk behind he woman, rather than dash across the disance to the lodge and find the phone on her wn. Evan took her hand as they walked, queezing it in a silent offer of support. They inally reached the phone, and Deanna dialed he familiar number with trembling fingers.

"Brian?" she yelled into the receiver, before ne had even said hello. "Is it a heart?"

"It's a heart!" Brian yelled back. "They're flyng it in from somewhere. Gloria's already left o take Sara to the hospital. Listen, she said it vas going to be hours, the surgery itself probbly not until morning sometime, for you not to ry to get back here tonight. She just knew you'd never forgive her if she waited until morning to et you know. She told me to tell you Georgia is vith her, and she'll see you tomorrow."

Deanna searched for a solid surface, her egs feeling suddenly weak. She sank into a nearby chair, grasping the receiver as if it were a lifeline.

"Is Dad there?" Brian asked.

Deanna relinquished the receiver to Evan, ner mind awhirl with everything they needed o do. She tried to figure out what they needed to do first. She wished they hadn't drunk so much of that stupid wine.

"We'll leave as soon as it's light," Evan said replacing the receiver. "Thanks," he said to the proprietor. "It was good news."

"What do you mean as soon as it's light?" Deanna asked, as they walked back toward their tent.

"I mean only a fool rides through these mountains at night when it isn't necessary, especially after consuming a bottle of wine."

"Then let's rent a car," Deanna said, not willing to wait until morning.

"We can't do her any good tonight, Deanna. Georgia's with her. We'll leave as soon as it's light enough to see. According to Brian, we'll be back long before Sara's out of surgery."

"There's no way I'm going to sleep," Deanna complained, leaning down to crawl back into the tent. "Can't we wait a couple of hours, until we sober up, then go?"

"It'll still be dark, and you'll be tired, a lethal combination coming down off a mountain in any vehicle, much less a motorcycle." She heard him strip out of his clothes, then slide into the sleeping bag. "Come on, Deanna. You can rest, even if you can't sleep."

Restless frustration roiled within her. She didn't want to lie down. She wanted to be with Gloria, with Sara. She wished she hadn't come on this trip, but Phil had told them it could be months before a heart donor was available. Now she was stuck on top of a mountain in the middle of the night instead of being at the hospital.

"What would you do if you were there?" Evan's voice asked in the dark, as if he were tuned in to her thoughts.

She supposed it didn't take a crystal ball to know what she was thinking about. She sat on the sleeping bag and unlaced her boots. "Waiting, I guess, like we did the last time. The first surgery took two hours, and it felt like a lifetime. This will be worse." She shucked her jeans and slid her legs into the sleeping bag.

"Here," Evan said, handing her a T-shirt. "Sleep in this if you're cold. I can't sleep with that fuzzy sweater."

She pulled the sweater over her head, took off her bra, and put on his T-shirt.

"You sleep in your pearls?" Evan asked, as she settled her body into the curve of his arm, her head pillowed on his shoulder.

"I'm not going to take them off and risk losing them in this tent."

Evan fingered them a moment, then released them to pull her more tightly against him. "I would bet money that you are the only HOG that wears pearls under her leather jacket."

Deanna's mind was back on Sara. "Evan, what if she doesn't survive the surgery?" She knew he couldn't answer that question, but it gnawed on her heart and demanded attention

"You're the one who said she was a fighter that her incredible will to live was one of the reasons you reached out to her."

"I know, but now I'm scared for her They're going to remove her *heart.*"

'And give her one that's whole. Does she have any chance without it, Deanna?"

"No, but she still had some time. The surgery may take that time away from her."

"I'm sure that's a risk Gloria has thought a lot about."

Deanna knew that she had. Evan let her talk let her worry, let her verbalize her fears and her frustrations. He stroked her back and listened, making an occasional comment when it was called for. Deanna talked for a long time, but still the restless frustration wouldn't go away.

"Evan?" she asked, after she had lain quiet for awhile, her mind still refusing to shut down

"Hmmm?"

She raised up to look at him, though she couldn't see a thing in the darkness. "Are you asleep?"

"Resting," he said, but his voice was thick.

Deanna slid back down, rubbing her breasts against him through the T-shirt. She stroked her hands over his thigh, nudging him suggestively. He made an appreciative sound in his throat and moved his body in response, but Deanna suspected he was still more asleep than awake. She continued to stroke and rub, placing slow, provocative kisses along his jaw. When she got to his ear, he flinched.

"What are you doing?"

"Well, I can't sleep. Do you think it would be awful if we made love while Sara's life is on the line?"

Evan rolled to where he could participate more fully in her plan. "No, I think it would be an affirmation of life. I've heard it's a common phenomenon in times of stress or even grief."

Deanna didn't want to think about grief. Mostly, she didn't want to think at all, but the thoughts were there, intrusive, cloying, keeping physical release just beyond her reach. Evan seemed to sense her ambivalence. He loved her with a sensitivity and patience that made the climax all the more poignant when it came. Deanna lay in his arms when it was over and felt the tears fall.

Deanna fought her way through a crowd of bikers, a television news crew, and half the women's auxiliary before she reached Gloria, surrounded by even more people in the surgical waiting area. Gloria saw her coming and stood up to receive her hug.

"They just started a couple of hours ago," Gloria told her. "They warned me it would be a long wait until we'd know anything."

Deanna pulled back to study Gloria. She wasn't wearing her makeup, and a night without sleep and several bouts of tears was evident on her face and around her eyes. Her short, blonde hair was disheveled, as if she'd spent the night running her hands through it in frustration. Deanna hugged her again.

"I should have been here," she admonished herself again.

"It wouldn't have mattered," Gloria consoled her. She studied Deanna's face, returning the assessment Deanna had given her. Deanna didn't imagine she looked much better than Gloria— no makeup, a night without sleep, several crying bouts, plus a three-hour motorcycle ride that had started at first light. Gloria smiled at Deanna's grim expression.

"I'm sorry I ruined your weekend."

"Stop that," Deanna scolded, taking Gloria's arms in a stern hold. "There are going to be lots more weekends, for all of us."

She looked around the waiting room, amazed at the familiar faces watching the two of them. Hank hovered the closest. Deanna smiled at him. "At least Hank was home."

Gloria extended her hand to him, bringing him into their circle. "He brought us in. I called Georgia and Brian from here. They're somewhere around here."

Deanna found them with Evan. In addition to half the women's auxiliary waiting with Gloria, half the North Georgia HOG chapter either stood inside the waiting room or milled around outside the building. The news program that had interviewed Gloria then covered the benefit in Buford stood by, waiting to tape the triumphant announcement. Deanna hoped someone had told Phil. Since he was doing this for free, he at least deserved to get the publicity.

"You always did know how to make an entrance," Georgia teased her, indicating her biking costume, complete with helmet in hand. "I guess the cat's out of the bag now."

"Yeah," Deanna agreed, wincing as she ran a hand through her hair. "At least no one will ever label me boring and predictable again."

Georgia grinned. "Phil was the only one who believed that, and we've already determined that he's a jerk."

"But he's a great surgeon," Deanna said. "I'm glad he's in there."

"Sherylyn's with him," Georgia told her.

"It doesn't get any better than that," Deanna said. Sara was in the best hands there were. The rest was up to powers out of their control, and Sara's own will to survive.

The groups paced, side-stepped each other, spoke in small clusters in low voices. Deanna alternated between sitting with Gloria and pacing with Evan. She didn't know whether the amount of time required was a good or a bad sign.

"You're going to strangle yourself on those pearls," Evan warned her, bringing her a third cup of coffee in as many hours.

Deanna forced her hands to release the pearls, accepting the styrofoam cup. "You were right," she told him. "It wouldn't have done us any good to have been here last night, except to have helped this throng do further damage to the carpet of the waiting room and hallway."

Evan put his arms around her, just holding her, offering his strength and his presence, knowing better than to offer her false assurances. Deanna watched Hank doing the same with Gloria, who looked more brittle as the hours passed.

"She's tougher than she looks," Evan said, seeing the direction of Deanna's focus and apparently sharing her thoughts. "No matter what happens, she'll survive."

"I know," Deanna agreed. "But life should

be more than survival. Do you know what she cried about last night?"

Evan didn't offer a suggestion but waited for Deanna to tell him.

"She cried for the baby who died and for his parents who gave his heart so that Sara might have a chance to live." The tears came again, as they had when Gloria had shared the story. Evan didn't say anything, just held her against him and let her cry.

A stirring moved across the room, catching Deanna's attention about the same time Evan pulled away from her. They looked toward the doors of the surgery, where Phil stood in his green scrubs, talking earnestly with Gloria and Hank. Deanna strained to see their faces, unable to hear their voices, seeking clues— good or bad?

Gloria cried. Copious tears flowed down her cheeks as she took Phil's hands and practically squeezed the life out of them. Then she turned into Hank's arms, and they both cried, Hank totally unashamed of the tears that coursed down his cheeks as he hugged Gloria to him, then kissed her. The news camera got the entire scenario.

"It must be good news. Right?" Deanna demanded, standing on tip-toe to see better. "Those are tears of joy, aren't they?"

"I think we're going to find out," Evan said,

as Phil faced the camera instead of returning to surgery.

"I've been asked by the family to thank everyone for their support and especially their prayers," Phil said to the camera, his voice strong and authoritative. "Baby Sara came through the surgery without any complications. The donor heart is doing well. Sara's color's good, and though her status will remain critical for these first several days, we're all very optimistic."

The crowd in the room went wild. It rivaled any New Year's Eve celebration Deanna had ever witnessed. It rivaled the Atlanta Braves winning the pennant. Barriers fell as the bikers and the women's auxiliary hugged each other in their jubilation. Deanna hugged Evan, the tears streaming again, this time with joy. She noticed his eyes were a little damp as well, then she was torn out of his arms and hugged by Ernest, who nearly broke her ribs in his exuberance.

"We did it, Miss Deanna! That little baby is gonna live!" He didn't wait for her response but turned to hug someone else. Deanna tried to make her way to Gloria. It took her ten minutes, between receiving hugs from people along the way and the crowd that thronged around Gloria and Hank.

Gloria saw her and helped create a path. The two women hugged, and the tears began all over again. "Thank you," Gloria said, between sobs. "I couldn't have done this without you."

"I think you had a lot more help than me," Deanna said, ineffectively wiping her own eyes. "Look at this mob."

They looked out over the packed waiting room, security trying to reduce the number without much effect. Deanna watched Ernest grab Georgia in a crushing bear hug. Georgia hugged him back. Deanna didn't think there was a dry eye in the house.

"Mrs. Randolph, these people can't all be in here," the security officer said, coming up to her through the crowd. "There's other patients and other families, not to mention fire codes. You understand how it is."

"Yes, Bruce, I know," Deanna said. She turned to Gloria. "If you and Hank can come outside, just for a minute, I think all these people will follow. They just want to share your joy, then they'll go home. I'd hate for our celebration to turn into a riot, especially with the news crew here."

It was late afternoon before Gloria finally got to visit Sara, and then only for a minute. The group that remained— Hank, Deanna, Evan, and Georgia— had moved into the intensive care waiting room. Only Gloria would be allowed to visit Sara, and then only for short periods.

When Gloria returned, fresh tears sparkled in her eyes, and a radiant smile covered her tired features. "Her toes are pink," Gloria said. "She's ten months old, and she's never had pink toes. They've always been dusky, or even blue from lack of oxygen." She looked at Deanna.

"Go home, Deanna. Take Georgia, and Evan and go home." She looked up into Hank's craggy face with adoration. "We're going to be fine. Sara's going to be fine. She has a strong healthy heart, she has pink toes, and for the first time since her birth, she has a future."

Deanna was amazed when they went back outside that the sun was still shining. She felt like they'd been inside the hospital for days, felt like she'd been awake for days, yet it was still the same day that had begun with a ride down the mountain.

Georgia walked them to where they'd parked the bikes, now the only two motorcycles left in the parking lot, then gave them each a hug goodbye. "You look pretty sharp sitting on that Harley," Georgia told Deanna, "but then you always do."

Evan straddled his bike and pulled on his helmet, leaving his visor open so he could breathe. "Where to?" he asked her.

Deanna looked at him, thinking about their night, thinking about their day, thinking about her life since she'd first entered a Harley-Davidson dealership with trepidation in her heart and a mission in her soul. She loved this man, loved the way he loved her, loved the way he believed in her, loved the way he shared her life. "Let's go to your house," she said, giving him a warm smile.

He studied her for a minute. "What's at my house?"

"Brian, Kyle, Ghost, the new puppy— what's his name?"

Evan grimaced. "Spot. That's what happens when you let a four-year-old name a dalmatian."

"Right, Spot."

He studied her a while longer. "Once I get there, I'm not driving all the way back in to Buckhead."

Deanna felt her smile widen. He was catching on. "I know."

He looked skeptical. "You'll stay at my house, all night, with Kyle there?"

"Um-hmm." She loved teasing this man. She didn't feel nearly as tired as she had a moment ago. She thought maybe she was up to teasing him a lot more, later, after she'd played with Kyle and his new puppy Spot.

"You're sleeping in my bed."

She still had to work on his bad habit o
making demands, but he was definitely show
ing progress. "Where else would I sleep?"

He was starting to smile, just a little one
pulling at the edges of his mouth. "It's been
a long day. Could you just give me a hint a
to what this means?"

"Do you think Kyle would like to call m
'Grandma'?" Deanna asked.

Evan grinned, a full-blown, self-satisfied
wholly masculine grin. He thumbed the starte
to his Softail, gunning the engine to life. "I'
race you home, Grandma!" he shouted, then
dropped his visor into place.

Deanna started the Sportster. Like Bab
Sara, they had a future— unknown, unpre
dictable, but bright with possibilities. She toe
the Sportster into gear and led the way out o
the parking lot.

About the Author

Fay Kilgore has a nursing degree from Wichita State University and has recently received her masters in Nurse Midwifery at Emory University in Atlanta. Writing fiction has always been a creative outlet. Her hobby is reading.

Fay has an excellent support system in her family. Her husband cooks, her daughter cleans the house, and her son, who just started driving, offers to run errands for her, especially if he can drive her car. Family time is usually spent in the boat on Lake Lanier.

Fay also loves cats, especially Siamese. "Writing and reading are both such solitary pastimes. I love the solitude, but it's better with a cat in my lap."

Thanks to writing this book, she also now owns a motorcycle, a Kawasaki Vulcan 500. It's as fantastic as Deanna describes it. I still want a Harley, so I can join the great folks in the North Georgia HOGs!"

Look for a Super-Special
To Love Again
romance
next month

DEAR EMILY by Fern Michaels

plus

Joyce C. Ware's third *To Love Again*,
COLORADO HIGH

Taylor—made Romance From Zebra Books

WHISPERED KISSES   (3830, $4.99/5.9‹

Beautiful Texas heiress Laura Leigh Webster never ima‹ ined that her biggest worry on her African safari would ‹ the handsome Jace Elliot, her tour guide. Laura's guar‹ ian, Lord Chadwick Hamilton, warns her of Jace's dange‹ ous past; she simply cannot resist the lure of his stror arms and the passion of his *Whispered Kisses*.

KISS OF THE NIGHT WIND   (3831, $4.99/$5.9

Carrie Sue Strover thought she was leaving trouble behir her when she deserted her brother's outlaw gang to live h life as schoolmarm Carolyn Starns. On her journey, h‹ stagecoach was attacked and she was rescued by handson T.J. Rogue. T.J. plots to have Carrie lead him to her brotl er's cohorts who murdered his family. T.J., however, soc succumbs to the beautiful runaway's charms and loving c‹ resses.

FORTUNE'S FLAMES   (3825, $4.99/$5.9

Impatient to begin her journey back home to New Orlean beautiful Maren James was furious when Captain Hav‹ delayed the voyage by searching for stowaways. Impatienc gave way to uncontrollable desire once the handsome ca‹ tain searched *her* cabin. He was looking for illegal passe‹ gers; what he found was wild passion with a woman ‹ knew was unlike all those he had known before!

PASSIONS WILD AND FREE   (3828, $4.99/$5.9

After seeing her family and home destroyed by the cru‹ and hateful Epson gang, Randee Hollis swore revenge. Sl‹ knew she found the perfect man to help her — gunsling‹ Marsh Logan. Not only strong and brave, Marsh had tl‹ ebony hair and light blue eyes to make Randee forget h‹ hate and seek the love and passion that only he could gi‹ her.

Available wherever paperbacks are sold, or order direct from t‹ Publisher. Send cover price plus 50¢ per copy for mailing ar‹ handling to Penguin USA, P.O. Box 999, c/o Dept. 1710‹ Bergenfield, NJ 07621. Residents of New York and Tenness‹ must include sales tax. DO NOT SEND CASH.

How I Played the Game

ALSO BY BYRON NELSON

Byron Nelson's Winning Golf
(available from Taylor Publishing)

Shape Your Swing the Modern Way

How I Played the Game

BYRON NELSON

AN AUTOBIOGRAPHY

FOREWORD BY **ARNOLD PALMER**

TAYLOR TRADE PUBLISHING
Lanham • New York • Boulder • Toronto • Oxford

Copyright © 1993 by Byron Nelson and Peggy Nelson
First paperback edition 2006

All photos are from the author's collection.

Published by Taylor Trade Publishing
An imprint of The Rowman & Littlefield Publishing Group, Inc.
4501 Forbes Boulevard, Suite 200
Lanham, Maryland 20706

Distributed by NATIONAL BOOK NETWORK

The hardback edition of this book was previously cataloged by the Library of Congress as follows:
Nelson, Byron, 1912–
    How I played the game / by Byron Nelson ; foreword by Arnold Palmer.
    p.   cm.
    1. Nelson, Byron, 1912– 2. Golf—United States—Biography. I. Title.
GV964.N45A3 1993
796.352'092—dc20
[B]   92-37339
                                                                                          CIP

    ISBN-13: 978-0-87833-819-1 (cloth : alk. paper)
    ISBN-13: 978-1-58979-322-4 (pbk. : alk. paper)
    ISBN-10: 0-87833-819-5 (cloth : alk. paper)
    ISBN-10: 1-58979-322-6 (pbk. : alk. paper)

∞ ™ The paper used in this publication meets the minimum requirements of American National Standard for Information Sciences—Permanence of Paper for Printed Library Materials, ANSI/NISO Z39.48-1992.

Manufactured in the United States of America.

To Peggy,
the joy of my life
since November 15, 1986
and my favorite golfing partner

ACKNOWLEDGMENTS

Always, ever since I've been in golf, I've been helped by many wonderful people. I believe you'll find I've thanked each of them in turn in this book, but as for the actual writing of it, I first must thank all those friends who insisted that I do it. Without their urging, I never would have thought of it myself. Even with their encouragement, though, I couldn't have begun without all the records, statistics, and so forth supplied over the years by my wonderful friend Bill Inglish of Oklahoma City. Bill knows more about my career than I do, I think. Pat Seelig, an excellent golf writer I've worked with numerous times, read the manuscript at various stages and offered many helpful suggestions. Yet, with all the help of Bill, Pat, and my many other friends, this book still wouldn't have been written without the help of my wife, Peggy. Peggy is a freelance writer who volunteered to be both interviewer and typist for my recollections, and who also spent hours researching old scrapbooks and other records of my career in golf. Finally, to my editor, Jim Donovan, I owe a debt of thanks for his assistance in putting the chapters in the best sequence, checking on the accuracy of my stories, and generally making the book readable. I'm happy so many people expressed an interest in my doing this book—and I'm even happier now that it's done.

CONTENTS

· · · · · · · · · · · · · · · · · · · ·

Twenty-four pages of photographs follow page 120

FOREWORD
· ·

Back in the late 1970s, when Cliff Roberts was in the process of handing over the chairmanship of Augusta National Golf Club to Bill Lane, they decided to create a private room for those of us who had won the Masters Tournament, a sanctuary where we could relax and have a bite to eat at our leisure during that always-exciting week in April. Appropriate wooden lockers were installed along one short wall of the room. By then, there were some twenty-four living Masters Champions and many more to come, so doubling up of active and inactive players was deemed proper. I have no way of knowing who decided who would share a locker with whom—very likely it was Cliff Roberts, who died before the project was completed—but nothing has ever pleased me more than when I walked into that new Champions Room upstairs in the main clubhouse and saw two plates on one of the lockers, one bearing my name and the other that of Byron Nelson.

It would certainly have been my choice if I had been asked, because Byron Nelson was an idol of mine long before I met that wonderful gentleman and magnificent player. I was in my impressionable teens and wrapped up in golf when Byron was accomplishing things on the pro tour that never have been and never will be even approached.

How many times have people in golf wondered out loud what Byron Nelson might have put into the record books if he hadn't retired from serious competition at such a relatively young age? As a player myself, I absolutely marvel at two of his greatest accomplishments on tour—the eleven consecutive victories he posted from March to August in 1945 and the eighteen tournaments he won that year. I have never won more than three in a row and was quite proud when I won eight times on the Tour in 1960. I can't think of any records that are farther beyond anybody's reach than those two.

I read Byron's first book back in the 1940s and used a lot of his instruction as a blueprint in the development of my own game. Later on, when I was on the Tour and got to know Byron pretty well, I always enjoyed it when we got together and talked about golf. I remember times when he was working as a television commentator that he would come out on the course and walk and talk with me while I was playing practice rounds at the major championships.

We never played together, of course, when Byron was competing on a full-time basis, just once or twice at the Masters, but I well remember the enjoyable day we had when Jack Nicklaus and I joined with Byron and Jug McSpaden—remember those years when the press revelled in calling them the "Gold Dust Twins"?—in an exhibition at Jug's Dub's Dread course in Kansas.

My father was a great influence on me in many ways, not the least of which was my behavior and treatment of others. That all sank in quite well, but I must say that observing and getting to know Byron Nelson reinforced every bit of that. Here has always been a man of the highest personal standards, a man we in golf can hold up as the epitome of a true golf champion.

—ARNOLD PALMER

INTRODUCTION

··

T here has been quite a lot written about me, and I've been fortunate that most of it has been accurate. But there have been
a few times when what was written wasn't quite factual enough to suit
me, such as the amount of my winnings in 1945, my so-called "nervous stomach," why I left the tour, and a few other things. This is the
best opportunity I'll ever have to put my two cents' worth in about
how I lived, how I played the game of golf, and to set the record
straight for anyone who wants to know.

I hope you'll enjoy reading it.

—BYRON NELSON
Roanoke, Texas
1992

ONE
·······

The Road to Glen Garden

I HAVE ALWAYS BEEN A BLESSED MAN, AND THE FIRST WAY I was blessed on this earth was by having wonderful parents. My father was John Byron Nelson. His family was from Virginia originally, but he was born in Texas in 1889. He was a quiet, gentle man, shorter than me, but his hands were even larger than mine. He was a hard worker, but not particularly ambitious, and my mother always felt he was too kindhearted to be a good businessman.

My mother, Madge Allen Nelson, was born in 1893. Her family came to Texas from Tennessee when she was a small child. She loved Texas, and lived here all her life till her death in 1992 at the age of ninety-eight. She was smart, spirited, ambitious, and full of energy. She taught school some before she married my father, who was five years older than she was. They were married on February 8, 1911, and I was born four days shy of a year later, on February 4, 1912.

I was born at home, out in the country, on our 160-acre cotton farm in Long Branch, in Ellis County outside of Waxahachie, Texas. I was named John Byron Nelson Jr. after my father. My father had inherited the farm when he was just six years old after his father died of tuberculosis. His mother had died of consumption—what we now call TB—when he was just six months old. My father had it too, before he got married, and it ruined one lung, but fortunately it never spread to the other one. My father was raised by two maiden aunts, and he was a fine, hardworking man, so I guess those two aunts did a pretty good job.

Back then, you know, no one ever went to the hospital to have a baby—mostly only if they were about to die. So there was nothing unusual about my being born at home, except for my size.

I'm told I weighed twelve pounds, eight ounces at birth. My mother had just turned eighteen two months before, and she was in labor such a long time that the doctor figured I couldn't have survived it. In fact, he had given up on me and was just trying to save my mother's life at that point. He finally had to use forceps to deliver me, and broke my nose doing so. I still have a few dents in my skull from it. After I was delivered, he just placed me on a table near the bed, thinking I was dead.

After a few minutes, though, my Grandmother Allen, my mother's mother, shouted, "Doctor, this child is alive!" Then my grandmother started working with me, and the doctor did too, and to everyone's surprise I did make it, thanks to an abundance of my mother's milk. It was such an ordeal for my mother, though, it took her quite a long time to recover; in that day and time, there was no medication. I don't know whether my size and the difficult labor had anything to do with it, but she had only two more children, at seven-year intervals. Both my sister Ellen and my brother Charles, though, were of normal size, fortunately.

Our house was very close to the dirt road we lived on, and we stayed there till I was five. The soil in that area was heavy black clay, and having a cotton farm always meant a lot of hard work. I can still remember seeing folks in their horse and buggy going down that road in wet weather, when it would be all the horse could do to pull the load, the road was that slow and sticky.

I guess from the time I could walk, I woke up when my parents did, and my mother had to make breakfast holding me on her hip. I walked when I was about ten months old, which is early, but then, I was about half grown when I was born.

I was always an outdoor child. I hated being in the house, and I never really played much—I "worked." I had a little old wagon, and

I'd take it out and fill it with rocks or dirt and haul it someplace and empty it, then go back for more. That was my idea of play.

Not only did I not like to be inside, but I hated shoes, and went barefoot all the time. I remember when I was about five my mother bought me one pair, for wearing on Sunday. When we came home after church the first time I wore them, though, I took them off as soon as I got in the house. My mother had gone to the kitchen to cook dinner, and there was a fireplace in our living room, and I took those shoes and threw them on the fire.

After a little bit, my mother smelled that leather burning, and came in to see what I'd done. She scolded me and said, "All right, if you don't want to wear shoes, I just won't buy you any more. You can just go barefoot everywhere, winter and summer alike." And that was just fine with me.

I was fair-skinned with blond hair, and because I spent so much time outdoors, I sunburned easily. One time when I'd gotten burned, my mother put a sunbonnet on me, and tied it so I couldn't get it undone. I went out to play in the front yard of our house, which was very close to the road, even though we were out in the country. I tried every which way to get that bonnet off, but I couldn't, and I was getting pretty hot out under that Texas sun. So first I took off my shirt, then I took off my pants, and pretty soon I had everything off but that bonnet.

My mother was back of the house, and every once in a while she'd notice folks driving by and laughing their heads off, so she got curious and came around to see what was going on. There I stood, naked as the day I was born, with that bonnet still on my head. I can't remember whether I got a licking for that, but I probably should have.

It was along about this time that I had the first serious injury of my life. My father had bought a fine team of horses, and while he was busy doing something else, I was feeding an ear of corn to one of the horses. Well, I let my fingers get too close to the horse's mouth, and it bit the tip of my forefinger on my left hand. My father and mother used kerosene, or coal oil, to keep it protected and it healed up pretty soon, but that finger is still shorter than the one on my right hand. And I've always been mighty careful of how I feed horses since then.

When I was six, we moved to San Saba County in southwest Texas, to a 240-acre cotton farm on the San Saba River. The cotton grew well there, and you could see the fields from our house above the river. Only problem was, there were an awful lot of rattlesnakes in that country. One summer, we killed sixty-five of them, just around our house. By this time I'd gotten used to wearing shoes, fortunately.

By the time I was eight, I'd become a pretty good field worker. I'd weed the cotton in the summer, and pick it in the fall. I'd pick it and put it in a canvas sack, and I was so little then that the sack would just drag in the dirt behind me. I can't say I ever liked picking cotton much, because it made your hands bleed and it was powerful hot, hard work. But my parents encouraged me to work hard, because they knew that our field hands would work harder when they saw a child my size working like I did. And their strategy worked.

My father was drafted for World War I, but because he had one punctured eardrum and one collapsed lung from having had TB as a youngster, he was turned down. Then in 1919 my sister, Margaret Ellen, was born. I asked my mother, "Are you going to love her more than you love me?" I guess I kind of liked being the only child.

Because we lived way out in the country, there was never any kind of school within reach till I was eight. In San Saba, the nearest school was fourteen miles away. My mother had been a schoolteacher before she married my father, so she taught me all the basics at home.

But finally they built a schoolhouse three miles away, and I rode a coal-black horse we had across the fields bareback to school. My grandmother used to tell my mother, "You're going to get that child killed." But my mother would tell her, "You couldn't *pull* Byron off that horse!"

I hated school about as much as wearing shoes. I guess it was because I was used to getting all the attention from my mother at home; at least, that's what my brother Charles told me later. But another thing was, the schoolhouse was too warm to suit me. I was always opening the windows and getting in trouble for it. But because I'd get too hot, then go outside in the cold air, I got a lot of bad colds.

They started me off in the first grade, of course. But since I already knew how to read and write, and knew my geography and history, plus my multiplication tables up to 12, I was quickly promoted to the third grade. I still didn't like it, though.

I was always brought up to be honest, and of course everyone back then had to be mighty careful with the material things they did have. I remember one time I was playing over at the house of my friend, J. T. Whitt, and I brought home a nearly empty spool of thread to play with. It was only the spool I wanted, and it just had about eighteen rounds of white thread left on it. But when my mother saw it, she asked if Mrs. Whitt had given it to me. When I said no, she told me I had to take it back, right then. Now, my friend's house was a mile away, and it was already getting on toward dark. I guess I was about five years old at the time, so I was afraid of having to walk all that way and come home in the dark. But my mother wouldn't hear of waiting till the next morning, so off I went. I got there and back as fast as my legs would carry me. And it taught me never to take anything that didn't really belong to me.

The house we lived in when I was very young, like a lot of the houses of country folk back then, was just one-walled. There wasn't any insulation or wallpaper—they were really more like cabins, in a way. And even though it was down in south Texas, it could get pretty cold of a winter. I remember one time it got so cold that when we came in the kitchen one morning, the fire had gone out, and a one-gallon milk can we had sitting in the kitchen had frozen solid during the night.

When I was nine, we moved to San Angelo. Ellen—that's what we called Margaret Ellen—was about two. Our grandfather and grandmother Allen lived there, because their son, our Uncle Benton, had TB, and was staying in the sanitorium. Uncle Benton died, and it turned out later that my sister had a light case of TB herself, probably due to exposure to Uncle Benton, who'd always pick her up and kiss her. Of course, that was before he knew he was sick, and besides, back then people didn't realize how contagious the disease was.

In San Angelo, my father worked for a mohair warehouse that was the largest in the country, and it was right on the Santa Fe railroad line. Santa Fe was one of the largest producers of mohair wool. He loaded and unloaded the wool, but could only work part-time, because jobs were so hard to find then.

I remember the warehouse caught fire one time, and everyone came running to see it and help put out the fire. My mother saw my Daddy up on top of the warehouse, trying to get the fire under control, and she started screaming, "He's going to be burnt up!" Fortunately, they did get the fire put out and my father was all right. But the smell from that mohair burning was awful, and it hung around for days.

We had a wonderful team of horses and a wagon, and part of the time Daddy hauled gravel for a highway that was being built quite a ways away. It was too far for him to come home except weekends, so he found an old wooden crate someone had shipped a piano in and slept in that when he couldn't come home. Our family knew what "poor" really meant.

Next, we moved to Alvarado, south of Fort Worth. Our neighbors, the Majorses, who lived one-quarter of a mile away, had thirteen children living with them. Some of them were Mrs. Majors' sister's kids. Her sister had died some time before we moved there. I played with one of the children quite a lot.

Our place backed up to my Grandfather Allen's. It's from Grandfather Allen that I inherited my woodworking ability, but fortunately I didn't inherit his disposition. Gran didn't like children much, though he and Gram had six of their own. Maybe that's why he didn't like them. Anyway, I was always such an active little child that he would offer me a nickel if I could sit still for five minutes, but I was such a wiggler, I never got that nickel. My mother used to tell him, "Gran, if Byron needs a licking, you tell me and I'll give it to him. But I don't want you to touch him."

One day we were over at their house and the grownups were all sitting inside talking and I went outside looking for something to do. I guess I was about five or six. Gran had a few turkeys he raised, and he'd just fed them, so they were out in the yard pecking at their food. I wanted to see if I could catch one, so I sneaked up behind this old turkey hen and grabbed her by the tailfeathers. She started jumping and flopping around, but I held on, and first thing you know, all her tailfeathers came out in my hands.

I was in trouble, and I knew it. I looked around for a place to hide the evidence, and saw Gram's washtubs sitting on a bench, turned upside down waiting for washday. I hid the feathers under them and went inside, never saying a word. Not too much later, Gran went outside and came back in with this puzzled look on his face and said, "That's the strangest thing—I just went out and checked on the turkeys, and there's one that doesn't have any tailfeathers. She's all right, not sick or anything, but there's not one feather in her tail!" Naturally, I kept real quiet, and no one suspected anything.

Well, it came washday, and Gram went to turn over those wash-tubs and found all those feathers, and told my mother. Mother came to me and said, "Byron, did you pull the feathers out of Gran's turkey's tail?" I knew I had to come up with something good, so I said, "No, ma'am, I didn't. I just grabbed hold of her and she pulled them out herself!" For some reason, this got my mother to laughing, and I never did get the licking I deserved, fortunately.

We're so used to all our shopping centers and supermarkets now, but I can still clearly recall when we'd go to town in our horse and wagon for supplies once a week. We'd get flour, beans, shortening, and so forth. If you ran out, you did without till the next Saturday. Of course, the Majorses had so many children, they'd run out of something every once in a while, and they'd come to us for oh, some flour, maybe. Mrs. Majors had to get up awful early of a morning to start her cooking, so most of the time the kids would come over before daylight. They'd stand out in the yard and holler "Hello!" until Mother or Daddy answered, then tell us what it was their mother needed.

But they'd always pay us for it, or bring back the amount they'd borrowed next time they went to town. People were like that back then.

It was in Alvarado that my mother developed mastoiditis—an infection in the mastoid bone behind the ear. I was just ten, and I was out plowing the fields with our team of horses and the cultivator. My father came and told me they were going to Fort Worth to see the doctor, and I had to take care of the place while they were gone. When they came back, it turned out Mother had to go back four days later for surgery, and so I was the "man of the house" again, taking care of the house, plowing the cotton fields and all.

A little later, we moved to Fort Worth from our place south of the city. We lived in a town called Stop Six, so-called because it was on the way to Dallas on the interurban bus line, and right near our place was the sixth stop—the interurban was sort of like a streetcar line.

My father got a job as a truck driver and a deliverer for White Swan Foods. I was surprised he even got the job, because he'd had no experience like that. Pretty soon the economy caught up with us and he was laid off. Then he went to work delivering feed for Dyer's Feed Store on 15th Street in Fort Worth. Mr. Dyer was a good boss, but he drank and used bad language, and my father didn't do either one. My father never said a word to Mr. Dyer about it, but pretty soon, Mr. Dyer stopped drinking, and then he stopped swearing, too. Mr. Dyer liked my daddy a lot, just like everyone else who knew him.

That fall, I started school, and pretty soon, I noticed quite a few of my friends would have an extra nickel or dime or quarter to spend. Doesn't seem like much now, I know, but back then, it was very unusual for a child to have any spending money. So I asked them where they got it, and they said, "Caddying at Glen Garden Country Club." I had no idea what caddying was, so I asked more questions, and when they started explaining about golf and what they did to earn that extra money, I decided I'd like to learn more about it. But before I could learn much, I had to learn about something else—rabies.

I have to back up a bit to tell this story. When we had lived at Stop Six, right across the street from us was a family named Wells, with six children. We'd occasionally go back to visit them and I'd play with the Wells children, and one time, they'd just gotten a puppy, so we'd all play with that puppy. The puppy was sniffing us and nipping at us a bit, just playing, and pretty soon we all had a scratch or bite here or there. Well, in a few days, the puppy got sick and started foaming at the mouth. Back then, rabies was rampant because there wasn't any vaccination done like there is now.

When they had the dog examined, he did have rabies, which meant all of us children had to get rabies shots. You don't see much about it now, but back then it meant you had to take one shot a day, in your abdomen, for twenty-one straight days. But if the place you were bitten was above your shoulders, you'd have to have two shots a day.

Mr. and Mrs. Wells decided it was too expensive to get the shots done in Fort Worth, so they took their children and me to Austin, where the state would do the inoculations free. They had gotten permission from my mother and father, naturally, and it was very nice of them to include me.

They rented a house with quite a few bedrooms, which they were lucky to find, because times were really tough then in 1922. Then, every day, we'd all go to get our shots at the insane asylum. You weren't in there with the residents, but that was where we had to go to get the shots. They used quite a large needle, and after a few days, you didn't feel very good, but you had to keep taking the shots so you wouldn't get rabies.

Along about the fifteenth day, I began to feel really bad, and was getting a lot of headaches, which I was not accustomed to. Mrs. Wells gave me some aspirin to keep my head from hurting so much, but she wasn't as alert to signs of sickness as my mother was. She didn't think there was anything else wrong except my reaction to the shots.

When the twenty-one days were up, we headed back to Fort Worth. We got back late in the afternoon, and both my parents were there to greet us. But when my mother put her arms around me—I'll never forget it—she right away held me back from her with her hands on my shoulders, and said to my father, "This child's got typhoid fever."

Of course, in that day and time, typhoid was very prevalent, too, because they didn't have plumbing and water systems like they do now, and I guess down in Austin they just got the water right out of the river. The reason my mother recognized mine was that my father had gotten typhoid right after they were married, and she recognized the odor from when he'd had it. Typhoid basically is an intestinal disease, and creates its own peculiar smell.

So they put me to bed right away and called the doctor, and he agreed with mother's diagnosis: typhoid fever. I weighed 124 pounds when I got it, and over the next few weeks I dropped to 65. They even wrapped me in a sheet one time and weighed me on a cotton scale, and it was true—I'd lost half my weight. I was about eleven at the time, and about 5'8" or so, so you know I was awful thin. I can remember lying in bed and seeing my hipbones sticking straight up so plain.

I also remember that I gave myself a relapse. You weren't allowed to eat anything, just take the small amounts of liquids and things that the doctor authorized, and I didn't realize how serious it was. But there was a bottle of Horlick's malted milk tablets on the windowsill near my bed, and I'd get so hungry, I just kept eating those, and no one ever saw me, so they didn't know what I was doing. It wasn't very much, but it was enough to make me even sicker. My temperature soared to 104, 105, even over 106. They were packing me in ice, and said I'd never live.

By now, the doctors had pretty well given up on me, and it was a Mrs. Keeter, a chiropractor and a member of the Church of Christ we attended, who saved my life. This may sound strange, but she was an expert on giving enemas—I guess they'd call it colon-cleansing now.

She told my mother, "I can help that child. It will take quite a while, but I can cure him." So she treated me once or twice a day, very gently and carefully, and after about ten days, I began to improve. It took me quite a while to regain my strength and get back to my normal weight, but I did. The high fever I ran, however, apparently caused some memory loss, because I have very little recollection of my childhood, other than what my family and friends have told me.

So by the time I got well, I was just barely twelve years old, and had twice been given up on by the doctors—once when I was born, and again when I had typhoid. The fact that I survived both experiences is one of the reasons why I feel I've always been a blessed man.

TWO

From Caddie to Pro

T HOUGH I WAS SO SICK WITH THAT TYPHOID, I WAS MORE
concerned about something else. My parents were both members of
the Church of Christ, and by this time I had been well-taught by them
about the Bible and God's laws. My mother, in fact, was a wonderful
Bible scholar who worked not only with me but with many other people in her lifetime, teaching God's plan of salvation and all the Bible
prophecies and such. I knew I needed to be baptized, and I was worried that I wouldn't have the chance. So as soon as I was recovered
enough to go to church, it so happened that we were having a gospel
meeting, preached by a man named Brother Hubbard. At that time,
people didn't have enough money to pay for a full-time preacher, and
Brother Hubbard had a regular job as a railway mail clerk who sorted
mail on the train as it went from town to town. He had to develop a
peculiar way of walking to balance himself as he did this, and when he
preached, he did the same thing. He'd kind of rock back and forth,
back and forth as he talked.

During that meeting, I took my opportunity to obey the gospel
and was baptized. It made me very happy to know my past sins had
been forgiven, and because of my early upbringing and teaching from

my parents, I have continued as a member of the Church of Christ and realize more and more that the Bible truly is the inspired word of God. My faith has been a great blessing to me all my life. In fact, I really feel the reputation I've enjoyed all my life, especially after becoming a champion golfer, came very much from that upbringing and my continued faithfulness to the Bible and the church. Even the fact that I never smoked or drank or used bad language, and have tried to treat others as I'd like them to treat me, comes from that.

It took quite a while for me to really recover from the typhoid, but pretty soon I began to think again about my friends at school and the extra money they'd gotten by caddying. I had pretty well determined that I wanted to find out more about being a caddie, because I already knew as much as I ever wanted to know about rabies and typhoid both. When I was well enough, and my parents said it was okay for me to walk over to Glen Garden one day, I started off. Of course, I knew nothing about golf whatsoever. But I'd talked to my mother and father about it, and they said it would be all right for me to do it. As it turned out, it was a pretty important step for me, even though at the time all I was concerned about was that extra change in my pocket.

It may not sound like much, a boy having a nickel or dime spending money, but in the mid-twenties, it was a lot more than most of us had. Families weren't destitute and they had plenty to eat and to wear, but they didn't have extra money to spare.

So when my friends said they caddied at Glen Garden Country Club, well, that gave me an idea that I wanted to caddie also. Of course, I knew nothing about golf whatsoever. But I walked over to the club, which is on the southeast side of Fort Worth, about a mile away from where we lived on Timberline, and I went to the caddiemaster and told him I'd like to become a caddie.

His name was Harold Akey, and he told me, "Well, we have more caddies now than we have players, but if you want to come over on the weekends or on holidays, why, that's fine, 'cause that's when most of the play is." I thanked him and went home, and that weekend, I went over there. It took about six times before I ever got to caddie for anyone, but in the meantime, the ones who weren't getting to caddie were getting caddying lessons from Mr. Akey. We were taught how to look out for the clubs' owner, how to carry the clubs over our shoulders, how to hunt golf balls and keep our eye on the ball, how to stay out of the way, and the other rules that caddies have to abide by.

I knew nothing about caddying at first, but it wasn't difficult to learn. The other caddies, though, didn't like to see any new ones, because that might mean they wouldn't get a job sometimes. So they had what they called a "kangaroo court." It was like a fraternity initiation. They'd form two lines, and we'd have to run between them while each one of them gave us a good hard lick with their belts as we ran by. Sometimes they'd get a barrel and put a new kid in it and roll it down this big hill the clubhouse sat atop of. That was even worse than running the gauntlet, but for some reason, they never did that to me. I don't know why. They did try to run the new boys off, but I didn't run off very well. After I became a regular caddie, I never did pick on the younger boys, because I hadn't liked it when they did it to me and didn't think it was right.

Finally I got a job one Saturday caddying for the Rotarians of Dallas, who had come over to play the Rotarians of Fort Worth. That long ago, there was just one club in each city. The caddie fee was fifty cents, and my golfer was a man named Mr. Shute. Mr. Akey told Mr. Shute that I was a new caddie but that he thought I'd do all right for him.

So we got on the first tee and Mr. Shute said, "You're a new caddie, the caddiemaster told me." I said, "Yes sir, I am. I'll try to do my best." He said, "All right, I'll tell you what. If you don't lose a ball for me, why, I'll give you an extra quarter." Well, he sliced the first ball off the first tee way into the right rough, and I lost sight of it and never did find it. So there went my quarter. But I didn't lose any more and I caddied all right, so he said I was okay, and I got my first fifty cents.

It was late fall when I started caddying, and the club let the caddies play at Christmas time, when they had a party for us. That was the first time I ever played. I borrowed a set of clubs that year, and I shot 118—but that didn't count the times I whiffed the ball completely.

I liked golf right away. I liked any sport where you could swing something like a baseball bat or a stick or anything. And soon I was beginning to practice a little bit. I didn't have any clubs at first, but I remember the first one I bought was an old Standard, a hickory-shafted mashie—what's now a 5-iron. Whenever I could find an old ball, I'd beat it around with that old mashie. Pretty soon I bought a few more clubs with my caddie money, and my game progressed quickly. I learned to play by trial and error, but as I caddied I also watched the people I caddied for and gradually acquired a general idea of how you should develop a swing. I also had one golf book, the great Harry Vardon's, that I studied until I felt confident enough to do a few things on my own.

The next spring, I took up caddying again. A lot of times, I would go to the club just to see if I could get a job. One Saturday, I met a man named Judge J. B. Wade and caddied for him. He knew my parents, and he liked me, so I got to caddie for him every Saturday. He had a regular foursome and one of the fellows that played in it was Mr. Cecil Nottingham, who worked as assistant auditor for the Fort Worth-Denver City Railroad. He helped me get a job with the railroad when I quit school—but more on that later.

One time when I was caddying for Judge Wade, I got myself in trouble. You see, we caddies weren't ever allowed to hit balls while we were working or use the member's clubs without their permission. This one day, though, I'd given Judge Wade his driver, then walked down the side of the fairway. While I was waiting, I just got an impulse and dropped a ball I had in my pocket on the ground, took out one of Judge Wade's clubs, and hit toward where their drives would land.

Don't you know, that clubhead came right off the shaft. There wasn't anything for it but to tell the judge, so I did, and he just said, "We'll have to tell the caddiemaster." I wasn't any too eager to see the end of that round, but I made sure I told the caddiemaster what I'd done before the judge got there. Doing something like this generally meant getting expelled from the caddie yard for a time, but fortunately, Mr. Akey liked me, and just said, "We'll put in a new shaft, and you'll have to pay for it." The new shaft cost $2, which meant three rounds of golf I'd have to caddie to pay for it. But I felt very lucky it wasn't any worse, and I never did that again. However, as I caddied more and more for the judge, he'd every so often have me hit a ball with one of his clubs—usually an iron, and that encouraged me that maybe I had a little talent for the game.

The judge was a large man, about 6'1", big but not fat. He was about a medium golfer, what you'd call a "businessman golfer." He told me I was a "pretty good ballhawk," so I guess I'd improved some from that first time I caddied.

My mother was about to have another baby along about this time, and my parents asked me if I wanted to help name it. I thought a lot of Judge Wade by then, so I asked if it was a boy, could one of his names be "Wade," so that's why he's now Charles Wade Nelson. I really did quite a bit to help raise him—fed him, changed him, took care of him in church, and so forth. He was a naturally good child; he never got mad at me but one time. I don't remember why he was angry, but I remember he was trying to hit me. I was 6'2" by then, so I just put my hand on his head and held him away from me, and he swung at the air until he got tired.

I caddied for some other members, too, including a woman named May Whitney, who was a pretty good golfer and a good friend of the club pro, Ted Longworth. I also caddied for a woman named Hetty Green—not the millionaire from New York, just Hetty Green from Fort Worth, Texas. Mrs. Green was nice to caddie for, and helped me out quite a bit in my amateur career, in a way.

During my amateur years, I sold Mrs. Green nearly all my trophies and prizes, to get enough money to go to my next tournament. Years later—in fact, after I'd left the tour—I contacted her and told her I'd like to buy some of them back. I wasn't interested in the golf bags and such, just the silver trophies for their sentimental value.

Well, she said she wanted to keep them a while longer, and wouldn't sell any of them right then. She said she'd leave them to me in her will. I was kind of disappointed, but they were rightfully hers, so I didn't have a whole lot to say about it. Some time later, I learned that she had died, a widow with no children, but I never was able to discover anything about a will or such, so I never have gotten any of those back.

By the spring of 1927, I'd started working for Ted in the pro shop, putting in new shafts, cleaning the clubs, and so forth. We didn't have chrome in those days, so the irons would rust badly, and we had to use a buffing wheel to shine them up halfway decent. The stuff we used to shine them would come off that buffing wheel as black dust, and it would get on my face and hands till they were practically coal black. I'd always have to make sure I washed up good before I ever went back outside.

I got good enough at working on clubs that Ted asked me to help him make the irons he was going to use to play in the U.S. Open at

Oakmont that year. He'd already qualified, so we got right to work on those clubs. He'd select the hickory shafts out of this barrel of shafts we had, making sure each one was good and straight and strong. Then I'd work down the end of the shaft so it would just fit good and tight in the hosel of the clubhead. I'd drive the shaft in with a maul, and put a metal pin or nail in through a small hole on the side of the hosel to hold it in place. He took those clubs with him to Oakmont and played pretty well, finished about fifteenth or so, I think. I felt real proud of him, and happy I'd been able to help with his clubs.

My first real thrill in golf happened that same summer. It was when they held the PGA Championship in Dallas at Cedar Crest Country Club. Ted took me with him, and I was pretty excited because I wanted to follow Walter Hagen, who was paired against Al Espinosa in the semifinals. I stuck real close to him—in those days they didn't have gallery ropes, so I was right beside him the entire match. It was late in the afternoon on the back nine, and the players were facing into the western sun. On one particular hole, Hagen was squinting to see where to hit his approach shot. He kept putting his hand up over his eyes, and I said, "Would you like to borrow my cap?" He looked at me, looked at my school baseball cap, and said "Yes." Then he took my cap and sat it on his head, just enough to block the sun from his eyes. Of course, he never wore a cap or hat while playing, and he did play to the gallery quite a bit, so I'm certain he was just being kind, but it gave me a good feeling anyway. After he played the shot—the ball landed about eight feet from the hole—he gave my cap back. He sank the putt and tied Espinosa, then won the match in one extra hole. The next day he beat Joe Turnesa to win his fifth PGA Championship. You'd think I would have kept that cap all this time, but I haven't. I've never kept clubs or balls I won tournaments with or anything like that. Just not sentimental that way, I guess.

That Christmas they had the Caddie Championship again, but this time it was just nine holes, not eighteen. By sinking a long putt on the last hole I tied with a small, dark-complected boy named Ben Hogan. Par was 37, and we both shot 40. The members decided since it wasn't dark and the weather was good, we would go another nine holes. The members caddied for us. My caddie was Judge Wade; I don't recall who caddied for Ben. There were even a few folks in the gallery. Since

I didn't yet have a full set of clubs, I borrowed Judge Wade's. I was fortunate and won by one shot, so that was the first time I played against Ben and beat him. I was fourteen then, and Ben would turn fourteen the following August. They gave us each a golf club—mine was a 5-iron, and he got a 2-iron. Well, I already had a five, and he already had a two, so we traded clubs. The club also gave us junior playing privileges, which meant we could practice at the club and play at certain times when the members weren't on the course. That really helped me develop my game a lot faster.

I had met Ben before, of course, but hadn't really gotten to know him. He lived across town and went to a different school, and I didn't see him except at Glen Garden. Though he was short, he had big hands and arms for his size. He was quiet, serious, and mostly kept to himself. The first time I was really aware of him was Christmas the year before, when the members put on a little boxing match for entertainment. Ben liked to box, and so did another caddie we called Joe Boy. They boxed for about fifteen minutes, I guess, but nobody got knocked down or hurt. I was just watching, because I never did like to box or fight. When the members decided it was over, they all gave Ben and Joe Boy a big hand.

I don't recall that Ben and I ever even caddied together. If we did, I hadn't gotten to know him yet, because I sure don't remember it. But that wasn't unusual, because on a weekend there might be at least forty or fifty caddies around, and since we were pretty busy when we were on the course, we didn't get to know everyone. I know for sure that when I was caddying, I was too busy to talk much, and when I wasn't caddying, I was in school, at home doing chores, or working on my game.

I kept at it, practicing whenever I could, especially my short game. I'd practice at home, pitching balls off the rug onto the bed and getting them to just stop dead. I've had several people tell me they've tried this little trick, and it's not as easy as it sounds. Fortunately, I never broke anything in the room when I did it.

There was a practice area at Glen Garden where we could hit balls to one end and then go hit them back. Sometimes, we'd get up a game where the one who hit the shortest shots had to go gather up all the balls and bring them back. I did see Ben out on the practice range quite a lot, even then. Being as short as he was, he had to go get those balls quite often. Well, of course he didn't like that, and he found that if he turned his left hand over on the club and gave himself what we call a strong grip, he could hook the ball and make it roll quite a way on that hard, dry ground. So he didn't have to go chase balls much after that.

I've heard it said a number of times that Ben started out playing left-handed. I don't really know about whether he might have tried playing with a left-handed club sometime, but I never saw him play left-handed, and when we traded our 2- and 5-irons, neither one was left-handed. So I don't know how that story got started, but in all the time I knew Ben, from when we were both about thirteen, I never saw him play that way.

Several of the caddies got to be quite good players. One of them, Ned Baugh, was better than Ben at that time, but he didn't progress as much, because he didn't work on his game as much as Ben or I did. I did run into Ned a little later on, though, at one of my first real amateur tournaments. It was the next spring, when I started to play in local amateur events around town, whatever ones I could get to. The first one I won was in March of 1928, at a course called Katy Lake, south of Fort Worth. There was a full field, it was match play, and in the finals, I was up against Ned, who by this time had another job and was a year or so older than me. I was really nervous, but I just barely beat him. Katy Lake was a short course, but not particularly easy. It's no longer there, but I still have the little silver trophy to prove I won.

Shortly after that Katy Lake victory, I got the worst shellacking I ever had, from another Texan named Ralph Guldahl. Most people don't realize it, but Ralph was from Dallas, where he caddied at Bob-o-link, which is gone now. The same people owned Katy Lake and Bob-o-link, and decided to have a caddie match between the two clubs. We drew straws, and I got picked to play against Ralph, 36 holes at each club, with the first 36 at Bob-o-link, the second at Katy Lake. Ralph was a much more experienced player than I, and after the two rounds at his club, I was 12 down. The next day, we went to Katy Lake, and after the first eighteen, I was down 6 more, so we didn't ever play the last eighteen. Years later, I beat Ralph in three tournaments that I can recall real well, but I never did make up for that awful drubbing he gave me.

We caddies couldn't play or practice on our course during the evenings, but late in the evenings, I would go down to the third green, which was out of sight of the clubhouse. That's where I'd practice pitching and chipping. I'd do it till I couldn't see the hole any more, then I'd spread my handkerchief over the hole and keep at it.

I thought nobody at the club could see me, but I'd forgotten about Mr. Kidd, the club manager. We all called him "Captain Kidd." He lived in a little apartment on the third floor of the clubhouse, and one evening, he saw me down there on the third hole. Naturally, I got called on the carpet the next day, and Mr. Akey told me if I'd promise him I wouldn't do it any more, he wouldn't expel me. The punishment for practicing on the course was one week's expulsion. I felt I had to be honest, so I told him he'd have to expel me, because I couldn't promise never to do it again. I took my punishment—and then I made sure nobody could see me the next time I went down to practice.

Glen Garden's golf course was the only one I'd ever seen at that time, and I never thought there was anything unusual about it. But on the back nine, the holes ran like this: par four, par four, par five, par five, par three, par three, par four, par three, par three. There were two pairs of par threes on the last five holes, which was pretty unusual.

Of those par threes, the seventeenth hole was the only one that was easy. Fourteen and fifteen were both over 200 yards long, and the 15th was a 213-yard blind shot to an uphill green. You couldn't even see the flag from the tee. I realized later that having four par threes on the back nine was unique, but I played there again a few years ago, and it's still exactly the same.

With all that—caddying, playing golf, and school—I still had quite a lot to do at home. We had over a hundred white leghorn chickens, and it was my job to sell the eggs. I sold quite a few to the chef at Glen Garden. We also grew vegetables—black-eyed peas, corn, green peas—and we'd take all our produce and eggs to the neighborhood grocery stores to sell.

I guess it was about this time that I completed my first woodworking project. I used to carry the eggs and vegetables to market in a little wagon, and I remember I built wooden rails for the wagon so it could hold more. I also had some other ways of making an extra few dollars, like selling magazines and other things door to door. One of the magazines was *Liberty,* and one of the products I sold was called Hand-Slick, which took greasy dirt off your hands and worked very well. We had a cow, which I milked, and when my brother Charles developed an allergy not only to my mother's milk but to cow's milk, we bought a goat, and that fixed him right up. So I had a cow and a goat to milk. I sure didn't have to wonder what to do with my spare time.

Of all the things I had to do, I enjoyed school the least. I didn't mind English and some of the other subjects, including regular math, but geometry really confused me. And as I become more and more interested in golf, I became less and less interested in school.

In that day and time, it wasn't as important as it is now for people to have very much formal education. Very few people went on to college, and it was possible to do pretty well for yourself with just a high school diploma, if you were smart enough and willing to work hard.

My history teacher, Miss Nina Terry, used to play golf occasionally. One time I was playing with her, and she told me, "Byron, if you don't at least open your history book, I'm going to have to flunk you." So that got me busy and I managed to pass history all right.

Another teacher I liked very much was Miss Martel, who taught English. A few years ago, my wife Peggy and I were at a dinner at Fort Worth's Colonial Country Club, and we found ourselves seated with Miss Martel. I hadn't seen her for over sixty years, but she still remembered me. She told Peggy that I was "a good student," which I thought was very kind of her, since I had hated school so much.

I finally got to where I not only wasn't doing my homework, I began to play hooky so I could go play golf. Well, of course the school called my parents, and finally, my father told me, "Son, you've got a choice—either go to school or go to work." I'd always liked to work anyway, so I said I'd go to work, and that ended my formal education, when I was about halfway through the tenth grade.

So I had to live up to my word and go to work. I looked everywhere, but since it was 1928, jobs were scarce. I was already working at Glen Garden, not only in the shop, but also mowing the greens. They had a single-reel mower, and you walked while you mowed. I had to start right after daylight, and make sure I guided the mower properly, not overlap too much. I did this the first summer after I left school, and it gave me the opportunity to play a lot of golf. I mowed seventeen greens while another man did the 18th green and the putting clock.

Fortunately, I had gotten to know quite a few of the members by then. Mr. Cecil Nottingham, who worked for the Fort Worth-Denver City railroad, told me that if an opening came up, he'd let me know, and pretty soon after that, he did. I started as a file clerk for Mr. Nottingham in the fall of 1928, and worked there most of 1929 as well. I enjoyed the work, which mostly was sorting waybills and filing them. Since Mr. Nottingham was a golfer, he understood my desire to work on my game, and if I had all my work done for the afternoon, he'd let me go play.

But jobs then were not only hard to come by—they didn't last very long. One day in the middle of the week Mr. Nottingham called me to his desk and told me, "Byron, I hate to tell you this. You've been a good employee, but things are tough and we have so many people. I'm going to have to lay you off." So I was looking for work again.

With or without a job, I kept playing golf whenever I could and working on my game. The following spring, 1930, I played in the Texas Open Pro-Am in San Antonio. In those days, pro-ams meant just one amateur (rather than four) and one pro per team. I was paired with the fine Scottish golfer, Bobby Cruickshank, who was a pro in New England.

The tournament was at Breckenridge Park. I knew the course, and I could putt common bermuda greens real well. We both played well and we finished second, and I kind of expected that Bobby would thank me or compliment my game some way. After all, he'd won fifty or sixty dollars, and I had another silver cup. But all he said was, "Laddie, if ye don't larn to grip the club right, ye'll niver make a good player."

That took the wind out of my sails a bit, but I thought a lot about what he'd said, and asked Ted Longworth, the pro at Glen Garden. I had what they called a typical caddie swing, long and loose, with a strong right hand. Ted made a couple of suggestions, and I paid close attention, because he was a fine player and had been the Missouri state champion. I read some books on the swing and the grip, too, and after I got it figured out, I never had to change it again. In fact, people have often said my grip was one of the best things about my game.

I've never lost a club at the top of my swing as so many players do. Actually, I never changed or had any trouble with it at all until I cut the end of my middle finger off woodworking when I was seventy-six years old.

I was soon playing a lot of local Monday morning pro-ams in Fort Worth with Jack Grout, who came to Glen Garden as assistant to his brother Dick. Dick Grout had recently replaced Ted. Ted had been a big promoter of golf at Glen Garden, encouraging the members to play more and to get involved in various tournaments, which he did himself. But in 1930, Ted left for the pro job at Texarkana Country Club, which had a bigger membership and a fine golf course, with lots of those tall East Texas pine trees.

Jack Grout and I got to be good friends and remained that way the rest of his life. Back then, we played every week or so in the pro-ams. Remember, it was just one pro and one amateur, and there were no handicaps involved. Prize money wasn't much, maybe $25 to the winner, but $25 went a long ways in the Depression. Of course, it was Jack who became Jack Nicklaus's coach for so many years. The Grout brothers also had a sister who was Oklahoma State Ladies' Amateur Champion, so they were a whole family of golfers.

Jack was the best pro around, and I had become one of the best amateurs. We won those pro-ams so many times that the other pros got together and made a rule that a pro could only play with the same amateur once a month. So that gave the other boys a chance.

As for work, I'd had to fill in with first one thing, then another. It was the summer of 1930 before I found another regular job. This time my boss was Mr. Lawson Heatherwick, who published *Southwest Bankers* magazine. I was just a flunky—I helped put copy together, answered the phone, and was the gofer. It tied me down more than the railroad job, but the hours were fairly short, and it was just a monthly publication. While any job was better than none, it had begun to worry me some that I hadn't any background for running a business, or plans for a future of any kind. And between working, playing golf, and still doing my chores at home, I hadn't any time for dating, either. I never had a date in my life, in fact, till I moved to Texarkana when I was twenty years old.

Fortunately, Mr. Heatherwick played a lot of golf and was also willing to let me play, as long as it wasn't the end of the month. I worked about thirty hours a week and my salary was fifteen dollars, though it varied some.

One time he called me from Eastland, where he was playing in a tournament. After checking to see if everything was caught up at the office, he asked, "Why don't you come out here and play?" I hopped on a bus and got there just in time to qualify, playing in the rain. Everyone else had already qualified, so they had to send a scorer with me. As it turned out, I won the tournament, so it was worth the trip.

At that point, I was winning something in nearly every tournament, usually a silver cup or plate or something like that. I'd sell most of the prizes to get enough money to get to the next tournament. I also played in a lot of local invitationals—every city had one back then. I guess I played in twenty or twenty-five tournaments in those two years, plus the pro-ams and such. I was nervous sometimes, but I really enjoyed playing. And of course in between I was working on my game and practicing as much as I could.

In the summer of 1931 I qualified to play in the U.S. Amateur at Beverly Country Club in Chicago, but it looked like I wouldn't get to go. I had enough money for train fare, but not enough to stay at a hotel while I was there. Only two golfers from my area qualified—Edwin McClure and me. His father had a little money, and they were going to stay at the Morrison Hotel in Chicago. They offered to let me stay in their room, so I did. I ended up sleeping on the couch.

I got to Chicago late in the afternoon the day before the tournament began and never had time to play a practice round. The next day I had to play 36 holes. I'd never seen bentgrass greens before, and I had thirteen 3-putt greens. I failed to qualify by one stroke. I remember very little else about that Amateur. The course was fairly hard. The club pro was Charlie Penna, Tony's brother, with whom I became very good friends in later years. The tournament was won by Francis Ouimet, though I didn't get to meet him while I was there, because I had to go back home the next day. I was nineteen, it was the first time I'd ever left Texas, and the only time I ever played in the National Amateur.

The rest of that summer and fall I continued playing in local amateur tournaments. There were so many of them back then, one nearly every weekend. Fort Worth was the clearinghouse for setting them up, so that's how I found out about them. Some of the amateurs I'd played with had turned pro by then, and I quite often would play as well as or better than some of the pros. I won the Rivercrest Invitational in September, and I was also medalist in the qualifying rounds. But for some reason I'd never thought about becoming a professional. That just goes to show you you never know what's around the next corner.

Ted Longworth had been at Texarkana for about two years when he got the members to hold a little Open tournament, with the prize money being $500. It drew a lot of fine players from four states—Missouri, Texas, Arkansas, and Louisiana. In November, Ted wrote me a note from Texarkana (we didn't have a phone yet), saying the club was having a tournament and he'd like me to come play in it. This was to be an Open tournament, with both pros and amateurs playing. The total prize money was $500, Ted said, but of course he thought I'd be playing as an amateur.

A week or so later I got on the bus with my clothes in a little suitcase and my golf clubs at my side. By then, *Southwest Bankers* magazine was defunct, and I was out of work again, living at home and just doing odd jobs here and there to earn enough to keep body and soul together. There were even fewer jobs available then, as you might guess, because it was about the middle of the Depression. On that long ride to Texarkana, I got to thinking about that prize money. I knew you couldn't make much of a living playing professional golf, but there was some pretty good money going at these tournaments, and I felt I was good enough to have a chance at some of it.

It was on that bus that I decided to turn pro. When I got there for the qualifying rounds, I asked the tournament officials what I had to do to turn pro, and they told me, "Pay five dollars and say you're playing for the money." It was as simple as that—no qualifying schools, no mini-tours like they have today. So I did it. I put my five dollars down and announced my intentions, and that was that. It was November 22, 1932.

I finished third and won $75. Boy, I thought that was all the money in the world. I'd never even seen that much money in my hand at one time in my entire life. The tournament was a pretty good one, really. You might be surprised at some of the other pros who were there. Hogan, who'd turned pro two years earlier, was third in the qualifying rounds but didn't finish in the money, which only went to six places. Jimmy Demaret and Dick Metz played, and Ky Laffoon finished second, three strokes back of Ted, who won. So I wasn't in such bad company for my professional debut. I don't have that $75 any more, but I do still have a newspaper clipping about it, sent to me by my good friend, Bill Inglish of *The Daily Oklahoman.*

You have to understand that my parents at the time didn't really approve of me playing so much golf. Golf pros then didn't have as good a reputation as they do now. But when I came home and told them what I'd done, Mother was real proud of me, and though my father didn't say much, they told me, "Whatever you do, do it the best you can, and be a good man." They always supported me, even though they didn't get much of a chance to come see me play.

I'd made my move. I had $75 in my pocket, but still no job. I knew enough, though, to realize my next step was to go on the tour in California that winter, if I could possibly get there. So that was what I set out to do.

THREE

Texarkana and a Girl Named Louise

AFTER I GOT BACK HOME FROM TEXARKANA, I STARTED reading about the tour in California. There were four winter tournaments in the Los Angeles area in the early thirties: the Los Angeles Open, the Long Beach Open, the Pro-Am at Hillcrest, and one at Pasadena's Brookside Golf Course, right next to the Rose Bowl. Of course I didn't have any money to get there, even with my Texarkana winnings. But some friends in Fort Worth decided to back me, and gave me $500—enough to get there, plus some extra. These were a couple of amateurs who'd won some money on me in Calcutta pools, where people would bet on their favorite golfers, and I guess they thought I was a better player than I was. In those days, a one-way train ticket was over $250, so I had to find a cheaper way to get there. Luckily, I found a ride with a man named Lee Davis, and we drove in his car. But I knew I had to win some money if I wanted to take the train back home.

Unfortunately, I didn't do very well. I didn't play all that badly, but most of the tournaments in my time only paid twelve, maybe fifteen places. Today, everyone who makes the cut—usually sixty or so—wins some money. I came close to the money, but didn't win a dime, and pretty soon I'd gone through about all my expense money. When I wired my backers that I needed more cash to continue on the tour, they told me they couldn't send me any more, not even enough for the train, and I'd have to get back home the best way I could. Thank goodness, there was a man I knew from Fort Worth in L.A. on business at the time, a fellow by the name of Charlie Jones. He was headed back to Texas right after the Pasadena tournament, and I got a ride back with him.

That was my first time in California, and I thought it was very pretty country. There were no freeways to speak of, and the traffic wasn't bad at all then. There was more interest in golf, more play at the clubs, and the courses were much harder than those in Texas. They were longer, and had more bunkers, more rough, and a different kind of rough from what I was familiar with.

By the end of January 1933 I was back home, practicing and playing at Glen Garden, helping around the house and garden, milking the cow, and so forth. It was kind of a dead time. I decided to write to Ted Longworth about my experiences in California. Along about the middle part of March I got a letter from him, saying he was leaving Texarkana for Waverly Country Club in Portland, Oregon. He said I might want to apply for the Texarkana job—I wouldn't make any money at it, just enough to eat regular. That was enough for me.

A man named Pharr who owned a general merchandise and hardware store was president of the club at the time, and I had played golf with his wife in an amateur tournament in Fort Worth in early '32. She was a fine player, about middle-aged, and had been both the Texas and Arkansas Women's Amateur champion as well as the club champion at Texarkana. So when I went there, I went to see Mrs. Pharr first before I talked to her husband. She told me she'd help me. I don't know if it helped or not, but I did get the job in the first week of April 1933.

My parents were happy about it in one respect, because they knew by now I had golf in my soul. They were sad to see me leave town, though, and told me to be a good pro, to take care of myself, to be good, and to go to church.

I only took a few things with me—my golf clubs and some clothes. I really didn't have much more than that, anyway. I found a place to live close by, about a par-five distance from the club. It was the home of Mr. and Mrs. J. O. Battle, and they gave me a nice room plus two good meals a day for $7 a week.

That sounds pretty inexpensive, and it was, but it took nearly half my earnings each month. I received no salary, just whatever I got for lessons and anything I made in the shop. I got $2 for a half-hour lesson, but not many people took lessons then—especially not from a young, inexperienced pro like me. We had about sixty sets of members' clubs at $1 per set monthly storage fee, and we sold balls, tees, new clubs, and golf bags. There were no golf shirts or other clothes like they have now. Besides, whatever you wanted to sell in your shop, you had to pay for first, out of your own money, not the club's. Ted left me the inventory, and over the next few months, I paid him what he'd had in it. So I netted about $60 a month. Like he'd told me, enough to live on.

After finding a room, the next order of business was finding a church. In the phone book I saw the Walnut Street Church of Christ, which was about three miles away. I started attending, and they had quite a large group of young people, so I placed my membership there right away. It was a very good influence for me, particularly since this was my first time away from home.

I had no transportation, of course, and even taxis were expensive. I could walk to the club, but had to ride a streetcar to church at first. There was a member of the club named Dyer who owned the local Ford dealership, and he took a liking to me after I'd been there about a month. We got to talking one day and I mentioned that I sure would like to get a car, but there was no way I could buy one on what I was making. He just said, "Come down to my office and we'll talk about it." When I went to see him, he showed me a '32 Ford Roadster, royal blue with cream wheels and top. Since it was already the middle of 1933, he'd had this car over a year. He was willing to let me have it for $500, paying whatever I could each month, with no interest. It didn't take me long to say yes. I worked pretty hard, and after a bit, things got better at the club, so by the time I left for Ridgewood in '35, I had that car pretty well paid for.

It wasn't too long after I got my car, about June of '33, in fact, that I met Louise, my wonderful wife of over fifty years. The way I roped that gal in is a story in itself.

One Sunday at Bible study, there was a new girl—a tiny brunette with pretty brown eyes who came up and introduced herself to me as Louise Shofner. She had been living with relatives in Houston until recently, learning to be a hairdresser—we called them beauty operators in those days. I liked her right away.

The young folks got to talking about the picnic they were having that evening after worship at Spring Lake Park, and they invited me along. Well, I was busy at the club and didn't get to go to evening church, but I went ahead to the park anyway. The food was great and after I'd had my dinner, I went and got a piece of angel food cake with some sort of delicious lemon-flavored butter frosting. After I took the first bite, I said, "Who made this cake?" and found out it was Louise's.

She was dating another boy at the time, so I went and took the seat out of my car—Fords then had seats that came out easily—and invited Louise and her date to sit with me on that car seat, rather than on the grass, while we had dessert. I had seconds, too. She impressed me as quiet and reserved, but friendly. She was about 5'2" and couldn't have weighed more than 100 pounds. The next day, I called and asked if I could have a date with her, but she told me, "No, I'm busy." But I called every day after that with the same question.

The following Sunday when I got to church, Louise was sitting there with her little sister, Irma Drew, who was just a little bitty child, seventeen years younger than Louise. I went up and sat right next to them on Louise's other side. The boy she'd been dating came in, saw me sitting there, got mad and went to sit someplace else.

After church, I asked if I might take Louise and her sister home, and she said yes, so I did, and got her to agree to a date the next Saturday. We went to a picture show—I think it was a musical—then to the drugstore for a sundae, and I remember I had to have her home by 10:30. I was twenty then, and she was nineteen. That was the first real date I ever had in my life, and once I met Louise, I never even thought about dating anyone else.

The next day, Sunday, I sat with Louise and her sister again, and I noticed how she was able to get that little child to behave, to sit up and pay attention to the preacher, even though Irma Drew wasn't but two or three. I drove the two of them home again, and we had to stop at a railroad crossing to let a train go by. While we were waiting, I looked over at Louise and said, "Are you going to make our children behave like you do your sister?" She looked at me a minute, then said, "I guess so." So she never had any more dates with anyone but me. In fact, she used to kid me that on our first date, I had this to say about the boy she had been dating, who worked at a bank: "If I ever catch him on the street, I'll run over him!" So it wasn't too long before everyone understood we were unofficially engaged.

I owe at least some of my success in courting Louise to Mr. Arthur Temple, the president of Temple Lumber Company. I would play in fivesomes with the club members sometimes, and Mr. Temple liked to bet me a dollar that he could beat me. I nearly always shot par or better, so when I played Mr. Temple, I could usually count on having a dollar to spend on a date with Louise. With a dollar, we could go to a movie and then go to the drugstore for what was called a "Stuttgart," kind of an ice cream sundae but with a whole lot of real thick chocolate syrup on top. Boy, that was good. If it weren't for Mr. Temple, most of the time we'd just have to sit on Louise's folks' front porch and talk the whole evening, and I wasn't very good at talking then. So, thank you, Mr. Temple.

Now I had more interest than ever in becoming a good player, because I wanted to impress Louise. My game was falling together well, but I still couldn't put four good rounds together, and I knew I needed to do that to get anywhere.

Texarkana was a good club, and had a great golf course. The original course was cut out of a forest, so there were lots of wonderful pine trees, and that was one of the things that made the place so beautiful. I had a certain spot where I parked my car each day, and I kept a nice soft chamois so I could keep all the dust off it. In fact, I kept it so clean I almost wore the paint off it, and every once in a while I'd wax it, 'cause I had plenty of time.

The course itself had a lot of bunkers, and the sand in them was more like fine gravel. The greens were stiff bermuda grass with a lot of contour to them. The course forced me to learn to hit the ball straight, to get out of deep bunkers, and to play to elevated greens. It was built by Langford and Monroe, who also did the Philadelphia Country Club at Spring Mill, where I won the Open in '39. Through the years, the course gradually got redone and basically ruined until Ron Prichard redid it in 1985. He restored it to its original design, only better, and he did a wonderful job.

The best thing about the Texarkana job was it gave me plenty of time to practice. They had a big practice area. Of course, there weren't any practice balls, you had to furnish your own. And in that day and time, I was not a prominent enough player, so I had to buy my golf balls. No manufacturer was going to give me any like they do with so many of the players today. I guess they did it even then with the prominent players, but I wasn't prominent at all. So I saved my money and bought a few, and eventually I had a good shag bag full of golf balls.

I'd go out to the practice area and—well, back then there were plenty of caddies around, but I couldn't afford a caddie to shag my balls, so I would shag my own. I'd hit 'em down the practice field, then I'd go down and hit 'em all back to where I'd hit 'em from. Then I'd hit them out again, then back. And it wasn't the 8-iron, it was the niblick, or mashie niblick, because we didn't use the numbers back then. I really got to practice a lot there, and it was very good for my game.

I finally did get to where I could afford to pay a caddie to help me practice, and the one I remember best was Miller Barber, who was about thirteen or fourteen at the time. He'd shag balls for me quite a bit, and for years, he's told people that the reason he's bald is because my shots hit him on the head so many times while I was practicing. I wish I could say I really was that accurate. He caddied for me some, too, and sometimes we'd play nine holes together. I'd play him for a dime, and give him four strokes. He told me the other night that he never did beat me, but I never took his dime. See—I wasn't such a bad guy.

I've always been glad Miller became such a good player, though I don't think I had anything to do with it, and I certainly wouldn't want to take credit for his swing. But Miller's a very nice man, loves to play golf, and his wife Karen is a wonderful lady. I feel very fortunate to count them as my friends.

I gave a few lessons at Texarkana, and I'll never forget the first lesson I gave. I think I got a dollar for it. It was a couple named Mr. and Mrs. Josh Morris. He was in the insurance business, and she was a very kindly, soft-spoken lady, and it was Mrs. Morris I was to give my first official lesson to. I told her that I was new at teaching, that I would work with her all she wanted, and I'd try to be as helpful to her as I could.

She was very kind and she thought I did okay. That encouraged me, and I always had a soft spot in my heart for her, and I gave her quite a few lessons. Then some other ladies started coming to me, and I got to where I was giving more and more lessons. Of course, back then people didn't have a lot of money for lessons. And you didn't give just thirty-minute lessons, you just kept on working with them until they got tired and quit, because there weren't all that many lessons to give back then.

Mrs. Morris never did make a very good player, so I guess I didn't really help her with her game. But I did sometimes work with Mrs. Pharr. She would take a lesson once in a while, but I think she did it just to kind of encourage me, because she was a fine player and really didn't need much in the way of lessons. I did teach both of her daughters some, though.

At that time, there was so little play that you could always play fivesomes or even more. I had no problem getting a game, and I usually didn't have too much to do in the afternoons so I could play quite a lot. Wednesday was "doctors' day," of course, but you could get a game Thursday, and then Saturday and Sunday, too.

Playing with these members, I never did gamble, but every once in a while, I would hit a pretty good shot, and these members would brag on me. It got to where I could shoot par or less—par was 73—most all the time after I'd gotten used to the golf course and had practiced a little bit.

By now, I was playing with steel shafts. In fact, I hadn't played with hickory shafts since 1930, because the new steel was so much better. I had a few clubs with hickory shafts in them, but I never did play with them again. I even had a putter with a hickory shaft, which you even see a few of today, modern ones, but by 1933, most everyone was playing with the steel, which had come out in 1931. It caught on very quickly.

There weren't very many club manufacturers back then. The main ones in the golf club business at the time were Spalding, Wilson, and MacGregor. There was another one, Kroydon, and those were the clubs I was playing then. I switched around quite a bit between Kroydon and Wilson.

In the summer of 1933 I had an interesting match with a fellow named "Titanic" Thompson. He was a very nice person, a handsome man, and he could play almost as well right-handed as left. He was a gambler, the kind of fellow who would bet on just about anything. Some friends in Fort Worth contacted me and said they wanted me to play a money match against him where they would be betting on me. I didn't care for betting-type matches, but they really wanted me to come to Fort Worth and do it, so I figured out when I could go home next and told them. We played at Ridglea, but I had nothing to do with the betting, all I did was play. They gave Titanic three strokes, which I wouldn't have done, but since I didn't have any money on it, I didn't have anything to say about it. Anyway, I shot 69 and he shot 71, so he beat me one stroke. You see, I knew Titanic was a better player than most people gave him credit for. He had the ability to do whatever he had to to win, and he always knew the percentages. But he was never quite good enough to play on the tour, and really, he only played where he knew or felt that he had the advantage, like most good gamblers. Several years before that, when I played in the Southwestern Amateur in 1930 at Nichols Hills, Titanic bet he could throw a grapefruit over the Skirven Hotel, and someone was silly enough to take the bet. The hotel was about six stories high, but there was a building right next to it the same height, so Titanic got up on top of that building and sure enough, he threw his grapefruit right over the hotel. So I was wise to Titanic before that match with him ever took place.

I met a fellow named Harvey Penick while I was at Texarkana. He was from Austin, and already was getting a reputation as a good teacher. I'd see him each year at the Texas Open in San Antonio, and he'd be at some of the other tournaments around every once in a while. He and I had quite a few discussions about the swing, and I always found it good to talk with Harvey about golf. He was a quiet, easy, shy sort of a man, a very good man to know and to help anyone understand the golf swing. He's credited me with sending him a lot of students, but I simply passed the word along that he was a good teacher, and quite a few of the younger players were smart enough to go look him up.

All the while I was still thinking quite a bit about the possibility of going to California and playing out there during the winter of '33. Of course, I hadn't said anything to anybody about it, because I hadn't done very well in California the year before.

During this time, I'd met J.K. Wadley, who'd taken an interest in me. He was an oilman and a lumberman at that time—mainly oil. He encouraged me with my golf; he knew quite a lot about the game, and thought I had a good rhythm to my swing. One of the first times we played together, he told me I had one of the best grips he'd ever seen. So I told him about the time I'd played with Bobby Cruickshank, and he really enjoyed that story.

Mr. Wadley hadn't taken up golf until his forties, but he'd become very enthused about it. He wanted to learn all he could about the game, and he already had a substantial amount of income, so one year he hired "Long Jim" Barnes, the 1916 PGA champion, to teach him. The way it came about was Mr. Wadley found out Barnes was going on a barnstorming tour. It was a series of exhibitions all around, wherever he could find someone to pay him to come, though what he got paid, I have no idea. Anyway, Mr. Wadley contacted him and contracted with him for Mr. Wadley to go along and watch the exhibitions, and Barnes would teach him everything he knew about golf.

Mr. Wadley learned a lot about golf this way and studied some more on his own, so he really was helpful to me. He'd say, "This is the way I used to do it," or "This is the way Jim Barnes did it," or "This is the way some of the older players did it." Of course, most of that was different from the way I was trying to do it, but he did encourage me and thought I had a lot of potential. He always liked me because I didn't drink or smoke or swear, and he thought I was a pretty nice young man.

He was going to finance me on the tour that winter in exchange for half my winnings, so I really went to work on my game, practicing and playing every chance I had. By the time fall arrived, I really was beginning to play quite well, though I knew I had a lot to learn yet and a lot of work to do. But in that day and time, you had to go on the tour and play on the tour to learn. Today you play through high school and college and get a lot of competition there, and then you can even go on the mini-tours, so you learn a lot before you actually qualify to go on the main tour. But in that day and time, we got our education and learned about competing on the tour itself.

By then, Louise and I were talking about when we might get married, and without telling me, she had talked to her father some about loaning me money to go to California. When Louise told Mr. Shofner what Mr. Wadley's offer was, her father said he'd loan me a little bit and we wouldn't have to split anything, that if Louise had that much confidence in me, that was good enough for him. I remember Louise telling me her father wanted to see me, and since I didn't know she'd talked to him about my going to California, it scared me a little at first.

But we had a very nice conversation. Mr. Shofner told me, "If Louise has confidence in you, I do, too." He arranged to loan me some money to get to California and get started. Well, I made a little bit, but I had to send back for a little bit more. I'd played in the Los Angeles Open, and then at Brookside Park in Pasadena, then in a pro-am at Hillcrest, and in a tournament in Lakewood, but I was still struggling, and still having to borrow a little bit of money.

I headed back to Phoenix, then to San Antonio for the Texas Open, which was one of the oldest tournaments on the entire PGA tour. After that, there was one more tournament, in Galveston, the only tour event ever played there.

When I got to San Antonio, I figured up how much money I had in my pocket. I knew how much it was costing me per day, and I figured, "Well, I've got enough money to play here and in Galveston, and then I'll go back to Texarkana and go to work." I would have no money left at all to repay Mr. Shofner, and by now I owed him $660. That was a lot of money for me or anybody else then.

At the Texas Open, I was introduced to the gallery on the first tee by a man named L.G. Wilson, who was a golf salesman but no kin to the Wilson company. He was full of hot air, and really built me up, calling me "a promising young player"—I thought he never was going to get through introducing me. The more he talked, the more nervous I got.

This was at Breckenridge Park, where the tournament was still played until just a few years ago. At that time, they had these rubber mats you hit from on every tee, and you didn't dare hit under it or behind it, because you could break your club, or even your hands. So I was being really careful not to hit behind it, and I came over the top of it instead. In fact, if there'd been one less coat of paint on the ball, I'd have missed it entirely. The ball just dribbled off the tee about forty or fifty yards. After that big buildup Wilson had given me, I was really embarrassed.

I did hit a good second shot with my brassie—now they call it the 2-wood. I put it about 125 yards from the green, got it close, and made the putt for a 4. And the thought just popped into my mind, "Well, you silly goose, if you can miss one that bad and make a par, if you ever hit it right, you might make a birdie!"

So sure enough, from then on I played real fine—shot 66 the first round and led the tournament. I got excited and nervous and everything else; it was the first time I'd ever led a tournament in my life. Then I kind of faltered around all the way through the rest of the tournament, even though I didn't play all that badly, and finished second. Wiffy Cox, the pro at Congressional in Washington, D.C. and a fine player, considerably older than me, won it. I was paired with him the final round.

But I won $450, and boy, I thought I was rich. So I figured, well, if I can go to Galveston and play pretty good in Galveston, I can get back home with a little money in my pocket, and pay Mr. Shofner back.

So I went to Galveston and finished second there, too, but there wasn't as much money—I only won a little over $300. Craig Wood won that tournament. Then I jumped in the car and headed for Texarkana. I don't think the wheels hardly hit the ground the whole way from Galveston to Texarkana. It was right around the first of March, 1933.

As soon as I arrived, I walked straight in to Mr. Shofner's grocery store and said, "Mr. Shofner, I owe you six hundred and sixty dollars," and I paid him in cash. Then I said, "How much interest do I owe you?" and he said, "You don't owe me any interest. I'm just glad you finished off your trip real good. I'm proud of you."

So that left me a hundred dollars. I went to Arnold's Jewelry Store (Mr. Arnold was a member at the club, so I knew him pretty well), and bought a hundred-dollar diamond ring, which was a pretty decent little ring in those days. I gave it to Louise and we became officially engaged. Then I was broke again—no money at all!

By now it was the spring of 1934. I kept working on my game, getting a little more recognition, giving quite a few lessons, and things were looking up, so Louise and I decided to get married. Actually, I seem to remember Mr. Shofner saying to Louise, "You and Byron are spending too much time together. I think you should go ahead and get married." We thought it was a fine idea, though of course I had no money saved up.

But that didn't stop us from going ahead with our wedding plans. We decided to get married on June 24, and I guess my first training in learning to be a good husband came a few weeks later, when I was in Mr. Arnold's store again. I noticed a set of blue-and-white dishes in a wooden barrel, and asked Mr. Arnold how much they were. He told me they were on sale, and it seemed like a pretty good deal to me.

So, being young and ignorant in such things, I went ahead and bought the whole set—144 pieces. I was real proud of myself for finding such a bargain, and drove straight to Louise's to tell her. I was in for a surprise. Louise didn't seem to be happy about it at all. Her eyebrows went up, and she said, "I want to see them, *right now.*" You have to understand that in that day and time, you didn't return something you'd bought like you can now. That just wasn't done very often, especially if it was sale merchandise. So if she didn't approve, I was in double trouble.

But back to the store we went, and fortunately, Louise did like the dishes, very much, so I was relieved, and felt I'd learned a good lesson at the same time. In fact, we kept those dishes for thirty-five or forty years, and she finally gave them to her niece, Sandy. In all that time, I think we broke only two of the 144 dishes.

Though my mind was more on my marriage than golf right then, I did have my first hole-in-one at that time. It was on the eleventh hole at the club, and it happened just two days before we were to be married. That golf course will also always be dear to me for another reason. Later that summer I was playing golf with Mrs. Pharr. It was 1934, about the middle of the summer, and the fairways were good and hard, so we were getting a nice amount of roll. The 16th hole then was 560 yards, and I hit a good drive downwind about 300 yards, then took my brassie, now called a 2-wood, and knocked the ball in the hole in two for my one and only double eagle. In fact, the next week I was playing with a foursome of men, knocked my second shot very close and made an eagle. That didn't happen very often to me either, so it was fun and seemed to impress the fellows I was playing with.

Louise and I had no money for a church wedding, so we were married in the living room of Louise's parents' home. No one in my family was able to come, with money being so tight then. But they had all met Louise, and they definitely approved of the match. Louise's sister Delle was maid of honor, and I had "Coach" Warren Woodson to stand up with me. He was a good friend and football coach at Texarkana Junior College at the time, and his wife Muriel played golf. They were club members, and we remained good friends with them both for all our lives.

Our honeymoon, if you can call it that, was a trip to Hot Springs, Arkansas, a nice resort about 120 miles north. But both of us were so nervous from the wedding and all that we got upset stomachs, only stayed one night, and came back home. We found a kitchenette apartment that was roomy enough, but its only drawback was there was no cross-ventilation—no air conditioning either, of course—and in the summer, it was mighty hot. Lots of times we went to her folks and slept outside on the front porch. Louise went back to work as a beauty operator, and did that for several months. She was good at it, and she liked it very much.

That winter, right after Christmas, Louise went with me to California for her first experience on the tour. Jack Grout traveled with us by car, and I remember his golf clubs wouldn't stand up in the back seat and kept falling on one or the other of us. By the time we'd reached L.A., Louise had had enough, and said, "Either the clubs go, or I go." So Jack had to find another way home, but he was very understanding about it. Jack had a wonderfully long, fluid, smooth swing and good rhythm, but he was too nice a guy, not a tough enough competitor, so he never did very well on the tour.

Traveling at night in my little roadster, Louise's feet and legs would get cold. Women didn't wear slacks hardly at all then, and always dressed nice, especially for traveling. But cars had no heaters in that day and time, so we'd heat bricks in the oven before we left home in Texarkana and wrap them in paper. Then she'd put her feet on them and wrap a lap robe around her, which helped a lot. We would stop the next night at her Grandmother Reese's in West Texas, heat the bricks again, and keep going. We were mighty glad when we got a car with a heater, I can tell you.

We stayed at the same place I'd stayed the year before, the Sir Launfels Apartments in Los Angeles. Also staying there were Al and Emery Zimmerman, brothers and pros themselves, and we invited them to dinner one night. After they'd tasted Louise's good cooking, Al said to Louise, "We've got a deal for you, Louise. We'll buy all the groceries if you'll cook for us." Louise liked to cook, and the idea of saving money appealed to her, so she agreed, and we've remained friends with the Zimmermans ever since. Another interesting thing about that apartment building—the owner was a nice lady with a cute daughter named Jean, whom golfer Dick Metz met and later married; they've been together ever since. So it was a pretty good place for us pros.

Fortunately, I did a little better on the tour that winter than I had the year before, although we barely made expenses. The high point of that winter, though, was how I played against Lawson Little in the San Francisco Match Play Open in January. Of course, I was still learning to play then, not prominent at all and not known very well. The tournament was held at the Presidio Golf Club, where Little's father was the commanding officer. At that time, Little had just won both the American and British Amateurs two years in a row, and had twenty-seven consecutive victories in match play.

I think I was paired with Little in the first round because I was the least-known player who had qualified. Since he was a local boy and it was his home club, I guess they figured I was the easiest player for him to play against.

Well, some of the other pros—in fact, I guess just about all of them—were steamed, because they had all had to qualify for one of the thirty-two spots in the tournament, and Lawson Little didn't. Back then, tournaments were often run by local committees, not necessarily by the PGA, so the rules might be different depending on where you were playing. As you might guess, I was pretty nervous about playing him, but the other pros encouraged me, and Leo Diegel told me before our match, "Kid, Little hates to be outdriven, so you just go out on that first tee and shake him up. You can do it."

That's exactly what I did. I was all pumped up anyway, with Leo's encouragement on top of it. Little drove first, and when I stepped up there, I just let one fly and it sailed right over where his ball had stopped. He gave me the old fisheye, but I birdied the hole to his par, and that was kind of key to the match. I was fortunate. I played very well and beat Little, and it got national publicity.

In fact, the headline in the paper the next day—well, the sports-writers didn't know anything about me, but since I'd gotten married the previous June, they wrote, HONEYMOONER BEATS LAWSON LITTLE! Louise was so embarrassed she wouldn't leave the hotel room the next day. You had to read half of the article before my name even appeared. I won all of $50.

I didn't do anything else spectacular that winter, but at least we didn't have to borrow anything from Mr. Shofner, and Louise was a mighty good cook, so we ate regularly and ate well. Still, I've always felt that my performance in San Francisco, plus a few other good rounds I had in '34, were the main reasons I was invited to Augusta to play in the second Masters tournament in 1935.

During the tournament—at that time called the Augusta Invitational—a man named George Jacobus, who was golf professional at Ridgewood Country Club in Ridgewood, New Jersey, and president of the PGA, came to see Ed Dudley, the golf pro at Augusta National. George told Ed, "I'm looking for a new young assistant, a decent sort of a fellow who has a good possibility of becoming a good player." Of course, you were hired then to play some with the members, and to do quite a bit of teaching, too.

Ed Dudley knew me, and had known me for some time. He was originally from Oklahoma, and with me being from Texas, well, I'd met him at a few of those golf tournaments in both states. Ed told George about me and then introduced us. George interviewed me one day and we had a long conversation, and he said he'd like to talk to me again the next day. So he checked back on my record and what the people thought of me at Texarkana where I was head pro. The next day he hired me to come to Ridgewood as his assistant after the Masters tournament.

My salary would be $400 for the summer, plus half of my lesson fees. Doesn't sound like much, I know, but it was considerably more than what I was making at Texarkana, and the season was shorter, which would allow me to play more tournaments in the winter.

I was very excited about going to Ridgewood, because I had known of Mr. Jacobus for some time though I hadn't met him before. Of course I didn't know anything about Ridgewood and hadn't ever played there. In fact, I'd never been east of the Mississippi until the

Masters. But the fact that George was a prominent pro and president of the PGA impressed me very much. He told me Ridgewood was a 27-hole layout designed by A.W. Tillinghast, which would make it an excellent place to practice and work on my game.

This all took place before and after the first round of the Masters that year. I finished ninth with a score of 291 and won $197. I remember I told Dudley then, "I want to win this tournament in about three years." I beat that forecast by one year.

My first impression of Augusta National was one of surprise—there was really no rough to speak of at all. The trees were not very tall then, either—today they're a good forty feet taller. But the flowers were just as beautiful then. I saw the great Bob Jones there, but didn't get to meet him that year. Most people called him Bobby, but those closest to him always called him Bob.

So I went back home to Texarkana and resigned, packed up, and drove to Ridgewood. It was the first time Louise had to leave home, but when I told her the news, she said, "That's fine." Louise was always very encouraging and supportive of me, and often told me I was a hard worker. She came to Ridgewood a little later, because she had to see after all our things and say goodbye to her family. After I left Texarkana, they hired Don Murphy, a fine pro who stayed there forever, practically, and is now pro emeritus.

I also knew Ridgewood would be an excellent stepping stone in my career, with many more opportunities for me. It would be easier to travel to and play in many of the tournaments in the North and Southeast, and would give me more experience playing in all kinds of weather. But if I had known then what awaited me during my time at Ridgewood, I don't know if I could have stood that much excitement.

FOUR

Ridgewood
and a
New Driver

Since George Jacobus wanted me to start at Ridgewood as soon as possible, I drove home to Texarkana right after the Masters, packed as much as my little Ford roadster would hold—which wasn't much—and drove straight to Ridgewood. The trip took two and a half days of hard driving, and I arrived about noon of the third day.

As I drove up to the clubhouse, I was pretty awed. I had never seen a clubhouse so imposing and elegant before, and I was very apprehensive about it all. But back then, to be successful in the golf business in any way, you had to get a club job in the East. You needed that type of experience, for one thing. Of course, making a living came first for me, so playing on the tour was secondary. One thing for sure, I knew I was very fortunate to be working for Mr. Jacobus, who was then and for quite a long time afterwards president of the PGA. At that time, the PGA was really struggling. There was no money to be made running it, and it wasn't anything like what the tour is today. But working for George gave me the chance to learn about all the tournaments ahead of time, and to see what went into running the PGA and its events. In the mid-thirties, like most folks and many other organizations, the PGA was having financial difficulties. They had very little income, hardly enough to operate the tournaments they were involved in. I remember at one point, just to make a little money for the PGA, George negotiated a deal with golf ball manufacturers. They made balls with their name on one side and "PGA" on the other, and the PGA got a small royalty for each ball sold. It wasn't much, but it helped.

When I walked into the clubhouse, George came to greet me and was very happy to see me. He immediately showed me the pro shop and introduced me to the other fellows I'd be working with. Then he told me about the house where I'd be staying, which he had sent me a telegram about before I'd left Texarkana. He even rode out there with me, knowing I was new in town and might have trouble finding my way.

I was anxious to see it, and make sure it would be all right. This was the first time Louise would be moving away from home, and I knew it was going to be hard on her, as she was very close to her family. Not only that, but I'd be away all day and working pretty long hours, so she'd have very little to do other than her hand work— needlepoint and so forth. She wouldn't even have cooking to occupy her time, because we would actually be boarders, with the cost of our food included in our rent. I believe it was between seven and nine dollars per week. That doesn't sound like much now, but remember, I only made $400 plus half my lessons for the whole season, which ran from April 1 to Labor Day. I got $2.50 for each lesson and gave over $50 a week, for a total of about $100. So my monthly income was a little under $400 per month. Whatever we could save had to help pay expenses while I was on tour in the winter.

You might wonder why we didn't find a place of our own, where Louise would have more to do. But even a small apartment back then was more than we could afford, and besides, when I'd go on the tour in late fall, it made more sense for us to go back to Texarkana for the winter, where Louise could be with her family, because I'd be gone for several weeks at a time.

The people who owned the house we lived in were Mr. and Mrs. W. W. Hope, and they were very nice folks. I remember when Louise arrived about two weeks later, Mrs. Hope chuckled because Louise was so small—5'2"—while I was a good foot taller. Mr. and Mrs. Hope were just the opposite, and when she saw Louise, Mrs. Hope said, "I knew you'd be tiny—tall men always marry little women!"

Our room was small but comfortable, with a ¾-sized bed. That's right, not even a double. It was mighty cozy, I can tell you, and we shared a bathroom with another boarder and the Hopes' son. But Mrs. Hope had put a small rocking chair in our room just for Louise. With all the hand work she did, it was great to have that chair.

Mrs. Hope took a liking to Louise, and it made a world of difference. She had her help with the cooking for all the boarders—there were three of us, plus the Hopes' son. That helped Louise quite a bit, because she was terribly homesick. She cried a lot at first, and had very little to do that could help pass the time. Her friendship with Mrs. Hope carried her through the summer, though—in fact, we came back to stay there the following year as well.

Louise didn't come to visit me at the club much. Back then, it was very rare for a pro's wife to come to his club. I don't think Louise came to Ridgewood more than a half-dozen times in the two years I was there. It just wasn't done then, and since she didn't play golf anyway, there was little reason for her to come by.

Getting back to my first day at work, after I unloaded what I'd brought along in the car, George and I returned to the club, which was about a ten-minute drive from the house. I was very much impressed with the pro shop. It was very adequate in size and well-stocked. Also, George had two employees besides me, which was unusual in those days. Most clubs then had just the pro and one man to take care of the clubs. Being just a young kid from Texas, I was very nervous about this new situation, and knew I was most fortunate to be working for George. The others working for him were Ray Jamison, who came to be my assistant and who is still a good friend; and Jules the caddy-master, who also took care of the clubs and the whole back end of the shop. He and I also became good friends.

The next day, Mr. Jacobus and I went over my duties and my teaching methods. George was a good listener, and wanted me to go over my new way of playing golf with him quite thoroughly. I was very pleased to find he agreed with the changes I was making, and that encouraged me considerably. He gave me permission to teach my ideas to my students, who were mostly juniors and younger players, plus a few women and beginners.

I was told that I was always to look neat, which meant wearing a shirt and tie every day. And of course, it was most important to be polite to everyone at all times. Fortunately, thanks to my parents, I didn't have too much trouble with that job requirement. I learned a great deal from George about how to merchandise and promote new clubs, shoes, balls, and clothing—mostly sweaters and argyle socks. It stood me in good stead later in my career as a club pro.

The weather in New Jersey was still pretty cool when I arrived the first week in April. At that time, the Masters tournament was still played the last week in March, rather than the first full week of April as it is now. So it wasn't really spring just yet. In fact, there was a slight snowfall the second or third day after I got there. Still, some people were already playing golf.

I was anxious to play the course myself. Though I hadn't heard of Ridgewood before I met Mr. Jacobus, I learned that Tillinghast was a good architect, and knew the course would be a challenge for me to play and would help sharpen my game.

For the first few days, until I got used to my duties, I only had time to play a few holes by myself in the evenings when my chores were done. There were three nine-hole courses, East, West, and Center, with the East and West being more difficult than the Center course. Though there was water only on the first hole of the Center course, I found Ridgewood to be as difficult to play as Augusta National. The bentgrass greens were slick, much faster than what I was used to in Texas, where we had common bermuda grass then. The whole time I was at Ridgewood, my best score was a 68. But after the '39 Open, which I was fortunate to win, I went back and played an exhibition there and shot a 63. I was happy about that. I also got to see Ladies' Champion Virginia Van Wie and Glenna Collett play while I was there, which was a real treat.

I met Tillinghast shortly after my arrival, because he spent a lot of time at Ridgewood. And I got to know him quite well, though he didn't play a lot and I never played with him. I don't really remember what kind of a game he did play, but he intrigued me. He always wore a loose-fitting tweed jacket and smoked a pipe, and was always very friendly. Of course, I wasn't thinking anything about golf course design then, so I never talked to him about it. But I've now played quite a few of his courses, and his are always among the best, in my opinion.

After a while, I began to meet and play with some of the younger members of the club. I was surprised to see so much play as compared to Texarkana, and especially to see so many women playing. I had to confine practicing to my spare time, which there wasn't much of at first. There were quite a few caddies, though, and we were on very friendly terms right from the start, so some of them would shag balls for me, which was a great help. As for teaching, I did very little until the members got to know me and were willing to take a chance on a young kid with new ideas.

By the time I arrived at Ridgewood, I had developed the style of play which I still use today. I'd take the club straight back from the ball, not pronating as used to be necessary with the old hickory-shafted clubs. After talking with me and watching what I was doing and trying to do with my game, George grew to like my ideas. Eventually, he incorporated some of them into his teaching as well. He was most encouraging to young players, and that's how he helped me the most.

George, who was in his early forties at the time, had a wonderful ability to know his membership. He knew which ones liked to argue, and which ones had to be handled with kid gloves. His shop sold quite a lot of clubs, and also some clothing, which was just starting to be made specifically for golf at that time. But service was the most important thing we offered, by far.

As you might guess, the difference in accents between Texas and New Jersey is pretty noticeable, and I had a little trouble at first understanding people, though I suspect they had more trouble with my Texas twang. But they didn't kid me about it or tell me I ought to change, so I never did.

There were quite a few members I remember well, including Ashe Clarke, Max Kachie, and Ernie Thomas, but the one I played with the most often was Chet O'Brien. Chet was a nice-looking young man, married to a Broadway actress-dancer named Marilyn Miller. I was very impressed with how nicely he dressed—always wore handmade long-sleeved silk shirts and ties, and dressed well all the time. I complimented him several times, and he eventually took me to his tailors, Arco and McNaughton. He had them make me a pair of slacks in a sort of a gabardine called buckskin. Even back then, they were $60 a pair, but I got spoiled real fast, and went back to them often. Later, when I went to Inverness in Toledo, I went to a tailor named Fromme who made all my slacks for a number of years, from that same Arco and McNaughton pattern.

This may make me sound as if I cared too much about clothes, but that was one reason I decided I wanted to be on the Ryder Cup team. The 1935 matches were held at Ridgewood, so I got to be part of all the preparations for the event. Mr. Jacobus was very involved in selecting the team's wardrobes, of course, and when the players arrived and got all dressed in their uniforms, I thought they looked mighty sharp. They had British tan slacks, brown-and-white shoes, brown gabardine blazers, and tweed coats, tan and brown. Their golf bags all matched, too.

It got me to thinking about getting to be a good enough player to make the team. I wanted it as much for the clothes as anything else, but it gave me that much more motivation for working on my game. It was about then I told the caddies one day that I was going to be on the next Ryder Cup team. They laughed and told me, "Quit dreamin', Byron," and that was even more motivation.

I was very excited about meeting the team, because they were the leading U.S. and British players at the time. Paul Runyan, Craig Wood, Walter Hagen, Henry Picard, Olin Dutra, Johnny Revolta, Gene Sarazen, Percy Alliss, Alf Padgham—I did meet them, of course, but I'm sure that few of them were aware of me at all, and no reason why they should be, really. I was just another assistant pro to them. I was even more enthused about seeing them play for the first time. That was great. I watched nearly all the matches, and learned a lot from watching those wonderful golfers play. The United States, by the way, won 9–3.

So I began practicing harder, and one evening I had come back from the practice range with my 3-iron. Some of the caddies were outside the pro shop, and there was a flagpole about a hundred feet away, over toward the first tee of the Center course. The caddies challenged me to see if I could hit that flagpole from the slate terrace in front of the shop, and each of them put down a nickel or a dime— about fifty-five cents total.

Now, hitting a ball off a stone terrace sounds pretty tough, but I'd had plenty of practice with bare lies in Texas. My first shot, I tried to fade the ball, and missed the pole about six feet on the left. But I drew the second shot, and it was right on the money. I hit that flagpole nice as you please. The caddies were standing there with their mouths still open when I picked up my fifty-five cents and went home.

Right after the Ryder Cup matches was the PGA championship. That year it was at Twin Hills in Oklahoma City, and something new had been added—expense accounts. If you qualified for the tournament, you could get ten cents a mile, which was a nice incentive. I had to qualify at a course in New Jersey. The 18th hole was a par 4, and when I got there I had to par to qualify. I put my second shot in the bunker short of the green, bladed it over the green, and made bogey. Most of the reason I missed that bunker shot was I had gotten a special sand iron just for bunker play in the Open at Oakmont just before that, and never learned how to play with it, at Oakmont or anywhere else. But I had foolishly left it in my bag, and it was the only sand iron I had. Just a ridiculous mistake on my part.

I missed qualifying by one shot. I got rid of that so-called "special club" as fast as I could, and never saw it again, nor did I ever see that ten cents a mile that year. The worst part, though, was when I had to tell Louise I hadn't qualified. That made her cry, because it meant we'd have to borrow money from her father to come home. If I remember right, Johnny Revolta beat Tommy Armour in the finals of the PGA that year.

I've never been one to keep old clubs or trophies much. But one thing I do have is a small black notebook that I kept all my tournament records in. It begins in 1935, when I finished second in the Riverside (California) Pro-Am and won $125. It ends after the Masters in 1947, when I finished second again—and won $1500. In that little book I recorded tournament names, dates, my scores, whether I won anything, and what my caddie and entry fees were. In 1944, I expanded on this recordkeeping a bit, and it came in very handy in 1945—but more about that later.

My 1935 record wasn't very good. I was still having trouble putting four good rounds together, and my putting was hit-or-miss an awful lot of the time. Greens were so different then. They were very inconsistent, for one thing. Because local committees were in charge of the tournaments, there wasn't anyone to oversee course conditions everywhere and make sure fairways, roughs, and greens were the same all across the country.

Even in one tournament, the committee might have only half of the fairways watered. Or the greens might be watered one day and not the next, or watered on the front half and not the back. Of course, they used different types of grasses, too. Common bermuda in the south and southwest, and rye, poa annua, bluegrass, or bent in the north and east. They used a particular type of German bent at Oakmont, Inverness, and Merion that I never saw anywhere else. Each type of grass behaved differently. Some had more grain, some were slower, some grew faster—all of which made a big difference depending on what time of day you played.

So with different grasses on the greens and inconsistent watering, when it came to the short game, most of the pros worked on pitching and chipping, and very little on putting. Because it just didn't pay to spend a lot of time on putting. We concentrated more on getting our approach shots as close to the pin as possible.

My biggest triumph in 1935 was winning the New Jersey State Open that August. I won $400 plus another $40 for the Pro-Am. I played in quite a few local pro-ams around and won a few—though sometimes it was hardly worth the trouble. One I have in my black book says that I tied for first and won $10.40. That wasn't good money even then, but it did give me a chance to practice—and it never hurts to win.

My most memorable failure in '35 was my play in the U.S. Open at Oakmont—my first time to play in it. I had a miserable 315, though the course was hard and the winning score was only 299. It was really disappointing. But there's another reason I remember that Open so well, and it's a good one.

When I got home the first night after we got there, I'd just finished my first practice round, and hadn't been driving the ball as well as I thought I should. Not that the rest of my game was flawless—far from it. But my driving was the most inconsistent of all. In the past year, I'd bought four drivers, and probably spent more than I should have, since money was very scarce right then. In fact, we were so poor we were staying in the basement of a parsonage while I played in the Open, so you know we weren't doing too well financially.

Anyway, that evening, I sat with Louise after dinner and thought about my driving, while she did some needlework. Finally I said, "Louise, I need to buy another driver. I'm driving terrible." There wasn't any reaction from Louise for a couple of minutes. Then she put her work down and said, "Byron, we've been married over a year. I haven't bought a new dress or a new pair of shoes or anything for myself in all that time. But you've bought four new drivers, and you're not happy with any of them. One of two things—either you don't know what kind of driver you want, or you don't know how to drive."

Well, that stopped me in my tracks. Because there was no denying what she'd said was right. So the next morning, early, I took one of the drivers I had, a Spalding, to the shop there at Oakmont as soon as they opened, and went to work. Dutch Loeffler, the pro there for many years, was very kind and let me use whatever I needed.

Nearly all the drivers then were made with a completely straight face—same as when they had hickory shafts. That straight face worked all right when you pronated and didn't use your lower body at all, but with the steel shafts, it was very unsatisfactory. Now, I'd had in my mind for quite a while what a driver should really look like. So I began shaving off, very, very gradually, a slight bit off the toe of the club, then the heel, and kept that up till it had a nice little rounded face—what's called a "bulge." When I got it to looking exactly like that picture in my mind, I smoothed it off, put the finish on, and went out to play. And I never had any trouble with my driving after that, even though I didn't score very well in that particular Open.

Eventually, when I went to work for MacGregor, I had Kuzzy Kustenborder, head of their custom-made club department, make a persimmon driver to those specifications, and that was the driver I used from 1940 throughout the rest of my career. It's now in the World Golf Hall of Fame. Today, Roger Cleveland of Cleveland Golf Company makes a driver with my name on it that's an exact copy of the one I used to win nearly all my tournaments. But I guess I might still be looking for the perfect driver if it hadn't been for what Louise said to me back in 1935.

I played in thirty-one tournaments that year, won money in nineteen of them, and my scoring average was a little over 73. My winnings were $3,246.40. Then I had my $400 from Mr. Jacobus, and $1500 from Spalding for selling their equipment in the shop and playing their clubs. Total income: $5,146.40. Net profit: $1200.

In 1936, things started to get a little better. I remember meeting Bob Jones at the Masters that year, though I don't remember anything about the way I played. I think they had built Jones' cottage by then, and I do recall noticing that he was following me some as I played, probably in a practice round. It pleased me to realize he thought I was worth watching, knowing his record and his popularity. I tied for twelfth and won $50, which wasn't as good as what I did in '35, so I wasn't any too happy about it. Just made me more determined to get better, though.

When I got back to Ridgewood, the weather was bad. It rained quite often, which kept most people from coming out to play, so I got to practice a lot, and worked on my game real hard. It paid off, because all of a sudden I stopped having those terrible rounds. Not that I never played badly again, but I quit having two or three bad rounds in a row. To me, a bad round was a 74 or 75, because I felt the key to becoming a really fine player was consistently playing well, shooting par or better all four rounds. And I was getting there.

The third week in May, I won the Metropolitan Open at Quaker Ridge on Long Island, put on by the Metropolitan Golf Writers' Association. At that time, this was considered a very important tournament, though the prize money wasn't big, $1750 total. I felt very fortunate to win it, for which I got $750. The field was great—Craig Wood, Denny Shute, Horton Smith, Paul Runyan—all of the top pros, and I won by three shots. Where were Snead and Hogan? Well, it's surprising to some people, but Sam Snead didn't come on the tour till 1937, and though Ben Hogan had turned pro in 1930, two years before me, he never made it to stay until 1938.

In that Met Open, we had to play thirty-six holes the last day. We had so little money, I couldn't afford to stay at a hotel or anyplace, so I had to commute every day. Got up about four or five and drove two hours, then drove home at night. In fact, I barely had enough for gas and caddie fees, which were about $5 a day then. I also didn't have enough money to eat in the clubhouse, so, wearing my knickers, I sat outside and ate a hot dog and a Coke. We still have that picture, too. And the argyle socks I was wearing in that picture were one of two pair that Louise had knitted for me. They were the same pattern and color, the only good ones I had, and when I'd play in a tournament, I'd have to wash one pair at night and wear the other pair the next day, because it would take them nearly a day to dry.

After winning the Met Open, I had my first real interview. Oh, I'd been asked a few questions the year before when I beat Lawson Little in San Francisco, but this time, it was for real. The newspaperman was George Trevor, and he asked me all sorts of questions. I was unused to this sort of thing, but I was polite as I could be; I answered yes and no and yessir and nosir, but never explained anything. He wrote the next day, "This young man can really play, but he sure doesn't know how to talk." He had also noticed my argyle socks, thought I wore the same pair every day, and wrote that I was superstitious. That wasn't true, of course, but he never asked me about my socks, just about my golf.

It was right after the Met Open that I had my first opportunity to do an endorsement—but it was certainly a mixed blessing. The company that made a cigarette called 20 Grand asked me if I would do an ad for them. I wouldn't have to be smoking or even say that I smoked, simply say that I had read the report saying that the cigarettes were low in tar and so forth.

Well, I had never smoked and didn't believe in it. In fact, I'd been told from childhood that no one in the Nelson family ever smoked or drank, and while my parents never asked me to promise that I wouldn't, it was simply a matter of family pride as well as health with me. I knew that to play well, I had to be in the best possible condition at all times.

To be truthful, I wasn't comfortable with doing the ad at all, but even with the money from the Met Open, we were really struggling financially. So I said I would. They paid me $500 for a six-month contract, and since I'd had quite a lot of publicity already saying I didn't smoke or drink or carouse, I thought it would be all right.

But it wasn't. As soon as that ad appeared, I began getting letters from Sunday-school teachers and all sorts of people, telling me how I had let them down, that the young people really looked up to me and here I was, more or less saying that smoking was all right. It really upset me. I hadn't realized till then that people, especially young people, were already looking to me as a role model. I found it more true than ever what my parents had always told me—that whatever you did would have some influence on someone.

I talked to the 20 Grand people and told them I'd give the money back if they'd stop the ad, but they either couldn't or wouldn't. I promised the good Lord that if he'd forgive me I'd never let anyone else down and try to be a good example, and I've worked very hard at doing that.

As a result, people have given me quite a bit of credit for not smoking or drinking, but quite honestly, I never was tempted to do either one. Alcohol, even in a small amount, always had a bad effect on my system, so drinking didn't appeal to me any more than smoking did. I've probably had no more than a dozen drinks in my life—a glass of wine now and then, and once in a great while a vodka and tonic. But I never liked it and it never agreed with me, so I never enjoyed it.

Louise tried smoking once, though, and it happened about this same time. She and Harold McSpaden's wife Eva had become good friends, and Eva smoked. One day when we were all together, Eva asked Louise if she'd ever smoked. Louise said no, but decided she wanted to try it, and Eva gave her a cigarette. As soon as I saw her put it in her mouth, I said, "No, you don't," but she lighted it anyway, and I reached over and knocked the cigarette from her lips. I didn't touch her or hurt her in any way, but she was upset with me for doing it that way in front of Eva, and I can see why. Still, I made my point, and it would have been her right to do the same thing if I had been the one to light up.

As for drinking, I had one bad experience with it that taught me a good lesson. It was during the Miami Open in 1940, and I was leading going into the fourth round. There was a party that night, and someone talked me into having a glass of champagne. Since I wasn't used to alcohol, I didn't really like the taste, but I drank it and it didn't seem to bother me much, though I could feel it some.

The next morning, I was thirsty when I got up, probably because of the champagne, and I had a glass of water. Right away, I got to feeling what it must be like to be either really drunk or hung over. I felt very bad, and when I got to the course, I hadn't improved much. I was mad at myself for it, and it really affected my game. I shot a 38 on the front, which was just terrible. But I started to feel better on the back, and had a 32, so I managed to win by one stroke over Clayton Heafner. It was a good lesson, and fortunately not a very expensive one.

To get back to my skill at being interviewed, I must have improved some, because when I won the Open in '39, Trevor wrote, "Not only can Nelson play better—he's also learned how to talk." I guess I can thank Mr. Stanley Giles at Reading Country Club for quite a bit of that, and I'll tell you more about him later. However, I must say that when I first talked with Mr. Trevor, I was mesmerized by his appearance. He had one good eye and a pretty sorry-looking patch over the other one, plus he kept a pipe in his mouth all the time, and he wasn't just real careful about keeping his chin dry. I found myself staring at him, I'm afraid, instead of concentrating on answering his questions like I should have. But he was a wonderful golf writer, one who understood the game very well.

When I played in the '36 Open at Baltusrol, Paul Whiteman, the orchestra leader, was walking down the fairway with Louise and me and her sister, Delle, who was visiting us. Now there was of course a family resemblance between Delle and Louise, but to me it wasn't all that strong. Anyway, Paul looked at both of them and said, "How in the world do you tell them apart?" I replied, "I've never had any trouble." I didn't mean anything by it, but something about the way I said it kind of upset Delle a little, and she never did let me forget it. I still had a lot to learn about women, I guess.

My second-best finish in 1936 was at the General Brock Open in July. It was held on the Canadian side of Niagara Falls. I finished second and won $600. There we were, Louise and I, hundreds of miles from home, and the tournament committee decided to pay us in cash from the gate receipts. It was all in ones and fives and tens. We were so nervous about it, we stashed it in a dozen places all around the car that night till we could get home and put it in a bank. None of it was stolen, but we hid it so well that when we got home, we had an awful time trying to find it all. Fortunately, most all the tournaments paid by check, so we didn't have any more stories like that to tell.

Where they held the General Brock Open was such a small town, there was no place for people to stay, and we never had enough money then to stay in a nice hotel. We drove all over the place looking for a room, and finally in desperation Louise said, "Let's try the hotel."

Since it was the General Brock Hotel that was sponsoring the tournament, she thought they might have special rates for the players. Sure enough, she was right—$2 a night. The bad part was that it was awfully hot, and the rooms had little or no cross-ventilation. Everyone was buying fans and ice and trying to keep cool any way they could think of. Air conditioning had only just been invented, so we had to put up with the heat and like it, most of the time.

Besides finishing second and winning all that money, the General Brock Open was when I had my second big thrill in golf—playing with Walter Hagen. I was leading the tournament going into the final round, and I was paired with Hagen himself. Here he was, the golfer who'd once borrowed my cap when I was just a kid, and I was going to actually play golf with him. It was toward the end of his career, and he was more or less just making appearances by that time, but I still was very excited about it.

They didn't have any regulations about making your tee time back then, and Hagen was at least forty-five minutes late, which was a little unnerving. The tournament committee knew he was on his way to the course, but told me I had the right to play with a marker if I wanted to. But I thought it might be my only chance to ever play with Hagen, so I said I'd wait. He finally arrived, and never apologized for being late, but said to me on the first tee, "I see you've been playing pretty well." I said, "Thank you. I'm very pleased to get to play with you today." Hagen himself didn't play very well, but joked and laughed with the gallery as we went along.

But the waiting had done something to me, or else I was just nervous playing with such a great champion, and I shot an awful 42 on the front, gathered myself together, and had a 35 on the back, which meant I ended up second. I didn't have any bad feelings about Hagen or my decision to wait for him, though; it was worth it, and he really was a pleasure to play with. Besides, I should have had enough self-discipline to control myself and play my usual game. He had quite a bit of gallery, so between my fans and his, we had a good group. He never mentioned borrowing my cap all those years ago, and I didn't bring it up, knowing he would have forgotten all about it. It was a great growing experience for me, to learn that a so-called celebrity like Hagen was really just a nice person, as most such folks are.

In the fall of 1936, Louise and I drove back to Texarkana. She stayed with her folks while I went on a tour of the Pacific Northwest. I had to go alone, because we couldn't afford train fare for Louise. I took the train and rode in an upper berth all the way.

I played Vancouver, Victoria, Seattle, and Portland. In the first tournament, I'd been playing my irons beautifully, but not putting particularly well. In the last round, I hit the first five greens in a row, never farther than ten feet from the pin, and never made a single putt. I guess my frustration just got the better of me, because something just flashed over me, and I threw my putter up in some big old evergreen tree back of the green. I thought that putter never was going to come back down, but it finally did. There weren't any people there, so no one was in danger, but I was really ashamed of myself. Then all of a sudden I started making birdies, one right after the other, shot 66, tied with Jimmy Thompson for first money, and won $975. Ken Black, an amateur who was the son of the pro at the club, won the tournament.

During the last two rounds, I had been paired with Horton Smith, who was about ten years older than me, and who took it upon himself to help the younger players learn the ropes on the tour. He never said a word when I threw my putter, but after the round, he said he wanted to take me to dinner that night. We ate at the hotel, and had a real nice meal. Then when we were about finished, Horton said, "Byron, I'd like to talk to you about throwing your putter today. I know you're a nice young man and you know you shouldn't have done that."

I said, "I know, it was terrible. I've never done anything like that before, and I promise I'll never do it again." Well, Horton talked to me a little bit about how being a professional golfer meant being a gentleman all the time, obeying the rules and etiquette of the game and such. Then he kind of smiled at me and said, "But you know, if you hadn't thrown that putter, I don't think you would have shot sixty-six!"

This Pacific Northwest tour drew all the top players—Harry Cooper, Ralph Guldahl, Jimmy Thomson, and Al Zimmerman, as well as Horton. My winnings in those four tournaments, plus what I'd won in the Western and St. Paul Opens, totaled nearly $2500 in just six weeks. After that, I never looked back.

The day after the Seattle tournament, I went out on a yacht for the first time and caught my first salmon. We ate it right on deck, and I still think that was the best-tasting fish I ever had. I've never been much of a fisherman, though, except for a couple of other salmon-fishing trips like that one. I'm not a good sailor, for one thing, but mainly, it's just that fishing's too quiet for me.

At this point, my game was really going well. I liked the flight of my ball and the way it landed softly, with no hook. Even with the smaller British ball, which was harder to control, I could do it. Now, instead of having two or three good rounds out of four, I was playing four good rounds each time. I was achieving the consistency that I needed, and I never changed my grip, my swing, or my game after that.

Following that Pacific Northwest trip, Louise and I stayed in Texarkana with her folks, where we fortunately didn't need to pay room and board. Then we started on the tour in California right after the Christmas holidays. My little black book says that in 1936 I won money in twenty-four out of twenty-seven tournaments, at a time when most tournaments paid only ten or fifteen places, and some of them less than that.

My total winnings for 1936 were $5,798.75. My salary and Spalding bonus and lesson fees added to that brought my annual income total to $7,898.75. I don't know what my net profit was that year, but I hope it was better than the year before. Because we weren't exactly in high cotton.

FIVE
· · · · · · · · ·

Reading and Some Major Wins

I N JANUARY OF 1937 I TIED FOR NINTH IN THE L.A. OPEN AND won $75. I wasn't quite as happy with that sum as I was back at the Texarkana Open in '32, I can tell you. Next, I tied for seventeenth at Oakland, out of the money, then I finished sixth at Sacramento and won $140. That was kind of the way it went. One week I'd do all right, the next they hardly knew I was there.

At the San Francisco Match Play Tournament, though, I met a fellow who'd just turned pro, a fellow my age from Virginia, name of Sam Snead. I played him in the first round and beat him 2 and 1, but even then, I figured he'd always be someone to contend with. What a smooth swing Sam always had—looked like he'd never worked at it at all.

I look at my scores for that winter tour, and they're kind of interesting. Most of them are in the low 70's, but then in the tournaments where I won some money, there'd be a 66 or a 68. So I was getting a little better and learning to play under different kinds of conditions in different parts of the country.

See, we'd start in California, play four tournaments there, then drive to either Houston or San Antonio (in '37 it was Houston), to

Thomasville, Georgia, then to Florida for four events there. Next, it was Charleston for their Open, and after that the North and South, which was always played at Pinehurst. This time I did better, finishing third and winning $500.

At this point, I'd played in twelve tournaments and had won about $1800—not a very good average, especially considering expenses. I was looking forward to getting back to my job at Ridgewood in April. I wanted to work on my game more and get closer to my goal of being consistent.

However, back in February, Mr. Jacobus had called and told me he'd been contacted by Stanley Giles, president of Reading Country Club in Reading, Pennsylvania. The club was looking for a head golf pro. Besides being club president, Mr. Giles was head of the committee to find a new pro, so he'd called George. He wanted a young man who gave promise of being a good player as well as a good teacher, someone who also knew how to conduct the business of a golf shop. In those days, running a shop well was more important to most clubs than whether or not the pro was winning tournaments.

Of course, all the time I was at Ridgewood, I wasn't just working on my game, because no one could make a living playing golf then. You had to have a club job. So I was also learning how to be a head pro at a good club. I'd had a lot of good experience under George, and I was definitely interested in the Reading job, because the main reason for working for someone else at a fine club was to eventually get a club of your own. I'd done a lot of teaching and my game was getting better. In short, I felt I was ready.

So, with a good reference from Mr. Jacobus, I drove to Reading from Pinehurst, which was about a three-hour drive, and had an interview with Mr. Giles. I could see he really knew what he wanted in a golf pro. Somehow, I convinced him I could fill the requirements he had, so we signed a contract. It was about two weeks before the Masters in '37, and I was guaranteed $3750 per year, plus whatever I could make from the shop and my lessons. That was considerably more than I was making at Ridgewood. It certainly looked as if we wouldn't have to borrow any more money from Louise's folks.

Naturally I was all excited about having a club of my own, so when I went to Augusta to play in my third Masters, I was high as a kite. That may be part of the reason why I played as well as I did. But

I also had a practical reason for wanting to play well. I didn't have any money to buy things for my shop at Reading. Ralph Trout was going to be my assistant there, and he would have my shop open by the time I got back from Augusta, so I needed to be able to stock it with new merchandise as quickly as I could.

With all the adrenalin flowing about my new job and playing the Masters for the third time, I managed to win it, with a great opening round of 66 and a great last round on Sunday. That 66 stood as the best opening-round score by a Masters champion for thirty-nine years, until Raymond Floyd topped me in 1976 with his 65.

Though the Masters was already considered a major tournament in the golf world in '37, none of us had any idea it would get to be as popular as it is today. To think of all these people today trying every way to get tickets, when back then they maybe charged $3 and hardly had enough gallery to count—well, it sure is quite a change. And in most ways I think it's good.

Getting back to that 66, though, it was the best I'd ever played any golf course in my life, tee to green. I hit every par 5 in two, every par 4 in two, and every par 3 in one, for 32 strokes. Add 34 putts to that— pretty average putting, really—and you have an easy 66. I was paired with Paul Runyan that round. He called himself Pauly, and I remember he'd talk to himself quite a bit. "Hit it, Pauly," or "Pauly, you sure messed up on that one." But I wasn't really paying a whole lot of attention to him. I was concentrating real well that day.

We were staying at the Bon-Air Hotel then, a large hotel with a big foyer. The dining room was just off the foyer, and when I came down for breakfast that first morning, there was a lady in the foyer demonstrating a Hammond organ. She was playing soft, quiet music, mostly waltzes like "The Blue Danube." I listened to her play for about thirty minutes while I ate, and never really thought much about it. But my rhythm was so good that day, I later thought listening to that waltz tempo might have had something to do with it. Funny, because I don't really like organ music.

In the second round, I shot even par 72, and in the third, 75. I'd now lost the lead. In the fourth round, I was still faltering—shot a 38 on the front nine, leaving me three strokes behind Ralph Guldahl. Walking down to the tenth hole, someone in the gallery told me Guldahl had already birdied the tenth. That meant I had to birdie it too, or

I'd be 4 back with eight holes to go. I put my second shot on the green about fifteen feet from the hole and made it. I was paired with Wiffy Cox, the pro at Congressional in Washington, D.C. When I sank that putt, he said, "Kid, I think that's the one we needed."

I parred 11, and next was the wonderful, difficult 12th hole, one of the most famous par threes in the country. Rae's Creek runs diagonally across the front of the green—on television, it looks like it's straight across, but it's not. If the pin's on the right, it plays one club longer. And with that Amen Corner wind, it's always a tricky shot, no matter where the pin is.

Standing on the tee, I saw Guldahl drop a ball short of the creek, which meant he'd gone in the water from the tee. If he got on and 2-putted, he'd have a 5. Watching his misfortunes, I suddenly felt like a light bulb went off in my head, like the fellow you see in the cartoons when he gets a brilliant idea. I realized then that if I could get lucky and make a 2, I'd catch up with Guldahl right there. Fortunately, I put my tee shot six feet from the hole with a 6-iron into the wind, and holed it. So now I was caught up, with six holes to go.

The 13th hole is a very famous par 5. I hit a good drive down the center of the fairway, just slightly on the upslope. I saw Ralph fooling around on the front of the green, and learned he'd made a 6. There was water in a ditch that runs just in front of the green, and there were a lot of rocks in it. Once in a while, if your ball landed in the right place, you could play out of it, but that day, Ralph didn't have any luck.

The green then had a real high left side, up on a ridge, making the left side much higher than the right. It's been changed since then. The pin that day was on that high left side. Waiting to play my shot, I knew I'd have to play a 3-wood to reach the green. If I played safe and got on in three, I'd probably make a 5, or could even make a 4. That would put me in the lead by one shot, but I knew that wasn't enough. So I said to myself, "The Lord hates a coward," and I simply tried to make sure my ball didn't go off to the right and into the water. I pulled it slightly, and it stopped just off the green, about twenty feet from the hole. I chipped in for a 3, which made me feel pretty good, because I was now three strokes ahead of Ralph.

I parred fourteen, then got on fifteen in 2 and three-putted for par. Guldahl had made a 4 at fifteen, and we both parred in after that, so I won by two shots, with a 32 on the back nine. That 32 did more for my career at that time than anything, because I realized my game could stand up under pressure, and I could make good decisions in difficult circumstances.

There was no green jacket then, but I got a great thrill out of winning, especially after leading, losing the lead, and finishing strong. The other thing that pleased me was having Bob Jones present me with the gold medal. He was the "King of Golf" then, so that was a real thrill. As I recall, Clifford Roberts and Jones made a few remarks each, and then presented medals to the first- and second-place players. And that was it.

I still have that medal, and when my playing career was over, I looked back and realized that was the most important victory of my career. It was the turning point, the moment when I realized I could be a tough competitor. Whenever someone asks me which was the most important win of all for me, I never hesitate. It was the 1937 Masters, the one that really gave me confidence in myself.

You know, in the early days of the Masters, it was the most enjoyable tournament to go to in the whole country, from the players' point of view. The tournament was small enough, and with the smaller number of players, you got to enjoy a lot of wonderful Southern hospitality. Every year, several members would host an early evening party, with country ham and all the trimmings. Everyone felt free and easy, and we all had a wonderful time. There was a black quartet that sang each year. They'd go to wherever the party was, and that was the entertainment. They were mighty good. But as the tournament grew, it got too big for folks to have parties for all the players. It wasn't done at all after the war.

Because the tournament was so small then, there were only a couple of hotels in Augusta. It was a small town and didn't have much going on the rest of the year. So even then it was difficult to find a place to stay. It wasn't too long before people began renting out their homes to pros and others who might want to entertain friends, customers, and so forth during Masters week.

Louise was there all week. She wasn't at the medal ceremony afterwards—wives were never included in such things then. But she was at the course, and up around the clubhouse. Wives then didn't follow their husbands much. Most of them didn't play golf at all, and the women dressed up more then than they do now, so it was difficult to walk such a hilly course.

Many people have wondered how I got the nickname "Lord Byron." Well, O.B. Keeler was a sportswriter for the *Atlanta Journal* and also for the Associated Press. He had one stiff knee but still went out and watched the play so he would know what questions he wanted to ask—he didn't just wait in the clubhouse for players to come in and talk to them afterwards. After I won in '37, he interviewed me in the upstairs locker room that the pros used during the tournament. Things had kind of quieted down by then, and he said, "Byron, I watched you play the back nine today, and it reminded me of a piece of poetry that was written by Lord Byron when Napoleon was defeated at the battle of Waterloo." We did the rest of the interview then, and the next day, the headline in his article for the Associated Press read, "Lord Byron Wins Masters," and the nickname stuck. Oddly enough, I was sort of named for Lord Byron, who unfortunately was not an admirable man and drank himself to death at a very young age. But my grandmother Nelson had liked Lord Byron's poetry, and she named my father John Byron. I was named John Byron, Jr. when I was born, but dropped the John and Jr. when I was twenty, and I've had good luck ever since then.

It wasn't too hard going off to Reading after that great week in Augusta. All we'd had in Ridgewood were our clothes, no furniture or anything, so all our personal belongings were in our car. Since I'd left Ridgewood in the fall of '36 and played the winter tour in California, then the spring in Florida and the Carolinas, we hadn't been back to New Jersey. But when George Jacobus heard the news, he called to congratulate me. It sure was good to hear from him and realize I'd come quite a ways from when I first arrived in New Jersey just two years before.

My first impression of Reading was quite a bit different, since by now I'd been to New Jersey and New York. It was a bigger city than Texarkana, of course, but not anything like Ridgewood. Reading sits in the foothills of the Blue Mountains, southeast of the Appalachians, and that means coal mining country. The roads were narrow and hilly, so the traffic was pretty slow. The weather was different, too—lots of lightning storms, which took some getting used to. Besides the coal industry, there were several large textile mills in Reading, including Berkshire Mills.

The people were more reserved than at Ridgewood, mostly Pennsylvania Dutch. But once they decided to take you in, they were very warm and hospitable. They loved desserts, and I remember we'd go to play bridge of an evening at someone's home, and afterward they'd have what amounted to a full, heavy meal, complete with several desserts. I'd really have to watch it not to gain weight.

I have to admit, at first we weren't very impressed with Reading, but once we got to know the people and their ways, we had a very good time. In fact, when we left for Inverness in '39, it was the first time Louise had cried over such a thing since she'd left Texarkana. Mrs. Giles, the wife of the club president, was especially nice to Louise and me. She'd have us over to dinner and they'd play bridge with us several nights a week, and my, she was a good cook. She was quiet, easy, didn't play golf but did all the usual housewifely things and did them very well. Mrs. Giles died in the summer of '92, at the age of ninety-nine, and I was fortunate to have had a good visit with her two years earlier.

The Reading clubhouse itself was done in English Tudor style, and was quite impressive. The course was fine—not as good as the Tillinghast design at Ridgewood, but very adequate. It had small greens, and while not really hilly, was quite rolling. I found out quickly that I wouldn't have as much time to play and practice, because my responsibilities were quite a bit different from Ridgewood, since I was the only pro and did all the teaching. One big difference was that Reading had no practice range or practice bunkers. I used to use the bunker on the ninth green, next to the clubhouse, for my sand practice. Mr. Giles was kind enough to give me permission to do that. But he was the only one I ever had to get permission from—I never had to go to a committee or anything like that.

They had to replace the sand in that bunker at least four times while I was there because I practiced so much. I got to where I could hit the ball out and deliberately spin it back in. And Mr. Giles used to get me to demonstrate that shot to his friends.

A few days after we arrived, Mr. Giles called me and said, "I've got a Rotary Club luncheon this afternoon, and I want you to go with me and give a talk."

"Give a talk?" I said, scared to death. "Mr. Giles, I don't know anything about giving a talk. I've never done anything like that in my life." I started crawfishing any way I could, trying to get out of it. But he said, "All you have to do is tell them how you won the Masters." I replied, "I shot the lowest score." He laughed and said, "Here's how we'll do it. You'll get up and tell them everything you can think of about how you won—the shots you hit on the last nine, and all that. Then when you run out of things to say, I'll be sitting right next to you, and I'll ask you questions and keep it going." So that was what we did, and it worked out fine.

Since that day, I've given more "talks" than I could count, and now people tell me what a good job I do. But if it hadn't been for Mr. Giles, I don't know that I'd ever have gotten started.

Another story about Mr. Giles concerns his golf, not mine. He was the most consistent 83–85 shooter I ever saw. He just never varied hardly at all above 85 or below 83. He had a good short game, and he was pretty good with his irons, but never could hit a wood very well—especially off the tee. He'd hit this little old pecky slice about 150 yards down the fairway every time. Just never could play his woods very well at all.

Well, he'd watched me play for quite a few months at Reading, and one day he told me, "Byron, if I could drive like you, I'd eat your lunch." I just looked at him and smiled a little and said, "You think so, Mr. Giles?" He said, "I sure could. If I had your drives, I'd just beat you all to pieces!"

I thought about it for a few days, then I called him. "Mr. Giles, I've been thinking about what you said the other day, and I've got a game worked out for us. We'll each hit our drives, then we'll switch balls, and play to the hole." You could feel him smiling into the phone. He said, "I can't get there quick enough!"

So he got a couple of his buddies and we played. But he didn't know he was playing right into my hands, because my long irons were about the best part of my game right then. I have to admit that playing his drives, I was on parts of the golf course I'd never seen before, and my score went up a few strokes. But his score didn't come down quite enough, so I beat him.

He couldn't believe it. We played that way two more times, and he never got below 77, while I never went above 75. After the third match, he'd had enough, and he told me, "If I'd been a betting man, I'd have bet a thousand dollars that I could beat you using your drives!"

And $1000 then was a lot of money, so I was glad he didn't bet it. He was a good sport about it, though.

The biggest surprise about Reading was the number of row houses. Being from the wide-open spaces out West, I was used to freestanding homes, so it was a little difficult, getting used to living that close to our neighbors. We rented a corner row house from a family named Corbitt. John Corbitt was the local Studebaker dealer, and he and his family moved out, come June, to their summer home on the Schuylkill River, where it was much cooler.

Since we'd arrived the first of April, we lived in the Berkshire Hotel until May 1. While we were living in the hotel, waiting for the Corbitts to move to their summer home, Mrs. Giles practically adopted us, realizing it was difficult for both of us, and especially for Louise. Then, after we moved into the Corbitts' home, Mr. Giles kept us in fresh cut flowers the entire time we were there. One of the best things about living in the Corbitts' home was that years before, they had befriended a young Polish Catholic girl, Josephine Brynairski, who lived there and did the cooking and housekeeping. Her room was on the third floor, and Louise and Josephine became very good friends during our time in Reading. Josephine also had a job as a waitress in a fine restaurant in Reading, so her cooking was very good, too.

The Corbitts would move back to town in mid-September, but we didn't leave for Texarkana till a little bit later. So back we'd go to the Berkshire Hotel for a few more weeks. On the first floor of the hotel were the offices of the Reading Auto Club, of which Mr. Giles was president, in addition to his floral business. So I got to see quite a bit of him during our hotel stays.

At Reading I got to teach players at all levels. One family, the Lutzes, was especially interesting. Mr. Lutz owned one of the leading mortuaries in Reading and had three young children—a son, Buddy, ten years old and two daughters, twelve and fifteen. Mr. Lutz was a pretty fair businessman golfer who loved to play and wanted his children to play too. He came to me one day and said, "If you can teach them to play, Byron, I'll buy each of them a set of clubs plus pay for all their lessons." That was certainly a good incentive for me to work hard with those children.

Now Buddy was a total beginner, but he caught on quickly, and his twelve-year-old sister was coming along pretty well, too. I started her with just a 7-iron and graduated on up, and she was getting the ball airborne all right. But the older girl, I never could get her to progress at all. This went on for quite a while, as the children were taking a lot of lessons because it was summer and they were all out of school. Well, Mr. Lutz came out one day and asked, "How are my children doing, Byron?" I told him, "Mr. Lutz, Buddy and your younger girl are doing quite well, but I haven't made any progress at all with your older daughter, and I feel ashamed." He smiled at me and said, "Do you want me to tell you what the problem is?" I said, "I sure do, because maybe I can correct it." He answered, "No, I don't think you can because it's your blue eyes—that's all she ever talks about!" I was amazed, because I'd had no idea anything like that was going on in that young girl's mind while I was trying to teach her how to play golf. So that was the end of that, but I did sell two sets of clubs, anyway, and in all the teaching I've done, that was the only time anything like that ever happened.

Obviously, when it came to women, I still had a lot to learn, and my next lesson in this area came from Ann Metzger, a lady in her mid-forties who was married to a dentist at the club, Dr. Paul Metzger. I had been working with Mrs. Metzger a little while and making some progress, but not getting her to do the things I really wanted her to do. I felt bad about it because she was nice and her husband was a pretty good player. Mrs. Metzger was a rather buxom lady, and one day she saw Louise and told her, "Louise, I've been taking a lot of lessons from your husband, and we're not getting very far. I wish you'd explain to him how we women are made, because I get in my own way and that's why I can't swing the way he wants me to!" So Louise gave me the message, and the next time I saw Mrs. Metzger I said, "I'm going to change my procedure today. From now on I want you to stick your back end out further, bend over a little more, and take your arms out a little further away from your body." She looked at me and said, "Louise must have talked to you," and I said, "Yes, she did." Fortunately, I was able to help her a lot after we'd gotten around the anatomy question, so to speak.

As the only pro, I was more restricted on how many tournaments I could play in, as well as not having as much time to practice and play at the club. I only had one boy in the shop to clean clubs on weekends. Fortunately, I didn't need to do much teaching on weekends, because that's when most of the men played. Also, we had "doctors' day" on Wednesdays. I remember Dr. Mike Penta, who was such an avid golfer that he took lessons from me twice a week—at sunrise. And there was Dr. Metzger and his wife, Ann. They were both good golfers. She followed me in all the local tournaments I played in, and walked down the fairway with the other folks in the gallery. When I'd get a little tense, she'd get up alongside me and just say, "Smile." That's all. And of course, when you smile, it relaxes the muscles in your face, and somehow it would help me relax with my game and play better, too.

My second win that first year at Reading was the International Match Play Championship in Boston at Belmont Springs that fall. Actually, though the Masters was considered more important and the Belmont Match Play doesn't exist anymore, I won quite a bit more money for that—$3000, according to my records. After qualifying with 141, I played John Levinson; he was a left-hander, but quite good. That match had kind of a strange ending. I was one down going to eighteen, and I hit a long drive down onto a gravel road that crossed the fairway. A spectator picked up my ball and threw it backwards several yards onto the fairway. The rule was that you could get relief from the gravel and drop back, but the official naturally and correctly ruled that I had to drop it myself, which I did. I ended up making par, while Levinson bogeyed. I then eagled the first extra hole to win the match 1 up. That seemed to help my game all of a sudden come together, and I went on to beat Frank Walsh 1 up, Lloyd Mangrum 2 up, Charlie Lacey 5 and 4, Harry Cooper 5 and 4, and Henry Picard 5 and 4 in the final. I remember it was one of the few times Dad Shofner ever got to come and see me play, and he became interested in watching Ralph Guldahl, who was known for being a slow player. Mr. Shofner told me later that it took Ralph five full minutes to play a shot. Anyway, I was very happy to win with Dad Shofner there, because by now, he knew for sure he hadn't made a mistake loaning me that money in Texarkana.

The funny thing about the whole tournament was that I hadn't planned on playing in it at all. Harold McSpaden, who was the pro at Winchester in Boston, had called and begged me to come; he even let Louise and me stay with him and Eva. I hadn't been playing very well and was awfully busy at the club, but I decided to go anyway. Like I've said before, you just never know . . . .

Also, I was medalist in the PGA Championship qualifying at Pittsburgh Field Club, which back then was played at the end of May. I was determined to qualify, because I'd missed by one stroke the year before. Then I kept going—beat Leo Diegel, Craig Wood, and Johnny Farrell before losing in the quarterfinals to Ky Laffoon, all of which netted me $200. The course had very high, very dense rough. I drove the ball straight most of the time, but when I got in that rough, I used a small-headed wood called a cleek, with extra lead in the head, to play out. I'd bought it specifically because of the rough there, and most of the other players had one like it.

It was a 36-hole qualifier—eighteen in the morning, eighteen in the afternoon. The course was interesting. You drove off the first tee into a valley, then played the entire course in that valley till the 18th. The fairway going up to the 18th green was so steep, there was a rope tow for the players to use, and by the time we'd played thirty-six holes, we weren't too embarrassed to use it, either. The photo that was taken of me for being the medalist in that qualifier is a good one, if I do say so, and it's when we still were wearing shirts and ties to play. I often wonder what it would be like for the boys today, playing in those kinds of clothes and conditions.

To back up a bit, it wasn't too long after the Masters that I learned I had been chosen for the Ryder Cup team. Boy howdy, was I excited. I'd never even been outside the United States before. I didn't think it was possible that the dream I'd had just two years before at Ridgewood could be coming true already. The PGA of America picked the team then, and they didn't keep any long-term, detailed records like they do now. They didn't pick anyone who wasn't playing well, naturally. But of course, if you won a major, that did have some effect on their decision, and so I was selected.

There were a few on our team who'd never played in a Ryder Cup before—myself, Snead, Ed Dudley. So we were inexperienced to some degree, and we also knew that the Americans had never beaten the British on their own soil before. But Walter Hagen would be our captain—that really was a thrill.

First, though, I had to see what I could do in the National Championship—what everyone now calls the U.S. Open. I did much better than in '35 and '36—finished tied for seventeenth, according to my black book, and won $50. The tournament was at Oakland Hills in

Birmingham, Michigan, a very tough course. Naturally, I wasn't thrilled with my performance, but I already had my mind on the trip to England.

Toward the end of June, Louise and I rode to New York with Mr. and Mrs. Giles, and met all the other fellows and their wives there. The PGA threw a big party for us before we left on the USS *Manhattan* the next day, June 24. I was kind of worried about the crossing, because I was a poor sailor. I'd only been out on a small boat on a lake once or twice in my life and it disagreed with me. Even swinging on a porch swing could make me queasy. So I wasn't looking forward to this part of the trip.

But as it happened, the ocean was smooth as a millpond the entire six days out. The captain himself, a veteran of twenty years' sailing, said he'd never seen it that calm. That made me feel quite a bit better, having that ocean trip go so well. The trip back was another story.

When we arrived in England, we were met by the British contingent—the Royal and Ancient representatives. Our accommodations were comfortable but not luxurious, adequate for the team and their wives, six of whom went along.

There's nothing as exciting in golf as playing for your country. In the first matches, we played a Scotch foursome, alternating shots. One player would drive on the odd holes, the other on the evens. Hagen had paired Ed Dudley and me against Henry Cotton and Alf Padgham, the reigning British Open champion. Hagen came to me before the match and said, "Byron, you've got a lot of steam, a lot of get-up-and-go. And Dudley needs someone to push him. So I'm going to put you two together. You can get him fired up."

We were unknowns in England, so the headline in the paper the next morning said, HAGEN FEEDS LAMBS TO THE BUTCHER. Well, we did get steamed up over that. I drove against Cotton all day, and on the par threes, I put my ball inside his every time, and we ended up winning the match. The next day, the headline read THE LAMBS BIT THE BUTCHER. It was a great thrill to win, especially against a player like Cotton.

The weather for the matches was fine except for the last day, when it turned terrible. Cold, windy, drizzly. And pros weren't as welcome at these clubs as they are now. We were just barely allowed in the locker room, and our wives weren't allowed in the clubhouse at all.

There they were, standing outside, freezing, all six of them huddled together, trying to stay out of the wind, when the mayor's wife saw them. She had enough compassion to invite them all into the club-house, and because she was the mayor's wife, no one could say no to her. Then she served them some 200-year-old port, and they warmed up quickly after that. They said later they'd never tasted anything as good as that port in all their lives.

Fortunately, despite the bad weather, we held on to win, 8 to 4. It was the first time we'd ever defeated the British on their home ground. It made all of us feel proud, especially since we weren't used to playing the type of golf courses they had at Southport and Ainsdale.

The next week, we went north to Scotland for the British Open at Carnoustie. The gallery walked with us there, just like in the U.S., and in the first practice round, I was walking along with my driver under my arm, when a fellow accidentally tripped me. I landed crooked because of having the driver tucked under my arm, and hurt my back pretty bad. In fact, I didn't think I'd be able to play at all. But the local people found me someone like a modern chiropractor, and he worked on me quite a while, using some strong liniment, and I was okay in a couple of days.

Carnoustie was a very different course from what I'd seen before. In the driving areas, even if you were a long hitter, you'd have to go right or left to avoid the bunkers in the middle of nearly every fairway. The bunkers had high lips, too, but at least they were clearly visible from the tee. And there was this small creek, called a "burn," that wandered through the course.

Carnoustie used to be one of the seven courses in the rotation for the British Open, but some years ago they had to take it out, because there simply wasn't room for all the people and the cars and so forth, golf had gotten so big. I understand they're trying to do something about that now, because it's a fine course and it would be good to see the Open played there again.

It was normal Scottish weather, cold, windy, and damp. In the third round, it turned worse, but I shot a 71 and came from way back to third place, with Cotton in the lead. The final round I shot 74, fin-ished fifth, and won $125. Our boat tickets came to $1020, plus I'd lost a month out of the summer in the shop with both the Ryder Cup and the British, so you can see why we didn't play in the British Open much back then. The PGA did cover some of our expenses, but I lost $700–$800 out of my own pocket. For the same reasons, the British players weren't able to play in our Open much, either.

Those British galleries—they were much different from Americans. They really knew their golf, and they'd applaud only for a really marvelous shot. If you hit an iron or chipped up eight or ten feet from the hole, they wouldn't make a sound. But a difficult pitch or a long iron to within a few feet or inches, they'd really appreciate that.

All in all, we had a very good time, and we were elated when we climbed back on that boat. It was a good thing, too, because the crossing coming home was bad. Most of the passengers stayed in bed nearly half the trip, it was so rough. And if we hadn't won, it would hardly have been worth it.

The food on our trip was also very different from what I was used to, and I'm afraid I can't say it was very good. There was a lot of mutton and a lot of thick porridge. About the only things I liked were the tea and cookies.

There was an even bigger party for us when we returned to New York, and though it had been a great experience to play in the Ryder Cup and the British Open, we were sure glad to get back to our home in Reading and return to a more normal life. I played very few other tournaments that summer, because I'd lost so much time out of my shop with the Ryder Cup trip.

An interesting sidelight to my time in Reading was the change in how club members saw the club professional. Louise and I played bridge and went to parties at the homes of several of the members. This was kind of a transition time for club pros, because up till then they were considered more in the lower working class. But we had quite a busy social life in Reading, and made many good friends during our stay. Of course, it didn't hurt that I'd won the Masters before I arrived and the Open a few months before I left.

One of my more interesting experiences as a teacher at Reading was with a young lady named Betty Pfeil. Her mother made an appointment for me to give Betty a lesson, and before I ever met Betty or her mother, several people had told me that Betty had the makings of a good player if someone could teach her not to overswing.

Well, Betty and Mrs. Pfeil came out for the lesson, and I watched Betty swing for a good forty-five minutes, talked to her a little about this or that part of her game, but never mentioned anything about overswinging. When I was done, her mother asked me why, and I said, "Mrs. Pfeil, Betty doesn't overswing. She's extremely supple, and she doesn't lose the club at the top or move her head, so she's not overswinging." That seemed to give Betty more confidence in her game, and she went on to be quite a good player. Won the Pennsylvania State Amateur several times, I believe.

Another fine woman player I became acquainted with while I was at Reading was Glenna Collett. She lived in Philadelphia, and though she was several years older than I, she liked to watch me play, so she'd come see me in quite a few local tournaments. I got to see her play quite often, too, and she was the finest woman golfer I'd ever seen at that time. Now, she couldn't have beaten Babe Zaharias or Mickey Wright or the good modern women pros, but she was a fine player, with a beautiful swing—and no one can argue with her record. In Glenna's day, it was still "ladies' golf," not women's golf as it became later and is today, and the ladies then didn't have the strength or the distance they developed later on.

In the fall of '37, I was invited along with Denny Shute and Henry Picard, who had played with me on the Ryder Cup team, to go to Argentina to do a series of exhibitions and play in the Argentine Open. Louise and I went back to Texarkana before the trip, and I worked steadily on my game. There was no one around to bother me and I wasn't working there, so I had the practice area all to myself most of the time. I shagged balls for myself, and just kept refining my swing and working on my short game. Don Murphy, the pro who had come in after me, would come out sometimes and we'd talk about the golf swing. He taught pretty much what I was doing. He continued there till he retired a few years ago, and now is pro emeritus. A good man.

We were in Texarkana for about a month before we flew to Argentina. Folks today would find this hard to believe, but it took, by actual count, seven days to fly there. We flew a combination of DC-3's and PBY's—planes that would land and take off on water. We'd start early each day and stop about the middle of the afternoon, because none of the airports or water landing areas had any lights or radar.

With those PBY's, when we'd take off, they'd have a speedboat go out ahead of us and create a wake for us to take off on. And you'd land between these floating logs they'd anchored on the water. It wasn't the most enjoyable thing, believe me. In fact, looking back on that trip, I'd say aviation has improved since then even more than golf!

The worst part of the trip down was going through the mountains. That was something, flying through the Andes in a cabin that wasn't pressurized, at 23,000 feet or more. The plane was dipping and shifting in the wind currents like a blue darter looking for a bug, and we had to take oxygen through these tubes you held in your mouth. Denny Shute got terribly sick, but it didn't seem to bother me much at the time. Years later, when I began to fly for ABC and found I would just about get the shakes every time, I realized that experience in '37 really had affected me. I finally had to go see a hypnotist—Dr. Charles Wysong, brother to Dr. Dudley Wysong, whose son now plays some on the Senior Tour. His office was in McKinney, Texas, and he cured me in about a half-dozen sessions. I've never had any more trouble with it.

Anyway, the airline had made advance hotel reservations for us, which helped. The mosquitoes were so bad that the beds had mosquito netting all around them, or we never would have gotten much sleep. A Mr. Armstrong of Armour Meat Packing Company had arranged the whole trip; he also made sure our meals were set up ahead of time. I believe he was the head man for Armour in Buenos Aires. We had very good food in Argentina, and as you might expect, wonderful steaks much of the time.

It took us a week to get there. We were there a month, and spent another week getting back. We were paid our expenses plus $1500— and nothing for the two weeks of travel time. We played in a couple of small tournaments, the Argentine Open and another match play event. I didn't negotiate the greens very well—they were stiff and wiry—so I didn't score well at all.

One interesting thing happened during one of those exhibitions— a plague of locusts. The air was so thick with them that every time you swung a club, you'd kill six or seven of them and have to wipe off the club before you could hit again. Kind of upset your stomach, really. You could hardly see for all the locusts in the air, plus you'd crunch dozens of them under your feet when you walked. We played three holes before they finally called a halt, and we had to wait about three days till the wind switched directions and the bugs flew off somewhere else and let us play. We have a photo of it, and it's amazing—people can't believe we even tried to play under those conditions.

One other note: I got the first case of hives in my life down there. Thought it was the stress of traveling or something, but a doctor determined that it was the avocados with hot sauce I was eating every day. He told me to quit eating them, and the hives cleared up. But I've never had any trouble with avocados since then, so maybe it was the hot sauce—who knows?

We played about four exhibitions a week, plus those other tournaments, then flew to Rio de Janeiro, heading home. We stopped to give an exhibition in Rio, but I was tired and homesick, so I came on home. It was a great homecoming. Louise was always glad to see me come back when I went off to play in tournaments, but this time, with me being so far away for six weeks and her worrying about me flying and all, she was happier to see me than I ever expected.

The whole effect of the trip was so negative, really, that a few years later I turned down an offer to go to South Africa and play with Bobby Locke. Sam Snead went instead and got beat fourteen out of sixteen matches, but he was paid $10,000 and they gave him a real nice diamond. Louise didn't want me to go, of course, but she said later that she wouldn't have minded having that diamond.

You could say that 1937 was a whirlwind year for me, with my first Masters win, my first Ryder Cup, first British Open, my win in the International Match Play Championships, and the trip to Argentina that fall. So it's no wonder that I only played in a couple more tournaments by the end of the summer, not doing particularly well in either one. The first was in Miami, and from there, McSpaden and I went on to play in Nassau. It's interesting to note that our trip there and back was paid for. That was long before the PGA developed the idea of not accepting expenses or appearance money, which I think is a good idea and has been good for the integrity of the game all the way around.

Before we left for Texarkana that fall, Mr. Giles drew up my contract for renewal. He didn't say anything about a raise, so I told him very politely that I felt I had earned one, that I'd done a good job in the shop and had played well for the club. He agreed, and without another word, he raised my guarantee from $3750 to $5000. That wasn't salary, you understand. It was simply that if I didn't clear $5000 from my shop, club care costs, lessons, clothing, clubs, balls, etc., then the club would make up the difference. Fortunately, I had no trouble meeting and even surpassing that guarantee each year, due to increased play and more lessons. I was fortunate in that there was very little cash involved, as nearly everything was charged to each member's account. Also, the club paid Ralph Trout, my assistant, so I didn't need to worry about that. In 1939, I didn't get another increase; it stayed $5000, but once again, I wasn't worried about making it. Naturally, if you didn't make your guarantee, the club wouldn't be very happy with your performance if they had to pay out a lot of money. It was more of a protection in case you had a lot of bad weather or some such thing. Still, that raise surely was some good news to take home to Louise that night.

My winnings in '37 were $6,509.50, and my caddy and entrance fees were a little over ten percent of that, $712. I did get a $500 bonus from Spalding for winning the Masters, but not anything else that I remember. I ranked seventh on the money list, which was by far the best I'd done yet.

In 1938, I played in twenty-five tournaments and won two of them. Finished well in several more, but I wasn't burning up the course anywhere. I did play in the second Crosby Pro-Am, at Rancho Santa Fe in California. My partner was Johnny Weissmuller, the movie "Tarzan" and Olympic swimmer. Originally, you know, the amateurs played without any handicaps at all. We didn't do very well, as I recall, but Weissmuller sure was fun to play with.

Another amateur who played in that tournament was Eddie Lowery, who had McSpaden as his partner. Eddie had been Francis Ouimet's caddie in the U.S. Open in 1913. He told me once that he'd had to play hooky from school to do it. He would hide out until just before the round started, because they had truant officers in those days, and they were tough. But they didn't bother him after he got on the course. I'd met Eddie before, but spent quite a bit of time with him that week, and it became the start of a wonderful, lifelong friendship. Eddie was also the one who started me working with Kenny Venturi and Harvie Ward.

One of the most interesting stories that year was the weather during the San Francisco Match Play Tournament. The wind was blowing so bad that there were hurricane flags up out on the bay, but we played anyway. I led after the first qualifying round with a 77, if you can imagine that. I don't believe they'd play in weather like that now, and I'm glad. It really was scary, and dangerous.

In '38, I won a little money in most of the tournaments I played, had a good mini-streak of two out of three wins in Florida that spring, and then finished fifth at Augusta. Maybe I didn't win the Masters because they weren't demonstrating the Hammond organ this time. It wasn't a bad year at all, but it would have been hard to equal '37 anyway, and I didn't expect to.

Ben Hogan had turned pro two years before I did, but he was a late bloomer. He had trouble with hooking the ball too much, and it took him quite a long time to get that under control. So it took him a long while to make it on the tour to stay. He'd come out for a while, run out of money and go back to Fort Worth, come out again, go back to Texas, and so on. He grew quite discouraged at times, but I could see that he had not only talent, but a kind of dedication and stubborn persistence that no one else did. I encouraged him to keep at it and keep working on his game, and he did all right, finally. Ben practically invented practice, because back then, most clubs didn't even have a practice area, but Ben would spend hours working on his game wherever he could find a place to practice, and it's a great part of the reason he was so successful.

But it did take a while before he was on the tour to stay. In the early days of the Masters, they had a Calcutta pool, and in 1938, I was there at the party because I was the defending champion and Mr. Roberts asked that I make an appearance. So Ben Hogan's name came up, and no one bid on him at all. They were about to put his name in a pot with a couple of other players when I decided to buy him, and I gave $100. The next day, Ben saw me and said, "I hear you bought me in the Calcutta pool last night for $100." I said, "Yes, Ben, I did." He said, "Could I buy half-interest?" So I agreed and he scrounged around and came up with fifty dollars. But he didn't play very well at all and finished out of the money, so at least I only lost $50.

In the '38 Masters, I was the defending champion, of course, and in the first round, by tradition, I was paired with Bob Jones. It was the second big thrill I had in golf, as far as playing with the legends was concerned. At that time, Jones always played the first round of the Masters with the defending champion, and the last with the tournament leader. He was very nice to play with, talked just the right amount, and encouraged me. He shot a 76 that day, and I had a 73, but it was quite a while after he'd quit playing publicly, and he was really serving as the host of the tournament more than as a player.

When he became too ill to play a few years later, he gave me a great honor by asking me to play the final round in his place, which I did from 1946 until 1956, when Kenny Venturi was the leader. Then the committee decided that since I had worked closely with Kenny, it would be unfair to the other players to have me paired with him, and they put Snead with him instead. After that, they changed to putting the leader with whoever was closest to him, like they do now.

On that spring tour I recall something else pretty unusual happening in a tournament at St. Petersburg, Florida—I whiffed one. That's right, flat missed the ball. It was in the last round, on a par five, and I drove over to the left side of the fairway, right in front of a nice, five-foot-tall palm tree. When I took a practice swing, my club just barely touched the leaves, so I figured I was okay. But when I took my 4-iron back and started down, the club hit a leaf just hard enough to kind of grab on to it, and I swung right over the top of the ball—never even moved it. No choice but to knock it out in three, and I hit my approach close enough to make my putt for a fairly unusual five.

One interesting thing about the North and South Open, which was always held at Pinehurst. For the money we were making, it was a very expensive place to play, since about the only hotel was the Carolina Inn, where you had to dress for dinner every night—black tie, the works. We never actually stayed there until '39, and they put all the golfers on the ground floor. Naturally, as we came in after our rounds, we'd be talking about how we'd played, and first one and then another fellow would come out of his room, and pretty soon we'd all be standing out in the hall, talking about golf. It was really fun. Louise and I felt we were living high on the hog in those early days at Pinehurst.

But in '38, I really was even busier at the club than I had been the year before, so I couldn't play in as many tournaments as I had at Ridgewood, particularly if they were very far away. One I did play in was the Cleveland Open, when a fellow named Babe Ruth played. After watching him, I thought it was good he played baseball and not golf, because I don't think he'd ever have made a good golfer. But the gallery loved seeing him.

The U.S. Open in '38 was at Cherry Hills. I finished fifth and won $412.50, but my clearest memory of that tournament was the rough. It was very inconsistent, and one time, I know it took me two shots to get out of it. Tough course. For the last thirty-six holes I was paired with Dick Metz, who was leading the tournament at the time. But he started leaving every approach shot short of the green, and leaving every putt short, too. I liked Dick very much, and felt sorry for him, but there wasn't anything I could do to help him. He had a terrible score and finished way out of contention.

The PGA was at Shawnee Country Club in Shawnee on the Delaware, Pennsylvania. Fred Waring, the wonderful bandleader, owned the course. He was also involved in the Waring Company, and as a result, all of the players were given a Waring blender. Quite a newfangled gadget at the time. Unfortunately, it was one of those times when I got hot too early. I beat Harry Bassler, a pro from California, 11 and 10 in my third match, but lost steam after that and got beat in the quarterfinals by Jimmy Hines, 2 and 1.

Runyan and Snead made it to the finals that year, and Runyan used a 4-wood to Snead's 6-iron and put his ball inside Sam's every time, nearly. He was already being called "Little Poison" then, and beat Snead 8 and 7. We didn't have match play tournaments very often—usually in the PGA Championship and a few other events. Even then, tournament organizers were realizing it was hard to predict whether the so-called big names would make it to the finals, and that really affected their ability to sell tickets and make money, or even break even. My own match play record was good, but it should have been better. I had quite a few early matches with what I would call less experienced players, but felt I had to play hard in those matches to keep myself fired up, and I'd peak too early. In the PGA at Pomonok in '39, for instance, I beat Dutch Harrison 10 and 9 in the semifinals, but I must have used up all my good shots, because I lost to Picard in the final on the 37th hole. Still, I was tenth on the money list that year, and got some sort of a bonus from Spalding, plus balls and equipment. Not a great year, but certainly nothing to be ashamed of.

1938 was also the year I got started in the golf shoe business. While McSpaden and I were at Pinehurst playing in the North and South, we got to talking with Miles Baker, a salesman for Field and Flint, who made wonderful men's street shoes. Miles was from Kansas City and a good friend of Jug McSpaden, and he liked golf. Lots of times he would arrange his schedule so he could be where the tour was. We saw him at quite a few of the tournaments. Anyway, this evening we were complaining to Miles about the sorry state of golf shoes. The soles were so thin you could feel the spikes almost right through the leather. And of course, when it rained or we had to play on a wet course, the shoes wouldn't hold up at all.

So we were telling Miles all this, and we said, "You make such excellent street shoes—'Dr. Locke' and 'Foot-Joy.' Why couldn't you make good golf shoes, too?" Miles asked us what we wanted, so we told him. We felt the sole needed to be thicker, and the shoes needed to be broader across the ball of the foot. A little while later, he had us come up to Boston to the factory there, and they made special lasts for us. Then they made up one pair for each of us to try—mine were British tan and brown with wingtips, and McSpaden's were white buck.

When we came out to the golf course in those new shoes, the players had a fit. "Where'd you get those shoes?" everybody was asking. So all of a sudden Field and Flint was in the golf shoe business, and McSpaden and I each received a 25-cent royalty per pair for quite a few years.

I shot my highest score ever, 434, in a tournament that year of '38, but I tied for third and won $950. For some reason I don't recall, we played 108 holes at Westchester, for a purse of $10,000. Guess they wanted to make sure the fans got their money's worth.

Toward the end of September in 1938, McSpaden and I went to do an exhibition in Butte, Montana, on our way to the Pacific Northwest. Louise came too, and we were to fly into Butte, but in those days you didn't fly very quickly. We took off right after playing in Tulsa and made a lot of stops; by the time we reached Butte it was about midnight. What was worse, though, was there was a snowstorm and we couldn't land, so we flew on and landed at Missoula. Then we caught a milk train from Missoula back to Butte that stopped at just about every little station to load five-gallon milk cans into the baggage car. It was terribly cold, but fortunately, there was one car that had a little old pot-bellied coal stove, and that's how we kept from freezing. The seats were just straight down and up with no padding, so they weren't very comfortable. We got to Butte about two and a half hours later and went straight to bed. When we woke up there was snow on the ground, but the man in charge said we still were going to play. At the golf course, thank goodness, there were just patches of snow, so we put on a clinic and then went out to play. Believe it or not, quite a few people had come out for this, but not being used to the cold weather, we were about to freeze. I finally noticed one man in the gallery who had on a beautiful, warm-looking down jacket. I said, "That sure looks good—I'd like to have that on me about now!" He said, "Well, I can't give you this one, but I'll send you one—what size do you wear?" Sure enough, he did send me one just like his, and though I don't get to wear it much here in Texas because we have such mild winters, it does come in handy once in a while.

That fall, we returned to Texarkana and Louise's folks' place. We'd been married over four years now, and we were beginning to wonder why we hadn't had any children. So Louise went to her doctor and was tested, and the doctor said there wasn't any reason he could find why she couldn't get pregnant. My turn was next, and that was when they discovered the high fever I'd had with the typhoid had made me sterile. Louise was very disappointed, naturally, and I was, too, but she took it very well, didn't brood about it, though it made her sad for quite a while. Some time later, she wanted to adopt a child, but I wasn't in favor of it. We had to travel so much, and it wasn't like it is on the tour now, with nurseries and special arrangements for babies. You almost never saw a tour player's children at any tournament, unless it was being played in his city. It was just too much trouble, driving from city to city as we did then, to have children along and try to bring them up that way.

The other problem was I'd seen so many adopted children who just didn't turn out right, for one reason or another. I was very reluctant to take that sort of a chance, and after a while, Louise gave up the idea and turned her energies instead to her nieces and nephews. I guess that in all our fifty years of marriage, that was the one regret she had. This may sound strange, but I never particularly regretted not having any children, except for Louise's sake, because I always wanted to please her and make her happy. She was a wonderful wife in every way, and I know she would have been a wonderful mother, too. As it turned out, when we moved back to Texas and settled in Roanoke in '46, we spent so much time with Louise's nieces and nephews that we almost felt we'd helped raise quite a few of them. That helped Louise tremendously, and I enjoyed it, too.

In 1938, though, we spent the fall in Texarkana, with me practicing quite a bit and Louise enjoying being with her family. We lived at her parents' home, since they had a spare bedroom. It was good to be free of the responsibility of running a club for a while, because it gave me more time to concentrate on my game. Really, those times in Texarkana were about the only vacations we had while I was on the tour.

I didn't do anything spectacular in California those first weeks on tour in '39. Probably the most interesting thing I did was play in a pro-am at Hillcrest in Los Angeles with Chico Marx. He was very animated and funny, though he didn't say much. When he signed the scorecard, he wrote, "I enjoyed it—bet you didn't." But I did tie for seventh in L.A., finished eighth in Oakland, and lost the first round in the San Francisco Match Play tournament. Then I tied for second in the Crosby Pro-Am, and was third in the Texas Open at San Antonio. In that Texas Open McSpaden and I played a practice round against Runyan and Ben Hogan, and McSpaden shot a 59. I helped four shots, making our best ball 55. Not everyone knows that the Texas Open is one of the oldest on the tour. Only the Western, the PGA, and the U.S. Open have been going on longer.

The next tournament in '39 was the Phoenix Open, and that was when I finally woke up. I won by twelve strokes. Mind you, that was a 54-hole tournament, so I had to be playing good to be leading that much after three rounds. I shot 64 in the Pro-Am, then 68-65-65. All that work for $700. Believe it or not, it snowed so much in Phoenix Friday and Saturday that we couldn't play either day, and had to play thirty-six on Sunday just to have a tournament at all. The two 65's I shot that Sunday were the record for one day for quite a few years.

I let up a little bit after Phoenix, and didn't play particularly well for the next couple of months. One thing of interest, though, was the Thomasville tournament in Georgia. The course was Glen Arven, and it had the oddest finishing hole I ever saw. It was a par 5, and horseshoe or U-shaped, so the green was no more than a hundred yards from the tee. The area within the "U" was considered out of bounds, and that wasn't so unusual, but they had a local rule that said you couldn't even cut across that out of bounds area. If you hit your drive to the right spot to try and go over the "U," they could rule your ball O.B., even if it landed on the green. Kept us all honest, I guess.

It's also interesting to realize that there was often quite a bit of difference in the purses among various tournaments, much more so than there is now. Most had a purse of $5000, and occasionally one would offer $10,000, but there were still quite a few of $3000 or less. And even the $10,000-purse events didn't pay everyone who made the cut—mostly only the top twenty places or so. We still played in every one we could get to, though. Obviously, we weren't playing just for the money sometimes, more for the fun of it and the chance to keep working on our games.

Back then, you learned to play winning golf by playing on the tour. None of us had college degrees or any other kind of jobs other than club jobs, and we hadn't had all the training that the young men and women have today on their tours. We had what I guess you might call on-the-job training. It was tough at times, but life was good, too.

In St. Petersburg that spring, I played with Frank Walsh, whose brother became president of the PGA some years later. Frank was a pretty good player himself, but had some odd ideas. For one, he always believed that good players carried their clubs in their left hand. Jimmy Demaret was the only one I knew of who did, and he was a pretty good hacker, but I never really noticed anyone else doing that consistently. Guess I had my mind more on my own game.

My next big target that year was the North and South Tournament at Pinehurst #2. I hadn't yet played as well there as I felt I should have, and I was hoping to do better this time. I played very steady, nothing really very unusual, shot 280 and won by two strokes. They say when you're playing well, you get a lot of breaks—or another way of putting it, the harder you work, the luckier you get. But on the seventeenth hole in the last round, I really did have a bit of luck—both good and bad.

The bad part was my tee shot buried in the face of the right-hand bunker on a fairly steep upslope with the pin cut on the right side. The good part was I holed out for a 2, and that birdie ended up being half of my two-stroke winning margin.

The reason I say I was fortunate was that I didn't putt very well through the entire tournament. In fact, after it was over, R.A. Stranahan, the president of Champion Spark Plug in Toledo, Ohio, and the father of Frank Stranahan, who later became a fine golfer, came to me in the locker room and said, "You made a liar out of me." Surprised, I said, "How did I do that?" And he replied, "I said no one could putt poorly and win this tournament." So I guess it's a good thing I didn't have to putt on the seventeenth. Mr. Stranahan was around golf a lot, involved in various golf organizations, and an avid golfer himself. To give him credit, he was right—it was very unusual for someone to putt poorly and still manage to win.

The North and South was a very important win for me, since it was considered a major at the time, and I felt very good about being able to win despite very average putting. I was very happy to have achieved another goal of mine, and the folks at Reading were, too.

In defense of my putting, though, the greens we played from city to city were so inconsistent that we mostly concentrated on getting our approach shots close enough to the pin that we wouldn't have to worry about putting much. Very few of the pros worked a whole lot on their putting. Made more sense to work on your irons or your chipping.

I played all right the next two weeks, finishing tenth at Greensboro and seventh at the Masters, then skipped Asheville, the Met Open, and the Goodall Round Robin. Not because I had to be at the club, but because I had been given another wonderful opportunity to advance in my career as a club professional.

Cloyd Haas, president of the Haas-Jordan Company in Toledo and a member at Inverness, had gone to George Jacobus, my good friend at Ridgewood, and told him Inverness was looking for a new pro. George told him about me, and also suggested he speak with Ben Hogan up the road at Hershey Country Club. Mr. Haas did exactly that, and I guess he liked the way I combed my hair better or something. Anyway, he invited me to come up to Inverness, which I did the next week, and I signed a contract with Ralph Carpenter, president of the club and of Dana Corporation, to come to Inverness in April 1940.

I would be paid $3600 in salary—basically about $600 a month for the time I'd be there, plus I got all the profits from the shop. The club paid the caddiemaster, Huey Rogers, and either all or part of assistant pro Herman Lang's salary. Even then, though I was playing well and winning money most of the time, I wasn't thinking about making a living on the tour. I knew I needed that club job to survive.

My Inverness contract was again an improvement over what I was making at Reading, but also a lot more responsibility, larger membership, and a well-known championship course. As you can imagine, I was flying pretty high. I also signed an endorsement contract with MacGregor in June 1939. Tommy Armour was the pro at Boca Raton, and his clubs were the main ones MacGregor was making then. We pros were all at Boca at the time for a meeting, and afterwards I went to Tommy's pro shop and picked out a set of his irons, called "Silver Scots." Two weeks later, I won the Open with those irons and kept them quite a while—at least till I had MacGregor make some with my own name on them.

The Open that year was held at Philadelphia Country Club, which at that time had two courses: Bala Cynwyd in town, and the Spring Mill Course out in the country, where the tournament was to be held. I felt I was playing rather well, hitting my irons great, and in the practice rounds, I scored close to par. It was normally a par-71 course, but the USGA wanted to make it more difficult, and changed two of the short par fives into par fours, which made it a par 69—about the only time such a "short" course has been an Open site. One of the redesigned holes was the eighth, and the other was the twelfth. This was in the days before clubs would spend money to change a course just for a specific tournament.

You might be interested to know that despite a par of 69, those par fours were far from easy. They were 480, 454, 453, 449, 447, 425, and 421 yards, so you know we were using those long irons a lot.

I was very nervous in the first round and played poorly for the first seven holes. The eighth was a long par 4, slightly uphill. I hit a good drive and a 2-iron on the green and almost birdied it. On the 9th I hit a long iron to within eight feet of the pin and made it, which encouraged me. I really did hit my irons well, though I never holed a chip or pitch the entire time. In the four regulation and two playoff rounds, I hit the pin six times with my irons, from 1-iron to 8-iron.

We played thirty-six holes the last day, and I was paired with Olin Dutra, who'd won in '34 at Merion. We were both well in contention. My friend from Texarkana, J.K. Wadley, was following us, and also knew Olin. After our first eighteen, he offered to buy us lunch. Dutra ordered roast beef with gravy, mashed potatoes and all the trimmings. I said, "I'll have the same," and Mr. Wadley said, "No, you won't." He ordered for me—a chicken sandwich on toast with no mayonnaise, some vegetables, iced tea, and half a piece of apple pie.

That afternoon, it was hot and muggy. Dutra played badly, and I shot a 1-under-par 68, which got me in a tie with Denny Shute and Craig Wood. That taught me a good lesson, not to eat too heavy a meal before going out to play, and I've abided by it ever since.

I was very fortunate to get into that playoff. Snead, who was worried about Shute playing behind him, made a poor club selection on eighteen. He thought he needed a birdie to win when he only needed a par, but he ended up with an 8, so he missed both winning and getting into the playoff.

In the first playoff, Shute struggled to a 76, while Craig and I tied at 68. On the last hole, Craig was leading me by a stroke and tried to reach the green at 18 in two, but hooked his second shot badly, and hit a man in the gallery right in the head. The man had been standing in the rough to the left, and the ball dropped and stayed there in the rough, about thirty yards short of the green. The fellow was knocked out, and they carried him across the green right in front of us while Craig waited to play his third shot. Of course, his ball would have been in even worse trouble if it hadn't gotten stopped, but that didn't make Craig feel any better. He hit a pitch shot then that left him with a six-footer for birdie, while my ball was eight feet away. I would putt first.

As I stood over my ball, suddenly the thought popped into my head of all the times when we were playing as caddies at Glen Garden and we'd say, "This putt is for the U.S. Open." Now I was really playing that dream out, and it steadied me enough that I sank my putt. But Craig left his just one inch short, so we were tied.

That meant another 18-hole playoff in those days, and the committee asked us before we played that afternoon whether we would be willing to go to sudden death if we tied again. We both said, "No, we'll go a full eighteen." They weren't real happy to hear that, because the folks working on the tournament had to get back to their jobs, and of course the members wanted their course back. But we both felt the same way, that we didn't want to win based on just one or two holes. So they agreed.

On the second playoff, I hit a bad second shot at the first hole and ended up in the deep right bunker, but I got up and down all right. On the second, a long par three, we had to use drivers, and had to carry the green. I pushed mine into some deep rough, while Wood's tee shot landed on the green. I got out with my sand wedge and saved par, and Wood two-putted. The next hole I birdied while Craig parred, and on the fourth, I hit a good drive, then holed a 1-iron for an eagle, while Craig made another four.

When I was lining up to play my second shot, I wasn't thinking at all about holing out. But I'd been striking my irons so well, had just birdied the third hole, and I felt I could hit this one close and make birdie again. Sure enough, the ball went straight up to the green and straight into the hole like a rat. There were a lot of folks in the gallery, and they whooped and hollered quite a bit, though they were still quieter than the fans are now. You know, when you're on the golf course and hear the spectators cheering, you learn quickly that the applause for an eagle is different from a birdie, and of course it's even louder for a hole in one. No matter where you are, you can tell by the applause just how good the shot was. What you don't want to hear the gallery do when you're playing is give a big groan—because that means you just missed a short putt.

Anyway, as I walked off the green, I remember thinking very vividly, "Boy, I'm three strokes ahead now!" But I knew it was no time to turn negative or quit being aggressive. I knew I had to continue playing well. As it happened, I then bogeyed a couple of holes but so did Craig, and that three-stroke lead proved to be my winning margin, 70 to 73.

Harold McSpaden—who was really the best friend I had on the tour—walked along with me through both of the playoff rounds, helping me get through the gallery and just being there. Naturally, he didn't say anything, but his presence and support sure were a big help to me.

Mr. Giles, my boss and friend from Reading, was there with quite a few of the members, so you might say I almost had my own gallery. George Jacobus was there too, and was nearly beside himself with excitement. He said to me afterwards, "You remember, Byron, we talked about this, and I said, 'You're going to be the National

Champion one of these days.'" I was kind of in a trance for a few days before I fully realized I was indeed the U.S. Open champion and had accomplished another dream.

After I got back home, the members of all three clubs—Berkleigh, Galen Hall, and Reading—gave Louise and me a wonderful party. They presented Louise with a large silver bowl that had her name engraved on it. Then they gave me a handsome, solid gold watch by Hamilton, engraved on the back "Byron Nelson, Winner U.S. Open 1939–40, Members of Reading Country Club." I still have both of them. They also gave me a Model 70 Winchester 30.06, a mighty fine rifle. That was arranged by Alex Kagen, a member at Berkleigh, who owned a sporting goods store and had once asked me if I hunted. When I told him all I had was a shotgun, he came up with the idea for the Winchester. I used it every time I went hunting, and kept it until just recently, when I sold it to my good friend, Steve Barley.

So there I was, the U.S. Open champion, with a contract I'd signed two weeks before to go to Inverness, just like when I signed the contract to go to Reading one week before I won the Masters. Some people would say I needed an agent to help me capitalize on my wins, but hardly anybody had one in those days. Hagen was the only one I knew of who did—a fellow named Bob Harlow, the golf writer who started *Golf World* magazine.

Shortly after the Open, Ben and Valerie Hogan came to visit and stayed a week. We practiced a lot and played some. I had to work, of course, but Ben played a couple of times with Mr. Giles, and he really enjoyed getting a chance to play with Ben, who was playing much better by then.

As it happened, my next tournament was the Inverness Invitational Four-Ball, which involved seven two-man teams. It was an interesting format, where you scored only plus or minus over seven rounds and four days of play. I was paired with McSpaden, and we tied for first at plus 6, then lost on the first playoff hole. This was my first real chance to see the course and the club where I'd be working the next year, and I enjoyed myself.

One week later, I won the Massachusetts State Open. McSpaden wanted me to come play in it because he knew the course real well, and because we were such good friends. I went, and in the last round,

Harold and I were battling it out pretty tight. Along about the middle of the last nine, there was a long par 3 with a bunker on the right. I pushed my tee shot into the bunker and holed it from there. That kept me going good and I won by four shots. I won $400 plus $250 appearance money. There weren't many events that paid appearance money then, and I'm glad the PGA stopped it, but it sure did come in handy back when most of us were just barely making ends meet.

The PGA that year was at Pomonok, Long Island. The World's Fair was in New York, and my mother came to see me play and see the fair, too. It was the only tournament she ever saw me play in. I beat Chuck Garringer, Red Francis, John Revolta, and Emerick Kocsis—brother to Chuck, a wonderful amateur who still shoots better than his age—to get to the quarterfinals. Then I went up against Dutch Harrison, and either I was playing awfully well or he was way off his game, but after the 26th hole, I was 9 up, and as we came to the 27th hole, Dutch said to me, "Byron, why don't you just birdie this one, too, and we won't have to go past the clubhouse." I thought it was a good idea. As it happened, I did birdie, and beat him 10 and 9.

In the finals, though, I had my hands more than full with Picard. I was one up coming to the last hole, and Picard laid me a dead stymie. It was a short par 4, and I had pitched to three feet. But Picard's shot stopped twelve inches from the hole directly in my line, and since we were playing stymies, you didn't mark your ball or anything—the other fellow had to figure out a way to get over or around you and in the cup. Unfortunately, I didn't make my shot go in, and we tied.

Picard won on the first extra hole, but there's a little story connected with how it happened. This was the first tournament ever that was broadcast on radio. It was just short-wave, and it was done by Ted Heusing and Harry Nash. Ted Heusing was an excellent broadcaster who my good friend Chris Schenkel admired a great deal, and Harry Nash was a fine golf writer for the *Newark Evening News*.

On that first extra hole, Picard hit his drive into the right rough, and Ted and Harry were riding in a sizable four-wheeled vehicle, right close by. They didn't see where Picard's ball had landed, and drove right over it. The officials ruled that he should get a free drop, which was only right, and he put his next shot twenty feet from the hole and made birdie to win.

I took the next week off, missing the tournament in Scranton, to make sure things were in order back at the club and to practice some for the Western Open, another major I had my sights set on. It was at Medinah #3, and I drove exceptionally well—seldom ever got in the rough at all. I won by one shot, and it meant even more to me because the trophy had been donated by my friend J.K. Wadley.

Though the North and South and the Western Open aren't considered majors now—the North and South doesn't even exist anymore—you knew then which ones were more important because the golf club companies would award bonuses for them. I got $500 from Spalding that year for the Western, which was always considered somewhat more important than the North and South because it drew from all around the country. The other was always played at Pinehurst, and a lot of the players from the western part of the country didn't go. Another reason the Western was ranked higher was that the tournament contributed money to the Chick Evans Scholarship Fund, which added prestige and publicity. Evans, an excellent golfer, was always there, too, and his name meant a lot of good things to golf. He'd won the Open himself, and had been a caddie like most of us, so I felt really good about winning the Western.

The next regular tour event I played well in was the Hershey Open several weeks later. The tournament was sponsored by Mr. Hershey himself, who was the president of the club and a very nice man. Par was 73. I was 5 under and leading going into the fourth round, and paired with Ed Dudley and Jimmy Hines. We came to the 15th hole, where you'd drive down the fairway and over a hill. Well, I drove right down the middle of it, but when we got to the place where my ball should have been, it was nowhere to be found. There wasn't any confusion about it, because my golf balls had my name imprinted on them, and everyone there had seen mine go absolutely straight down the fairway and disappear over the hill.

I had no choice but to go back and hit another ball. But with that two-stroke penalty I ended up in fourth place. Afterwards, I was talking to the press in the locker room and told them what had happened. Fred Corcoran was managing the tour then, and always trying to get publicity, so he got all the papers he could to pick up the story.

About ten days later, I received an anonymous letter stating that the writer's guest and friend at the tournament, a young woman who knew nothing about golf, had picked up my ball and put it in her purse. After the tournament, as they returned to New York on the train, the woman opened her purse and showed him the ball she'd found on the course, and the gentleman realized then what had happened. Since these were the days before gallery ropes, people walked all over the course in front of you and in back of you and right alongside you. The young lady had apparently been walking across the fairway at the bottom of the hill after I drove, saw the ball lying there, and simply picked it up.

The letter was postmarked from the New York Central Post Office, and the man included money orders totaling $300—the difference between third prize in the tournament and fourth, where I finished. The money orders were signed "John Paul Jones"—clearly fictitious. I never did find out who did it, but whoever it was, it was a nice thing to do.

I guess I got a lot of media attention for that time but it was very little compared to what goes on now. I was glad for the attention, but since I hadn't talked to the press much after beating Lawson Little in San Francisco in '35 and winning the Masters in '37, it took some getting used to. I was even being interviewed on radio now, though we always had to go downtown to the station to do it.

I've always been fortunate with the publicity I received, and have had very little inaccurate reporting. Might be because I was always a little on the shy side, and didn't really talk very much or very fast, so the reporters couldn't get much wrong. I'd have to say, overall, that I enjoyed the attention. After I won the Open especially, people in the gallery would say, "Boy, you're sure hitting your irons good," or some such thing, and that would encourage me. Then I'd try even harder, because I didn't want to let them down.

With three majors to my credit, 1939 was definitely my best year so far. My official winnings were $9444, making me fifth on the money list. My stroke average was 71.02, good enough to win the Vardon Trophy, which was an added bonus.

The year I'd have in 1945 was a little more unusual, but with the quality of the tournaments that I won—three majors—and the way I played, 1939 was right up there with '45. And naturally, I had no idea what would happen in '45 was even possible. No, at that point, I was simply looking ahead to the winter tour and wanting to do my best for the folks at Inverness the next spring.

So Louise and I packed up and went back to Texarkana, where I practiced and played some with my friends or with the pro there, Don Murphy. Looking back on the whole year, I was more than satisfied with my accomplishments.

SIX
· · · · ·

Inverness
and the
War Years

W ITH MY JOB AT INVERNESS—A WONDERFUL CLUB
and wonderful golf course—waiting for me the next spring, I guess I
was a little nervous going out on the tour that winter of 1940. I certainly didn't get my game going very quickly. For some reason I can't
recall, I skipped several tournaments early that year. I didn't play at
Los Angeles, Oakland, or the Crosby Pro-Am; I lost in the quarterfinals at San Francisco, and finished out of the money at Phoenix. Not
a very good start.

Back then the tour was different than it is now. A lot of us pros
drove from tournament to tournament in a kind of caravan, and right
after Phoenix, which happened to end on my birthday that year, we all
headed for Texas. Ben and Valerie Hogan and Louise and I liked to
stick together, so we'd follow each other pretty closely on the road.
You kind of had to do that, because if you had car trouble, it was good
to have a buddy nearby to help you fix a flat or whatever.

There was a place in Las Cruces, New Mexico, where we liked to
stop for lunch. They had the best tamales and chili we'd ever tasted,
with real authentic Mexican flavor. One particular time, we decided to
ask if we could buy some to take along with us. The waitress told us,

"Well, the tamales come in a can, and they're made by the Armour Meat Company in Fort Worth." All four of us just looked at her. Then at each other. Somehow, those tamales had suddenly lost their appeal, and we never ordered them again.

On that same trip, the wives of Ed "Porky" Oliver and Harold McSpaden weren't along, so Ed and Harold were driving together. It was a good hard day's drive from Phoenix to Van Horn, Texas, where most of us stopped for the night. McSpaden drove pretty fast, but Oliver was a lot more cautious. They were going along down this two-lane road and had to go through a tunnel at one point. Ed kept telling McSpaden to slow down, but Harold just kept saying, "I know this road like the back of my hand." They got into this tunnel, and the tunnels then were always narrower than the road, and halfway through, barreling along at full speed, they met this fellow driving a wagon pulled by two big old mules. They just barely squeaked by, with McSpaden not slowing down hardly at all, and when they got through, Oliver yelled, "Don't tell me you knew that wagon and those mules were going to be there, too!" I don't know that they ever rode together after that, because it scared Ed pretty bad.

We all made it to Van Horn, including Oliver and McSpaden, and stayed at the El Capitan Hotel, which we always liked because they had wonderful hot biscuits and their food was very good. About dinnertime, we noticed that Oliver had disappeared. When he showed up about five hours later, everyone wanted to know where he'd been. He'd gone to a double feature movie the entire evening. Imagine— after sitting in a car from dawn till dark, he goes and sits in a theatre for four hours more. We couldn't believe it. But it was all part of life on the road, and even though we had to do a lot of driving, we all stuck together and had a lot of fun.

As far as tournaments go, though, the first good thing I remember about that year was the Texas Open at Brackenridge Park. Ben Hogan and I tied at 271. I beat him in the playoff, 70–71, and broke 70 all four regulation rounds. It seems as if I played better against Ben on the average than I did against anybody else. I tried harder against him, because I knew I had to.

After we tied, we were told that a San Antonio radio station wanted to interview us. There wasn't any such thing as a remote broadcast then, so they had to take us downtown to the station. I was asked how I felt about tying for the tournament and being in the playoff with Ben, and I said, "Anytime you can tie Ben or beat him, it's a feather in your cap, because he's such a fine player." Then they asked Ben the same thing, and he said, "Byron's got a good game, but it'd be a lot better if he'd practice. He's too lazy to practice." Ben never did think I practiced enough. But I did manage to beat him the next day, practice or not.

The next tournament was the Western Open at River Oaks in Houston. On the morning of the first round, my head hurt and I felt terrible. I shot a 78. The next day, I tried to play, because I hated to withdraw, but I shot 40 on the first nine and nearly passed out, and just had to quit. It turned out I had the flu and ended up in bed four days. I didn't get the flu often, but whenever I did, it really laid me flat. Jimmy Demaret won the Western that year in a playoff with Toney Penna.

We went on to New Orleans, and I must have still been weak, because I finished fifteenth and won $146. I don't remember much else about that week, except that we were staying at the St. Charles Hotel, and Louise and I were having breakfast in the dining room when she realized she'd left her aquamarine ring in our room. She went up to get it, but it was gone. We called in the manager and house detective and everyone, but it was never found. Louise was very upset about it. The ring wasn't all that expensive, but I had brought it back from my trip to South America in '37, and it had a lot of sentimental value for her.

The spring of 1940 was my first chance to play in the Seminole Invitational, one of the pros' favorite tournaments. In the pro-am, if you won, you got 10% of the money in the Calcutta pool. The pros loved to get invited, because not only was it a wonderful golf course, but they had great food—a buffet every night that had more good food than any of us had ever seen before.

Next was the St. Petersburg Open. I made an eight-footer on the last hole for a 69, finished second to Demaret and won $450. Demaret was two years older than Ben and I, but he never would admit it until it was time for him to collect social security. He always claimed, in fact, that he was actually younger than we were.

In the Miami Four-Ball that year at the Biltmore Hotel golf course, McSpaden and I were partners. In the first round, we beat Johnny Farrell and Felix Serafin, 7 and 6, and then got trounced in the second round by Paul Runyan and Horton Smith, 5 and 4. They were a fine partnership team and outputted us that day. They were always wonderful putters, both of them.

In the Thomasville Open at Glen Arven Country Club in Georgia, I finished second again, this time to Lloyd Mangrum, though I broke 70 all four rounds. Next was the North and South, where I was defending champion. I finished second again at 2 under, won another $450, and lost to Hogan, who had two very fine first rounds and held on to win.

The Greensboro Open was played then at two courses, Starmount Forest and Sedgefield. I shot 68–68 the last two rounds and was third at 280. My philosophy at this point was not to have a bad round, and to have at least one hot round each tournament. I didn't always do it, but that was what I knew I had to do to win or finish near the top.

Next was the Masters. Even then, just a few years after Bob Jones and Clifford Roberts started this wonderful tournament, it was a very prestigious one, and everyone coveted the title. I always loved going, seeing the flowers and Jones and Cliff. Just being at the Masters always got me excited and I nearly always played well there. That year, I finished third at 3 under and won $600. This was when the greens were not only as fast as they are today, but they were hard as rock, too. If you landed an iron shot on the green, it would bounce six feet in the air and roll off nearly every time. You couldn't back the ball up no matter how much spin you put on it. Being able to back the ball up or land it on the green and stop it came about in later years.

Immediately after the Masters, Louise and I drove straight to Toledo. I was a little anxious about how I would do at Inverness. I felt I could handle it, but there were so many more active members compared to what I was used to. At Reading, I had less than a hundred sets of clubs to care for, and not all of those members were real active golfers. At Inverness, I had 365 sets of clubs, all quite active. I replaced Al Sargent, whose father was pro at Atlanta and had been Bob Jones's pro when Jones was a young man. The golf shop at Inverness was in a separate building, about seventy-five yards from the clubhouse and right next to the first tee. In fact, it had been the clubhouse at one time. It was built when the original clubhouse had burned down years before, and served as a temporary clubhouse until the new one was completed. Then it became the golf shop. The caddies' room was in the back, then there was my office, and then the shop itself. It was a nice building with high ceilings, though the shop was a little smaller than I would have liked.

One of the first things I did was to stock shoes. I brought in eighty-four pairs of men's shoes, both street and golf, by Foot-Joy, selected with the help of my friend Miles Baker. Miles told me I was really the first pro to do this. Most pros would have sample pairs of different styles, but the members had to order them and then wait several weeks to get them. My eighty-four pairs covered all the styles in just about all the sizes and widths, which made it very convenient to sell the shoes on the spot.

Next, I talked to Mr. Carpenter and got his permission to put up an 8 × 8-foot square mirror on the wall across from the door. It not only made the shop look bigger, but when the weather was bad or I had time, I'd use that mirror to check my swing. When I had lessons scheduled during rainy weather, I'd put the students in front of that mirror and work with them, have them check their shoulder alignment, grip, stance, where they placed the ball, and so forth. It was really quite helpful.

When I arrived they gave me a locker upstairs, right where a group of the most prominent and influential members' lockers were. That was a big help, because I got acquainted with them more easily. Another thing that helped me greatly was that Huey Rodgers, the caddiemaster, would stand at the door of the shop, and when he'd see the members coming from the clubhouse, he'd tell me who they were. That way, I got to know the members by name very quickly, and it impressed them that I could learn their names so soon—I don't guess they knew Huey was helping me.

One of the first things I found to be different at Inverness was bookkeeping. At Reading, I had been fortunate in this regard. I just kept all the members' charge slips and simply turned them in to the club bookkeeper each month. But at Inverness, it was a whole new world. It was so much busier, for one thing, and then I found I was expected to do my own bookkeeping, which naturally took quite a lot of time. Actually, I didn't know how to go about it at all, and in about six weeks, I had all these boxes full of slips and charges and merchandise orders and no idea how to organize them. I was terribly confused. Finally I asked one of the members what to do, and he recommended

Roy Bowersock, a fine CPA with the accounting firm Wideman and Madden, who got my books straightened out and taught me how to keep them myself. His firm was bought out by Ernst and Young some years later, and they moved Roy to Tulsa about the time I moved back to Texas in 1946. A year later, Roy was transferred to Fort Worth, and did all my bookkeeping and accounting for many years afterwards. I've been pretty good about it ever since—in fact, good enough to get me out of trouble with the IRS many years later.

About this time I was advised I needed to have an official domicile for tax purposes, and I figured Texas would be the best place, because it was one of the few states that had community property laws to protect Louise in case anything happened to me. It was also my home state, and Louise and I had felt for some time that if I ever left the tour, we wanted to settle near Fort Worth, because my family was all there and her sister Delle had married and moved there by this time.

Just as important to me was the fact that I'd wanted to do something for my folks for some time. They were living in Handley, Texas, and my father was running a feed store there. My brother Charles, about fourteen, was helping out, lifting those hundred-pound sacks of feed and doing the deliveries, but it was still awfully hard work for my father. He had bought the feed store some time before from Mr. Magee, the banker, with whom he'd become good friends. Magee was a widower, and talked my mother and father into moving into his home where my mother could keep house and cook for him, and they had lived with him for a few years. But I wanted them to have their own place.

We eventually found a fifty-four-acre farm for sale southeast of Denton. We bought it, and they moved there in October of 1940 and lived there six years. It was a good place for them. The farm gave both my parents plenty to do without overworking them, and made it easier for Charles and my sister Ellen to go to college as well. Louise and I never actually lived there, though it was my official domicile for tax purposes until I left the tour in '46 and moved back to Texas permanently.

But back to Inverness and golf. Naturally, I was so busy those first few months that between the Masters and the Open, I only played in one 72-hole tournament, the Goodall Round Robin. It was at Fresh Meadow Country Club in Flushing, New York; I tied for sixth at plus

2 and won $300. Hogan played beautifully and won with plus 23. Besides being busy, my contract only allowed me to be gone six weeks out of the six months I would be at the club, so unless a tournament was close by that summer, I couldn't play in it. The pros' club contracts differed quite a bit back then. Some pros could go play in tournaments every week, and simply "played out of" a certain club rather than working there every day, while others worked a full week, like me. But I was enjoying my new job and the club a lot more than traveling on the tour, and making more and steadier money most of the time besides. I did play in one local tournament, the Ohio Open at Sylvania Country Club just northwest of Toledo. I shot 284 and won $250, but it wasn't an official PGA event, so it doesn't count on my record. But it served as a nice warm-up for the National Championship two weeks later.

The Open was at Canterbury Country Club in Cleveland that year, about a two-hour drive from Toledo. Not quite close enough to commute. I tied for fifth with 290, but felt very good about how I'd performed, all things considered. Lawson Little and Gene Sarazen tied at 287, and Little won in a playoff. The week after, I played in the Inverness Invitational Four-Ball. I was paired with Walter Hagen, long after the peak of his career. The sponsors then did everything possible to get more people to come watch the tournament, and in those days they didn't invite just the players on the tour, necessarily. Hagen was in his fifties and playing no tournament golf at all, but they invited him to help draw more gallery. Because I was the host pro, they had me play with Hagen because it would have been unfair for the other players to be paired with him as his game wasn't very sharp. We had to walk, naturally, and Inverness was a tough course, so it was a bit much for Hagen. The ninth hole there comes right by the side of the clubhouse, the tenth tee is at the men's entrance to the locker room, and the 13th hole comes back to the clubhouse again. So after we played the front nine, Hagen would say to me, "Play hard, Byron, and I'll see you at the fourteenth tee." This was the only tournament I finished last in after becoming an established player (we tied for last, actually, at minus 14), but it was all for a good cause and it was fun to see Hagen play even then, so I didn't really mind.

The PGA was at Hershey in 1940, but busy as I was at the club, I hadn't played in a tournament for two and a half months. I was playing well, however, playing quite a bit with the members and giving lots of lessons. I had arranged in my contract with Mr. Carpenter that I could play in fivesomes with the members. What that meant was on Saturdays I'd go play a few holes with one foursome and a few holes with the next and so on. It was a good way for me to get to know each of the members, plus I could see what condition their clubs were in and how they were playing, and help them decide what kind of clubs, putters, new bags, or whatever they needed. It helped my sales in the shop, and it helped the members, too. They seemed to like it that I played with them.

About a month or more before the PGA, I started to get in shape for the competition by taking on three members at a time and playing against their best ball. They gave me a one-putt maximum on the first green, so I always started with par or birdie, but after that, I had to really play hard. We'd play once a week. These fellows all shot in the 70's, and their best ball would be 65 or 66. It was tough competition, but I held my own and won most of the time. Some of the fellows I played with were Ray Miller, Eddie Tasker, Bob Sawhill, Alan Loop, and Tony Ruddy. A great group of golfers and good friends.

So I felt I was in good shape when I arrived at Hershey. I did all right in the qualifying and early matches, and made it to the semis without too much trouble. I remember how difficult it was for me to play in the semifinal against Ralph Guldahl, who was a wonderful player and a tough competitor, but who was also very slow and deliberate, while I played very quickly. I had to work at staying calm and not becoming impatient, and I managed to do it, fortunately. Then, in the final against Sam Snead, on the third hole in our afternoon round, Sam laid me a dead stymie* and thought he had the hole won. But I

---

* We played stymies into the late forties. You see, we weren't allowed to mark, lift, clean, and replace the ball on the greens then like we all do today. So in match play, if the other player's ball was in your way, that was just bad luck. You played around it or pitched over it or whatever you could do to get in or near the hole. A lot of luck was involved, naturally, because you didn't think about trying to stymie your opponent when you were pitching from sixty yards off the green or more. But that was the reason scorecards then were exactly six inches long and had an arrow pointing in both directions at the bottom. If your ball was quite close to your opponent's, you placed the scorecard between yours and his, and if it touched both of them, one of you had to mark the ball. Otherwise, it was a stymie. You didn't think about laying someone a stymie when you were well off the green, but if you had to play over someone's ball, you'd try to.

chipped over his ball with my pitching wedge and holed it and we halved the hole instead with birdies. By the time we reached the 16th tee, I was one down with three to play. On the 16th, I hit a good drive and a fine iron and holed a six-footer for birdie to catch up with Sam. On the 17th, a short par 4, you drove out on to a hill and pitched to a small green. I pitched three feet from the hole and made another birdie to go one up.

Then we came to the 18th, a long par 3, and it was my honor. I'll never forget it. I took my 3-iron, almost hit the flag, and went about ten feet past the hole; I'd be putting downhill. Sam put his tee shot about twenty-five feet to the left of the hole and putted up close, so he had three. So all I had to do was make three to win the match one up. I coasted that putt down the hill very gently and made my three to beat Snead and win the PGA Championship.

As a nice sidelight to that victory, a couple of years ago I received a very kind letter from a man named Charles Fasnacht in Pennsylvania. He wrote that the boy who had caddied for me at Hershey had been a good friend of his, and when I sank that last putt to win, his buddy tossed Charles the ball and he had kept it all this time. He felt bad about it and wanted to send me the ball, but I wrote and told him that if it had meant that much to him to keep it all these years, then I couldn't think of anyone who deserved to have it more.

That PGA was where the story got started about my so-called nervous stomach. Mr. and Mrs. Cloyd Haas came over when I had to play Guldahl in the semifinals. Mr. Haas had gone to the locker room with me before this 36-hole match, and while he was there, I lost my breakfast. He went right out and told Louise and Mrs. Haas. Louise said, "Good!" which Mr. Haas at first thought was very cruel, but he later found out that it was a good sign, because it meant I would play well. I didn't do it all that often, but somehow the story got started in later years that this was why I left the tour. Actually, it was a little more complicated than that, which I'll tell you about later.

A few other members from Inverness had come with the Haases—Hazen Arnold, Mr. Carpenter, the Bargman brothers, and several others, and after I won, I learned they'd made reservations for me and Louise to return to Inverness on the train that night. After dinner, they gave us a wonderful celebration party in the dining car on the way home.

I'd now won every major American tournament plus the Ryder Cup, but had not won the Los Angeles Open, which was considered a big tournament then. But I just didn't feel yet that I'd completed my record. I wanted to win the PGA again, and had hopes of winning the national championship again as well. So I still had some golf to play.

The week after the PGA, I played in the Anthracite Open at Scranton and was second, with Snead winning. Then it was back to Inverness and no more tournaments until after I left the club in the early fall and went back to Texarkana. I finished the year well, though, winning the Miami Open and $2,537.50 at Miami Springs. I shot 69-65-67-70— 271 and beat Clayton Heafner by one shot.

One thing I should mention about that year was how I got Cloyd Haas started in the golf umbrella business. Golf umbrellas then were about as bad as golf shoes had been before Foot-Joy started making them for me and McSpaden. Our umbrellas were flimsy, the cloth they used wasn't waterproof and would leak, and if it was windy, the things would turn inside out and the ribs would break all to pieces.

Mr. and Mrs. Haas had taken Louise and me in like their own children, and we went over to their home for dinner quite often. Summers in Toledo were famous for mosquitoes, but they had a nice big screened-in back porch where Mr. Haas and I would go after dinner to sit and talk. We'd talk about first one thing and another, and one evening, I said, "Mr. Haas, you make such wonderful street umbrellas. Why couldn't you make a good golf umbrella, too?" He said, "What kind of a golf umbrella do you need?" I told him, and he got to thinking about it. A few weeks later, I was at the Goodall Round Robin tournament in Fresh Meadow, New York. Mr. Haas was up there in New Jersey at the same time, visiting the factory he ordered his umbrella frames from, so he asked me to come out and meet him there. We talked with the manager about what we needed, and we settled on a double rib design and birdcloth for the fabric. They used my size to decide how big to make it, and it was quite adequate. Those first ones turned out to be a little heavy, but they were so much better than what we'd had before. I had mine made up in British tan and brown, and had one made for McSpaden in green and tan. When we brought them out to the course, all the boys wanted to know where they could get one, too. So Haas-Jordan got into golf umbrellas from then on, and theirs are still the finest, in my opinion.

I worked with Haas-Jordan for several years after that. Mr. Haas made me vice president of marketing, and each tournament I'd go to, I'd visit the large department stores—Neiman-Marcus, Macy's, Bullock's—and give them my card, and just introduce myself. I didn't really do any selling, it was more of a public relations thing. But I got $25 for each call I made, which was nice, plus a generous bonus check each year, which was even nicer. Mr. Haas also had special ties made up for his staff to wear, with all kinds of different designs of umbrellas. I soon became known as "The Umbrella Man," and it stuck for quite a while.

My connection with the Haas family continues to this day. I gave some lessons to Mr. Haas's daughter, Janet, when she was just a college student, and she and her husband, H. Franklin "Bud" Waltz, became two of our dearest friends. Bud has been on the PGA advisory committee for many years.

I started to teach right away at Inverness, and found that I was teaching more of the better players now. I gave lessons almost constantly while I was at the club, and I enjoyed it. It was much easier to make the better players understand what I was saying, because they had a better grasp of the basics of the game.

One of the first good young golfers I met at Inverness was Frank Stranahan, R.A.'s son. He was quite an admirer of my accomplishments, and as he got better at his own game, he began to think he was as good as I was, which led to some interesting stories.

At one point, Mr. Stranahan had signed Frankie up for some lessons with me. Well, I soon found out that this young man wouldn't listen to anything I had to say. He just wanted me to watch him hit balls, and wouldn't change anything or take any of my suggestions seriously. After a few weeks of this, I told him, "Frankie, I'm not going to give you any more lessons. You won't listen to me, and you're wasting my time and your father's money."

Naturally, it didn't end there. A few days later, Mr. Stranahan came into the shop with Frankie in tow, and said to me, "Frankie says you won't teach him any more." I was really on the spot. I certainly didn't want to get Mr. Stranahan mad, because he was very influential at the club. But I had to tell the truth, too.

"Mr. Stranahan," I said, "that's not exactly what I said. Frankie won't listen to me or change anything about the way he plays, and he's wasting your money and my time. That's why I told him I wouldn't teach him any more." Mr. Stranahan looked at Frankie and asked, "Is that true?" Frankie nodded and said, "Yes." So Mr. Stranahan said to me, "If you'll continue to teach him, I'll make sure Frankie does what you say." I agreed to give him another try, and he fortunately changed his attitude as well as his golf swing, and became a very fine player.

I had three assistants during my time at Inverness—Tommy Sullivan, Herman Lang, and Ray Jamison, who I hired from Ridgewood. Ray was an excellent golfer and teacher, and after I left Inverness, he moved on to be head pro at Hackensack Country Club in New Jersey, where he worked for many years. Herman Lang was a wonderful pro too, and was later hired to be head pro at Inverness until he retired and was succeeded by their present pro, Don Perne, also a fine man.

I had quite a few bad last rounds in '40 that cost me some tournaments. I became conscious of this, and it wasn't because I was nervous or choking or freezing up, but I gave some thought to it, and changed my philosophy. Regardless of whether I was behind or ahead going to the last round, I tried to really charge and go all out—not foolishly taking chances, but building myself up for the last round mentally. That's why I began to play the fourth round the best later in my career.

1940 was a little like 1938. I had won four tournaments and added another major, the PGA, to my record, but I couldn't expect it to be as big a year as '39 had been. I was enjoying life in Toledo and my job at Inverness. I finished second on the money list, and I felt very fortunate. It was really a wonderful year, considering how little golf I played.

Louise and I left Toledo for Texarkana at the first cool spell, about the middle of September. I left my assistant in charge of the shop until it actually closed around the first of October. In December, we drove to Miami for the Miami Open again, which I managed to win for the second year in a row. That put another $2,537.50 in the bank, so my total winnings for the year, according to my little black book, were $9696. No, we weren't having to borrow from Dad Shofner any more.

I went deer hunting that November in Uvalde, Texas, with Hogan, Demaret, and the new Winchester rifle I'd received from the folks at Reading the year before. I bagged a beautiful buck with a twelve-point rack of horns, but the game warden decided that since I had an Ohio driver's license and Ohio plates on my car, my official domicile in Denton and my Texas hunting permit didn't count, so he confiscated the deer and I had to pay an $80 fine. It really upset me, because I'd obeyed all the rules, but this fellow didn't agree. And $80 was a lot of money in those days, especially for us.

Very few people today realize what it was like to be on the tour then. You didn't make enough money even if you were a fine player to make a living or ever accumulate anything just playing in tournaments, so it was necessary to have a club job. Certainly, the better you played and more tournaments you won, the better your chances of getting a job at a fine club. Especially if you were toward the end of your career and wanted to settle down and not travel any more, having a good tournament record was a really big help. Being a good player also helped you get more lessons, because people thought if you could play that well you certainly should know something about the game and be able to impart your knowledge to your pupils. That wasn't always true, because some of the touring pros didn't ever spend much time teaching or become good teachers. The best teachers in my opinion were those who had taught themselves how to play, and who also had the ability to take it slow and easy with amateurs and be very patient. A top touring pro could also help increase membership and playing activity. Ridgewood was pretty full when I arrived, but Reading wasn't, because there were a lot of golf clubs in Reading and it wasn't that large a town, so my coming there after winning the Masters and then winning the Open two years later really did increase the membership. Inverness was always a famous club ever since 1920, when they held the U.S. Open there for the first time, so Inverness was also full when I arrived, but I did give quite a few more lessons than the pro before me had done. A couple of other examples of fine touring pros getting jobs at good clubs were Craig Wood at Winged Foot and Claude Harmon after him. No doubt their playing ability helped a great deal, in both their getting the jobs and helping to improve the clubs as well.

There were a few pros, like Hogan and Snead, who were registered at a club such as Hershey for Ben and Greenbrier for Sam, but who never worked there full time, really, though the club got the benefit of their names and the prestige associated with their wins.

But my situation was more like the rest of the fellows out there. I was very busy at Inverness and extremely happy there. I did enough traveling during the winter in California and the southeast that by the time the Masters was over, Louise and I were happy to get back to Toledo and spend the relatively cool summer there. Plus, I was making more money at the club—from salary, lessons, and shop profits—than I could count on making on the tour anyway.

Still, it was hard to keep my game in shape, and essentially, my golf suffered the first three years I was at Inverness. For instance, I started out 1941 pretty rough. Played badly the first two events, with a 302 at the L.A. Open and a 290 at Oakland, and just plain failed to qualify for the San Francisco Match Play tournament. Then I tied for fifth at the Crosby Pro-Am and for second in the Western Open at Phoenix Country Club. On the last hole, I hit a high 6-iron to the pin, which was cut fairly close to the front, over a bunker. I made that eight-footer to tie for second.

We pros always enjoyed playing in Phoenix, because Barry and Bob Goldwater would invite quite a few of us pros out to Barry's house for a steak cookout during the tournament. This was long before Barry ever became Senator Goldwater. In fact, the two brothers owned Goldwater's department store, a wonderful store which they ran quite well. The Goldwaters were very nice people—Barry was a natural leader, a good thinker, and good at speaking. Louise and I always looked forward to that party, and since I had won the tournament in '39, I was on the list of invitees the rest of the time I was on the tour. This must sound at times as though all we pros thought of was our stomachs. The truth is, traveling the way we did, sometimes the food we'd get was all right, sometimes it wasn't very good at all, and once in a while, it would be excellent. We'd all had enough lean times that we really appreciated good food when we could get it, and that wasn't any too often.

The Texas Open was next, and that year it was played at Willow Springs in San Antonio, a tough little course. We had terrible weather, both snow and hail, but we went ahead and played in it. Lawson Little shot a 64 the final round—none of us could believe that—and I tied for fourth, mainly due to my putting. I had streaks of poor putting then; I remember after I'd played in the British Open, someone said that if I had putted well, I could have set a new scoring record. Well, that may be or may be not, but as I've said before, we didn't work on our putting much because of the inconsistency of the greens. We concentrated on getting our approaches close to the pin, which was a lot more effective.

I didn't do too well in New Orleans, either, tied for eighth. Then we went on to Miami for the Four-ball. My partner was McSpaden again, and again we lost to Runyan and Smith in the second round. Maybe that's why Jug and I were called the Gold Dust Twins—because we didn't get the gold, just the dust.

Next was the Seminole Invitational Pro-Am—not an official PGA event, but we loved the course and the food and loved to get to go. My partner that year was a fine amateur named Findlay Douglas. He was sixty-six years old and the 1898 National Amateur Champion. He still carried a 6 handicap, and he was a pleasure to play with. On the last hole, we needed a 3 to win, and a 4 to tie. Well, I made the 3, so that made Findlay pretty happy. Interestingly enough, though my winnings weren't considered official, I did get $232.50 for my two rounds of 64-71, and $571.79 for my share of the Calcutta pool for a total of $803.29. Not bad pay for two rounds of golf, back then.

Then Louise and I headed back to Toledo so I could get things ready in the shop. The golf course wouldn't really open until the middle of April, and there wouldn't be much activity until after Decoration Day—what's now called Memorial Day. But I needed to get things ordered and see that things would be running right when I did return after the Masters.

The next tournament was the North and South at Pinehurst. I played all right, tying for fourth, but had a bad last round of 76. I don't remember what caused it now—sometimes it's a blessing not to have a perfect memory. But the Greensboro tournament started the very next day, and I did better. I had a hot second round of 64 and won, so I was real pleased. A round of 64 can almost make you forget a 76. Another reason I was pleased to win there was that the weather was real bad, and the courses weren't in good condition at all. Playing well in conditions like that gives you confidence. Of course, we pros didn't complain about course conditions then—we were just glad to get to play.

You know, looking over my record for '41, I'm surprised to see how many bad last rounds I had. It's understandable that I didn't win much until I got those last rounds turned around some. The next week at Asheville, North Carolina, I tied for tenth on a very hard course and never scored better than 72, though at the Masters I played very steady and finished three shots back of Craig Wood, who won.

Because my contract limited me to six weeks away from the club, I skipped the Goodall Round Robin in favor of playing in the U.S. Open, which was at Colonial in Fort Worth. They had put new sod on two greens and the course was in terrible shape. There had also been a lot of rain, which didn't help anything. People didn't know what to do then for golf courses like they do now, so we all just played and tried our best. I had another terrible final round of 77, tied for seventeenth, and won $50. You could say I was disgusted with myself. So the next few weeks I worked hard and finished second three times in a row, at Mahoning Valley, the Inverness Four-Ball with McSpaden, and the PGA at Cherry Hills.

A couple of interesting things happened at that PGA championship. I remember in my second match, with Bill Heinlein, I was coasting along through the front nine. Then all of a sudden he got hot and pretty soon I was 2 down going to the 13th. I managed to pull myself together and won 2 up. Next, I dispensed with Guldahl 2 and 1, and faced Hogan in the quarterfinal. I was 1-up going to the final hole. He had a fifteen-foot putt and I had a twelve. He missed his, I made mine, and that was the match. Remember, all of these were 36-hole matches, and the qualifier was thirty-six holes as well.

Next was the semifinal against Gene Sarazen, always a tough competitor. Fortunately I won, 2 and 1. Later he came over to me in the locker room and said, "Nelson, you double-crossed me." Surprised, I looked at him and said, "How did I do that, Gene?" He said, "I've been playing my irons so well, I decided I'd let you outdrive me, then put my ball close to the pin and it would bother you. But you just put yours inside me all day!"

Next came the final against Vic Ghezzi, and one of the most unusual things happened that I ever saw or heard of in golf. I played wonderfully well the first twenty-seven holes and was leading 3 up going to the back nine. But I'd had such tough matches before this one, all of a sudden I just felt like all the adrenalin went out of me. I tried to fight it, but it didn't do any good. After thirty-six holes Vic and I were dead even.

The playoff was sudden death. On the 2nd hole, we drove, then hit our approach shots close to the green. We both chipped past the hole about forty-six inches, and our balls were fairly close together, though mine was about a half-inch further away and his was about eight inches to the left. The referee, Ed Dudley, asked if Vic's ball was in my way, and I said no. But when I took my stance, I accidentally moved his ball one inch with my foot. Well, of course, that was a penalty. In match play, it meant loss of the hole and in this case the match. Naturally, I conceded.

But Vic said he didn't want to win that way, and there was quite a discussion. They decided that I should go ahead and putt, but I knew the rules. In my mind I'd already lost the match and knew it wasn't right to let me putt. I didn't want anyone ever to say I'd won by some sort of fluke. So of course I wasn't concentrating real well and missed the putt, and Ghezzi won, which was only right.

The next tournament I played in was the St. Paul Open at the end of July. It was a six- or eight-hour drive from Toledo, so it was reachable. I tied for seventh and won $278. You see, I really did make more money at Inverness than I could count on on the tour. With my salary, all the income from my lessons, and shop profits, I did pretty well, with the exception of winning the occasional big tournament. This was why, with my commitment to Inverness, I had to pretty much concentrate on the majors and big money tournaments, because anything less would cost me time at Inverness, plus lesson fees and shop income. And if I didn't play well, I could end up losing even more.

So I worked until the first week in September, when I drove to Chicago for the Tam O'Shanter. This was a new tournament put on by George S. May, a "business engineer." That meant he advised other companies how to run their businesses. He was the first to put up a lot of money for a tournament. The first year, 1941, the first prize was $2000, the next year $2500, and it kept going up.

I played well in that first Tam O'Shanter and won the $2000. No, I didn't make that much each week in the shop, but that was just one tournament of four or five that had big purses, and I sure couldn't count on winning all of them. I always did well at the Tam, though. I wish the course were still there—it was turned into a development some years after George May died. The course was fairly hard, and the fairways were narrow. I played well there for two main reasons:

one, it was a big money tournament so I tried harder, and two, I played those clover fairways well. Not that they planted the fairways in clover, but there was a lot of it on the course, and there were no chemicals to control it back then. Having learned to play on Texas hardpan, I always clipped the ball off the fairway and didn't take much turf like some of the other boys. That clover had a lot of sticky juice if you hit very much of it, which would cause you to hit fliers. Fliers have little or no spin and you never can be sure what they'll do, except it's usually something you don't want.

After the Tam, I played in a couple of little events near Inverness, the Hearst Invitational and the Ohio Open just outside Toledo, where I had a final-round 62, one of my lower scores in competition. Then Louise and I took our annual trip back to Texarkana. In December, we drove to Florida again, where I won the Miami Open for the second year in a row. That brought me $2000 prize money, plus an extra $537.50 in pro-am and low-round awards. It was a tough little course and the greens were stiff bermuda with a lot of grain. But in the practice round, I noted which way the grain ran on each hole, and most of the time, I didn't pay as much attention to where the pin was as to which way the grain ran on that green and where I wanted to be when I putted. I was hitting my irons well, so I was able to place most of my approach shots where I would be putting downgrain, because that was the easiest putt you could have on that type of grass.

Right after Christmas, I played in the Beaumont Open and tied for seventh, then won the Harlingen Open with 70-65-70-66. The Beaumont course had the narrowest fairways of any course I ever saw. They were lined with trees, and Chick Harbert, who had trouble keeping his drives straight anyway, would tee his ball up as high as he could and hit toward wherever the green was. He'd say, "If I'm going to be in the trees, I'd rather be closer to the green." Even as straight as I was, I had trouble staying in the fairways. They were the talk of the week.

I finished up 1941 playing in 27 tournaments, and my black book says I won $11,819.12, though Bill Inglish's records say it was a little more, $12,025. The difference wasn't enough to worry about, that's for sure.

Of course, the whole year of '41, there had been a lot of talk and worry over the situation in Europe, and we knew it was just a matter of time before the United States would get involved. Sure enough, that

December we jumped in with both feet, and everyone's lives changed almost overnight. Most people thought we'd lick both Germany and Japan in six months, come home victorious, and get on with business as usual—but of course, it didn't turn out that way.

All of the men who were able to signed up for the draft, and then we tried to go about our business whatever way we could until our number came up. You know, it's a good thing we really can't see into the future, because if we'd been able to back then, I don't think many folks could have stood it.

Starting out in '42, I tied for sixth in Los Angeles, which kept the L.A. Open on my list of important tournaments I still wanted to win. Then in Oakland I did win, by five shots. This is how I did it: The greens there were quite soft, and all eighteen had a definite slope from back to front. I noticed that we were all hitting at the flag, and our balls were spinning back, sometimes off the green. I changed tactics after the last practice round, and aimed for the top of the flag. Then, when my ball spun back, it ended up closer to the hole. That's the main reason I won. I remember the pro there was Dewey Longworth, brother to my good friend Ted Longworth from Texarkana. He was a good player and a nice man, just like Ted.

Our next stop, the San Francisco Open, was played at the California Golf Club where my friend Eddie Lowery was a member. I played well but putted very poorly and finished eighth. I've already said that most of us pros didn't spend much time on putting, because of the difference in the greens and so on, but I had another reason. I had originally learned to putt on stiff bermuda greens, where you had to hit the putt rather than roll it. I never really got over that, and I didn't work on it enough because we tend not to work on things we're not good at, and that certainly was true for me. I didn't three-putt much, but my bad distance was eight to fifteen feet. Those were the ones I didn't make as often as I should have.

Hogan won at San Francisco, though he was still hooking quite a bit then. On the 18th, which was a dogleg right, Hogan hooked a 4-wood high up over the trees and back into the fairway, because he just couldn't fade the ball or even count on hitting it straight then. Though he hooked it, he used the same swing and did the same thing every time, so he got to be pretty consistent.

At the Crosby and the Western I didn't do very well. I'd occasionally have several weeks when I wasn't chipping or putting well, either one. But I practiced some, and by the Texas Open, I was doing better, finished eighth, then sixth at New Orleans, and second at St. Petersburg. Still couldn't make much headway in the Miami Four-Ball, though—got knocked out in the second round again, this time with Henry Picard as my partner. But at least it was someone else beating us—Harper and Keiser instead of Runyan and Smith.

My game was getting better all along, but of course, so was everyone else's. Our on-the-job training was working for quite a few of the players, from those who had loads of natural talent to those who had some talent and a lot of persistence. There still were no real teachers to go to like the boys have today. Most of the older club pros were still making the transition to steel shafts, or even teaching the old way of pronating and all, so they really couldn't help anyone much. We had to figure things out on our own for the most part, and some fellows were better at it than others. But it was getting more and more important to have most of your rounds under 70, if you wanted to have a chance to win.

After Miami, I played in the Seminole Invitational again, enjoyed all their good food and being with the other players, and won $50. Well, at least the food was free, there was no entry fee, and my caddie only cost $8, so I had $42 more when I left than I did when I arrived.

I did better in the North and South, but had a bad last round of 73, tied for third, and won $500. At Greensboro, I had another poor last round of 74 and tied for fourth. Back then, they sometimes had prizes for low round of the day, and I tied in the third round with a 68, so I got another $25. Then I finished third at Asheville, and won $550. In my last five tournaments, I'd finished second once, third twice, and fourth once. I was definitely getting steadier, despite final rounds I wasn't very happy with.

During that Asheville tournament, I realized there hadn't been any pictures or publicity about me. It seemed the articles were all about the other players. I figured the press had gotten tired of writing about me, and I had gotten just enough used to all the attention that I kind of missed it. Anyway, about the third round, I was playing just so-so and was tied for the lead or leading. On the 16th hole, I put my ball in the left bunker, which was over six feet deep. I got in there and was trying to figure out how to get out and close enough to one-putt, and stuck my head up and looked over the bank to see the pin. Right above the bunker, on the green to my left, was a photographer, getting ready to photograph me as I played my shot. I said to him, "Where have you been all this week? Just get out of my way!" I did get up and down, but I felt bad about what I'd said, so I looked the fellow up afterwards and apologized, and he said, "That's no problem, I shouldn't have been where I was."

Along about this time, McSpaden and I were on a train together, talking about the money to be made on the tour. We figured then that with an interest rate of about 10%, if we could make $100,000 during our careers, we could retire and live quite comfortably on that annual interest of $10,000. That seemed quite reasonable at the time, but it's a ridiculous idea now.

Next was the Masters, but before the tournament started, I played a match there with Bob Jones against Henry Picard and Gene Sarazen. We were all playing well that day, including Bob, and on the back nine, Henry and Gene made seven straight birdies—but never won a hole from us. Jones shot 31 on the back nine that day. Amazing.

Then the tournament began, and fortunately, I played very well, ending the first round with 68. Paul Runyan led nearly the whole first round, and ended up tied with Horton Smith at 67. Sam Byrd was tied with me at 68, and Jimmy Demaret was behind us with 70. The second round, Horton led by himself for one hole, then I tied him with a birdie at the second hole. It was kind of huckledy-buck between Paul, Horton, and me for the next five holes, but I pulled ahead of them both with a birdie at the par-5 eighth. I was leading then for the rest of the second round, when I shot 67, and all through the third, but lost a little steam in the fourth when I bogeyed six, seven, and eight. Hogan had caught up with me when he birdied the eighth himself. He was several groups ahead of me, of course, so I couldn't see how he was doing. I birdied 9 to lead again, and led till the last hole despite bogeying 17.

When I stepped up to hit my drive on 18, I noticed the tee box was kind of soft and slick. As I started my downswing, my foot slipped a little and I made a bad swing, pushing my tee shot deep into the woods on the right. By now I knew Ben had shot 70, and I had to have a par just to tie. When I got to my ball, I was relieved to find I had a clear swing. The ball was just sitting on the ground nicely, and there was an opening in front of me, about twenty feet wide, between two trees. I took my 5-iron and hooked that ball up and onto the green fifteen feet from the pin and almost birdied it—but I did make my par. So you can see why I felt very fortunate to tie.

Then came the playoff. This was one of the rare occasions when I was so keyed up my stomach was upset, even during the night. I lost my breakfast the next morning, which I thought might be a good sign, because I had always played well when I became that sick beforehand, and it always wore off after the first few holes. When I saw Hogan in the clubhouse, he said, "I heard you were sick last night," and I said, "Yes, Ben, I was." He offered to postpone the playoff, but I said, "No, we'll play." I did have half of a plain chicken sandwich and some hot tea, which helped a little, but you can see in the picture that was made of Ben and me when we were on the first tee that I was very nervous and tense.

This was probably one of the most unusual playoffs in golf, in that at least twenty-five of the pros who had played in the tournament stayed to watch us in the playoff. I don't recall that ever happening any other time. Ben and I were both very flattered by that.

Flattered or not, though, I started poorly. On the first hole, I hit a bad drive into the trees and my ball ended up right next to a pine cone, which I couldn't move because the ball would move with it. On my second shot, the ball hit more trees in front of me, so I ended up with a 6 while Ben made his par. We parred the second and the third. Then, on the fourth, a long par 3, I thought the pin was cut just over the bunker, but my long iron was short and went in the bunker, so I made 4 while Ben made 3. We'd played four holes and I was 3 down.

The 5th hole had a very tough pin placement at the back of the green, but we both parred it. The par-3 6th, I began to come alive a little and put my tee shot ten feet away, while Hogan missed his to the left and made 4. I put my ten-footer in for birdie, so I caught up two shots right there.

We both parred the 7th. Next, I eagled 8 and Ben birdied, so now we were even. I picked up three more shots on the next five holes, including a shot on 12 that rimmed the hole and stopped six inches away. But Ben didn't get rattled much. Though his tee shot stopped short on the bank, his chip almost went in for a 2.

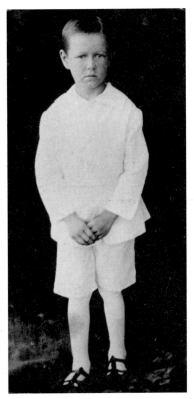

Byron Nelson, about eight months old.

At age 5 ^{1}/$_2$.

Byron with his mother, Madge Nelson, and her parents, M.F. and Ellen Allen.

Byron in 1934. *Louise Shofner Nelson.*

Louise and Byron on their wedding day in 1934, leaning against Byron's 1933 Ford roadster.

Byron leading in the first round of the Texas Open at San Antonio's Brackenridge Park. He finished second behind Wiffy Cox.

Byron playing Lawson Little at San Francisco's Presidio in January 1935.

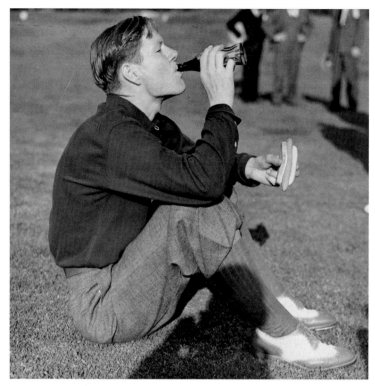

Taking a lunch break on the final day of the 1936 Metropolitan Open, which he eventually won.

A locust swarm during an exhibition at the Jockey Club in Argentina in 1937. After 3 holes the match was called off.

Byron with winner Tom Watson sometime in the late seventies at the Byron Nelson Classic…

…and in May 1992 at the same event.

A publicity shot taken in 1981 at Augusta.

Byron and wife Peggy at a local charity tournament in 1992.

Vice president Dan Quayle, Sam Snead, Gene Sarazen, Peggy Nelson, and President George Bush watch as Byron putts on the White House lawn in May 1992.

The 1992 Masters Champions Club Dinner. ***First row:*** *Byron, Tom Watson, Gene Sarazen, Jack Stephens, Ian Woosnam, Henry Picard, Herman Keiser, Sam Snead.* ***Second row:*** *George Archer, Nick Faldo, Doug Ford, Gay Brewer, Bob Goalby, Art Wall, Ray Floyd, Bernhard Langer, Arnold Palmer, Seve Ballesteros.* ***Third row:*** *Ben Crenshaw, Craig Stadler, Larry Mize, Tommy Aaron, Sandy Lyle, Jack Nicklaus, Gary Player, Fuzzy Zoeller, Charles Coody.*

Byron after shooting a course-record 66 at the 1937 Masters.

The 1937 Ryder cup team. **Standing:** PGA President George Jacobus, Ed Dudley, Byron, Johnny Revolta, Horton Smith, Henry Picard. **Sitting:** Gene Sarazen, Sam Snead, Ralph Guldahl, Denny Shute, Tony Manero.

Harold McSpaden (with seat cane) accompanies Byron on his way to victory in the 1939 U.S. Open in Philadelphia...

...and Byron accepting the trophy from USGA President Archibald M. Reid.

Teeing off at the 1939 PGA Championship in Flushing, New York. Byron lost to Henry Picard on the 37th hole of the finals.

A sand shot on the 7th hole on the way to winning the 1939 U.S. Open.

Sam Snead waits his turn at left as Byron drives from the third tee in the final round of the 1940 PGA Championship in Hershey, Pennsylvania. Byron won on the last hole.

Byron, Jimmy Demaret, Jimmy Hines, and Tony Penna look over the $10,000 prize money at the 1940 Miami Open, won by Byron.

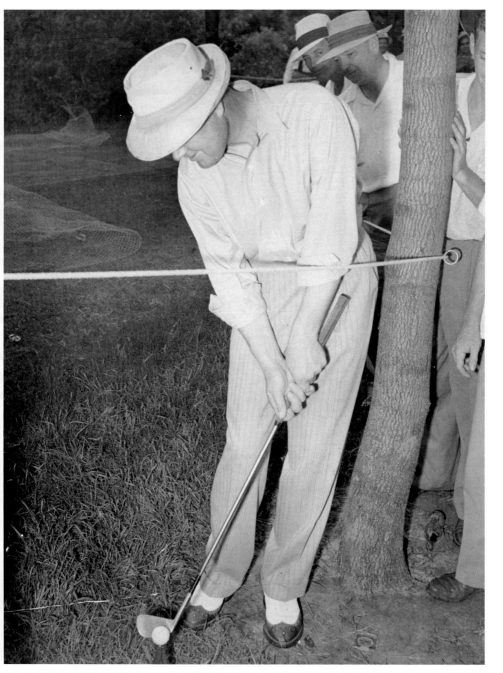

Playing in a 1941 exhibition match for British relief, Byron nearly holed out after Olin Dutra picked up his ball and placed it on a pop bottle lying nearby.

The Gold-Dust Twins: Byron with his longtime golfing partner, Harold McSpaden, in the early 1940s.

Bob Hope, Bing Crosby, Byron, Johnny Weissmuller, and Jimmy Demaret have a little fun in Houston during a wartime Red Cross/USO tour.

(Left to right) Ben Hogan, Byron, Bob Jones, and Jimmy Demaret at Augusta National Golf Club in 1942.

Playing out of the rough on the way to victory at the 1945 PGA Championship.

Celebrating a world record 259 at the 1945 Seattle Open.

At the 1944 Tam O'Shanter in Chicago, Byron holes one in a playoff win over Clayton Heafner.

Teeing off at the San Francisco Open in 1946. Byron won by nine.

Byron with his mother and father on his Denton farm in the early forties.

Feeding the hogs in Denton.

This Ford tractor from the 1940s is still running.

The Masters Champions for the first dozen years, excluding the war years: Horton Smith, Byron, Henry Picard, Jimmy Demaret, Craig Wood, Gene Sarazen, Herman Keiser. (Ralph Guldahl is missing.)

The 1947 Ryder Cup team. **Standing:** *Dutch Harrison, Lloyd Mangrum, Herman Keiser, Byron, Sam Snead.* **Sitting:** *Herman Barron, Jimmy Demaret, Ben Hogan, Ed Oliver, Lew Worsham.*

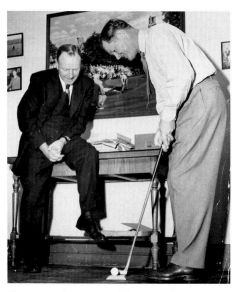

*Byron putting in good friend Eddie
Lowery's office in San Francisco.*

*Byron with Babe Didrikson Zaharias
in 1946.*

Ben Hogan, Byron, and Herman Keiser at Augusta in 1946, just before the final round.

Byron and Louise with two half-Tennessee walkers presented to them by the mayor of Denton on the courthouse steps in 1946.

Byron receiving some tips from Ed Sullivan in the early fifties.

With Bob Hope at Pebble Beach in the late sixties.

Byron with President Eisenhower, Ben Hogan, and Cliff Roberts at Augusta in the late fifties.

Arnold Palmer, Byron, Doug Sanders, and Gene Littler at the 50th anniversary of the LA Open in the mid-seventies.

Presenting Ken Venturi with the Sportsman of the Year award after he won the U.S. Open in 1964.

Byron with longtime ABC "Wide World of Golf" partner Chris Schenkel doing a Masters tournament broadcast in the early sixties.

At President Ford's tournament in Vail, Colorado. The president's birdie putt has just lipped out.

Ken Venturi and Byron doing a clinic at Jasper Park Lodge in Canada in 1980.

When we arrived at the 18th tee. I was leading by 2, and Ben's approach shot ended up way at the back of the green, with the pin way at the front. I played short of the green on purpose, not wanting to take a chance on the bunker, because in those days, a ball landing in the bunker would bury, and then you really had your hands full. But I figured I might chip up and make par, or no worse than 5, while I was pretty sure Ben couldn't make his putt from up on the top ledge. I was right—he two-putted, I made 5 and won by one shot.

Louise and Valerie had stayed together up at the clubhouse during the playoff, and they were both very happy for me. Valerie was a very gracious lady, and Ben was always fine whether he won or lost. It was a great victory for me, and more so because I'd been able to beat Ben, who by then was getting to be a very fine player. The fact that he had come from well behind everyone else here showed that he had a lot of determination and persistence.

Then it was time for us to head back to Toledo and Inverness, where we stayed for six weeks before I played again. The PGA that year was at Seaview Country Club in New Jersey, and I was up against Jim Turnesa, one of the wonderful Turnesa brothers, in the semifinal. Jim was in the service, and naturally, the gallery was pulling for him, which I could well understand. I was 1 up when we came to the 18th hole, and I was short of the green, but chipped up two feet from the hole. Jim putted his stone dead and I gave it to him. The gallery gave him a tremendous round of applause because he'd played so well, and I thought it was one of the nicest things I'd ever seen a gallery do, to applaud like that when they thought he'd lost. I felt I had taken enough time over my putt, but maybe I hadn't waited long enough for the noise to die down and lost my concentration. Anyway, I missed my putt, so we were tied. On the first playoff hole I hit a terrible drive and pulled it into the sticks. I made bogey, so Turnesa won, but ended up losing in the final to Snead. I was very disgusted with myself, feeling I'd just thrown the match away.

Back home, the Inverness Four-Ball was two weeks later, and my partner was Jimmy Thomson. We made a pretty good team, because I was playing well generally, able to make pars most of the time, and he was a good partner because he was so long. I'd hit a good drive and he'd be twenty to forty yards ahead of me. We managed to finish fourth and won $454.

The next week was the Hale America Open at Ridgemoor in Chicago, where I finished fourth and won $475. I skipped the Mahoning Valley tournament the next week in favor of the Tam O'Shanter again, and managed to win it—but just by the skin of my teeth. I was leading by five shots going into the fourth round and playing very well in beautiful weather. It seemed I had the tournament won, though I certainly didn't feel that way. Anyway, on the first hole, I left my approach shot short and the green had a ridge on it with the pin on top. I three-putted for a 5. On the second hole, I hit an excellent drive that landed in a divot. But it was sitting all right and I was sure I could reach the green in two, though there was a creek just in front. Well, I hit it thin, it went in the creek, and I three-putted for a 7. The 3rd was a par 3 with a lake in front of the green; I hit a 6-iron that landed on the edge of the green but rolled back into the water. I'd made one bogey and two doubles, and was five over after three holes. I was out in 42—just terrible. But I pulled myself together and played the back in 35, which put me in a tie with Clayton Heafner after starting the day five shots ahead of the field. You think I don't feel for the boys today when the same thing happens to them? I surely do.

We had the playoff the next day—all playoffs were eighteen holes in medal tournaments, and there were just about as many playoffs then as there are now. But the beautiful weather had gone—it was windy, rainy, and miserable. However, I was steamed up enough to play well, shot a 67 to Heafner's 71, and won the Tam again. That was a good comeback for me, particularly because of the way I'd lost in the PGA just a few weeks before.

I won two other small tournaments that year, the Ohio Open and the Charles River Invitational, but neither of them were official events, so they don't count on my record, though they were good experience for me, and it never hurts to win, even if you're just playing a casual round with friends.

What did happen that year—in fact, the next month—was my professional baseball debut. Growing up, I liked to play baseball and was a good outfielder. At one point, I thought quite a bit about which one I wanted to concentrate on, and chose golf. But I still loved baseball and went to watch a game whenever I had the chance. In Toledo, that meant the Mudhens, a farm team for the St. Louis Browns. Fred Haney was their manager, and he and I had played golf some at Inverness. The

Mudhens had an exhibition game coming up against the Browns, and Fred got the idea of having me play in it to get more people out to the game, which was going to benefit the Red Cross. He advertised it as "Golf Night," and gave me ten days to practice with the team. I remember that catching the ball in the type of glove we had then was making my hand really sore. He told me I could fix it by sitting and tapping my palm with a pencil over and over to toughen the skin, and it worked.

In the practice sessions, I did all right on everything but batting. You just can't believe how fast that ball went past the plate. You really had to be ready to hit before it left the pitcher's hand, and I never quite caught on. Then they got me suited up, and Fred told me it was fortunate I was the size I was, because I wasn't too hard to fit.

The game began, and I started in right field in place of a fellow named Jim Bucher. Milt Byrnes was the center fielder, and he said, "Byron, if you get the ball, just toss it to me and I'll come running and throw it in," because he knew I'd have trouble throwing accurately the distance to second or third or home. Well, the first thing you know, someone hits a grounder right at me. I scooped it up and threw it to second, which kept the runner on first and got me a big round of applause from the fans.

Then it was my turn to bat, and I whiffed. The fans started hollering, "Better stick to golf, Nelson!" and "Put Bucher back in!" Fred kept me in till the fourth inning, though, and then he said, "Byron, you've had enough fun, and I really would like to win this game, so I'm taking you out." That was fine with me. So Bucher goes back in, and strikes out his first time at the plate. Now the fans start yelling, "Put Nelson back in!" And then when we took the field, Bucher tried to catch a fly ball and dropped it, which really got the fans yelling even louder, "Put Nelson back in!" It was a lot of fun for me, but not so much for Bucher.

There's a good follow-up to this story, though. The Ohio Open was a few days later in Cleveland. Marty Cromb, the pro at Toledo Country Club, rode on the train with me to Cleveland, and was criticizing me severely for being so foolish as to play baseball. "You could have hurt yourself—broken a finger, ruined your career," he said. When we got to Cleveland, we were met by a friend of his, Bertie Way, a Scottish pro. Marty got to telling Bertie how crazy I was to play baseball, and how it was going to hurt me playing in the tournament.

Well, Bertie got all fired up and went to see some buddies of his, making bets against me, even though I was the favorite. We had no time to play a practice round, so I went out when the tournament started, scrambled around on the first hole and made par, scrambled again on the second, then settled down and started playing. To make a long story short, I birdied 6, 7, 8, 9, 10, 11, and 12, shot 63, and won the tournament. Bertie was so mad at Marty I thought he was going to kill him. He really thought Marty had set him up.

By this time the war was getting worse, and many of the pros were already in the service. It was becoming more difficult to put on tournaments, and at the end of '42 the tour just plain stopped.

There would be no Masters or U.S. Open for the duration of the war, and none of the regular events were played for all of '43. We did have just a couple of tournaments that had pretty good fields, but most of the boys were either in the service in some capacity or doing exhibitions for the Red Cross or war bonds.

Back in the spring of '42, when the draft was in full swing, I'd had a conversation with Colonel Woolley from the artillery training base at Camp Perry, near Toledo. He had played golf with me several times and thought I had a great eye for judging distance. He knew I had registered for the draft, and wanted me to let him know when my number was coming up, because he wanted to get me to teach his men how to judge distance. I went down to enlist soon after he talked to me, but I failed the physical because of my blood condition. It was not hemophilia, but what was called "free bleeding"—my blood didn't coagulate within the normal amount of time. Later that year my number did come up, and I failed the physical again for the same reason. They could have put me in a desk job of some sort, of course, but I still would have to go through basic training, and the Army didn't want to take a chance on me getting hurt out in the field and not being able to get help soon enough. After I failed the physical the second time, they didn't call me any more. So I was out of it. McSpaden was rejected too, because he had severe allergies and sinusitis. So there we were, looking as healthy as could be, but not in uniform like the rest of the boys. It was an uncomfortable feeling, believe me.

But it wasn't too long after we were rejected that Ed Dudley, who was president of the PGA then, asked if we could do some exhibitions for the war effort, visiting rehab centers and so on. He and Fred Corcoran, who had been managing the tour, wanted golf to do its part. So Jug and I began in late '42 and did exhibitions all through '43 and part of '44. David Fay, president of the USGA, told me recently that we did 110 of them, traveling back and forth across the country. We actually criss-crossed the United States four times doing Red Cross and USO shows, and going to the camps where they had rehabilitation centers for the soldiers. A lot of the camps had putt-putt courses and par-3 courses for the boys. Sometimes we'd go on military planes, sometimes on trains. We got no money, but MacGregor helped pay my expenses and Wilson paid some of McSpaden's. The people at Inverness really supported me during that time too, making sure my shop was being run right while I was gone.

We started in the early spring, working with the Red Cross and the USO to help the boys' morale. There were very few golf facilities, so we didn't do a lot of exhibitions, but we did visit the hospitals and camps and shook hands with the soldiers and told them how much their sacrifices meant to us and to the whole country. Most of the patients were ambulatory, so when there were golf facilities available, we'd show the soldiers the fundamentals of grip, stance, and so forth, or hit some drives and other types of shots to demonstrate the basics. One time we went to a camp near a rocket-testing site in New Mexico, I believe, and they shot off a few rockets for us to see. It was impressive—and scary.

Because of all the gas rationing, we traveled on restricted types of orders. We'd be put on troop trains or planes where they'd always feed the servicemen first, which was only right. We weren't neglected, you understand—just hungry a lot. Once, I remember they ran out of food before they got to us, so when we stopped at a little station near El Paso, Jug and I jumped out and ran in to see if we could get a sandwich. Well, the man said, "These are for the soldiers," but after we explained what we were doing and why we were on the train, he finally let us have one sandwich apiece.

It was tougher on McSpaden than on me in a way, because he really did love to eat and could eat a lot more than I could. Once, in Seattle, we stayed at a hotel and at breakfast, McSpaden had half a cantaloupe with ice cream, ham, eggs, toast, and tea. I had what you'd call a more normal breakfast. When he was done, he asked the waitress to bring him another half cantaloupe with ice cream. The waitress said, "Are you kidding?" and Jug replied, "That's what I ordered, isn't it?" She brought the cantaloupe, put it down on the table very carefully, and then backed away like she was expecting him to explode any second. That fellow really could eat.

On the trains, once in a while we'd have a berth to sleep in, but mostly we just slept sitting up like a lot of the soldiers. Even though we were pretty young ourselves, most of the servicemen seemed like kids away from home for the first time. But their morale was quite good. I'd have to say the whole experience was enjoyable for us, but very tiring with all the travel, and it wasn't easy to see those young boys going off to war or coming back all busted up.

In the middle of July, we did have a tournament called the All American, played at George May's Tam O'Shanter course. The purse was $5000. I tied for third, thanks to a final-round 68, and won $900. I was one shot back of McSpaden and Buck White, a pretty good player who wasn't around too long on the tour. McSpaden beat Buck in the playoff. In August, I played in the Chicago Victory Open. I started off with a 68, then did three 72's in a row and finished fifth. I didn't win any money because they paid only the first four places. Then there was the Minneapolis Four Ball at Golden Valley, which I played with McSpaden. We finished second at plus 8. They also had the Miami Open in December, but I didn't play in it, most likely because I was doing an exhibition somewhere to raise money for the war or the Red Cross.

I did, however, play in and win the Kentucky Open that year. It was played at a course called Whittle Springs, and I remember it well because I was presented with my winning check by Sergeant Alvin York, the much-decorated hero of World War I. That was quite an honor for me.

We also had sort of a substitute Ryder Cup tournament that summer, called the Ryder Cup Challenge. I was selected to be on the Ryder Cup team, and Walter Hagen captained the "Challengers." We played at Plum Hollow in Detroit. McSpaden and I tied Willie Goggin and Buck White in the foursomes, plus I beat Goggin in the singles, 4 and 3. We beat Hagen's team overall $8\frac{1}{2}$–$3\frac{1}{2}$.

Sometimes we'd pick up other people who'd play these exhibitions with us—people from golf or the entertainment field like Bob Hope or Bing Crosby. We didn't always play eighteen holes, usually only nine, but they'd build a platform near the clubhouse at whatever course we were at, and whoever was in charge of raising the money for the Red Cross or selling the war bonds would get up on the platform, and it would be almost like an auction. A man would say, "I'll give ten thousand dollars if Bing will sing 'White Christmas.'" Or "I'll give five hundred if Hope will tell a joke." We'd raise tens of thousands that way. It was exciting at times, and I really believe we contributed more to the war effort that way than if we'd been accepted for service. Another benefit was that it kept my game in tiptop shape for when the war was over and the tour started again. Fortunately for some of the pros who were in the service, they had the opportunity to play quite a bit, too. Sam Snead was in the Navy, stationed at La Jolla, California, and he played nearly every day with the admirals and such. Horton Smith, Ben Hogan, and Jimmy Demaret also had quite a few opportunities to play—not just at the bases where they were stationed, but in whatever tournaments there were, too. By the end of '43, we'd played at quite a few camps where our fellow pros were stationed. So despite the fact that the tour was canceled, we did get to see the fellows from time to time and play with them a little.

Once we did nineteen days in a row with Hope and Crosby, who were great. Bing would sing and Bob would tell jokes, and the crowd loved it. They were both just as you imagine them, born entertainers. Bob was always telling jokes, and Bing was quick-witted, too, plus he was completely natural at all times. The people loved them both. On one of these stops we were staying at a hotel and to avoid the crush of autograph seekers they ushered us in through the back door and up the elevator. But some of the fans had seen the elevator going up and where it had stopped, and they all trooped up six flights of stairs to our floor. Bob and Bing were so impressed with the fact that these kids would climb all those stairs just for an autograph that they signed every single one of them.

One other time, I was with Hope and we were on an Army plane. Sometimes there wouldn't be any seats—we'd sit on a bucket or a box or just on the floor. Anyway, they had picked us up in Alabama and we were going to Memphis. Ed Dudley was going to meet us and we were to put on a show there. When we landed, the runway was very narrow, plus it had rained a lot, the ground there was very muddy, and the plane slipped off the runway and into the mud up to its hubcaps. It took forty-five minutes for them to get a vehicle big enough to pull that plane out of the mud. But we got there and did the show just a little late and everyone seemed happy.

I did have one pretty scary experience during this time. I was with Bing Crosby in San Antonio, and a man picked us up at the train station and took us to an army base—I don't quite remember which one—where Bing was to perform. There were a lot of restrictions then, and when we arrived at the gate, there were two sentries with rifles guarding it. But this fellow who'd picked us up just drove past them without even stopping. There was another pair of sentries a little further on, and when they saw us drive past the first sentries they immediately raised their rifles and ordered us to stop. I was in the front seat and Bing was in the back, and when we saw those rifles go up, Bing hit the floor and I ducked as best I could. We truly thought we were going to get shot at. Of course, the driver had to stop then and explain who we were and what we were doing there, and they finally did let us through, but they really gave that fellow a tongue-lashing for not stopping at the first gate. And you know, that man never did even apologize to us. Just acted like nothing had happened at all.

I've been asked whether we got much criticism for not being in the service, and I have to say we got far less than I expected. Mainly, I think it was because what we were doing for the war effort with our Red Cross and USO exhibitions and so forth got plenty of publicity, and every write-up that I can recall was sure to mention that we had been rejected for military service for physical reasons. We were fortunate to have that kind of positive press; there were plenty of other men who had also been refused for physical reasons that no one else could see who were unfairly criticized.

The only complaints I did get were about gas rationing. I was still the full-time pro at Inverness all through 1944, but because I had to travel so much to do all these exhibitions, I needed more gas stamps than most people. Fortunately, I was able to get them without too much difficulty, because the people in charge of the various exhibitions would take care of it for me most of the time. But sometimes people would see me driving along here and there and think I was doing something wrong. Once the rationing board called me in about it because a man in Toledo had complained, but when I explained what I was doing and showed them my stamps, which were all legal and proper, they said it was all right.

Naturally, Louise couldn't be with me on any of these Red Cross or USO exhibitions. She mostly stayed at her folks' place in Texarkana, her sister Delle's in Fort Worth, or else in Denton at the farm I'd bought for my parents in 1940. It was a difficult time for her, and I sure didn't appreciate the separation myself, but fortunately it didn't last forever.

By 1944, the tour was alive again with twenty-three events, not quite as many as there had been before the war. Still, many of you who read this will be surprised that there were even that many. I was, too, really. The PGA had used golf in any way they could to help the war effort, but the people interested in golf had reached a point where they were hungry for news of any sports, including golf. Ed Dudley and Fred Corcoran deserve a lot of credit for not only what they did during the early war years, but for getting the tournament back on its feet again in '44. Many of the tournaments in '44 were renewals of ones that had been going on before the war, but a few were new ones, and some of the older and bigger ones still weren't back in operation, including the Masters and the U.S. Open. What Louise and I were happiest about was the fact that we could travel together again. McSpaden was okay as a traveling partner, but I definitely preferred Louise.

As I said earlier, my game was in good shape because of all the work I'd done during 1943, so I started out in '44 with some good pro-ams. We still played pro-ams then with just one partner and used no handicaps, which meant we always got good partners. Just like today, your partner would be someone who had helped sponsor the tournament. Anyway, at the pro-am at Hillcrest I won with 65. Then I won with 67 at San Gabriel Country Club in Los Angeles, and with 64 in Phoenix.

Another thing worth noting about the Phoenix tournament was that it was the only time my good friend Harold McSpaden beat me head to head. It was in an 18-hole playoff and we were even, going to the 17th. He had a twenty-footer, I had an eighteen-footer; he made his, I missed mine, and we both birdied the last hole, a par 5, so he beat me by one shot. I think that's the happiest I ever saw him in golf, because the rest of the time, I just happened to be fortunate enough to sneak out on him one way or another.

Of course, I was still at Inverness all this time and working hard, but I was playing every tournament my contract would allow. By now, Frankie Stranahan had become a pretty good amateur golfer, and from time to time wanted to take me on. I was too busy with the shop and my own tournaments, so I turned him down a few times. Well, one day he came in the shop with a couple of the boys he usually played with, and wanted me to play him. Something about the way he said it intimated that I was afraid to play him, and I guess it kind of got under my skin, because I said, "Okay, Frankie, I'll play you. Not only will I play you, but I'll throw in your two buddies and play all three of you, right now, best ball!" I was hot. We got out on the course and I was nicely steamed up and shot a 63, a new course record, beat Frankie and his friends, and Frankie never bothered me again.

So much has been written about 1945 and what I did then that my performance in '44 has been kind of overlooked. I played in twenty-one of the twenty-three tournaments and won eight of them—some record books don't include the Beverly Hills Open—which is a little better than a third. I was second five times, third five times, fourth once, and sixth twice. My winning margin was from 1 to 10 strokes, and I was also runner-up in the PGA. So '44 was a good year for me also.

One of my most memorable wins that year was the Dallas Victory Open at Lakewood Country Club where I won by 10 shots, which was a pretty nice margin of victory for me. It was the tournament's first year, and it drew a very good field. I won it the first year, Snead the second, and Hogan the third. Hogan was in the military in 1944 but played in the tournament, though I don't recall where he finished. Then it wasn't held again until 1956. I did some writing for the tournament during my newspaper years and always kept my eye on it, and it turned out to be the predecessor of the Byron Nelson Classic that is still going strong today.

Another interesting note about '44 was that I won twice in San Francisco, once in January and once in the fall, and both times at the same club, Harding Park. It was a fine municipal facility, and the pro there was Kenny Venturi's father, a good pro and a nice man. This was where Kenny learned to play as a young boy, and I guess he was about twelve at the time. I won by six strokes in January and by one in the fall. Kind of unusual, I thought.

Something else kind of unusual happened in that tournament. Seeing Nick Faldo with his ball up in the tree at Pebble Beach in 1992's U.S. Open reminded me of it. It was the last round, and I was fighting it out with Jim Ferrier. Ferrier was a pro from Australia and his wife was unusual among the pros' wives of that time in that she followed him every time he played, walked the course every hole with him. Anyway, we were on the 16th hole at Harding Park. The hole goes downhill and doglegs right. I was one stroke up and hit a good drive. Jim pushed his tee shot and his ball went into a tree, where it stayed. But you could see where it was, just kind of resting on this big branch. After a bit, Jim decided to try and play it out, and got someone to boost him up. He knocked it off that branch and out into the fairway, then onto the green, where he holed his putt for one of the most unusual pars I've ever seen.

That year Jug McSpaden and I played together in the Golden Valley Invitational in Minneapolis. It was a round-robin type of tournament, with seven teams. We played eighteen holes Thursday, then thirty-six holes Friday, Saturday, and Sunday for a total of 127. It was best ball of the team, but they gave plus or minus scores, plus being good and minus being bad. So if you lost the first round 5 down and won the second 6 up, you'd be plus 1. McSpaden and I had a wonderful tournament and finished 66 under par for the 127 holes, which is an average of a little better than a birdie every other hole. Not bad hacking around, but still we only won by three shots, so the other boys were playing pretty well too. My back was very bad that week, but somehow it didn't bother me when I played, and it even seemed to help me play better, because I played like gangbusters.

The next week after Golden Valley was the Beverly Hills Open, which I also won with a score of 277. Then came the PGA, where I started off well by being medalist with 138. In those days there was some extra money if you were medalist, so many of the boys would play in the qualifying rounds even if they didn't have to in order to have a chance at that extra prize money. I then made it to the finals against Bob Hamilton but lost on the 36th hole. He played very well and holed a great putt for birdie on the last hole after I had made a birdie trying to get even. There were some players still in uniform, and some who were just about done with their tour of duty. Lloyd Mangrum was the only pro I know of who actually saw combat. He was injured and awarded the Purple Heart, I believe.

Yes, 1944 was a good year. My average score was 69.67, and I was over par only three times in the twenty-one tournaments I played; my total was under 280 ten times. I was reasonably well satisfied with my performance, and very happy about winning over $37,000, which was more than twice as much as anyone had won before then. I was also given a great honor by being voted the Athlete of the Year by the Associated Press writers, and that topped it all off, for sure.

There was a major change in my job situation that fall—one that made it possible for me to have more freedom and play even better in '45. What happened was that some of the members at Inverness were becoming uncomfortable over how much money I was winning as well as what I was making at the club. This was along about the fall of the year, and fortunately, Mr. Haas warned me about it ahead of time. I must admit I was a little surprised by it, because I had worked hard at the club and the members had seemed pretty well satisfied with me. It was the first time I had had any problems in my working life as I had moved from Texarkana to Ridgewood to Reading and then to Inverness. Most people understood that young folks wanted to better themselves in those days.

Well, I was thirty-two, I had already realized I didn't want to play tournament golf forever or be a club professional all my life, and I'd been thinking about leaving Inverness before this came up, so it gave me a perfect excuse to resign, which I did.

Though I had done well that year on the tour, I also had another source of income besides Inverness. Mr. Haas had made me a vice president for Haas-Jordan. I had been able to be of great help to Mr. Haas during the war years when they were unable to get material for their umbrellas. On one occasion I happened to be playing golf with a fellow in the East who owned a fabric company, and I put him in touch with Mr. Haas. That made it possible for Haas-Jordan to get the material they needed.

Leaving Inverness made it possible for me to enjoy for the first time the freedom the pros in the sixties and later knew, of being able to play in as many tournaments as you wanted and concentrate solely on your game, with few distractions and worries. It was another part of what made the year to follow as memorable as it was.

SEVEN

1945 and the Streak

PEOPLE HAVE ASKED ME A LOT OF QUESTIONS ABOUT 1945. What happened? How did you come to play so well? How bad was the pressure? and so forth. There were several reasons for my good play that year. Mainly—and this seems unconnected to my golf, but it's not—I had thought for quite some time that I wanted to have a ranch someday. It had been my dream for years, really. And since Louise and I had grown up and lived through the Depression, we didn't want to borrow any money to buy a ranch. We wanted to pay cash for it. Actually, Louise didn't really like the idea of a ranch at all, because I didn't know very much about ranching, and she was afraid we couldn't make a go of it. But it was my dream, and she knew I'd done well in everything else I'd tried, so she decided to go along with me as long as we didn't have to borrow any money. That meant I had to make enough from my golf, and 1944 was the first year that I made enough to think I could make my dream of a ranch come true within a few years. All I had to do was continue to play well enough to keep winning or at least finishing in the top ten.

The second reason I did so well in '45 had a lot to do with something I did in '44, when I won nearly $38,000, played in twenty-one of twenty-three tournaments, won eight, and averaged 69.67 per round. During that year, I kept a record of my rounds and whether I played badly or what club I used, also whether I chipped badly, drove bad, putted terrible, or whatever. When I got through with the year, I went back over that book—which I don't have anymore, though I wish I did—like a businessman taking inventory.

I found two things that were repeated too often during the year, and they were "poor chipping" and "careless shot." The word "careless" was written in there quite a few times, which often was due to poor concentration. Or sometimes I would have a short putt and walk up to it and just kind of slap at it and miss it. So I made up my mind, like a New Year's resolution, that for all of 1945 I would try very hard to avoid a careless shot.

One other thing I should mention. My game had gotten so good and so dependable that there were times when I actually would get bored playing. I'd hit it in the fairway, on the green, make birdie or par, and go to the next hole. The press even said it was monotonous to watch me. I'd tell them, "It may be monotonous, but I sure eat regular." But having the extra incentive of buying a ranch one day made things a lot more interesting. Each drive, each iron, each chip, each putt was aimed at the goal of getting that ranch. And each win meant another cow, another acre, another ten acres, another part of the down payment.

Finally, I had one other incentive. I wanted to establish some records that would stand for a long time. I wanted to have the lowest scoring average—lower than when I'd won the Vardon Trophy in '39, when it was 71.02. And though I'd won eight tournaments in '44, I knew that the way some of these boys played, that number wouldn't stand up very long. I also wanted the record for the lowest score for an entire tournament. At that time, the record was 264, held by Craig Wood and a few others. I also wanted to be the leading money winner again. So you see, I had a whole collection of goals I wanted to reach, and every good shot I hit supported all of them. I guess I was fortunate to have so many goals, because to focus on just one, like a tournament scoring record, probably wouldn't have worked for me. But the ranch was my number-one, overriding dream, and that was what kept me going even in tournaments where I didn't play particularly well or finish where I wanted to.

Actually, I had played so well in '44 that it gave a great boost to my confidence, and it would have been unusual for me not to have done the same the next year. So I started off very positively in '45. In January I was second at the L.A. Open by one shot; that just gave me more determination to try and win it next year. At the start of the tournament, Bing Crosby—who by now I considered a good friend—was there on the first tee. I asked him, "You going to go with me some?" And he said, "I'm going to follow you till I feel you've made a bad shot." He was with me the whole first round when I shot 71, which was par, and he showed up again on the first tee the next day. On the 11th hole, I hit a drive and a 6-iron to the green, but pushed the ball to the right, and it landed short in the bunker. I happened to look around then and saw Bing leaving, waving his hand and saying, "I'll be seeing you!"

The next week I won the Phoenix Open by two, then was second—again by one shot—at both the Tucson and Texas Opens. My second win of the year was by four shots in the Corpus Christi Open in early February, where I also tied the low tournament scoring record of 264. While it was nice to have played so well and tied Craig and the others, I couldn't help but feel it would be even nicer to set a new record, so that remained one of my goals. Then I won my third tournament of '45 the next week at the New Orleans Open, this time by five shots in an 18-hole playoff with Harold McSpaden. Actually, Jug had a chance to beat me. In the last round, he had to birdie the 18th to win, but he hit a bad drive and we ended up tied. By the way, a lot of people don't know this, but McSpaden set a record that year himself—he finished second thirteen times.

I dropped back to second the next week, losing at Gulfport, Mississippi, by one shot in a sudden death playoff—one of the few times sudden death had been used on the tour at that point. I had tied with Sam Snead, who was just back on the tour. (Both he and Ben Hogan were released from the military early in the year and played quite a few tournaments. Hogan played in at least eighteen, and Snead twenty-six.) The playoff was to begin on the first hole, which had a creek running across the fairway at just about driver range. All through the tournament, we'd all been laying up in front of the creek with 3-woods. Well, I didn't realize that my adrenalin was up, and I hit that 3-wood absolutely perfect and it rolled into the creek. When Snead saw my ball go in, he put his 3-wood back in his bag and laid up with a 1-iron. I made bogey to his par and that was that.

I slacked off a little more the next week at Pensacola, finishing second to Snead by seven shots, though I played pretty well, shooting 69-69-71-65. Then at Jacksonville I played just plain terrible—for me—and tied for sixth, nine shots back, mostly because of a bad third round of 72, which was par there. Well, that must have gotten me a little steamed up, because it was the next week that I got started on what everyone today calls my streak, though of course I didn't have any idea at the time it was going to happen or keep my name alive in golf for so long.

It began with the Miami International Four-Ball the second week of March. I was paired with McSpaden again in what had never been a good tournament for either one of us. But it must have been our turn, because we finally did win. We beat Willie Klein and Neil Christman 6 and 5, Hogan and Ed Dudley 4 and 3, Henry Picard and Johnny Revolta 3 and 2. Then to finish it off, we walloped Sammy Byrd and Denny Shute 8 and 6. Harold and I were 21 up in our four matches, so we weren't exactly squeaking by.

Next was the Charlotte Open at Myers Park a week later. Snead and I had tied after 72 holes. This time it meant an 18-hole playoff, and on the 18th hole of that playoff, a long par 3, Sam was leading me one stroke. He put a 1-iron just on the front edge of the green, which was two-tiered and quite long. So he was a long way from the hole. Now, I was getting a little tired of having Sam beat me, and I thought, "There's a chance he just might three-putt from there." So I reversed what had happened at Gulfport. I changed from a 1-iron to a 3-wood and knocked the ball onto the upper level of the green about twenty feet from the hole. Sure enough, Sam three-putted and I parred, so we were tied and went into another 18-hole playoff the next day. This time I really concentrated and played better than Sam, shooting a 69 to his 73; I knocked in a thirty-foot putt for a birdie 2 on the final hole. That gave me a lot of confidence and made me feel my game was in tiptop shape. I was driving very well and putting even better than I had the year before. From there on, I just kept going and playing well and it seemed everything was going my way.

Of course, it wasn't going as well for some of the other players, and it was common knowledge that some of them were unhappy that

McSpaden and I were winning so many of the tournaments and so much money. During the Charlotte Open, in fact, Willie Goggin, one of the older pros, suggested that the PGA redistribute prize money in the tournaments so that there would be more money available for players who finished farther down the list. I could see his point, but I have to admit I sort of liked things the way they were.

The next tournament was the Greensboro Open, which the press would one day call "Snead's Alley," after he won it a record eight times. Sam had a wonderful following, and there were times that if it looked as if his ball was going over the green, the gallery would just stand there and let it drop right in the middle of them, which often made the ball end up closer—though sometimes his lie might not be as good where the grass was all trampled. However, I felt real good that week, and managed to win by eight shots to go three in a row. That particular year the tournament was played completely at Starmount, which was nice for the players, because the other course, Sedgefield, was clear across town, so it saved us all a lot of driving.

The following week we were at the Durham Open playing the Hope Valley course, which was a very good one. We played two rounds the last day, and the 18th hole was a slightly uphill par 3 of about 210 yards. In the morning round, I used a 1-iron, put the ball four feet from the pin, and made birdie. In the afternoon, I started out one shot behind but shot 65 to win by 5. Toney Penna finished five strokes behind me at 270. The icing on the cake was when I reached 18, got out my 1-iron and made another birdie.

Talking about that tournament reminds me that in 1990, the 45th anniversary of my streak, I was greatly honored by a party at Durham. My good friend Buddy Langley, then head of GTE Southwest, got together with the folks at Hope Valley, who in turn contacted the other nine clubs still in existence (Tam O'Shanter was gone, unfortunately—it had been sold and made into a development), and invited them all to come and celebrate. They had a beautiful plaque made to commemorate the event and installed it at the 18th tee. There was a little scramble tournament and a party that night, and everyone had a very pleasant day. I'm always amazed that people think so much even today of what I did so long ago. I guess it's a good thing they do, or I might think I dreamed it all up.

By now, having won four tournaments in a row and tying the record set by Johnny Farrell, I of course wanted to break that record, too. My concentration had gotten so good that I was in sort of a trance much of the time. That's about the only way I can really explain it. When I did hit a bad shot, I never thought anything about it, just went ahead and played the next one and it never bothered me or upset my ability to focus. I wasn't hooking at all, just had a good, normal flight to the ball that landed it softly on the greens. I was swinging just enough from the inside, and the ball flew straight until its velocity slowed to a certain point and it would fall slightly to the left, though I could go right if I needed to.

Next in line was Atlanta, a par-69 course, where I finally broke the scoring record with a 263. But I could have done better. The last hole was a long par 3, and I put my tee shot on the green, tried too hard to make birdie, and three-putted. That's a funny thing about golf—even when we play well, we know there are shots we missed. I remember that even Al Geiberger, when he shot his 59, said he missed a couple of short putts or he would have had a 57. Still, I had also broken the record of four consecutive wins and I won pretty decisively—by nine shots—so I didn't feel like I should complain very much.

After I'd won the fifth tournament in a row, someone from the company that made Wheaties approached me about doing an ad for their cereal, which was of course known as the "Breakfast of Champions." I never had an agent so I just talked to them myself and they put my picture and some statistics about me on the box and paid me $200 plus a case of Wheaties a month for six months. I had to give most of the cereal away; because although I liked Wheaties fine, you can only eat so much of it. I don't know if any of those boxes are still around—I sure don't have any, and back then, people didn't collect or save such things like they do now. Even during my streak, for instance, I signed very few autographs, though you might find that hard to believe.

To add a little to my story, a few years back I went to WFAA's studio in Dallas to talk with Bryant Gumbel on the morning news show. We chatted a bit about my record and the Nelson Classic, then Bryant asked if I had done any commercials in those days. I told him about the Wheaties ad and he said, "Pete Rose just signed a contract with Wheaties for $800,000." Well, we both had a good laugh. But considering where Pete Rose is today, I think I was better off with my $200.

But after Atlanta in early April, pressure from the press and fans was starting to build. Up to that point, there had been only a couple of other players who had won four in a row, so when I passed four, the writers and fans started saying, "He's got four, can he make it five?", then "He's got five, can he make it six?" One way I dealt with the pressure was to simply not play practice rounds, which kept me away from the press and the fans to some extent. That sounds foolish, but many times I played my best golf when I hadn't even seen the course, just went out and played. I was blessed with wonderful sight for many years and was an excellent judge of distance, which was a great help on an unfamiliar course. I'd just look down the middle of the fairway and try to hit it there, and I wasn't worried about getting into trouble because I didn't know where the trouble was. But by this time, too, I was familiar with most of the courses on the tour anyway.

Quite often, I'd play an exhibition at another town on the way to where the next tournament was and make $200–$300 for one round of golf, which was nice and helped a lot. That kept my game going well, besides helping me get closer to my goal of buying a ranch one day. That was another reason why I might not get to some tournaments until it was time to actually start playing.

There was a two-month break on the tour at this time—I have no idea why, just that no one was holding a tournament. So Louise and I went back home, worked on my parents' farm in Denton some, and visited her folks in Texarkana. That's where I practiced, hitting a bucket of balls every day or so. I wasn't working on anything in particular, just keeping my muscles limbered up.

I also did a couple of exhibitions during this time, and even played in something called a "Challenge Match" against Snead. There was a lot of talk going around then because Sam and I were both playing so well. Some folks thought Sam was better, some thought I was, so they had this match to supposedly decide the thing once and for all. It was in Upper Montclair, New Jersey, and it was a 36-hole match, with the first 18 being medal play and the second 18 match play. Sam shot 69 and I had 70 the first day, but the second day I beat him 4 and 3, so they figured I won.

But back to the streak. Next, in June, came the Montreal Open at Islesmere Golf Club in Montreal, where I finished 20 under par and won by 10 shots. Jug came in second with 278. I made just one bogey the entire tournament, on the par-3 14th hole in the last round, when I hit a 1-iron through the green and took three to get down. At that party in Durham in 1990, the nice folks from Islesmere gave me a beautiful silver tray that was engraved, "The greatest display of sub-par golf ever witnessed on a Canadian course." That made me feel pretty good, even forty-five years later.

Now I had won six in a row, and I was enjoying myself despite the pressure. The next week we were playing in the Philadelphia Inquirer Invitational. McSpaden lived there, and Louise and I were staying with him and Eva. We were both playing well, but starting the last round, McSpaden was leading by two shots. At that time, remember, they always didn't pair according to who was leading going into the last round. They tried to spread the gallery out among the players. That was why very often the leader might be playing a couple of groups or more ahead of the ones going off last. That was true in this case, because McSpaden was leading the tournament starting the fourth round, but was several groups ahead of me.

Now, Leo Diegel was a club pro who also lived in Philadelphia, and he had always liked me, called me "Kid," in fact. He came out to see how I was doing that afternoon, and I was getting ready to drive on 13. He said, "How you doin', kid?" And I said, "Well, I've got par in for 68." And he said, "That's not good enough." I said, "Why isn't it good enough?" He replied, "McSpaden just shot 66." He was leading me two shots before we started, so standing there on the tee I said, "That means I have to birdie nearly every hole but one to beat him." He laughed, and I did too, not thinking very much about it.

But as it happened, I did birdie all but one hole on the way in, shot 63, and beat Jug by two. On the last hole, I'll never forget it, I hit a driver and 6-iron and knocked the ball one foot from the hole, made my birdie, and Jug was right there watching me. He was so mad at me he called me every dirty name you can think of. When he accepted his check, he said, "You not only beat my brains out, but you eat all my food, too!" Still, he'd beat me in that playoff in '44 at

Phoenix, so I couldn't really understand what he was so upset about. That 63 was the most unusual thing I did that whole year—knowing I had to birdie the last five holes to win, and being fortunate enough to be able to do it.

The eighth tournament in my streak was the Chicago Victory Open at Calumet Country Club at the end of June. I don't remember a lot about it, except that I played very steady there, though the fairways were quite narrow and the rough pretty heavy. I shot 69-68-68-70— 275, 13 under par, and won by 7 shots. McSpaden came in second again, tied with Ky Laffoon at 282. Sometimes people are surprised I don't remember more about all these tournaments, but as I said, I was in a trance of sorts, so a lot of the events and people and so forth were all kind of a blur to me.

However, the next tournament is one I remember quite clearly— the PGA Championship at Moraine in Dayton, Ohio, a city that would prove to be very important to me some time later. First of all, I tied for medalist with John Revolta in the qualifying rounds. I didn't have to qualify because I was a former champion, but in those days they gave a cash prize for medalist, and I wanted that money—all of $125—to go toward another acre or two for my ranch.

Some people think of match play as being easier than medal play, but there was a whole lot of pressure every round. And most of the PGA championships were 36-hole matches after the qualifying rounds. You had to sometimes play ten rounds of good golf just to make it to the finals, and it was nearly always played in August, the hottest time of the year. It was tough.

In my first match I took on the Squire himself, Gene Sarazen, and managed to top him 3 and 2. I was told later that he had asked Fred Corcoran to pair the two of us in the first round, because he wanted to either get beat early or stay a long time. I guess he got half his wish, but I don't think it was the half he really wanted.

My second match was against Mike Turnesa, one of that great family of golfers. He was playing well too, and putting beautifully. So well, actually, that he had me 2 down going to the 15th tee in the afternoon round. The 15th was a par 3, about a 4-iron shot, and he put his ball on the green about ten feet from the hole. The way he was putting, I thought, "Man, if I'm ever going to get out of this match, I've got to get the ball closer than where he is." And I did it, put mine just inside of Mike's. He putted first and I thought sure he'd made it, he hit such a beautiful putt. But it rimmed the hole on the high side and stayed out. I was fortunate to get mine in, so I got one back.

Now I was one down with three holes to go. On the 16th at Moraine, you drive over a hill and pitch up to a little old dinky green. It's a tough little shot. The hole is short, but you have to hit the ball straight and have it in the right position. Well, I made a birdie there while Mike parred, so I got even.

The 17th was a par 5. I'd outdriven Mike a little bit, and he put his second shot just on the front of the green. I put mine closer, about twenty-five feet from the hole. He putted up very close, and I gave it to him, so he had a birdie. Well, I scrambled around and made my putt for an eagle. Now I was one up, and the last hole is a drive and 2-iron par 4. Fortunately we halved that one, so I managed to beat Mike one up. His brother Jim was playing another match the same time we were playing ours, and he lost, too. They were Italian, and afterward they were kidding around in the locker room, saying, "We'll have to eat our spaghetti without the meat sauce for dinner tonight."

Then I played Denny Shute, who'd won the PGA twice, and beat him, too. That gave me confidence, because if I could beat those three fine players, I might have a chance to win. Next came the semifinals, where I played Claude Harmon, a wonderful player who became one of the greatest teachers of the game, and who had won the Masters as well as several other tournaments. But I shot 65 and Claude shot 68, and afterwards he said, "I know what you've got to do to win a match—you've got to shoot better than I've been doing. Because when I shoot 68 and lose three down, the game's too tough for this old man."

Now I was up against Sam Byrd, a wonderful player who was making a career out of golf after being a fine baseball player for the Yankees. In the morning, he finished with four birdies in a row, then chipped in from about forty yards off the green on the last hole to put me 2 down at noon. Starting off in the afternoon, he birdied the fourth and I was 3 down. Everybody said it looked like I was going to lose in the finals again. The wind was 35 miles an hour that day, so besides playing a tough opponent, I was playing under tough conditions as well. But I had grown up in Texas and was a much better wind player than Sam, fortunately. I managed to make a two at the next par 3, and from there to the 14th hole, where the match ended, I was 6 under par.

That PGA was one of the best match play tournaments ever for me, because I played some very difficult matches and very wonderful players. It was the most strongly contested championship of match play in my career. These were all 36-hole matches, remember, so by the time I won, I had played 204 holes and was 37 under par. That was a lot of golf, especially in July in Ohio, and there were more than 30,000 in the gallery. Fortunately, for the first time, each hole was roped off and the crowds were controlled with the help of soldiers from nearby Wright Field.

My back was beginning to bother me some by then, and I was having heat and massage and osteopathic treatments every night during the championship. A couple of weeks later, I went to the Mayo Clinic and had them check me out, which took about three days. All they told me was that I had a lot of muscular tension, which wasn't much of a surprise, and they recommended that I find some way to relax, which was next to impossible right then.

But bad back or not, I was on the tour again two weeks later at the Tam O'Shanter All-American Open in Chicago and shot 269. I won by 11 shots, adding $10,200 to our savings for the ranch. It was one of my best tournaments that whole year—including my 259 at Seattle. The course was tough and the prize money of $10,200 brought out all the top players, including Hogan and Sarazen, who tied for second at 280. I may have said this before, but one reason I always did so well at the Tam was that I had learned to nip the ball off the fairway—I didn't ever take much turf. This was important in Chicago because the Tam O'Shanter fairways were nearly solid clover, and when that clover got between the ball and the club, the clover had a lot of slick juice in it. You never knew where the ball would go, but most of the time, you'd hit a flier. Because of the way I nipped the ball, I didn't ever hit many fliers, especially not at the Tam O'Shanter.

An interesting sidelight to that victory concerns George May, the fellow who put on the Tam. He liked to drive around the course in a cart and be very prominent in front of the spectators, doing whatever he could to promote interest in the tournament. In the first round that year, I had a 34 on the front nine, and George was waiting for me on the 10th tee. He bet me 100 to 1 that I couldn't shoot 34 on the back.

I could only lose a dollar, so I took him on. I started with an eagle 3 at 10 and a hole in one at 11, so I was four under after two holes. I parred the rest of the way, shot 32, and got my $100.

George loved to make those kinds of bets, and he especially loved to bet with Joe Louis, the great prizefighter. Joe was a pretty good golfer, but was really too muscular through the chest and shoulders to be as good as he wanted to be. One time on the first tee at the Tam, which was just to the left of the clubhouse—a long, low building about twenty yards away—May came up and bet Joe he couldn't break 80 that day. So Joe got all fired up and took a swing at the ball, hit under it and off the toe, and we all watched it sail right over the clubhouse. So there went his chance to break 80 and make a little money off George.

Getting back to my streak, by this time the pressure from the press and the fans really was getting to me. Another thing that added to it was that I was expected to make a talk at some sort of civic club luncheon nearly every city I played in, since I was a leading player and these folks were doing the pros a favor by putting on the tournaments. I didn't get paid, just got a free lunch, but it all added to the pressure, believe me. I got so sick of it that I just wanted to get it over with. Before I went out to play the first round at the Tam, I told Louise, "I hope I just blow up today." When I came back in, she asked, "Did you blow up?" I replied, "Yes, I shot 66."

So it went on. A week after the Tam O'Shanter I played in the Canadian Open, and that was really a test. The Canadian PGA had gone to work to make the Thornhill course really difficult, and they succeeded. Snead said the first seven holes were the hardest seven holes in a row he'd ever seen. According to an article written before the tournament, those seven holes were lengthened specifically because of me—and some of the other fine players, I'm sure—and par was changed from 71 to 70. I guess a few of our friends across the border weren't happy about my playing so well at Islesmere in June. My friend George Low, a pro famous for his wonderful putting, even bet that no one would break 70. But I shot 68-72-72-68—280 and won by four shots, ahead of Herman Barron at 284 and Ed Furgol at 285. So I think I gave everyone their money's worth—except maybe the folks who bet against me.

As you can imagine, though I was playing very well, I was also getting very tired. The next week we went to Memphis, and that was where the streak was broken by an amateur named Fred Haas—no relation to my friend Cloyd Haas of Toledo. I read recently that Fred was supposed to have been wearing shorts during the tournament, but I surely don't remember that he was. We weren't allowed to then any more than the boys are now. But regardless of what Fred was wearing, I had gotten very tired and made some foolish mistakes and ended up fourth at Memphis.

Now comes a strange thing. I was definitely and genuinely relieved when the streak was broken, because it took so much pressure off me from the media and the fans. But the fact that I had played poorly at Memphis made me kind of hot, and I went out and won the next two tournaments. One of them, the Spring Lake Invitational in New Jersey, doesn't count as an official tournament now, but I played and won $684.74 in the pro-am and $1500 in the tournament itself, so it counted as far as Louise and I and our bank account were concerned.

I went back to work at Knoxville, winning the pro-am with a 66 and the tournament by 10 shots with 67-69-73-67—276. Sammy Byrd was second with 286 and Ben Hogan was third with 287. After that came Nashville and the Chickasaw Country Club. I shot 70-64-67-68 and finished second. I had a good caddie, and in the first round on the back nine, I pulled my tee shot into the trees. When I got to the ball, my caddie was there ahead of me. I saw that I had a clear area for my swing and a clear shot to the green, so I said, "That's all right." The caddie said, "I was praying it would be all right." Now, I have to explain that I've been a member of the Church of Christ since I was twelve, and quite a few of the fans knew that I was. We preferred to be called simply Christians, but sometimes were referred to as Campbellites, because a man named Alexander Campbell had begun the Restoration movement that resulted in the Church of Christ being brought back to life as we feel it was begun in the Bible. Anyway, a man in the gallery overheard the caddie and me, and said, "Your caddie must be a good Campbellite, too." It made me feel good to realize I'd gained a reputation for not only being a good golfer, but also for being a Christian.

Next I played the Dallas Open, where I was third, then Southern Hills in Tulsa, where I was fourth. I didn't drive well there, and at Southern Hills, you must drive well. The greens were bermuda, but for some reason I wasn't negotiating them well. I was getting a little weary and feeling a little burned out by all the excitement and pressure of the whole year. Things were slipping a little, more than I liked, so I decided to try and put a stop to it when the tour went to the Pacific Northwest the next week. I did a little better in the Esmeralda Open at Indian Canyon Country Club in Spokane, sponsored by a local hotel called Esmeralda. I shot 266 and won by seven shots— McSpaden was second with 273—but there's more to that story. Before Louise and I arrived in Spokane, I had made reservations at the Davenport Hotel. We got in very late, nearly midnight, and they didn't have our reservation. The night clerk told me, "All our rooms are reserved for the golfers." Obviously, he didn't recognize me as being a golfer, which I could understand, but we were tired and I was somewhat put out by the confusion and the fact that they had no rooms at all. We called Fred Corcoran, who was staying at the other large hotel in town, the one that was actually sponsoring the tournament, and he managed to get us a room there. Louise was even more upset than I was at the situation, and before I went out to play the next day she said, "I just have one favor to ask. I want you to play well enough in this tournament that they'll know who you are!" Fortunately, I did— though we never went back to that hotel anyway, so I'll never know if they figured out who I was or not.

At the Portland Open the next week, Ben Hogan played the best tournament of his life and shot a new all-time record of 261, 27 under par. He obviously was playing quite well, and had been that entire year. I might have been happier for Ben if I hadn't finished 14 shots out, even though I was only in second place. I remember the press asked me how long I thought Ben's score would hold up, and I said, "Well, you don't know in this game. It could be forever, or it could be broken next week." As it turned out, I was two weeks off.

The next tournament was at Tacoma, Washington, the first weekend of October, on a course called Firecrest. I wasn't on fire at all, finishing third, 8 shots back. I was still fuming at how I'd played the week before and that upset my concentration so much I had my worst finish all year, ninth place. Tacoma and Tulsa were the only two tournaments that whole year that I finished over par, by a total of seven shots. But that wasn't much comfort right then. I was getting steamed about the way I was playing, and I really got hot the next week at Seattle, when I shot the easiest 259 you ever saw, 62-68-63-66. Jug

McSpaden was again second, tied with Harry Givan at 272. I liked the Broadmoor Golf Club's course, and I drove well and played my irons exceptionally well. Didn't have to hit many putts of any length at all, and in the first round I had two eagles. The last round, I was leading by so many shots that someone said, "All he has to do is make it to the clubhouse and he'll win." But I knew by the middle of the last round I had a chance to go for the record, and I was able to keep focused and do it. I really was pleased, especially after the drubbing I'd taken from Ben at Portland. In fact, I was so embarrassed by having Hogan beat me by 14 that I might not have played as well at Seattle if I'd only been two or three shots back at Portland. That 259 held up for ten years, till Mike Souchak shot 257 at Brackenridge in the Texas Open.

The tour was still going on, but I was pretty tired at that point and needed a good, long break. After all, by this time I'd won seventeen official tournaments and the pressure from the press was constant. After we got back from the hunting trip, I worked quite a bit at the farm in Denton and kept busy with first one thing and another, but my only other tournament that year was the Fort Worth Open at Glen Garden, my old stomping ground, and I was fortunate enough to win it.

It was in December of '45, just a week before Christmas. We were on our way to Glen Garden from our place in Denton. On the way there was a bridge with some ice on it, and a car was stopped on the bridge. As I started to go around the other car, mine skidded off the road into the ditch and turned over. We weren't hurt, but in the back seat we'd had a box of about 140 eggs we were taking to Louise's family and some friends. When the car rolled over, it threw all those eggs into the front seat on Louise. She was a mess, with eggs dripping off her hair and everywhere. Fortunately, a man with a wrecker was coming down the road to help the car that was stuck on the bridge, so first he turned ours over and fortunately, it was driveable. Another man came along then, and he kindly took Louise back to Denton and straight to her beauty shop. Her hairdresser said, "This is one time you've really gotten an egg shampoo." But we never could get the smell of those eggs out of that car, so we didn't keep it for very long. Guess that's why I played so well in the tournament—I knew we'd have to be getting another car soon.

It was actually the worst golf I'd played to win that whole year. The sub-freezing weather was terrible, and the greens were frozen each morning and hard as rock. The first round, you absolutely had to run the ball up because if you landed it on the green it would bounce as high as if you'd hit the sidewalk. There was a cold wind that blew nearly all the time, and it never did get very warm. I did have a 65 in the second round, though, with a 30 on the back nine. I finished with five straight 3's—remember, there are four long, tough par 3's the last five holes—by birdieing the par-4 16th and parring all the par 3's, so it made an interesting finish to that round. Jimmy Demaret, in his first tournament since his discharge from the Navy, was second with 281, and Harold was third at 282. The local paper the next morning called me "the Man O' War of golf," one I'd never heard before.

Really, it was a remarkable year. My scoring average was 68.3, I had eighteen official wins, eleven in a row, finished second seven times, and had nearly 100 official sub-par rounds, my best being 62. I set new records for most wins in a row, most in one year, lowest tournament score, and lowest scoring average. Not too many "careless shots"—in fact, my New Year's resolution had knocked off $1\frac{1}{3}$ strokes per round. Looking back, I realized that even though I had all those goals in mind, I never expected to do so well, especially against the competition I had. And despite the fact that some of the boys were still in uniform for part of the year, most of them were playing at least part of the time. Snead played in twenty-six events, Hogan eighteen, Dutch Harrison at least thirteen, and so forth. But beyond the fields I played against most of the time, I think that 68.3 speaks for itself.

Louise was very happy about what I had done and very happy for me, though she was realizing one thing about our situation that didn't especially please her. Because I had become something of a celebrity, Louise became simply "Byron Nelson's wife" to a lot of people, rather than Louise Shofner Nelson, and at times that was a little awkward for her. It's a shame the way the world can be about such things, though on the other hand, when she wasn't with me, she could go wherever she wished anonymously, while I no longer had that option very much—and that's become even more true today.

One thing that helped her feel better happened late that fall. The city of Denton wanted to honor us for all the good publicity we had brought to Texas and especially Denton, so they surprised us one day by presenting us with a pair of beautiful horses on the courthouse steps. They were half Tennesee Walkers, so they made good riding horses for our 54-acre place there in Denton and eventually for the ranch in Roanoke. But Louise definitely got the better part of the deal. Her horse, Linda, was not only beautifully gaited; she had a wonderful disposition. You could do just about anything with her. My horse, Rex, a gelding, never was anything like Linda; he was quite fractious at times and we eventually had to sell him. But Linda was a joy to us for a long time, and it was certainly a wonderful honor from the folks in Denton.

It was now December. I had begun my career with the goal of winning every important tournament in the United States at least once. I already had the Masters, the U.S. Open, the PGA, the North and South, the Western, and the Tam O'Shanter. The only one left was the L.A. Open, which once again had eluded me in 1945. I ended the year feeling very satisfied in some respects, but I still had at least one goal left in golf—and still had to save up enough money to buy that ranch I'd been dreaming of.

Speaking of money for the ranch . . . . in 1945, I made more than I ever had before, but because so much of it was in war bonds, it's been reported in the press for years and years that I won much more than it actually turned out to be. You see, Fred Corcoran, who was running the tour at the time, wanted golf to do as much as possible toward the war effort, and we were all glad to help. So he got the various tournament committees to have the prize money in war bonds. In case anyone doesn't know, they were similar to our savings bonds and CD's today. You bought, say, a $1000 bond for $750, and if you held on to it for ten years, it would actually be worth $1000. Most of the tournaments paid totally in war bonds, a few paid in a combination of cash and bonds, and once in a while one would pay totally in cash.

Well, none of us were making the kind of money where we could hold on to those bonds for ten years, so we cashed them in immediately, which meant at about 75% of their face value. When you look at the official records and see where I won $1,333.33, for instance, that meant it was actually $1000 in cash. According to the press, I won somewhere between $60,000 and $66,000 in '45, but according to my black book where I kept records of each tournament played and what I really won, my winnings were closer to $47,600. In fact, my IRS records for that year show that I made $52,511.32 from golf, but that includes such things as exhibitions and pro-ams and sometimes a portion of the gate receipts, which once in a while you would get if you were in a playoff. It's very confusing for anyone trying to get all those figures to make sense, because the PGA didn't keep the best records then, and sometimes even the press reported things inaccurately. But that's about the best I can do at straightening it out as far as my own golf winnings are concerned. I know for sure that Louise and I didn't hold on to any of those war bonds—we couldn't afford that luxury!

EIGHT

Golf for the
Fun of It

E VEN THOUGH I'D HAD A WONDERFUL YEAR IN 1945, I still had that goal of winning every important tournament in America at least once. But that Los Angeles Open had gotten away from me every year. I felt I'd just plain thrown it away a couple of times. All golfers have certain areas of the country where they play better— especially on the greens—than others. I negotiated the greens beautifully in Chicago, where I won six tournaments, and San Francisco, where I won three. So I was always comfortable playing in both those cities. But I never could get the hang of the greens in Los Angeles. They were poa annua then, and everyone told me the greens always broke toward the ocean, but half the time I couldn't figure out which way the ocean was. We had caddies, but they were just kids, most of them, and in that day and time, nearly all the players depended on themselves to judge distances and read greens.

So the Los Angeles Open was still on my list to win, and I set myself to win it that next January, just a couple of weeks after I'd won the Fort Worth Open at Glen Garden. I was still hitting my irons very well, and I remembered that the 10th hole at Riviera was a very demanding one. It was more than a dogleg, it just went dead right at the landing area. You had to drive on the left side of the fairway, because the green sloped to the left and you had to approach it from the left to have any chance to make par. So I was very sure to drive to the left, and I believe I even made a couple of birdies. Fortunately, I played very steady on the other 17 holes as well, shot 284, and won by 5 strokes. That was very satisfying, to win a tournament that had escaped me so many times. I was bent on playing well, of course, and I was leading going to the last round anyway, but I finished five shots ahead of Sam Snead, thanks to a birdie on the 18th hole. That birdie gave me a great deal of satisfaction, being in front of quite a large gallery and coming at the end of a tournament that had eluded me so many times. Maybe it meant more to me because southern California was where I'd done so poorly when I first turned pro, and I was determined to make up for it. In any case, it was an excellent tournament for me, and another goal checked off on my list.

At the San Francisco Open the next week, my score was one shot better—283—than at L.A., but I got a little more distance between me and the field, partly because of the course conditions. It was terribly wet and cold all through the tournament. The ball did not roll at all; in fact, the players were allowed to lift, clean, and drop the ball if it plugged in the fairway. I hit some of the best iron shots of my career in that tournament, and beat Ben Hogan by nine. What I liked best about it was the tenth hole, a very demanding par four. I hit driver and 1-iron all four rounds and made two birdies and two pars, and won by 9 shots. Under those conditions, that was pretty good. The other satisfying thing was that the tournament was held at the Lakeside Course of the Olympic Club, which is my favorite course outside of Riverhill in Kerrville, Texas.

I was scheduled to play at Richmond just outside San Francisco the next week, but by now I was starting to think about retiring. I really felt I had played all I wanted to play. I'd achieved all my goals and then some, and the traveling was getting pretty old. I wanted to settle down and do something different with my life. I'd been doing nothing but golf since I was twenty, and it's a hard life in many ways, even though it has its exciting and glamorous aspects—especially if you're playing well. But fourteen years was enough.

During December of '45, Louise and I had talked some about my quitting golf someday, and she said that would be fine with her. I knew she was as tired of the travel and so forth as I was. But we had to talk seriously, because this was a complicated decision. I had a contract with MacGregor, we hadn't found the ranch yet that we wanted to buy—there were a lot of things to consider. But at least we had quite a bit in the bank, and we needed to stop and think about what we wanted to do and how we would do it.

So I withdrew from the Richmond tournament and telephoned Louise. She and Eva McSpaden had already caught a train to Phoenix for the next tournament, and Jug and I were to meet them there after we played San Francisco and Richmond. The girls were staying at the Westward Ho Hotel, and when I reached Louise and told her I had withdrawn from the tournament at Richmond, she was really worried. She asked me three or four times if I was all right. When I finally convinced her I was, I told her I was catching a train and would pick her up in Phoenix and that I wanted us to go home and do some serious talking about the tour. I asked her not to say anything about it, even to Eva.

We started talking as soon as we both were on the train in Phoenix and began figuring things out. The first thing to think about was my contract with MacGregor. It was a pretty good one, and in all fairness to the company, when I decided to quit I would have to renegotiate it, which would naturally mean less income we could count on. We finally decided I would have to go back and play on the tour until all the problems were worked out. So as soon as I got home, I called Henry Cowan at MacGregor and told him I wanted to talk to him. I went up to Cincinnati and told him I was going to retire and needed to renegotiate. He was upset that I was leaving the tour, but we worked out an agreement where I would take the same amount of money for the three-year period of the contract and spread it out over ten years. Then I went back out to play.

One very funny thing happened after I withdrew from the Richmond tournament. I didn't find out about it until nearly forty-five years later, but Prescott Sullivan, a fine sportswriter for the *San Francisco Examiner,* had written a column about me after I'd left San Francisco after winning there in '46. He talked about how the other players were pleased that I wasn't playing at Richmond because I'd been winning all the money on the tour, it seemed like, and they were tired of it. In fact, Willie Goggin, who'd brought this up before, had again tried to get the tour to change the prize distribution. The article ended by saying that I was "knee-deep in greenbacks" down there in Texas. My good friends Bud and Janet Waltz of Haas-Jordan showed me the article just a couple of years ago, and I don't know if I ever laughed so hard in my life as when I read that.

Knee-deep in greenbacks or not, I skipped not only Richmond, but Phoenix and Tucson too. So my first tournament after that was at San Antonio on the Willow Springs course. We had terrible weather— it snowed and hailed. I was third, which wasn't bad considering all that was going on in my head. One big distraction was that we had found the ranch we wanted to buy. It was 630 acres in Roanoke, a small town 22 miles north of Fort Worth. There was already a bid on it, but this was to be a cash sale, and our agent didn't think the buyer could come up with that much money that fast. He said we would know in a month.

So, all excited about buying this ranch, off I went to New Orleans, where I pulled myself together and won by five strokes. We played City Park again, a fine municipal facility that I always liked. I always played well there, and especially liked the long par threes, since I was a good long-iron player. I was a little behind Hogan starting the last round, and birdied the first six holes, as I remember it, to pull ahead of him, so that felt good. Now I was really counting the extra acres and cattle that I could get with my winnings if we were able to buy that ranch.

Next was Pensacola, but with everything on my mind and being all keyed up about the ranch and all, I played terrible. I shot 286, tied for thirteenth, and won $152.50. That wouldn't buy much ranch. But this was the first of March. My real estate agent back in Texas, Mr. Ray, was supposed to have called me by this time and I hadn't heard from him at all, so it was upsetting me. Louise and I got packed and she was sitting in the car, waiting for me to drive us to St. Petersburg, when I decided to call Mr. Ray right then and there. When I got him, he told me he was just getting ready to call me. He'd just found out that the deal hadn't gone through, so I had the opportunity to buy it. I told him, "I have to leave right now for St. Petersburg, but I'll call you as soon as I get there." I was really excited.

All the way on that six-hour drive, Louise and I talked it through. Louise was willing to go along with the idea of the ranch, but she insisted—and I agreed—that we shouldn't dip into any of our investments to buy it. We had to do it strictly with our cash savings, and the purchase price was $55,000, which we were still somewhat short of. We figured if I did well enough through the rest of the year, we'd have just enough to buy the ranch, plus a little to live on and buy cattle with and so forth. When we got to our hotel room in St. Petersburg, my mind was made up. I didn't even unpack, just got on the phone immediately and told Mr. Ray I'd send him the check for the escrow money right then.

With that load off my mind, I played a little better at St. Petersburg, finishing fifth and winning $650. Now my winnings meant more than a ranch "someday"—they meant "very soon." I played in the Miami Four Ball next partnered with McSpaden, but we weren't as lucky as we had been in '45. We did make it to the semifinals, though, and won $300, which was better than getting poked in the eye with a sharp stick.

After that, I took a few weeks off to come home and begin to get some loose ends tied up. Earlier in the year, Otis Dypwick, a sportswriter from Minneapolis, had contacted me about writing an instruction book to be called *Winning Golf,* and I'd agreed to do it, so now it was the middle of March and warm enough in Texas to take the pictures we would need. We did them out at Colonial, and after they were done, I worked with Otis on the copy to go with each picture. One funny thing—in quite a few of the pictures, my hands look darker than you would expect, especially for that time of the year. It's because I'd been painting fences just before we did the pictures, and we didn't have products like they do today for taking paint off your hands, so I still had quite a bit of that red paint on my hands. But red hands or not, I've always been proud of that book. I call it "the primer of golf," because it's quite simple and easy to understand.

Another thing I needed to do was to find out whether my parents were willing to move to the ranch, because I knew I would need a lot of help, and my father was a good hard worker. When I talked to them, my father was willing to move, but my mother wasn't too eager about it. But she agreed to do it and it worked out fine. There was a smaller house next to the ranch house where they could live, along with my brother Charles. Ellen, my sister, had married and moved out by that time.

Finally, I had to start learning how to be a rancher. I wasn't about to jump into buying cattle or much of anything for the ranch until I really had some idea of how to go about it. I set myself to studying and working on it the whole rest of that year. I read everything I could get my hands on, and talked to anyone I could find who had some knowledge on the subject.

But in the meantime, it was back to work on the golf course. My next tournament was the Masters, where I finished seventh. I wasn't very happy with that performance, but my heart just really wasn't in it anymore. I had achieved my goals as far as the Masters and the other majors were concerned, though I still hoped to win the Open again.

For several months then, I would go out and play a tournament, then go back home and study up on ranching. A month after the Masters, I played at Houston and won by two shots, adding another $2000 to our savings. That tournament was interesting in that it was the only one I can recall of all the times we played together through the years that Hogan, Snead, and I finished in the top three spots. I was first, Hogan second, and Snead third. You'd think, as well as we all played then, that something like that would have happened more often, but it didn't. There really were quite a few fine players around then, and they didn't just let us walk all over them much. I think part of the reason I played so well was that, except for Houston, I had won every important Texas tournament, and some not-so-important ones as well. I'd won at Dallas, San Antonio, Fort Worth, Beaumont, even Harlingen, but never Houston. So that was sort of a minor goal for me, and now I had achieved it, which made me feel good.

The following week I played in the first Colonial National Invitational in Fort Worth and finished in a tie for ninth place. That whole year, I would have a spurt of being able to get fired up for a tournament or two, and then run out of steam. The excitement and tension of 1945 had taken more out of me than I had actually realized. But I never did play well at Colonial—my best finish was a tie for third with Harvie Ward some years later, and I really was making just a guest appearance to help the tournament get going and receive some publicity. It's a fine course, but I just never was able to play it very well, though it's difficult to say whether I might have done better had the Colonial gotten started before I'd made up my mind to leave the tour.

It was about this time that Louise and I closed the deal on the ranch. Because the owner had cattle to sell and equipment to get rid of and so forth, we wouldn't be moving in till the end of August, so it was back on the tour for a few more weeks.

Next was the Western Open in St. Louis. I didn't play well, shot 280, and only won $516.67. Then I went to Winged Foot in Connecticut for the Goodall Round Robin, but before the tournament started, I played a 36-hole exhibition called the "International Challenge Match," against Richard Burton, the British Open champion. My good friend Eddie Lowery was the referee, and I beat Burton 7 and 6 and won $1500. Then, in the tournament itself, I finished third at plus 22, and won $1150. Not a bad week, all things considered.

I didn't play at Philadelphia, because I wanted to save my energy for the U.S. Open at Canterbury in Cleveland, which came right afterwards. Also, by this time I was making quite a few appearances promoting *Winning Golf,* which had just been published, and that took quite a lot of time. You might be interested to know that I got 25 cents for each book, which sold for $2.50. That doesn't sound like much, but it was on the best-seller list for several weeks and sold 130,000 copies, and that 25-cent royalty enabled me to buy my first fifty head of Hereford cattle when I did finally get to start ranching.

Canterbury was a good course, and as usual for the national championship, it was tough. The rough was long, the fairways narrow, and I knew inside that this was going to be my last shot at really trying to win it again. I was playing well, hitting my irons as well or better than ever before, including the Open in '39. In the first round, on the front nine I never missed a fairway or had a putt more than ten feet for birdie, but I two-putted every one and had nine straight pars.

In the second round, Cliff Roberts and the great writer Grantland Rice were in my gallery. On the 15th hole, you drove into a valley and had a blind shot to the green. I got up there in good position for birdie, hit my putt perfect, but the ball swung in and out of the hole. I was walking toward it thinking I'd made it, and couldn't believe it didn't go in. I was told later that Rice said to Cliff right then, "He'll never win." When Cliff said, "Why? He's playing beautifully." Grantland said, "Yes, but the ball's not rolling right for him. He's not getting any breaks at all." As it turned out, he was right, but not because the ball wasn't rolling right.

In the third round, on the par-5 13th hole, I hit a good tee shot and a good second, but I laid up on it a little because if you hit it too far you'd be on a downslope. As soon as I hit it, naturally, the caddie went quickly toward it. Remember now, they didn't have the fairways roped off then for most of the tournaments—the only ones I recall for sure were the '45 PGA and the Masters. The spectators would walk right along with you till you got to your ball, and the marshals would then put a rope up to hold the fans back just enough to give you room to swing, really. Sometimes, if the crowd moved too fast, the marshals couldn't get there ahead of them, and that's exactly what happened this time. My caddie got there and ducked under the rope the marshals were holding, but the rope was too close to my ball; my caddie didn't see it, and he accidentally kicked it about a foot. Since I was leading the tournament at the time, Ike Grainger, one of the top USGA officials, was there as my referee, and we talked about the situation and what it meant. We were both pretty sure it meant a penalty stroke, but Ike said he preferred to talk to the committee before he made a ruling, though he said I had the right to have the decision right then. I said it was okay to wait, which was my mistake, and in my mind that was what cost me the tournament, not the delay itself. Because then I was trying to play with all that on my mind. I was pretty sure I would receive a penalty stroke, but not having it settled right then, I played two over par from there in, and then had the penalty stroke added on besides.

I didn't make up any ground the last round, though I had a good chance or two. On the 17th, a long par 3, I hit my 3-wood just beautifully, but it went over the green and ended up on the fringe—actually, in a lady's hat she had put on the ground next to her. Back then, they allowed people fairly close to the green itself, much closer than they do now. They ruled that I could pick up the ball so the woman could remove her hat, then replace it with no penalty, but the lost time and distraction of all this made me lose my concentration again. I chipped from there and it rimmed the hole, spun out three and a half feet, and I missed the putt. I was a little upset by that, and my tee shot on 18 went down the left side of the fairway, where it landed and bounced further left and into the rough, which was really tall and thick. It was only about a foot into the rough, but it was so thick that I had to use an 8-iron to get out. Then I got to the green and missed a twelve-footer for par, so I ended with two bogeys to tie with Lloyd Mangrum and Vic Ghezzi.

One other unusual thing happened there—we three were in and already tied, but on the 72nd hole, Ben Hogan and Herman Barron were on the green with medium-long putts for birdie to win. Both of them three-putted, but if they'd even two-putted, there would have been a five-way tie.

Now we were in the playoff, and on the 4th hole, the first par 3 on the course, Vic and Lloyd both had thirty-footers. They both made theirs while I missed my own ten-footer. I made up that stroke, but we all played very steady golf and ended up tied again at 72. In the second playoff, on the par-5 9th hole, Mangrum hit his drive out of bounds on the left. He got disgusted with himself, hit again, then put a fairway wood on the green and made an 80-foot putt. He ended up with a 71 to Vic's and my 72's. I'd have to say it was the best I played to lose a tournament my whole life. My concentration was probably not as good as it should have been, because I'd made up my mind ahead of time that if I won I would announce my retirement then and there, so that may have been too much on my mind.

One thing I'd like to say here is that Lloyd Mangrum was the most underrated player of my time. He won twenty-one tournaments, including the '46 Open. He was a fine player, but he had a kind of unusual, funny sarcasm that he used, and if you didn't know him and understand it, it made him sound kind of tough. Some years ago, Susan Marr was doing some radio during the tournament at Westchester, and she asked me to go on the air with her. She said, "I've been asking people all day who are the seven pros who've won twenty-one or more tournaments, and nobody's been able to name them all. Can you?" I said, "I'll try." I'd been doing a little studying for my own broadcast work and got through all of them, including Lloyd, and she said I was the only one who'd remembered Mangrum. I won the prize, which was a "Thank you."

Here's a funny story about Lloyd that most people don't know. He was born in Grapevine, Texas, near where I live now in Roanoke, and he was delivered by the father of my good friend Dr. Dudley Wysong. One time, "Dr. Dud" and his mother were visiting us and discussing that fact, and Mrs. Wysong said, "His daddy ain't paid for it till yet!" The next time I saw Lloyd, I told him what she'd said and he almost died laughing. He thought maybe he should go ahead and send her a check for $25, which was what it cost for a delivery in those days.

The next week in Toledo, back in my old stomping grounds, Mc-Spaden and I played together again—for the last time, really—at the Inverness Invitational Four-Ball. We played pretty well, finished second at plus 14 to Hogan and Demaret, and collected $850 apiece.

I took a week off, then played the Columbus Invitational at Columbus Country Club in Ohio and won it, adding another $2500 to our bank account, which came in very handy. Next week, at the tournament in Kansas City, I tied for third (Frank Stranahan came in first) and won $1,433.34.

Here's a very curious story that I hope someday we find the answer to. As I recall, in the summer of '46 I was playing in a tournament in Kansas City at Hillcrest Country Club. There was an electrical storm going on but we kept playing because the rules said we had to. I was standing on the ninth tee with Horton Smith and Jug McSpaden, when we saw lightning hit back of the ninth green and kill several spectators. I was checking on this story recently with my good friend Bill Inglish though, and he said there was no account in the papers of any such thing happening. So I called Tom Watson, who asked his father, Ray Watson, about it. Ray remembered it distinctly, because he was sitting on the clubhouse porch across from the first tee, which was right next to the ninth green, and Ray saw the lightning hit. Only trouble was, Ray said it happened in 1938, and so does the written history of Hillcrest Country Club. This got my curiosity going, so I called McSpaden, who remembered it the same way I did and also said it was much later than '38, because he was at Winchester in Boston then and never got to play in Kansas City that year. I wasn't in Kansas City in '38 either, according to Bill Inglish's records.

However, it wasn't until 1948 that the USGA made the rule about being able to stop play as soon as any of the players see lightning. Up to that point, even though lightning was visible, you couldn't stop playing until the tournament officials said you could, which wasn't very satisfactory. Still, it's a mystery to me why there's no record anywhere of that other lightning strike, when both McSpaden and I have such a clear memory of it. But wherever we were, if our memories are right, Horton Smith birdied that ninth hole, which really impressed me. Guess he wanted to get out of there as fast as he could.

Louise and I had been on the road now for six out of the last seven weeks, and we were both homesick. As soon as I finished playing in Kansas City, we drove all the way home, had one full day there, then drove all the way to Chicago the Wednesday before the Chicago Victory Open tournament started. With all that driving, it was amazing I played as well as I did, but I managed to win. It was played on Medinah #3, which everyone knows is a very tough course. I drove exceptionally well, shot 279, and won by 2 shots. What I remember best about it, though, was that in the first round I was paired with Tommy Armour, the famous Scottish pro. Tommy and I were having breakfast, and he was known to have too much to drink now and then and he was a little hungover that morning. So before he ate anything, he fixed himself a Bromo-seltzer and drank that. It was the first time I'd ever seen anyone do that before breakfast, and I never forgot it.

The Tam O'Shanter that year was called the All-American for some reason, and I genuinely didn't want to play in it. For one thing, I'd already won there four times, and for another, that year they had begun a promotion deal where the winner was almost duty bound to play at least fifty exhibitions the next year, at $1000 apiece. Well, the money was nice, of course, but that type of thing can be hard on your game. Lloyd Mangrum did it one year, and never played as well afterwards. Anyway, I tied for seventh, winning $1,233.34, so I didn't have to worry about it.

I took off again the next two weeks and then played in the PGA at Portland. I won three matches and made it to the quarterfinals against Porky Oliver. We were tied going to the 18th hole, a long par 5 that had a lot of left-to-right slope on the green. I was thirty feet from the hole and Ed was forty. He had to borrow five feet or more for his putt to break, and he made it, while I missed mine. So much for the defending champion.

I went home again after that, and the first thing that happened was we moved to the ranch on August 26. It took only two carloads to get all our things from Denton to the house in Roanoke. We had no furniture of our own, because we had rented already furnished homes the entire time I played on the tour. Fortunately, Louise's sister Delle had some things of hers in storage because her husband was still in the service and Delle was living at home in Texarkana. We used her stove and refrigerator and a few pieces of furniture till we could get started with our own, and when everything was settled, we found we had $2500 to live on, which we figured we could make last six months.

This was also when I prepared to formally announce my retirement. I did it a few days before I played in something called the "World's Championship" at the Tam O'Shanter course in Chicago. I had mentioned a couple of times already that I was thinking of gradually retiring, but hadn't said anything definite yet. I told the press then that I was formally retiring from tournament golf, that after 1946, I would make only a few token appearances, mainly at Augusta and at the Texas PGA.

Now comes a strange thing. After I made my announcement, I played in a "World's Championship" with Snead, Mangrum, and Barron. It was just two rounds, and I finished second two shots behind Snead, but apparently it was a winner-take-all event, because Snead won $10,000, and the rest of us didn't get anything but our expenses. But the most amazing thing is that I don't recall one single thing about playing in it whatsoever. I guess the fact that I didn't win a dime kind of made me want to forget the whole thing.

At this point, taking a break from everything, Jug and I went on a wonderful hunting trip with Seattle businessman Ralph Whaley, one of the most remarkable men I ever met in my life. We had gotten acquainted with Ralph the year before when I had that 259 in Seattle, and during the tournament he'd invited McSpaden and I and our wives to his house for dinner. Ralph was 6'4", a strong-looking man with a wonderful engineering background. He had helped build Hoover Dam, but mainly he was an outdoorsman and a hunter. He'd bagged various wildlife specimens for the Smithsonian, and in his home there, he had a room fixed up exactly like a cabin where he'd spent a lot of time in the Rockies when he was doing a lot of hunting and trapping. He also was a wonderful shot; he did a lot of exhibition shooting for Winchester and he got so good at it that it got boring, so he started hunting with a bow and arrow instead.

As you might guess, he wasn't bashful at all and started telling us about some of his hunting trips and so forth. He said he was very good with a tomahawk, that he could throw one a long way and stick it in a tree or cut a man's head off if he needed to. To prove it, he took us into this "cabin" room, and hanging on the wall was a tomahawk. Ralph took that down and threw it clear across the room. It landed deep into a wooden post between two big picture windows that looked out over the Broadmoor golf course. Next, because it wasn't dark yet, he took his bow and arrows and we walked outside, where he shot several arrows into the air. We couldn't see any of them after they went off, but he told us exactly where each one would land in the fairway, and he was exactly right. Later, he told us about playing a round of golf against a couple of very prominent pros where he played their best ball. But on each hole, instead of hitting a wood or iron, he would shoot an arrow to the green, then chip or putt from wherever it landed. He played in fifty-seven "shots," so it was no contest.

We were quite impressed with Ralph, and that's why we ended up going hunting with him. He'd already arranged an exhibition in Moscow, Idaho, for which we got no money, but the people putting on the exhibition paid for all the stuff we needed for a hunting trip to this secluded area of Idaho. The amazing thing about Ralph was that when you listened to him talk, you thought he was exaggerating, but when you got out into the woods with him, you found he could actually do everything he said and more.

We hunted elk and I killed one. These elk were on the mountain across from us, and I sighted on this big bull and pulled the trigger. I didn't think I'd hit him, but Ralph said, "You got him—I saw his legs buckle." The bull then took two or three steps and all of a sudden raised up on his hind legs and fell backwards so hard his antlers stuck in the ground. I had his head mounted and shipped to Louise's father, and Dad Shofner hung it on a big post in his grocery store for many years.

My final tournament that year was the Fort Worth Open, which I'd won the year before at Glen Garden. I was somewhat obligated to be there since I was defending champion, but I didn't do well at all and finished seventh. It was the last money I won that year, $550, and brought my total to $22,270.

What a relief it was to have it all over with. I packed up my clubs, sent them to MacGregor, and told them to keep them till I asked for them, which wasn't going to be for a long time. That way, if someone asked me to play even a casual round of golf, I could just tell them I didn't have my clubs, and that would get me off the hook.

Now I could get serious about my ranch. Besides the studying I was doing, I had to do quite a bit of repair work. The fences on the place were in pretty sad shape, so all that winter I worked on rebuilding them. If you've ever done fence work, you know it's hard, but I enjoyed it. I enjoyed everything I did at the ranch—except raising hogs.

I had figured I could make some money on porkers, and I'd read enough about it and gotten enough advice to feel like I could do it. So as soon as I got some of the fences fixed, I bought thirty-eight piglets and fed and watered them till they weighed 220 pounds, the proper weight you had to get before you took them to town to sell. I loaded up those hogs and took them to Fort Worth. Well, it so happened that the price on pork wasn't too good right then, and I made exactly one dollar per animal—$38.00 for thirty-eight hogs. Those were the last hogs I ever raised.

Once I'd left the tour, I really expected that people would more or less forget about me, but that didn't prove to be the case. Oh, I knew at least a few of my records would stand for a good long while, but I was very much surprised and gratified, really, to find that people still wanted me to be involved in golf. I knew I wasn't going to make enough money off my ranch to really live on, and I had planned to continue doing exhibitions and making appearances, so it was fortunate for me that folks still did want me to be part of golf.

For the next few years, I began to spend my time doing a whole variety of things. I did a series of instructional articles for *Popular Mechanics* magazine which dovetailed nicely with my *Winning Golf* book. And after the Masters in '47, I also began to do quite a few exhibitions. As much as I wanted to get away from tournament golf, I did want to remain involved with the game, and to give something back to the sport that had done so much for me. Leaving the tour made it possible for me to do that.

For instance, I'd already been doing a little work with Fred Cobb, the golf coach at North Texas State in Denton, and now I could do more. I worked with the team up there quite a bit over the next few years, and they brought along some pretty good players like Don January, Ross Collins, and Billy Maxwell. Cobb was the best thing that ever happened to golf up there. He had the ability to get the best out of every player he had. Unfortunately, he died at a relatively young age in 1953, and the golf program there has never reached that level since.

I also began to do an occasional appearance or exhibition for MacGregor, and I can honestly say I enjoyed it. Playing exhibitions without the pressure of the media and thousands of fans, but with everyone relaxed and enjoying themselves, was quite a different thing, and a lot of fun as long as there wasn't too much of it.

About six weeks before the '47 Masters I received my invitation to play. I'd had enough time off from golf that I was looking forward to it. I called MacGregor, had them send my clubs back, and started practicing. As part of my routine, I would go play at Brookhollow in Dallas with my good friends Jim Chambers and Felix McKnight. I worked at the ranch till noon, then drove over and played. They used to laugh at me because I'd complain about being so sore and I played just terrible at first. They said, "You think you can be digging post-holes all morning and come over here and not be sore trying to play golf?" We played at Brookhollow so much that the club finally made me an honorary member, which was a great privilege.

But I got tuned up well enough for the Masters, at least so I wouldn't embarrass myself, and off Louise and I went. We stayed at the Richmond Hotel, and I can still remember the hot biscuits and country ham you could get there every morning. I didn't have the ham a lot because it was too salty, but it sure was good.

It was an unusual tournament for me in a way. Everyone at Augusta National was glad to see me, and I surprised myself by playing as well as I did. I was 14 under par on the par fives, and I had three eagles: one on 15 in the third round, and two on 13, in the first and second rounds. It was a record at the time, and held up till 1974. I don't recall who I was paired with or very much about the tournament, but I finished tied with Frank Stranahan for second, so I was very pleased. There was a point during the tournament when I realized I was playing well enough that I had a chance to win, but it really didn't matter to me one way or another, which may be why I didn't try harder. Though I played well on the par fives, I played the par threes poorly and putted badly, so there wasn't one particular hole where I could say, "That was where I lost it." The fact was, I really didn't care anymore. I enjoyed seeing our friends there, and Augusta will always be a special place for me, but playing there in '47 showed me once again that I was definitely through with the tour. I had no desire to go back out there. It was behind me.

But I did start to do more in other areas of golf soon after the Masters. In June, I went to St. Louis for the Open, but instead of playing, I wrote for one of the press services. That was interesting and fun, kind of being on the inside and the outside at the same time. Less than two weeks later, I played an exhibition at my old post, Ridgewood Country Club in New Jersey, where I proceeded to set the course record of 63. The next month, I began a series of exhibitions in cities like Flint, Michigan; West Bend, Wisconsin; Elgin, Illinois; and even Chisel Switch, Kansas. I did thirty-five exhibitions in two months, shot between 63 and 68, averaged 67, and made enough to keep the ranch going a while longer. Besides being a nice relaxed way to make some decent money, exhibitions made me realize I really enjoyed putting on a show for the fans, especially doing the clinics. Without the pressure of an upcoming tournament to worry about, I could laugh and joke with the crowd, and I found out I actually had a sense of humor.

All that exhibition work also prepared me well for the Ryder Cup matches that year in Portland. It was a great honor to be selected for the team again. I had been selected a couple of other times since 1937, when I'd first played in the Ryder Cup. But with the war on, we never really played until '47, so it was gratifying to get to do it again, since I had a feeling it would be the last time I would get picked for the team. It was an interesting situation. The British, who were just barely starting to recover from the war and all the bombing, were not allowed to take any money out of England. A man named Robert A. Hudson, a successful businessman in the Pacific Northwest and a golf nut, paid the expenses for the British team himself. In fact, the great British player Henry Cotton was able to come and play in the Masters that year only because Eddie Lowery loaned him the money—which Henry paid back immediately.

I remember one funny thing about that Ryder Cup. Herman Barron and I were playing in our alternate-shot match. I was the captain of our twosome, and we were one up going to the 17th, a par 3. I put my tee shot eight feet from the pin, and the British were fifteen feet away. Herman was a wonderful putter and I had complete confidence in him, so when we walked on the green, I got this idea in my head that I would give the other guys their putt, which I did. Barron looked at me like I was completely crazy, and said as much to me. But I just said, "Herman, I have no doubt at all that you'll make this putt." Which of course he did, and we ended up winning the match nicely.

After '47, my appearances in tournaments such as the Masters, the Colonial, and occasionally the U.S. Open were purely ceremonial. With only a few exceptions, I never did play particularly well in any of them, though I certainly enjoyed seeing the people and knowing that they liked seeing me again. For quite a while, I enjoyed playing in a tournament without having the pressure. I could relax, just amble along and enjoy the good shots, but sit back and realize it didn't matter to me if I finished fifth or twenty-fifth. And of course, I didn't play in any of these beyond where I could put on at least a good show. I was the first to play 100 rounds at the Masters, though, which I'm pleased about.

So from that point on, my career in golf is of little interest to most folks except for an occasional story. One funny thing happened in 1948, at the National Celebrity tournament at Columbia Country Club in D.C. I was paired with Snead, who happened to hate cameras. Snead would always look around the gallery before he hit to see if anyone was taking pictures. Well, that day some guy was following us. He was standing about thirty yards down the fairway, and had this camera hanging around his neck—there weren't any rules then about cameras on the course during a tournament. Sam saw him and watched him every hole, though he never once took a picture or even acted like he was going to, so Snead could never say anything to him. But Sam played poorly and I shot 67 and was low pro. I always wondered whether that fellow knew how much Snead hated cameras and had bet against him that day.

Then came one of the most moving experiences of my life. It was the summer of '48, and my brother Charles had been married to Betty Brown of Gainesville, Texas, for several years. Charles had just gotten out of the service, and Betty was seven months pregnant. Then Charles came down with a fever. For a few days we thought it was the flu, but they finally diagnosed it as polio. We took him to the Veterans' Hospital in Dallas, but we didn't feel he was receiving the best treatment. I wanted to take him out of there myself and get him to a civilian hospital. But Charles refused; he knew they wouldn't release him, then he'd be AWOL and that would cancel his Army benefits, so he stayed. My parents drove over there from Denton every single day. They didn't think he'd ever live because he had bulbar polio, the most serious kind.

Well, he did live. After their baby was born, which they named Byron III, Louise invited Betty to come live with us. When Charles finally got out of the hospital, he lived at the ranch with Betty and the baby until he could find work. Now, Charles had a wonderful singing voice, a beautiful, deep, bass-baritone. He had been song leader at the Pearl Street Church of Christ in Denton and when he got well enough, they told him he could come back. When it was announced that he was going to start leading the singing again, the church was packed full, and our whole family was there. He was sitting on a bench with his crutches, behind the podium, but when he got up, he fell. Absolutely flat on his face. But he told everyone not to help him. Then he crawled to the podium and pulled himself up, while the whole church was silent. When he finally stood up, Charles hit the first note of the first song full bore, and off he went. There wasn't a dry eye in the house, and I don't know if any of us were singing very well right then. Even though he's my little brother, Charles has always been an inspiration to me, and I can never remember that moment without getting pretty emotional.

I bought my first herd of Herefords for the ranch in the fall of '48. I bought the cows from a Dr. Wiss in Keller, and the bull from Dr. Alden Coffey in Fort Worth. The bull was from the bloodline of Prince Domino Returns, one of the greatest Hereford bulls ever. As far as I was concerned, the day those Herefords arrived was a lot more important than any tournament I played in that year. My father and I did a lot of the work on the ranch ourselves. We had one hired hand most of the time, and the three of us hauled manure, cut and baled hay, dug post holes, and built fences—whatever there was to do, we did. It was also during these years that I started raising turkeys. Two things started me on them. I knew I wasn't going to be able to make much money on our cattle because the ranch was really too small for that. But I knew you could make money on either turkeys or chickens. We had eaten store-bought turkeys the year before and remembered they hadn't had much flavor because they were too lean. A fellow I knew, Claude Castleberry, was in charge of all the food for the Texas State College for Women in Denton. He played golf, and also had a cafeteria in the school where townspeople could come and eat. When I asked him where he got his turkeys, he said mainly just big producers like Armour and Swift. I was going to raise a few just for our friends and us, but when I told him I was thinking of raising turkeys he said, "If you do, I'll buy them." Between the college and the cafeteria, he would use 400–500 a year. So I got going and built a turkey building right next to my cattle barns, and some roosting racks outside for when they outgrew the building. Then I fixed some brooders in the cattle barn, and raised about a thousand turkeys at a time. They were called "Texas Bronze" because of the bronze coloring at the end of their feathers. I passed the word around to our friends, and I finished the turkeys on corn the last couple of months to fatten them up. The toms weighed an average of over twenty-four pounds, and the hens fourteen. Back then, you could take them to regular eviscerating plants to get them cleaned and dressed, which I did. Then I would deliver them myself, door to door, to our friends and family in Fort Worth and Dallas.

You'd have to use a big pan to roast them because they were so juicy, and everyone said those were the best turkeys they ever ate. I did make a little money on those birds, but I worked hard for my dollar. Things went along all right for a few years, but then in '53, Claude Castleberry left TSCW and someone else took over the buying. Their policy had changed and now they had to take bids, but naturally I had to get more money than the big poultry producers who didn't finish their birds on corn. So I couldn't compete, and I got out of the turkey business. But I have to say you can buy a better turkey now than you could then. Today's turkeys are excellent.

The chicken business was next. Again from playing golf, I'd met Joe Fechtel, president of Western Hatcheries in Dallas. I knew he was in the chicken business and he knew about my turkeys, so one day he asked me if I'd ever thought about producing fertile eggs to sell to a hatchery. He told me his company would furnish the chickens and roosters and show us what to do, then they'd buy the eggs from us. They would pay 65 cents a dozen, cleaned and cased. Then they'd put the eggs in an incubator under my name, and for every percentage point above 65% fertility, I'd get an extra penny, but if I was under

65%, I'd get docked a penny. I'd always liked chickens, and my mother knew a lot about them, so I liked the idea. I invested over $20,000 in the buildings, the refrigerated egg house, and all the automatic feeders and waterers we needed. We had over 17,000 laying hens at one time, and in all the ten or so years we had those chickens, we never had less than 65% fertility. More than any other one thing I did with the ranch, the chickens always made me a little money, enough to fool with, anyway. But in the early sixties, things began to change again. The chicken business started moving to Arkansas, where the summers weren't so hot. Joe told me when he was going to move, and my operation was the last one he closed out with before he moved.

All this chicken talk reminds me of a golf story. One day in June of 1949, I got a call from my good friend Eddie Lowery in California. Eddie had been a fine amateur player as a youngster. In fact, he got started as a caddie, just like I did, only about a dozen years earlier. And Eddie always was serious about golf. He was small, about 5'9" or so and 150 pounds, but he had very large hands. He won several championships in New England, from the time he was sixteen on, and by the time I met him, he knew everyone in golf. He served on the USGA board for many years, and was an amazingly energetic man. He didn't always use the best language, but you couldn't help liking him, he loved golf so much.

Anyway, after we'd chatted a bit he said, "How are you playing, Byron?" I'd been playing well, so I told him, "I'm playing pretty good, Eddie." He talked a little more then said again, "Are you really playing good?" I replied, "Yes, I'm playing good, Eddie—why?"

He said, "I've been playing out here at Santa Rosa Country Club with the Buzzini brothers, and they're picking me like a chicken. I want you to come out here and play them with me. I'll set up a few exhibitions for you, but first we'll play these guys." George Buzzini and his brother worked as the pro and assistant at Santa Rosa. George especially was a pretty good player and did well in all the local tournaments, though neither he nor his brother ever played on the tour as far as I know. But I told Eddie I'd come out there.

Louise and I got there, and after dinner we went to Eddie's house. He took me up to his bedroom where he had this practice putting gadget and a whole bunch of putters lined up against the wall. Now, Eddie never did think I was a very good putter. He was right to some degree, as I've explained before. He just never thought I was as good as I ought to be. So he picked out this putter, a MacGregor Spur, and had me start hitting some putts with it. I had a little trouble at first, but then started hitting it pretty good. Eddie said, "That's the putter I want you to use tomorrow against the Buzzinis." I said, "Eddie, I've got my own putter and I'd rather use it." But Eddie said, "It's my money we're playing for, so you use that putter, not yours." I finally agreed, so we were set.

The next morning, I started off a little slowly and scrambled around and made a par, then another par, then pretty soon I started making birdies. The Buzzinis began pressing, but I kept on making birdies with that putter. To make a long story short, they finally quit pressing, because I made 12 birdies and six pars and shot 60. Eddie got all his money back—with interest.

He had me take that putter home and said, "If you ever use anything but that putter, you're nuts." I used it for two more months and never made another putt outside of four feet, and finally sent it back to him. When he got it back, he phoned me and called me every name in the book, but I told him, "Eddie, I think I used up all the putts in that club when we played the Buzzinis!"

A couple of years ago I got a call from a young man who'd been hired to do a book on the history of the Santa Rosa Country Club. He'd come across a clipping about my 60 and couldn't believe it, wanted to know all the details. It *was* pretty unbelievable—particularly since that putter quit working so soon after that match.

While I was working on getting the ranch going and keeping it going, Louise was very busy getting the house in shape. It was quite a mess when we moved in. The previous owners had dogs that they apparently kept inside the house, and the first night we were there, we had to sleep on a mattress on the living room floor. The first thing we knew, we were getting bitten by all these fleas that were in the carpet, so we had to get the whole house treated the next day. As soon as we could afford to, we hired an excellent architect and set about making the place over. We did it pretty much room by room, starting with the back porch, which we made into a good-sized kitchen, then taking what was the kitchen and dining room and making it just one big dining room. What's now the den or trophy room used to be the bunkroom for four children. It had a little old metal shower in the corner and a fake fireplace and just a couple of little bitty windows. It was quite a project those first few years, but Louise loved it. She had a real talent for decorating and an eye for beautiful things, and because it was our first real home, it made me happy that I could finally afford for her to make our home exactly the way she wanted it to be.

We were so busy with ranching and redecorating that I wasn't thinking about golf much at all. But my friend Eddie Lowery didn't seem to ever think about anything *but* golf. One day in the late forties, Eddie called and had this idea that he'd like me to go on Ed Sullivan's television show and give some brief golf instructions. Back then, the show was sponsored by Lincoln-Mercury, and Eddie, who was a very successful Lincoln-Mercury dealer, was on the panel that coordinated the advertising. I'd known Sullivan and had played golf with him since my early days at Ridgewood. In those days, Ed was a sports-writer and did a radio show called "The Talk of the Town."

So off I went to New York to try this out, and what I did was go on stage with a golf club chosen for whatever the tip was going to be about. The first time we had only two minutes, and of course you can't say much in two minutes. Remember, this was all live TV. Ed introduced me, then he stood very close to me, so close I could hardly swing the club. He apologized later and explained that many newcom-ers on the show would freeze up when they got out in front of the audience and had all those bright lights nearly blinding them. I didn't have that problem, fortunately.

That first golf tip was reasonably well received, and a few months later, Ed had me on for five straight weeks. They didn't use real golf balls, but light plastic ones, sort of like the wiffle balls they have to-day, and on one show, Ed saw a friend of his sitting in a box seat not too far from stage, so Ed asked me to hit one of the balls to his friend. I hit it too hard and a little thin, and it hit a lady in about the third row right on her forehead. She wasn't hurt or anything, but after the show she brought the ball up to us and you could still see the dimple on her forehead from where it had hit. Fortunately, in those days we didn't have to worry about being sued, but still I decided to start practicing with those balls, and learned if you didn't hit it hard it would go a lot farther. After that, Ed would often have me hit to someone or a cer-tain place in the audience, and I did all right—at least, I didn't hit anyone else in the head. I enjoyed it, but I enjoyed more getting to see the performers backstage and how they got made up and their nervousness and all they'd go through to get ready to go on stage. It was something to see.

During that five-show stint, one day Louise and I were walking down the street in Manhattan after a show I'd done the night before. We happened to pass by a group of about five men standing together who didn't see us because they were arguing about the way I'd said to do something on Ed's show. Louise said, "Why don't you go over and interrupt them?" but I was a little shy yet about doing such things, so we just kept going.

Along about this time, when I wasn't doing something with or because of Lowery or working on the ranch, I was often invited by Cliff Roberts to play at Augusta. One time in '49 or '50, I was there playing when a fellow named General Dwight David Eisenhower walked in. As it happened, Augusta's pro, Ed Dudley, was Ike's teacher, and Ike was there to take some lessons from him. Cliff set it up for us to play together, and it was fun. Ike was a good man to play golf with. He liked to chat, was very friendly-like, and when he'd hit a good shot, that expressive face he had would just beam all over. But when he hit a bad shot, he'd fuss at himself just like the rest of us. He hit a lot of good shots and was good around the green, but had trouble on his long shots, which faded off to the right a lot.

One of the best compliments I ever had came a few years later when President Eisenhower asked Cliff if I had time to come down to Augusta and play with him, shortly after the election in 1952. Of course, I made time whether I had it or not, and we played several rounds together, one of which made the President very happy. On the second hole, the left side of the fairway slopes downhill toward the green pretty severely. I had driven to the right where it was flat, while Eisenhower drove to the left. It was quite a good drive and when his ball did stop, he had outdriven me a good bit. On the 10th, the same thing happened, and he outdrove me again. I never thought anything about it, but some months later, after he was in the White House, he had a dinner one night for a few of us pros. All of us were in the dining room waiting for him, and he came in and asked us to sit down. Then, before he sat down himself, Ike pointed at me and said, "I want you all to know that I played golf with that man last year and outdrove him *twice!*"

Usually he'd ride in a cart at Augusta, and I would drive. But he was like a cricket, he'd jump out of the cart before it stopped, every time. It made me nervous, so I finally said, "Mr. President, I wish you'd wait till I stop the cart before you get out, because it would look terrible in the newspapers if it said, 'Byron Nelson Breaks President's Leg.'" He laughed and said he would, and he did wait the next time, but after that he never waited again. I didn't mention it again, though.

One other time, Louise was at Augusta with me and wanted to meet him, so when she saw us coming to the 18th, she went out and sat down there by the clubhouse. She had practiced and had it all set what she was going to say to him when I introduced her, but when he saw Louise, he surprised us both by rushing right up to her and introducing himself and saying how glad he was to meet her. She did fine, said something or other to him, but she told me later, "I know I just stood there with my mouth hanging open." That evening, we had an early dinner because we had to leave, and as we got in our car outside the clubhouse, Ike came out to our car. He asked how far we had to drive and told us to be careful. That's how warm and nice he was.

Then, in the fall of 1950, Jim Shriver, a salesman for MacGregor's Northwest territory, called just before he was starting on his fall sales tour. He said he'd like to book me for some exhibitions in his area the next spring. He thought he'd be able to book quite a few and I'd get $300 each, so I said, "That sounds all right, Jim." Unfortunately, when he got back from his fall tour, he called and said, "Byron, I booked a few, but not enough for you to come out for." Well, I was disappointed, because the money sure would have come in handy.

Fortunately, Bing Crosby called me that December and wanted me to come play in his pro-am in January of '51 with Eddie Lowery, George Fazio, and Bill Ford of the Ford Motor Company. I said I would, and as soon as I hung up, I remembered my conversation with Shriver. I realized that I hadn't been doing anything to get publicity and my name was fading fast out there. I made up my mind right then that I was going to try hard to make people aware I was still around.

We flew out to Pebble Beach on Thursday before the tournament started, and I went out and practiced—but only from 100 yards in.

My long game was fine, but my short game wasn't as sharp as it ought to be. By the time the tournament started, my short game had jelled and I was doing quite well. I won with three good rounds, 71-67-71. The weather was very poor that year, with both wind and rain, so one round was washed out completely.

My strategy worked, though. Two weeks after the Crosby, Jim Shriver called again and said, "I've got twenty-six matches booked for this spring. Every town I talked to wants you to come out and play." Well, that was great, so I went on the road for a month. But just to show the difference between then and now, here's what I did for that $300. I had to go to a luncheon at the country club or Kiwanis headquarters or whatever, then go to the course, put on a clinic for thirty minutes and play eighteen holes with the local pro, top amateur, or whoever was trying to beat me that day. Finally, I'd stay and have dinner with everyone that evening, give a talk, then jump in my car and drive that night or in the morning to the next town. So I earned every penny of that $300. I played quite well too.

The next fall, Jim wanted to know if I'd do it again in '52, so I did. I played exactly the same places, twenty-six matches in thirty days. That spring I played some of my best golf ever. My highest score was 68 and my lowest 59. The 59 was at Olympia Country Club in Olympia, Washington. It was a par-72 course, and I shot 31-28. I was playing real well, and was 5 under on the first nine. Then on the 10th, I hit driver and an 8-iron and holed it for a 2. On the 11th, a par 3, I made 2. On the 12th, a good par 4, I had a good drive and 6-iron and holed my putt for a 3. The 13th was a par-5, 520 yards, and I hit driver and 2-wood and holed my putt for eagle, so I used ten shots for four holes.

When I did these exhibitions, as I came to the 18th green I always stopped and thanked the people before putting out. This time they were really enjoying the show, so I said, "You may not know it, but I have this putt to make for 28, and if I do that I'll have a 59, which I've never shot before in my life." Then I sank the putt, fortunately, and they really did cheer me.

While I was playing those Pacific Northwest exhibitions in '52, The National Amateur was being played at Seattle. Eddie Lowery called me and said there was a young boy named Kenny Venturi who had qualified for the Amateur and Eddie wanted me to take a look at him. Eddie felt Ken showed great promise, which was enough recommendation for me. I went out and watched him play his first match with Mason Rudolph, and Mason beat him. Eddie introduced us after the match was over, and I asked Ken when he was going back to San Francisco. I told him I was going there too, and said for him to have Eddie get in touch with me and we'd have a game. We played at San Francisco Golf Club, where Kenny played a lot. He shot 66 but didn't play very well—he made a lot of bad swings. But he pitched and putted great and shot a better score than I did. He was expecting me to brag on him (I knew that from my own experience playing with Bobby Cruickshank when I was Kenny's age), but instead I said, "Kenny, Eddie said he wanted me to work with you and if you're not busy tomorrow, you come out early, because we've got six things we've got to work on right away." He looked at me kind of funny but said, "Okay, I'll be there." Kenny proved to be an excellent pupil. He listened very well and paid close attention, which wasn't easy because we talked about quite a few things.

Not too long after that, Eddie told me he had a fellow working for him, another amateur golfer, Harvie Ward—a young man who could hit the ball a long way and basically had a very good game. But Eddie told me, "He can't work the ball left or right." So I worked with him a few times on it. He could draw or fade after a fashion, but he wasn't going about it right, and was doing too many things wrong to get the results he wanted. When I showed him how to do it correctly, he caught on real quick and told me, "I didn't know the game could be so easy." This was before he won the American and British Amateur Championships. Later, when we were paired together in the Colonial tournament in '54, he was trying really hard to beat me, but in the last round he faltered on a few holes and we came to 18 even. I put my ball inside of his, and Harvie walked up, looked at me and smiled, and knocked his ball right in. Then I did the same thing, only I smiled *after* I made my putt.

Now for a story about a horse of a different color. It was also that summer of '54 that Waco Turner, an oilman in Ardmore, Oklahoma, called me. He wanted me to come up and play in his tournament there. It was a pretty big money event for those days, plus Waco was offering extra money for birdies and eagles and such. I wasn't really interested, but then he said he'd give me a beautiful palomino horse just for coming up and playing. I'd always thought palominos were awful pretty, so that got my attention and I agreed to go. As it turned out, I played very poorly, didn't make hardly any birdies at all, let alone eagles. So I didn't get much extra money.

But sure enough, I did get that horse. When the tournament was over, the sheriff of Ardmore rode up to me at the 18th green on this beautiful palomino mare. I got up on her, but I could tell right away she and I weren't going to get along. Still, my father knew a lot about horses, and I thought he could work with her. When I got back to the ranch he took one look at her and said, "Son, she'll never have a decent disposition." She was wall-eyed, and that's never a good sign in a horse. I kept her for a year, but she wasn't ever any good. Once, I took her to a plowed-up field and worked her and worked her, but it never helped a bit. Finally, I gave her—with fair warning—to a good friend who lived south of Fort Worth, and a month later he told me, "You were right—we can't handle her either." She probably ended up as dog food. What's that they say about not looking a gift horse in the mouth? Well, I sure should have thought twice about that one. It was the last time I played for Waco Turner, I can tell you.

Every once in a while in golf you run up against an odd ruling situation. In October of 1954, I was playing in the Texas PGA at Oso Beach Country Club in Corpus Christi, Texas. I had shot 63 the first round, but in the second for some reason I was just helpless and ballooned up to an 81. That just happens sometimes, as every golfer knows. Still, I had a good third and fourth round and had a chance to win when I ran into this peculiar situation. It was the 18th hole, and a fellow named Jack Hardin had to make a four to beat me. He hit his drive way to the right, over by the equipment barn, and everyone said it was off club property, which meant it would have been out of bounds. But there were no OB stakes, so the committee ruled his ball wasn't out of bounds. Jack managed to scramble for his par and beat me one stroke. I didn't have any bad feelings about it, though later the committee said they should have had stakes there, because without them no one can determine whether your ball is out or not.

I was the captain of the Texas Cup matches several times, and one time I remember very well was in '54. That's the year when Don January and Billy Maxwell, who were in college and still amateurs, were

11 under par for the first ten holes against me and Fred Hawkins at Dallas Country Club. I shot 66 and Fred helped me some, but with January and Maxwell playing like they were playing, we both felt like we weren't doing very well at all. They had two eagles, and it seemed like they were birdieing or eagling every hole.

In January 1955, Eddie and I were partners again in the Crosby Pro-Am. In those days you played at Monterey the first round, and this time we had a good score, 64. We played Cypress the second round, and because we'd started so well, we were right in the thick of the tournament. We came to the 17th hole, where the wind was blowing very strong off the ocean, quartering from the right. Eddie had pulled his drive way left, and mine ended up back of a group of trees, about 175 yards short of the green. I was too close to the trees to go over them, so I was looking at my ball, trying to figure out what to do. Then Eddie missed his second shot and was in the trees on the left and short of the green, so there was no way he could make par. With that strong wind blowing, I decided I could hit my ball against it, hook it, and let it draw back over the ocean to the green. As I took my stance, Eddie could see where I was aiming, and he started yelling and running toward me, but I couldn't hear him because of the wind. I went ahead and hit, and my ball sailed out over the ocean pretty as you please and landed about 15 feet from the hole. Eddie never congratulated me or anything, he just jumped all over me and swore at me and said I was crazy for taking such a chance. He must have decided I couldn't be trusted, because in the third round, which we played at Pebble Beach, Eddie was sensational. He used every one of his eight strokes despite the fact that there was terrible rain all day, and we shot 63 and won.

That must have given him a lot of confidence, because shortly after the Crosby, Eddie called and said he was going to go over and play in the British Open at St. Andrews. He wanted me to play too, and wanted Louise and me to go with him and his new wife, Margaret—it was their delayed honeymoon. (Eddie's first wife, Louise, had died of cancer several years before, and he had recently remarried.) I said, "Well, that sounds okay, Eddie, but you need to talk to Louise." Louise got on the phone then and she told Eddie, "We'll go on one condition—that after the Open we do some sightseeing, maybe even go to Paris." So we went.

We flew over and back on a TWA sleeper plane. At that time I was bothered by claustrophobia some, plus we ran into a bad electrical storm with hail and the whole works. Also, I wasn't a good flier then because of that experience in South America way back in '37, so I was really miserable. I couldn't stay in bed, I just lay there and shook. I was so scared I finally got up and sat and watched the pilot the whole rest of the way. The trip took fourteen hours, and though there really were no problems as far as the plane and the pilot went, it was just a terrible trip for me. Fortunately, when we came back home the weather was fine, and we returned in the daytime, which made it even better.

When we got to St. Andrews, Eddie had set up a practice round with Leonard Crawley, who had been a wonderful player and then became a good golf writer. I'd met Leonard before and Eddie thought he knew more about St. Andrews than anyone. As it turned out, Leonard didn't play, but he did walk the course with us and told us where to go on every hole, what you had to know about the many blind shots, and where the best place to approach the green was.

Now, I had heard and read all my life how hard and fast the greens were at St. Andrews, but even though it rained the first part of the week, I negotiated those greens all right and qualified with 143. Unfortunately, Eddie didn't make it. Then it turned hot—81–82 degrees, which was very hot to those folks—and people were getting sunburned and almost having heatstroke. But the worst part was that the grass started growing real fast, which made the greens very slow, and I never could get that through my head. I averaged 37 putts per round and finished twelfth. I played great from tee to green, hit more greens than anybody, but hitting greens doesn't mean that much on St. Andrews. Peter Thomson won by 5. That was my second and last showing in the British Open.

Now comes the good part. Unbeknownst to Louise and me, Eddie had entered both of us in the French Open the next week when we were going to be in Paris. He'd done it during the British Open after talking to a good friend of his, Jacques L'Eglise, who was president of the French Federation of Golf and was there at St. Andrews. Eddie didn't have the nerve to tell us what he'd done until the day the tournament ended, and with good reason. Louise was very upset with him, but he promised that we really would do some sightseeing after the

French Open—and he did finally keep his word. So we flew to Paris the next day and checked in at the Ritz, where we had a two-bedroom suite. Eddie was paying a lot of our expenses, so I made a deal with him that since I had to play in the tournament, whatever I won we'd put on the hotel bill.

When I went to register at the French Federation of Golf, it was on a street called Rue Byron, which made me feel lucky. As it turned out, Eddie didn't qualify, but I played very well. I broke 70 every round until the first nine of the fourth round, when I shot 38. Eddie was gone that morning; he'd had some business meetings and he got back just as I had turned nine. I wasn't playing well at all and was only a shot or so in the lead, with Weetman and Bradshaw chasing me. I was whining about how bad I was playing, and Eddie jumped all over me and called me all sorts of names. He made me so mad that if we hadn't been such good friends I'd almost have wanted to hit him. But what he said must have helped, because I shot 32 on the last nine and won—the first time an American had won the French Open since Walter Hagen in 1922. My prize money was 10,000 francs, but it wasn't even enough to pay our hotel bill!

Then we finally got to do some sightseeing. Of course, Eddie and Margaret were on their honeymoon, and they wanted to go out every evening. One night we went to the Folies Bergere, where the show was full of half-naked women, and the next night we went to another place where it was the same thing, though the food was good. But after that, Louise said, "Byron, I've seen all the naked women I want to see." I agreed with her, so that was the end of our nightclubbing. All in all, though, it was a very good trip, and that really was the last time I played golf to amount to anything much.

We got back home and settled down a little bit—as much as my life ever settled down, I guess—till that fall. For most of '54 and '55 Kenny Venturi had been in the army, but he got out that October of '55. As soon as he came home, Eddie took him out to Palm Springs to play. When he saw what Kenny was doing, Eddie called me and said Kenny was scoring pretty well but his swing was all off. Eddie wanted me to come out to Palm Springs and work with him, so I agreed. First, we went out and played a round at Thunderbird. Kenny played terrible, scored in the mid-high 70's. So we started practicing that day and worked hard the next three or four days, and the last round we played before I came back, he shot 65. One of Kenny's greatest strengths as a player was that he had the ability to make sudden, fast changes in his game when it was necessary. I felt pretty confident when I left that his game was back where it should be, which gave me an idea.

That year, the former Masters champions had the right to invite one player of their choice, pro or amateur, and I knew Kenny hadn't been able to play at Augusta in '55 because he was in the service. So I began canvassing the former Masters winners about Kenny, and they agreed that he ought to be invited to the Masters the next year, so I was happy about that.

It was early March of '56, and Harvie and Kenny had just played in the San Francisco city championship at Harding Park, where Kenny beat Harvie 6 and 4. There were at least 15,000 in the gallery at that tournament. Shortly after that, Eddie and I were in Pebble Beach for the Crosby Pro-Am, and so were Kenny and Harvie, playing as amateurs, of course. Louise and I and the Lowerys were invited to dinner one evening at George Coleman's home before the tournament started. During dinner, George said to Eddie, "Your two kids really played well in San Francisco." Eddie was feeling pretty good and he said to George, "Yes, they can beat anybody, those two kids." Then they got into a discussion. George said, "Anybody?" Eddie replied, "Anybody—yes, they can beat anybody!" George kind of baited Eddie a little bit and said, "Including pros?" And Eddie fired right back, "Yes, including pros." So George said, "Well, I've got a couple of pros I'd like to have play them." And Eddie said, "That's fine, they can beat anybody." George said, "What do you want to bet on that?" And Eddie said, "Five thousand."

Now all this time, Eddie hadn't yet asked Coleman who his players were. When he finally said, "Okay, George, who are your players?" George looked straight at him and said, "Nelson and Hogan." Well, that sure took me by surprise. But Coleman knew I had worked with both Kenny and Harvie and that I'd love to play with them anytime, so it was fine with me.

Eddie kind of swallowed and looked at me, and finally said, "They'll beat them, too!" Well, Ben wasn't at the dinner, so George first had to call Ben, and he said yes, he'd play. The match was on for the first thing in the morning. By the time we got to the course—which happened to be Cypress Point—the bet had gone down from

$5000 to just a friendly wager, fortunately. But word had gotten out that we four were playing, and we had quite a gallery, about a thousand people. We didn't waste any time getting started—the birdies started at the first hole. They made them, we made them, and sometimes we all made them together. We finally went one up at the 10th, when Ben holed a full wedge on a par 5 that you couldn't reach in two. Then I made a 3 with a drive and 2-iron and one-putt at the 11th, but they birdied too, so we halved that. Starting at 14, the hole up the hill through the trees, we both made 3, and we both made 3 at 15. At 16 I made 2, so we were two up at 17, and they birdied but we didn't. Now we were one up. They birdied 18, but so did Ben, so we won 1 up. The four of us were a total of 26 under par, and many of the people who were there said later that it was the greatest four-ball match in history. It would be interesting to see a couple of the good pros and amateurs play a match like that today.

As for the Masters that year, Kenny played wonderfully well and was leading the tournament four shots going to the last round. I had been paired with the last-round leader since 1946, but Cliff Roberts and Bob Jones decided I shouldn't play with Ken because I was his teacher and it might cause controversy. They had him play with Snead instead. Whether it was just because he couldn't play with me, or simply the pressure of being the one and only amateur to ever have a chance to win the Masters, he stumbled badly that last round; he shot 80 and lost. Four years later, in '60, Ken was in the clubhouse and they already had him in the winner's circle when Arnold Palmer birdied 17 and 18 to beat him by one stroke. So he just missed winning the Masters two times.

Somewhere about this time, I was in Wichita Falls for a large junior tournament. One night at a party, I got to talking with Rufus King, a fine amateur golfer, and his brother Charley, who was in the film business. Rufus was saying, "You know, Byron, you ought to do some instructional films—short ones, for television." Charley agreed and added, "If you could do about thirteen of them, that would be a good package to work with, and maybe I could find someone to help finance it." We all knew that Bob Jones had done some many years before that were sometimes shown in theaters in the early thirties. We talked about it two or three other times and I suggested that Rufus have Charley get in touch with Eddie Lowery. Rufus and Eddie knew each other from amateur golf, so Charley called Eddie and he did help finance it. We called the series "Let's Go Golfing," and did all the filming up at Wichita Falls, Texas. We had a very small crew—just a cameraman who also did the directing, and a couple of assistants. I enjoyed making the films. I'd talk and hit a few shots and talk some more—it wasn't much different from giving a clinic or a lesson except for the part where I'd be indoors, introducing the show or signing off. I never did know whether they really weren't any good or were just ahead of their time, but unfortunately, they didn't sell very well at all.

My golf by now was all right for the most part, though I continued to play just for the fun of it, and at the Masters in 1957, I had almost more fun than I could stand. On the 16th hole in the fourth round, I put my 4-iron tee shot in the water. So I went up to the front of the tee box, about thirty yards closer, and hit my 7-iron good and solid. The ball was sailing towards the hole just perfect, but it hit the flagstick on the metal section about a foot above the cup—back then Augusta had wood-and-metal flagsticks—and it bounced straight back into the water. It was the only time in my whole career that I hit the pin and ended up in the water. Next I went to the drop area, where the gallery sits now, got on, and two-putted for a 7. When I finally did get my ball in the hole, I got the biggest round of applause you ever heard anybody get for a quadruple bogey.

The next year, 1958, I began a minor career as a consultant on golf course design. It started at Brookhaven in North Dallas with Bob Dedman, who now owns Club Corporation of America and is successfully running more than 200 golf clubs. For Brookhaven, I was hired to help the architect, Press Maxwell, shape the fifty-four greens on the course. I greatly enjoyed it, and was able to rely on my experience in playing so many courses across the country. We used what natural landscape there was, didn't move a lot of dirt, and ended up with three good golf courses. I received $10,000 for the whole job.

That was the good news about 1958. The bad news was I had to have back surgery. You know, the peculiar thing about golf is that most golfers who have back problems find it begins bothering them when they're putting more than any other time. In April of '58, I was on the practice green at Augusta, and when I straightened up it hurt quite a bit, though it didn't bother me in the tournament other than when I was putting. After the Masters, my back kept on hurting and getting worse. The pain was going down my right leg; it was so painful to walk on that I could hardly stand it. I finally went to Dr. Brandon Carrell, a golfer and a wonderful orthopedic surgeon. He took X-rays and told me I had a disc problem in my lumbar vertebrae, numbers three, four, and five. Next, he made an appointment for me to see Dr. Albert Durrico, a fine neurosurgeon. Dr. Durrico tested my right leg and found I had lost about 50% of the feeling in it; I couldn't raise my toes on my right foot at all. So in August, they both operated on me at Baylor Medical Center in Dallas. It was then they discovered I'd hurt my back falling off that roof when I was a kid. But I got along just great, and the sixth day after surgery, I walked down the hall to the elevator and out to the car and Louise drove me home. It was good to be free of that pain, though I knew I had to be very careful and couldn't play any golf for a while.

After I'd recovered quite a bit, I called Dr. Carrell and asked him when I could play golf again. He told me I could start with a few little short shots, and work my way up gradually to the longer clubs. A few weeks later, he asked me to meet him at Brookhollow and watched me hit for a little while. Then he said, "I think you're ready to play—and I'll play with you." I'd always given him three strokes but he said, "It's been so long since you played, I'll play you even." Well, I shot 73 and beat him and he said, "Byron, if I ever get you on the operating table again, you'll never beat me any more!"

There was some more bad news that year, but it turned out all right in the end. In '55, when we'd won the Crosby, Eddie Lowery had bought us in the Calcutta pool. He won quite a nice amount of money, which he didn't keep for himself but gave away to his family and friends. Eddie was always a very generous man, and quite often when I went to a tournament he'd pay my expenses and those of others he'd invited, too. He was also quite generous to his brother and sister. The only problem with the money he'd won in that Crosby Calcutta was that he didn't report it to the government.

As it happened, about that time Eddie had a salesman who also played golf. This fellow got to where all he wanted to do was play golf and not work. Eddie called him on the carpet a few times, but finally had to let him go. Then the man got mad and told the IRS that Eddie had made all this money at the Crosby and hadn't reported it. The government picked up on it and in 1958 Eddie was called in on a special

IRS investigation and charged with fraud. Naturally, since my name had been connected with his for many years and I had played with him in the Crosby, they subpoenaed me for the trial. But the day before the trial began, Eddie's attorneys took me to dinner. They never mentioned what they wanted me to say or anything like that, but said, "We see no reason why we can't use you for a witness, too." I said, "Fine." They said, "You need to start thinking about all you want to say, because you'll be asked a lot of questions." When the trial began the next day, the defense was the first to call witnesses, and they called me as a witness first thing, which made the prosecution come right up off their chairs. Then they all had a confab with the judge, who decided I could be used as a general witness, rather than just for either the prosecution or the defense. They questioned me most of that day and the next. It was difficult, but luckily I could recall a lot of what Eddie had done for me and all the particulars, and my testimony helped to clear him. He had to pay the tax on that money plus a penalty, but he was cleared of fraud.

You'd think that would have been the end of it, but the next year I got called in on a special investigation because of my testimony, and the IRS went back five years into all my financial affairs. Fortunately, I was able to identify every deposit in my checking account and every check, and the agent said he'd never seen that done before. But even though they never found anything of any importance, every year they did a special audit on me, until finally my wonderful CPA, Jon Bradley, told them they were harassing me and threatened to take them to court. Things have been fine ever since.

I owe a lot of my financial success in life to golf. Not just because of the money I won—in fact, that was the least part of it—but because of all the wonderful people I met who have helped me in so many ways. Really, it's one of the best things about the game, that you can meet so many excellent people. As I said earlier, I've been a blessed man all my life, and one of the greatest blessings I have is my friends. And it just has always kept getting better and better.

NINE

·········

Television
and My Own
Tournament

AS YOU CAN SEE, THOUGH I'D RETIRED FROM TOURNA-
ment golf, I was just about as busy as I ever wanted to be, what with
one thing and another. I was still doing exhibitions and a little radio,
raising cattle, farming hay, working those eggs, writing for the *Dallas
Times Herald* with my friend Jim Chambers, and occasionally helping
to build a golf course somewhere. Then too, I was still working for
MacGregor; that continued until 1962, when I switched to Northwest-
ern and stayed with them for sixteen years. So I wasn't exactly finding time hanging on my hands.

I'd even done a little film work. Besides the instructional films I
did in Wichita Falls that never got off the ground, I'd had a very small
cameo part in a Dean Martin-Jerry Lewis movie back in the fifties.
When I say "small," I mean a long-distance shot of me off hitting a
ball somewhere, and I never heard anything about it after I did it,
though they did put my name in the credits. Ben Hogan was in it, too,
but he had a larger part than me, because his name was more prominent at the time.

By then, television was already showing sports such as football,
baseball, and basketball. They had even begun doing the golf majors

then—the U.S. Open, the PGA, and the Masters. I'd never thought about being part of all that. But in 1957, all of a sudden I was.

As I found out later, Cliff Roberts was having a discussion early that year with Frank Chirkinian, who produces CBS golf and has always produced the Masters telecast. They got to talking about the color commentator Cliff and Bob Jones wanted to use for the Masters. Frank had used various ones, both on radio and then on the first telecast in '56, but Cliff wasn't satisfied with any of them. Cliff and Bob wanted to keep the Masters from sounding as commercial as some of the other tournaments, so there were some restrictions an announcer needed to abide by. For instance, they didn't ever want you to mention the size of the gallery, the prize money, or how much money any of the players had won. You had to keep all that sort of thing toned down. So Frank asked Cliff, "Well, who do you want to use?" And Cliff finally said, "I know Nelson pretty well. He won't go off half-cocked and he'll do what you tell him to do. Why don't you ask him?" Frank called right away and asked me and I said yes, though I was quite nervous about it. Live broadcast announcing wasn't anything like the film work I'd done, nor was it really very much like radio. I knew they had used Vic Ghezzi, Gene Sarazen, and some others before, but I was out on the course playing and had never heard or watched them, so I didn't have an opinion of how they did or the opportunity to learn from them what I would be expected to do. It wasn't going to be easy, and I didn't want to let Cliff or CBS down. But one thing did make me feel better, and that was when they told me I would be working with Chris Schenkel. Chris was already quite well-known for his wonderful ability on television and as a speaker and master of ceremonies at dinners and so forth. Really, he was much more of a celebrity than I ever thought of being, and he still is today. I felt Chris would be good to work with and would help me a lot.

What I didn't realize was that Chris would help me get started on a whole new career. Even better, this became the start of my long friendship with Chris. It was another fortunate thing in my life that came about simply because I'd played good golf some years before and had gained a reputation for knowing something about the game. But when I first talked to Chris about it, I told him, "I'm afraid I won't know what to say." He encouraged me. "All you have to do is tell what's going on in the picture on the television screen in front of you, and you know golf well enough to be able to explain what the player is doing or has to do. You just do the golf, and I'll do the announcing." He helped me tremendously, and instead of being so nervous, I found I really did like doing the Masters because of being at Augusta and working with Chris.

That first year, 1957, we were in the tower back of the 16th green. I don't really recall any outstandingly good or bad shots on that hole, but I remember Doug Ford won when he holed out of the bunker on the 18th. The hardest thing to learn was not to talk about the play on 16 right in front of me, but rather to discuss the play being shown on television. Another difficult thing was to be talking on the air with the earpiece in my ear and Frank talking to me at the same time. Frank would say, "In two minutes we'll go to the twelfth and it'll be so-and-so on the screen." It was hard to remember at first and very disconcerting, but I got used to it reasonably easily.

Since I was just starting in television, I was very fortunate to have Frank Chirkinian as executive producer. When I first met Frank, he struck me as a man who was never at a loss for words, but also had good intuition about when to "move"—from one camera shot to another—to pick up a certain player. He could move from one player to another more quickly and smoothly than anyone I ever worked with. Most people have never seen him, but Frank is short, with dark skin, brown eyes, and very curly hair. He speaks very fast and is very pleasant to work with if you do your job, though if you don't, you're liable to catch a few choice words. But because he moved and spoke so fast, you really had to keep alert. If you weren't tuned in every minute to what was going on in your ear and on the screen, you could easily get caught flat-footed. It took a lot of energy.

We always prepared for the actual show on the weekend by doing a rehearsal during the practice rounds, which in a way was more complicated than the actual telecast. The public didn't hear or see this because it wasn't on the air, but Frank took it just as seriously as if it was. He'd say, "All right, you guys, we're going to do this short and sweet, but we're going to do it like we're on the air, only very fast. So be on your toes, because I don't want to have to tell you twice." He'd get uptight sometimes—you could hear his voice get a little more high-pitched, but you couldn't tell it unless you knew him real well.

The thing that helped me so much, even more than Frank's expertise, was that when the show would be thrown to us, Chris would lead me in at the right time and make it very simple. Also, if I were talking and he needed to say something, he'd just tap my leg to signal me that he needed to take over. I really feel that if I had not been assigned with Chris and later worked with him so long at ABC, I never would have been on television the length of time I was. He really did train me and helped me tremendously.

Apparently Cliff Roberts and Bob Jones weren't unhappy with my performance, because they asked me to come back the next year. This time, though, Chris and I were at the 18th hole, the command center for the tournament, which was considerably different from being at the 16th. After that we did the Masters together for several more years. In between, I also did a little freelance work for NBC and ABC, and in 1963, I signed my first full-year contract with ABC. Chris stayed with CBS till 1964 when he came to ABC. I was very happy about that, because I'd enjoyed working with him so much. Chris told me recently that I was the first professional golfer to do television commentary on a regular basis, so I guess I pioneered in that area, too.

When I first started, Arnold Palmer was on his way up; by the early sixties, he was in his heyday. I felt just like the gallery did. He was one of the most exciting golfers I ever saw. He really was a charger—he hit quite a few bad shots, but he had a knack of recovering with some wonderful shot to make up for his mistakes. Chris and I would always go watch him whenever we could. It was always fun to watch Arnold play.

I was still getting my feet wet in television work, just doing the Masters with Chris, when another film opportunity came along called "Shell's Wonderful World of Golf." Fred Raphael, who helped start the first seniors tournament in Austin—now called the Legends—was the producer for the Shell series, and he called me in the summer of 1961. He explained what the series was all about, that the matches were to be played with various players on courses around the world, and that he'd like me to play the first one with Gene Littler, the U.S. Open champion that year. The match would be at Pine Valley in New Jersey, and the winner would get $3000, the loser $1500. It sounded like fun, so I agreed to play.

Since this was the first match, the film crew was still learning what was involved, so it was very slow. They had a station wagon with a camera on top of it and some other small vehicles with cameras on them so they could get around where the wagon couldn't go. Gene Sarazen was the commentator for our match; he alternated on the series with Jimmy Demaret.

I played rather well, but Gene had a lot of trouble at the fifth hole, which is one of the most difficult par threes I know. You play uphill across a ravine, and a gravel road runs across the fairway quite a little ways short of the green. It was a driver for me from the back tee, about 227 yards, but I put it nicely on the green. Gene missed his tee shot badly and his ball went into these short, thick, stubby oak trees at the bottom of a hill to the right of the green. After he'd hit three times, I still couldn't see him. Finally I hollered, "Are you still down there, Gene?" He said, "Yes, but I'm not making much progress." Finally, he put his next shot on the bank at the side of the green and made 7. I had a pretty nice putt for a birdie but missed it and made 3, so I gained four strokes on Gene there. He shot 42 on the front and I shot 37.

They talk a lot about slow play today and it is a problem, but this match was ridiculous. We started as soon as it was light enough, but it took all day—ten solid hours—to film ten holes, and most of the next day to do the other eight. Slowest round of golf I ever heard of in my life. It bothered me some even though I played all right.

When we were finished for the day, Gene and I went in to shower and change clothes. I'd known Gene a while and after we'd already started to undress he said, "Man, I played badly today, Byron. What in the world was I doing?" He had respect for my knowledge of the golf swing, and I told him that when he played well, he set the club perfectly at the top of his swing. But that day, because of the slowness of the filming, he rushed his swing and wasn't getting set at the top. He asked me, "Do you mind if we go hit some balls?" I said, "Sure." So we got dressed again and went out to the practice tee, and the next day when we played the final eight holes, he put the charge on me and ended up with 34 on the back nine. I played the back nine well, but he made quite a few putts and came within two strokes. On the last hole, a tough par four, they had to stop filming for one thing or another three different times. Then the whole thing had taken so long that they ran out of film. When they finally got the film changed, it was time to hit my second shot, but I hit it real thin, put the ball in a deep bunker in front of the green and made five, while Gene made four. For the full eighteen I had 74 and Gene 76, which wasn't too bad considering it was the longest round of golf either one of us had ever played.

The way the series worked, whenever you won a match you'd play another one. So the next year, I had the pleasure of going to Holland and playing Jerry DeWitt, Holland's champion and a fine player. Unfortunately I had the flu and felt terrible, which isn't an excuse for the way I played, but Jerry did beat me that day. Before the match Sarazen, Demaret, Raphael and I had a wonderful luncheon with the president of Dutch Shell in his private suite. Gordon Biggers, the man from Shell who was responsible for arranging and producing all the shows, was also at that luncheon, and I got very well acquainted with him. After Shell stopped doing the series, I asked Gordon why and he said, "It was very well-liked, but Shell didn't sell any more gasoline because of the show, so we had to drop it." I've had many people tell me about seeing that match because so many golfers like Pine Valley, and they really did enjoy all the shows. Besides being about golf, they were kind of travelogues, showing the sights to see in the area around the golf courses where the matches were played—and of course, they always promoted Shell's products.

In 1963, the year after my match with Littler was shown on television—which incidentally was on my fiftieth birthday—I signed my first contract with ABC. As anyone who's ever heard me talk knows, I have a fairly strong Texas accent, and when I first started doing television, I not only had the accent but a lot of Texas expressions and pronunciations to go with it. Roone Arledge, our producer, right away started telling me I needed to change the way I spoke and quite a few of my expressions. But Chris told me, "Don't pay any attention, Pro. People who know you know the way you speak, and you speak very plainly. It wouldn't be you if you tried to speak like an Easterner." So I pretty much ignored Roone and only changed the way I pronounced one word, bermuda, which Texans used to pronounce "bermooda." No one seemed to mind that I didn't change much, and even Roone kind of got used to me after a while.

That first year with ABC, 1963, the PGA Championship was played at Dallas Athletic Club. I was working with Jim McKay and doing the color commentary. Jack Nicklaus won; it was his first PGA championship, and I remember the 18th hole well. Jack drove in the rough to the left and had to make a 4 to win. There was water in front of the green and he had a bad lie, so he played a smart shot and laid up in front of the water, knocked his third stiff and made 4. Besides it being Jack's first PGA, the other unusual thing about the tournament is that it was and still is the hottest week on record in Texas. The temperature hit 113 degrees and even the air conditioning in the clubhouse went out. There were people fainting everywhere; some almost had heatstroke, and it was very serious. I know the heat hurt attendance to some degree.

The next year, 1964, a couple of great things happened. The first was that Chris Schenkel came to ABC and I got to work with him again. Chris and I had a lot of wonderful times working together, and one of the funniest happened when we were doing the World Series of Golf at Firestone Country Club in Akron, Ohio. I was still pretty new to television, and one of the problems I had in those early days was keeping my voice low enough so the players on the green in front of us wouldn't be bothered as they tried to putt. Both of our voices carry quite well, but Chris had more experience at lowering his voice almost to a whisper, while I never really did learn to do it like he could. Quite often, the players or their caddies would be looking up at us on the tower and waving for us to hush.

But sometimes they listened real well. This particular year, Billy Casper was getting ready to putt for a birdie on eighteen, with his ball twelve feet back of the pin. I was describing the putt and spoke into the mike as quietly as I could, "No one has played quite enough break on this putt. Everyone has missed it on the low side." Billy was standing over his putt, but suddenly backed away, looked at it again, then walked up and knocked it in. I saw him later in the clubhouse and he said, "Thanks, Byron." I said, "What for, Billy?" He said, "I heard you talking about my putt on eighteen and I'm glad I did, because I didn't see that much break. I would have missed it otherwise." Shortly after that I suggested they put a plexiglass screen in front of Chris and me, so we could talk in a more normal tone of voice without the players being able to hear us.

Besides getting to work with Chris again, the second great thing that happened to me in '64 was Ken Venturi winning the U.S. Open after a terrible struggle. In the early part of the year, I'd had a few conversations with Ken about his golf game. He was playing very well then and I'd encouraged him and told him he was doing great. I didn't work with him at all, just talked with him on the phone. That June, the Open was at Congressional Country Club in Washington, D.C. Kenny did well the first two rounds despite the heat and humidity, which were very bad. But the real test came when they had to play the last thirty-six holes on Saturday. Kenny wasn't used to that kind of weather, living in San Francisco and having already had some recent health problems that had seriously affected his golf game for a while. Chris and I thought even during the third round that Ken wasn't going to make it. It looked like he was out on his feet just walking down the fairways. After he played the morning round, a doctor took care of him all during his break for lunch and followed him quite closely the rest of the day.

When he went back out in the afternoon, Kenny just played absolutely automatic, thinking more about just finishing than what he was doing as far as playing was concerned. Fortunately, he was playing with Ray Floyd, an excellent man to be paired with and a super nice person. I can still see how Ken looked on that television monitor. I couldn't believe he was still on his feet. When he made his putt on the last hole, I don't think he could have gone another step. Ray Floyd was so moved by Kenny's performance that there were tears in his eyes when he picked Kenny's ball out of the hole. I'd have to say that those 36 holes were the two most unusual rounds of golf I ever saw. What's more, they proved what a great player Kenny really was.

It wasn't very long after the Open, though, that Ken began to have trouble with his hands. A golfer's hands are pretty important, and Kenny's hands got so bad that he finally had to have them both operated on in June of 1965. I was concerned about what this might mean to Kenny's career in golf, and my concern became considerably stronger when Kenny was selected to be on our Ryder Cup team. The rest of the team included Julius Boros, Billy Casper, Tommy Jacobs, Don January, Tony Lema, Gene Littler, Dave Marr, Arnold Palmer, and Johnny Pott.

It was a good team, I felt, and I had just begun to wonder who the captain would be when I got a call from Warren Cantrell, president of the PGA, who happened to be from Amarillo, Texas. Warren said,

"Byron, I talked to the players on the team and asked if they would like you as captain, and they said 'Absolutely!'" There wasn't one dissenting vote, which made me feel very happy and very honored. Warren's call took me right back to the days of the 1935 Ryder Cup at Ridgewood when I was assistant pro. While I knew then that I wanted to be on the team one day, I never dreamed about being captain. This wasn't even on my list of goals when I was on the tour.

It was certainly one of the greatest honors in my career, but I wanted it to be more than an honor—I wanted it to be a victory. The Americans had held sway for quite a while, but I knew the British players were getting stronger and were looking forward to the chance to trim our sails. In those days, the captain had nothing to say about the selection of the team—it was all done on the basis of points earned by winning or playing well in various events over the two-year period between the matches. When my captaincy was announced, it was only three months before the matches, so I didn't really have much time to work with the team.

Because of the lack of time, right away I began thinking about what I could do to help the team before we went over to England. Our opponents were still using the smaller British ball and we would have to use it too, so I got some for the team to practice with when we all met in New York before flying to England. I made arrangements with the good folks at Winged Foot, and as soon as the team arrived, we went out there to practice. They were amazed at how differently that British ball behaved. Because it was smaller, you didn't get as much ball on the face of the club, so it didn't have as much backspin and it wouldn't fly as high as the American ball. Also, the heavier, wetter air they would encounter in England would affect the ball even more. I'd always felt that was why the British played more pitch-and-run shots than we did, because the small ball lent itself to that type of shot more.

I already had Venturi's hands on my mind, and then during the practice round that afternoon, Johnny Pott got a stitch in his right side that was hurting quite a little bit. But we had a doctor examine him who decided it was only a pulled muscle and shouldn't be a problem. That relieved me considerably, because Venturi had only recently gotten back to playing and was just now at the point where he could play without gloves, so he was somewhat of an unknown quantity.

There were several parties for us before we left, and the biggest one was on the last night, when the PGA gave a wonderful one at the Waldorf-Astoria. There we were, dressed in our dark blue suits, white shirts, and striped ties, all matching, and each of us had a complete Ryder Cup wardrobe right down to our golf bags, shoes, and windbreakers, just like when I'd been on the team in '37 and '47. Bob Hope was there, I think Bing Crosby was too, plus the Governor of New York, the Mayor, and many golf dignitaries from all across the country. Everyone wanted to give us a big sendoff and encourage us to play well, which we all appreciated.

We had a good flight over on BOAC and landed in London, then boarded a smaller plane which took us to Southport, near the Royal Birkdale course. When we'd recovered from the trip and began practicing, it soon became apparent that Johnny Pott's side wasn't any better. As it turned out, he never so much as hit a ball. That cut me to nine players, and I knew Venturi's hands wouldn't allow him to play every match, so I had to figure very carefully how I would use him and the rest of my team. What's more, Tony Lema had not come over with us because he'd been competing in the Canada Cup matches in Madrid, where he'd played poorly because of a sore elbow. That didn't reassure me any, but during the practice rounds, Tony came to me and said, "Byron, I'm driving the ball badly—I need help." He had a lot of confidence in me because he'd watched me play a lot at the California Golf Club when he was the assistant caddiemaster there in the fifties, and we'd played some together, too. I went out on the course to watch him, and I saw right away he wasn't setting the club right at the top of his backswing. We had a little discussion about it, I told him what he was doing, and he began playing better immediately.

Despite our situation with Pott and Venturi, when there was a press conference that afternoon, I was not about to let the British know my concerns. The British captain, Harry Weetman, had his say first. By now, we had become the underdogs in the British press, so Harry announced that the British definitely had the stronger team and would win the match. Then it was my turn. I got up, looked at him and said, "Harry, we didn't come three thousand miles to lose."

It's very awe-inspiring to represent your country in the Ryder Cup, and I'll never forget the feeling of pride and excitement as I raised our country's flag at the start of the matches. The Prime Minister, Harold Wilson, was there and welcomed us, Harry Weetman and Warren Cantrell made some remarks, and the match was on.

Most of the matches were very exciting and quite close, except for Davey Marr and Arnold Palmer's showing in the morning foursomes on the first day. It was Dave's first time to play in the Ryder Cup and he was very nervous. I watched him and he hardly got the ball off the ground the first seven holes. Obviously, even Arnold couldn't overcome that and they lost to Dave Thomas and George Will, 6 and 5. However, I'd noticed that Dave finally settled down and was playing real well at the end, so I got an idea. Since this was the second match that morning, I figured Harry would move Thomas and Will to the first match that afternoon, so I did the same thing with Dave and Arnold. When I announced at lunch that Palmer and Marr would be playing Thomas and Will again, Arnold and Dave didn't even finish their food, they jumped up from the table and charged off to the practice tee. My guess was right, because in the afternoon they shot 30 on the front nine—a remarkable score at Royal Birkdale, where par is 73—and they turned the tables completely, winning 6 and 5. We were all pretty happy about that, and I think it was the most exciting match of the whole tournament.

Though Tony was playing well and Arnold and Davey had come back, at the end of the first day we were tied at 4 points apiece. Kenny had not played well in his first two matches, so I had him rest during the morning of the second day. That was when we played the alternate shot format properly known as four-ball. In the morning we won two matches, lost one, and halved one, so we were needing to do better in the afternoon. For the last match of the afternoon I decided to pair Ken with Tony because they were good friends; they were both from San Francisco, and I knew they enjoyed playing together. They went up against Hunt and Coles and came to the last hole, a par five, deadlocked. It was Kenny's turn and he hit a good drive, then Tony pulled the second shot and the ball ended up left and short of the green, back of a small shallow bunker. I was standing back of the green and knew we needed a point badly. The British players left their second shot short but on the right side, with only a simple chip to the green. Prime Minister Wilson was standing next to me and he said, "I say, sir, it appears as though we have the advantage." I answered,

"Yes, Mr. Prime Minister, it appears that way, but of all the people on my team, I'd rather have Venturi playing this shot than anyone else." Then Kenny gripped down on the club, used a little short firm motion, and chipped close to the hole. The British chipped short and missed their putt and we won, 1 up. At the end of the second day we had taken the lead, 9 to 7, and went on to win decisively.

When the matches were over, I was talking to some of the British golf officials. They were wondering why it was that the Americans seemed to play better golf and a different type of golf. I told them it was in great part due to the different ball we used, and after I explained my ideas, quite a few of them agreed. A year or so later, they changed their ball to the same specifications as ours, which was a good thing for the game altogether.

It was a very emotional moment when the matches were over. The bugle corps played "Taps" as Harry Weetman and I lowered our country's flags, and everyone had tears in their eyes. We had a beautiful flight home and we were a very happy group, believe me. The PGA officials had a celebration party for us when we arrived, and it was an occasion I will always remember, for a very good reason.

All through the matches, I had wanted so much to do a good job and help our team win that I moved around more those three days than for any other tournament in my life. I tried hard to see at least part of every match and was very visible at all times. The team must have appreciated that, because unbeknownst to me they got together and had a duplicate made of the actual Ryder Cup trophy and presented it to me when we arrived back in New York. It's a beautiful piece, and of all the trophies I've won, that is one of my most prized possessions.

One final note about our team. Except for Tony Lema, who was killed in that tragic plane crash in July 1966 after winning the Oklahoma City Open, and Julius Boros, who is now in his seventies and has had some health problems the last several years, all of those fellows are still active in golf, either on the senior tour, in television, or at good club jobs. I feel that's a good recommendation for golf.

In 1967, two years after the Ryder Cup, I got to participate in something that was a lot of work, a lot of fun, and made many new friends for me I never expected to have. It was called the Lincoln-Mercury Sports Panel, and it was the brainchild of Gar Laux, the head of Lincoln-Mercury. Gar was very sportsminded. He knew a lot of people in various sports, and got the idea that a good promotion for Lincoln-Mercury would be to form a panel of top people in various sports and use them to generate publicity and goodwill. The head of his promotion department was Bernie Brown, and Bernie took the ball and ran with it. He started out with Arnold Palmer, the great professional bowler Billy Welu, Detroit Tigers outfielder Al Kaline, tennis great Tony Trabert, Jesse Owens, the great track star and the first ever to win four gold medals in the Olympics, hockey star Gordie Howe, Chris Schenkel, and me. What a great lineup.

Part of our job was to go to the big auto shows, sit on the stage at the Lincoln-Mercury display, and answer questions from people, then hand out our pictures. We would be on for thirty minutes and then take a break to sign pictures backstage, and we did that four hours each day of the weekend. Another thing we did was to help entertain Ford's top dealers from all over the country. We'd go to Las Vegas, Los Angeles, or sometimes Hawaii, and I'd play golf with the folks while Tony gave tennis lessons and clinics. They used Tony and me mainly, but some of the others would come along and socialize with the dealers at the parties they had in the evenings.

One time we were in Hawaii at Mauna Kea, and Ford had three different groups of a hundred dealers come in for three days apiece. It was nine days' work total, and though much of it was enjoyable it was also very tiring. But it had its moments. One time, Tony had just finished doing a clinic with some of the tennis players and I was watching him. He saw me and asked, "Byron, you ever play tennis?" I said, "Tony, I never have. Haven't even hit more than a half-dozen tennis balls in my life." He replied, "Well, you've got pretty good coordination—let me hit some easy ones to you and you hit them back, just for fun." I had on my rubber-soled teaching shoes so I thought I'd try it. I got a few back to him but missed some entirely, and he said, "Byron, you have to keep your eye on the ball in tennis the same as in golf!" I got a little better then, and out of curiosity I said, "Tony, serve three balls to me just like you would if you were playing in a championship." He wound up and let go, and I never saw any of those three serves, much less had a chance to hit them back. It made me very glad I'd played golf instead of tennis.

But the next day we both went out on the course. Tony was a good golfer and liked to play, but I was familiar with the course we were playing, and he'd never seen it before. On the first hole, he was on in two and had about a 25-foot putt. I could tell from the way he was lining up he wasn't playing very much break, because you couldn't see it, just looking at it. I said, "Tony, that putt breaks six feet to the right." He backed off and looked at it, then shook his head and said, "Well, Byron, I know tennis and you know golf, so I'll believe you." He played it where I told him and made his birdie, so he did a lot better at golf than I did at tennis.

I had a little better luck at bowling. Once we were doing a show with Billy Welu, and I watched Billy give a clinic. Suddenly Billy said to me, "Byron, have you ever bowled any?" I told him, "There used to be a bowling alley in the basement of the Texarkana Country Club, Billy, and I guess I bowled about a half-dozen games." So he said, "Come on out here!" I stepped up, threw one ball and made a strike. Then I said, "Thank you very much, Billy, that's enough for me!" People today don't know much about Billy Welu. He bowled twenty-seven 300 games, which was absolutely amazing, especially considering how young he died.

To get back to my television career, Chris and I did around fifteen tournaments a year, and I usually got there well ahead of time. The only way I felt I could do a good job as a commentator was to go out on the course and study it, so I would know each hole and where the trouble was. I actually walked the course as if I were playing it myself, paying special attention to the holes we were showing on the telecast. I would then determine in my own mind what it would take to win each tournament. I didn't always make this mental prediction for regular tournaments, but I always did it for the majors, and one time, I got in trouble for it.

It was just before the 1967 U.S. Open at Baltusrol. Jim McKay and I were taping a preview of the tournament to be shown two weeks before the Open started. It included a history of the tournament and the course, and was done to increase interest for the audience we hoped to have. I had gone out on the golf course, scorecard in hand, and spent two hours walking hole after hole, figuring what I thought a good player would shoot on that course. When we started the filming, McKay did the introduction and talked about the course some, then turned to me and said, "Byron, how does the course look to you?" I told him, "The course is in great shape. They've had a drought in the area so the rough is not very bad and the greens are perfect. The whole course is in excellent condition." Then Jim asked me, "What do you think they're going to shoot?" And I replied, "I've walked the entire course and totalled up all four rounds the way I think a good player should play this course, and I think they'll shoot 275." We were right there on the porch of the Baltusrol clubhouse, with several members of the club and some USGA people nearby. Well, as soon as we were done, the club president and tournament chairman approached me and used a lot of strong words and said, "Don't you know this is Baltusrol? No one's ever burned the course up like you just said they would!" and I said, "Yes, I played Baltusrol when I was an assistant pro in Ridgewood, New Jersey. I know the course pretty well." They were very upset about it, because Baltusrol has the reputation of being a tough course generally; when the Open was held there in 1954, Ed Furgol won with 284. Well, I didn't say anything else about it, but Jack Nicklaus saved my skin when he holed a 30-footer for birdie on the 72nd hole and won with 275. Those same two gentlemen who had jumped all over me later wrote me a very nice letter apologizing for coming on so strong about what I'd said, which I did appreciate.

One interesting match I played took place twenty-two years after I retired, on Monday, August 12, 1968. Harold McSpaden and I played Palmer and Nicklaus in Kansas City at McSpaden's course, Dub's Dread, which was rated then as one of the toughest courses in the world. It was an exhibition, and it was set up this way: Because McSpaden's and my ages added together totaled 116 and Palmer's and Nicklaus's totaled 66, we got a fifty-yard advantage on every hole. I told Jug they'd still outdrive us but he didn't think so, and sure enough he was right. I was driving very well and they didn't outdrive us on but one hole. The problem was their putting was so much better than ours. We were scared to death playing against them and hadn't been competing any or playing in front of a gallery in so long. Not only that, but there was so much more of a gallery than we'd expected, and the course wasn't roped off or anything, so it was too much for us and we lost, 3 and 2. But I did have one thing to brag about—the 17th hole was a long par 3, and I decided to play it even though the match was over. I took out my driver and put my ball on the green from the back tees, so that made me feel good and helped take the sting away.

Besides doing the men's tournaments on TV, Chris and I also got to do the commentary on some of the women's championships. I always enjoyed watching the ladies play because as a group they had better basic fundamental swings than the men did. One tournament I remember particularly well was the USGA Women's Open in 1967 on the Cascades course at Hot Springs, Virginia. It was won by a French amateur, Catherine Lacoste, and it was the only time I ever saw the ladies upset about a tournament. They weren't upset with Catherine at all, but the fact that she was an amateur and not an American, they felt, would set women's professional golf in this country way back. Some of them talked to me about it, but I told them they shouldn't worry about it because they had played very well. Maybe I should have reminded them of how close Kenny Venturi had come to winning the Masters when he was an amateur just a few years earlier. That hadn't upset the men pros—in fact, it generated more interest than ever in professional golf and golf at all levels.

In 1969, we covered the tournament when Donna Caponi won the Women's Open at Scenic Hills Country Club in Pensacola, then again when she repeated the next year at Muskogee Country Club in Muskogee, Oklahoma. Everyone liked Donna because she was so friendly and wonderful with the gallery. A funny thing happened in Pensacola, something that very much impressed me about Chris Schenkel. In those days we sat out in the open, at the top of a metal scaffolding tower sometimes two or three stories tall. Most of the time, all we had over our heads to keep off the sun and rain was a canvas tarpaulin. Well, that year, 1969, a terrible rainstorm came up. There was no lightning so the ladies were still playing. Chris and I were very busy. I was keeping score, figuring out if the player on the screen was four over, eight over, or whatever, and Chris was doing all his work, so we had all these sheets of paper spread out on the table in front of us. What we didn't realize was that all this rain was collecting on the tarp over our heads, and it was getting fuller and fuller and sinking lower and lower.

All of a sudden it gave way completely, and a couple of barrels of water poured all over us. It ran off our faces and soaked all our clothes. Worse yet, the papers on the table in front of us with all our scores and so forth were deluged. But Chris never missed a lick, and after a couple of minutes I got back on track too, so we went ahead like nothing had happened.

We didn't know it then, of course, but Bob Jones himself had seen the telecast. When we went to the Masters the next spring, Bob said to us, "I never laughed so much in my life, seeing you sitting there with water all over your faces and everything, but you just kept on talking like nothing had happened. I felt sorry for you but I couldn't help laughing." By then we thought it was pretty funny too, though it sure wasn't at the time.

That same year, 1970, I was working with Jim McKay at Pensacola on the men's tournament when there suddenly came up another rainstorm, with terrible lightning like we'd never seen before. Believe it or not, there were no provisions made for us to get down from the tower, which was all metal, and Jim got so terribly upset he told me, "I'm getting off this tower, I'm going straight to the clubhouse!" He took off right then, and during the next commercial break the rest of us did, too. We ended up doing the remainder of the telecast in the clubhouse. We could look out the window at that tower, and the wires on it were just frying. It was the worst experience of bad weather we had during my nearly twenty years in television.

It was interesting how the tournament officials sometimes handled these sorts of things, too. During the U.S. Open at Medinah in 1975 when Lou Graham won, Ben Crenshaw was finishing up his third round and was walking to the 17th hole. But just as he got to the green, lightning flashed nearby, and it scared him so he just flat ran off the course. We were doing the telecast, which is why I remember this so well. After he left the course, we learned that a couple of USGA officials were saying Ben would have to be disqualified. But as they started out the door to talk to him, several bolts of lightning hit next to the clubhouse and they scurried right back inside. That convinced them to call a delay, so Ben didn't get disqualified, fortunately. Thank goodness the lightning detection systems they have now are so much better, and improving all the time. It's a great game, but it's just not worth risking your life for a round of golf.

In addition to whatever the weather brought our way, those early days of televised golf meant a lot of equipment problems, especially when the weather was wet. Our cables were just lying on the ground then, and rainwater would get in the cable connections and short them out. We'd be talking but there'd be no picture, or there'd be picture but no sound. It was frustrating, but now you have practically none of that because the equipment is so much better.

In 1966, we were doing the British Open live via satellite for the first time. This was quite an advance in television broadcasting, because prior to this, we would film the day's play, fly the film back to the U.S., and show it a day late. With the satellite, we still filmed the day's play, then added our live commentary and so forth later when the American audience would be watching. Naturally, the difference in time zones, six hours at least, meant we were doing the live portion at some pretty odd times. McKay and I would be out there at the course in the middle of the night, up in the tower and very cold, talking to a camera but with no one else there besides us, the crew, one sentry, and a guard dog. Jack Nicklaus won the tournament, and because he played rather slowly, they had to cut and edit it very tightly before we went on the air. The result was we showed Jack driving and then immediately playing his 3-iron to a par 5. There wasn't time to show him walking or anything but playing his shots, which was rather unusual.

One thing I felt was very important in order to do televised golf well was having a producer and director who knew how to play the game. Once in a while we would have someone who didn't, and boy, could you tell it. He'd use the wrong terminology, saying "chip" for a long pitch, or calling a 150-yard shot "long," and he usually didn't know the players' names very well. Fortunately, this didn't happen very often and never for the majors, but when it did, it sure made things interesting.

In 1971, the year after we got dumped on at Pensacola, we were to broadcast the Women's Open at Kahkwa Country Club in Erie, Pennsylvania, where a very strange thing happened. When I got there, I went to the pro shop as I always did at these tournaments. I introduced myself to the pro and was telling him how glad I was to be there and so forth when he said to me, "Byron, I'm glad to see you again." I didn't recognize him so I said, "When did you see me?" He said, "You played an exhibition here several years ago." I looked at him and said, "I sure don't remember it." He went into his office a minute and came out with a scorecard in his hand. My signature was on it, and apparently I had not only played there, but had set what was then a course record of 66. It was the oddest thing, because usually my memory is pretty good, but I didn't remember a single thing about having played there. Even when I went on out to study the course before the tournament started, none of it looked familiar to me at all. In fact, I didn't remember ever having been in Erie before except with Louise on our first anniversary in 1934, when we stopped briefly beside the road there and waded out into Lake Erie. I still have the photo of that—but as for playing that golf course then or any other time, my mind is a complete blank. Very strange. So many people are amazed at my memory, and I like to think it's pretty good most of the time, but when something like that happens it really makes you wonder about yourself.

As for that ladies' tournament at Kahkwa, you know, we men sometimes think the ladies don't hit the ball very far. But I remember one hole on the back nine, about the 15th or 16th, where a little road went across the fairway 235 yards from the tee the ladies were playing. Joanne Gunderson Carner hit the ball a long ways, and she carried over that road twice during the tournament. Kathy Whitworth, the winningest golfer on any tour, was second to Joanne that year. On the other hand, while some people didn't think women could hit the ball very far, others thought the women's touch and feel on the greens would be better than the men's, which led to some big-money putting contests between the two sexes. I remember Sam Snead was involved in a few of them. Invariably the men won, but they'd been competing on their tour and against larger fields much longer than the ladies. Since then, the women have really improved, especially in their ability to read the greens.

When we televised women's tournaments, I also walked the course so I would know what I was talking about, but I didn't ever try to predict scores, at least not in public. I'd have in my mind an idea of what I felt the winning score would be, but I wasn't real close most of the time. What fooled me was that the women's short game was not as good as it is now, nor as good as you'd expect it to be. Their long game was excellent and they got in very little trouble except around the greens, but of course that part of their game is also much improved today.

While Chris and I enjoyed doing the women's championships, I'd have to say that of all the broadcasting I did, the most exciting golf I saw was in 1971 when Lee Trevino won the Open at Merion, won the Canadian Open in Montreal the very next week, then flew to England and won the British Open at Royal Birkdale. He won three majors in nineteen days and Chris and I got to see all of it. That really was an amazing accomplishment.

I guess the most exciting single shot I saw during my broadcasting years happened the next year. It was Jack Nicklaus's 1-iron on the 17th at Pebble Beach in the 1972 U.S. Open. He had to hit against a strong wind, and the ball just ticked the flag and dropped right down by the edge of the hole—as close to a hole-in-one as I've ever seen in a major tournament.

Chris and I also covered some of the men's amateur championships, and one in particular I recall vividly was the next year, 1973, at Inverness. Having been pro there in the forties, I was really looking forward to working on that tournament. I was also interested to see how we would broadcast it, because the format had gone back to match play that year, which is far more difficult to televise and keep interesting. What they did was to film some of the earlier matches, such as the quarterfinals and semifinals, and show some of that as we waited for the two players in the final to get to each shot. I felt it worked very well, and Chris did a good job with it.

I really enjoyed doing the broadcast, especially because it was the first time I ever saw Craig Stadler play. He beat David Strong 6 and 5 in the final, and he behaved just the same then when he missed a shot as he does now, getting all disgusted with himself. The only thing different now is that he's a little older and a little heavier, but he still hits that nice, high fade. Fortunately, he didn't have to get very upset with himself then, because he sure wasn't missing many shots that day.

Another great memory from those years was the fifteen-pound salmon I caught during the 1970 U.S. Amateur in Portland. I brought it back to the hotel for the chef to prepare for dinner that night, then invited Chris and quite a few other friends for the feast. The chef did a marvelous job and I believe it was the greatest salmon dinner any of us ever had. Chris kidded me when I told him I'd caught our dinner myself, because he knew I wasn't much of a sailor, but it was true. In case you're wondering, a fellow named Lanny Wadkins won the tournament, and the runner-up was another promising youngster, Thomas O. Kite, Jr.

One other thing I owe to television is that it was responsible for my meeting Tom Watson. It happened in 1973 when I was doing the telecast at Doral, where they play the infamous "Blue Monster," which is what they call the Blue Course because it's so tough and has so much water. I was walking the course during the pro-am to familiarize myself with it. I was outside the ropes, so I didn't walk with people who had a lot of gallery because I wouldn't be able to see enough. Walking the back nine on about the 14th hole, I was minding my own business when a pretty brunette walked up to me and said, "Aren't you Mr. Nelson?" I said "Yes," and she said, "I'm Mrs. Tom Watson." I'd never met Tom though I'd heard a little bit about him from Bob Willits, a good amateur player from Kansas City I'd met at various tournaments. I watched Tom play from there on in, and Linda introduced him to me when he finished his round. I was very impressed by his demeanor and I liked the quick, aggressive way he played, so I began to watch for him on the tour each week. He had just finished playing well in the Hawaiian Open, and then won his first tournament, the Western Open, the following spring. In 1975 he won something called the Byron Nelson Golf Classic—his second victory—and gave the Salesmanship Club who sponsored the tournament a $1000 check, which was a kind and very generous thing to do when he was really still just becoming successful on the tour. After that, I kept even closer track of how he was doing, but I never worked with him until after he lost the Open at Winged Foot to Hale Irwin in 1975.

I was doing the telecast, and Tom was leading after the third round. He wasn't a real well-known player at the time, and the press was all over him, trying to find out more about him. I wondered how well he'd handle it, because I knew he hadn't had much experience in that situation. The next day he had a bad last nine, but not because he was choking. It was just that he'd not had that kind of pressure before and didn't quite know how to handle it. Having been in golf so many years, I knew Tom would be very discouraged, so after he left the press room I went to see him. He was in the players' locker room upstairs, sitting with John Mahaffey and having a Coke. I sat down and told him, "Tom, I'm sorry you had such a bad day. I've seen quite a few people who've been in the lead but not played good the last round until they had a few tries at it." He was still pretty down, which was natural, but he was nice and very polite to me and thanked me for what I'd said. When I left, I told him, "I'm not working with anyone right now, and if any time you'd like me to work with you, I give you permission to call me. No one else has that privilege." Well, of course he went out and won the first of his five British Opens at Carnoustie the next month, so that proved he had a winning attitude despite losing the month before.

After I'd offered to work with Tom, I became even more interested in his progress. I could see he had the makings of a great player, and that's why I especially enjoyed doing the telecast of that British Open at Carnoustie in 1975, when Tom won in a playoff against Jack Newton. Of course, Tom and I were good friends by then, and the first day, he stopped by to say hello as Chris and I were having some tea and Scottish shortbread in the press tent. It just so happened that Tom played well that first round, so he took his visit as a sign of good luck or something, and continued to stop and see us every day. The last round, however, proved what Scotland is famous for. It was a typical horrible Scottish day, windy, rainy, and cold. I knew Tom had never played there in that type of weather, so I said, "Tom, I played this same course under these same conditions in 1937. Now, even if you make three bogeys in a row, don't think anything about it, because everybody will be making bogeys. You'll be amazed at how different the course will play today." At one stretch he did make three bogeys in a row, but he remembered what I'd said, didn't let it bother him, wound up tying Newton and then beat him in the playoff. Nice man that he is, Tom then gave me a lot of credit for his victory—more than I deserved—just because of what I'd told him before that last round.

The next fall, 1976, he did come to see me and we began working together three or four times a year. We'd also have conversations at the tournaments I was working on, and when he came to the Nelson each year I'd work with him every day. Not that I would tell him what to do, but it encouraged him to know I was there and he could call on me if he needed me. It was mainly a confidence-builder for him.

The U.S. Open that year, when Jerry Pate won, was when I did my last television commentary, just a few months before Tom and I began working together. After nearly twenty years of traveling almost as much as I had on the tour, I was beginning to look for a good reason to retire. As it happened, the people at ABC had decided to change what they were doing and begin using player-commentators on the course, like Bob Rosburg, Ed Sneed, Judy Rankin, and Gary McCord today. They also wanted whoever was at the 18th to do diagrams like the football coach-commentators were doing. I tried that once, but I was very poor at it, so I told Roone Arledge and Chuck Howard that I really didn't think I'd enjoy making all those changes—I was sixty-four at the time, after all—so we ended our relationship by mutual agreement on a quite friendly note.

Every so often during my television career, someone would say to me, "Byron, don't you wish you were out here playing today, with the money so great?" It was considerably more money than what I had played for, though nothing like it is today. But I never once felt, "Boy, if I were still playing I could have some of that." I still had no desire to be in that situation again, even though the money was better and tournaments bigger. I was glad to be doing just what I was doing, glad to be in golf and participating, and especially glad not to have the pressure.

One of the things I was happiest about as far as my television work was concerned was how the players reacted to what I said. They seemed to accept it quite favorably, because I was never very critical. I called the shot and when they missed it I said so, but I didn't jump all over a player or talk negative about anyone. I knew exactly how hard it was out there, and I couldn't see any reason to talk that way about anyone, particularly someone having a difficult time playing this most difficult game.

My years in television were great, really, but I never dreamed in my wildest imagination when I started doing broadcasting that it would do for my name what it did. People even today recognize me and speak to me who never saw me play, and tell me how much they enjoyed the work I did with Chris on ABC. Many people have recognized me in a restaurant or other public place just by my voice. They say, "Aren't you Byron Nelson?" And when I say, "Yes," they say, "I recognized your voice." I'm always amazed by that. And it makes me feel good.

There is something that makes me feel lots better than having people recognize me because of my television work, though. It has to do with a group of men called the Salesmanship Club, a couple of golf courses, and children who need a lot of help. But I'll need to start at the beginning.

In 1962, I was asked to help build a golf course in North Dallas at a place the owners had decided to call Preston Trail. I worked with golf course architect Ralph Plummer, who was from Texas and had caddied at Glen Garden about ten years before me. At that time Preston Trail was so far from the heart of Dallas—seventeen miles, actually—that everyone thought we were crazy for doing it. But Pollard Simon, Jim Chambers, John Murchison, and Stuart Hunt, who owned the property, felt the natural direction for Dallas to grow was north—and time has proved them right. The course opened in 1965, but because of its distance from the city, selling memberships wasn't too easy. I had a lot of kidding from my friends about it. The first fifty members were the toughest to get, though after that people figured it was safe and began signing up. Preston Trail was designed from the beginning as a men-only course, which might have been part of the reason it was slow getting started, because the men also continued their memberships at other clubs where their wives could play.

About the time Preston Trail opened, I began doing radio commentary for the Dallas Open, a tournament that never had done real well. I had won the first one in '44, Snead in '45, and Hogan in '46, but then it was discontinued and didn't start up again till 1955 when Jim Ling of Ling-Temco-Voight (LTV) got it going. It still wasn't what you would call a real strong event on the tour, though. Even after '55 there were a couple more years when it wasn't held at all.

But things began to change in the early part of 1967. I was slated to do the Dallas Open on radio that year at Oak Cliff Country Club, and the tournament this time was sponsored by the Salesmanship Club of Dallas, an organization that sponsored a highly successful, year-round outdoor camp for troubled boys. Quite a few days before the tournament started, I was talking to several of the Salesmanship Club's top members who were concerned because ticket sales had been very slow. At this point, Arnold Palmer hadn't yet entered the event, and they asked if I would be willing to call him. They told me if he would agree to play, they'd have a plane come pick him up wherever he wanted. I liked these fellows and I knew their camp program was a very good cause, so I called Arnold. He agreed to come, and I went along when they picked him up. The next two days, after it was announced that Palmer would play, they sold 5000 tickets. It showed what a difference a big name like Palmer's could make—and I felt good that I was in a position to help bring it about.

Maybe that was what gave those Salesmanship Club guys their next big idea. Because it wasn't too long after the Dallas Open that they came and talked to me again. Felix McKnight, a newspaperman I'd known since my amateur days, talked to me first and told me the Salesmanship Club knew they could make money for their camp program by sponsoring a tour event, but felt they needed to have a well-known golfer connected with it. They were thinking of changing the name of the tournament to reflect that, and were also considering moving the tournament to Preston Trail. Felix asked if I would entertain the idea of having my name used instead of calling it the Dallas Open. I said I would, and he said, "I'll be back in touch with you soon."

A few days later, Felix called and said the whole tournament committee wanted to talk to me as soon as possible. I said, "That's fine, Felix, I'll be coming to Dallas in a couple of days," and Felix interrupted me with, "No, we'd like to come out to the ranch and talk to you right now." Well, that was okay with me, and forty-five minutes later Felix, W.L. Todd, Frank Anglim, and Jim Chambers pulled in the driveway and proceeded to give their whole presentation. They wanted to call the tournament the "Byron Nelson Golf Classic," and Preston Trail had already agreed to host the tournament. Before that call from Felix, though, I had done my own homework on the Salesmanship Club and found them to be a dedicated group of men with the most successful children's rehabilitation program that I'd ever heard of. So I agreed to do it, and it's become the best thing that's ever happened to me in golf, better than winning the Masters or the U.S. Open or eleven in a row. Because it helps people.

The committee also told me they'd already started to plan a big kickoff party for the tournament the next spring, and were going to invite all the dignitaries and celebrities they could think of. Well, they did just what they said they would, and the next April, 1968, at the Southland Center Hotel, there was a terrific party, over 1300 people. Chris Schenkel was the master of ceremonies, my mother and Louise's father were there, Governor John Connally, Bob Hope, Glen Campbell, Sammy Davis, Jimmy Demaret, Ben Hogan—the list went on and on.

It really was a very wonderful occasion and a great way to start the tournament. To top it all off, the final event of the evening was when Gar Laux, the head of Lincoln-Mercury, presented me the keys to a beautiful red Lincoln Mark II, right there at the party. That really put the icing on the cake.

One interesting thing about the evening was seeing how nervous Sammy Davis was before he sang. He really was a wreck. I'd never imagined that such an accomplished performer and someone so accustomed to being in front of people would be that way. He told me it was because there were so many important people there. But when he started on stage, you would never have known that he was nervous, and of course he performed beautifully.

That first year, Louise and I got to visit the Salesmanship Club's outdoor camp a couple of times, which was an eye-opening experience for us. These boys weren't just from poor families—they came from all sorts of backgrounds, but had somehow gotten off the track and into trouble, first at home, then school, and often with the law. While it was sad to learn how troubled they had been, it was also a good feeling to see the great progress they were making in the camp program. Several years later, they started a separate camp for girls, and one year at the Christmas party, I told one girl camper that I had recently given Louise a fur coat. She said, "What did you expect to get for that?" I was amazed at her question. I answered, "Nothing. I just wanted to make her happy." That told me a lot about how sad the lives of these children were—not because their parents might not have money for fur coats or other luxuries, but because they didn't know what loving and caring for people really meant, until they came to the camp and learned it firsthand.

Right away, the Salesmanship Club fellows and I started having a lot of meetings about the Dallas Open. We talked about its pluses and minuses, and how to make it better. Having been a pro and around tournaments all my life, I told them, "The only way you're going to have a successful tournament is for the pros' wives to be happy." Because Preston Trail was a men-only club, there were no facilities for women, so we had to do something about that. I also suggested to them, "No event on the tour has a nursery, and a lot of the pros have little children they need to bring along, so we need to start one— that'll help a lot." They got going immediately on those ideas, and when it came time for the tournament to start, they had moved in trailers and set up one for the pros' wives and another for the nursery, both of them staffed by wives of Salesmanship Club members. This arrangement worked very well, and the pros and their wives really did appreciate it.

It was amazing to me to see how the club members, several hundred of them, threw themselves into putting on this tournament. One of their traditions is to "Never say no" when asked to do something for the club, the tournament, or the kids, and they really do abide by it. It was very inspiring to me to realize my name was connected with such a great group of people, and over the years, that feeling has grown. Overall, I feel the Salesmanship Club and the tournament have done far more for me than I have for them, because they really have kept my name alive.

Another wonderful thing about being part of this bunch and having my name on the tournament was that I got to work with Chris for ABC on the telecast, from 1968 until I retired from television work in '76. For those first eight years, I worked full time as a color commentator up in the booth for the entire broadcast, and that was a special kind of fun for me, doing the broadcast for my own tournament.

As it happened, that first tournament in '68 was won by Miller Barber, which really made me feel good since he'd started as a caddie at Texarkana where I had been pro so many years before. What with the big kickoff party we had and Miller winning, it was a very good beginning year. We even got all four rounds in, and since the Nelson has been plagued with rain nearly every year of its existence, that was another fortunate happening for our inaugural year. In fact, in the past twenty-five years we've only had one or two that didn't have rain interruptions or cancellation of a round.

The tournament had immediate and full acceptance by everyone in the area. Despite the fact that the course was still quite a ways away, people really wanted to come and see the pros play, and fortunately, we drew nearly all the big names right away. In fact, the third year we had an unusually exciting finish. Arnold Palmer—the crowd favorite still—had finished his last round and shot 274. Right behind him, Jack Nicklaus came to the 18th green needing a four for a score of 273 to beat Arnie by one shot. Jack hit a good drive but his approach shot was a little strong and went over the green. His ball was on a downslope and in a slight little bit of rough, making for a very difficult little chip. The people loved Arnie so much that they were afraid Jack would chip close, make his par and win. They didn't want to see the tournament end just yet, so when Jack chipped short, the gallery applauded, figuring he would make five and tie and they would get to watch a playoff, which is exactly what happened.

The playoff started on the 15th hole, a long par 5, and it took two very long, very good shots to reach the green in two. Arnie and Jack both hit good drives, but Arnold left his second shot short of the green about thirty yards, chipped short and made five, while Jack put his second shot hole high and just off the green to the right. Jack chipped stone dead and made four to win. It was our first playoff, a great finish for both players, and one of the most exciting ones we've had. For some reason, we have had quite a few playoffs in the history of the tournament, more so than the average, but the gallery sure does love it.

One rather unusual thing happened at the tournament in 1974. Chris and I were doing the telecast, and there had been a rain delay. Because most of the fourth-round leaders wouldn't be able to finish before we went off the air, we had to televise some players way down the leaderboard who were on the course right then. It wasn't the best situation for our broadcast, but as it happened, one of those players was Brian "Buddy" Allin, a short, little-known fellow who shot a 65 that round, finished with a 269, and ended up winning the tournament. It was the lowest 72-hole score of the whole fifteen years the tournament was at Preston Trail, though Tom Watson matched it the next year. The entire ABC crew congratulated Buddy for winning—and then thanked him for saving our show, which he most certainly did.

Our most winning player so far is Tom Watson, who won for the first time in 1975, then went on to win again in '78, '79, and '80. The next year, 1981, Tom tied with Bruce Lietzke at 281 and Bruce won the playoff on the first hole, or Tom would have set a new record of winning our tournament four years in a row. As you might guess, those particular years were a great deal of fun for me, especially since I was no longer doing television by 1978 and could enjoy going out on the course and watching Tom in person, instead of just seeing him on the monitor.

With such wonderful players and exciting finishes, the tournament continued to grow and enjoy greater support each year from the people in the Dallas-Fort Worth area. By 1980, we knew it wasn't going to be long before we would outgrow Preston Trail. There was the problem of not having any facilities in the clubhouse whatsoever for the ladies, and the trailers we had for the pro wives and their children were quickly becoming too small. But more important, we were running out of space to park cars, which really was a serious situation. The club itself only had room for 250 cars, and there had been so many large homes built around the course that we could no longer use that space. In 1982, the last year we played at Preston Trail, several members of the Salesmanship Club bought a piece of property close to the club so we could park there. They later sold it at a nice profit, which all went to the club's camp program. That incident is a good example of their tradition of never saying no, because I'm told that when these fellows were asked to go to the bank and sign a note to buy the land, they weren't told how much it was for. When one of them got to the bank and learned the note was for several million dollars, he called the club president and said, "That note I just signed is for four million dollars. Could I ask what it's for?"

Knowing we were running out of room, the committee had already been searching over a year for a place where we could go. They finally contacted Ben Carpenter, the founder and developer of Las Colinas, a fast-growing master-planned community in Irving, just north of Dallas and northeast of Fort Worth. Part of Ben's development was a place called the Las Colinas Sports Club, a wonderful athletic facility that happened to have a golf course already on it. When the committee began looking at the course, they asked me to go along and see if it would be all right for the tournament. It was, just barely; it had been made just for a resort course and really wasn't going to work very well for national tournament play with as large a gallery as we expected to have. The front nine was on one side of a busy four-lane residential street, MacArthur Boulevard, and the back nine was on the other side. Neither golfers nor spectators could get to the other side except by way of a pedestrian underpass, which wasn't really very satisfactory. Still, we decided to go ahead with it, worked out a deal with Mr. Carpenter, and the next year, 1983, we held the tournament there. The course was originally designed by Trent Jones's son, Bob, so we worked with him on making a few changes such as reducing the size of some of the bunkers and lengthening the course by adding tournament tees.

We played the tournament on that course for three years, but the tournament was growing so fast that it quickly became apparent we couldn't continue that way. Mr. Carpenter and the Salesmanship Club then came up with a plan to completely redo the place. What they were going to do was to completely tear up the nine holes on the east side of MacArthur, build a brand-new 18-hole Tournament Players Course there, and add nine holes on the west side of the boulevard. At the same time, Ben had already started to build the resort hotel that had been part of his original plan. When completed, the hotel would be right next to the TPC course, which would work out perfectly for the players as well as for the hotel guests the rest of the year.

It was quite a project. We called in Ben Crenshaw and a wonderful golf course architect, Jay Morrish, with me in the background as sort of an unofficial consultant. Then, the day the tournament was over in '85, we had 'dozers and all sorts of equipment ready to move in the next morning. My good friend Steve Barley masterminded the entire job, working with as many as twenty different contractors at once, and not once did any of those contractors get in another company's way. It all went incredibly smoothly and our brand new TPC course was ready for major tournament play exactly one year later. I've never heard of anything being done like that before or since. Still scares me to think about it.

The course wasn't bad that first year. The players understood the situation and appreciated the improvements over what we'd had before. Now, besides having a far better course all in one place, they had a beautiful new hotel to stay in, and their wives and children could use the Sports Club next to the hotel during their free time, so everyone was pretty happy. Several years later, the Four Seasons took over management of both the hotel and the club, and they've done a beautiful job with it. What's also nice is that sometimes the Tour's schedule permits the players to play our tournament one week and the Colonial the next week in Fort Worth, which the players really like.

What pleases me most about the tournament is not that I have my name on it or that we draw such a good field or even that the PGA Tour says ours is the best-marshaled event all year, but that all of the proceeds go to charity. We raise more than a tenth of all the charity money on the tour, and in 1992, we netted over three million dollars for the Salesmanship Club programs, which now include our camp for both boys and girls in Hawkins, Texas, and an education center in Dallas where troubled children go to school and they and their families get counseling. The club is now planning its own Community School, and if it works as well as the camp and counseling programs do, we will be able to help even more people.

I believe the main reason we've always gotten such good support for the tournament is because people realize that every cent of the profits goes to these children and their families and no one takes any money out for themselves. I don't get a penny, never have, nor does the club president or the tournament chairman. I've always been fortunate to be connected with people who are substantial, who know how to get things done and who do them honestly and properly. And the Salesmanship Club is the best example I've ever seen of these kinds of qualities.

Not only has the Salesmanship Club been wonderful for me to be associated with, but the people with GTE, our title sponsor, and the folks at the Four Seasons Resort and Sports Club have too, as well as the good folks at USAA who now own the entire place. In fact, in 1992, General Robert F. McDermott, who heads USAA, really put the icing on the cake as far as I was concerned. But I have to back up a bit to tell the whole story.

From 1980 on, the Salesmanship Club people had wanted to have a life-size bronze made of me to have installed at the course. At that time, though, when they told me what it was going to cost, I told them it was too expensive and I felt the money could be better spent on the children the tournament was designed to help. I thought that would be the end of it, but after USAA took over the hotel, club, and golf courses, the idea came up again. Early in the fall of '91, Mike Massad, chairman of the club's executive committee, made a presentation to General McDermott and a group of USAA and Four Seasons people, hoping to find someone to finance both the bronze and a wall to list the names of the tournament champions, which together would enhance the whole facility. After a long discussion, Mike said they had not been able to find anyone to do it. The general hadn't said anything to this point, just listened. Finally, he looked at me and said some very complimentary things, then announced, "I'll go back to our headquarters in San Antonio and see if we can't do it."

Well, he not only could, but did, and the statue was unveiled at my eightieth birthday party in February 1992, and installed in front of the wall of champions the next week. It really overwhelms and almost embarrasses me, but it truly is one of the greatest things that's ever happened in all my life. The sculptor, Robert Summers from Glen Rose, Texas, who also did the statue of John Wayne that stands in the Orange County airport in Los Angeles, did a wonderful job, right down to the wing-tip shoes I'm wearing and my name on my driver. It's over nine feet tall so it's a little bigger than me, but it really looks more like me than I do.

How can anyone say thank you enough for the things that have happened to me? I've never felt I was any different from or any better than anyone else just because I used to play a little golf fifty years ago, but people treat me that way, and all I can do is be grateful and enjoy it and try hard to deserve it. And that's what I do.

TEN

·······

Golfers I've Known Over the Years

I N NEARLY SEVENTY YEARS IN THE GAME, I'VE PLAYED WITH and watched quite a few golfers. From the best on the tour to the 40-handicappers, I've seen some amazing things and some just plain strange ones. Here are a few stories about some of my favorites.

Tommy Armour. Tommy was a Scottish pro who came to the United States and became a wonderful player, especially with his irons. He won the U.S. Open in 1927 and the British in 1931 despite the fact that he had very poor vision in one eye because of an injury he got during World War I. Tommy was about twenty years older than me, and we first met in Boca Raton on June 1, 1939, when I signed with MacGregor and he was head man on their staff, playing his Silver Scot clubs. After I'd signed, I went to Tommy's shop and picked out a set of his irons, which I used to win the U.S. Open two weeks later. I used those same irons for a long time, until MacGregor made me get a new set.

I played with Tommy a few times myself, and something that always impressed me about him was the size and strength of his hands. He could take an iron and hold it with his arm outstretched and the club held between only his forefinger and middle finger. Try it some-time if you think it sounds easy.

Tommy had the greatest gift of gab of anyone I ever knew. He was simply a wonderful storyteller who could take the most uninteresting hole or shot or round of golf and make it sound fascinating, and be-cause of the way he could talk, he became a wonderful teacher. He'd sit down at Boca Raton under the shade of an umbrella with a toddy on the table next to him, and he'd teach until he just ran out of energy to talk.

Besides playing and teaching golf, Armour liked to bet a little bit, especially when he felt he knew what he was doing. In 1942, when Hogan and I tied for the Masters, he bet on me against Hogan because by this time I had also developed a reputation as a good long-iron player, and he liked that. In the playoff, when I started so poorly and was three over after the first four holes, the man he'd made the bet with came to him and said, "Looks like Byron's having a bad day—I'll settle with you fifty cents on the dollar," but Tommy looked at him and said, "The game has just started." Fortunately I did win, which made Armour think I was greater than I really was.

Roone Arledge. Chris Schenkel and I were playing with Roone, our producer at ABC, at Prestwick during the British Open one year. Unfortunately, I had to quit after six holes because I had something I had to do. On the very next hole Roone made a hole-in-one, and he was quite upset that I didn't get to see it. I may have had to leave early due to the fact that we were playing so slowly, because in those days, Roone was an unusually deliberate player.

Another time—in fact, during the first part of the British Open at Carnoustie in 1975—Roone asked Chris and me to play with him at St. Andrews early of a morning. What made Roone so slow was that while he walked quickly enough, he would get to his ball, take a prac-tice swing, pull up his glove, take another swing, then another tug at his glove, and do that two or three times on every shot of any length at all.

Chris and I are both very fast players, and we were getting further and further behind the group in front of us, but Roone didn't really seem to notice. I guess because of who we were, the marshal didn't say anything for a while about the way we were holding up play, but finally on the 14th hole, here he came on his bicycle. He walked up to Roone, pulled out his Big Ben watch, held it up where we could all see it, and said, "I say, sir, you should be on the eighteenth green by now." Roone was embarrassed, and so were we. He did speed up some, but then when we were finished he wanted us to play with him again the next day. Chris and I looked at each other, and finally replied, "Only if you'll play fast enough so we don't get in trouble."

Herman Barron. He was pro at Fenway Country Club in Westchester County, Long Island, and he had a funny little short, flat swing that wasn't very effective. Harold McSpaden and I played quite a bit of golf with him, and we got to kidding with him about that swing. Then we started working with him some till he finally got a little more upright and became a good player. He won the Tam O'Shanter one year and a couple of other tournaments, and the three of us became lifelong friends. One year the pros had a 108-hole tournament there at Fenway, and the sixth hole, a long par three, came right by the clubhouse porch, where a lot of people were watching the play. Herman used a wood off the tee and his ball ended up short and to the right. He stepped up and pitched it into the hole, and the noise went through the whole clubhouse. "Hermie did it!" they yelled. I got quite a kick out of it because doing that at your own club was a lot of fun. Another thing about Herman was that he was an excellent card player, especially gin rummy and bridge. He was so good, actually, that he had to quit playing with the members because he was about to get in trouble for taking too much of their money.

Bill Campbell. One of the best amateurs I ever saw play, and he's been good for years. Bill is a good friend of Sam Snead's because they come from the same area of West Virginia, and Bill has a long, fluid swing—not like Sam's, but it makes you think of Sam because of the rhythm Bill's swing has. Because of his wonderful way of conducting himself, Bill has become known as a true amateur, and that's a great compliment. He was U.S. Amateur Champion in 1964 and won the U.S. Senior Amateur championship in both '79 and '80. A few years ago, he was also selected to be Captain of the Royal & Ancient Golf Club of St. Andrews, which is a great honor. A few years ago during a USGA Museum Committee meeting at the Chicago Golf

Club, they unveiled a painting of Bill in his uniform as honorary Captain. It was very well done, and a proud moment for Bill, but he was very humble about it all. He doesn't consider himself important because of his accomplishments in golf, he just has so much respect and love for the game, and a very humble spirit about it. I've always admired that about him.

Joanne Carner. Joanne always hit very long for a woman—especially in her earlier years—which is part of the reason why she won the women's amateur five times and the Open twice. In fact, a few years back I played in an exhibition with her in Kansas City with Tom Watson and Fuzzy Zoeller. They had her drive from the members' tees, and besides outdriving me consistently, she drove almost up with Tom and Fuzzy all day as well. She surely thrilled the gallery that day.

Fred Cobb. Fred was the golf coach at North Texas State in Denton, and I worked with his teams up there for several years until shortly after Fred's death in 1953. Fred was very likable and would do anything for his team, which was a big part of why they worked so hard for him. To me, Fred was the one who really started good college golf in Texas. His work at North Texas State was remarkable for a man who had no funds, no scholarships to offer, and not even much of a golf course to play on. But not only did he teach his boys how to play the game, he taught them to be gentlemen. He'd be out watching them through his binoculars when they didn't know he was even on the course, and if he saw anyone throw a club or knew they were using bad language, he'd let them know right now that such behavior wasn't acceptable. He had quite a few fine players during his time there, including Don January, who has done so well on the senior tour. He loved those boys and they loved him. After he died, the golf program there never came close to what it was back in the late forties and early fifties.

Charlie Coe. Besides Ken Venturi, Charlie is the only other amateur who in my opinion should have won the Masters. He was so thin it looked like a strong wind could blow him away, but he could really hit the ball. During the Masters in '61, everyone who watched the play on the last nine saw him put his approach shots closer than Player's on nearly every hole, but he just never made a single putt. Charlie won the amateur championship in 1958 and several other big amateur tournaments. He's still a member at Augusta and is greatly respected whenever folks talk about fine amateur players.

Henry Cotton. After Cotton came over from England to play in the Masters in 1947 (courtesy of a loan from Eddie Lowery), he then went to San Francisco to do a few exhibitions Eddie had arranged. I was out there also, and one day the three of us went to play at the California Golf Club. He and Eddie got to talking and Henry said, "I understand you're a pretty good bunker player, Eddie." Eddie said, "Yes, I guess I am." So Henry said, "Let's have a contest." That was fine with Eddie, so they headed to the bunker by the practice green. Cotton was very confident in his game and thought he could win some easy money from Eddie, who of course was an amateur, though a very good one. They bet $5 a ball for whoever got closest to the pin, and the one who lost got to pick the next spot to hit from. But Eddie was so good out of the bunker that after about fifty shots he was winning most every time, and Henry finally gave up. Eddie really was the best out of a bunker that I ever saw.

Bing Crosby. Bing loved golf and scored in the mid- to high 70's a lot. His swing was easy and smooth, with no rushing or jerking ever. Bing always conducted himself very well and was very cordial with the golfers who came to his tournament. But one time during the Crosby, he did get on me a little. He and I were supposed to do a little sketch for television, and though my part was very small I never could get it right. After I'd tried to do it a number of times he finally said, "Byron, if you can't remember three lines of dialogue, I don't know how you can ever remember how to hit a golf shot!"

Another thing that impressed me about Bing was that when I won the Crosby in '51, he had to leave before the tournament was over and go to Los Angeles to get treatment for kidney stones. Bing didn't like to fly, so he rode a train, and on that trip, though he was in terrific pain, he wrote a very kind letter congratulating me.

My last Bing story happened some years ago, when Bing's wife Kathy played on my team in our Lady Nelson pro-am two weeks before my tournament. Bing couldn't come because he was still recovering from a fall off a stage, but after we were done, Kathy wanted to call him, so we did. After she'd talked with him for a few minutes she handed the phone to me, and Bing said, "How'd Kathy do?" I told him she'd helped us on both a par five and a par three. Then he asked, "When she was out of the hole did she pick up?" I laughed and said, "No," and he asked, "When she missed a shot did she want to play another one?" I laughed again and said, "Yes," and he finally said, "Byron, you are a patient man!"

Jimmy Demaret. One of the most colorful pros in the history of golf. Jimmy was from Houston, so I got to know him when I was still quite young, and I knew him very well. He had a funny, quick wit about him, which I admired because I don't feel I have any whatsoever. The people at Augusta named their three bridges for Sarazen, Hogan, and me, and Jimmy used to joke, "Hey, I won it three times and I never even got an outhouse!" Jimmy played a nice, high fade, and he certainly proved you could win at Augusta without hooking, even though people said you couldn't.

Jimmy used to use a golf ball with a steel center made by a company in Chattanooga, Tennessee. He called them "Steelies." One year at the Masters he put two balls in the water, at 12 and 15, and when he came in, before anybody could say anything, Jimmy announced, "I found out one thing today—that old Steelie won't float!" He used to wear these big old tams that flopped down the side of his head, and the most outlandish colors. He'd often choose colors that clashed on purpose, just to create interest and get attention. He laughed at himself and people laughed with him—everybody kidded him and he really had a lot of fun with it.

President Eisenhower. Besides loving to play golf, Eisenhower was a fine bridge player, and one time I was asked to fill in for a couple of hands with him, Cliff Roberts, and Bob Woodruff, who was head of Coca-Cola. I was scared to death because I knew what good bridge players they all were, and I was really not much more than a beginner. In one hand, I wound up bidding four hearts but messed up somehow and didn't make it. When the hand was over, I said to Cliff, "I know I should have been able to make that bid some way," and Cliff said, "All you had to do was lead the two of hearts, Byron." I was glad when their fourth arrived. But it certainly was fun to watch them play, which I got to do nearly every evening after we'd played golf. They'd play just three or four cards, then everyone would lay their cards down and that was it. They were so good at knowing exactly where all the cards were. It just amazed me.

James Garner. Jim Garner is not only a fine actor, but loves to play golf and plays well, though he has back problems from time to time. One time I played an exhibition in Chicago with Jim and we had the oddest combination I'd ever seen. It was the two of us, Doug Sanders, and LPGA pro Laura Baugh. Garner hit the ball a long ways, and he was kidding Doug Sanders especially that day, because he was driving the ball very well. He'd hit a great drive and say, "Okay, Doug, try to catch that one." He outdrove Doug nearly all day long. Jim is very outgoing, especially when his back isn't bothering him, and it wasn't that day. Really, he was the long driver most of the time in our group, though he might go east or west sometimes instead of down the middle. He was about an 8 handicap, so he was definitely a good-caliber player.

Ralph Guldahl. Though Ralph was one of the slowest players on the tour, from 1936 to 1938 he was also a great player, winning the Western Open three times and the U.S. Open twice. I have to admit that after Ralph beat me so bad when we were both kids in Texas, it was nice to be able to top him at the Masters in '37, after Ralph had been leading me by three shots going to the last nine. In my own mind, I figured that made us about even. And then when I beat Ralph again during the International Match Play Championship at Belmont Springs that fall, I did kind of smile to myself, "And that makes me one up."

I believe the most unusual thing I ever saw a player do was in the U.S. Open in '37 at Oakland Hills in Birmingham, Michigan. Ralph was on the eighteenth green in the final round. He had the tournament won, all he had to do was hit his putt. He was all lined up and ready when he stopped, backed away, and took a comb out to comb his hair. I think he suddenly realized that they'd be wanting to take pictures and he wanted to make sure he looked good, but it was a little strange for someone to do that during the most important tournament we have.

He finished with his hair, two-putted, and that was that. I don't recall if the press said anything about how nice his hair looked.

Ralph won exactly $1000 for winning that Open, and the very next week his wife, Laverne, spent every penny of that thousand dollars on a fine riding horse. That was all right, I guess, but the third time she rode it, she fell off, broke her arm—and gave the horse away. I believe that was even more unusual than Ralph combing his hair on that final hole.

Walter Hagen. He was one of the best showmen I've ever seen, and the first pro golfer who really entertained the gallery. Besides entertaining the fans, though, Hagen also had the ability to politely intimidate his opponents. I watched him play in the semifinals against Abe Espinosa in the PGA Championship at Cedar Crest in Dallas in 1927, and Hagen was one down going to the last hole. Espinosa drove into some shallow rough while Hagen was nicely in the fairway. Hagen walked over to Abe's ball, looked at it, looked up at the green, didn't say a thing, then walked back to his own ball. So Abe went a little long and his ball ended up on the back of the green with Hagen's ball inside his. Now Hagen walks over behind Abe's ball again, lines it up as if he were going to putt it, then moves back out of the way. Of course, all this broke Abe's concentration and he three-putted; Hagen won on the first extra hole. He would do things like that whenever he needed to. In this day and time that wouldn't work at all, but back then no one thought much about it.

Hagen also had a knack of making a big production out of what was really a very easy shot. If he had a simple little chip, say, he would really look it over and make it look like it was very tough. Then he hit it well, of course, but the gallery would all think it was something great. On the other hand, when he had a really difficult shot he would walk up, hardly look at the ball, and just hit it. I guess the other thing people always liked about Hagen was that he always dressed immaculately and drove a handsome new car. That impressed everyone and allowed him to get away with things that the rest of us might not have. I may have said this before, but Hagen was also the first one that I knew of to ever have an agent—Bob Harlow, who started *Golf World* magazine.

Ed Haggar. Ed's father started the Haggar clothing company in Dallas, and he and his wife Patty are very dear friends of ours. A few years ago we were playing golf with them at Castle Pines. Ed and I had a pretty big bet going, a dollar nassau, and I had beaten him one down on the first nine. On the back, we came to the par-three eleventh hole, which is all downhill. I put my tee shot on the green but Ed hit a bad shot to the right, into all this brush and trees. His caddie said, "You'd better hit another one, Mr. Haggar," but Ed said, "No, we'll find it." Well, they went down in there and beat around in the brush awhile but didn't have any luck—which was a good thing, as it turned out. Because Ed went back to the tee, played another one, and his ball landed twenty feet back of the hole almost at the top of this big ridge that ran across the green. Then his ball started rolling back down and ran straight into the hole for a three. It was the only time I ever saw that happen in all the years I've played golf.

Ben Hogan. Back in our early years when neither one of us had much money at all, Ben and I were playing in the Oakland Open at Sequoia and staying at the Lehman Hotel. I was going to ride to the course with Ben for a practice round, so we went out to the parking lot, got to his car, and found it sitting there jacked up on cement blocks with all four wheels gone. Ben just couldn't believe it and said, "I sure hope whoever took them needed them worse than I do." We used my car instead, and I don't remember where he got the money to buy new wheels, but fortunately he did.

Ben has never liked being around a lot of people and that's fine. It's his business and I respect that. But I always thought it was a shame in a way because he missed so much. People idolized him so and to a certain extent that can be a very good thing. I know the way people feel about me has always made me feel good and made me want to try hard to be a better person. It's difficult for people to get a chance to interview Ben so they ask me about him a lot, but I just don't particularly like to talk about him. I feel like that's invading his privacy, so I don't say much. We've always gotten along fine and we've always liked each other very much. We're simply different personalities, and there's nothing wrong with that.

Bob Hope. Bob is and always has been a very funny man. Actually, he was more serious on the golf course than at any other time, and is one of the best goodwill ambassadors that golf ever had. Until his later years, Bob was a pretty steady player and scored in the mid-80's all the time, though he didn't start to play till he was older.

One time in the late thirties or early forties, I was in Los Angeles to play in the L.A. Open, and Bob wanted me to come out and go on his New Year's Eve show. I was pleased he wanted me to be on the show, so Louise and I flew out. We had a rehearsal and then went to the Rose Bowl game at Pasadena—Bob and Dolores, Louise and I, and Chester Morris and his wife. Bob was driving, and halfway to the Rose Bowl we ran into a terrible traffic jam. Of course, everyone knew Bob, including the policemen. All of a sudden Bob pulled out of line, and began driving on the wrong side of the road, telling policemen, "I'm late for a show!" Fortunately there was no traffic coming the other way, but it was still scary. We finally got to the stadium, and as soon as we got out of the car Louise said, "I don't care how we get back, I'm not going back with him." Fortunately, Cliff Roberts was there and sitting right where we were, so we rode back in his car instead.

When I went on the show that night, I didn't remember my lines very well. I never was much at memorizing. I was supposed to say something complimentary about Miss America, who was also on the show, but I couldn't remember my lines at all. Bob said to the audience, "This man's older than he looks, isn't he?" And they really laughed. But in case anyone wants to know, that's why I never became a movie star.

Bob Jones. Jones had the greatest name in golf in his time, of course, and is still considered great today. He was a wonderful man, with great knowledge about the history of the game and the best way to play. His ability to judge players and know what they needed to do to play good golf was excellent. Very educated and quite articulate, Jones wrote many articles and letters and several books on golf. He also made some instructional films that are selling quite well as videotapes today. I was fortunate to have played with Bob a number of times at Augusta, and always enjoyed it very much. You felt in awe when you played with him, regardless of what kind of game you played yourself. His attitude toward everyone was very friendly, but he was kind of quiet, really, and didn't have a lot to say most of the time. One time at the Masters Club dinner—the one attended originally just by the Masters winners plus Bob Jones and Clifford Roberts—the players were criticizing the way the pin had been placed on the third hole because it was nearly impossible to make a birdie. All of a sudden Jones said, "You guys make me sick. You think you've got to birdie every hole. You birdie a lot of them as it is, and there are going to be some tough pin placements out there that if you want a birdie, you're really going to have to earn it."

One of the great honors of my career was when Jones asked me to play in his place with the Masters tournament leader the last round, which I did until Ken Venturi was the leader in 1956. Since I was Venturi's mentor, Cliff and Bob decided that it wouldn't be right for me to play with Kenny, so they put me with someone else and Kenny played with Snead and lost. From then on, they began pairing the players according to their score only, which was really the best way.

Bobby Knight. Bobby and Chris Schenkel were very good friends, and one time I was playing in a tournament called the Mad Anthony in Ft. Wayne, Indiana, near Chris's home town. Bobby had played in the morning while Chris and I were scheduled for the afternoon. Before we started off, Bobby asked Chris if I would mind him following me around. What he wanted was for me to tell him what I was trying to do with each shot as I played, which was fine with me. I had a good day, fortunately, and most of the time was able to do exactly what I told him I was going to do. When we came in he said, "Boy, if I could get my basketball team to do that, we could sure win a lot more games!"

Chuck Kocsis. Chuck is from Michigan and is a fine amateur player who was runner-up to Harvie Ward in the 1956 U.S. Amateur. He's in his late seventies and still shoots his age or less on a regular basis. One summer in the early forties when I was pro at Inverness, Bobby Locke came over from South Africa to play some exhibitions for five straight days, all through Michigan. One of these exhibitions was at Red Run in Detroit, and I was invited to play with Bob Gaida, the pro there, Chuck, and Locke. Chuck was having a very good day and shot 33 on the front, while I had 34. We were good friends, but as we started the back nine, I said to him, "You'd better get going, because I'm not going to let any amateur beat me." As luck would have it, I shot 30, so I did manage to get past him.

Ky Laffoon. Ky was on the tour mostly in the early part of my career and was the most unusual golfer, personality-wise, that I ever knew. He was always doing something interesting. I first became acquainted with him when I was in California that first winter, 1933, because we were both staying at the Sir Launfels apartments in Los Angeles. Ky was part American Indian, and had a brother, Bill, who caddied for him and traveled with him all the time. Bill was the first traveling caddie I ever knew of. One day, Ky and I were playing two brothers, Al and Emery Zimmerman, in a practice round for the Pasadena Open at Brookside Park right by the Rose Bowl. At that time there was no restriction on the number of clubs you could have in your bag, and it was amazing how many people had clubs that were numbered between an 8 and a 9-iron—especially pitching clubs. On the ninth hole, I'd outdriven Ky and was watching as he put his second shot on the green. I hollered, "What club did you use, Ky?" He hollered back, "A three-quarter seven-and-a-half."

Ky chewed tobacco and used to squirt the juice between his front teeth. You had to stay out of the way because sometimes it went quite a few feet. But in spite of that unattractive habit, Ky felt he was really good-looking. I'd be in his room sometimes when he was getting dressed, and he'd preen in front of the mirror, slick his hair back, and say, "Boy, you're the best-looking man in the world. I don't know how you stand it!" Ky was a good player, but he was never satisfied just to play, no matter what the tournament was. He always had to have some kind of small side bet going about what he'd shoot or whether he'd win. One time he was playing in a tournament in Cleveland, Ohio, and was using a mallet-head putter with a wooden shaft that he usually did very well with. He was on the last hole and winning the tournament, but he had to two-putt to win his own bet on what he said he'd shoot. Now when Ky hit a bad putt, he'd always kick the putter head. Well, he putted past the hole and missed it coming back, which meant he lost his bet. So he got mad and kicked his putter as usual. Unfortunately, this time the head fell right off the putter, but Ky reached over quick, grabbed the putter head, and knocked the ball in the hole—one stroke too late.

Most of the time, though, he'd win those little old bets. Ky really was the best player for his own money of anyone I ever saw. There were quite a few younger players coming on the tour then, and he would play as many as three at a time, best ball, for a $5 nassau. All in all it was fun, knowing and playing golf with Ky Laffoon.

Tony Lema. When I first met Tony, he was the assistant caddiemaster at California Golf Club when I played in tournaments there and many other times when I played with my friend Eddie Lowery. Tony then became caddiemaster before he turned pro. He would watch me every time I played or practiced, and I always felt that of all the golfers out there, Tony used his feet and legs more like I did than anyone else. When Tony was a member of the Ryder Cup team I captained in 1965, that was a real bonus for me, and he did very well. After we'd won the Cup, our team was in the locker room waiting for the official award ceremony, and Tony opened up a case of champagne. He loved champagne and had been nicknamed "Champagne Tony" by the press because he bought it for everyone when he won a tournament. I let them all have a glass, but then had them put it away for later, because I wanted to be sure we'd behave all right during the ceremony, with Prime Minister Wilson there and all.

Tony was very well liked by the other players and very outgoing, but kind of shy around me. Before the Ryder Cup, he had decided he wanted to live in Texas and asked to use my name as a reference when he applied for an apartment in Dallas over on Turtle Creek, which is a pretty nice area. They called me about it, and I had to tell them everything I knew about Tony, nearly. He was approved, fortunately, and once he'd moved in, he would bring his mother out to the ranch quite often to visit Louise and me. In fact, he was living in Texas when he was killed in that terrible plane crash.

Lawson Little. Lawson was a fine player who won the American and British amateurs and many other amateur tournaments before he turned pro. While he was still an amateur he got a job writing for

King Features Syndicate, and that was how he could afford to travel to tournaments and play. In 1936, the year after I beat him in the San Francisco Match Play tournament when I was just starting, I was heading out to play the Pacific Northwest tour, the one where I really got going good. I was riding the train from Seattle to Portland, and on the way to the dining car I heard a typewriter clicking away in the drawing room. I saw Lawson in there working, and when I said hello, he said, "Byron, come here a minute and guess what I'm writing about." I said I had no idea, and he said, "I'm writing about how you trounced me good last year in San Francisco!"

Bobby Locke. Not only was Bobby a fine player, but he was also considered one of the great putters of all time. In six exhibitions I played with him one long week in Michigan in the early forties, he never missed one putt under five feet. It was when we got off the course that the trouble started. I was acting as his host and after each round we'd talk to the people awhile, then go get changed and go out to eat. Now I wasn't particularly rushing, but I'd have my shower and be all dressed and ready to go and Bobby would still be about half-dressed and not showered, sitting there having a beer. I'd say, "Bobby, c'mon, let's go." "All right, laddie," he'd say, "I'll be ready in a few minutes." Happened every time. Bobby had a certain speed he moved, and he never varied, never rushed, just always moved at that same tempo. He was very deliberate in everything he did, particularly in the way he played golf. He even walked with a very deliberate gait. When he played, though, he played very well. He'd hit a little draw hook every shot, exactly the same every time. When Sam Snead went over to South Africa to play him in the late thirties, Bobby beat Sam fifteen out of sixteen matches. Made me glad I didn't go.

Jim McKay. One time when Jim and I were on a plane going to the British Open, we got to talking about golf, and he complained he wasn't putting very well. I didn't think I'd be able to help him right then and there, but sure enough, someone on the plane had a putter and I gave Jim a lesson right in the aisle. What was wrong was he wasn't looking straight at the ball, which made it impossible to keep the putter on line going back and through. So I showed him how to correct that, and everyone on the plane got a kick out of it. Of course, planes then were not as crowded as they are now, and fortunately we had a smooth flight. Once we landed and he got out to play, he did putt quite well and told me later that was the best putting lesson he'd ever had.

Harold McSpaden. Harold and I played a lot of golf together and played well as a team, though we had very different personalities. I was easygoing and kind of shy, but there was nothing shy or easygoing about Harold. He wasn't mean at all, but kind of rough and gruff and he would tell you how he felt right quick, so you never had to wonder what he was thinking. I had a number of players ask me, "Doesn't McSpaden bother you?" and I said, "No, I like to play with him." Besides having a strong personality and being honest and forthright, Harold was a better player than anyone ever gave him credit for. Another difference between us was that he had exceptionally long arms. Though he was one and a half inches shorter than me, he wore a 36-inch sleeve while I took a 33. I believe the reason we were such a good team was because I played a different type of game from Harold. I was very steady—in the fairway, on the green, and no more than two putts—while he might get into trouble on a few holes but could also make a lot of birdies, so we "brother-in-lawed" it pretty good most of the time.

Harold was very strong, with a kind of loose-jointed walk. With his long arms, for most of his career he used only a 42-inch driver. He was barrel-chested and had hazel eyes and dark hair he combed straight back, sort of in the style the young folks are bringing back now. For sure, he certainly was a better player than most people know. He once said to me, "Byron, if you hadn't been born, I would have been known as a wonderful player!" In fact, during my wonderful year of 1945, Harold finished second thirteen times, which has to be a record.

Eddie Merrins. Quiet and easy but always getting the job done, Eddie is one of the absolute top club professionals ever. He's called "The Little Pro" because he is so small, but he's a wonderful teacher and was recently named club pro of the year for his work at Bel Air in Los Angeles, where he's been pro for thirty years. There are a lot of movie stars and bigwigs at Bel Air, so you know it's not the easiest place in the world to work. Besides running the golf program at his club, Eddie served as the golf coach for UCLA, which has graduated such fine players as Steve Pate, Corey Pavin, and quite a few others. He's also a great organizer. Some years ago he began the Friends of Golf (FOG) tournament to raise money for golf scholarships for UCLA. The tournament has been very successful and has expanded to benefit other college and junior golf programs around the country.

Francis Ouimet. I first met Francis through Eddie Lowery, who caddied for him when Francis won the Open in 1913. Francis lived in Massachusetts and I played with him and Eddie a few times at the Charles River Country Club when Francis was in his fifties. Quiet though not shy, he was a beautiful player and a wonderful long-iron player. Francis had what today would be called an abbreviated swing—the club never even quite reached horizontal. But he was effective because he had a very smooth, flowing action and his rhythm was excellent. It was pretty to watch and I was very impressed with his game. He was impressed with mine also, so we had sort of a mutual admiration society. He was on the USGA committee in 1939 when I won the International Match Play Championship in Boston. That was the first time I actually met him, though he had such a strong New England accent I could hardly understand anything he said. Besides winning the Open in 1913, Francis won the Amateur in 1914 and again in 1931, and was also Captain of the Royal and Ancient Golf Club of St. Andrews, which meant our friends across the ocean appreciated him too.

Arnold Palmer. Arnold is the most popular golf professional that's ever been and he deserves it. I've never seen anyone sign as many autographs or be as nice to the public as he is. But besides being so popular and the most exciting golfer I ever saw, Arnie is an excellent pilot and flies his own plane, which impresses me. I flew with him a number of times and always felt completely at ease. One time, though, I was visiting him at his home in Latrobe, Pennsylvania, in the late fifties when he called President Eisenhower at Gettysburg to see if he would come play golf with us if Arnie would go pick him up. There was a prediction of rain, but Arnie said, "Yes, the weather looks a little bad but I think it'll be all right." Both of us got in

Arnie's plane and headed towards Gettysburg, but about halfway there the weather got terrible, with lots of rain and fog. To be honest, I was getting a little scared—not about Arnie's flying, but because the weather really was pretty bad. Arnie called the airport we were to land at and they told him we could come in, so he had them call Eisenhower, but Ike told them, "I'm not going up in this—I don't want to and Mamie wouldn't let me anyway!" Well, you couldn't argue with either one of them, so we just had to turn around and go back.

At his home in Latrobe, Arnie has a good-sized basement, with pigeonholes all along the walls for the golf clubs he loves to fool with—and he's got hundreds of them. He always liked to take clubs, put them in a vise, take them apart, and work them over. He put some of the strangest facings I'd ever seen on his clubs. Sometimes they'd be real straight and other times he'd have the face cut back almost even with the hosel. And he liked to bend iron clubs around some, experimenting. He never played with any of them that I know of but he loved to fool with them; it was sort of therapy for him. I've seen Arnold go to the practice tee with three drivers, trying to make up his mind which one to use, and he'd do the same thing on the putting green. That was so foreign to what most other players did, but it didn't make much difference what he used. The way he played and scored, he always did great.

Judy Rankin. Johnny Revolta was a fine player on the tour who became an excellent teacher and was pro at Evanston Country Club in Illinois for many years. A number of years ago, Johnny and I were discussing the golf swing and teaching and he said, "Have you ever seen Judy Torluemke?" That was Judy's maiden name. I said, "Yes, I've seen her play but only from a distance." He told me, "I want you to look at her grip and tell me if you ever want to teach anybody again." The next chance I got, I did get a closer look and I was quite surprised, to say the least. Judy's left hand position was so strong that the back of it almost faced up at the sky. Her right hand was quite good, but her left was far too strong for anyone to say she could ever be a good player. But her success—she won at least twenty-five tournaments—shows that if you practice and repeat the same motion you can overcome anything, because she played very well despite her unorthodox grip. Very probably she developed it to gain extra distance, because she was quite small. Judy also understands the game very well and does a good job today as an on-course commentator for ABC.

Clifford Roberts. Cliff and I had become friends from the time I'd won the Masters in 1937. I had made a little money in '38 and the first part of '39, and I'd bought a few shares of five or ten different stocks. Cliff was one of the top officials in Reynolds Securities, so I asked him some questions about the stocks I'd bought, but he just kind of grunted and didn't say much. Then one day I was at Augusta in '39 and he called and said, "Byron, I want you to come down to my office at nine a.m." When I arrived, he had just finished his breakfast and was drinking some tea. He said, "You asked me some questions about stocks, so I want to talk to you about it." He added, "I like you, Byron, but you're never going to make any money in golf. And if you keep fooling around buying stocks on your own, you're going to lose what you do make."

Then he said, "I don't handle any account under a million dollars, but because you've been good to us here at Augusta, I would like to handle your account, under the condition that I have power of attorney, so I can buy and sell what and when I want to. But I assure you I will handle your account very much like it was a bank. You won't make an awful lot of money, but you will make a little. Also, whenever you have a thousand dollars or five thousand saved up, you send that to me and I'll continue to invest it. I'll also take the stocks you have now and sell them—I don't know where you got those dogs anyway." Financially, it was the best thing that ever happened to me.

Cliff was from New York, was a great friend of Bob Jones, and was also the best executive that I ever heard of. He really knew how to get things done, but he talked very slowly and thought things out before he said anything at all. After Bob Jones became somewhat incapacitated because of his illness, Cliff did an excellent job of conducting the tournament and seeing to it that things gradually improved. One year, they had put out the gallery ropes—this was when they first started roping the golf course off like they do now—and the ropes were all white. I was out on the course with Cliff, and he looked around at the white ropes and said, "That doesn't go in this place at all. The ropes should be green." This was just before the tournament was to start, but in a couple of days, the ropes were changed to a twist of white and green. That was a big improvement;

you could see them all right, but they didn't stand out so much. Cliff was always alert to seeing that everything was done right.

I also recall one time during the early years when admission to the Masters was very cheap—three dollars—and there had been a big discussion about it. Cliff wanted to raise the fee to five dollars, but the others on the tournament improvements committee said that was too much. Then Cliff said, "We went to New York recently and saw Beau Jack fight. [Beau Jack was a shoeshine boy in the locker room at Augusta who some of the members had backed financially to further his boxing career.] We had ringside seats to watch just two men in a prize fight. Here, you've got a field of the best golfers in the world, and the people are paying just three dollars while we paid fifty dollars for those ringside seats. That's ridiculous." They agreed with him then and raised the ticket price to five dollars.

In those days the Masters was still small enough that everyone drove down Magnolia Lane to the clubhouse and then to the parking lots. One morning during that year's tournament, I happened to walk out on to the porch and folks were coming in, just streaming down Magnolia Lane. Cliff was standing there, and he smiled at me as he watched the people driving by and said, "five dollars, five dollars, five dollars. . . ."

Quite a few years later, Cliff spent a night at our ranch on his way back to Augusta from California. We had dinner and talked until late in the evening. He asked me quite a few questions about my ranch, what I'd paid for it and other things, and the next day I took him to the airport and didn't think any more about it.

Well, some time after that I got a call from Cliff at 10:30 at night. He was in Freeport in the Bahamas, so it was 11:30 where he was. He said, "I understand that Mr. Hogan is building a golf course about three miles from you." I said, "Yes, that's right." And he said, "I understand they have 2500 acres and they paid $3500 an acre for it." I replied, "That's right, too, Cliff." Then he said, "I remember you telling me you paid $82 an acre for your ranch in '46." And I said, "Your memory's very good, Cliff." Then there was a long pause. Finally, he said, "Remind me to treat you with more respect."

Barbara Romack. Back in the mid-fifties I was in Sacramento visiting my friend Tommy Lopresti who was pro at Hagen Oaks. He said, "Byron, I have a little fourteen-year-old towheaded girl out on the course playing with a bunch of boys. I've been trying to get her to change her grip a little and she won't listen to me, but I think she'll listen to you." I said okay, so we got in his car, went out, and found her. She had on blue jeans rolled up above her knees and a shirt with the sleeves rolled up. She looked like a real tomboy, but she also had a good-looking swing. We watched her play a couple of holes and when she came in, Tommy and I talked to her about her grip. I liked Barbara right away, she had a very warm, pleasing personality, and fortunately she did listen to what I had to say. A few years went by and I didn't see anything more of her until she turned pro, and then one day I saw an article in the paper where she'd won an award for being the best-dressed lady on the LPGA tour, so she apparently wasn't such a tomboy anymore.

One year, the LPGA began playing a tournament in Dallas at Glen Lakes Country Club and Barbara contacted me. I helped her a little then, and the next year I worked with her quite a lot over at Brook-hollow Golf Club in Dallas. After we'd practiced, she and I would play with some of my men friends. We'd play from the men's tees, she'd shoot 75, and since she liked to bet a little bit, she'd always take some of their money. Then she'd turn around, go play in the ladies' tournament from the white tees and shoot in the high 70's or low 80's. I'd say, "Barbara, how can you shoot 75 from the men's tees at Brookhollow and then not do nearly as well when you play with the ladies?" She told me, "I learned to play with men most of the time, and it's so different playing with women that I just haven't gotten used to it. They talk so much it drives me crazy sometimes!" I still get a card from her every Christmas, and she's doing a lot of teaching at Atlantis, Florida, so I'm sure she's doing well and still dressing great.

Gene Sarazen. When I first started on the tour, Gene was very active in golf and very outspoken. I had come on the tour with a new style of play where I used my feet and legs a lot. He said then, "Byron will never make a good player because he has too much move-ment in his knees and legs." I never resented it because he hadn't learned to play the way I did and no one else was doing it besides me, so I understood why he said it. I've played a lot of golf with Gene, and always respected his ability, since he's one of only four players in the history of the game who have won the modern or professional

"Grand Slam"—the Masters, the PGA, and the U.S. and British Opens.

For quite some time after I first knew Gene, I never saw him wearing anything except knickers, which of course look quite good on him. But I began to wonder why he never wore slacks at all, and then one time I did see him in a suit and I figured it out. Gene is quite short, but somehow knickers make him look taller, while a suit seems to emphasize his small stature. But he was always plenty big enough to beat just about anybody when he wanted to.

Everyone knows about Sarazen's double eagle at Augusta in 1935, but very few people really saw it happen. Today Gene says he's been told by at least 25,000 people that they saw it, but we both know there were only about 5000 people total in the gallery that day and not all of them were following him, because Craig Wood was leading and was in the clubhouse. However, I was one of the few who did get to see Gene's shot. It was my first Masters ever, and I was playing 17 while Gene was on 15 and the two fairways ran parallel to each other. I had driven to the right and had to wait to hit my second shot till Gene hit his and his gallery moved out of the way. Naturally I watched Gene's shot, because I was excited to have the opportunity to see him play, so I did actually see his ball go in the hole. The unfortunate thing was that Craig Wood thought he had it won, because he was three shots ahead of Gene. But after the fifteenth hole Gene parred in and tied him, and then won the playoff.

Gene, Sam Snead, and I were invited to be the honorary starters for the Masters a few years ago. We were going along all right the first few holes, though Snead had mentioned his back was bothering him some on the first tee. I really thought he was trying to hit the ball too hard, and then he really flinched on his tee shot at the fourth hole. Finally, when he hit his drive on 5, his back went out completely and he could hardly move. He said, "I've got to quit," got in the cart, and went back to the clubhouse. So Gene and I finished the fifth hole and were walking to the sixth tee when Gene said, "We're doing pretty well, Byron. We've played five holes and only had one casualty."

This past spring, 1992, we were on the first tee again. Sam had had an automobile accident and hurt his shoulder so he couldn't play, and I hadn't played in two years because of my hip surgery. But Gene, who's ninety, was in great shape. He warned us, "I'm only going to hit one shot," stepped up and hit it absolutely perfect 180 yards straight down the center. He turned to us and said, "That's the best drive I've hit this year!"

Chris Schenkel. Playing golf with Chris was always fun. He never once worked on his game, but had a good grip and was the fastest golfer I ever played with, faster even than Chi Chi Rodriguez, and just about that fat, too. Chris would tee it up and hit it almost before you could get out of his way. If he'd ever had time to work on it, he would have made a pretty good player. He had good coordination, but because he didn't work on it, he'd hit that old banana ball a lot. Of all the friends I made in golf, Chris is the closest. He likes me a lot and has always done and said so many nice things it almost embarrasses me, but I love it.

In 1984, Abilene Christian University started a golf endowment fund in my and Louise's name. They had a huge party at the Anatole in Dallas with over 1200 people, and Chris was the master of ceremonies. I'll never forget as long as I live when he said, "I have one last, heartfelt wish, and that is this: If the Lord would grant me another brother, I'd want him to be you." Thank you, Chris.

Randolph Scott. Besides being one of my favorite actors, Randy Scott loved golf and was a beautiful player with a wonderful putting stroke. One year we played in the Pro-Am at Thunderbird in Palm Springs before it became the Bob Hope tournament, and Randy shot the easiest 68 you could imagine. Randy was always so nice and conducted himself so well; in fact, he was one of the few actors ever allowed to be a member of the Los Angeles Country Club. One day I was playing there on the south course with Randy, Lee Davis, and my good friend J.K. Wadley, and I shot 61—a course record at the time. I must have learned something from watching Randy putt, because I did putt very well that day.

Lefty Stackhouse. Lefty was in some ways the most unusual golfer that I ever knew. He had an almost uncontrollable temper when he played golf, and the peculiar thing was that he actually was a good player. But as soon as he'd miss a shot or do something he considered stupid, he'd get so mad that he'd actually do himself bodily harm. I was playing with him in the Odessa Pro-Am one year, and Lefty's partner was Billy Erfurth, the Texas State Amateur Champion. We were playing best-ball and on the eighth hole, Lefty was just short of the green, while Billy was nicely on. Lefty decided to pick his ball up and let Billy play the hole, but Billy three-putted. Then Lefty realized that if he'd continued to play, he could have chipped close and made par. He was so mad he hit himself with his fist on the side of his cheek, which bled considerably; he had to go in and get bandaged up. There were many stories like that and worse about Lefty, and it was a shame because he really was a good player.

I always wondered what caused him to do this, but after he quit trying to play golf on the tour or compete in any kind of tournament, he became very quiet and good-natured. He went on to do more work for the juniors in his area down around Seguin, Texas, than anyone I ever heard of. Obviously the reason he got so mad was that competition put so much stress on him, because he never did it after he quit playing in tournaments.

Payne Stewart. One of my favorite golfers because he looks so great in the outfits he wears, and I think that's really good for the game. I also like Payne because of the way he came back and won my tournament after losing in a playoff several years before that. A few years ago, I played with Payne, D.A. Weibring, and Bruce Lietzke in Quincy, Illinois. It was a fun exhibition and I was holding my own all right, which was kind of a surprise. On the last hole, Payne was twenty feet away and I was fifteen. He nonchalantly knocked his in for birdie, then smiled at me and said, "That just made yours longer, Byron." As luck would have it, I made mine right on top of his, so we both got a kick out of that.

Ed Sullivan. Ed loved to play golf but he was extremely slow, slower than Roone Arledge ever thought of being. He was bad about taking several practice swings, getting over the ball, then moving away from it and starting over. What's more, he was always talking; he never acted like he was thinking about golf at all. Everybody playing with him would say, "Come on, Ed, it's your turn," but he never seemed to get much better. He was such a good guy, though, that you couldn't help but like him.

Ken Venturi. One of the reasons Kenny's short game is so good is his bunker play, and he and I both learned that from Eddie Lowery. We were at Palm Springs, where I was working with Kenny one time, and back of Eddie's house was a green and a sand bunker which he and three neighbors had paid to have built there. Guess they played a little golf, too. Anyway, one evening after dinner Eddie, who was about an 8-handicapper, challenged us, "I'll play your best ball out of the bunker, twenty-five cents a shot." We did this three evenings in a row and lost a lot of quarters, but from then on we both became excellent bunker players, thanks to Eddie. He really was phenomenal out of the sand, and when we asked him how he got so good at it he said, "I had to learn how to play out of bunkers because I used to be in so many of them."

Johnny Weissmuller. Johnny was almost as much fun on a golf course as he was in his Tarzan movies, because he was always getting in trouble. Johnny could hit the ball a long ways, but a lot of times it went the wrong direction. When he hit a good one, though, he'd do his Tarzan yell and you could hear it all across the golf course. The first time I played with him was in the 1938 Crosby at Rancho Santa Fe; it was a big thrill for me after seeing him in the movies. Also, in case I haven't mentioned it already, Johnny joined Bing and Bob and me on many of those Red Cross and war bond exhibitions during the war. It was a lot of hard travel and hard work, but we had a great time doing it together.

Lawrence Welk. The most amazing thing about playing golf with Lawrence Welk was that he never started playing golf till he was sixty-two, but still did remarkably well for having started that late in life. You remember that when leading his orchestra he'd always go "a-one and a-two," and he did the same thing on the golf course. He'd take one quick little practice swing, then another quick little practice swing, and then he'd hit, using the same rhythm as he did in his music. Years ago, we played a charity tournament in Nashville, Tennessee. It was me, Lawrence, and Minnie Pearl, and it was really fun. Minnie played a pretty fair game, but what I liked was that she was just as funny on the golf course as she is on stage. My brother Charles was living in Nashville then and came out to watch us play. Lawrence really got a kick out of meeting him and was impressed enough by his voice to invite Charles on his show to sing a little while after that. Another time I played with Lawrence at Bel Air in Los Angeles, along with the comedy team Shipstad and Johnson, and you couldn't hardly play golf for laughing. They didn't care whether they had a four or an eight on a hole, and it was mostly somewhere in between.

Kathy Whitworth. The first time I saw Kathy play was when I was working for ABC. I was impressed first of all by the fact that all of her fundamentals were excellent—grip, stance, swing, the way she stayed down to the ball, everything. You couldn't win eighty-eight tournaments as she has without having all those things right. The second thing that impresses me about Kathy, though, is that she has always been a real lady. I've never heard anyone say a single thing against her. She now lives two miles east of me at Trophy Club, Texas, and I see her at the local grocery store or the post office every now and then. It's always good to see her and realize what she has done for women's golf.

Craig Wood. Craig, who by the way was pro at Winged Foot when he played on the tour, was called the "Blond Bomber." He was a very natty dresser, and always drove a fancy car, but he did a lot more than just look good. I played with and against Craig in many tournaments, and I always knew that if I were to beat him I really had to play my absolute best. Because of the '35 Masters and the '39 Open, it seemed for a while that something unlucky always happened to him, kind of like Greg Norman today. But in 1941 Craig won both the Masters and the U.S. Open at Colonial in Fort Worth, so it apparently didn't bother him too much.

People used to feel sorry for Craig because of what happened to him in the '35 Masters. He was already in the clubhouse and they had taken him into the so-called "Champion's Room" with Gene Sarazen and I and a few others still out on the course. Sarazen was the closest to Craig, but he was still three shots back and no one thought there was any chance he could catch up, when he made that wonderful double eagle on the fifteenth hole. Sarazen went three under right there and tied Craig, then beat him in the playoff the next day. But Craig never grumbled. Then in the '39 U.S. Open, when I had that eagle two on the fourth hole, he just said to me, "That was a fine shot, Byron," and kept on playing his best, trying to win. He was a fine player and a gentleman, and it was a shame he died at a relatively young age.

Mickey Wright. Mickey was one of the best ball strikers and had the best golf swing of anyone I ever saw, man or woman. She played so well and won so often she got kind of bored with it and left the tour early. Besides, just like on the men's tour when I quit, the ladies weren't making much money in the sixties, so Mickey decided to do something else and became a stockbroker.

When Chris and I were broadcasting the Women's Open at Pensacola, I rode out to the course with Mickey and some other ladies during one of the practice rounds. I was going out to study the course for the broadcast, and during the ride I asked Mickey how she was playing. She said, "Byron, I'm playing terrible." I said, "I can't believe that, Mickey," and she said, "How much time do you have?" So I watched her play the first nine, and she hit it dead solid, the middle of every fairway and every green except for the last hole, when she pushed her 4-iron about four feet to the right of the green and almost chipped it in. When she finished I went over to her and said, "Yes, Mickey, I see how badly you're playing." She smiled then and protested, "But I only made one birdie, Byron!" That's how much of a perfectionist she was.

One time, during the ladies' tournament at Glen Lakes in Dallas, Mickey arranged an exhibition with her coach Earl Stewart, Marilynn Smith, and me, playing an 18-hole match for charity. The ladies played from their tees and Earl and I from the men's, and Mickey put her ball inside of Earl and me all day long. Marilynn played very well also, but fortunately I made a couple of putts at the end and we eked it out, two up. It was a close thing, and I said to Earl when we were done, "Earl, don't you ever get me in a trap like this again!"

Babe Zaharias. In Texas we call someone like Babe Zaharias "a piece of work," but as brash as she could be at times, she sure did have the talent to back it up. I first heard about her when she was fourteen and was running in a track-and-field event in Fort Worth. Babe ran in all the girls' events and won every one, then started competing in the boys' events, but the officials wouldn't allow it. If they had, I'm sure she would have won at least a few of those events too, because she was one of the greatest athletes the world has ever known.

When she took up golf, people said, "This is one game the Babe won't be so good at." But they didn't know her. She practiced till her hands bled and goodness alive, she could play—and she had such perfect balance. In the late thirties I saw her play against Leonard Dotson at St. Augustine, Florida. They had a bet going and set up this kind of crazy match where they had to play each shot standing on just one foot. Try it sometime. Anyway, Babe shot 75 and won easily, and if that doesn't prove something, I don't know what does.

ELEVEN

Today

As I said at the beginning of this book, I am a blessed man. I was born into a loving family, married a wonderful woman, and was very fortunate to do all I did in golf—playing, teaching, broadcasting, and even helping build golf courses. You would think that as I got older my life would have slowed down, but it seemed to get still busier. By the time I turned seventy, I was still running a few cattle on the ranch, being involved in my own tournament, playing in an occasional charity or celebrity event around the country, giving clinics, traveling to the majors and a few other tournaments, and even doing a little woodworking.

Louise was happy, too. She'd continued to fix up our home till she'd gotten it about where she wanted it, and finally was getting to spend a lot of time with her family, who by now all lived in Fort Worth. We weren't doing a lot of traveling, but most of what we did do we did together, and we enjoyed it. One of our favorite trips always was to the Masters, and on April 1, 1983, that was where we were planning to go next.

It was Good Friday; we were to leave for Augusta the following Monday. Louise had already laid out all the clothes we would need, and we were both looking forward to seeing our many friends there. A month before, Louise had been feeling a little tired and had a checkup, but the doctors hadn't found anything, and for all the past week she'd been feeling fine. Late that afternoon, both of us were doing chores and running errands so we'd be ready for our trip. Louise had gone to the post office in town just a mile away, and I was working at my desk. About the time I expected her back, something made me look out the window, and that's when I saw Louise's car in the ditch in the front of our house. The wind was blowing very hard that day, as much as sixty miles per hour, and at first I thought maybe the wind had blown her car off the road. I jumped up and ran out the door—it seemed like my feet only hit the ground twice getting to her. The car was kind of sideways up against the fence, and Louise's door was still closed when I came up. I yanked the door open and said, "What's wrong, honey?" But as soon as I saw her face I knew something was very wrong. She never moved or looked at me. The only thing moving was her left foot and left hand, and I knew she'd had a stroke. Apparently, it had happened just as she started to turn into the driveway. I yelled next door to my sister and brother-in-law to call an ambulance, then went with her to the hospital and stayed that night.

Our family physician, Dr. Jim Murphy, called in a neurosurgeon right away, and the two of them told me Louise's condition was very serious and they might have to operate. At first they thought she'd had an aneurysm, but after they'd taken X-rays, they determined it was a very serious stroke and she would probably not live more than two weeks. Well, Louise did live, but after a few weeks the doctors said she'd probably never know me or anything else. She continued to improve, though, and then they told me, "She'll know you, Byron, but her disposition will change—she'll never be like she was." By this time, Louise had survived a month and four days, and they were amazed, because the damage to the left side of her brain was so severe. Once it was clear she was going to live, they moved her to the rehabilitation unit of Harris Hospital, which was the best rehab area for stroke victims in Fort Worth, and she was there four months. During all that time and throughout her therapy, she never was able to speak again, except to say, over and over, "Home, home, home." The head of the unit, Dr. Bickel, finally told me they'd keep her another six weeks and after that they wouldn't be able to help her any more.

When it was time for Louise to come home, her primary nurse, Linda Buchanan, and Dr. Bickel, head of the rehab unit, came to our house and determined what changes I would need to make to take care of Louise properly. We had to have ramps built so her wheelchair could navigate the several floor levels we had, we made our master bedroom into a room just for Louise, complete with a hospital bed and so forth, and I hired two nurses who worked alternating week-long 24-hour shifts. Fortunately, we had just added a wonderful garden room to our home the year before, and it was there that my beautiful Louise spent most of her time after she came home from the hospital.

When she did come home, it was very hard for her to adjust to the realization that she was always going to be paralyzed and unable to talk. She had loved to cook so much and was such a good cook, but she never went back into her kitchen again, and one day, shortly after I brought her home, I found her crying and pushing her wheelchair in circles all around our dining room table. She did it for the longest time, until she just plain wore herself out. After that, she gradually got to where she accepted things as they were, but it was so sad to see her that way.

Though Louise never spoke again except to say, "Home," she did sing once or twice when we went to church shortly after I brought her home, but then she apparently had another small stroke and never sang again. She learned to feed herself, but could never write or walk, and pretty much needed to be cared for totally. Yet her personality didn't really change that much. She was still there, although it was like she was in a prison, and her main way of communicating was through me. Even though she couldn't talk, we had been married so long and were so close to each other that I could nearly always figure out what she wanted or needed. One time, about the middle of the summer, she was trying very hard to communicate something to me when I finally realized she wanted to go to our favorite fruit farm in Weatherford, about forty-five miles away, for fresh peaches. Another time, she wanted to visit her niece, Sandy, in Fort Worth. It made me feel good to know I could help her in those ways, because there was so little else I really could do, though I took care of her myself at times on weekends or when one of the nurses was sick.

In many ways, Louise's mind was still quite normal, yet in other ways she became very fearful, probably because of having to be so dependent on everyone else and having no way to communicate. She became very fearful of fire, for instance. That first fall, as soon as it got cold, I started to build a fire in the den, because we had always enjoyed having a cozy little fire of an evening. But Louise became so agitated I had to put it out, and never even tried to have a fire the whole rest of the time she was alive. She also would get quite worried in the car. The Salesmanship Club had very kindly given me a special van with a hydraulic lift for Louise's wheelchair, but although she was strapped in very securely, she would still watch the speedometer closely and let me know right away if she thought I was going too fast.

To their everlasting credit, our best friends stayed in close touch. For instance, Jim and Betty Chambers came over from Dallas nearly every Sunday afternoon and visited with us. Also, Chris Schenkel and Tom Watson came to see Louise quite often during her illness, and I can never thank them enough for taking so much trouble. Louise always recognized everyone and was happy to see them. Sometimes it was frustrating for her not to be able to talk, though Chris and Tom would talk to her as though she could, which wasn't easy for them to do. Chris was excellent at it, and she really enjoyed that.

But after spending five months in the hospital and rehab, Louise never really made any more progress. She lived for twenty-five months more. Then, on September 14, 1985, she had another very bad stroke while sitting in our garden room just after breakfast one morning. I rushed her to the hospital, but after waiting several days, the doctors said she was now brain-dead and there was no chance for recovery at all. Now came the hardest decision of my life—telling the doctors to disconnect the life support systems they had Louise on. She and I had talked about this situation years before and had both agreed we didn't want to be kept alive that way, but it still is a difficult thing to do. Even so, it was amazing how strong her body was physically, because she lived another two weeks and finally died October 4, 1985. I still went to visit her every day and sat holding her hand when she died. We had been married fifty years and four months.

You know, I don't think it's possible for a man to be as successful as I was and not have a wife like Louise to help support me through the bad times as well as the good ones. It must have been very difficult for her during my streak, for example, because I was going through so much. She never said "I wish it would end," even though I

knew all the pressure I was having was affecting her, too. In my earlier career, too, she always seemed to know when I needed encouragement and when I needed a little push—when to be politely forward
enough to get me to do what I should to become a better player and a
better person. She never minded being "Mrs. Byron Nelson" and taking a back seat regarding all the publicity I was getting, but I was so
eternally grateful when the ladies of the Byron Nelson Classic gave
her a party one year. It showed Louise that they understood how important she was to me, but more important, that they loved and appreciated her for herself, not just because she happened to be my wife.
Another thing that happened along this line was that Abilene Christian University established a golf scholarship endowment fund in both
our names, and gave an enormous party for us to get it started. It
made both of us feel very good—there were over twelve hundred people, and it was a wonderful evening.

Of course, Louise's illness wasn't easy for me, either. It was hard
to feel so helpless. I did everything I could for her and was glad to
have the opportunity to make up for all the years when she had sacrificed so much for me, but there was only so much I could do. The
strain of it all made me start to lose weight, and when I got down to
160 Dr. Murphy told me I had to do something about it or I'd end up
in the hospital too. I had prayed and all the church and our friends
were praying for me, but nothing seemed to help much until one day I
decided to go for a walk. I took off and went a mile or so down our
country road, and by the time I got back I felt better. I began to walk
nearly every day, and besides being good exercise, it seemed to give
me more of a sense of having some control over my life again. I started
to eat better and put on a little weight, and all of that helped me take
better care of Louise.

But after she died, I felt so lost. Now I had no one to take care of
and it didn't seem like I had much reason to go on living. I started to
go downhill again, losing weight and pretty much just feeling sorry for
myself. Once again, Dr. Murphy told me, "Byron, we're going to have
to get you turned around some way, or we're going to lose you." But I
didn't care a whole lot one way or the other, till one day the next
March, when I got a call from my good friend Cy Laughter.

Cy ran a tournament in Dayton, Ohio, called the Bogie Busters,
sort of a fun tournament with some celebrities like Johnny Bench and

Glen Campbell, President Gerald Ford, and quite a few well-known people in business and politics from around the country. I had gone to it several times before, and when Cy invited me to be his special guest, I agreed to go.

As soon as I hung up the phone, I remembered a young woman I'd met the last time I was at Cy's tournament, in 1981. Her name was Peggy Simmons, and she was an advertising writer. She had impressed me, though at that time she was just starting to play golf and didn't really know a lot about it. We'd talked quite a bit at the course the two days of Cy's tournament, and she had sent me a nice note afterwards, telling me she'd appreciated getting to meet me. That was in 1981, and I'd never seen or even thought about her again until I got that call from Cy in March of '86, five years later.

Well, I had an idea I'd like to have her come out to see me play again, so I dug up her address and wrote to her. She wrote back, then I called her, and pretty soon we were writing and calling every day, nearly. Six months later she moved to Texas, and we were married on November 15. Living with Peggy has been a great joy for me. Despite the difference in our ages—nearly thirty-three years—and our different backgrounds, we get along amazingly well and have a lot of fun together. I've helped her improve her golf game so much that now she's about a 15 handicap, so I refuse to give her any strokes, and I have to work hard to stay ahead of her.

I truly feel that if it hadn't been for Peggy, I wouldn't be alive today, and many of our friends tell me the same thing. She had led a pretty quiet life before, so being married to me was quite a change, but she's adjusted very well to being the wife of this old broken-down pro. I just hope we'll have a lot of years together, because I'm enjoying every moment of it.

At least, I'm enjoying every moment when I'm not being operated on. I've had two hip surgeries in the past two years, cataract surgery, a hernia repair, and my eyelids fixed because they were drooping so much I was having trouble seeing. In addition to all that, I also managed to cut a finger off out in my shop, doing some woodworking. The doctor sewed it back on, fortunately. It made me a lot more cautious in my shop, but it wasn't enough to make me quit.

I'd started fooling around with wood about 1976, and my first projects weren't much to look at. But I kept at it, studied some books, talked to some friends, and with constant encouragement, first from Louise and now from Peggy, I've improved a little. Grandfather Allen, my mother's father, was a carpenter and helped build some of the homes in Waxahachie that are now on the city's historic homes tour each year, so that must be where I got it from. I still struggle with it, but I have made some nice things over the years—teak trivets, cherry end tables, an oak barrister's bookcase, parquet top tables, koa wood serving trays, honduras mahogany hope chests, and a lot of other things. I've never gone in for carving or fancy work because I don't have that kind of talent and my hands are too big to do a lot of detail work, but I enjoy making useful things and especially Christmas presents for our friends. Really, most of the time I'd rather do woodwork than play golf anymore, because I can't play golf all that well these days and when I do play, it makes me hurt just about everywhere. But when I work in my shop, I have something to show for my time, and beautiful wood is really satisfying to work with. I love it.

Since the late fifties I've also had occasion to help design several golf courses—kind of a third profession and one I've enjoyed quite a bit. Not that I could actually design one all by myself—I have no engineering background, and there's a lot of that involved—but after playing golf for sixty-five years I've observed some things about what makes a really good golf course, and I'll work with the architect on all phases of the layout, the direction of the holes, the size of the greens, and things like that. Well, eventually someone thought because I'd played pretty good golf about a hundred years ago, I might have something to contribute in that area. I've worked on quite a few throughout the country, many with my good friend Joe Finger, but my favorite golf course involves the work I'm proudest of.

It all began in 1978, when I was at Augusta for the Masters. I was on the General Improvements Committee, and during our meeting the subject of the par-five eighth hole came up. You see, Cliff Roberts had died in 1977, but quite a few years before his death he had decided to change the eighth green. He didn't like the mounds around the green because he felt they made it too hard for spectators to see the play. These weren't viewing mounds like on today's stadium courses; they were small but strategic mounds the player had to work around for his approach shot. Cliff had those mounds almost completely flattened, and the result was that it ruined the hole. He realized it himself eventually, and before he died he said that he wished they would put it back the way it used to be.

The only problem was no one could remember what the original green looked like, nor could anybody find any pictures of it. They'd asked several of the players, and one thought there had been a bunker or two, one thought something else, but no one was sure at all. Then they asked me. I described it to them and I was quite sure I remembered it exactly, so they offered me the job of developing a scale model of the hole and bringing it back the next spring to show them.

When I got home, I called Joe Finger and told him what I'd gotten myself into, and fortunately he was willing to help. We were working on another course at the time, so when he came up for that project, we sat down and he started drawing a picture of the green as I described it. Then we got Baxter Spann, one of Joe's partners and an expert at building models, to go to work on it, and the next spring, back we went to Augusta. When we showed our model to the committee, they said, "Go ahead." As soon as the course closed at the beginning of the summer we went to work, and in six weeks, we had it all ready— the mounds all around the left and back of the green exactly like I remembered it.

One day the men were just putting on the finishing touches and spreading the grass seed when we looked up and here came Frank Christian, the photographer for the club, in his car. Frank's father had been the club photographer before him, and when he reached us, Frank said, "I found a picture of the old green up in my attic!" Joe and I just stared at each other. Then Joe took the picture from Frank, looked at it, looked at the green, looked back at the picture, and said, "I don't believe it—it's exactly the same!" Fortunately, that was one time my memory worked pretty well. It would have been a lot easier on us if Frank had found that picture sooner, but if he had, we might not have gotten the job and I wouldn't have this story to tell.

Today my life is still busy. Sometimes it's busier than I want it to be, so I'm having to say no to people quite a lot, but when you're this old there's only so much energy left, and I simply can't do everything I used to be able to do. In the past few years, however, I've been given quite a few honors that I never expected or dreamed of, and though it meant a lot of travel, it was fun and made me feel very good. First, in

1990, my friend Buddy Langley wanted to celebrate the forty-fifth anniversary of my streak in '45. Buddy was head of GTE Southwest at the time, and of course GTE has been our tournament's title sponsor for the past several years. Buddy happened to be a member at Hope Valley Country Club in Durham, North Carolina, where I'd won the fourth tournament in the streak, so he got together with them and they invited folks from all of the clubs where I had won the other ten tournaments to come for the party. It was great—there were people from Montreal, Atlanta, Philadelphia, Toronto, Dayton, and the Carolinas. They even put up a wonderful plaque for me at the 18th tee, that great little par three where I made those birdies.

Also, I was asked that year to be Honorary Chairman for the U.S. Senior Open at Ridgewood, my old stompin' ground, and it was a great feeling to go back there. They gave a wonderful party for me one night and a lot of the senior pros came and said so many nice things about me it was almost embarrassing. But I have to admit I enjoyed it.

Then in May of '91, USGA's Golf House museum did a special exhibit of my life, calling me golf's "master craftsman." They not only displayed all my trophies and golf memorabilia, but also some of my woodworking projects, which really surprised and pleased me. It was a lot of work for us and the Golf House staff to collect all the stuff for the display, but while we were doing it, we came across an old spelling test book I had from the fifth grade. I was a pretty good speller back then, and we noticed there were quite a few 100's in that little old book, so we got to counting them. Turns out I had an even longer streak of wins than my eleven in a row in golf, because when I was in the fifth grade, I had thirty-seven straight 100's in spelling. I'm not sure I could spell all those words right today, in fact.

Now I'm eighty, almost eighty-one. Except for a sore hip and some arthritis in various places, I have excellent health and still manage to get around all right. Peggy and I travel a little, go to the majors, play golf together, take a vacation now and then, and also spend time at our home in Kerrville whenever we can. I sign more autographs now than I did when I won all those tournaments in '45, and when I look back on it all, I'm completely amazed at all that has happened to me.

I hope this book answers some of the questions I'm asked so often. No, I didn't have hemophilia or bleeding ulcers, and I left the tour because I wanted to, not because of "poor health," as is even stated in the *Encyclopedia Britannica,* I discovered recently. I've had a wonderful life with many blessings, and I guess the best one came on my birthday last year, when the Four Seasons Resort where my tournament is held gave me a tremendous party. My buddy Chris Schenkel was the emcee and we invited about 150 of our family and closest friends. We had a wonderful dinner, then a beautiful birthday cake with fireworks on it, and for the climax, they unveiled the nine-foot bronze statue of me by Robert Summers, which now stands near the first tee. It makes me feel so humble, because I feel I can never be as good as people think I am. But I try hard to be a Christian and do right, and all I can really do is to say "Thank you."

APPENDIX

The Records of Byron Nelson

BYRON NELSON'S AMATEUR RECORD

1928—Winner, Glen Garden CC Caddie Championship over Ben Hogan in 9-hole playoff

1928—Winner, Katy Lake Amateur, Fort Worth, Texas

1929—Runner-up in Fort Worth City Amateur, Meadowbrook Municipal GC, Fort Worth, Texas

1930—Winner, Southwestern Amateur, Nichols Hills G&CC, Oklahoma City, Oklahoma

1931—Failed to qualify by one shot in USGA National Amateur, Beverly CC, Chicago, Illinois

BYRON NELSON ON TOUR

Event	Finish	Score	Won	Purse	Winner
1932					
Texarkana*	3	296	$ 75	$ 500	Ted Longworth
1933					
Los Angeles	T-16	294	$ 34.50	N/A	Craig Wood
Western	T-7	295	N/A	N/A	Macdonald Smith
1934					
Los Angeles	T-26	297	$ 36	$5,489	Macdonald Smith
San Francisco Match Play		Qualified with 72			
Lost second round to Bill Mehlhorn			$ 55.75	$4,049	Tom Creary
Agua Caliente (Mexico)*	T-23	294	$ 33	$7,274	Wiffy Cox
Texas Open	T-2	284	$ 325	$2,346	Wiffy Cox
Galveston	2nd	293	$ 325	$1,849	Craig Wood
U.S. Open	MC	162	$ 0	$5,000	Olin Dutra

Event	Finish	Score	Won	Purse	Winner
1935					
Riverside Pro-Am*	T-2	64	$ 137	$992	Charles Guest
					Al Barbee
San Francisco Match Play					
1st round—Defeated Lawson Little, 5 & 4					
2nd round—Defeated Vic Ghezzi, 4 & 3					
Quarterfinal—Lost to Harold McSpaden, 5 & 4					
			$ 150	$3,250	Harold
					McSpaden
Agua Caliente					
(Mexico)*	T-6	291	$ 257	$5,175	Henry Picard
Phoenix	T-10	290	$ 75	$2,373	Ky Laffoon
Charleston	6	284	$ 100	$2,750	Henry Picard
North & South	12	292	$ 65	$3,951	Paul Runyan
Atlanta (54 holes)	3	215	$ 250	$2,000	Henry Picard
Augusta National					
Invitation (Masters)	T-9	291	$ 137	$5,000	Gene Sarazen
Metropolitan Open	OM	306	$ 0	$1,250	Henry Picard
U.S. Open	T-32	315	$ 0	$5,000	Sam Parks, Jr.
Western Open	3	296	$ 200	$2,153	Johnny Revolta
Medinah	T-12	301	$ 62	$2,150	Harry Cooper
General Brock Open	T-2	292	$ 600	$4,000	Tony Manero
New Jersey*	1	288	$ 400	$1,500	Nelson
Hershey	T-6	296	$ 143	$3,829	Ted Luther
Glen Falls	T-12	290	$ 56	$3,500	Willie
					MacFarlane
Baltimore	T-10	295	$ 25	$2,374	Vic Ghezzi
Louisville	T-4	289	$ 362	$5,000	Paul Runyan
Miami Biltmore	T-29	294	$ 37	$9,888	Horton Smith
1936					
Riverside	T-3	286	$ 300	$3,000	Jimmy Hines
Los Angeles	7	287	$ 200	$5,000	Jimmy Hines
Sacramento	3	287	$ 350	$3,000	Wiffy Cox
San Francisco Match					
Play	DNQ	147	$ 52.50	$4,479	Willie Hunter
Catalina (Short					
course–Par 66)	T-6	259	$ 208.33	$5,000	Willie Hunter
St. Petersburg	T-8	292	$ 55	$2,500	Leonard
					Dodson
St. Augustine					
Pro-Am*	Won 1 match		$ 50	$2,300	Sarazen-
					Reynolds
Charleston	T-11	296	$ 75	$3,000	Henry Picard

Event	Finish	Score	Won	Purse	Winner
Augusta National					
Invitation (Masters)	T-12	298	$ 50	$5,000	Horton Smith
Metropolitan Open	1	283	$ 750	$5,000	Nelson
U.S. Open	MC	153	$ 0	$5,000	Tony Manero
Shawnee	T-4	290	$ 226	$4,000	Ed Dudley
General Brock Open	10	296	$ 140	$4,100	Craig Wood
Western Open	3	278	$ 200	$2,145	Ralph Guldahl
St. Paul	T-5	281	$ 306	$5,248	Harry Cooper
Vancouver	T-2	278	$ 975	$4,994	Ken Black
Victoria	2	272	$ 450	$3,000	Horton Smith
Seattle	7	293	$ 270	$4,996	Macdonald Smith
Portland	T-7	282	$ 250	$5,054	Ray Mangrum
Glen Falls	3	284	$ 400	$3,700	Jimmy Hines
Hershey	T-9	293	$ 180	$5,000	Henry Picard
Canadian Open	T-10	287	$ 41.66	$3,000	Lawson Little
Augusta	T-13	289	$ 86	$5,000	Ralph Guldahl

1937

Event	Finish	Score	Won	Purse	Winner
Los Angeles	T-9	285	$ 75	$7,905	Harry Cooper
Sacramento	6	287	$ 140	$3,000	Ed Dudley
San Francisco Match Play					
1st Round—Defeated Sam Snead, 2 & 1					
2nd Round—Lost to Henry Picard, 3 & 2					
			$ 150	$4,760	Lawson Little
Houston	T-4	285	$ 250	$3,000	Harry Cooper
Thomasville	T-14	292	$ 32	$3,000	Dick Metz
St. Petersburg	T-14	291	$ 15	$3,000	Harry Cooper
Florida West Coast	T-2	289	$ 400	$3,000	Gene Sarazen
Hollywood (Florida)	T-5	277	$ 200	$3,000	Dick Metz
Miami Four-Ball					
(with McSpaden)	Lost, 1st Round		$ 0	$4,000	Picard-Revolta
North & South	3	292	$ 500	$3,980	Horton Smith
Augusta National					
Invitation (Masters)	1	283	$1,500	$5,000	Nelson
PGA Championship	Qualifying medalist with 139				
1st round—Defeated Leo Diegel, 2 & 1					
2nd round—Defeated Johnny Farrell, 5 & 4					
3rd round—Defeated Craig Wood, 4 & 2					
Quarterfinals—Lost to Ky Laffoon, 2 down					
			$ 200	$9,200	Denny Shute
U.S. Open	T-20	295	$ 50	$6,000	Ralph Guldahl
British Open	5	296	$ 125	$2,532	Henry Cotton
Central Pennsylvania*	1	140	$ 150	N/A	Nelson (won in playoff)
(36 holes)					

Event	Finish	Score	Won	Purse	Winner
Hershey	OM	306	$ 0	$ 5,000	Henry Picard
Belmont Match Play	1	—	$3,000	$12,000	Nelson
Miami Biltmore	11	289	$ 125	$10,000	Johnny Revolta
Nassau	T-13	285	$ 47.50	$ 3,500	Sam Snead

1938

Event	Finish	Score	Won	Purse	Winner
Pasadena	3	279	$ 350	$ 3,000	Henry Picard
Sacramento	T-8	294	$ 100	$ 3,000	Johnny Revolta
San Francisco Match Play					
Qualified with 158					
1st round—Lost to Paul Runyan, 1 down			$ 75	$ 5,000	Jimmy Demaret
New Orleans	DNQ	79	$ 0	$ 5,000	Harry Cooper
Thomasville	1	280	$ 700	$ 3,000	Nelson
St. Petersburg	3	283	$ 350	$ 3,000	Johnny Revolta
Hollywood (Florida)	1	275	$ 700	$ 3,000	Nelson
Miami Four-Ball (with McSpaden)					
1st round—Defeated Willie Klein & Johnny Farrell, 1 up					
2nd round—Defeated Frank Moore & Denny Shute, 2 & 1					
Semifinals—Lost to Dick Metz & Ky Laffoon, 3 & 2					
			$ 150	$ 4,000	Metz-Laffoon
North & South	T-3	286	$ 400	$ 4,000	Vic Ghezzi
Masters	5	290	$ 400	$ 5,000	Henry Picard
U.S. Open	T-5	294	$ 412.50	$ 6,000	Ralph Guldahl
PGA Championship					
1st round—Defeated Clarence Yockey, 5 & 4					
2nd round—Defeated Al Krueger, 20 holes					
3rd round—Defeated Harry Bassler, 11 & 10					
Quarterfinals—Lost to Jimmy Hines, 2 & 1					
			$ 250	$10,000	Paul Runyan
Cleveland	T-20	291	$ 100	$10,000	Ky Laffoon
Hershey Four-Ball					
(with Ed Dudley)	T-3	Even	$ 325	$ 4,600	Ghezzi-Hogan
Westchester					
(108 holes)	T-3	434	$ 900	$12,500	Sam Snead
Columbia					
(South Carolina)	T-6	293	$ 0	$ 5,000	Johnny Revolta
Augusta	T-8	288	$ 0	$ 5,000	Craig Wood
Miami	DNQ	—	$ 0	$10,000	Harold McSpaden
Houston (54 holes)	T-5	219	$ 186.66	$ 3,000	Harold McSpaden
Central Pennsylvania*					
(36 holes)	2	141	$ 90	N/A	N/A

Event	Finish	Score	Won	Purse	Winner
1939					
Los Angeles	T-7	286	$ 129.25	$ 5,500	Jimmy Demaret
Oakland	9	280	$ 230	$ 5,000	Dick Metz
San Francisco Match Play		Qualified with 143			
1st round—Lost to Ben Coltrin, 2 & 1			$ 75	$ 5,000	Dick Metz
Crosby Pro-Am	T-2	139	$ 300	$ 3,000	Dutch Harrison
Phoenix (54 holes)	1	198	$ 700	$ 3,000	Nelson
Texas Open	3	274	$ 550	$ 5,000	Dutch Harrison
New Orleans	T-5	291	$ 650	$10,000	Henry Picard
Thomasville (54 holes)	T-4	215	$ 183.34	$ 3,000	Henry Picard
St. Petersburg (54 holes)	T-4	211	$ 250	$ 3,000	Sam Snead
Miami Four-Ball (with Frank Walsh)					
1st round—Lost to Dutch Harrison & Ray Mangrum, 4 & 2					
			$ 50	$ 5,000	Snead-Guldahl
North & South	1	280	$1,000	$ 4,000	Nelson
Greensboro	10	290	$ 170	$ 5,000	Ralph Guldahl
Masters	7	287	$ 250	$ 5,000	Ralph Guldahl
U.S. Open	1	284	$1,000	$ 6,000	Nelson
Inverness Four-Ball (with McSpaden)	T-2	Plus 6	$ 425	$ 5,200	Picard-Revolta
Massachusetts Open*	1	283	$ 400	$ 1,500	Nelson
PGA Championship		Qualified with 143			
1st round—Defeated Chuck Garringer, 4 & 2					
2nd round—Defeated Red Francis, 3 & 1					
3rd round—Defeated Johnny Revolta, 6 & 4					
4th round—Defeated Emerick Kocsis, 10 & 9					
5th round—Defeated Dutch Harrison, 9 & 8					
Finals—Lost to Henry Picard on 37th hole					
			$ 600	$10,600	Henry Picard
Western Open	1	281	$ 750	$ 3,005	Nelson
St. Paul	T-10	281	$ 205	$ 5,003	Dick Metz
Dapper Dan	T-8	291	$ 391.66	$ 9,825	Ralph Guldahl
Hagen Anniversary* (with Dick Metz)	3	Plus 4	$ 375	$ 2,700	Dudley-Burke
Hershey	4	287	$ 450	$10,050	Felix Serafin
Miami	5	278	$ 600	$10,000	Sam Snead

Event	Finish	Score	Won	Purse	Winner
1940					
San Francisco Match Play	Qualified with 144				
1st round—Defeated Rod Francis, 1 up					
2nd round—Defeated Charles Klein, 3 & 2					
Quarterfinals—Lost to Willie Goggin, 3 & 2					
			$ 150	$ 5,000	Jimmy Demaret
Phoenix (54 holes)		215	$ 0	$ 3,000	Ed Oliver
Texas Open	1	271	$1,500	$ 5,000	Nelson
Western Open	WD	78	$ 0	$ 5,000	Jimmy Demaret
New Orleans	T-15	295	$ 146	$10,000	Jimmy Demaret
St. Petersburg (54 holes)	2	212	$ 450	$ 3,000	Jimmy Demaret
Miami Four-Ball (with McSpaden)					
1st round—Defeated Farrell & Serafin, 7 & 6					
2nd round—Lost to Runyan & Smith, 5 & 4					
			$ 75	$ 5,000	Burke-Wood
Thomasville (54 holes)	2	205	$ 450	$ 3,000	Lloyd Mangrum
Greater Greensboro	T-3	280	$ 412.50	$ 5,000	Ben Hogan
Asheville	T-7	284	$ 230	$ 5,000	Ben Hogan
Masters	3	285	$ 600	$ 5,000	Jimmy Demaret
Goodall Round Robin	6	Plus 2	$ 300	$ 5,000	Ben Hogan
Ohio Open*	1	284	$ 250	N/A	Nelson
U.S. Open	T-5	290	$ 325	$ 6,000	Lawson Little
Inverness Four-Ball	T-7	−14	$ 350	$ 4,800	Guldahl-Snead
PGA Championship					
1st round—Defeated Dick Shoemaker, 4 & 3					
2nd round—Defeated Frank Walsh in 20 holes					
3rd round—Defeated Dick Metz, 2 & 1					
Quarterfinal—Defeated Eddie Kirk, 6 & 5					
Semifinal—Defeated Ralph Guldahl, 1 up					
Final—Defeated Sam Snead, 1 up					
			$1,100	$11,050	Nelson
Anthracite Open	2	278	$ 750	$ 5,000	Sam Snead
Miami	1	271	$2,537.50	$10,000	Nelson

(Prize money includes $25 daily award for low round plus one tie.)

Event	Finish	Score	Won	Purse	Winner
1941					
Los Angeles	OM	72-77-75-78-302	$ 0	$10,000	Johnny Bulla
Oakland	OM	290	$ 0	$ 5,000	Leonard Dodson
San Francisco Match Play	DNQ	147	$ 0	$ 5,000	Johnny Revolta
Crosby Pro-Am	T-5	68-71-139	$ 125	$ 3,000	Sam Snead
Western Open	T-2	68-69-67-74-278	$ 600	$ 5,000	Ed Oliver
Texas Open	T-4	71-71-69-71-282	$ 325	$ 5,000	Lawson Little
New Orleans	T-8	75-69-69-72-285	$ 210	$ 5,000	Henry Picard
Thomasville	T-6	73-70-74-217	$ 170	$ 3,000	Harold McSpaden
St. Petersburg	T-13	144-65-77-286	$ 40	$ 5,000	Sam Snead
Miami Four-Ball (with McSpaden)	Lost, 2nd Round		$ 75	$ 5,000	Sarazen-Hogan
Seminole Pro-Am*	1	64-70-134	$ 803.29	N/A	Nelson
Florida West Coast (54 holes)	2	72-67-67-206	$ 450	$ 3,000	Horton Smith
Lost in playoff with Horton Smith, 68-69					
North & South	T-4	69-71-69-76-285	$ 350	$ 4,000	Sam Snead
Greater Greensboro	1	72-64-70-70-276	$1,200	$ 5,000	Nelson
Asheville	T-10	74-76-74-72-296	$ 155	$ 5,000	Ben Hogan
Masters	2	71-69-73-70-283	$ 800	$ 5,000	Craig Wood
U.S. Open	T-17	73-73-74-77-297	$ 50	$ 6,000	Craig Wood
Mahoning Valley	2	67-70-73-67-277	$ 750	$ 5,000	Clayton Heafner
Inverness Four-Ball (with Jimmy Thompson)	2	Plus 8	$ 600	$ 6,000	Hogan-Demaret
PGA Championship	2	N/A	$ 600	$10,600	Vic Ghezzi

Event	Finish	Score	Won	Purse	Winner
St. Paul	T-7	73-70-70-68-281	$ 278	$ 7,500	Horton Smith
Tam O'Shanter	1	67-69-72-70-278	$2,000	$11,000	Nelson
Philadelphia	T-6	72-71-74-68-285	$ 160	$ 5,000	Sam Snead
Ohio Open*	1	68-69-72-62-271	$ 125	$ 500	Nelson
Miami	1	70-67-66-66-269	$2,538	$10,000	Nelson
Harlingen	4	65-70-70-66-271	$ 450	$ 5,000	Henry Picard
Beaumont	T-7	71-69-74-72-286	$ 225	$ 5,000	Chick Harbert

1942

Event	Finish	Score	Won	Purse	Winner
Los Angeles	T-6	72-70-74-72-288	$ 350	$10,000	Ben Hogan
Oakland	1	67-69-69-69-274	$1,000	$ 5,000	Nelson
San Francisco	8	287	$ 200	$ 5,000	Ben Hogan
Crosby Pro-Am	T-13	70-72-142	$ 57	$ 5,000	Johnny Dawson
Western Open	T-11	285	$ 105	$ 5,000	Herman Barron
Texas Open	T-8	74-67-73-70-284	$ 162	$ 5,000	Chick Harbert
New Orleans	6	74-73-69-71-287	$ 300	$ 5,000	Lloyd Mangrum
St. Petersburg	T-2	68-76-75-70-289	$ 585.33	$ 5,000	Sam Snead
Miami Four-Ball (with Henry Picard)	Lost, 2nd round		$ 100	$ 5,000	Harper-Keiser
North & South	T-3	69-70-69-73-281	$ 500	$ 5,000	Ben Hogan
Greater Greensboro	T-4	72-68-68-74-282	$ 412.50	$ 5,000	Sam Byrd
Tied for low 3rd round, won $25					
Asheville	3	69-73-66-70-278	$ 550	$ 5,000	Ben Hogan
Masters	1	68-67-73-72-280	$1,500	$ 5,000	Nelson
Won in playoff with Hogan, 69-70					

Event	Finish	Score	Won	Purse	Winner
PGA Championship	Semifinalist		$ 150	$ 7,550	Sam Snead
Inverness Four-Ball					
(with Jimmy					
Thomson)	T-4	Plus 5	$ 454	$ 7,650	Little-Mangrum
Hale America	T-4	69-70-69-70-278	$ 475	$ 6,000	Ben Hogan
Tam O'Shanter	1	67-71-65-77-280	$2,500	$15,000	Nelson
Won in playoff with Heafner, 67-71					
Toledo*	1	N/A	N/A	N/A	Nelson
Ohio Open*	1	273	N/A	N/A	Nelson

1943

Event	Finish	Score	Won	Purse	Winner
All-American	T-3	72-72-71-68-283	$ 900	$10,000	Harold McSpaden
Chicago Victory	5	68-72-72-72-284	$ 0	$ 2,000	Sam Snead
Money awarded to first four finishers only					
Minneapolis Four-Ball					
(with McSpaden)	2	Plus 8	N/A	$ 5,000	N/A
Kentucky Open	1	N/A	N/A	N/A	Nelson

1944

Event	Finish	Score	Won	Purse	Winner
Los Angeles	T-3	68-72-71-72-283	$1,125WB	$12,500	Harold McSpaden
Won Pro-Am at Hillcrest with 65 and won $150WB					
San Francisco					
Victory	1	68-69-68-70-275	$2,400WB	$10,000	Nelson
Won Pro-Am at San Gabriel with 67 and won $127					
Phoenix	2	71-66-71-65-273	$ 750	$ 5,000	Harold McSpaden
Won Pro-Am with 64 and won $150					
Texas Open	2	75-63-68-68-274	$ 650	$ 7,000	Johnny Revolta
New Orleans	2	71-78-71-70-290	$ 750	$ 5,000	Sam Byrd
Gulfport	3	73-70-69-71-283	$ 550WB, $187.50 cash	$ 6,000	Harold McSpaden

Event	Finish	Score	Won	Purse	Winner
Charlotte	3	70-70-73-66-279	$ 1,000WB	$10,000	Dutch Harrison
Durham	2	68-67-69-70-274	$ 750WB	$ 5,000	Craig Wood
Knoxville War Bond	1	69-68-66-67-270	$ 1,000	$ 6,666	Nelson
Philadelphia	6	70-71-69-79-289	$ 675WB	$17,500	Sam Byrd
New York	1	N/A	$ 500	N/A	Nelson
New York Red Cross	1	69-69-66-71-275	$ 2,667WB	$13,333	Nelson
Chicago Victory	3	65-74-68-69-276	$ 1,350WB, $ 422 cash	$10,000	Harold McSpaden
Minneapolis Four-Ball (with McSpaden)	1	Plus 13	$ 800WB, $ 250 cash	$ 8,800	Nelson-McSpaden
Utah Open*	2	67-65-72-69-273	$ 450	$ 2,500	Harold McSpaden
Beverly Hills	1	71-69-68-69-277	$ 1,500	$ 5,000	Nelson
PGA Championship	2	N/A	$ 1,500	$14,500	Bob Hamilton
Tam O'Shanter	1	68-70-73-69-280	$10,100	$30,100	Nelson
Nashville	1	64-67-68-70-269	$ 2,400WB	$10,000	Nelson
Texas Victory	1	69-69-70-68-276	$ 2,000	$10,000	Nelson
Portland	T-4	73-74-75-74-296	$ 1,025WB	$13,600	Sam Snead
San Francisco	1	72-71-69-69-281	$ 2,667WB	$13,333	Nelson
Oakland	T-6	66-72-72-73-283	$ 380WB	$ 7,500	Jim Ferrier
Richmond (California)	T-3	73-69-68-70-280	$ 668WB	$ 7,500	Sam Snead

Event	Finish	Score	Par	Won	Purse	Winner
1945						
Los Angeles	2	284	E	$ 1,600WB	$13,333	Sam Snead by 1
Phoenix	1	274	−10	$ 1,333WB	$ 6,666	Nelson by 2
Tucson	2	269	−11	$ 700	$ 5,000	Ray Mangrum by 1
Texas Open	2	269	−15	$ 700	$ 5,000	Sam Byrd by 1
Corpus Christi	1	264	−16	$ 1,000	$ 5,000	Nelson by 4
New Orleans	1	284	−4	$ 1,333WB	$ 6,666	Nelson by 5
Won in playoff with McSpaden, 65-70						
Gulfport	2	275	−9	$ 700	$ 5,000	Sam Snead
Lost in playoff with Snead						
Pensacola	2	274	−14	$ 933WB	$ 5,000	Sam Snead by 7
Jacksonville	T-6	275	−13	$ 285	$ 5,000	Sam Snead
Miami International Four-Ball (with McSpaden)	1	21-up in 4 matches		$ 1,500WB	$10,000	Nelson & McSpaden
Charlotte	1	272	−16	$ 2,000WB	$10,000	Nelson by 4
Won in playoff with Snead, 69-69-138 to 69-73-142						
Greater Greensboro	1	271	−13	$ 1,333WB	$ 7,500	Nelson by 8
Durham	1	276	−4	$ 1,333WB	$ 6,666	Nelson by 5
Atlanta	1	263	−13	$ 2,000WB	$10,000	Nelson by 9
Montreal*	1	268	−20	$ 2,000	$10,000	Nelson by 10
Philadelphia	1	269	−11	$ 3,333WB	$17,500	Nelson by 2
Chicago Victory National	1	275	−13	$ 2,000WB	$12,300	Nelson by 7
PGA Championship	1		−37 for 204 holes, 17 up in five matches			
				$ 5,000WB	$14,700	Nelson
Tam O'Shanter	1	269	−19	$13,600WB	$60,000	Nelson by 11
Canadian Open	1	280	E	$ 2,000	$10,000	Nelson by 4
Spring Lake Pro-Member*	1	140	−4	$ 2,100	$ 2,500	Nelson by 1
Memphis	T-4	276	−12	$ 1,200	$10,000	Fred Haas by 5
Knoxville	1	276	−12	$ 2,666WB	$10,000	Nelson by 10
Nashville	2	269	−15	$ 1,600WB	$13,333	Ben Hogan by 4
Dallas	3	281	−7	$ 1,000	$10,000	Sam Snead by 4
Tulsa	4	288	+4	$ 800WB	$ 7,500	Sam Snead by 9
Esmeralda	1	266	−22	$ 2,000WB	$ 7,500	Nelson by 7

Event	Finish	Score	Par	Won	Purse	Winner
Portland	2	275	−13	$1,400	$14,500	Ben Hogan by 14
Tacoma	T-9	283	+3	$ 325WB	$ 7,500	Jimmy Hines
Seattle	1	259	−21	$2,000WB	$10,250	Nelson by 13
Fort Worth	1	273	−11	$2,000WB	$ 7,500	Nelson by 8

1946

Event	Finish	Score	Par	Won	Purse	Winner
Los Angeles	1	284		$2,666.67 WB	$13,333	Nelson by 5
San Francisco	1	283		$3,000WB	$15,000	Nelson by 9
Texas Open	3	273		$ 750	$ 8,000	Ben Hogan
New Orleans	1	277		$1,500	$ 7,500	Nelson by 5
Pensacola	T-13	286		$ 152.50	$ 7,500	Ray Mangrum
St. Petersburg	5	277		$ 650	$10,000	Ben Hogan
Miami Four-Ball (with McSpaden)	Semifinalists			$ 300	$ 7,500	Hogan-Demaret
Masters	T-7	290		$ 356.25	$10,000	Herman Keiser
Houston	1	274		$2,000	$10,000	Nelson by 2
Colonial National Invitation	T-9	285		$ 520	$15,000	Ben Hogan
Western Open	T-6	280		$ 517	$10,000	Ben Hogan
Goodall Round Robin	3	Plus 22		$1,150	$10,000	Ben Hogan
U.S. Open	T-2	284		$ 875 + $333.33 (Playoff)	$ 8,000	Lloyd Mangrum
Inverness Four-Ball (with McSpaden)	2	Plus 14		$ 850	$10,000	Hogan-Demaret
Columbus Invitational	1	276		$2,500	$10,500	Nelson by 2
Kansas City	T-3	276		$1,433.34	$15,000	Ed Stranahan
Chicago Victory	1	279		$2,000	$10,000	Nelson by 2
All American	T-7	287		$1,233.34	$45,000	Herman Barron
PGA Championship	Quarterfinalist			$ 500	$17,700	Ben Hogan
World's Championship	2	140		$ 0 (Winner take all)	$10,000	Sam Snead
Fort Worth Invitational	T-7	277		$ 550	$10,000	Frank Stranahan

* Not an official PGA tournament.

Nelson retired at the end of 1946. Over the next twenty years he made infrequent starts on the PGA Tour. His wins during that time include the Texas PGA Open in 1948; the Crosby Invitational in 1951; and the Crosby Pro-Am (with Eddie Lowery) and the French Open in 1955.

BYRON NELSON'S CAREER HIGHLIGHTS

Tournament Victories—61, including 54 PGA-sanctioned events and the French Open in 1955

The Masters—1937, 1942

U.S. Open—1939

PGA Championship—1940, 1945

Member of the Ryder Cup Team in 1937 and 1947. Selected for team in 1939 and 1941. Also served as captain of victorious Ryder Cup team in 1965.

Records Nelson still holds:

Most tournament wins in a row—11, in 1945: Miami Four-Ball, Charlotte Open, Greensboro Open, Durham Open, Atlanta Iron Lung Tournament, PGA Canadian Open, Philadelphia Inquirer Invitational, Chicago Victory Open, PGA Championship, Tam O'Shanter Open, Canadian National Open

Most tournament wins in one year—18, in 1945

Lowest scoring average—68.33, in 1945

Most consecutive rounds under 70—19, in 1945

Most consecutive times finishing in the money—113

Nelson was named Athlete of the Year in 1944 and 1945 by the Associated Press; he won nine tournaments in 1944 and six in 1946, just prior to his retirement from tournament play; and in 1945, in addition to winning 18 PGA-sanctioned events, he also finished second in seven others. He was also the first pro to play 100 rounds in the Masters.